# UNDERSTANDING ASATRU

## REV. SIMON ROBERT WAKE

Published by

# PRAYERS

MAY THE GODS OF ASGARD GUIDE YOUR STEPS TOWARDS THEIR GATES,

IN YOUR JOURNEY MAY IT BE FILLED WITH LIGHT, MAY YOU FIND STRENGTH FROM THOR IN YOUR DARKEST HOURS, MAY YOU FIND WISDOM FROM ODIN IN TIMES OF CONFUSION.

MAY YOU FIND BEAUTY AND LASTING BONDS FROM FREYA AND FREY.

MAY YOUR WEB BE SPUN TIGHTLY WITH THAT WHICH MAKES YOU STRONGER HAPPIER AND WISE.

MAY THE GODS ALWAYS LOOK UPON YOU WITH GRACE.

_____

LO THERE DO I SEE MY FATHER, LO THERE DO I SEE MY MOTHER, AND MY SISTERS AND MY BROTHERS.

LO THERE DO I SEE THE LINE OF MY PEOPLE BACK TO THE BEGINNING.

LO THEY DO CALL TO ME, THEY BID ME TO TAKE MY PLACE AMONG THEM IN THE HALLS OF VALHALLA WHERE THE BRAVE MAY LIVE FOREVER.

_____

WE DO NOT BEND OUR KNEE IN SUPPLICATION TO THE GODS AND GODDESSES NOR DO WE BEG THEM TO DO FOR US, RATHER WE ASK THEM TO EMPOWER US DO  FOR OURSELVES.

WE NEITHER NEED, NOR ASK FOR OUR GODS FORGIVENESS, WE WERE NOT EVER BORN INTO SIN, WE WERE BORN TO BE THE BEST THAT WE CAN BE.

_____

ODIN FAR WANDERER, GRANT ME YOUR WISDOM, COURAGE AND VICTORY.

FRIEND THOR GRANT ME YOUR STRENGTH.

AND BOTH BE WITH ME.

****

A special thank you is owed to my stepson **Noah** for the book cover art, Cheers kid.

****

# ABOUT THE AUTHOR

The Reverend Simon Robert Wake, born in Northumbria, England, now resides in the United States, embodying a life rich in exploration and achievement. A voracious reader, Simon has read over 20,000 books, fueling his success in fields ranging from the British Military to municipal government, photography, and cruise ship adventures.

As an ordained minister, he has united over two dozen couples in matrimony, reflecting his compassionate nature. At home, he cherishes life with his wife, Megan, their three children—Kristian, Leah, and Noah—and their three loyal dogs, Tika, Nilla, and Finnegan.

Simon's adventurous spirit is evident in his travels to 137 countries and a lifetime of experiences, from excelling in judo and track and field to his  military service. His story is a celebration of curiosity, versatility, and the joy of embracing life's possibilities.

# DEDICATION

I dedicate this book to my father **Joseph Robert Wake**, my wife **Megan wake** and all those who, like me, have embarked on a quest for knowledge about the enigmatic Asatru religion. Our journey has not been easy, with information scattered across various sources, like runes hidden in the depths of a forgotten forest. But, like the rays of the Summer Solstice sun, the truth emerged in Iceland in 1972 with the founding of the Íslenska Ásatrúarfélagið, officially recognized a year later. Soon, the flame spread, and the Asatru Free Assembly was kindled in the United States, later evolving into the Asatru Folk Assembly. Our religion is not one that is simply handed to us in a single, convenient volume. Instead, we must piece together ancient texts, oral traditions, and our own personal experiences to understand the divine. To my brothers and sisters on this path, I raise a horn in salute. Hail Odin, the Allfather, who guides us on our quest for knowledge. Hail the Ancestors, whose wisdom echoes through the ages. And Hail the Folk, who keep the ancient ways alive in our modern world. May our struggle bear fruit, and may the spirit of Asatru illuminate our path.

# CONTENTS

Celebrating the Old Ways: Rituals and Festivals in Asatru

Wisdom of the North: Unraveling the Havamal's Teachings

Reconstructing the Past: A Guide to Norse Paganism for the Modern Seeker

Sacred Seasons: Celebrating the Festivals of Asatru

The Allfather and His Kin: A Comprehensive Guide to Odin, Thor, and Freyja

Beyond the Void: Ginnungagap and the Birth of the Cosmos

Realms of Wonder: Exploring Norse Mythology

Heimdall's Watch: Guardian of the Nine Realms

Living the Nine Noble Virtues: A Practical Guide for Everyday Life

Threads of Destiny: Unraveling the Web of Wyrd in Norse Mythology

Wisdom Through Sacrifice: Odin's Journey to Enlightenment

Odin's Call: Invoking the Allfather Through Prayer and Offerings

From Odin to Today: Tracing the Asatru Revival

Unlocking the Secrets of Viking Runes: A Comprehensive Guide to Their Meaning and Use

Echoes of the North: Unraveling the Icelandic Sagas

Echoes of Asgard: Analyzing the Prose Edda's Mythological Tapestry

Beyond the Shield Wall: Disentangling Asatru from Racism

# INTRODUCTION

As I delved into the depths of the Asatru religion and Norse Paganism, I felt like a stone skipping across a pond, briefly touching on the myriad facets of this fascinating faith. I could have easily penned a far weightier tome several thousand pages long, but I showed restraint and kept it to a modest (ahem) almost six hundred pages. So, dear reader, if you emerge from this book with your sanity intact, I encourage you to dive deeper into the rabbit hole—it's a wild and wonderful ride! And now, without further ado, let us embark on this journey together, exploring the realms of the Norse gods and the ancient ways that continue to captivate and inspire and the modern iteration of the old pagan religion in practice today. May your reading bring you joy and enlightenment.

# Celebrating the Old Ways: Rituals and Festivals in Asatru

## Chapter 1: Introduction to Asatru

### Understanding Asatru

Asatru, a contemporary pagan faith rooted in Norse traditions, emphasizes a deep connection to both the ancient gods and the natural world. Its practitioners, often referred to as Ásatrúar, engage with a rich tapestry of history, mythology, and cultural practices that date back to the Viking Age. Understanding Asatru involves exploring not only its spiritual dimensions but also its ethical frameworks, community structures, and rituals that celebrate the cycles of nature. Each of these elements contributes to a holistic understanding of how Asatru manifests in the lives of its practitioners today.

Central to Asatru is the veneration of the Norse pantheon, which includes deities such as Odin, Freya, and Thor. These gods are not merely mythological figures but are seen as archetypes that embody various aspects of existence, offering guidance and inspiration. The myths themselves serve both as sacred stories and as metaphors for human experience, illustrating the values of bravery, wisdom, and honor. Practitioners often engage with these stories through study and storytelling, allowing them to deepen their connection to the divine and to their own personal journeys.

Rituals and celebrations form the heartbeat of Asatru practice, marking significant moments within both the natural world and the practitioner's personal life. Seasonal festivals, such as Yule and Midsummer, are celebrated with specific rites that honor the cycles of nature and the gods. These gatherings foster a sense of community among practitioners, reinforcing bonds and shared beliefs. Rituals can vary widely in form and complexity, from simple offerings at personal altars to large, organized gatherings that include communal feasting, music, and storytelling, all of which help to create a vibrant spiritual atmosphere.

Asatru also emphasizes the importance of ethics and values derived from ancient traditions. Concepts such as honor, hospitality, and respect for nature guide practitioners in their daily lives and interactions with others. The Nine Noble Virtues—courage, truth, honor, fidelity, discipline, hospitality, self-reliance, industriousness, and perseverance—serve as a moral compass for individuals navigating modern society. This ethical framework not only shapes personal conduct but also fosters a sense of responsibility toward the community and the environment, promoting sustainable practices and a deep reverence for the earth.

In the contemporary context, Asatru has developed into a diverse and dynamic community that spans the globe. Practitioners connect through local groups, online forums, and social media, sharing knowledge, resources, and experiences. This networking fosters a sense of belonging and support, making it easier for newcomers to find their place within the tradition. Additionally, Asatru's presence in popular culture has sparked interest and curiosity, prompting discussions that bridge ancient beliefs with modern values. As practitioners continue to explore and express their faith, Asatru remains a living tradition, continually adapting while honoring its roots.

## The Historical Roots of Asatru

The historical roots of Asatru can be traced back to the ancient Norse and Germanic peoples, who practiced a polytheistic faith deeply intertwined with their cultural identity and social structures. This belief system was characterized by a veneration of a pantheon of deities, such as Odin, Thor, and Freyja, each embodying distinct aspects of life, nature, and human experience. Archaeological evidence, including burial sites, rune stones, and sacred groves, highlights the significance of these deities and the rituals performed in their honor. The connection to the land was paramount, as many practices revolved around seasonal changes, agricultural cycles, and the natural world, which were integral to the survival of these communities.

With the advent of Christianity in the Scandinavian regions during the late first millennium, many of the traditional practices of the Norse were suppressed or transformed. Despite this, elements of Asatru managed to persist in folk traditions, folklore, and local customs. The syncretism of Christian and pagan beliefs resulted in a rich tapestry of cultural practices that maintained a connection to ancient traditions, albeit in altered forms. The transition from a pagan to a predominantly Christian society did not extinguish the reverence for the old gods; instead, it led to a gradual transformation of the understanding and expression of these beliefs.

The revival of Asatru in the 20th century marked a significant reawakening of interest in Norse mythology and ancient practices. Influenced by movements such as Romanticism and the broader revival of folk traditions, practitioners sought to reconnect with their ancestral heritage. This modern resurgence was fueled by a growing appreciation for pagan spirituality and a desire for alternative belief systems that resonated with contemporary values. Asatru became a means for individuals to explore their identity, heritage, and connection to the natural world, leading to the establishment of various groups and organizations dedicated to the practice and promotion of these ancient traditions.

Today, Asatru is practiced by individuals and communities around the world, emphasizing personal spirituality and the importance of ethical living in accordance with ancient values. The principles of honor, courage, and respect for nature are central to Asatru ethics, guiding practitioners in their daily lives. Rituals and celebrations often draw from historical practices, reimagining them in a way that is relevant to contemporary society. Festivals such as Yule and Midsummer not only celebrate the seasonal cycles but also reinforce community bonds and shared values among practitioners.

The historical roots of Asatru serve as a foundation for its modern expressions, ensuring that while the practice evolves, it remains deeply connected to its ancestry. This interplay between history and contemporary practice allows Asatru to flourish as a living tradition, inviting practitioners to honor their past while embracing the potential for personal and communal growth. As the Asatru community continues to expand and diversify, it is essential to acknowledge and respect the historical influences that shape its practices, ensuring that these ancient ways are celebrated and preserved for future generations.

## Core Beliefs and Values

Core beliefs and values form the foundation of Asatru, guiding practitioners in their spiritual journeys and social interactions. At the heart of Asatru lies a deep reverence for the natural world, reflecting the ancient Norse understanding of the interconnectedness of all beings. Nature is not merely a backdrop for human existence but a living entity imbued with spirit and significance. This belief fosters a sense of responsibility towards the environment, encouraging practitioners to honor and protect the land, animals, and elements as sacred expressions of the divine.

Another core value in Asatru is the emphasis on honor and integrity. Practitioners are encouraged to uphold their word and act with sincerity in all endeavors. This principle is often expressed through the concept of "Hamingja," which refers to the luck and fortune that is carried by individuals and families. A person's actions can impact their Hamingja and that of their kin, creating a moral framework that emphasizes personal responsibility and accountability. This belief in ethical living not only shapes individual character but also strengthens the communal bonds within the Asatru community.

The practice of hospitality, or "gestaþórr," is another significant value in Asatru. It reflects the importance of welcoming guests and treating them with respect and generosity. This tradition harks back to the Viking Age, when sharing food and drink was a vital aspect of social life. In modern practice, hospitality fosters community connections and nurtures relationships, creating a supportive environment where individuals can share experiences and grow together. It reinforces the idea that the Asatru community is a collective of diverse individuals united by shared beliefs and values.

Asatru also places a strong emphasis on the importance of ancestry and heritage. The veneration of one's forebears is a key aspect of the tradition, as practitioners recognize the influence of their ancestors on their lives and identities. This connection to the past is celebrated through rituals that honor the dead, such as ancestor veneration and the observance of seasonal festivals. By acknowledging and learning from the wisdom of those who came before, Asatru practitioners deepen their spiritual understanding and reinforce their personal and communal identities.

Finally, the values of courage and resilience are integral to Asatru. Practitioners are encouraged to face challenges with bravery and to embrace the struggles of life as opportunities for growth and learning. This perspective is rooted in the Norse myths, which often depict gods and heroes overcoming adversity. By embodying these qualities, Asatru practitioners cultivate a spirit of perseverance, finding strength in their faith and community. This empowerment through belief not only enriches their personal spiritual paths but also contributes to a vibrant, dynamic Asatru community that thrives on shared values and collective strength.

# Chapter 2: The Cycle of the Year

## Seasonal Festivals and Their Significance

Seasonal festivals hold a central place in Asatru, serving not only as markers of time but also as profound expressions of the faith's connection to nature, community, and the cycles of life. Each festival corresponds to the changing seasons and reflects the rhythms of the earth. For Asatru practitioners, these celebrations are opportunities to honor the gods, ancestors, and the land itself, fostering a sense of belonging and continuity with the past. Understanding the significance of these festivals offers insights into the values and ethics that underlie Asatru practice, emphasizing the importance of living in harmony with the natural world.

The major seasonal festivals in Asatru include Yule, Ostara, Midsummer, and Winternights, among others. Each of these festivals encapsulates specific themes and rituals that resonate with the seasonal changes they celebrate. Yule, for instance, marks the winter solstice and symbolizes rebirth and renewal, as the days begin to lengthen after the longest night. Rituals during Yule often include lighting candles and sharing feasts, which serve to bring warmth and light into the darkest time of the year. Such practices not only honor the gods but also reinforce community bonds as practitioners gather to celebrate the returning sun.

Ostara, celebrated during the spring equinox, embodies themes of fertility, growth, and balance. This festival is a time to recognize the awakening of nature, making it a fitting moment for planting seeds, both literally and metaphorically. Rituals may include blessing seeds and honoring the earth, reinforcing the Asatru commitment to nature worship and stewardship. The emphasis on renewal and fertility during Ostara serves as a reminder of the interconnectedness of all life, echoing the core Asatru belief in respecting and nurturing the natural world.

Midsummer, or Litha, celebrates the peak of summer and the abundance of life it brings. This festival is characterized by bonfires and feasting, symbolizing the height of the sun's power. Midsummer rituals often involve honoring the gods and goddesses associated with fertility and prosperity, and they encourage practitioners to reflect on their own lives and the growth they wish to cultivate. The communal aspect of Midsummer fosters connections among practitioners, allowing individuals to share their personal journeys and aspirations as they align themselves with the natural cycles.

Winternights, marking the onset of winter, is a time to honor the ancestors and reflect on the past year. This festival emphasizes gratitude and remembrance, encouraging practitioners to acknowledge the lessons learned and the blessings received throughout the year. Rituals during Winternights often involve creating altars for ancestors and sharing stories, thus reinforcing the values of respect and gratitude that are foundational to Asatru. By engaging in these seasonal festivals, practitioners not only connect with their heritage but also cultivate a deeper understanding of their spiritual path, grounding their practices in the cycles of nature and the wisdom of their ancestors.

## The Wheel of the Year in Asatru

The Wheel of the Year in Asatru encompasses a cycle of seasonal festivals that honor the natural rhythms of the Earth, resonating deeply with the beliefs and practices of Norse paganism. Central to this concept are the eight festivals, known as the Sabbats, which mark significant points in the agricultural calendar and reflect the changing seasons. These celebrations serve as a way for practitioners to connect with the land, the gods, and the ancestors, reinforcing a sense of community and continuity with the past. Each festival is imbued with its own unique significance and rituals that celebrate the life cycles of nature and the divine.

The Wheel of the Year begins with Yule, the winter solstice, a time of reflection and renewal as the days begin to lengthen. This celebration honors the rebirth of the sun and the promise of new growth. Following Yule, the festival of Imbolc marks the gradual awakening of the earth as the first signs of spring emerge. This time is often associated with the goddess Brigid and involves rituals that emphasize purification and the rekindling of creativity and inspiration. As the Wheel turns, practitioners engage in rituals that foster gratitude for the returning light and the fertility of the land.

Ostara, celebrated during the spring equinox, symbolizes balance and the flourishing of life. Rituals during this time often focus on planting seeds, both literally and metaphorically, as individuals set intentions for personal growth and development. Asatru practitioners often incorporate the themes of fertility and renewal into their celebrations, invoking gods and goddesses of agriculture and prosperity. This festival serves as a reminder of the interconnectedness of all life and the importance of nurturing both the earth and one's spiritual path.

As the year progresses, the festivals of Midsummer and Lammas bring attention to the height of summer and the abundance it offers. Midsummer, or Litha, is a vibrant celebration of the sun's power, often featuring bonfires and communal gatherings that honor the light and warmth. Lammas, or Lughnasadh, follows closely, marking the first harvest. This festival emphasizes gratitude for the fruits of one's labor and the importance of community, as shared meals and offerings to the gods become focal points of the celebration. These rituals reinforce the values of cooperation and reciprocity within the Asatru community.

The Wheel of the Year culminates with the darker seasons, beginning with Samhain, a time for honoring ancestors and reflecting on the cycle of life and death. This festival encourages practitioners to acknowledge their lineage and the wisdom of those who have come before. As the year comes full circle, the celebration of Yule returns, completing the cycle and inviting reflection on the lessons learned throughout the year. Engaging with the Wheel of the Year offers Asatru practitioners a structured way to connect with nature, honor their heritage, and cultivate a deeper understanding of their personal spirituality within the context of community and tradition.

# Celebrating the Solstices and Equinoxes

Celebrating the Solstices and Equinoxes holds a significant place in Asatru, reflecting the cyclical nature of life and the deep connection practitioners have with the rhythms of the earth. The solstices, marking the longest and shortest days of the year, and the equinoxes, representing the balance of day and night, are pivotal moments in the seasonal calendar. These events provide opportunities for reflection, gratitude, and connection to the divine, rooted in the ancient practices of our ancestors. For adult practitioners of Asatru, these celebrations are not merely commemorative but serve as a means to align personal spirituality with the natural world.

The Winter Solstice, or Yule, is a time of rebirth and renewal. As the darkness reaches its peak, practitioners often gather to celebrate the return of the sun. Rituals may include lighting candles or a Yule log, symbolizing the warmth and light that will gradually increase as the days lengthen. This celebration can also involve storytelling, sharing the lore of gods and heroes associated with the season, such as the rebirth of Baldur. Participants may express gratitude for the past year and set intentions for personal growth in the coming months, reinforcing the ethical values central to Asatru.

In contrast, the Summer Solstice, or Midsummer, embodies abundance and vitality. This celebration often focuses on the fertility of the earth and the bountiful gifts of nature. Rituals may include feasting with seasonal foods, dancing, and honoring deities associated with growth and harvest, such as Freyja and Freyr. Community gatherings during this time encourage networking among practitioners, fostering relationships and shared experiences that strengthen the Asatru community. The joy and energy of Midsummer serve as a reminder of the interconnectedness of life and the importance of nurturing both the land and each other.

Equinoxes, occurring in the spring and fall, represent balance and transition. The Spring Equinox, or Ostara, heralds the arrival of new life and the awakening of the earth from winter's slumber. Rituals during this period may include planting seeds, symbolizing hope and renewal, and celebrating the fertility of the land. Practitioners reflect on personal transformation, using the energy of this time to set goals and intentions aligned with the cycle of nature. The Fall Equinox, or Harvest Home, is a time of gratitude, acknowledging the fruits of labor and the changing seasons. It emphasizes the value of community support and sharing the bounty with others.

Celebrating these seasonal markers fosters a profound connection between Asatru practitioners and the natural world, enhancing personal spirituality and reinforcing ethical values. By honoring the solstices and equinoxes, practitioners engage in a historical reconstruction of ancient rites, making them relevant in modern society. These celebrations not only connect individuals with their heritage but also cultivate a sense of belonging within the Asatru community. As participants embrace these sacred moments, they nurture a deeper understanding of their role within the larger tapestry of life, celebrating the old ways while adapting them to contemporary practices.

# Chapter 3: Rituals in Asatru

## The Importance of Ritual Practice

Ritual practice holds a central place in Asatru, serving as a bridge between the sacred and the mundane. For adult practitioners, engaging in rituals provides a structured way to honor the gods, ancestors, and the natural world, reinforcing a sense of connection to both the past and present. Rituals act as a means of expressing devotion and gratitude, allowing practitioners to articulate their beliefs through symbolic actions. By participating in these communal or solitary rites, individuals can cultivate a deeper understanding of their spirituality and the traditions that inform their practice.

The significance of ritual is not merely historical; it remains a vital aspect of contemporary Asatru practice. Rituals create a rhythm within the lives of practitioners, marking the passage of time through seasonal celebrations, life events, and personal milestones. Festivals such as Yule and Midsummer not only honor the cycles of nature but also foster a sense of community among practitioners. These gatherings provide opportunities for networking and sharing experiences, allowing individuals to build connections that reinforce their commitment to the Asatru path.

Rituals often draw from Norse mythology, serving as a means to engage with the stories and values of the gods and heroes. By incorporating mythological themes into their practices, practitioners can explore the moral and ethical teachings embedded in these ancient narratives. This connection to mythology not only enriches the spiritual experience but also encourages practitioners to embody the virtues exemplified by the gods, such as courage, wisdom, and honor. Such engagement with myth fosters a deeper appreciation of the cultural heritage that shapes Asatru today.

Moreover, the practice of ritual allows for personal spiritual growth and introspection. Through the intentionality of ritual actions—whether lighting a candle, offering mead, or creating a sacred space—practitioners can create moments of mindfulness that invite reflection and deeper connection to their personal beliefs. This aspect of ritual practice emphasizes the importance of individual spirituality within the broader framework of the Asatru community. Each person's unique experiences and interpretations contribute to the richness of the tradition, promoting a diverse yet unified practice.

In modern society, where the pace of life can often be overwhelming, ritual practice serves as an essential counterbalance, inviting individuals to slow down and engage with their spirituality thoughtfully. By establishing a regular practice, whether through daily offerings or seasonal celebrations, practitioners can reinforce their values and beliefs. This commitment to ritual not only strengthens one's personal practice but also honors the historical roots of Asatru, ensuring that these ancient traditions continue to thrive in contemporary contexts. Ultimately, the importance of ritual practice lies in its ability to weave together the threads of community, mythology, personal growth, and cultural heritage, creating a tapestry that reflects the vibrant spirit of Asatru today.

# Common Asatru Rituals

Common Asatru rituals are an integral part of practicing this ancient faith, providing a framework for connecting with the gods, the spirits of the land, and the community. Among the most well-known rituals is the blot, a sacrificial offering to the deities. This ceremony often involves the gathering of practitioners who come together to honor a specific god or goddess, such as Odin, Freyja, or Thor. Offerings can include food, drink, or crafted items, and these are presented with reverence, accompanied by prayers or poetry that express gratitude and intentions. The communal aspect of the blot fosters a sense of unity and shared purpose, reinforcing bonds within the Asatru community.

Another prominent ritual is the sumbel, a drinking ceremony that emphasizes the sharing of mead or other beverages in a ceremonial context. This ritual typically involves three rounds, where participants make toasts to the gods, ancestors, or each other. Each round allows for personal reflections, affirmations, or the recounting of heroic deeds. The sumbel serves not only as a means of honoring those who have come before but also as a way to strengthen the social ties among practitioners. It is often seen as a rite of passage, enabling individuals to articulate their intentions and aspirations within the supportive environment of their peers.

Seasonal festivals play a vital role in Asatru practice, aligning rituals with the rhythms of nature. Events such as Yule, Ostara, and Midsummer celebrate the turning of the seasons and various agricultural cycles. Yule, for instance, marks the winter solstice and is a time for reflection and renewal, while Ostara heralds the arrival of spring and rebirth. These festivals often include feasting, storytelling, and the decorating of sacred spaces. By engaging in these seasonal rituals, practitioners cultivate a deeper connection to the land, the cosmos, and the cycles of life, reinforcing the importance of nature within Asatru.

Rituals of personal devotion, such as daily prayers or offerings at home altars, are also common among Asatru practitioners. These intimate practices allow individuals to establish a personal relationship with the divine and create a sacred space in their everyday lives. Offering small tokens, lighting candles, or reciting verses from the Eddas can enhance one's spiritual experience and serve as reminders of one's commitments to the gods and the values of Asatru. Personal rituals provide a foundation for spiritual growth and reflection, enabling practitioners to navigate their paths with intention and mindfulness.

Finally, the act of storytelling is a ritualistic practice that holds significant value in Asatru. The recounting of myths, legends, and personal experiences serves to preserve cultural heritage and impart wisdom from the past. Storytelling can occur during gatherings, rituals, or even in solitary moments, allowing for the transmission of knowledge and the reinforcement of community identity. By sharing narratives that celebrate the deeds of gods and ancestors, practitioners can inspire one another and weave a rich tapestry of shared beliefs and experiences that continue to evolve within the modern context of Asatru.

## Creating Personal Rituals

Creating personal rituals within the framework of Asatru allows practitioners to connect deeply with their spirituality and the natural world around them. Personal rituals can serve as a means to honor the gods, celebrate the cycles of nature, and reflect on one's own life journey. By integrating elements from Norse mythology, historical practices, and individual values, these rituals foster a sense of belonging and personal significance. As practitioners seek to navigate modern life while maintaining their connection to ancient traditions, the creation of personal rituals becomes an essential avenue for expression and spiritual growth.

To begin crafting personal rituals, it is important for individuals to reflect on their intentions and what they wish to honor or achieve. This may involve contemplating personal milestones, seasonal changes, or specific deities that resonate with one's spiritual path. Drawing inspiration from historical sources, such as sagas or archaeological findings, can provide a solid foundation while allowing for personal interpretation and adaptation. The goal is to create a ritual that feels authentic and meaningful, serving as a bridge between ancient customs and contemporary life.

Incorporating natural elements into personal rituals is a vital aspect of Asatru practice. Nature is not only a source of inspiration but also a manifestation of the divine. Practitioners can use items such as stones, herbs, or flowers that hold significance to them, creating an altar or sacred space that reflects their connection to the earth. Seasonal changes can also inform ritual timing, aligning personal practices with events such as solstices, equinoxes, or the changing of the leaves. This harmony with nature fosters a deeper understanding of one's place within the cosmos and enhances the spiritual experience.

Rituals can also incorporate aspects of personal ethics and values inherent in Asatru. By reflecting on principles such as honor, hospitality, and personal responsibility, practitioners can develop rituals that reinforce their commitment to these ideals. For instance, a ritual could involve sharing a meal with friends and family, symbolizing the importance of community and connection. Alternatively, a personal reflection on one's actions and intentions may be performed during a quiet moment of solitude, providing an opportunity for growth and accountability.

Lastly, sharing personal rituals with the broader Asatru community can enhance the experience for both the individual and others. Networking with fellow practitioners allows for the exchange of ideas, fostering a deeper understanding of diverse practices within Asatru. Participating in group rituals or celebrating festivals together can create a sense of unity and shared purpose. By blending personal expressions of spirituality with communal celebrations, practitioners can cultivate a richer and more inclusive Asatru experience that honors both individual and collective paths.

# Chapter 4: Major Festivals in Asatru

## Yule: The Midwinter Festival

Yule, celebrated around the winter solstice, embodies the essence of midwinter traditions in Asatru. This festival marks not only the longest night of the year but also the rebirth of the sun, symbolizing hope and renewal. For practitioners of Asatru, Yule is a time to honor the cycles of nature and the resilience of life amidst the cold and darkness. This celebration invites participants to reflect on the themes of light overcoming darkness, mirroring the natural world where the days gradually begin to lengthen following this pivotal point in the yearly cycle.

Central to Yule festivities are rituals that honor the gods, ancestors, and the spirits of nature. Many Asatru practitioners create altars adorned with seasonal greens, candles, and symbols of fertility and rebirth. The Yule log, traditionally burned in the hearth, serves as a focal point for rituals, representing warmth, light, and the nurturing aspects of the earth. As the log burns, participants may offer prayers or blessings, asking for the return of the sun's warmth and the abundance it brings. This practice not only connects individuals with their heritage but also fosters a sense of community as families and friends gather to share in the celebration.

Traditional Yule feasts play a significant role in the festival, reflecting the importance of hospitality and abundance in Asatru culture. Foods such as roasted meats, root vegetables, and spiced drinks are common, often prepared with care and shared among loved ones. The act of sharing a meal is deeply rooted in Norse tradition, symbolizing unity and the bonds of kinship. Additionally, many practitioners incorporate storytelling, sharing tales of the gods, heroes, and the history of their ancestors, thereby passing down wisdom and reinforcing cultural values.

Yule also serves as a time for personal reflection and setting intentions for the coming year. Practitioners may engage in quiet contemplation, journaling, or meditative practices to connect with their inner selves and the natural world around them. This introspective aspect of the festival encourages individuals to consider their goals, aspirations, and the lessons learned throughout the previous year. By aligning personal intentions with the energies of renewal and growth embodied in Yule, practitioners can foster a deeper spiritual connection to their path in Asatru.

As modern Asatru continues to evolve, Yule remains a vital festival that bridges the past with contemporary practices. Many individuals and groups incorporate elements from historical sources while also adapting rituals to fit their personal beliefs and community dynamics. This flexibility allows Yule to resonate with a diverse audience, fostering inclusivity within the Asatru community. Through the celebration of Yule, practitioners not only honor their heritage but also reinforce the values of interconnectedness, gratitude, and resilience that are essential to the practice of Asatru in today's world.

## Ostara: The Spring Equinox Celebration

Ostara, celebrated at the Spring Equinox, marks a pivotal moment in the Asatru calendar, symbolizing renewal, rebirth, and the balance between light and dark. This celebration often aligns with the arrival of spring, as the days grow longer and the earth begins to awaken from the slumber of winter. Ostara is not only a time to honor the goddess Eostre, known for her association with fertility and spring, but also an opportunity for practitioners of Asatru to connect deeply with nature and the cycles of life. The festival emphasizes the importance of balance, reflecting the moment when day and night are of equal length, a theme that resonates with the values of harmony and equilibrium in Asatru.

Rituals during Ostara often involve the planting of seeds, symbolizing new beginnings and the potential for growth. This practice serves as a reminder of our connection to the earth and our responsibility to care for it. Many Asatru practitioners engage in outdoor ceremonies, where they may create altars adorned with symbols of fertility such as eggs, flowers, and spring herbs. These rituals can also include offerings to the spirits of the land, acknowledging the sacredness of nature and the importance of living in harmony with it. By performing these rites, practitioners reaffirm their commitment to the earth and its cycles, embodying the Asatru principle of honoring nature as a living entity.

In addition to individual and communal rituals, Ostara is an opportunity for storytelling and sharing wisdom. Gathering with fellow practitioners allows for the exchange of experiences and insights, reinforcing the sense of community that is vital in Asatru. Participants may recount tales of the gods and goddesses, particularly those related to renewal and fertility, drawing inspiration from Norse mythology. This communal aspect of Ostara not only strengthens bonds within the Asatru community but also provides a platform for learning and growth, essential elements for practitioners, especially those new to the path.

Traditional foods play a significant role in Ostara celebrations, emphasizing the bounty of the season. Dishes made with seasonal ingredients, such as eggs, greens, and root vegetables, are common, reflecting the themes of fertility and sustenance. Sharing a meal together fosters a sense of unity and gratitude among participants, aligning with the Asatru value of hospitality. This act of breaking bread also serves as a reminder of the interconnectedness of all beings and the importance of nurturing relationships within the community and with the natural world.

As Ostara unfolds, practitioners are encouraged to reflect on their personal journeys and the changes they wish to manifest in their lives. This introspection aligns with the broader Asatru belief in personal responsibility and the power of intention. By setting goals or intentions during this time of renewal, individuals can harness the energy of the season to foster growth and transformation in their lives. Ostara becomes not just a celebration of the external world but also an internal journey, allowing practitioners to align their personal paths with the rhythms of nature and the wisdom of their ancestral traditions.

# Midsummer: Celebrating the Summer Solstice

Midsummer, or the Summer Solstice, represents a pivotal moment in the Asatru calendar, symbolizing the peak of the sun's power and the height of summer's warmth. Traditionally celebrated around June 21st, this festival honors the sun's life-giving energy, which is vital for the fertility of crops and the flourishing of nature. The solstice has deep roots in Norse mythology, with associations to figures like Baldr, the god of light and purity. For adult Asatru practitioners, this time of year not only serves as a celebration of nature's bounty but also as a moment for reflection on one's personal spiritual journey and connection to the earth.

Rituals during Midsummer often incorporate elements that celebrate the sun and the earth's abundance. Common practices include lighting bonfires, which symbolize the sun's intensity and serve as a means to ward off darkness and evil spirits. Participants may gather around these fires, sharing stories and songs that honor the gods and the natural world. Offerings of mead, flowers, and herbs might be presented, invoking blessings for prosperity and protection. Engaging in these rituals not only strengthens the bonds within the Asatru community but also deepens the individual's connection to the divine and the cycles of nature.

The Midsummer celebration also emphasizes the importance of nature worship within Asatru. Practitioners are encouraged to spend time outdoors, engaging with the land and its energies. Many choose to hold rituals at sacred sites, such as groves or near bodies of water, where the natural world can be fully appreciated. This immersion allows for a deeper understanding of the interconnectedness of all life, reinforcing the Asatru value of living in harmony with nature. The solstice is a reminder to honor the earth as a living entity, deserving of respect and reverence.

In modern society, Midsummer offers a unique opportunity for practitioners to reconnect with ancestral traditions and to share these practices with newcomers to Asatru. Community gatherings during this time often feature educational components, where more experienced members can guide beginners in the significance of the rituals and the mythology surrounding the solstice. By fostering an inclusive environment, the celebration serves to strengthen community ties and encourage the sharing of knowledge, ensuring that the wisdom of the past continues to flourish in the present.

As adults participating in Midsummer festivities, Asatru practitioners are also called to reflect on the ethical implications of their celebrations. This includes considering the impact of their actions on the environment and striving to practice sustainability. The solstice is not just a moment for revelry but also a time to commit to the principles of stewardship and respect for nature. By embodying these values, practitioners not only honor their heritage but also contribute to a more conscientious and connected world, reinforcing the relevance of Asatru in contemporary life.

## Harvest Festivals: Celebrating the Bounties of Autumn

Harvest festivals hold a significant place in Asatru, reflecting the deep connection between the community and the cycles of nature. As autumn approaches, the days grow shorter, and the air becomes crisp, signaling a time for gratitude and celebration. These festivals serve as a reminder of the abundance the earth has provided throughout the growing season. They are occasions to honor the land, pay homage to the gods and goddesses associated with agriculture and fertility, and to come together as a community to share in the fruits of labor.

The historical roots of harvest festivals in Norse culture can be traced back to ancient traditions that revolved around the agricultural calendar. Asatru practitioners often look to the sagas and Eddas for inspiration, where tales of gods like Freyr and Sif highlight the importance of fertility and the harvest. These narratives not only celebrate the abundance of the earth but also reinforce the relationship between human beings and the natural world. Rituals during this time often include offerings to these deities, thanking them for the bounties received and asking for blessings for the coming winter months.

In modern Asatru practices, harvest festivals can take on various forms, from small family gatherings to larger community celebrations. One common practice is to hold a blót, a ritual offering that may include fruits, grains, or even mead, dedicated to the gods. Participants may also engage in storytelling, sharing myths and personal experiences that resonate with the themes of gratitude and abundance. Additionally, feasting becomes a central aspect of these celebrations, where the community comes together to enjoy seasonal foods, reflecting on the hard work that went into the harvest and fostering a sense of connection among participants.

Harvest festivals also provide an opportunity for practitioners to engage with the land in a more profound way, emphasizing the values of stewardship and sustainability inherent in Asatru. As modern society often distances individuals from agricultural practices, these festivals encourage a reconnection with nature. Activities such as apple picking, visiting local farms, or participating in community gardens can be integrated into the celebrations, reinforcing the importance of mindful living and respect for the earth. This connection to the land is not only a celebration of abundance but also a recognition of the responsibilities that come with it.

Ultimately, harvest festivals serve as a multifaceted celebration within Asatru, bridging historical traditions with contemporary practices. They highlight the importance of community, gratitude, and the sacredness of nature. By honoring the cycles of the earth and the deities associated with the harvest, practitioners cultivate a deeper understanding of their spirituality and their place within the world. These gatherings remind us to cherish the bounties of autumn, fostering a sense of unity and purpose as we prepare for the changing seasons ahead.

# Chapter 5: Norse Mythology and Its Influence

## Key Deities in Asatru

Key deities in Asatru represent a vital aspect of the tradition, serving as focal points for worship, ritual, and personal connection. At the forefront of these deities is Odin, the Allfather and god of wisdom, war, and poetry. Revered for his relentless pursuit of knowledge, Odin embodies the quest for understanding and personal growth. Practitioners often seek his guidance through rituals, invoking his presence in various ceremonies, especially those related to wisdom and inspiration. His role as a creator and transformer makes him a significant figure in Asatru, inspiring practitioners to explore their own paths to enlightenment.

Another central deity is Thor, the god of thunder and protector of mankind. Known for his strength and bravery, Thor symbolizes resilience and protection against chaos and destruction. His hammer, Mjölnir, is a powerful emblem in Asatru, often worn as a talisman by practitioners to invoke strength and safeguard their homes. Rituals honoring Thor typically focus on themes of courage and community protection, making him a beloved figure within the Asatru community, particularly during gatherings and festivals that celebrate kinship and collective strength.

Freyja, the goddess of love, fertility, and war, holds a prominent place in Asatru as well. Her dual nature encompasses both nurturing and fierce qualities, reflecting the complexities of life and relationships. Freyja is often called upon in rituals that celebrate love, fertility, and the cycles of life. Practitioners may honor her during seasonal festivals, invoking her blessings for growth and abundance. Her association with the Vanir, a group of deities connected to nature and prosperity, highlights the importance of harmony with the Earth, a value central to many Asatru practitioners.

Loki, the trickster god, while often viewed with caution, plays a crucial role in the Asatru pantheon. His complexity allows practitioners to explore themes of change, adaptability, and the duality of existence. Loki's presence in rituals can serve as a reminder of the unpredictable nature of life and the importance of embracing challenges. By acknowledging Loki, practitioners can engage with the more chaotic aspects of their own journeys, allowing for personal growth and resilience in the face of adversity.

The relationships between these deities and their worshippers form a rich tapestry of spirituality within Asatru. Each god and goddess embodies specific qualities and lessons, providing practitioners with diverse avenues for exploration and connection. Celebrating these deities through rituals and festivals not only fosters a deeper understanding of Norse mythology but also reinforces community bonds among practitioners. As Asatru continues to evolve in modern society, the reverence for these key deities remains a cornerstone of practice, guiding individuals on their spiritual journeys while honoring the ancestral traditions that shape their beliefs.

## Myths and Their Lessons

Myths serve as the backbone of Asatru, offering profound insights into the human experience, nature, and the divine. The tales of gods, goddesses, and legendary heroes encapsulate not only the beliefs of our ancestors but also the values they held dear. Each story carries lessons that resonate with contemporary practitioners, providing guidance on living harmoniously with oneself, others, and the natural world. By exploring these myths, modern Asatru practitioners can find a deeper connection to their spirituality and a richer understanding of their identity within the faith.

One prominent myth that illustrates the importance of wisdom is the story of Odin, who sacrificed himself on Yggdrasil, the World Tree, to gain knowledge of the runes. This narrative underscores the value of self-sacrifice and the pursuit of wisdom, inviting practitioners to reflect on their own journeys towards understanding and insight. In a world filled with distractions, the lesson of Odin encourages a commitment to personal growth and the importance of seeking knowledge, whether through study, experience, or community engagement. This myth serves as a reminder that true wisdom often comes at a cost, urging practitioners to value the lessons learned through hardship and sacrifice.

The myth of Thor and the Midgard Serpent reinforces the concept of bravery and the struggle against chaos. Thor's battles with Jörmungandr highlight the eternal conflict between order and disorder, a theme that resonates with many in today's society. Asatru practitioners can draw upon this narrative to inspire resilience in the face of life's challenges. The myth encourages individuals to confront their fears and uncertainties, emphasizing that courage is not the absence of fear but the determination to face it. This lesson resonates throughout the Asatru community, fostering a spirit of support and camaraderie among practitioners as they navigate their personal and collective struggles.

Another significant aspect of Norse mythology is the depiction of the relationship between gods and nature. The reverence shown to the land, animals, and natural cycles in these myths reflects the core principles of Asatru's nature worship. Stories of deities like Freyja, associated with fertility and the harvest, remind practitioners of the interconnectedness of life. By honoring these myths, Asatru practitioners are encouraged to cultivate a deeper relationship with the natural world, recognizing that their well-being is intricately tied to the health of the environment. This connection fosters a sense of responsibility towards nature, prompting modern practitioners to engage in sustainable practices and environmental stewardship.

Ultimately, the myths of Asatru are not merely relics of the past; they are living stories that continue to impart wisdom and guidance. By examining these narratives through a contemporary lens, practitioners can uncover valuable teachings that apply to modern life. From the pursuit of knowledge and bravery in adversity to the reverence for nature, these lessons shape the ethical framework of Asatru and inform how practitioners engage with themselves, their communities, and the world around them. As adults in this spiritual path, embracing these myths enables a richer, more meaningful experience of Asatru, fostering a culture of learning, reflection, and connection.

## The Role of Ancestors in Modern Practice

The reverence for ancestors holds a significant place in the practice of Asatru, reflecting a deep connection to heritage and lineage. For modern practitioners, honoring ancestors fosters a sense of identity and continuity with the past. This practice serves not only as a way to pay respect to those who came before but also as a means to draw strength and wisdom from their experiences. Rituals that include invoking ancestors during gatherings or personal ceremonies can create a powerful atmosphere of shared history and collective memory, reinforcing the idea that practitioners are part of a larger tapestry that spans generations.

Incorporating ancestral reverence into contemporary Asatru practice can take various forms, from creating altars adorned with photographs and mementos to performing specific rituals that invoke their guidance. Many practitioners choose to celebrate a dedicated day of remembrance, where family stories are shared, and ancestral connections are honored. This focus on ancestry cultivates a sense of belonging within the Asatru community, allowing individuals to explore their roots and share their unique heritages with others. Such practices not only enhance personal spirituality but also contribute to a collective understanding of the diverse backgrounds that enrich Asatru.

The role of ancestors extends beyond mere remembrance; it also invites practitioners to engage in ethical reflection. By considering the values and choices of ancestral figures, modern Asatru practitioners can derive lessons that inform their own lives. This ethical framework encourages individuals to reflect on the responsibilities they carry as members of their families and communities. Engaging with ancestral wisdom can inspire practitioners to make decisions that honor their heritage while addressing contemporary moral dilemmas, thus bridging the gap between ancient values and modern ethics.

In addition to personal benefits, recognizing the ancestors also strengthens community bonds within Asatru. Shared rituals and celebrations that honor forebears can serve as powerful communal experiences, fostering relationships among practitioners. These gatherings often encourage storytelling and the exchange of personal histories, thereby knitting a tighter social fabric. The act of honoring ancestors collectively not only reinforces individual identities but also builds a sense of unity and purpose among members of the Asatru community, promoting a shared commitment to uphold the traditions and values that shape their practice.

As modernity continues to evolve, the importance of ancestors in Asatru remains steadfast. Practitioners today find themselves at a crossroads where ancient traditions meet contemporary life. By embracing the role of ancestors, Asatru practitioners can navigate the complexities of modern society while remaining grounded in their cultural heritage. This connection to the past offers guidance and resilience, allowing practitioners to celebrate the old ways with renewed vigor and purpose. As such, honoring ancestors becomes an essential aspect of Asatru, reinforcing the enduring significance of lineage, legacy, and communal identity in a rapidly changing world.

# Chapter 6: Asatru Practices in Modern Society

## Integrating Asatru into Daily Life

Integrating Asatru into daily life involves a conscious effort to weave its principles and practices into the fabric of everyday activities. For adult practitioners, this means recognizing the significance of rituals, symbols, and values inherent in Asatru and finding ways to embody them in a modern context. Simple acts such as greeting the day with gratitude to the gods, or taking a moment to appreciate nature, can set a tone of reverence and mindfulness. Each day offers opportunities to honor the old ways, whether through personal reflection, engaging with the community, or participating in seasonal celebrations that align with the cycle of the year.

One effective way to integrate Asatru into daily life is through the establishment of personal rituals. These rituals can be as formal or informal as one chooses and can include lighting a candle for a specific deity, creating a daily offering of food or drink, or setting aside time for meditation and prayer. Personal altars can serve as a focal point for these practices, offering a space where practitioners can connect with the divine and reflect on their spiritual journey. By incorporating these rituals into daily routines, practitioners can cultivate a deeper awareness of Asatru's teachings and foster a sense of connection to their ancestors and the natural world.

Nature worship is a fundamental aspect of Asatru that can be embraced in daily life. This can be manifested through simple actions such as taking walks in nature, observing the changing seasons, and recognizing the sacredness of the earth. Engaging with the environment allows practitioners to appreciate the interconnectedness of all living things, reinforcing the Asatru belief in the divine presence within nature. Activities like gardening, foraging, or even just spending time outside can serve as expressions of reverence and gratitude for the gifts of the earth, aligning daily life with Asatru values.

Community plays a vital role in the practice of Asatru, and integrating this aspect into daily life can enhance one's spiritual journey. Finding or forming groups that share similar beliefs fosters a sense of belonging and support. Participating in community events, whether they are gatherings for festivals, seasonal rituals, or simply sharing meals, helps strengthen bonds with others who are on a similar path. Additionally, engaging in online forums or social media groups can provide a platform for sharing experiences, resources, and encouragement, allowing practitioners to feel connected even in modern society's fast-paced environment.

Finally, ethics and values rooted in Asatru can guide daily decision-making and interactions with others. Emphasizing principles such as honor, loyalty, and hospitality can shape one's behavior and relationships, creating a life that reflects Asatru's teachings. Practitioners might strive to live in harmony with their values by being mindful of their choices, whether in personal relationships, professional environments, or community involvement. By embodying these ethical principles, individuals not only enrich their own lives but also contribute positively to the larger Asatru community and society at large, creating a living expression of their faith.

## Community Involvement and Public Events

Community involvement and public events are vital components of Asatru practice, serving as opportunities for practitioners to come together, share experiences, and deepen their connections to their beliefs and each other. These gatherings often play a central role in fostering a sense of belonging among members of the Asatru community, especially for those who may be new to the faith. Public events range from seasonal festivals to community service initiatives, allowing practitioners to celebrate their heritage and values in a communal setting.

Seasonal festivals, such as Yule, Ostara, and Midsummer, are significant in Asatru, marking the cycles of nature and honoring the gods. These events often include rituals, feasting, storytelling, and traditional games, emphasizing the importance of nature and the changing seasons. Engaging in these festivities not only strengthens individual spirituality but also provides a platform for practitioners to bond over shared rituals and customs. Such gatherings are often open to the public, serving as an introduction to Asatru for those interested in learning about the faith.

In addition to seasonal celebrations, community service initiatives reflect the Asatru commitment to ethics and values, particularly the concept of community responsibility. Practitioners might organize clean-up efforts in local parks, food drives, or charity events, embodying the principle of "community first." These activities not only benefit the wider community but also enhance the reputation of Asatru as a positive force, dispelling misconceptions that may exist about the faith. By actively engaging in public service, Asatru practitioners demonstrate a dedication to the well-being of their communities, aligning their actions with their beliefs.

Networking and social interaction are also crucial aspects of community involvement. Many Asatru groups utilize social media and online forums to connect with others, share resources, and plan events. This virtual engagement can help practitioners build relationships with like-minded individuals across geographical boundaries. Furthermore, local gatherings often feature workshops, lectures, and discussions on various aspects of Asatru, offering opportunities for education and personal growth. Such interactions cultivate a supportive environment where individuals can explore their spirituality in a communal context.

Ultimately, community involvement and public events serve to reinforce the interconnectedness of Asatru practitioners. They provide a space for shared experiences and collective learning, fostering unity within the diverse expressions of the faith. By participating in these activities, practitioners not only celebrate their traditions but also contribute to the ongoing evolution of Asatru in modern society. Emphasizing the importance of community, these events help ensure that the old ways are honored and preserved, while also adapting to contemporary realities and fostering a vibrant spiritual community.

## Challenges and Misconceptions

Challenges and misconceptions surrounding Asatru can pose significant barriers to both seasoned practitioners and newcomers alike. One of the most prominent challenges is the misunderstanding surrounding the nature of the faith itself. Many individuals still associate Asatru primarily with neo-paganism, often overlooking its historical roots and the depth of its traditions. This lack of understanding can lead to misrepresentations in popular culture, where Asatru is sometimes portrayed solely as a whimsical or superficial form of spirituality. For practitioners, this can be frustrating as it detracts from the rich, serious nature of their beliefs and rituals.

Another significant challenge is the diversity within the Asatru community itself. Asatru is not a monolithic belief system; it encompasses a wide range of practices and interpretations. Some practitioners may lean towards a more historical reconstructionist approach, while others may adopt a contemporary interpretation that resonates with modern values. This diversity can create friction within the community, as different factions may struggle to find common ground, leading to misunderstandings or feelings of exclusion among practitioners. It is essential for individuals to engage in open dialogue and foster inclusivity to navigate these differences effectively.

Misconceptions about Asatru often extend to its relationship with nature and the environment. Many outsiders view Asatru as solely focused on ancient gods and mythologies, neglecting the profound connection practitioners have with the natural world. Nature worship is a vital aspect of Asatru, encouraging followers to recognize the sacredness of the earth and its cycles. This connection can inspire practitioners to engage in eco-friendly practices and advocate for environmental conservation. However, the failure to acknowledge this aspect can lead to the belief that Asatru is disconnected from contemporary environmental issues, which is far from the truth.

Moreover, the ethics and values espoused in Asatru can be misconstrued, particularly when it comes to issues of race and identity. Some factions within the community have been co-opted by extremist ideologies, leading to a skewed perception of Asatru as being inherently exclusionary or racist. This misunderstanding can deter potential practitioners who might otherwise find meaning and community within the faith. It is crucial for adherents to actively promote the core values of Asatru, which emphasize honor, integrity, and respect for all individuals, regardless of their background.

Finally, the challenges of navigating Asatru in a modern, often skeptical society cannot be understated. Practitioners may face scrutiny or ridicule, which can discourage open expression of their beliefs. This societal pressure can lead to feelings of isolation among followers, particularly those who practice Asatru in regions where it is less understood. Building a supportive community through networking and shared practices can help mitigate these feelings. By celebrating their traditions and fostering a sense of belonging, practitioners can create a resilient space that honors the old ways while adapting to contemporary life.

# Chapter 7: Nature Worship in Asatru

## The Connection Between Nature and Spirituality

The connection between nature and spirituality in Asatru is deeply rooted in the traditions and beliefs of our ancestors. As practitioners of this ancient faith, we honor the natural world as a manifestation of the divine. The elements—earth, air, fire, and water—are not merely physical substances but are imbued with spiritual significance. They serve as conduits through which we can connect with the gods, goddesses, and the spirit of the land itself. This connection fosters a profound respect for nature, encouraging us to engage with the environment in a way that reflects our values and beliefs.

In Asatru, nature is often seen as a living entity, filled with spirits and energies that can be felt and experienced. Each tree, river, and mountain holds its own unique essence, and many practitioners find solace and inspiration in the quiet beauty of the natural world. This perspective invites us to participate in a reciprocal relationship with our surroundings, where we not only draw strength and wisdom from nature but also offer our gratitude and respect in return. Rituals often incorporate natural elements, grounding our spiritual practices in the very landscape that nourishes and sustains us.

Seasonal festivals in Asatru provide an opportunity to celebrate the cycles of nature, aligning our spiritual practices with the rhythms of the earth. Events such as Yule, Ostara, and Midsummer are not only markers of the changing seasons but also times for reflection on the interconnectedness of all life. These celebrations often involve rituals that honor the spirits of the land and invoke the blessings of the gods, creating a sense of unity with the natural world. By participating in these observances, we reaffirm our commitment to living harmoniously with nature, recognizing its vital role in our spiritual journeys.

The historical reconstruction of Asatru has brought a resurgence of interest in nature worship among contemporary practitioners. By examining the practices of our ancestors, we can draw inspiration for our own rituals and celebrations. This exploration often leads to a deeper understanding of the sacredness of the earth and the need to protect it. Many Asatru practitioners today actively engage in environmental stewardship, recognizing that honoring the natural world is an essential aspect of our spiritual path. This commitment to sustainability and respect for nature reflects the ethical values central to Asatru.

Ultimately, the connection between nature and spirituality in Asatru is a powerful reminder of our place within the greater tapestry of existence. By embracing this connection, we cultivate a sense of belonging and purpose that transcends the individual self. As we honor the land and the spirits that dwell within it, we weave our personal stories into the rich narrative of our ancestors. In doing so, we not only celebrate our heritage but also forge a path toward a more sustainable and spiritually fulfilling future.

## Sacred Spaces and Natural Sites

Sacred spaces and natural sites play a pivotal role in the practice of Asatru, serving as physical manifestations of the spiritual beliefs that underpin this ancient faith. For practitioners, these sites are not merely locations; they are imbued with significance, acting as focal points for rituals, celebrations, and personal reflection. The reverence for natural elements—such as trees, rivers, mountains, and sacred groves—aligns seamlessly with the Asatru ethos, which emphasizes a deep connection to the earth and its cycles. Understanding the importance of these spaces is crucial for modern practitioners looking to deepen their spiritual practices and connect with their ancestors.

In historical contexts, sacred sites often served as places for communal gatherings and rituals, where Norse gods and goddesses were honored through offerings and celebrations. The remnants of ancient temples, burial mounds, and other archaeological sites continue to inspire contemporary Asatru practitioners to reclaim these traditions. Visiting these historical locations can provide a sense of continuity and belonging, as well as a tangible link to the values and practices of past generations. Modern practitioners may find themselves drawn to these sites, not only to honor their ancestors but to forge a personal connection with the divine.

Nature worship is deeply embedded in Asatru, reflecting a worldview that sees the divine in the natural world. This perspective encourages practitioners to cultivate relationships with local landscapes, recognizing the spirits that inhabit trees, rivers, and mountains. Many Asatru rituals incorporate elements of nature, such as using branches from sacred trees or collecting stones from a riverbed for altars. By honoring the natural world, practitioners reinforce their commitment to environmental stewardship, recognizing that the health of the earth is integral to their spiritual well-being.

For those new to Asatru, exploring sacred spaces and natural sites can serve as a gateway to understanding the broader principles of the faith. Engaging with these environments fosters a sense of respect and awe for the world around us, which is fundamental to Asatru ethics. Whether it is a solitary walk through a forest or a community gathering at a local hilltop, these experiences allow practitioners to embody the values of interconnectedness and reverence for all living things. This connection can enrich personal spirituality, providing a foundation for deeper exploration of Asatru rituals and beliefs.

The community aspect of Asatru is also enhanced by shared experiences in sacred spaces. Group rituals often take place in natural settings, creating a sense of unity among participants as they collectively honor the gods and the earth. Networking within the Asatru community can lead to the discovery of local sacred sites, allowing practitioners to come together for festivals and observances that celebrate their shared heritage. These gatherings not only revitalize ancient traditions but also foster a sense of belonging that is essential for the growth and sustainability of Asatru in modern society.

# Environmental Ethics in Asatru

Environmental ethics within Asatru reflect a deep-seated reverence for nature, rooted in the traditions and cosmology of Norse mythology. Asatru practitioners often view the natural world not merely as a backdrop for human activity but as a living entity imbued with spiritual significance. This perspective is informed by the belief in the interconnectedness of all beings, including the land, animals, and the elements, which are all considered to be manifestations of the divine. This holistic view fosters a sense of responsibility among practitioners to care for the environment and to honor the sacredness of the earth.

Central to the environmental ethics of Asatru is the concept of "övergång" or transition, which emphasizes the cycle of life, death, and rebirth. This principle encourages practitioners to recognize their role within these cycles, promoting sustainable practices that honor the earth's resources. Asatru encourages a mindful approach to consumption and resource management, advocating for practices that sustain the land and its ecosystems. From foraging to responsible land stewardship, these values highlight a commitment to living in harmony with nature rather than exploiting it.

Rituals and celebrations in Asatru often reflect this environmental consciousness. Seasonal festivals, such as the solstices and equinoxes, not only mark the passage of time but also serve as opportunities to honor the earth and its cycles. During these observances, practitioners may engage in activities that promote ecological awareness, such as planting trees or cleaning local natural spaces. Such practices reinforce the belief that reverence for nature should be an integral part of spiritual life, bridging the gap between the ritualistic and the everyday.

Asatru's historical roots also provide insight into its environmental ethics. The Norse peoples had a profound connection to their surroundings, often reflecting their understanding of the land in their mythology and daily lives. The reverence for deities associated with nature, such as Freyja and Njord, underscores the importance of respecting and protecting the natural world. By looking to these ancient traditions, modern practitioners can draw lessons on sustainability and environmental stewardship, creating a continuity of values that respects both heritage and the present-day ecological challenges.

In contemporary society, Asatru practitioners have the opportunity to engage in broader environmental movements, advocating for policies and practices that align with their values. By forming networks within the Asatru community, practitioners can collaborate on initiatives aimed at environmental conservation, education, and activism. This collective effort not only strengthens community bonds but also amplifies the message that reverence for the earth is a fundamental aspect of Asatru practice. In this way, environmental ethics within Asatru are not just a personal commitment but a communal responsibility, embodying the spirit of living in accordance with nature.

# Chapter 8: Historical Reconstruction of Asatru

## Sources and Research Methods

In the study of Asatru and its associated rituals and festivals, a diverse array of sources and research methods are essential for practitioners to gain a comprehensive understanding of these ancient traditions. Primary sources, such as the Eddas and Sagas, serve as foundational texts that provide insight into Norse mythology, cosmology, and the practices of early Germanic peoples. These literary works, while written in a different historical context, offer valuable information on deities, rituals, and the cultural significance of festivals. Additionally, archaeological findings, including artifacts and burial sites, play a crucial role in reconstructing the practices and beliefs of our ancestors, contributing to a more nuanced understanding of Asatru.

Secondary sources, including scholarly articles and books by historians and practitioners, complement primary texts by providing analysis and interpretation of the data. These works often synthesize current research and present different perspectives on the development and practice of Asatru in both historical and modern contexts. By engaging with these materials, practitioners can not only learn about the historical roots of their faith but also explore how these traditions have evolved and adapted over time. This engagement fosters a deeper connection to the rituals and celebrations that are central to Asatru practice today.

Field research is another vital method for understanding Asatru rituals and festivals. This approach involves participating in or observing gatherings, celebrations, and individual practices within the Asatru community. Through direct involvement, practitioners can experience the significance of these rituals firsthand, gaining insights that may not be captured in written sources. Networking with other Asatru practitioners allows for the exchange of ideas and practices, enriching one's understanding of how different groups interpret and implement Asatru traditions. Such firsthand experiences can reinforce a sense of community and shared spirituality among practitioners.

The integration of modern technology also enhances research methods within Asatru. Online forums, social media groups, and digital archives provide platforms for practitioners to share resources, discuss interpretations, and collaborate on research projects. This connectivity fosters an environment where individuals can learn from one another, regardless of geographic location. Moreover, the accessibility of online materials allows for a broader dissemination of knowledge, making it easier for beginners to engage with Asatru practices and history.

Finally, the ethical dimension of research in Asatru is paramount. Practitioners must approach sources with respect and integrity, acknowledging the cultural significance of the traditions they study. This includes being mindful of the diverse interpretations and practices within the Asatru community. As practitioners explore the historical and modern contexts of their faith, it is essential to appreciate the multiplicity of voices and experiences that contribute to the rich tapestry of Asatru. By employing a variety of research methods and maintaining an ethical approach, practitioners can celebrate the old ways with authenticity and reverence.

## Balancing Tradition and Modern Interpretation

Balancing tradition and modern interpretation in Asatru is essential for practitioners who seek to honor their ancestors while navigating contemporary life. This balance is not only about preserving the rituals and beliefs passed down through generations but also about adapting these practices to resonate with today's cultural and social landscapes. Asatru, rooted in Norse mythology and the values of the ancient Germanic peoples, offers a rich tapestry of traditions that can be explored and reinterpreted in a way that remains relevant for modern practitioners.

Traditionally, Asatru rituals were deeply tied to the natural cycles of the year, marked by seasonal festivals such as Yule and Midsummer. These celebrations honored the gods and goddesses, as well as the spirits of the land and ancestors. In today's fast-paced world, practitioners often find it challenging to engage with these traditions in their original form. Therefore, many have begun to incorporate modern elements that reflect contemporary values while still respecting the core tenets of Asatru. This can involve creating new rituals that emphasize community and personal spirituality, allowing practitioners to forge meaningful connections with each other and the divine.

The historical reconstruction of Asatru plays a critical role in this balancing act. Many practitioners delve into archaeological finds, texts, and folklore to better understand the traditions of their ancestors. However, strict adherence to historical accuracy can sometimes overshadow the personal significance of these practices. It is crucial for modern practitioners to remember that Asatru is not merely an academic pursuit; it is a living tradition that thrives through personal experience and expression. By weaving historical insights with contemporary interpretations, individuals can create a practice that is both rooted in the past and relevant to their lives today.

Nature worship is another vital aspect of Asatru that benefits from a balanced approach. The reverence for the natural world is a fundamental principle within the tradition, reflecting the beliefs of the Norse people who lived closely with their environments. In modern society, where urbanization and technological advancement often disconnect individuals from nature, Asatru practitioners can find ways to reestablish that connection. This may involve organizing community events that celebrate the changing seasons or participating in environmental stewardship projects that honor the land. Such activities not only align with traditional values but also respond to contemporary ecological concerns.

Ultimately, the journey of balancing tradition and modern interpretation in Asatru is deeply personal and varies from one practitioner to another. It requires a thoughtful engagement with both the past and the present, allowing for the evolution of practices that reflect current realities without losing sight of their historical roots. By fostering an open dialogue within the Asatru community about these themes, practitioners can support one another in crafting a vibrant, meaningful spiritual path that honors their heritage while embracing the future. This dynamic interplay between old and new ensures that Asatru remains a living tradition, vibrant and relevant for generations to come.

## The Role of Archaeology in Understanding Asatru

The role of archaeology in understanding Asatru is significant, as it provides tangible evidence of the beliefs, practices, and rituals of our ancestors. Through the study of ancient artifacts, burial sites, and sacred locations, archaeologists have uncovered essential insights into the spiritual lives of the Norse people. These findings help contemporary practitioners connect with their heritage, allowing for a deeper appreciation of the traditions that inform modern Asatru practices. By examining the material culture of the past, practitioners can draw parallels and inspirations for their rituals and celebrations today.

Archaeological discoveries, such as altars, stone circles, and household shrines, have illuminated the ways in which ancient Norse communities engaged with their gods and the natural world. These sites often reveal a rich tapestry of ritual activities, including offerings, feasting, and communal gatherings. By understanding the context in which these artifacts were used, practitioners can recreate similar experiences in their own celebrations, fostering a sense of continuity with the past. The study of these ancient practices not only enriches the spiritual lives of Asatru practitioners but also creates a shared historical narrative that strengthens community bonds.

Moreover, the examination of burial customs and grave goods offers profound insights into the beliefs surrounding death and the afterlife in Norse culture. The way our ancestors honored their dead speaks volumes about their values and ethics, highlighting the significance of honor, legacy, and remembrance. By integrating these insights into modern practices, Asatru practitioners can cultivate a more profound connection to their ancestry, ensuring that the lessons of the past influence their current spiritual journeys. This connection to history fosters a deeper understanding of the moral frameworks that guide Asatru ethics today.

Archaeology also plays a crucial role in the ongoing discussion of authenticity and reconstruction within Asatru. As practitioners strive to honor the traditions of their forebears, they often face the challenge of distinguishing between historical fact and modern interpretation. Archaeological evidence serves as a foundation for these discussions, providing a reference point for what practices may have looked like in the past. This evidence can help practitioners navigate the sometimes murky waters of reconstruction, allowing them to create rituals and celebrations that are both meaningful and respectful of their heritage.

In conclusion, the integration of archaeological insights into the practice of Asatru is invaluable for adult practitioners seeking to celebrate their spirituality authentically. By engaging with the physical remnants of the past, Asatru practitioners can deepen their understanding of their traditions, foster connections within their communities, and cultivate a more meaningful relationship with their spiritual path. As we continue to explore the ancient ways, the lessons drawn from archaeology remind us that our practices are not only rooted in history but are also living traditions that evolve and adapt to the needs of contemporary spiritual seekers.

# Chapter 9: Building Community and Networking

## Finding and Creating Local Groups

Finding and creating local groups within the Asatru community can greatly enhance the practice and understanding of this ancient faith. Asatru is not only a personal journey but also a collective experience that thrives on shared rituals, discussions, and celebrations. To begin this process, practitioners should first explore their local areas for existing groups. Online platforms, social media, and community forums can serve as valuable resources for discovering groups that align with one's values and interests. Participating in online discussions can also provide insights into the nature and practices of these groups, helping individuals assess whether a particular community resonates with their personal beliefs and goals.

When searching for local groups, it's important to consider the values and ethics that are central to Asatru. Different groups may interpret the traditions and teachings of Asatru in various ways, so understanding the foundational beliefs of each community is crucial. Look for groups that emphasize inclusivity, respect for nature, and a commitment to the ethical teachings of Asatru. Engaging in conversations with group members before attending a gathering can provide clarity on the group's approach to rituals, celebrations, and overall community dynamics. This preliminary research can help ensure a positive and enriching experience for all involved.

If existing groups do not meet your needs or if there are none in your area, consider creating your own. Start by gathering like-minded individuals who share an interest in Asatru, whether they are beginners or seasoned practitioners. Hosting informal meetings in public spaces can allow for the development of a supportive network where members can share knowledge, discuss rituals, and celebrate key festivals together. Establishing a clear purpose and set of values for your group will help attract individuals who resonate with your vision. As the group evolves, consider organizing activities that promote learning and connection, such as workshops on Norse mythology, nature-based rituals, or discussions on ethical practices within Asatru.

In creating a local group, it is also essential to foster a welcoming environment. Ensure that newcomers feel comfortable participating and sharing their thoughts, regardless of their level of experience. Incorporating a variety of perspectives can enrich discussions and deepen the collective understanding of Asatru. Regularly scheduled gatherings can help solidify the group, providing members with a sense of belonging and continuity. Encourage open dialogue about practices, beliefs, and personal experiences, as this can lead to deeper connections and a more robust community.

Lastly, consider the role of technology in enhancing local group dynamics. While in-person gatherings are invaluable, digital platforms can help maintain connections between meetings, facilitate discussions, and share resources. Creating a private online forum or group chat can allow for ongoing communication, where members can share insights, plan future events, and engage with a wider audience. This blend of local and digital interaction can help sustain interest and enthusiasm, making the journey through Asatru a shared and celebrated experience. By finding or creating local groups, practitioners not only enrich their own spiritual paths but also contribute to the broader Asatru community.

## Online Communities and Resources

Online communities and resources play a significant role in the modern practice of Asatru, providing a space for practitioners to connect, share, and learn from one another. These platforms often facilitate discussions that span a wide array of topics, including rituals, celebrations, folklore, and the nuances of Norse mythology. For adult Asatru practitioners, engaging with these online groups can enhance their understanding of traditional practices while also fostering a sense of belonging within a broader community. Social media platforms, forums, and dedicated websites have become invaluable tools for individuals to explore their spirituality and connect with others who share their interests.

One of the primary benefits of online communities is the accessibility they provide for beginners navigating their path in Asatru. Individuals who may feel isolated in their local environments can find support and guidance through these digital spaces. Many forums offer resources such as beginner guides, articles on rituals, and discussions about the ethical values inherent in Asatru. This knowledge-sharing aspect helps newcomers feel more confident in their practices and encourages them to engage with their spirituality more deeply. Additionally, many experienced practitioners contribute their insights, enriching the collective knowledge and helping to demystify complex aspects of the faith.

Asatru rituals and celebrations often vary widely between practitioners, influenced by personal preferences and regional customs. Online communities serve as a melting pot of ideas, where practitioners can exchange rituals they have created or adapted. This collaborative spirit fosters creativity and innovation, allowing members to experiment with new ways to honor the gods and the natural world. Furthermore, virtual gatherings and live-streamed ceremonies have emerged, enabling practitioners to participate in communal celebrations regardless of geographical distance. This accessibility not only enriches individual practices but also strengthens the bonds within the Asatru community.

Norse mythology is a cornerstone of Asatru, and online resources provide an expansive repository of information for practitioners seeking to deepen their understanding of the sagas and lore. Websites, podcasts, and video channels dedicated to Norse mythology can offer insights into the rich tapestry of gods, goddesses, and historical narratives that shape Asatru beliefs. Engaging with these resources allows practitioners to draw connections between ancient stories and their personal spiritual journeys, reinforcing the relevance of these myths in contemporary life. Moreover, online discussions often lead to deeper exploration of how these mythological elements can be integrated into modern rituals and celebrations.

The ethics and values central to Asatru, such as honor, respect for nature, and community, are often discussed in online forums. These conversations can help practitioners navigate the complexities of living out their faith in today's world. Ethos discussions also provide a platform for addressing contemporary issues, such as environmental stewardship and social justice, through the lens of Asatru principles. By engaging with these topics online, practitioners can cultivate a more informed and responsible practice that honors both the old ways and the needs of the present. Ultimately, the online landscape serves as a dynamic resource for adult Asatru practitioners, offering a space for growth, connection, and celebration of their shared heritage.

## Events, Gatherings, and Festivals

Events, gatherings, and festivals play a crucial role in the practice of Asatru, serving as opportunities for practitioners to come together, share experiences, and reinforce their commitment to the Old Ways. These occasions foster community bonds, allowing individuals to connect not only with one another but also with their ancestral traditions. Celebrations in Asatru are often tied to the cycles of nature, reflecting the importance of the changing seasons and the rhythms of the earth. By participating in these rituals, practitioners engage in a collective act of honoring the gods, goddesses, and the spirits of the land.

One of the most significant gatherings in Asatru is the blot, a sacrificial rite that pays homage to deities. During these ceremonies, offerings are made, which can include food, drink, or other gifts. This act of giving reinforces the reciprocal relationship between humans and the divine, emphasizing gratitude and respect. Blots are often held during major festivals such as Yule, which celebrates the winter solstice, and Midsummer, marking the height of summer. Each of these festivals has its own unique customs and practices, deeply rooted in Norse mythology and agricultural cycles, providing a framework for community and personal reflection.

In addition to blots, sumbels are another important aspect of Asatru gatherings. A sumbel is a ritual toasting ceremony that symbolizes unity and the sharing of blessings among participants. Attendees take turns making oaths, sharing personal goals, or honoring loved ones, often raising their horns or cups in a show of solidarity. This practice not only fosters a sense of belonging but also reinforces the ethical values of Asatru, such as honor, loyalty, and mutual support. Through these gatherings, practitioners can cultivate a sense of personal spirituality that aligns with their communal experience.

Seasonal festivals offer a chance to celebrate the changing aspects of nature, reflecting the interconnectedness of the Asatru practitioner's spiritual life with the earth. Events like Þorrablót in winter and Freyfaxi in autumn highlight the importance of agricultural cycles and the reverence for the land that sustains the community. These festivals often include traditional foods, music, and storytelling, creating a rich tapestry of cultural heritage. Engaging in these seasonal practices allows practitioners to deepen their connection to the natural world, reinforcing the concept of nature worship that is essential to Asatru.

Asatru events also provide opportunities for networking and community building, essential for individuals seeking to navigate their spiritual path in a modern context. Workshops, retreats, and local gatherings allow practitioners to share knowledge, experiences, and resources while fostering a sense of belonging within the wider Asatru community. By participating in these events, individuals can explore their beliefs, learn from one another, and strengthen their commitment to the Old Ways. Ultimately, the celebration of events, gatherings, and festivals in Asatru not only honors ancestral traditions but also nurtures a vibrant community that thrives on shared values and experiences

# Chapter 10: Ethics and Values in Asatru

## The Nine Noble Virtues

The Nine Noble Virtues serve as the ethical foundation for practitioners of Asatru, encapsulating the values that guide conduct and decision-making in daily life. Rooted in ancient Norse culture, these virtues provide a framework that emphasizes personal development and community responsibility. The virtues are: Courage, Truth, Honor, Fidelity, Discipline, Hospitality, Self-Reliance, Industriousness, and Perseverance. By embodying these principles, Asatru practitioners cultivate a lifestyle that honors both their heritage and the interconnectedness of all beings in nature.

Courage, the first of the Nine Noble Virtues, encourages individuals to face challenges with bravery and resilience. This virtue is not merely about physical bravery but also encompasses moral courage—the strength to stand up for one's beliefs and values in the face of adversity. In the context of Asatru, this involves not only confronting personal fears but also advocating for one's community and the environment. Practicing courage can manifest in various ways, from participating in community events to engaging in discussions about Asatru in wider societal contexts.

Truth is essential in Asatru, as it builds trust within the community and fosters genuine relationships. This virtue underscores the importance of honesty, not only in words but also in actions. Practitioners are encouraged to seek out knowledge and understanding, ensuring that their beliefs are informed and authentic. Upholding truth cultivates an environment where individuals can engage openly with one another, share experiences, and learn from both successes and failures, thereby strengthening community bonds.

Honor, as the third virtue, emphasizes the significance of reputation and integrity. In Norse culture, honor was closely tied to the concept of 'wyrd,' or fate, highlighting how one's actions can affect not only personal destiny but also that of future generations. Asatru practitioners strive to live honorably by keeping their word, respecting commitments, and showing loyalty to family and kin. This virtue also compels individuals to acknowledge and learn from the past, ensuring that their actions today contribute positively to their legacy and the community's collective memory.

The virtues of Fidelity and Discipline further reinforce the importance of loyalty and self-control in Asatru. Fidelity encompasses loyalty to family, friends, and the Asatru community, fostering a sense of belonging and mutual support. Discipline, on the other hand, encourages individuals to cultivate self-control, allowing them to pursue their goals with determination and focus. Together, these virtues promote a lifestyle that values commitment, whether to personal aspirations or to the well-being of the broader community, ultimately contributing to a more harmonious and interconnected existence.

Asatru practitioners are called to embody the remaining virtues of Hospitality, Self-Reliance, Industriousness, and Perseverance. Hospitality reflects the importance of community and generosity, inviting others into one's home and life. Self-Reliance emphasizes independence and personal responsibility, while Industriousness encourages hard work and dedication to one's craft. Finally, Perseverance embodies the spirit of resilience, urging individuals to remain steadfast in their pursuits despite obstacles. Together, these virtues provide a comprehensive ethical compass that guides practitioners in their spiritual journey and daily lives, fostering a rich and meaningful engagement with the world around them.

## Personal Responsibility and Honor

Personal responsibility and honor are foundational concepts within Asatru, deeply rooted in the traditions and values of Norse culture. In the context of Asatru, personal responsibility refers to the acknowledgment of one's actions and their consequences, both in the physical and spiritual realms. Each practitioner is encouraged to take ownership of their choices, fostering a sense of accountability that extends beyond the self and into the community. This creates a strong ethical framework that encourages individuals to act with integrity, ensuring that their behavior reflects both their beliefs and their commitment to the Asatru way of life.

Honor, closely tied to personal responsibility, is a guiding principle in interpersonal relationships and community interactions. In Norse society, honor was not merely a personal attribute but a societal expectation that influenced one's reputation and standing within the community. Asatru practitioners today are encouraged to uphold their honor through actions that demonstrate respect, loyalty, and trustworthiness. This commitment to honor not only enhances one's personal integrity but also strengthens the bonds within the Asatru community, fostering an environment where mutual respect and support can flourish.

The interplay between personal responsibility and honor can be seen in the practice of rituals and celebrations within Asatru. These rituals often serve as a means to reaffirm one's commitment to ethical living and community values. For instance, during seasonal festivals, practitioners may engage in acts of reflection and gratitude, acknowledging the interconnectedness of their actions and the impact they have on the world around them. This reinforces the idea that each individual's honor is tied to the collective well-being of the community, emphasizing that personal responsibilities are not isolated but rather part of a larger tapestry of shared values and traditions.

Moreover, the emphasis on personal responsibility and honor in Asatru encourages practitioners to embrace their roles as stewards of nature and culture. Asatru promotes a deep respect for the natural world, urging individuals to act in ways that honor the land and its resources. This stewardship is a direct reflection of one's personal responsibility, highlighting the importance of sustainability and ethical practices in daily life. By integrating these principles into their spirituality, practitioners can cultivate a profound connection to the earth and its rhythms, reinforcing both their personal and communal obligations to honor the traditions of their ancestors.

In a modern context, the principles of personal responsibility and honor in Asatru can help guide practitioners in navigating the complexities of contemporary life. As societal norms shift and evolve, maintaining a commitment to these values can provide a solid foundation for ethical decision-making. By actively engaging in practices that honor both personal and communal responsibilities, Asatru practitioners can foster a vibrant and supportive community that celebrates the old ways while adapting to the challenges of the present. This balance between tradition and modernity allows for a dynamic expression of Asatru, rooted in the timeless values of honor and responsibility.

## Asatru and Social Justice

Asatru, rooted in ancient Norse traditions and mythology, is not only a spiritual path but also a framework for ethical living that can resonate with modern social justice movements. Those who practice Asatru often find that its values encourage a deep sense of community, respect for the earth, and a commitment to personal and collective responsibility. These principles can be thoughtfully applied to contemporary issues of social justice, fostering a practice that is both relevant and impactful in today's society.

At the heart of Asatru is the concept of community, or "fellowship," which emphasizes the importance of individuals working together for the greater good. Many Asatru practitioners embrace the idea of "hearth" as a metaphor for both physical and social spaces where individuals come together to support one another. This sense of belonging and mutual aid can extend beyond the individual community, encouraging practitioners to engage with broader societal issues such as inequality, discrimination, and environmental degradation. By participating in social justice initiatives, Asatru practitioners can embody the values of their faith while contributing positively to the world around them.

Moreover, the ethical teachings found in Norse mythology often spotlight themes of loyalty, honor, and justice. Deities such as Tyr, known for his association with justice and sacrifice, serve as powerful symbols for standing up against wrongdoing. Asatru encourages adherents to embody these values in their daily lives, promoting a culture of accountability and respect for all individuals, regardless of their background or identity. This ethical framework can inspire practitioners to advocate for marginalized groups, ensuring that the principles of fairness and equality are upheld in both personal interactions and larger societal structures.

Nature worship, a significant aspect of Asatru, further intertwines with social justice by fostering a profound respect for the earth and its resources. As practitioners engage in rituals and celebrations that honor the natural world, they are reminded of their interconnectedness with all living beings. This awareness can motivate Asatru practitioners to address environmental injustices and advocate for sustainable practices that protect vulnerable communities disproportionately affected by ecological degradation. By integrating environmental stewardship into their spiritual practice, Asatru adherents can contribute to a more equitable and just society.

In conclusion, the intersection of Asatru and social justice offers a rich tapestry of opportunities for practitioners to engage meaningfully with both their faith and the world. By recognizing the potential for their spiritual beliefs to inform their actions in the realm of social justice, Asatru practitioners can foster a community that not only celebrates ancient traditions but also champions modern ideals of equity, respect, and environmental responsibility. The ongoing dialogue between Asatru practices and social justice not only enriches the spiritual experience but also empowers individuals to become agents of positive change in their communities.

# Chapter 11: Personal Spirituality in Asatru

## The Individual Journey

The concept of the individual journey in Asatru is an essential aspect that reflects the deeply personal nature of this spiritual path. Each practitioner embarks on a unique voyage shaped by their experiences, beliefs, and connections to the ancient Norse traditions. This journey is not merely about adopting rituals or celebrating festivals; it is about forging a relationship with the gods, ancestors, and the natural world. As practitioners delve into their individual paths, they often discover that their understanding of Asatru evolves, influenced by personal insights and the wisdom gleaned from historical texts and modern interpretations.

Central to the individual journey is the exploration of one's ancestry and heritage. For many Asatru practitioners, this involves researching family history and connecting with the cultural roots that resonate with Norse traditions. This exploration is often accompanied by a sense of responsibility to honor those who came before. By understanding ancestral ties, practitioners can cultivate a deeper sense of belonging within the broader Asatru community. This connection to the past serves as a foundation for personal spiritual growth, enabling individuals to navigate their paths with a greater appreciation for the values and ethics that underpin Asatru.

Asatru rituals and celebrations play a significant role in personal journeys, offering opportunities for individuals to express their spirituality. Whether it is a simple offering to a god, a formal blot, or a seasonal celebration like Yule or Midsummer, these acts of devotion create a space for reflection and gratitude. Through these rituals, practitioners often find a sense of empowerment, as they actively engage in the practices that resonate with their beliefs. The importance of community cannot be understated; however, the rituals undertaken alone can provide profound insights and a deeper connection to the divine.

Nature worship is another vital component of the individual journey within Asatru. The natural world holds great significance in Norse mythology, and practitioners are encouraged to foster a relationship with the land, trees, rivers, and animals. This connection can manifest in various ways, such as spending time outdoors, observing the changing seasons, or participating in nature-based rituals. Engaging with nature not only enhances spiritual practices but also reinforces the understanding of interconnectedness within the cosmos. Many practitioners find that their individual journey is enriched by a profound respect for the environment and a commitment to its preservation.

Ultimately, the individual journey in Asatru is about personal spirituality and the ongoing quest for meaning. Each practitioner must navigate their beliefs, ethics, and practices, drawing from both ancient wisdom and contemporary interpretations. This journey may include moments of doubt, joy, and discovery, all of which contribute to a richer understanding of oneself and one's place in the world. Embracing the diversity of individual experiences within the Asatru community fosters a vibrant tapestry of beliefs and practices, encouraging practitioners to celebrate their unique paths while remaining connected to the ancient traditions that inspire them.

## Meditation and Reflection Practices

Meditation and reflection practices hold a significant place in the spiritual journeys of Asatru practitioners, offering a means to connect deeply with the gods, ancestors, and the natural world. These practices allow individuals to cultivate a heightened sense of awareness and appreciation for the traditions that have been passed down through generations. By engaging in meditation and reflection, practitioners can create sacred spaces for contemplation, fostering a personal relationship with the divine and enhancing their understanding of Asatru's core values and teachings.

Incorporating meditation into Asatru practice can take various forms, from guided visualizations that explore the realms of Norse mythology to silent contemplation of the runes and their meanings. Practitioners may find solace in focusing on specific deities, seeking their guidance through introspection. This process not only strengthens one's connection to the gods but also encourages the integration of their wisdom into everyday life. Reflection practices can also include journaling about personal experiences and insights gained during meditation, allowing for a deeper exploration of the self and one's path within Asatru.

Nature plays an essential role in Asatru, and meditation practices often utilize the beauty and tranquility of the natural world. Practitioners are encouraged to find a quiet spot in a forest, by a river, or in their own garden to meditate. This connection to nature enhances one's ability to reflect on the cycles of life and the interconnectedness of all beings. By attuning to the rhythms of the earth, practitioners can cultivate a profound sense of gratitude and reverence for the land and its spirits, thereby reinforcing the importance of nature worship within Asatru.

Moreover, group meditation and reflection practices can foster a sense of community among Asatru practitioners. Gathering with others to meditate or share reflections on personal experiences creates bonds that strengthen the network of support within the Asatru community. These shared practices can also lead to collective insights, enriching the understanding of Asatru traditions and facilitating discussions around ethics, values, and personal spirituality. By engaging in communal practices, practitioners contribute to the historical reconstruction of Asatru, ensuring that these sacred rituals are not lost to time.

In modern society, where distractions and fast-paced living can overshadow spiritual practices, meditation and reflection serve as essential tools for grounding oneself in Asatru. They provide a sanctuary for individuals to reconnect with their roots, explore their beliefs, and nurture their personal spirituality. As practitioners embrace these practices, they honor the old ways while adapting them to contemporary life, ensuring that the spirit of Asatru remains vibrant and relevant. Ultimately, meditation and reflection practices are invaluable for cultivating a deeper understanding of oneself and one's place in the world, reinforcing the bonds between the past, present, and future within the Asatru tradition.

# Connecting with Deities and Ancestors

Connecting with deities and ancestors is a core aspect of Asatru practice that enriches spiritual life and fosters a deep sense of community. In Asatru, deities such as Odin, Thor, and Freyja are not distant figures but present forces that can influence our lives and provide guidance. Establishing a connection with these gods involves both understanding their myths and engaging in rituals that invite their presence. Practitioners often create altars adorned with offerings that honor these deities, incorporating symbols that resonate with their attributes. This tangible expression of reverence serves as a focal point for personal devotion and communal celebration.

Equally important is the connection with ancestors, who are viewed as guiding spirits in Asatru. Recognizing and honoring one's lineage establishes a profound link to the past, allowing practitioners to draw strength and wisdom from those who came before. Ancestor veneration can take many forms, including the creation of a memory altar, where photographs and mementos serve as reminders of family heritage. Rituals such as sumbel, a traditional toasting ceremony, provide opportunities to acknowledge ancestors, share stories, and invite their presence into the gathering. Through these practices, practitioners reinforce the idea that the past is a living part of the present.

Cultivating a personal relationship with deities and ancestors often involves individual contemplation and community ritual. Meditation, prayer, and offerings allow practitioners to develop a deeper understanding of the divine and the roles these figures play in their lives. This personal connection can be enhanced by studying the lore associated with each deity, allowing practitioners to align their intentions with the characteristics and stories of the gods. Likewise, sharing experiences and insights within the Asatru community fosters a collective sense of purpose and belonging, reinforcing the shared values and ethics that bind practitioners together.

Nature plays a significant role in connecting with both deities and ancestors in Asatru. The belief that the natural world is imbued with spiritual significance encourages practitioners to engage with the environment during rituals. Seasonal celebrations, such as Yule and Midsummer, not only honor the cycles of nature but also serve as times to invoke the favor of the gods and pay homage to ancestors. By aligning rituals with the rhythms of the earth, practitioners can experience a greater sense of interconnectedness, deepening their spiritual practice and fostering respect for the natural world.

Ultimately, connecting with deities and ancestors in Asatru is a dynamic and evolving process. As practitioners navigate their spiritual journeys, they may find that their relationships with these spiritual beings shift and grow. Embracing this fluidity allows for a more authentic practice, one that honors tradition while accommodating personal experiences and insights. Through ongoing engagement with the divine and the ancestral realm, Asatru practitioners cultivate a rich spiritual tapestry that informs their daily lives, strengthens community ties, and honors the legacy of their forebears.

# Chapter 12: Asatru in Popular Culture

## Representation in Literature and Media

Representation in literature and media has played a significant role in shaping the perceptions and understanding of Asatru and its associated practices. As the resurgence of interest in Norse mythology and pre-Christian traditions grows, it is crucial to examine how these representations influence both practitioners and the broader public. In recent years, various forms of media, from novels to television series, have attempted to depict the rich tapestry of Norse mythology, often blending historical accuracy with creative interpretations. This interplay can lead to a deeper appreciation of Asatru's values and ethics, but it can also misrepresent essential aspects of the faith.

Literature serves as a powerful medium for exploring the complexities of Asatru, allowing writers to delve into themes of nature worship, community, and personal spirituality. Many contemporary authors draw from historical texts and sagas, weaving narratives that honor the traditions while making them accessible to modern readers. These works can act as gateways for beginners seeking to understand Asatru's core principles. However, it is essential for practitioners to critically engage with these stories, discerning which elements resonate with their personal beliefs and practices and which may stray from authentic representation.

In the realm of popular culture, films and television shows often romanticize or oversimplify Norse mythology, leading to a dilution of its significance. While these portrayals can ignite interest and curiosity, they may also perpetuate stereotypes or misconceptions about Asatru. For instance, characters depicted as one-dimensional warriors or mystical beings may overshadow the depth and diversity of the faith. It is vital for Asatru practitioners to articulate their experiences and beliefs, providing a counter-narrative that emphasizes the richness of their traditions and the ethical values that guide their practices.

The digital age has further transformed representation, as social media platforms allow practitioners to share their rituals, celebrations, and personal journeys directly with a global audience. This democratization of content creation enables community building and networking, fostering a sense of belonging among Asatru practitioners. Through blogs, podcasts, and online forums, individuals can explore Asatru's historical reconstruction and its application in modern society. This grassroots representation not only bolsters the community but also serves as an educational tool for those interested in learning about Asatru.

Ultimately, the representation of Asatru in literature and media can significantly impact how the faith is perceived and practiced. As adult practitioners, it is important to engage with these representations critically, celebrating authentic portrayals while challenging those that misrepresent the traditions. By amplifying their voices and sharing their experiences, Asatru practitioners can contribute to a more nuanced understanding of their beliefs, ensuring that the old ways are honored and accurately reflected in contemporary discourse.

# Influence on Modern Paganism

Modern Paganism, particularly Asatru, has been shaped by a confluence of historical tradition and contemporary reinterpretation. The revival of ancient Norse beliefs and practices has sparked a vibrant community that integrates old-world spirituality with modern values and lifestyles. This revitalization is not merely a return to the past; it is a dynamic adaptation that resonates with the lives of contemporary practitioners. Asatru today is marked by a diverse array of rituals and celebrations that reflect both individual beliefs and communal identity, fostering a sense of belonging among its adherents.

One significant influence on modern Asatru is the growing emphasis on personal spirituality. Many practitioners are drawn to the tradition for its focus on individual experience and connection to the divine. This personal approach encourages practitioners to engage with the gods, ancestors, and nature in ways that are meaningful to them. Rituals may be adapted or created anew, allowing for a personal expression of faith that honors the essence of Norse mythology while reflecting contemporary values. This flexibility supports the idea that spirituality can be both a personal journey and a shared experience within the community.

The relationship between Asatru and nature worship is another crucial aspect of its modern expression. Rooted in ancient practices that revered the natural world, contemporary Asatru emphasizes environmental stewardship and the sacredness of the earth. Rituals often incorporate elements of the natural world, such as seasonal celebrations that align with the cycles of nature. These practices not only honor the gods and goddesses associated with the earth and its elements but also foster a deeper connection to the environment, encouraging practitioners to respect and protect the planet in their daily lives.

Community plays a vital role in the practice of Asatru, with networking and shared celebrations strengthening bonds among practitioners. Modern technology has facilitated the formation of online communities, allowing individuals from diverse backgrounds to connect, share resources, and participate in rituals together, regardless of geographical limitations. These networks have become invaluable for newcomers seeking guidance and support, as well as for seasoned practitioners looking to deepen their understanding of the tradition. The communal aspect of Asatru fosters a sense of unity and collective identity, reinforcing shared values and ethics that are central to the practice.

Lastly, the influence of popular culture cannot be overlooked in the shaping of modern Asatru. The portrayal of Norse mythology in literature, film, and gaming has sparked interest in ancient practices and beliefs, drawing new followers to the tradition. While some representations may stray from historical accuracy, they often ignite curiosity and discussion about the rich tapestry of Norse lore and its relevance today. This cultural engagement serves as a bridge for individuals exploring Asatru, providing a familiar entry point into a deeper understanding of its rituals, values, and community, thereby ensuring the tradition remains vibrant and accessible in a rapidly changing world.

# The Future of Asatru in Contemporary Society

The future of Asatru in contemporary society appears promising, as the revival of interest in ancient traditions continues to gain momentum. As the world becomes increasingly disconnected from nature and historical roots, many individuals seek solace and meaning in the rich tapestry of Norse mythology and the values espoused by Asatru. This resurgence reflects a broader cultural trend where people yearn for authenticity and community, and Asatru offers both through its rituals, celebrations, and ethical frameworks. The integration of these ancient practices into modern life provides a pathway for personal spirituality that resonates deeply with many practitioners.

Asatru's emphasis on nature worship aligns closely with the growing environmental consciousness of today's society. Practitioners often find inspiration in the natural world, viewing it as a manifestation of the divine. This connection fosters a sense of responsibility toward the environment, leading to initiatives that promote sustainability and ecological preservation. By incorporating rituals that honor the earth and its cycles, Asatru offers a framework for addressing contemporary environmental issues, encouraging practitioners to actively engage with and protect the world around them.

Moreover, the historical reconstruction of Asatru plays a significant role in its future. As practitioners delve into historical texts and archaeological findings, they strive to create a practice that is both authentic and relevant to contemporary life. This ongoing research not only enriches the community's understanding of its roots but also allows for the adaptation of rituals and values that resonate with modern sensibilities. Asatru's flexible nature encourages innovation while maintaining a respect for tradition, enabling practitioners to forge a path that honors both the past and the present.

Community and networking are essential components of Asatru that contribute to its future growth. The establishment of local kindreds and online platforms fosters connections among practitioners, facilitating the sharing of ideas, resources, and experiences. This sense of belonging is crucial for individuals seeking to explore their spirituality in a supportive environment. As the Asatru community expands, it also becomes increasingly diverse, bringing together individuals from various backgrounds and perspectives. This inclusivity enriches the practice and opens up new avenues for collaboration and understanding within the community.

In popular culture, Asatru is gradually gaining visibility, which further shapes its future. Representations in literature, film, and art create opportunities for dialogue and education about Norse mythology and Asatru practices. As more people become aware of these traditions, there is potential for a more profound appreciation of their values and ethics. This cultural integration not only helps to demystify Asatru but also invites new practitioners into the fold, ensuring that the old ways are celebrated and adapted for future generations. By embracing both the ancient and the contemporary, Asatru stands poised to thrive in the modern world.

# Chapter 13: Conclusion

## The Ongoing Journey of Asatru

The ongoing journey of Asatru is marked by a continuous engagement with its ancient roots while adapting to the modern world. Practitioners today find themselves in a unique position, where they can draw from the rich tapestry of Norse mythology, traditional practices, and contemporary values. This duality creates a dynamic landscape for Asatru, where rituals and celebrations are not merely reenactments of the past but are infused with personal significance and relevance in today's society. As followers explore their spirituality, they are often faced with the challenge of balancing historical authenticity with the evolving needs of their communities.

Understanding Asatru requires an appreciation of its historical context. The revival of Asatru in the 20th century was fueled by a growing interest in pre-Christian traditions and a desire to reconnect with ancestral roots. This revival has seen practitioners engaging in historical reconstruction, aligning their practices with what is known about ancient Norse customs, while also acknowledging the gaps in historical knowledge. This approach fosters a sense of continuity, honoring the traditions of the past while recognizing that Asatru is not a static belief system but one that thrives through adaptation and reinterpretation.

Asatru rituals and celebrations serve as focal points for community bonding and personal spirituality. Events such as blóts and sumbels are not only opportunities to honor the gods, ancestors, and nature but also occasions for practitioners to come together, share experiences, and forge connections. These gatherings often blend traditional elements with contemporary practices. The integration of modern ethical considerations, such as inclusivity and environmental stewardship, reflects a conscious effort to create a vibrant and relevant Asatru community that resonates with the values of today's practitioners.

The relationship between Asatru and nature worship is another essential aspect of this ongoing journey. For many practitioners, nature is not just a backdrop for rituals but an integral part of their spiritual practice. The reverence for the natural world, as embodied by deities such as Njord and Freyja, encourages a deeper connection with the environment. This relationship promotes a philosophy of stewardship, urging practitioners to engage with and protect the earth. In this way, Asatru practitioners contribute to broader ecological movements, demonstrating that ancient beliefs can inform modern actions in meaningful ways.

Asatru is also increasingly finding its place in popular culture, which presents both challenges and opportunities. The portrayal of Norse mythology in literature, film, and art can spark interest and curiosity, drawing new practitioners into the fold. However, it also necessitates a critical examination of how these representations align with authentic Asatru practices and values. As practitioners navigate the complexities of modern influence, they are tasked with ensuring that their expressions of faith remain true to their spiritual and ethical foundations. This ongoing journey invites both reflection and action, as Asatru continues to evolve in a world that is constantly changing.

## Embracing the Old Ways in a Modern World

In today's fast-paced and technology-driven world, the relevance of ancient traditions can sometimes feel overshadowed. However, for practitioners of Asatru, embracing the old ways is not merely a nostalgic inclination but a vital part of personal and communal identity. The rituals and festivals that have been passed down through generations serve as a bridge connecting modern practitioners with their ancestors, reinforcing a sense of belonging and continuity. By engaging in these ancient customs, Asatru practitioners can create a space where the wisdom of the past informs their approach to the challenges of contemporary life.

The practice of Asatru emphasizes a deep connection with nature, an aspect that is often lost in modern society. Festivals like Yule and Blot are not just celebrations but opportunities to honor the cycles of nature, fostering a reverence for the earth and its rhythms. As practitioners gather to celebrate these seasonal events, they reaffirm their commitment to living in harmony with the natural world. This alignment with nature encourages mindfulness and an appreciation for the environment, which is crucial as contemporary issues such as climate change become increasingly pressing.

Incorporating old ways into modern life also promotes a sense of ethical responsibility. The values embedded in Asatru, such as honor, truth, and courage, provide a moral framework that is particularly relevant in today's world. Practitioners are called to reflect on these principles in their daily lives, making decisions that honor their heritage while addressing contemporary ethical dilemmas. By actively engaging with these values, Asatru practitioners can contribute positively to their communities, fostering connections and encouraging a culture of respect and understanding.

Community is a cornerstone of Asatru practice, and embracing the old ways can strengthen bonds among practitioners. Networking within the Asatru community allows individuals to share experiences, celebrate together, and support one another in their spiritual journeys. Events like sumbels and blot ceremonies not only honor the gods and ancestors but also reinforce social ties among participants. In a world where isolation is common, these gatherings are vital for fostering a sense of belonging and collective identity, as they echo the communal practices of our forebears.

Finally, the celebration of old ways in a modern context can also enhance personal spirituality. By engaging with ancient rituals, practitioners are invited to explore their own beliefs and experiences deeply. This exploration often leads to a greater understanding of self and a more profound connection with the divine. The stories, symbols, and practices of Norse mythology resonate on a personal level, enabling individuals to find meaning and purpose in their lives. Embracing these traditions not only honors the past but also enriches the spiritual journey of each practitioner, allowing them to weave the wisdom of the ancients into their modern existence.

# Resources for Further Exploration

For practitioners of Asatru seeking a deeper understanding of their faith and traditions, a wealth of resources is available to enhance knowledge and practice. Books dedicated to Norse mythology, ancient texts, and modern interpretations provide a foundation for both beginners and seasoned practitioners. Essential texts such as the Poetic Edda and the Prose Edda offer insights into the lore and deities of the Norse pantheon. Additionally, contemporary authors like Diana Paxson and Hilda Roderick Ellis Davidson provide accessible interpretations that bridge ancient wisdom with modern practice, making these texts invaluable for personal study and reflection.

Online platforms and forums serve as vital spaces for Asatru practitioners to connect, share knowledge, and engage in meaningful discussions. Websites dedicated to Asatru offer articles, podcasts, and videos that cover a wide range of topics, from ritual practices to ethical considerations within the community. Social media groups and online forums provide supportive environments for practitioners to ask questions, share experiences, and explore the diverse expressions of Asatru. Engaging with these communities can foster a sense of belonging and encourage the exchange of ideas and resources.

Workshops and local gatherings play a crucial role in the experiential aspect of Asatru. Many regions host events that focus on rituals, seasonal celebrations, and educational sessions about Norse mythology and historical practices. Attending these gatherings allows practitioners to participate in communal worship, learn from experienced leaders, and connect with like-minded individuals. Additionally, these events often provide opportunities to explore nature, which is a central element of Asatru, reinforcing the relationship between the practitioner and the natural world.

For those interested in the ethical dimensions of Asatru, numerous resources delve into the principles that guide practitioners. Texts exploring Norse ethics and values can illuminate how these ancient teachings apply to modern life, addressing topics such as honor, hospitality, and the importance of community. Asatru practitioners can also find organizations that emphasize ethical practices and community service, promoting engagement with broader societal issues while staying true to their values.

Finally, the intersection of Asatru and popular culture can be an intriguing area for exploration. Numerous films, television shows, and literature draw inspiration from Norse mythology, often sparking interest in the actual practices and beliefs of Asatru. Engaging with these cultural representations can lead to critical discussions about authenticity, representation, and the ways in which ancient traditions evolve in contemporary society. By exploring these varied resources, practitioners can deepen their understanding of Asatru and enrich their spiritual journeys.

# Wisdom of the North: Unraveling the Havamal's Teachings

## Chapter 1: Understanding the Havamal

### Origins and Transmission

The origins of the Havamal trace back to the oral traditions of the Norse peoples, where wisdom and knowledge were transmitted through generations. This collection of verses, often attributed to Odin, encompasses a variety of themes, including ethics, social conduct, and practical wisdom. Scholars believe the Havamal was compiled during the late Viking Age, drawing from earlier oral traditions and possibly influenced by Christian texts. It serves as a valuable source for understanding the moral framework and social dynamics of Norse culture, reflecting the values held by the society that produced it.

Transmission of the Havamal occurred through a combination of oral recitation and later written manuscripts. As with many ancient texts, the oral tradition played a crucial role in preserving the Havamal's teachings before they were committed to writing in the 13th century. The most notable manuscript, the Codex Regius, provides insight into its reception and adaptation over time. This transmission process highlights the interplay between cultural practices and the preservation of knowledge, emphasizing how the Havamal has evolved while maintaining its core philosophical principles.

The Havamal's influence on Norse mythology and culture is profound, as its verses encapsulate the ethos of a society deeply connected to nature, honor, and community. The text provides guidance on various aspects of life, from the importance of hospitality to the nature of wisdom and the value of friendships. These teachings resonate within Norse mythology, where characters often embody the virtues extolled in the Havamal. The interplay between the text and mythological narratives illustrates how the Havamal served not only as a moral compass but also as a cultural artifact that shaped the identity of the Norse people.

In contemporary life, the teachings of the Havamal find practical applications that extend beyond historical context. Modern readers can draw on its insights to navigate personal relationships, ethical dilemmas, and social responsibilities. The verses encourage introspection and foster a sense of community, urging individuals to cultivate meaningful connections and act with integrity. As contemporary society grapples with issues of isolation and disconnection, the Havamal's wisdom provides a timeless framework for building healthy relationships and fostering resilience.

Comparative analysis of the Havamal with other ancient texts reveals both unique qualities and shared themes, enriching our understanding of its place in the broader tapestry of wisdom literature. The ethical and moral lessons found in the Havamal resonate with teachings from other cultures, including those of the Bible, the Tao Te Ching, and various philosophical works. By exploring these connections, readers can appreciate the universal nature of its insights and the ways in which the Havamal contributes to our understanding of human experiences and relationships across time and cultures.

## Structure and Composition

The structure and composition of the Havamal reveal the intricate design of this ancient text, which serves both as a poetic anthology and a guide to ethical living. The Havamal is traditionally divided into several sections, with the most prominent being the "Words of the High One," which contains wisdom attributed to Odin himself. This structuring highlights the importance of the teachings, presenting them as divine insights meant to guide individuals in their daily lives. The verses are often succinct and aphoristic, embodying a blend of poetic beauty and practical advice that resonates across generations.

Each stanza of the Havamal is characterized by its use of alliteration and parallelism, elements commonly found in Old Norse poetry. This stylistic choice enhances the memorability of the verses, allowing them to be easily recited and transmitted orally. The rhythmic quality of the poetry invites reflection and contemplation, encouraging readers to ponder the deeper meanings behind the seemingly simple advice. The use of metaphor and imagery throughout the text also enriches the reader's understanding, as the wisdom is often cloaked in vivid representations of nature and human experience.

The composition of the Havamal reflects a blend of cultural influences, drawing from both pre-Christian and early Christian ideologies. This interplay underscores the text's role within the Norse tradition as a repository of communal values and beliefs. The ethical teachings often align with universal themes found in other ancient texts, such as the importance of friendship, hospitality, and the pursuit of wisdom. Such comparisons highlight the shared human experience across cultures, revealing both the uniqueness of the Havamal and its commonalities with global philosophical traditions.

Moreover, the Havamal's structure allows for a rich exploration of themes such as social relationships and morality. The text emphasizes the significance of loyalty, trust, and the mutual responsibilities inherent in friendships. These teachings remain relevant today, offering insights into the dynamics of modern relationships and the importance of community. As readers engage with the verses, they can draw parallels to contemporary life, applying the lessons of the Havamal to navigate their own social interactions and ethical dilemmas.

In conclusion, the structure and composition of the Havamal are integral to its enduring impact and relevance. Through its poetic form and carefully crafted verses, the text communicates profound wisdom that transcends time and cultural boundaries. The Havamal serves not only as a historical document but also as a living guide, inviting individuals to reflect on their own lives and the values they uphold. As such, it continues to inspire and inform, encouraging a deeper understanding of both personal and collective ethical frameworks.

## Key Themes and Concepts

The Havamal, an essential text in the Norse literary canon, encompasses a range of key themes and concepts that mirror the values and beliefs of ancient Scandinavian society. At its core, the Havamal conveys lessons on wisdom, ethics, and the complexities of human relationships. It serves as a guide not only for personal conduct but also for navigating the social fabric of life. The text emphasizes the importance of discretion, foresight, and the value of counsel, highlighting how wisdom is not merely the accumulation of knowledge but the application of that knowledge in practical situations.

Historical context plays a vital role in understanding the Havamal's teachings. Emerging from a time when oral traditions were paramount, the Havamal encapsulates the worldview of the Norse people, blending mythological elements with everyday life. Its verses reflect the harsh realities of the Viking Age, where survival depended on cooperation, honor, and a deep understanding of human nature. This historical backdrop enriches the interpretation of its poetry, as the text resonates with the struggles and aspirations of a society that valued strength, loyalty, and the wisdom gleaned from experience.

The influence of the Havamal extends beyond its immediate cultural context into Norse mythology and broader Scandinavian folklore. Many of its themes are echoed in various myths, where the pursuit of wisdom and the consequences of folly are central narratives. The Havamal's reflections on the nature of gods, heroes, and the moral dilemmas faced by individuals provide insight into the values that shaped Norse identity. This intertextual relationship invites a comparative analysis with other ancient texts, revealing shared human concerns across cultures regarding morality, social order, and the quest for meaning.

In contemporary life, the practical applications of the Havamal's teachings are increasingly relevant. The text encourages readers to cultivate virtues such as patience, humility, and resilience—qualities that resonate in modern discussions about personal development and mental health. Furthermore, the Havamal's insights into friendship and social relationships emphasize the importance of trust, reciprocity, and the strength found in community. Such lessons encourage individuals to forge meaningful connections, fostering a sense of belonging in an increasingly fragmented world.

The psychological insights drawn from the Havamal's wisdom offer a profound understanding of human behavior and relationships. The text delves into the intricacies of social dynamics, warning against deceit and emphasizing the importance of authenticity. Its ethical and moral lessons challenge readers to reflect on their own values, urging a commitment to honesty and integrity. Through symbolism and imagery, the Havamal not only articulates the human experience but also provides a framework for navigating the complexities of life, making it a timeless source of guidance for individuals seeking wisdom in their own journeys.

# Chapter 2: Historical Context of the Havamal

## The Viking Age and Its Influence

The Viking Age, spanning from the late 8th century to the early 11th century, marked a significant period of exploration, trade, and cultural exchange across Europe and beyond. This era not only reshaped the geographical landscape of the continent but also influenced the spiritual and philosophical frameworks of the societies involved. The Havamal, a collection of Old Norse poems attributed to the god Odin, emerged from this dynamic backdrop, reflecting the values and wisdom of the Norse people while simultaneously drawing upon the cultural exchanges that characterized the Viking Age.

During the Viking Age, Norse society was deeply intertwined with maritime activities, leading to encounters with various cultures. These interactions contributed to a rich tapestry of ideas, merging the distinct philosophies of the Norse with those of the Celtic and Christian traditions they encountered. The Havamal encapsulates this synthesis, offering insights into the ethical and moral lessons that were vital for navigating relationships and social hierarchies in a rapidly changing world. It serves as a testament to how cultural exchanges can inform and enhance traditional wisdom.

The poetry of the Havamal is marked by its practical insights into human relationships, particularly regarding friendship, loyalty, and the importance of wise counsel. These themes resonate with the values upheld during the Viking Age, where social bonds were essential for survival and success. The teachings found within the Havamal emphasize the significance of fostering strong connections and the role of wisdom in guiding one's actions, reflecting the collective consciousness of a society that valued interdependence.

In examining the Havamal alongside other ancient texts, one can identify both unique and shared themes that reveal universal human concerns. The ethical lessons found in the Havamal resonate with those in texts such as the Tao Te Ching and the Analects of Confucius, suggesting a common exploration of virtue and morality. This comparative analysis highlights the timeless nature of the wisdom contained within the Havamal, affirming its relevance not only in the context of Norse mythology but also in broader philosophical discussions.

The influence of the Havamal continues to be felt in contemporary pagan practices and modern interpretations of ancient wisdom. Its teachings offer psychological insights into the complexities of human interactions, encouraging individuals to reflect on their relationships and ethical choices. The Havamal's enduring legacy lies in its ability to provide guidance that transcends time, offering practical applications for navigating the challenges of modern life while remaining rooted in the rich historical context of the Viking Age.

## The Role of Oral Tradition

The role of oral tradition in the transmission of the Havamal is fundamental to understanding its teachings and cultural significance. Before the advent of written texts, oral tradition served as the primary means of sharing knowledge, values, and narratives among the Norse people. The Havamal, a collection of wisdom poetry attributed to the god Odin, was likely recited and memorized in communal settings, allowing its lessons to penetrate the fabric of daily life. This oral transmission ensured that the teachings were not only preserved but also adapted to the changing contexts of society, reflecting the evolving moral and ethical landscapes of the time.

Oral tradition also played a crucial role in the formation of the Havamal's poetic structure. The use of alliteration, rhythm, and repetition made the verses easier to memorize and recite, which was essential for preserving the content in a largely illiterate society. The poetic devices employed in the Havamal not only enhanced its memorability but also added layers of meaning, inviting listeners to engage with the text on multiple levels. Each recitation could evoke different interpretations based on the audience's experiences, thus allowing the wisdom of the Havamal to resonate deeply within the community.

Furthermore, the communal aspect of oral tradition contributed to the Havamal's role in shaping social relationships and cultural norms. As people gathered to hear the verses, they not only absorbed the teachings but also participated in a collective ritual that reinforced shared values. The moral lessons contained within the Havamal, such as the importance of hospitality, friendship, and wisdom, were disseminated through these gatherings, fostering a sense of unity and identity among the Norse people. This communal reinforcement would have been vital in maintaining social cohesion in a society that faced numerous external challenges.

As the Havamal transitioned from oral to written form, the essence of its teachings remained rooted in the traditions of storytelling and communal sharing. The written texts, while providing a more permanent record, could not replicate the dynamic interplay of audience and reciter that characterized oral performances. Nevertheless, they served to preserve the wisdom for future generations, allowing scholars and practitioners to explore its significance in both historical and contemporary contexts. The enduring popularity of the Havamal in modern pagan practices and its influence on contemporary ethical discussions underscore the importance of its oral origins.

In analyzing the role of oral tradition in the Havamal, one must also consider its impact on the psychological insights derived from its verses. The act of sharing wisdom orally fosters a sense of connection between the speaker and the listener, creating an intimate space for reflection and personal growth. As individuals engage with the teachings, they are encouraged to internalize the wisdom of the Havamal and apply it to their own lives. This process highlights the transformative power of oral tradition, not only in preserving cultural heritage but also in promoting individual and communal well-being through the timeless teachings of the past.

# The Havamal in Historical Records

The Havamal, often translated as "The Words of the High One," is a collection of Old Norse verses that has been preserved through various historical records. Its origins can be traced back to the Viking Age, when oral tradition played a crucial role in the transmission of knowledge. The Havamal is not merely a standalone text; it exists within a broader context of Norse literature and mythology. Manuscripts such as the Codex Regius and the Flateyjarbók are critical in understanding how the Havamal was compiled and transmitted through generations. These historical records highlight the significance of the Havamal in shaping the moral and ethical framework of Norse society.

The Havamal's teachings revolve around themes such as wisdom, friendship, and the importance of social relationships, which resonate with the values held by the Norse people. Its verses often serve as practical advice for daily life, offering insights into human behavior and the complexities of interpersonal relationships. Historical context reveals that the Havamal was not just a philosophical text but a practical guide that informed social conduct and decision-making. The wisdom encapsulated in its lines suggests a deep understanding of human psychology and the social dynamics of the time, making it relevant to both ancient and modern audiences.

The influence of the Havamal on Norse mythology and culture cannot be overstated. It reflects the values of the Norse pantheon and provides a lens through which we can understand the ethical and moral code of the time. The Havamal's verses are interwoven with references to gods and mythological figures, illustrating how these teachings were integral to the cultural identity of the Norse people. The text not only served as a source of wisdom but also reinforced the societal norms and values that underpinned Norse mythology, offering a glimpse into the worldview of those who revered these teachings.

In contemporary times, the Havamal continues to inspire various pagan practices and spiritual paths. Its teachings promote mindfulness, ethical behavior, and the cultivation of meaningful relationships, making them applicable to modern life. As individuals seek guidance on navigating the complexities of contemporary society, the Havamal provides timeless wisdom that can be adapted to current challenges. The principles found within its verses encourage self-reflection and personal growth, aligning with modern psychological insights that emphasize the importance of social bonds and ethical living.

Comparative analysis with other ancient texts reveals that the Havamal shares commonalities with philosophical traditions from around the world. The ethical lessons found within the Havamal resonate with those in texts such as the Tao Te Ching and the Analects of Confucius, highlighting universal themes of wisdom and morality. This cross-cultural exploration not only enriches our understanding of the Havamal but also emphasizes its relevance in the broader tapestry of human thought. By examining the Havamal alongside other ancient writings, we can appreciate the depth and complexity of its teachings, affirming its place as a significant work of wisdom in both historical and contemporary contexts.

# Chapter 3: Interpretation of Havamal's Poetry and Verses

## Literary Analysis Techniques

Literary analysis techniques serve as essential tools for dissecting and understanding the complex layers of meaning within the Havamal. By applying various methods of literary critique, readers can unveil the intricate interplay of themes, symbols, and structures that characterize this ancient text. Close reading encourages a detailed examination of individual verses, allowing for a deeper appreciation of the language and poetic devices employed by the authors. This technique reveals how the choice of words and the rhythm of the verses contribute to the overarching messages of wisdom and morality, providing insights into the cultural and philosophical context of the Norse tradition.

Contextual analysis enriches the understanding of the Havamal by situating it within its historical and cultural framework. Recognizing the societal norms, values, and beliefs of the Viking Age illuminates the text's teachings on friendship, honor, and personal conduct. By exploring the historical background, readers can grasp how the Havamal not only reflects the ethos of its time but also offers timeless wisdom that resonates with contemporary audiences. This perspective highlights the relevance of the Havamal in modern life, as its lessons on ethics and relationships continue to guide individuals in navigating their social environments.

Symbolism and imagery are central to the poetic nature of the Havamal, and analyzing these elements can yield profound insights into its teachings. The use of metaphor and allegory in the verses invites readers to delve deeper into their meanings, revealing the multifaceted nature of the text. For example, the recurring imagery of the path and journey reflects the human experience and the choices individuals must make. By unpacking these symbols, one can draw connections between the Havamal's content and broader themes found in other ancient texts, thus situating it within a larger literary tradition that explores the human condition.

Comparative analysis provides a framework for examining the Havamal alongside other ancient works, such as the Epic of Gilgamesh or the Tao Te Ching. This technique facilitates a dialogue between texts, highlighting both shared themes and unique perspectives. By contrasting the ethical teachings found in the Havamal with those in other cultures, readers can appreciate the universality of certain moral principles while also recognizing the distinct cultural influences that shape each text. Such analysis deepens the understanding of the Havamal's influence on Norse mythology and its enduring legacy in contemporary pagan practices.

Psychological insights derived from the Havamal's teachings can be explored through thematic analysis, which focuses on the core ideas presented within the text. Themes of wisdom, humility, and the importance of social bonds are prevalent throughout the verses. By examining these themes in relation to modern psychological concepts, such as emotional intelligence and interpersonal relationships, readers can find practical applications of the Havamal's wisdom in their daily lives. This integration of ancient teachings with contemporary psychological understanding not only enriches one's appreciation of the Havamal but also demonstrates the timeless relevance of its insights into human behavior and social dynamics.

## Common Interpretations

The Havamal, a significant collection of Old Norse wisdom, has been interpreted in various ways throughout history, reflecting the cultural and philosophical milieu of its readers. Common interpretations often focus on the text's practical advice on living a virtuous and meaningful life. Many scholars emphasize the pragmatic nature of the Havamal, viewing it as a guide for behavior and social interaction. This perspective highlights the text's emphasis on prudence, moderation, and the importance of maintaining one's reputation within the community.

Another prevalent interpretation centers on the Havamal's spiritual and ethical dimensions. Readers often find profound moral lessons embedded in its verses, particularly concerning friendship, loyalty, and the dynamics of social relationships. The text is frequently cited as a source of ethical guidance, advocating for integrity and the cultivation of strong bonds among individuals. This interpretation resonates with contemporary audiences seeking frameworks for personal conduct and social harmony, linking ancient wisdom with modern ethical dilemmas.

In the context of Norse mythology and culture, the Havamal is frequently analyzed for its portrayal of the divine and the heroic. The text features a blend of practical wisdom and mythological elements, suggesting that the cultural identity of the Norse people was intricately tied to their understanding of the cosmos and the moral order within it. Interpretations that focus on this aspect explore how the Havamal reflects the values and beliefs of its time, providing insights into the worldview of the Norse societies that revered it.

Moreover, the Havamal's influence on contemporary pagan practices has led to new interpretations that seek to reconcile ancient teachings with modern spiritual paths. Many practitioners of Norse paganism draw upon the Havamal for guidance in rituals, communal gatherings, and personal development. This interpretation underscores the text's ongoing relevance, as individuals seek to integrate its wisdom into their spiritual practices and everyday lives, thereby bridging the gap between past and present.

Finally, the psychological insights derived from the Havamal's teachings offer another layer of interpretation. Readers often highlight the text's reflections on human nature, the complexities of relationships, and the pursuit of happiness. The Havamal's verses can serve as a source of introspection, encouraging individuals to navigate their emotions and interactions thoughtfully. This approach not only enriches the understanding of the Havamal itself but also demonstrates its potential as a tool for personal growth and self-awareness in the modern world.

## Challenges in Interpretation

Challenges in interpretation of the Havamal arise from a variety of factors, including the historical context in which it was written, the complexities of Old Norse language, and the cultural nuances that have evolved over time. The Havamal, a collection of wisdom literature attributed to the Viking Age, is steeped in the traditions and values of a society that operated under different moral and ethical frameworks than those of contemporary readers. This disconnect can lead to misinterpretations of its verses, as modern individuals may project their own values onto the text instead of understanding it within its original context.

The ambiguity of language presents another significant challenge. Old Norse, with its rich vocabulary and idiomatic expressions, often lacks direct equivalents in modern languages. Readers must navigate various translations, each reflecting the translator's interpretations and biases. Different scholars may emphasize disparate meanings based on their understanding of the words and phrases, which can lead to divergent interpretations of the same verse. This linguistic challenge is compounded by the fact that many verses in the Havamal employ metaphorical and symbolic language, requiring a deeper level of analysis to uncover the intended wisdom.

Cultural differences also play a critical role in interpretation. The societal norms and practices of the Norse people were vastly different from those of today. Concepts of honor, loyalty, and wisdom were intertwined with a worldview that included a belief in fate and the supernatural. As such, the lessons conveyed in the Havamal can be challenging to apply to modern life without careful consideration of these cultural contexts. Misunderstanding these social dynamics can lead to oversimplified or inaccurate applications of the text's teachings.

Moreover, the Havamal's influence on Norse mythology and culture further complicates its interpretation. As a text that sits at the crossroads of folklore, mythology, and practical wisdom, it is essential to recognize the intertextual relationships between the Havamal and other ancient Norse texts. This web of connections can enrich understanding but also introduces additional layers of complexity, as readers must discern which cultural references are relevant and how they shape the meanings of the verses.

Finally, the role of the Havamal in contemporary pagan practices poses both opportunities and obstacles for modern interpreters. While many practitioners draw on its teachings for guidance in their spiritual lives, the varying interpretations can lead to conflicting applications within different pagan communities. This diversity reflects the adaptability of the Havamal's wisdom but also highlights the need for thoughtful analysis to bridge the historical and cultural gaps. Engaging with the text requires not only an appreciation of its poetic beauty but also a commitment to understanding its deeper meanings amid the challenges of interpretation.

# Chapter 4: Havamal's Influence on Norse Mythology and Culture

### The Havamal and Norse Cosmology

The Havamal, a significant text in Norse literature, serves as a vital bridge to understanding Norse cosmology, the framework that underpins the worldview of the ancient Norse people. This collection of wisdom poetry, attributed to the god Odin, encapsulates a variety of teachings that reflect the values, beliefs, and social structures of the time. Within its verses, the Havamal offers insights into the nature of existence, the relationship between gods and humans, and the moral principles that guided societal interactions. The cosmological perspectives embedded in the text reveal how the Norse perceived their world as a complex interplay of order and chaos, where wisdom and prudence were essential for navigating life's challenges.

Central to Norse cosmology is the concept of Yggdrasil, the World Tree, which connects the nine realms of existence. The Havamal engages with this imagery, emphasizing the importance of knowledge and experience in understanding one's place in the universe. The text advocates for a life lived with awareness, where the acquisition of wisdom is paramount. This understanding is mirrored in the depiction of Odin himself, who sacrificed much in pursuit of knowledge. The verses encourage readers to seek wisdom, not only for personal growth but also as a means of fostering harmony within the community, reflecting the intertwined nature of individual and collective well-being in Norse thought.

The ethical and moral lessons found in the Havamal resonate with broader themes in Norse mythology, notably the importance of honor, loyalty, and the bonds of friendship. The text underscores the value of social relationships, asserting that wisdom is best cultivated in the context of community. Through practical advice on how to interact with others, the Havamal illustrates a cosmology where human connections are sacred and integral to a balanced life. This perspective on social ethics is not only relevant to understanding ancient practices but also provides a foundation for modern interpretations of community and personal responsibility.

In comparing the Havamal with other ancient texts, such as the Tao Te Ching or the Analects of Confucius, we find parallels in the pursuit of wisdom and the ethical treatment of others. Despite cultural differences, these texts share a common thread of promoting virtue and understanding the deeper truths of existence. The Havamal, with its poetic form and rich symbolism, offers unique insights that reflect the specific challenges and values of the Norse people, while also contributing to a universal dialogue on morality and the human experience.

The contemporary relevance of the Havamal is evident in its application to modern life, particularly in the realms of personal development and social ethics. The teachings of the Havamal encourage individuals to reflect on their values, relationships, and responsibilities, fostering a sense of mindfulness that is increasingly sought after in today's fast-paced world. As contemporary pagan practices draw upon the wisdom of the past, the Havamal remains a vital resource for those seeking to integrate ancient knowledge into their spiritual and ethical frameworks. Its verses continue to inspire, reminding us that the quest for wisdom is timeless and essential to the human experience.

## Figures and Deities in the Havamal

The Havamal, a foundational text in Norse literature, is rich with references to figures and deities that embody the values and teachings of the Old Norse worldview. At its core, the Havamal serves as a guide, imparting wisdom through the voices of gods and legendary figures. Odin, the chief deity, emerges as a central figure, embodying the archetype of the seeker of knowledge and wisdom. His quest for understanding is reflected in the verses that encourage self-awareness, humility, and the pursuit of wisdom. The teachings attributed to Odin resonate with the values of courage and foresight, urging individuals to navigate the complexities of life with both pragmatism and insight.

The presence of other deities and figures also enriches the Havamal's narrative landscape. Figures such as Freyja and Tyr illustrate various aspects of human experience and morality, offering lessons on love, sacrifice, and justice. Freyja's association with love and fertility juxtaposes Odin's more stoic pursuit of knowledge, highlighting the balance between emotional and intellectual pursuits. Tyr, the god of war and law, represents the importance of honor and integrity, reinforcing the idea that strength must be tempered with righteousness. These characters serve not only as embodiments of divine qualities but also as mirrors reflecting the values that were essential to Viking society.

The symbolism woven throughout the Havamal connects the figures and deities to broader themes of existence, ethics, and interpersonal relationships. Each reference to a deity or legendary figure offers a lens through which the teachings can be interpreted. For example, the imagery of Odin sacrificing himself on Yggdrasil to gain wisdom underscores the theme of personal sacrifice for greater knowledge. This symbolism extends to the ethical lessons imparted in the text, where the complexities of human relationships are explored through the lens of divine interactions. The interplay of these figures invites readers to consider how mythical narratives inform moral and ethical decision-making in their own lives.

The influence of the Havamal's figures extends beyond its poetic verses into the realm of contemporary culture and spirituality. Modern pagan practices often draw on these ancient teachings, utilizing the wisdom of figures like Odin and Freyja to navigate contemporary challenges. By embracing the lessons derived from these deities, practitioners can cultivate a deeper understanding of their own lives and the world around them. The Havamal thus becomes not just a historical text but a living guide that informs practices and beliefs, allowing individuals to connect with their ancestral heritage.

In understanding the Havamal's figures and deities, one can appreciate how these elements contribute to the work's overall ethical and moral framework. The interplay of divine wisdom and human experience offers a rich tapestry of insights applicable to modern life. As readers engage with the text, the teachings of these figures can inspire personal growth, ethical reflection, and a deeper appreciation for the interconnectedness of all beings. By examining the roles of these deities within the Havamal, individuals can extract timeless lessons that resonate across the ages, affirming the relevance of this ancient wisdom in today's world.

## Cultural Practices and Traditions

Cultural practices and traditions serve as a vital lens through which the teachings of the Havamal can be understood. Rooted in the Norse cultural milieu, the Havamal reflects the values and norms that shaped the daily lives and social interactions of the Viking Age. This text, often seen as a manual for living wisely, emphasizes the importance of community, hospitality, and the bonds of kinship. These cultural practices are not merely historical artifacts; they continue to inform contemporary interpretations of the Havamal, illustrating how ancient wisdom can be relevant in modern contexts.

Hospitality is a central theme in the Havamal, encapsulated in verses that extol the virtues of generosity and the duty to welcome guests. This practice was deeply embedded in Norse society, where the honor of a household was often measured by its willingness to host travelers. The teachings of the Havamal emphasize that sharing resources and providing shelter fosters communal ties and reinforces social cohesion. Such cultural imperatives not only reflect the practical necessities of survival in a harsh environment but also reveal a profound ethical framework that prioritizes human connection and mutual support.

Another significant aspect of the cultural practices illuminated by the Havamal is its perspective on friendship and loyalty. The text provides guidance on the qualities of a true friend, emphasizing reliability, trust, and the importance of standing by one's companions. In a society where alliances were essential for both personal and communal security, these teachings underscore the value placed on social relationships. The Havamal's insights into friendship resonate with modern audiences, offering lessons on the nature of trust and the dynamics of interpersonal relationships that remain relevant today.

Rituals and ceremonies also play a critical role in the cultural landscape described in the Havamal. The text reflects the significance of rites of passage, seasonal celebrations, and communal gatherings in reinforcing shared values and collective identity. These traditions were not only important for the community's social fabric but also served as opportunities for the transmission of wisdom and moral lessons across generations. Understanding these practices allows contemporary readers to appreciate the Havamal as a living document that speaks to the human experience, bridging the gap between the past and present.

The influence of the Havamal extends beyond its historical context, shaping contemporary pagan practices and spiritual explorations. Modern practitioners often draw upon its teachings to create rituals that honor the values of the past while adapting them to contemporary life. This blending of tradition and modernity highlights the enduring relevance of the Havamal's wisdom, encouraging individuals to cultivate ethical living, meaningful relationships, and a sense of belonging within their communities. As such, the cultural practices and traditions encapsulated in the Havamal serve not only as a reflection of Norse life but also as a timeless guide for navigating the complexities of human existence.

# Chapter 5: Practical Applications of Havamal Teachings in Modern Life

### Wisdom for Daily Living

The Havamal, a collection of Old Norse poetry, offers timeless wisdom that resonates with the complexities of modern life. Its verses provide practical guidance on how to navigate daily challenges with discernment and integrity. The text serves as a manual for personal conduct, emphasizing values such as humility, prudence, and the importance of fostering strong relationships. By exploring these teachings, individuals can find a framework for making decisions that align with both personal ethics and the well-being of their communities.

Central to the Havamal's teachings is the notion of wisdom as a guiding principle. The text underscores the significance of learning from experience, advocating for a thoughtful approach to life's dilemmas. It encourages self-reflection and the pursuit of knowledge, suggesting that true wisdom emerges not only from age but also from the lessons learned through observation and interaction. This perspective is particularly relevant today, as individuals are often faced with rapid changes and complex social dynamics that require a grounded approach to decision-making.

The Havamal also places considerable emphasis on the nature of friendship and social relationships. The poetry highlights the importance of loyalty, generosity, and trust, which are essential for cultivating meaningful connections. In a world where social media often replaces face-to-face interactions, the Havamal's teachings remind us of the value of sincerity and the need to invest in genuine relationships. It encourages individuals to be mindful of their actions and words, reinforcing the idea that the quality of one's relationships greatly impacts overall happiness and fulfillment.

Furthermore, the ethical and moral lessons embedded in the Havamal provide a compass for navigating the complexities of modern life. The text advocates for a balanced approach to living, where one must weigh personal desires against the collective good. This moral framework fosters a sense of responsibility, urging individuals to act with integrity and to consider the consequences of their actions. In contemporary society, where ethical dilemmas are commonplace, these teachings can serve as a source of guidance for making choices that reflect one's values while contributing positively to the community.

Incorporating the wisdom of the Havamal into daily life can lead to a more intentional and meaningful existence. By embracing its teachings on wisdom, relationships, and ethical conduct, individuals can cultivate a lifestyle that not only honors the past but also enriches their present and future. The Havamal's insights remain relevant, offering a pathway for personal growth and social harmony in an ever-evolving world.

## Decision Making and Leadership

Decision-making in leadership, as illuminated by the teachings of the Havamal, emphasizes the importance of wisdom, experience, and the ability to reflect on the consequences of one's choices. The Havamal, a collection of Norse wisdom poetry, offers valuable insights into the qualities that define a good leader. It advocates for a thoughtful approach to leadership, where decisions are made not in haste but through contemplation and understanding. This guidance is particularly relevant in today's fast-paced world, where leaders are often pressured to make quick decisions without fully considering their implications.

The Havamal underscores the significance of knowledge and learning in decision-making. It suggests that those who seek wisdom from various sources, including personal experiences and the teachings of others, are better equipped to navigate the complexities of leadership. This notion aligns with contemporary theories of leadership, which emphasize the importance of continuous learning and adaptability. By drawing on the rich historical context of the Havamal, modern leaders can appreciate the value of gathering diverse perspectives and insights before making pivotal decisions.

Moreover, the text highlights the necessity of integrity and ethical considerations in leadership. The Havamal teaches that a leader's character is crucial in fostering trust and loyalty among followers. Ethical decision-making, grounded in moral principles, not only enhances a leader's credibility but also promotes a positive organizational culture. This principle resonates across various ancient texts, where the virtues of honesty and accountability are often celebrated as essential leadership qualities. The comparative analysis of the Havamal with other wisdom literature reveals a shared understanding of the moral imperatives that guide effective leadership.

In addition to moral integrity, the Havamal emphasizes the importance of social relationships in decision-making processes. It recognizes that a leader does not operate in isolation but rather within a network of relationships that influence outcomes. The Havamal's teachings on friendship and community highlight the importance of collaboration and support in leadership contexts. Effective leaders are those who cultivate strong relationships, enabling them to solicit advice, gain insights, and foster a sense of belonging among their followers, ultimately leading to more informed and balanced decisions.

Finally, the psychological insights derived from the Havamal's wisdom suggest that emotional intelligence plays a pivotal role in leadership decision-making. Leaders who are attuned to their own emotions and those of others can navigate the complexities of interpersonal dynamics more effectively. The Havamal encourages leaders to reflect on their thoughts and feelings, promoting a deeper understanding of themselves and their impact on others. In practicing these teachings, modern leaders can enhance their decision-making capabilities, ensuring that their choices are not only wise but also compassionate and considerate of the broader community they serve.

## Building Resilience and Mindfulness

Building resilience and mindfulness are essential themes woven throughout the Havamal, providing a framework for navigating life's challenges with grace and fortitude. Resilience, the capacity to recover from difficulties, is mirrored in the Viking ethos, which emphasized strength in the face of adversity. The Havamal offers practical wisdom, urging individuals to cultivate an inner strength that allows them to withstand life's trials. This resilience is not merely about enduring hardship but involves learning from experiences, adapting, and emerging stronger, echoing the notion that each challenge is an opportunity for personal growth.

Mindfulness, on the other hand, involves being present and aware of one's thoughts, feelings, and surroundings. The Havamal encourages a mindful approach to living, emphasizing the importance of thoughtful speech and action. Its verses often reflect the significance of being conscious of one's environment and relationships, promoting a deep awareness of the interconnectedness of all beings. By practicing mindfulness as advocated in the Havamal, individuals can enhance their emotional intelligence, fostering healthier relationships and a greater appreciation for the present moment.

The teachings of the Havamal encourage individuals to reflect on their choices and the consequences that arise from them. This reflective practice is a cornerstone of resilience, as it promotes self-awareness and personal accountability. By understanding the impact of one's actions, individuals can cultivate a mindset that not only embraces resilience but also fosters a sense of purpose. The Havamal's focus on ethical decision-making and the importance of integrity serves as a reminder that resilience is intertwined with moral fortitude, guiding individuals to act in ways that are both courageous and principled.

Moreover, the historical context of the Havamal enriches its teachings on resilience and mindfulness. Emerging from a culture that valued bravery and wisdom, the text encapsulates lessons learned from the harsh realities of Norse life. The emphasis on communal bonds and the wisdom of elders highlights the importance of social support in building resilience. The Havamal acknowledges that individuals do not face their struggles alone; rather, they are part of a larger community where shared experiences and collective wisdom can fortify one's resolve.

In contemporary applications, the teachings of the Havamal can inform modern practices of resilience and mindfulness. Those seeking to integrate these principles into their lives can draw upon the text's insights to navigate personal and professional challenges. By embracing the Havamal's call for ethical living, self-reflection, and mindful interaction, individuals can cultivate a robust resilience that not only empowers them but also enriches their communities. The timeless wisdom of the Havamal serves as a guiding light, offering valuable lessons that remain relevant in today's fast-paced and often tumultuous world.

# Chapter 6: Comparative Analysis of Havamal and Other Ancient Texts

## Similarities with Other Wisdom Literature

The Havamal, a collection of Norse wisdom sayings attributed to the god Odin, shares notable similarities with other ancient wisdom literature, reflecting universal truths and moral teachings across cultures. Texts such as the Proverbs in the Bible, the Tao Te Ching in Taoism, and the teachings found in ancient Greek philosophy reveal parallels in their approaches to ethics, interpersonal relationships, and the pursuit of knowledge. These commonalities suggest that despite cultural differences, the human experience often leads to similar conclusions about living a virtuous life.

One significant area of similarity lies in the focus on practical wisdom. The Havamal emphasizes the importance of knowledge gained through experience, advising individuals to be cautious, observant, and wise in their decisions. Similarly, the Proverbs delineate practical guidelines for daily living, often highlighting the value of wisdom and understanding in navigating life's challenges. These texts encourage readers to cultivate discernment and self-awareness, underscoring the notion that wisdom is not merely theoretical but should manifest in actionable insights applicable to everyday life.

Moreover, the themes of friendship and social relationships resonate throughout the Havamal and other wisdom literature. The Havamal stresses the importance of loyalty, trust, and reciprocity in friendships, echoing sentiments found in the works of Confucius, who emphasized the significance of virtue in relationships and the collective responsibility towards one another. Both texts advocate for the development of strong, supportive bonds, illustrating the role of community and the impact of social connections on individual well-being and moral conduct.

Ethical teachings also serve as a common thread linking the Havamal with other ancient texts. The Havamal provides guidance on virtues such as humility, generosity, and integrity, paralleling the moral imperatives found in Greek philosophy, particularly in the dialogues of Plato and Aristotle, where the cultivation of virtue is central to the good life. In these texts, the pursuit of ethical living is portrayed as essential for personal fulfillment and societal harmony, reinforcing the interconnectedness of individual actions and the broader community.

Lastly, the use of metaphor and imagery in the Havamal resonates with the stylistic elements present in other wisdom literature. The poetic structure of the Havamal, rich with vivid imagery and symbolic language, serves to convey deeper meanings and insights, akin to the allegorical narratives found in texts like Aesop's Fables or the parables of Jesus. This artistic approach not only enhances the memorability of the teachings but also invites readers to engage in reflective thought, allowing for a personal interpretation of wisdom that transcends cultural boundaries.

## Contrasts with Eastern Philosophies

Contrasting the teachings of the Havamal with Eastern philosophies reveals significant differences in worldview, ethical frameworks, and approaches to personal development. While the Havamal, rooted in Norse tradition, emphasizes individual strength, honor, and pragmatic wisdom, Eastern philosophies such as Buddhism and Taoism advocate for interconnectedness, inner peace, and the transcendence of the self. This divergence reflects broader cultural attitudes towards existence, morality, and the nature of wisdom. The Havamal's focus on personal agency and social bonds stands in stark contrast to the Eastern emphasis on detachment from desires and the collective nature of human experience.

The Havamal's teachings on friendship and social relationships illuminate the value placed on loyalty, honor, and reciprocity within Viking culture. In contrast, Eastern philosophies often approach relationships with an emphasis on compassion and the reduction of ego. For instance, in Buddhism, the concept of "metta," or loving-kindness, guides interactions, promoting an altruistic outlook that prioritizes the well-being of others over personal gain. This difference elucidates how cultural contexts shape the understanding of interpersonal dynamics, with the Havamal advocating for a strong, individualistic bond among friends, while Eastern traditions encourage a broader compassion that transcends personal ties.

Ethical and moral lessons within the Havamal stress practical wisdom, often presented as proverbs that provide guidance for navigating life's challenges. The verses advocate for a clear-headed approach to decision-making, emphasizing the importance of foresight and the consequences of one's actions. Conversely, Eastern teachings, particularly in Confucianism, emphasize the cultivation of virtue and moral integrity through social harmony and respect for hierarchical relationships. The Havamal's pragmatic view can be seen as a reflection of the harsh realities of the Norse environment, where survival hinged on individual competence and social bonds, whereas Eastern ethics often arise from a communal perspective, seeking to maintain societal balance.

Symbolism and imagery in the Havamal draw heavily on nature and the harsh realities of the Northern climate, using metaphors that resonate with the Viking experience. This contrasts with

Eastern texts, which often employ more abstract and philosophical imagery, focusing on concepts like the Tao or the cycle of samsara. The Havamal's use of vivid, concrete examples serves to ground its teachings in the practical, while Eastern philosophies may invite deeper contemplation on the nature of reality itself. This difference not only highlights cultural preferences in depicting wisdom but also reflects the distinct approaches to understanding life's complexities.

Finally, the practical applications of Havamal teachings in modern life resonate with those seeking clarity and actionable advice in an increasingly complex world. Its focus on self-reliance, ethical behavior, and the importance of community relationships provides a framework for navigating contemporary challenges. In contrast, Eastern philosophies often encourage introspection and meditative practices aimed at achieving inner peace. The integration of both perspectives can enrich an individual's journey by blending the Havamal's actionable wisdom with Eastern insights on mindfulness and interconnectedness. This comparative analysis not only enhances our understanding of the Havamal but also illustrates the rich tapestry of human thought across cultures.

## The Havamal in a Global Context

The Havamal, a collection of Old Norse poetry, serves as a window into the values and beliefs of the Viking Age, but its teachings resonate far beyond that historical context. In a global perspective, the Havamal can be seen as part of a larger tapestry of wisdom literature found in various cultures. Its verses echo themes that are universally relevant, such as the importance of wisdom, the complexity of human relationships, and the necessity of ethical behavior. By comparing the Havamal with texts like the Tao Te Ching, the Bible, and other ancient philosophical works, one can appreciate the shared human quest for understanding and the moral frameworks that guide societies across time and geography.

The ethical lessons embedded in the Havamal are particularly notable when viewed alongside contemporary moral philosophies. The text emphasizes virtues such as prudence, humility, and the significance of friendship, reflecting values that are equally cherished in various cultures worldwide. For instance, the Havamal's thoughts on the nature of friendship and social bonds resonate with Confucian ideals of relational harmony and responsibility. This common ground underscores the Havamal's relevance, illustrating how ancient insights remain applicable in navigating modern interpersonal dynamics and ethical dilemmas.

Moreover, the Havamal offers psychological insights that align with contemporary understandings of human behavior. Its verses emphasize self-awareness, the importance of reflection, and the need for emotional intelligence in relationships. These principles can be paralleled with modern psychological approaches, such as cognitive behavioral therapy, which stresses the value of understanding one's thoughts and emotions. By integrating these ancient teachings into modern psychological practices, individuals can find guidance in their personal development and interpersonal interactions, highlighting the Havamal's enduring significance.

The influence of the Havamal on Norse mythology and culture cannot be overstated. The text not only informs the understanding of Norse gods and their interactions but also provides a moral compass for the society that revered these deities. The imagery and symbolism found in the Havamal, such as the portrayal of wisdom as a gift to be cultivated, enrich the narrative of Norse mythology, thus deepening our comprehension of the cultural context in which these stories were told. This interconnectedness between the Havamal and mythology illustrates the text's role in shaping the ethical landscape of Norse culture.

In contemporary pagan practices, the Havamal continues to serve as a source of inspiration and guidance. Modern practitioners often turn to its verses for wisdom on personal conduct, community building, and spiritual growth. The Havamal's teachings on the importance of hospitality and generosity resonate with communal values, fostering a sense of connection within contemporary pagan communities. As these groups seek to revive and reinterpret ancient traditions, the Havamal remains a vital text, offering timeless wisdom that encourages individuals to reflect on their values and their roles within the broader tapestry of human experience.

# Chapter 7: The Role of the Havamal in Contemporary Pagan Practices

## Rituals and Ceremonies

Rituals and ceremonies hold a significant place in the cultural landscape described by the Havamal, serving as vital expressions of community, belief, and the human experience. Rooted in the ancient Norse worldview, these practices were not merely ceremonial but deeply intertwined with the social fabric and moral lessons imparted by the Havamal's verses. The text emphasizes the importance of actions and communal gatherings, illustrating how rituals can reinforce social bonds and convey shared values, thereby fostering a sense of belonging among participants.

The rituals outlined in Norse traditions often revolved around key life events such as birth, marriage, and death, as well as seasonal changes and agricultural cycles. Each ceremony was imbued with significance, drawing upon the wisdom encapsulated in the Havamal. For instance, the act of toasting with mead during feasts is not just a celebration but a ritual steeped in the principles of friendship and loyalty, themes that resonate throughout the Havamal. These gatherings provided opportunities for individuals to reaffirm their connections to each other and to the divine, highlighting the text's emphasis on the interconnectedness of human relationships.

In exploring the historical context of the Havamal, it becomes evident that rituals served both practical and spiritual purposes. They were essential for marking the passage of time and the cycles of life, while also acting as a means of transmitting cultural knowledge and ethical teachings. The Havamal encourages reflection on the importance of wisdom and the values that underpin societal norms, suggesting that the ceremonies performed were not only acts of faith but also opportunities for moral education. Participants would engage with the teachings of the Havamal during these rituals, reinforcing ethical behavior and communal responsibility.

The influence of the Havamal on contemporary pagan practices can also be seen in the way modern practitioners incorporate ancient rituals into their spiritual lives. These ceremonies often draw upon the themes of wisdom, courage, and mutual respect found within the Havamal, reflecting a desire to connect with ancestral traditions. By adapting ancient rites to suit modern contexts, practitioners create spaces where the teachings of the Havamal can be actively engaged with, allowing for a renewed exploration of its ethical and moral lessons in today's world.

Moreover, the psychological insights derived from the Havamal's teachings can be observed in the way rituals promote mental well-being and community cohesion. Engaging in ceremonial practices can foster a sense of purpose, belonging, and identity, which are crucial for psychological health. The Havamal emphasizes the value of friendship and social relationships, and rituals serve as a powerful reminder of these principles. By participating in communal ceremonies, individuals not only honor their ancestors and traditions but also reinforce the bonds that contribute to a supportive and resilient community, echoing the timeless wisdom found in the text.

## The Havamal as a Spiritual Guide

The Havamal, a cornerstone of Old Norse literature, serves as a profound spiritual guide that transcends the boundaries of time and culture. Its verses, rich in wisdom, offer insights into the human experience, emphasizing themes such as ethics, friendship, and the pursuit of knowledge. The text reflects a worldview deeply intertwined with the spiritual and practical aspects of daily life, urging individuals to cultivate virtues that foster personal growth and harmonious relationships within their communities. By understanding the Havamal, readers can uncover timeless teachings that resonate with contemporary spiritual and ethical dilemmas.

Historically, the Havamal is situated within the broader context of Norse mythology and culture, emerging from a tradition that values wisdom and knowledge as paramount virtues. The text is believed to have been composed during the Viking Age, a period marked by exploration, conflict, and the quest for understanding the cosmos. The verses encapsulate the values of the Norse people, integrating their experiences and observations into a cohesive framework that addresses the complexities of life. By examining the historical context of the Havamal, readers gain insight into how its teachings were shaped by the societal norms and spiritual beliefs of the time.

The poetic structure of the Havamal enhances its capacity as a spiritual guide, employing vivid imagery and symbolism to convey deep philosophical concepts. Each stanza invites interpretation, allowing readers to engage with the text on multiple levels. This interpretative richness is one of the reasons the Havamal has maintained its relevance across centuries. The verses not only provide practical advice on social conduct and personal integrity but also encourage introspection and self-awareness. The interplay of language and meaning in the Havamal invites comparative analysis with other ancient texts, revealing universal themes that resonate across different cultures and belief systems.

In contemporary life, the teachings of the Havamal can be applied to modern ethical dilemmas, offering guidance on issues such as friendship, loyalty, and the pursuit of wisdom. The text encourages individuals to cultivate meaningful relationships, emphasizing the importance of trust and reciprocity. As a spiritual guide, the Havamal advocates for a balanced approach to life, where one seeks knowledge while maintaining respect for others. This balance fosters a sense of community and belonging, which is often lacking in today's fast-paced, individualistic society.

The influence of the Havamal extends into contemporary pagan practices, where its teachings are embraced for their spiritual depth and moral clarity. Practitioners draw upon its wisdom to navigate their spiritual journeys, finding relevance in its discussions of ethics and social relationships. The psychological insights embedded in the Havamal's verses encourage self-reflection and personal growth, allowing individuals to explore their values and beliefs in a structured way. By engaging with the Havamal, modern readers not only connect with their historical roots but also find a source of inspiration for cultivating a more meaningful and ethically sound life.

## Community and Identity

Community and identity are central themes in the Havamal, reflecting the interconnectedness of individuals within the fabric of Norse society. This ancient text emphasizes the importance of social bonds and the roles individuals play in their communities. The verses convey a deep understanding of the dynamics that govern relationships, highlighting that identity is not solely an individual construct but is significantly shaped by one's interactions with others. The teachings urge individuals to cultivate virtues such as loyalty, generosity, and wisdom, which are essential for fostering a cohesive community.

In the historical context of the Havamal, the Viking Age was characterized by a strong sense of kinship and loyalty. The social structure of Norse society relied heavily on familial ties and alliances forged through shared experiences and mutual support. The Havamal articulates these values, illustrating how one's identity is often intertwined with the roles one fulfills within the community. This perspective is crucial for understanding how the Norse people viewed themselves and their place in the world, as the text serves not only as a guide for personal conduct but also as a foundation for collective identity.

The poetry and verses of the Havamal offer rich imagery that speaks to the significance of social relationships. The metaphor of the strong tree with deep roots is frequently used to illustrate how individuals can thrive when they are well-connected to their community. This symbolism extends to the notion of friendship, which is portrayed as a vital component of a well-lived life. The Havamal advises that true friends are those who support one another through both triumphs and hardships, reinforcing the idea that identity is often defined through these critical social connections.

Moreover, the influence of the Havamal on Norse mythology and culture cannot be overstated. The text's teachings resonate through various myths and legends that emphasize communal values and the importance of social integrity. Many of the ethical and moral lessons found in the Havamal have permeated Norse folklore, shaping cultural norms and practices that prioritize community well-being over individual desires. In this way, the Havamal serves as a cultural touchstone, preserving the wisdom of the past while continuing to inform contemporary understandings of identity and belonging.

In modern life, the teachings of the Havamal on community and identity offer practical applications that resonate with contemporary challenges. As individuals navigate increasingly fragmented societies, the emphasis on fostering strong relationships and a sense of belonging is more relevant than ever. By drawing on the wisdom of the Havamal, individuals can find guidance for building supportive networks and cultivating a sense of identity that honors both personal aspirations and communal responsibilities. This duality reflects the enduring legacy of the Havamal, reminding us that our identities are shaped not only by who we are alone but also by who we are together in community.

# Chapter 8: Psychological Insights from the Havamal's Wisdom

## The Psychology of Ancient Wisdom

The Havamal, a foundational text of Norse wisdom, offers profound insights into human psychology that resonate through the ages. Ancient wisdom often reflects a deep understanding of human nature, and the Havamal is no exception. Its verses delve into the complexities of human behavior, relationships, and the ethical dilemmas faced by individuals within their communities. By examining these teachings, we can gain a clearer perspective on our own psychological frameworks and the implications of the choices we make in our lives.

Central to the Havamal's teachings is the theme of self-knowledge and restraint. The text emphasizes the importance of understanding oneself before engaging with others, suggesting that personal introspection is essential for healthy relationships. This aligns with modern psychological theories that underscore the significance of emotional intelligence and self-awareness as foundational elements for establishing meaningful connections. The Havamal instructs individuals to reflect on their motivations and actions, advocating for a balanced approach to personal conduct that acknowledges both strengths and weaknesses.

Friendship and social relationships are pivotal themes in the Havamal, framed within the context of loyalty, trust, and mutual respect. The text provides guidance on the nature of companionship, highlighting the necessity of discernment in choosing friends and the moral obligations that arise from those relationships. This perspective is particularly relevant in contemporary discussions about social dynamics, where the quality of friendships is often seen as a reflection of one's character. The Havamal encourages individuals to cultivate relationships that are not only beneficial but also ethically grounded, facilitating a deeper understanding of community and social responsibility.

Additionally, the ethical and moral lessons embedded within the Havamal offer a rich source for psychological reflection. The text addresses the consequences of actions and the importance of integrity, which resonates with modern psychological concepts such as cognitive dissonance and moral reasoning. By exploring these lessons, individuals can better navigate the complexities of moral choices in their own lives, drawing on ancient wisdom to inform contemporary ethical dilemmas. The Havamal serves as a reminder that our decisions are intertwined with a larger moral framework, guiding us toward a more conscientious existence.

Finally, the symbolism and imagery used in the Havamal enrich its psychological insights. The metaphors and poetic devices employed throughout the text evoke powerful emotions, allowing readers to engage with the material on a deeper level. This artistic expression not only enhances the memorability of the teachings but also provides a canvas for personal interpretation and emotional resonance. By reflecting on the symbolic language of the Havamal, individuals can uncover layers of meaning that speak to their own experiences, fostering a personal connection with this ancient wisdom that remains relevant in our modern psychological landscapes.

## Emotional Intelligence and Relationships

Emotional intelligence plays a vital role in shaping relationships, and the teachings of the Havamal provide profound insights into this aspect of human interaction. The Havamal, often regarded as a foundational text of Norse wisdom, emphasizes the importance of understanding oneself and others to foster meaningful connections. Throughout its verses, it advocates for self-awareness, empathy, and effective communication, all of which are critical components of emotional intelligence. By promoting a deeper understanding of our emotions and those of others, the Havamal underscores the necessity of emotional intelligence in nurturing strong, resilient relationships.

One of the key themes in the Havamal is the significance of trust and loyalty in friendships. The text illustrates that emotional intelligence is not merely about recognizing emotions but also about valuing the bonds formed through mutual respect and loyalty. The Havamal teaches that true friends are those who support each other in times of need, highlighting the importance of empathy in understanding the challenges faced by others. This perspective aligns with modern psychological insights that suggest emotional intelligence fosters stronger social networks, ultimately leading to more fulfilling relationships.

Moreover, the Havamal emphasizes the wisdom of restraint and measured responses in interactions. It advises against impulsive reactions, suggesting that individuals should take time to reflect before expressing their feelings or making judgments about others. This principle resonates with contemporary approaches to emotional intelligence, where self-regulation is seen as essential for maintaining harmony in relationships. By advocating for thoughtful communication and the careful consideration of one's words and actions, the Havamal provides a timeless framework for developing emotional intelligence that remains relevant in today's fast-paced world.

The text also explores the dynamics of power and vulnerability within relationships. Emotional intelligence involves recognizing the balance of these elements, as the Havamal suggests that true strength lies in the ability to be vulnerable and to show compassion. The wisdom found in its verses encourages individuals to embrace their emotions and to be open to the feelings of others, fostering an environment where authentic connections can flourish. This understanding is crucial in both personal and professional relationships, as it creates a foundation of safety and trust that allows for deeper engagement.

In conclusion, the teachings of the Havamal on emotional intelligence and relationships invite readers to reflect on their own interactions and the underlying emotions at play. By emphasizing the importance of self-awareness, empathy, loyalty, and vulnerability, the Havamal offers a rich resource for understanding and improving our relationships. Its insights not only illuminate the significance of emotional intelligence in forging connections but also provide practical guidance for applying these principles in modern life, ensuring that the wisdom of the North continues to resonate across time and culture.

## Coping Strategies in Modern Contexts

Coping strategies derived from the teachings of the Havamal can be particularly relevant in the fast-paced and often chaotic modern world. The Havamal, a collection of wisdom and proverbs attributed to Odin, emphasizes the importance of prudence, patience, and perspective in facing life's challenges. These ancient teachings encourage individuals to cultivate resilience, suggesting that one should remain grounded and composed even amid adversity. By incorporating the Havamal's insights into daily life, individuals can find practical ways to navigate stress and uncertainty, thereby fostering mental and emotional well-being.

One of the central themes of the Havamal is the value of moderation and self-control. In contemporary contexts, where impulsivity and instant gratification are prevalent, embracing moderation can serve as a powerful coping strategy. The Havamal urges readers to reflect before acting, promoting thoughtful decision-making. This practice can mitigate feelings of regret or anxiety that often accompany rash choices. By adopting this principle, individuals can develop a more balanced approach to their desires and challenges, leading to healthier relationships and a more fulfilling life.

Another vital aspect of the Havamal is its emphasis on the significance of social connections and friendships. In a modern context, where many face isolation and disconnection, nurturing relationships becomes a crucial coping mechanism. The Havamal teaches that true friends are invaluable, providing support and understanding during difficult times. By fostering these connections, individuals can create a network of support that helps them navigate life's tribulations. Engaging with others in meaningful ways not only enhances emotional resilience but also enriches one's life experience, echoing the Havamal's teachings on the importance of community.

The Havamal also offers insights into the acceptance of fate and the inevitability of change. In the face of life's unpredictability, the ability to adapt and embrace change is essential for coping effectively. The teachings encourage individuals to recognize that while one cannot control external circumstances, they can control their responses. This shift in perspective aligns closely with modern psychological practices, such as cognitive-behavioral therapy, which emphasize the importance of reframing thoughts to better cope with stressors. By internalizing these lessons from the Havamal, individuals can cultivate a more adaptable mindset, enhancing their capacity to cope with life's challenges.

Finally, the Havamal speaks to the importance of reflection and self-awareness as tools for coping. In a world filled with distractions, making time for introspection can lead to greater clarity and understanding of one's emotions and reactions. The wisdom of the Havamal encourages individuals to ponder their experiences, learn from them, and apply those lessons moving forward. This practice not only fosters personal growth but also equips individuals with the skills necessary to face future adversities with confidence and wisdom, reinforcing the timeless relevance of the Havamal's teachings in modern life.

# Chapter 9: Havamal's Views on Friendship and Social Relationships

## The Nature of Friendship

The nature of friendship, as explored in the Havamal, reflects deep cultural values that resonate through Norse mythology and the ethical frameworks of the time. In this ancient text, friendship is depicted not merely as a social bond but as a vital component of one's moral fabric. The verses convey that true friendship requires mutual respect, loyalty, and a commitment to support one another in times of need. This understanding emphasizes the importance of trust and reliability, suggesting that friendships are not only beneficial but essential for personal and communal well-being.

The Havamal provides practical wisdom that illustrates the dynamics of friendship, urging individuals to be discerning in their relationships. It advises against superficial connections, advocating instead for friendships rooted in genuine understanding and shared values. The text underscores the significance of reciprocity; a true friend is someone who not only offers assistance but also expects the same in return. This reciprocal nature of friendship fosters a sense of responsibility, encouraging individuals to nurture their bonds with care and intentionality.

Historically, the context of the Havamal reveals how friendships were viewed in Viking society, where alliances could determine social standing and survival. The text serves as a guide for navigating the complexities of social relationships, highlighting the necessity of forging strong, reliable connections. In a landscape where trust was paramount, the wisdom imparted in the Havamal illustrates that friendships were often forged in the crucible of shared experiences, whether in battle or communal endeavors. This historical lens enriches our understanding of the ethical implications surrounding friendship in Norse culture.

Moreover, the Havamal's teachings on friendship extend beyond mere social interactions, inviting readers to consider the psychological dimensions of these relationships. The verses reflect an awareness of human emotions and the need for companionship, portraying friendship as a source of strength and resilience. This perspective aligns with contemporary psychological insights that highlight the importance of social support in mental health and well-being. By emphasizing the value of meaningful connections, the Havamal provides timeless guidance relevant to modern life, where the challenges of loneliness and disconnection are increasingly prevalent.

In conclusion, the nature of friendship, as articulated in the Havamal, offers profound insights into the ethical and moral lessons that can be gleaned from this ancient text. It encourages individuals to cultivate friendships that are rooted in loyalty, reciprocity, and mutual respect, reflecting a universal truth about the human experience. As we delve into the teachings of the Havamal, we not only honor its historical significance but also embrace its relevance in fostering genuine connections in our contemporary lives, reinforcing the idea that friendship remains a cornerstone of human existence.

## Social Obligations and Community

Social obligations and community are central themes within the Havamal, reflecting the intricate web of relationships that bind individuals to one another in a shared social fabric. In the Norse worldview, the strength of a community often determines the resilience and success of its members. The verses of the Havamal emphasize the importance of mutual support, highlighting that individual well-being is deeply intertwined with the welfare of others. This understanding fosters a sense of responsibility among individuals to contribute positively to their communities, reinforcing the idea that social obligations are not merely duties but vital components of a flourishing society.

The Havamal articulates various social responsibilities that individuals owe to their kin, friends, and wider community. It emphasizes the significance of hospitality, urging individuals to extend generosity and kindness to guests and strangers alike. This principle not only strengthens communal bonds but also creates a culture of trust and reciprocity. The act of sharing resources, stories, and wisdom is portrayed as a sacred duty, elevating the act of community-building to a moral imperative. Such teachings resonate with contemporary practices, where the principles of hospitality and generosity remain integral to fostering healthy relationships, both personally and socially.

Moreover, the Havamal's insights into friendship reveal the intricate dynamics of social relationships. It advocates for loyalty and sincerity among friends, underscoring the importance of choosing companions wisely. The text warns against superficial connections, promoting instead deep, meaningful relationships that withstand the tests of time and adversity. In a modern context, these teachings serve as a reminder of the value of nurturing genuine friendships and the impact these relationships have on one's emotional and psychological well-being. By fostering strong social ties, individuals can create a supportive network that enhances their resilience in the face of life's challenges.

The ethical and moral lessons embedded within the Havamal also extend to the responsibilities individuals have toward their communities. The text encourages active participation in communal life, urging individuals to engage in actions that promote collective prosperity. This ethos aligns with contemporary movements advocating for social responsibility and communal engagement, where individuals are encouraged to contribute to their society through volunteerism, civic participation, and the promotion of justice. The Havamal's teachings thus find practical applications in modern life, inspiring individuals to reflect on their roles within their communities and to act in ways that foster collective well-being.

In essence, the Havamal serves as a timeless guide to navigating the complexities of social obligations and community interactions. Its teachings encourage a balance between individual aspirations and communal responsibilities, highlighting that true wisdom lies in understanding one's place within the larger tapestry of society. By embracing these principles, individuals can cultivate a sense of belonging and purpose that enriches their lives and the lives of those around them. The enduring relevance of the Havamal's perspectives on community and social obligations invites readers to reflect on their values and to engage meaningfully with the world, fostering a spirit of cooperation and mutual respect in contemporary society.

## Conflict Resolution and Loyalty

Conflict resolution is a theme intricately woven into the fabric of the Havamal, showcasing a pragmatic approach to interpersonal disputes that highlights the importance of loyalty. In the ancient Norse worldview, loyalty was not merely a personal virtue but a societal necessity, underpinning familial ties, friendships, and alliances. The Havamal emphasizes that maintaining harmony within relationships often requires direct confrontation of conflicts, advocating for open communication and mutual respect. This perspective offers timeless wisdom that resonates with modern readers facing similar challenges in their personal and professional lives.

The teachings of the Havamal suggest that conflict, while often uncomfortable, can be a catalyst for strengthening bonds if approached with the right mindset. Loyalty, as portrayed in the verses, is not blind allegiance; rather, it is an informed commitment that allows individuals to navigate disagreements without sacrificing integrity. The text encourages individuals to weigh their loyalties carefully, advocating for a balance between personal values and the expectations of relationships. This nuanced understanding of loyalty promotes a healthy dynamic in which conflict can lead to growth and deeper connections.

In the historical context of the Havamal, loyalty was pivotal in the Viking Age, where communal survival often depended on the strength of alliances. The poetry reflects a society where conflicts could arise from competition for resources, social standing, or honor. The Havamal's insights into conflict resolution were essential for maintaining peace within communities and ensuring that disputes did not escalate into violence. This historical perspective informs our understanding of loyalty as a social contract, where individuals are expected to uphold their commitments for the greater good of the group.

Practical applications of the Havamal's teachings on conflict resolution can be seen in contemporary settings. Modern readers can glean insights on how loyalty informs decision-making processes during conflicts. The principles of open dialogue, respect for differing viewpoints, and the willingness to compromise are highlighted in the text, offering a roadmap for navigating disputes in a way that preserves relationships. By applying these ancient teachings, individuals can foster environments of trust and cooperation, which are essential in both personal relationships and organizational dynamics.

Furthermore, the exploration of loyalty in the Havamal extends beyond interpersonal relationships to encompass broader societal implications. The text positions loyalty as a cornerstone of ethical behavior, encouraging individuals to reflect on their commitments to family, friends, and community. This ethical framework invites readers to consider the consequences of their actions and decisions within a larger context, reinforcing the idea that loyalty, when rooted in wisdom and understanding, not only resolves conflicts but also cultivates a sense of belonging and shared purpose.

# Chapter 10: Exploration of the Havamal's Ethical and Moral Lessons

## Core Ethical Principles

The Havamal, a collection of Old Norse poems attributed to the wisdom of Odin, embodies core ethical principles that resonate through its verses. These principles serve as a guide for personal conduct and interpersonal relationships, reflecting the values of Norse society and offering timeless wisdom applicable in today's world. At the heart of the Havamal lies the emphasis on the importance of honor, loyalty, and the pursuit of wisdom, which are essential for fostering a just and harmonious community.

One of the most prominent ethical principles in the Havamal is the concept of honor, which is closely tied to one's reputation and the respect one commands within society. The text underscores that honor is not merely bestowed by birthright but earned through actions and integrity. It advocates for a life led with courage and a commitment to one's word, emphasizing that a person's honor is paramount in establishing trust and social bonds. This principle encourages individuals to act in ways that uphold their dignity and the dignity of others, fostering a culture of mutual respect.

Loyalty emerges as another foundational ethical tenet within the Havamal. The text eloquently speaks to the significance of loyalty in friendships and alliances, illustrating that true companionship is rooted in steadfastness and mutual support. The Havamal advises individuals to choose their friends wisely and to remain loyal to them, suggesting that loyalty is a reciprocal bond that strengthens community ties. This principle not only enhances personal relationships but also extends to the collective, encouraging a sense of belonging and shared responsibility among individuals.

Wisdom, as articulated in the Havamal, is not only an intellectual pursuit but also an ethical imperative. The text teaches that acquiring knowledge and understanding should be a lifelong endeavor, as wisdom enables individuals to navigate the complexities of life with discernment. The Havamal encourages the reader to seek counsel, learn from experiences, and reflect upon one's actions, thus reinforcing the idea that the pursuit of wisdom is essential for ethical living. This principle resonates deeply in modern contexts, where critical thinking and informed decision-making are vital for personal and societal progress.

Finally, the Havamal asserts the importance of community and social relationships, highlighting that ethical living is inherently relational. The text emphasizes that one's actions impact not only oneself but also the wider community. It advocates for kindness, generosity, and the importance of maintaining harmonious relationships, suggesting that a well-functioning society is built on the foundation of ethical interactions. By promoting these core ethical principles, the Havamal not only provides insights into the values of its time but also offers practical guidance for cultivating a more ethical and interconnected modern life.

## Moral Dilemmas and Guidance

Moral dilemmas are a central theme within the Havamal, reflecting the complex interplay of ethics and human behavior in the context of Norse culture. The verses provide insights into the struggles individuals face when confronted with difficult choices, often highlighting the tension between personal desires and societal expectations. The Havamal's teachings encourage readers to navigate these dilemmas with wisdom, emphasizing the importance of foresight and consideration for the consequences of one's actions. By examining these moral quandaries, we can glean valuable lessons that resonate even in contemporary society.

The historical context of the Havamal informs its moral teachings, as the text was shaped by the values and norms of the Viking Age. In a world marked by uncertainty and conflict, individuals were often faced with choices that tested their integrity and honor. The Havamal advises prudence and self-restraint, urging individuals to weigh their options carefully before acting. This historical backdrop enriches our understanding of the moral dilemmas presented in the text, as it mirrors the real-life challenges faced by its original audience, making the verses relevant across ages.

Interpretations of the Havamal's poetry reveal a nuanced approach to moral guidance. The verses often employ metaphor and symbolism, allowing for multiple readings that can resonate with diverse audiences. For instance, the imagery of the traveler seeking wisdom can be seen as a metaphor for the journey through life, where one must confront various ethical decisions. This layered approach encourages readers to engage with the text on a personal level, drawing from their own experiences and dilemmas to extract meaningful insights.

Practical applications of the Havamal's teachings in modern life can be seen in how individuals navigate personal and professional relationships. The emphasis on loyalty, honesty, and respect mirrors contemporary ethical standards, making the moral lessons of the Havamal particularly applicable today. By applying these teachings, individuals can cultivate healthier relationships and make decisions that reflect a commitment to ethical behavior, reinforcing the text's relevance in a modern context.

The exploration of ethical and moral lessons in the Havamal serves as a bridge to understanding its broader implications within Norse mythology and culture. The text not only provides individual guidance but also contributes to the collective moral framework of Norse society. By examining the intersection of personal dilemmas and cultural values, we can appreciate the Havamal's lasting influence, offering a rich tapestry of wisdom that continues to inspire ethical reflection in both individual and communal contexts.

## Relevance to Modern Ethics

The Havamal, a collection of ancient Norse wisdom, offers profound insights that resonate with modern ethical considerations. Its verses impart lessons on personal conduct, social relationships, and the importance of wisdom and prudence. In a world characterized by rapid technological advancement and social change, the principles articulated in the Havamal provide a framework for navigating contemporary ethical dilemmas. The text encourages individuals to reflect on their actions and the impact they have on others, fostering a sense of responsibility that is increasingly relevant in today's interconnected society.

Central to the Havamal's teachings is the emphasis on the importance of honor, respect, and reciprocity in human relationships. The text underscores the value of trust and loyalty, essential components of ethical interactions. As modern society grapples with issues of betrayal and disconnection, the Havamal's insistence on maintaining strong social bonds serves as a reminder of the ethical obligations we hold towards one another. By promoting virtues such as generosity, hospitality, and wisdom, the Havamal aligns closely with contemporary values that prioritize community and interpersonal support.

Moreover, the Havamal's reflections on the nature of knowledge and its application resonate with modern ethical discussions surrounding the responsible use of information. In an age where misinformation can proliferate rapidly, the Havamal advocates for discernment and critical thinking. The text teaches that true wisdom involves not only acquiring knowledge but also understanding its implications and using it judiciously. This perspective is crucial in guiding ethical behavior in areas such as media consumption, decision-making, and leadership, where the consequences of knowledge can have far-reaching effects.

The ethical lessons found in the Havamal also extend to the realm of personal integrity and self-awareness. The text encourages individuals to engage in self-reflection and to cultivate an understanding of their own motivations and desires. This introspective approach is vital in today's world, where external pressures can lead to decisions that conflict with one's core values. By advocating for self-examination and the pursuit of inner wisdom, the Havamal provides a philosophical foundation for ethical living that emphasizes authenticity and moral clarity.

Finally, the Havamal's relevance to modern ethics is evident in its exploration of the balance between individualism and communal responsibility. In contemporary society, where personal freedom is often prioritized, the text reminds us of the interconnectedness of our actions and their impact on the larger community. By fostering a sense of ethical obligation to others, the Havamal encourages a holistic approach to ethics that integrates personal growth with social well-being. This synthesis of individual and collective responsibility is essential in addressing the moral challenges faced in modern life, making the teachings of the Havamal not only timeless but also urgently applicable today.

# Chapter 11: Symbolism and Imagery in the Havamal's Verses

## Key Symbols and Their Meanings

In the Havamal, a collection of Old Norse poems offering wisdom and guidance, symbols play a crucial role in conveying deeper meanings and moral lessons. One of the most prominent symbols is the "raven," often associated with Odin, the god of wisdom and knowledge. Ravens in Norse mythology are seen as messengers, bridging the gap between the human and divine realms. Their presence in the Havamal signifies the importance of seeking knowledge, understanding the world around us, and being open to the lessons that life offers. This symbol encourages readers to be observant and to cultivate wisdom through experience and learning.

Another potent symbol found in the Havamal is the "axe," which represents both the potential for conflict and the necessity of resolution. The axe can be interpreted as a metaphor for the challenges and adversities one faces in life. It serves as a reminder that while conflict is often unavoidable, how one chooses to wield their axe—whether in defense or aggression—determines the outcome. This duality emphasizes the importance of temperance and deliberation in decision-making, urging individuals to approach conflict with a sense of responsibility and foresight.

The "fire" is yet another significant symbol within the Havamal, representing warmth, community, and transformation. Fire is integral to Norse culture, symbolizing both the light of knowledge and the destructive potential of unchecked passions. In the context of the Havamal, fire invites readers to reflect on the balance between nurturing relationships and the dangers of uncontrolled emotions. It encourages the cultivation of inner strength and resilience while remaining mindful of the potential consequences of one's actions in both personal and social contexts.

The concept of "fate," often linked with the Norns in Norse mythology, serves as a recurring symbol in the Havamal. Fate represents the inevitability of certain life events and the acceptance of one's circumstances. This symbol underscores the importance of recognizing and embracing the things we cannot change while focusing on what we can influence. The Havamal teaches that understanding fate allows individuals to navigate life's challenges with grace and wisdom, fostering a sense of peace amid uncertainty.

Lastly, the symbol of "friendship" permeates the Havamal's teachings, highlighting the value of camaraderie and loyalty in personal relationships. The text stresses that true friendship is built on mutual respect and understanding, encouraging readers to cultivate bonds that are both supportive and enriching. This symbol serves as a reminder that relationships are foundational to a fulfilling life, urging individuals to invest time and energy into fostering connections that contribute to personal growth and collective well-being. In a world that often prioritizes individualism, the Havamal's emphasis on friendship reinvigorates the importance of community and shared experiences.

## Imagery in Context

Imagery in the Havamal serves as a powerful vehicle for conveying its teachings and philosophies. The verses are rich with metaphorical language, drawing upon the natural world and everyday experiences to illustrate deeper truths about human existence. This vivid imagery not only enhances the aesthetic quality of the text but also facilitates a more profound understanding of its moral and ethical lessons. The use of tangible symbols from nature, such as the raven, the wolf, or the oak tree, allows the reader to connect with the teachings on a visceral level, bridging the gap between the ancient context of the Havamal and modern interpretations.

The historical context in which the Havamal was composed also plays a significant role in the imagery presented. Rooted in the traditions of the Norse people, the text reflects their environment, societal norms, and values. The imagery often evokes the harsh realities of Viking life, where survival depended on wisdom, resourcefulness, and the strength of social bonds. For instance, the depiction of the communal feast not only highlights the importance of hospitality but also serves as a reminder of the social structures that underpin human relationships. These images resonate with the collective memory of the Norse culture, grounding the teachings in a context that is both specific and universally relevant.

In examining the imagery within the Havamal, one can draw parallels with other ancient texts, revealing a shared human experience across cultures. Similar themes of wisdom, friendship, and ethical conduct can be found in the works of philosophers from different traditions, such as the Tao Te Ching or the Analects of Confucius. This comparative analysis highlights the universality of the Havamal's teachings, as the imagery employed often mirrors the symbolic language found in these texts. The imagery serves not only to convey the specific values of Norse culture but also to engage with a broader, timeless dialogue about the human condition.

The psychological insights offered through the Havamal's imagery provide practical applications for contemporary life. The verses encourage readers to reflect on their inner lives and relationships, promoting self-awareness and empathy. The imagery of the wise man, who observes and learns from his surroundings, serves as a guide for personal development. By engaging with the symbols and lessons of the Havamal, individuals can cultivate a deeper understanding of their own values and behaviors, fostering healthier social interactions and a more mindful approach to life.

Finally, the role of imagery in the Havamal extends to contemporary pagan practices, where these vivid symbols are often invoked in rituals and teachings. Practitioners draw upon the powerful imagery of the text to connect with the wisdom of their ancestors, using it as a source of inspiration and guidance in their spiritual journeys. The imagery not only enriches the practice but also serves to keep the teachings of the Havamal alive in a modern context, demonstrating the text's continued relevance and the enduring nature of its wisdom. Through this exploration of imagery, readers can appreciate the depth and richness of the Havamal, recognizing its potential to inform and enhance both personal and communal experiences.

# The Role of Metaphor in Understanding

Metaphor serves as a vital tool in the realm of understanding, particularly within the rich tapestry of the Havamal's teachings. In this ancient text, metaphors are not merely decorative language but are foundational to conveying complex ideas about life, morality, and human relationships. By employing metaphors, the Havamal transcends the limitations of literal language, allowing readers to explore deeper meanings and insights into the human condition. These figurative expressions create layers of interpretation, inviting readers to engage with the text on both intellectual and emotional levels.

The historical context of the Havamal further underscores the significance of metaphor in its verses. Composed during a time when oral traditions dominated, metaphors served as mnemonic devices that facilitated the transmission of wisdom across generations. This poetic technique was essential in a culture that valued storytelling and the oral recitation of knowledge. By embedding profound truths within metaphorical frameworks, the Havamal ensured that its teachings would resonate with listeners, prompting reflection and discussion that extended beyond the immediate surface meaning.

In examining the Havamal's influence on Norse mythology and culture, it becomes evident that metaphors have shaped not only personal understanding but also collective identity. The metaphoric language often draws on natural elements, animals, and daily experiences familiar to the Norse people, fostering a sense of connection between the individual and the cosmos. Such imagery reinforces the notion that wisdom is intertwined with the natural world, emphasizing the importance of living in harmony with one's surroundings. This relationship between metaphor and cultural identity is crucial in appreciating how the Havamal informs contemporary pagan practices, where these metaphoric insights continue to inspire rituals and ethical frameworks.

Practical applications of the Havamal's teachings in modern life also benefit from the metaphorical language woven throughout the verses. By unpacking metaphors, individuals can extract relevant lessons for personal growth, interpersonal relationships, and ethical decision-making. For instance, the metaphor of the "noble oak" may symbolize strength and resilience in the face of adversity, encouraging readers to cultivate these qualities in their own lives. This adaptability of metaphor allows the wisdom of the Havamal to remain pertinent, providing guidance that resonates with the challenges faced in contemporary society.

Lastly, the psychological insights derived from the Havamal's metaphors reveal the depth of human experience, showcasing the intricate interplay between thought, emotion, and behavior. By engaging with metaphorical expressions, individuals can gain a more nuanced understanding of their own motivations and relationships. The ethical and moral lessons embedded in these metaphors challenge readers to reflect on their values and choices, promoting self-awareness and personal transformation. Ultimately, the role of metaphor in the Havamal enriches its teachings, making them an enduring source of wisdom that continues to illuminate the path of understanding in both ancient and modern contexts.

# Chapter 12: Conclusion: The Enduring Legacy of the Havamal

## Summary of Key Insights

The Havamal serves as a profound reservoir of wisdom that transcends its historical context, offering insights that remain relevant in contemporary society. This ancient Norse text, often considered a foundational piece of the poetic Edda, intertwines practical advice with philosophical musings, allowing readers to glean valuable lessons on ethics, relationships, and personal conduct. The teachings found within the Havamal provide a comprehensive understanding of the values and beliefs of the Norse people, and they continue to influence both modern pagan practices and the broader cultural landscape.

One of the key insights from the Havamal revolves around the importance of social relationships and the ethical principles that govern them. The text emphasizes the value of friendship, loyalty, and mutual respect, underscoring how these principles foster a sense of community and belonging. In a world increasingly marked by individualism, the Havamal's teachings on interpersonal dynamics serve as a reminder of the significance of maintaining strong bonds with others. The advice on choosing friends wisely and nurturing those relationships is particularly pertinent, as it encourages individuals to cultivate supportive networks that contribute to personal and communal well-being.

Moreover, the Havamal's exploration of moral lessons and ethical conduct provides a framework for navigating the complexities of modern life. Its verses advocate for integrity, moderation, and wisdom in decision-making, echoing themes found in other ancient texts such as the Tao Te Ching and the Analects of Confucius. This comparative analysis highlights a universal human quest for guidance in ethical living, suggesting that the Havamal's insights are not only relevant to its own cultural context but also resonate across diverse philosophical traditions. The text's pragmatic approach to ethical dilemmas encourages readers to reflect on their values and the implications of their choices.

Symbolism and imagery play a vital role in conveying the Havamal's teachings, enriching its poetic verses with layers of meaning. The use of nature as a metaphor for human experience invites readers to draw connections between the external world and their internal lives. This intricate symbolism enhances the text's psychological insights, allowing individuals to engage with the Havamal on a deeper level. By interpreting these symbols, readers can uncover personal meanings that inform their understanding of self and society, fostering a more profound connection with the wisdom encapsulated within the verses.

In summary, the Havamal offers a wealth of insights that are both historically rooted and universally applicable. Its teachings on friendship, ethical conduct, and the importance of community resonate deeply in contemporary life, encouraging individuals to reflect on their relationships and moral choices. The symbolic richness of the text invites ongoing exploration and interpretation, ensuring its relevance across generations. As both a historical artifact and a living guide, the Havamal continues to inspire those seeking wisdom in the complexities of modern existence.

## Future Directions for Study

As the interest in the Havamal continues to grow, it is crucial to explore innovative methodologies for analyzing its verses and their implications. Future research should focus on interdisciplinary approaches, combining literary analysis, historical context, and cultural studies. By investigating the Havamal through these various lenses, scholars can enhance our understanding of its significance within Norse mythology and cultural practices. This multifaceted approach can also uncover deeper psychological insights, allowing for a richer interpretation of its teachings on human relationships and moral lessons.

Moreover, the Havamal's influence on contemporary pagan practices presents an exciting avenue for exploration. Future studies could examine how modern practitioners interpret and apply the wisdom contained in the text. This might involve fieldwork, interviews, and participant observation within contemporary pagan communities. By understanding how the Havamal informs rituals, beliefs, and ethical frameworks today, researchers can bridge the gap between ancient wisdom and modern spirituality, illuminating the text's enduring relevance.

A comparative analysis of the Havamal with other ancient texts can yield valuable insights into universal themes and cultural distinctions. Scholars should look into how themes of wisdom, morality, and social relationships are expressed in other traditions, such as the Tao Te Ching, the Bible, or the Analects of Confucius. Such comparative studies can reveal shared human experiences and values while also highlighting the unique aspects of the Havamal's teachings. This broader context can enrich our understanding of the text's place within the global literary canon.

The Havamal's rich symbolism and imagery deserve further scholarly attention. Future studies could delve into the metaphors and symbols employed in its verses, exploring how they convey complex ideas about existence, community, and the human condition. Understanding the symbolic language of the Havamal can enhance our appreciation of its poetry and provide insights into the cultural mindset of the Norse people. This exploration can also inform contemporary applications of its teachings, as individuals seek to find meaning and connection in their own lives.

Lastly, the psychological insights derived from the Havamal's wisdom hold significant potential for modern applications. Future research can investigate how the text's teachings on friendship, social relationships, and ethical behavior can inform contemporary psychological practices. By integrating the Havamal's perspectives into modern therapeutic approaches, practitioners can offer clients a rich resource for personal growth and relational understanding. The enduring wisdom of the Havamal can serve as a guide for navigating the complexities of modern life, making its study not only relevant but essential in our quest for understanding and meaning.

## The Havamal's Place in Modern Discourse

The Havamal, a revered collection of Old Norse poetry, holds a distinctive place in modern discourse, bridging the gap between ancient wisdom and contemporary life. Its verses, often viewed as a guide to ethical living, friendship, and social conduct, resonate with individuals seeking insights into their personal and communal relationships. The text's practical advice, such as the importance of hospitality and the value of wisdom, offers relevant lessons for modern readers navigating the complexities of interpersonal dynamics and moral dilemmas. This relevance has sparked scholarly interest and public engagement, leading to a resurgence of interest in the text within various cultural and philosophical contexts.

In understanding the Havamal's historical context, one must recognize its origins in a period steeped in Norse tradition and mythology. Composed in a time when oral storytelling was paramount, the Havamal encapsulates not only the values and beliefs of the Viking Age but also the communal spirit of its people. This historical backdrop enhances the appreciation of its teachings, as they emerge from a society that revered bravery, loyalty, and wisdom. The interplay of these values within the text invites modern readers to reflect on how such principles can be integrated into contemporary life, particularly in a world where traditional social structures have evolved.

The interpretation of the Havamal's poetry reveals layers of meaning that continue to inspire comparative analysis with other ancient texts. Scholars frequently draw parallels between the Havamal and works such as the Proverbs of the Bible or the Tao Te Ching, highlighting common themes of wisdom, ethical conduct, and the nature of human relationships. This comparative approach not only enriches the understanding of the Havamal itself but also situates it within a broader discourse on moral philosophy and human behavior. By examining these similarities, modern readers can find a universal thread of wisdom that transcends cultural boundaries and historical contexts.

The influence of the Havamal extends beyond academic circles into contemporary pagan practices, where its teachings are often invoked in rituals and spiritual reflections. This revival of interest in Norse paganism has led to a renewed engagement with the text, as practitioners seek to embody its principles in their daily lives. The Havamal's insights into friendship, loyalty, and the ethical treatment of others resonate deeply within these communities, serving as a foundation for moral conduct and interpersonal relationships. This practical application of the Havamal's teachings reflects a desire for authenticity and connection in a modern world that often feels fragmented.

Lastly, the psychological insights derived from the Havamal's wisdom offer valuable perspectives on self-awareness and emotional intelligence. The text's emphasis on moderation, the importance of listening, and the recognition of one's limitations encourages a reflective approach to personal growth. By internalizing these teachings, individuals can cultivate healthier relationships, navigate conflicts with greater ease, and foster a sense of community grounded in mutual respect. As modern society grapples with issues of isolation and disconnection, the Havamal provides a framework for understanding and improving social relationships, ultimately affirming its enduring relevance in today's discours

# Reconstructing the Past: A Guide to Norse Paganism for the Modern Seeker

## Chapter 1: Introduction to Norse Paganism

### Historical Context

The historical context of Norse paganism is essential for understanding its development and the ways in which it has been reconstructed in the modern era. Emerging from the ancient Germanic traditions, Norse paganism was deeply rooted in the cultural and social practices of the Norse people, who inhabited Scandinavia and parts of Northern Europe from around the 8th to the 11th centuries. This period, commonly referred to as the Viking Age, saw the flourishing of a rich tapestry of beliefs centered around a pantheon of deities, nature, and ancestral spirits. The primary sources of information about these beliefs come from sagas, poems, and archaeological findings that illustrate the spiritual life of the Norse people, including their rituals, cosmology, and community structures.

Central to Norse paganism are the deities, each embodying various aspects of life and nature. Gods such as Odin, Thor, and Freyja played significant roles in the spiritual lives of the Norse, representing wisdom, strength, and fertility, respectively. These deities were worshipped through a variety of rituals and ceremonies, often conducted at sacred sites, such as groves or altars. The historical practices of the Norse were not only religious but also communal; they reinforced social bonds and cultural identity within Viking society. The transition to Christianity in the late first millennium marked a significant shift in these practices, leading to the gradual decline of traditional worship and the adaptation of old customs into new Christian contexts.

The remnants of Norse beliefs can be traced through various historical sources, including the Eddas and sagas, written in the 13th century but reflecting much older oral traditions. The Prose Edda and the Poetic Edda provide rich narratives about the gods, creation myths, and hero tales, which are crucial for modern practitioners seeking to reconnect with these ancient beliefs. Additionally, archaeological evidence, such as burials, rune stones, and artifacts, offers insights into the spiritual practices and daily lives of the Norse, revealing how they interacted with their environment and the divine. These sources serve as a foundation for reconstructionist approaches to Norse paganism, emphasizing authenticity and historical accuracy in contemporary practice.

Norse runes, another significant aspect of the tradition, were not merely an alphabet but also held deep spiritual and magical meanings. Each rune is associated with specific concepts, deities, and natural elements, making them powerful tools for divination and personal reflection. Modern seekers often incorporate runes into their spiritual practices, using them to gain insights and guidance. This practice reflects a broader trend in contemporary Norse paganism, where individuals draw upon historical elements while adapting them to fit modern contexts. The distinction between reconstructionist and eclectic approaches highlights the ongoing dialogue within the community, as some practitioners prioritize historical fidelity while others embrace a more fluid interpretation of Norse spirituality.

In recent years, Norse paganism has found a place in popular culture, influencing literature, film, and art, which has, in turn, sparked renewed interest in its historical roots. This cultural resurgence has led to the establishment of communities and gatherings, where practitioners come together to celebrate their shared beliefs and practices. Such gatherings often include rituals, storytelling, and discussions about the environment, reflecting the Norse view of humanity's interconnectedness with nature. As modern seekers navigate their spiritual paths, the historical context of Norse paganism serves not only as a guide but also as a reminder of the enduring power of these ancient traditions in contemporary life.

## Key Concepts and Beliefs

Norse paganism, often referred to as Ásatrú or Heathenry, is a contemporary spiritual path that seeks to revive and reconstruct the ancient beliefs and practices of the Norse peoples. At its core, Norse paganism centers around a pantheon of deities, including Odin, Thor, Freyja, and Loki, each embodying distinct aspects of life and nature. These gods and goddesses not only represent various human experiences but also serve as archetypes that practitioners can relate to in their personal journeys. Understanding these deities and their stories, drawn from sources like the Poetic Edda and the Prose Edda, is fundamental to grasping the essence of Norse spirituality.

Another critical aspect of Norse paganism is its emphasis on rituals and ceremonies. Traditional Viking practices, such as blóts (sacrifices) and sumbels (ritual toasts), play an integral role in community bonding and personal devotion. These rites serve not only to honor the gods but also to connect individuals with their ancestors and the natural world. Modern practitioners often adapt these ancient rituals to fit contemporary contexts, ensuring that the spirit of the traditions remains alive while also being relevant to today's seekers. This adaptability demonstrates the resilience of Norse paganism as a living tradition.

Norse runes, the ancient alphabet used by the Germanic peoples, hold significant spiritual meaning within the Norse pagan framework. Each rune is associated with specific concepts, deities, and energies, making them powerful tools for divination and personal reflection. Practitioners often engage with runes in various ways, whether through casting, carving, or meditative practices. Understanding the meanings and symbolism of runes allows practitioners to tap into their deeper insights, fostering a connection with the cosmos and the divine.

The relationship between Norse paganism and the environment is also a vital area of focus. Many modern practitioners emphasize the importance of nature and the interconnectedness of all living beings. This ecological awareness stems from ancient Norse beliefs that viewed the natural world as infused with spirit and divinity. Rituals and practices often include offerings to land spirits, honoring the earth's cycles, and promoting sustainable living. Such commitments reflect a broader trend within Norse paganism that recognizes the urgency of environmental stewardship in today's world.

Lastly, the tension between reconstructionist and eclectic forms of Norse paganism highlights the diversity within the community. Reconstructionists strive to adhere closely to historical sources and practices, while eclectic practitioners may blend elements from various spiritual traditions. This dynamic fosters discussions about authenticity and the evolution of spiritual practices. Furthermore, the influence of Norse mythology in popular culture has brought renewed interest in these ancient beliefs, inspiring community gatherings, workshops, and festivals that promote shared experiences and learning. Ultimately, the key concepts and beliefs of Norse paganism invite modern seekers to explore their spirituality while engaging with their heritage and the world around them.

## Importance of Reconstructing the Past

The reconstruction of the past plays a pivotal role in understanding and practicing Norse paganism today. Engaging with historical sources, such as sagas, eddas, and archaeological findings, allows modern seekers to connect more authentically with the beliefs and customs of their ancestors. These texts and artifacts provide a lens through which practitioners can interpret the spiritual practices, rituals, and values of the Norse people. By studying these materials, individuals can gain insights into the worldview of the Vikings, including their relationship with nature, the divine, and the community, fostering a deeper appreciation for the historical context of their spiritual path.

Reconstructing the past also emphasizes the importance of accuracy and authenticity within Norse paganism. The rise of eclectic practices, while offering a broader range of spiritual experiences, can sometimes dilute the core tenets that define Norse beliefs. By grounding their practices in historical accuracy, practitioners can maintain a sense of continuity with the past, ensuring that their rituals and ceremonies resonate with the original intentions and meanings. This commitment to authenticity not only honors the legacy of the Norse people but also strengthens the spiritual foundation upon which modern practitioners build their own beliefs and practices.

Furthermore, the exploration of Norse mythology and its deities through a reconstructive lens reveals the complexities of these ancient belief systems. Each deity represents not only specific attributes and domains but also the cultural values and societal norms of the time. By understanding these mythological figures and the stories surrounding them, seekers can draw parallels to their own lives, finding guidance and inspiration in the narratives that have shaped Norse spirituality. This connection to mythology enriches personal spiritual practices, allowing individuals to engage with the divine in a way that feels both rooted in tradition and relevant to contemporary life.

The relationship between Norse paganism and the environment is another critical aspect that emerges from reconstructing the past. The Vikings had a profound respect for nature, viewing it as a living entity imbued with spirit and significance. By revisiting these ancient perspectives, modern practitioners can cultivate a more sustainable and harmonious relationship with the environment. This alignment with nature not only enhances spiritual practices but also encourages a collective responsibility towards ecological stewardship, reflecting the values of the Norse traditions in the context of today's environmental challenges.

Lastly, community building is a vital component of reconstructing the past within Norse paganism. Gathering with others who share similar beliefs fosters a sense of belonging and connection, echoing the communal practices of the ancient Norse. By forming groups that emphasize historical accuracy and collective rituals, practitioners can create spaces that honor the traditions while also adapting them to modern contexts. This communal approach reinforces the shared values of reverence for the past, respect for nature, and the importance of interpersonal relationships, ultimately enriching the spiritual journey of each individual within the community.

# Chapter 2: Norse Mythology and Its Deities

## Overview of Norse Mythology

Norse mythology encompasses a rich tapestry of stories, beliefs, and practices that originated among the ancient Norse people. At its core, it describes a complex cosmology featuring a pantheon of gods, goddesses, and various mythical beings, each playing a pivotal role in the interplay of creation, destruction, and the human experience. Key figures such as Odin, the all-father and god of wisdom; Thor, the thunder god known for his strength; and Freyja, the goddess of love and fertility, serve as central characters in these narratives. These deities are not merely distant figures; they embody various aspects of life, nature, and human emotion, providing adherents with archetypes through which to understand their own lives.

The historical sources that document Norse beliefs are varied and often fragmentary, stemming from a mix of poetic verses, sagas, and archaeological findings. The Poetic Edda and the Prose Edda, both composed in medieval Iceland, remain the most significant texts for understanding the mythology and its cultural context. These texts not only recount the adventures and attributes of the gods but also reflect the values and societal norms of the time. In addition to these literary sources, artifacts such as runestones and burial sites offer invaluable insights into the rituals and practices that accompanied the worship of these deities, highlighting the deep connection between the Norse people and their environment.

Rituals and ceremonies within Norse paganism were integral to community life, often serving as a means to honor the gods, seek their favor, or mark significant life events. Blóts, or sacrifices, were commonly performed to celebrate the changing seasons, ensure successful harvests, or commemorate the dead. These gatherings fostered a sense of community and belonging, reinforcing the social fabric of Norse society. In contemporary practice, many Norse pagans seek to revive these ancient rituals, adapting them to modern contexts while maintaining their spiritual significance. This revival not only honors historical traditions but also strengthens the bonds among practitioners today.

Runes, the ancient script used by the Norse, carry profound meanings and are often employed in various spiritual practices and divination. Each rune symbolizes specific concepts, energies, or deities, allowing practitioners to connect with deeper layers of their spiritual journey. The practice of rune casting has become a popular form of divination among modern seekers, providing insights into personal challenges or guidance for future endeavors. This blend of historical significance and contemporary application illustrates the dynamic nature of Norse paganism, where ancient wisdom finds relevance in today's world.

As Norse paganism continues to evolve, it occupies a unique space within the broader landscape of modern spirituality. From the reconstructionist approach, which emphasizes historical accuracy and fidelity to ancient practices, to the eclectic methods that incorporate diverse influences, practitioners navigate their spiritual paths in various ways. Moreover, Norse mythology has permeated popular culture, appearing in literature, film, and art, thus influencing contemporary perceptions of the ancient Norse worldview. For many, engaging with this mythology is not merely an academic pursuit but a way to connect with a broader narrative of humanity, identity, and the natural world, fostering a deeper appreciation of both the past and the present.

## The Aesir and Vanir: Major Pantheons

The Aesir and Vanir represent two of the most prominent pantheons in Norse mythology, each embodying distinct aspects of the cosmos, culture, and human experience. The Aesir, often associated with power, war, and governance, include well-known deities such as Odin, Thor, and Frigg. They are typically portrayed as the ruling gods of Asgard, the celestial stronghold, and their narratives often reflect themes of conflict, authority, and the quest for knowledge. In contrast, the Vanir are linked to fertility, prosperity, and the natural world, featuring gods like Njord, Freyr, and Freyja. This pantheon emphasizes balance, sustainability, and harmonious relationships with the earth, making their role crucial in the context of Norse beliefs about the environment.

The relationship between the Aesir and Vanir is complex and multifaceted, marked by both cooperation and conflict. The most significant event in their history is the Aesir-Vanir War, which stemmed from misunderstandings and differing values between the two groups. Ultimately, this conflict culminated in a peace treaty that led to a mutual exchange of deities, symbolizing a blending of their powers and attributes. This integration highlights the importance of unity and coexistence in Norse cosmology, suggesting that both pantheons are essential for maintaining balance in the universe.

Understanding the characteristics and roles of these deities can enrich one's practice of Norse paganism. The Aesir, with their emphasis on strength and honor, inspire rituals focused on courage and protection. Celebrations may center around seasonal changes, such as the winter solstice or the summer solstice, and invoke Aesir deities for guidance and support. Conversely, the Vanir's association with fertility and abundance invites practitioners to engage in rituals that honor the earth and promote sustainability. Ceremonies dedicated to the Vanir often involve offerings to nature, reflecting a deep respect for the environment and the interdependence of all life.

The historical sources that recount the tales of the Aesir and Vanir serve as vital resources for modern seekers of Norse paganism. Texts such as the Poetic Edda and the Prose Edda provide a wealth of information about the gods, their attributes, and their interactions. Additionally, archaeological findings and sagas reveal how these beliefs were woven into the daily lives and practices of the Norse people. This rich tapestry of history allows contemporary practitioners to reconstruct authentic rituals and ceremonies, ensuring that their spiritual practices are grounded in tradition while remaining relevant to modern life.

In contemporary culture, the fascination with the Aesir and Vanir has found expression in various forms, from literature and films to games and art. This resurgence highlights a growing interest in Norse mythology and its deities, prompting individuals to explore their significance in today's world. For those involved in community building, understanding the dynamics between these pantheons can foster connections with others who share similar interests. Whether through gatherings, workshops, or online forums, engaging with the stories and values of the Aesir and Vanir can inspire collective spiritual practices and a deeper appreciation for the interconnectedness of all beings within the cosmos.

## Lesser-Known Deities and Their Roles

Lesser-known deities in Norse mythology play crucial roles that often go unrecognized in mainstream discussions about the pantheon. While figures like Odin, Thor, and Freyja dominate the narrative, numerous other gods and goddesses significantly influence the spiritual landscape and rituals of Norse paganism. These deities embody specific aspects of life, nature, and human experience, offering unique insights into the beliefs and practices of the Norse people. Understanding their roles can enrich one's spiritual journey and deepen the connection to the Norse tradition.

One such deity is Skadi, a goddess associated with winter, hunting, and the mountains. Skadi is often depicted as a fierce and independent figure, representing the strength and resilience required to thrive in harsh environments. Her story, which includes a marriage with Njord, the god of the sea, symbolizes the balance between the wilderness and civilization, land and water. In Norse pagan rituals, invoking Skadi can be particularly relevant during the winter months or when seeking guidance in matters related to survival and the natural world.

Another lesser-known deity is Bragi, the god of poetry and eloquence. Although he may not be as widely recognized, Bragi's influence permeates the cultural fabric of the Norse world. He embodies the importance of storytelling and the arts, serving as a muse for poets and bards. In modern practice, honoring Bragi can manifest through rituals that celebrate creativity, such as gatherings where participants share stories, poems, or songs, thereby fostering community and preserving the oral traditions that are central to Norse heritage.

The goddess Idun, known for her role in maintaining the youth of the gods through her golden apples, represents vitality and renewal. Idun's association with spring and rebirth highlights the cyclical nature of life, making her an essential figure in rituals that celebrate the changing seasons. Invoking Idun during spring equinox celebrations can serve as a reminder of the importance of rejuvenation and growth, both in nature and within oneself, aligning with the broader themes of Norse paganism that emphasize the interconnectedness of all life.

Lastly, the figure of Forseti, the god of justice and reconciliation, plays a significant role in maintaining harmony among the gods and humans. Forseti's wisdom in resolving disputes and promoting fairness is particularly relevant in today's world, where community and cooperation are vital for spiritual and social cohesion. Engaging with Forseti in personal or communal practices can inspire followers to seek justice and understanding in their interactions, reinforcing the values of community and ethical conduct that are central to Norse pagan beliefs. By acknowledging these lesser-known deities and their unique attributes, practitioners can cultivate a more holistic understanding of Norse mythology and its relevance to modern spiritual practice.

# Chapter 3: Viking Rituals and Ceremonies

## Sacrificial Practices

Sacrificial practices in Norse paganism were deeply rooted in the cultural and spiritual fabric of the ancient Norse societies, serving as vital expressions of devotion and community. These rituals were not merely acts of offering but were imbued with profound significance, reflecting the relationship between humans, the divine, and the natural world. Sacrifices were seen as a means to maintain balance between these realms, ensuring favor from the gods and securing prosperity for the community. The traditions surrounding these offerings varied widely, influenced by local customs, the availability of resources, and the specific deities being honored.

Historically, sacrifices could take various forms, including offerings of food, animals, and even, in some accounts, humans. Animal sacrifice, particularly of domesticated animals such as sheep and cattle, was common during festivals and important events. The blood of the sacrificed animals was often used in rituals, sometimes sprinkled on altars or participants as a means of purification and connection to the divine. These offerings were typically accompanied by prayers and invocations aimed at specific deities, such as Odin, Frey, or Thor, each of whom had their own attributes and domains that the sacrifices aimed to appease.

The concept of blóts, or sacrificial feasts, was central to these practices. A blot involved the ritualistic killing of an animal, followed by a communal feast where the community would gather to share in the meal and give thanks. These gatherings strengthened social bonds and reinforced communal identity, allowing participants to reconnect with their ancestors and the wider spiritual world. The act of sharing food was seen as a means of sharing life force, creating a spiritual communion that transcended the physical realm.

In modern Norse pagan practices, reconstructionist approaches to sacrificial rituals emphasize historical accuracy and cultural authenticity. Practitioners seek to recreate these ancient rites based on historical texts, archaeological findings, and ethnographic studies. This focus on tradition contrasts with more eclectic practices, which may incorporate a range of influences from various spiritual traditions, often leading to a more individualized interpretation of sacrificial offerings. While both approaches can coexist, the tension between maintaining historical integrity and embracing personal spiritual expression is an ongoing discussion within the community.

As contemporary practitioners navigate the landscape of Norse paganism, the environmental aspect of sacrificial practices cannot be overlooked. Many modern seekers are increasingly aware of their ecological footprint, seeking to honor the land and its resources through sustainable practices. This has led to a revival of more nature-based offerings, aligning with the Norse belief in the interconnectedness of all life. By integrating these values into sacrificial practices, modern Norse pagans strive to honor their ancestors while also being mindful stewards of the earth, creating a bridge between the ancient traditions and contemporary ecological consciousness.

## Seasonal Celebrations

Seasonal celebrations hold a significant place in Norse paganism, reflecting the cyclical nature of life and the interconnectedness of humanity with the natural world. These observances are deeply rooted in ancient traditions, celebrating the changing seasons and their impact on agriculture, livestock, and the community's well-being. Each celebration corresponds with specific seasonal markers, such as the winter solstice, spring equinox, summer solstice, and autumn equinox, and is often accompanied by rituals that honor the deities associated with these times, such as Odin, Freyja, and Thor. The rhythms of nature not only guide agricultural practices but also shape spiritual beliefs and community interactions.

Yule, celebrated during the winter solstice, is one of the most prominent seasonal celebrations in Norse paganism. Traditionally, it marks the rebirth of the sun and the gradual return of light. Celebrants engage in rituals that include lighting fires, feasting, and honoring deities associated with fertility and rebirth. The Yule log, a central symbol of this festival, is often decorated with runes and herbs, representing a connection to the earth and ancestral spirits. This time of reflection and gratitude fosters a sense of community, as families and friends gather to share stories, exchange gifts, and rekindle bonds that may have waned during the harsh winter months.

As the seasons shift toward spring, the celebration of Ostara emerges, emphasizing renewal and growth. This festival corresponds with the spring equinox, representing balance and the return of fertility to the earth. Rituals during Ostara often involve planting seeds, honoring the earth, and invoking the blessings of deities such as Freyja and Idunn. Celebrants may incorporate symbols of fertility, such as eggs and hares, into their rites, echoing ancient practices that celebrate life and abundance. The emphasis on community during Ostara is also vital, as individuals come together to prepare for the season of growth, fostering a spirit of cooperation and shared purpose.

Summer solstice, or Midsummer, is another key celebration that highlights the power of the sun and the height of life on earth. This festival celebrates the longest day of the year, symbolizing vitality and abundance. Rituals may include bonfires, singing, dancing, and honoring the gods of the sun and nature. The community aspect of Midsummer is particularly important, as people gather to share food, stories, and merriment, reinforcing social bonds and collective identity. The vibrant energy of this time encourages participants to connect with their surroundings, invoking gratitude for the warmth and growth that the sun provides.

As autumn approaches, the festival of Harvest or Blót offers a time of thanksgiving. This celebration focuses on gratitude for the bounty of the earth and the preparation for the coming winter months. Rituals often involve the offering of food and drink to the gods, ancestors, and land spirits, acknowledging the gifts received throughout the growing season. Community gatherings during this time foster a sense of unity, as individuals come together to share their harvest, tell stories, and reflect on the cycle of life and death. The cycle of seasonal celebrations in Norse paganism reinforces the profound connections between the community, the land, and the divine, inviting modern seekers to engage with these traditions as a means of fostering spiritual and communal growth.

## Life Cycle Rituals

Life cycle rituals in Norse paganism serve as profound markers that celebrate the various stages of human existence, from birth to death. These rituals are rooted deeply in the understanding of the interconnectedness between individuals and the wider cosmos, reflecting the Norse belief in fate, the influence of the gods, and the importance of community. Each life stage is recognized not only as a personal milestone but also as an opportunity for communal reinforcement of shared values, beliefs, and traditions. Rituals such as naming ceremonies, coming-of-age rites, weddings, and funerals are integral to fostering a sense of belonging and continuity within the community.

Naming ceremonies, or "vörðr," often take place shortly after a child's birth. This ritual not only welcomes the new life into the world but also establishes a connection between the child and the divine. In these ceremonies, family members and the community gather to invoke the blessings of the gods and ancestors, often through the use of runes, which are believed to hold significant power and meaning. The choice of a child's name can reflect ancestral lineage or desired traits, thus embedding the individual within a larger narrative. This practice emphasizes the importance of identity and heritage in Norse culture.

As individuals transition into adulthood, coming-of-age rituals mark the shift from childhood to responsibility. These ceremonies often involve tests of bravery, skill, and wisdom, reflecting the qualities valued in Norse society. Young men and women may undertake quests or challenges that symbolize their readiness to take on adult roles. Community support during these rites reinforces social bonds and highlights the collective investment in each individual's growth. These rituals serve not only as a personal milestone but also as a statement of readiness to contribute to the community.

Marriage ceremonies in Norse paganism are rich with symbolism and tradition. These rituals often include the exchange of vows before the gods and the community, emphasizing the importance of partnership and familial alliances. Elements such as the "handfasting" ritual, where the couple's hands are bound together, symbolize their commitment to each other and their shared path. The involvement of family and community underscores the belief that marriage is not just a union of two individuals, but a joining of families and social networks, reinforcing societal cohesion.

Death and funerary practices are perhaps the most poignant of life cycle rituals, reflecting the Norse view of life, death, and the afterlife. Funerals often incorporate elements that honor the deceased's journey to the afterlife, which may include offerings, feasting, and the recitation of poetry or sagas that celebrate the individual's life. The ritual act of sending the deceased off, whether through burial or cremation, signifies a final transition, but also a continuation of their legacy within the community. These rituals serve to provide closure for the living while reaffirming the cyclical nature of existence—birth, life, death, and rebirth—as understood in Norse cosmology.

# Chapter 4: Understanding Norse Runes

## History and Origin of Runes

Runes, the characters of the ancient Germanic alphabets, have a rich history that intertwines with the cultural and spiritual practices of the Norse peoples. The origins of runes can be traced back to the early centuries of the Common Era, with the earliest known inscriptions appearing around the 2nd century. Scholars believe that the runic alphabet, known as the Futhark, was influenced by the Latin and Etruscan scripts, adapted to suit the phonetic needs of the Germanic languages. This adaptation was more than a mere linguistic exercise; it marked the beginning of a unique system that held profound significance in the social and spiritual life of the Norse.

The term "rune" itself is derived from the Proto-Germanic word "rūna," meaning "secret" or "mystery," indicating that these symbols were not only tools for communication but also held esoteric meanings. Runes were often associated with magic and divination, as evidenced by their use in various rituals and ceremonies. The Norse believed that the runes possessed inherent power, capable of influencing fate and connecting practitioners to the divine. This belief system is reflected in the sagas and Eddas, where runes are frequently mentioned in association with gods like Odin, who is said to have discovered the runes through self-sacrifice and enlightenment.

Throughout the Viking Age, runes served multiple purposes, from marking graves and memorials to inscribing objects and talismans. This versatility underscores their significance in both daily life and spiritual practices. The inscriptions often conveyed messages of honor, identity, and the connection to the cosmos, serving as reminders of the intertwined nature of existence and the divine. As Norse society evolved, so too did the use of runes, with later variants emerging, such as the Anglo-Saxon Futhorc, which was adapted to accommodate the specific sounds of the English language.

The decline of runic use in favor of the Latin alphabet coincided with the Christianization of Scandinavia. This transition led to the loss of many traditional practices and beliefs surrounding the runes, relegating them to the shadows of history for centuries. However, the 19th century saw a resurgence of interest in runes during the Romantic movement, where they were reinterpreted as symbols of national identity and cultural heritage. This revival paved the way for modern Norse paganism, where runes are once again embraced as tools for spiritual practice, divination, and connection to ancestral wisdom.

Today, the study and practice of runes continue to thrive within the context of Norse paganism. Enthusiasts engage in varied interpretations of their meanings, drawing from historical sources while also incorporating contemporary insights. This blend of reconstructionist and eclectic approaches allows for a dynamic exploration of runes, fostering community building and gatherings that celebrate both the ancient traditions and their relevance in the modern world. As seekers delve into the history and significance of runes, they uncover a profound legacy that connects them to the past while enriching their spiritual journeys in the present.

## Rune Meanings and Interpretations

In Norse paganism, runes serve as a powerful symbol system, each imbued with unique meanings and interpretations that resonate deeply with the beliefs and practices of this ancient tradition. The runes, often associated with the god Odin, are not merely letters but magical symbols that convey profound spiritual insights. Each rune encapsulates a specific concept or force of nature, providing practitioners with a means to connect with the divine and the natural world. Understanding rune meanings is essential for anyone seeking to engage with Norse paganism authentically, as they serve as tools for divination, personal growth, and ritualistic practices.

The Elder Futhark, the oldest form of runic alphabets, consists of 24 characters, each accompanied by a name and a set of meanings. For instance, the rune Fehu represents wealth and prosperity, but it also speaks to the importance of sharing and the transient nature of material possessions. Similarly, the rune Kenaz symbolizes enlightenment and creativity, suggesting a flame of inspiration that can light the path toward personal transformation. By studying these meanings, practitioners can gain insights into their own lives and the world around them, using the runes as guides in their spiritual journeys.

Interpretation of runes can vary based on context, which makes their study a dynamic process. When drawn in a divination spread, for example, the significance of each rune can shift depending on its position and the surrounding symbols. This flexibility allows for a personalized approach to divination, where individuals can seek answers tailored to their unique circumstances. Moreover, practitioners are encouraged to develop their own interpretations over time, drawing on personal experiences and intuitive insights to deepen their understanding of each rune's essence.

The meanings of runes are also deeply intertwined with Norse mythology and the stories of the gods and goddesses. Many runes are linked to specific deities, reflecting their attributes and domains. For instance, the rune Tiwaz, associated with the god Tyr, embodies the principles of justice, honor, and sacrifice. Understanding these connections enriches the practice of Norse paganism by situating the runes within a broader mythological framework, allowing practitioners to engage with the narratives that inform their beliefs. This interplay between runes and mythology fosters a more holistic understanding of the spiritual landscape of Norse paganism.

Finally, the study of runes extends beyond individual interpretation to foster community building and shared practices within the Norse pagan community. Rituals involving runes, such as rune casting or creating rune stones, can bring practitioners together, reinforcing bonds through shared beliefs and experiences. These gatherings often serve as spaces for learning and exchange, where individuals can share their insights on rune meanings, engage in discussions about their historical significance, and explore their relevance in contemporary spiritual practices. As such, the exploration of rune meanings and interpretations becomes not just a personal journey, but a collective endeavor that strengthens the ties between practitioners of Norse paganism.

## Using Runes in Modern Practice

Runes, the ancient alphabets of the Germanic peoples, have transcended their original purpose as mere writing systems to become profound symbols of spiritual and magical significance in modern Norse pagan practices. In today's context, runes serve as tools for divination, meditation, and personal development, allowing practitioners to connect with the wisdom of their ancestors while navigating contemporary challenges. By engaging with runes, seekers can tap into the rich tapestry of Norse mythology and its deities, gaining insight into realms both seen and unseen.

The use of runes in divination mirrors ancient practices, where each symbol is imbued with specific meanings and energies. Modern practitioners often employ rune stones or cards to receive guidance on personal dilemmas or spiritual inquiries. This method of divination not only fosters a deeper understanding of oneself but also promotes a dialogue with the natural world, echoing the Norse belief in interconnectedness. As seekers draw runes, they engage in a ritual that honors the past while making sense of their present, allowing for a unique fusion of history and personal experience.

In addition to divination, runes can be integrated into various rituals and ceremonies, enhancing the spiritual atmosphere of gatherings and celebrations. By invoking specific runes associated with particular deities or natural forces, practitioners can focus their intentions and energies. This practice not only enriches communal experiences but also reinforces a sense of identity within the Norse pagan community. Rituals that incorporate runes can serve as powerful reminders of heritage, bridging the gap between ancient traditions and modern expressions of faith.

The exploration of runes also highlights the distinction between reconstructionist and eclectic approaches to Norse paganism. While reconstructionists strive to adhere closely to historical sources and practices, eclectics may adapt rune meanings and uses to fit their personal beliefs and lifestyles. This dynamic creates a vibrant landscape where diverse interpretations coexist, challenging practitioners to reflect on their own relationship with the symbols. Such discourse encourages a broader understanding of spirituality within the Norse context, illustrating how ancient wisdom can be relevant today.

Lastly, the cultural resurgence of Norse mythology and runes in popular media influences modern practices, often romanticizing or simplifying their meanings. However, this exposure can serve as a gateway for individuals to explore deeper aspects of Norse paganism, prompting them to seek authentic connections with their spiritual roots. By critically engaging with these representations and grounding their practices in historical and cultural contexts, modern seekers can cultivate a meaningful relationship with runes that honors both their ancestral heritage and contemporary spiritual needs

# Chapter 5: Norse Paganism and the Environment

## The Connection to Nature

The connection to nature is a fundamental aspect of Norse paganism, deeply woven into its rituals, beliefs, and worldview. The Norse people viewed nature as a living entity, imbued with spirit and significance. This reverence for the natural world is evident in the myths surrounding the deities, such as Freyja, who is associated with fertility and the earth, and Njord, the god of the sea and winds. The cycles of the seasons, the changing weather, and the rhythms of wildlife were not merely backdrops to human existence but integral components of their spiritual practice. Understanding this connection provides a vital framework for modern seekers looking to reconnect with their spiritual roots.

Norse mythology teaches that the world is a complex web of interconnected beings, including gods, giants, elves, and spirits. This interconnectedness extends to the land, water, and sky. Sacred sites, often natural features like mountains, rivers, and groves, were places of worship and offerings. The reverence for these spaces reflects a worldview where humans are part of a larger ecosystem, fostering a sense of responsibility toward the environment. Modern practitioners of Norse paganism can draw inspiration from these ancient beliefs, cultivating a spiritual practice that honors not only the divine but also the earth itself.

Rituals and ceremonies in Norse paganism often align with the cycles of nature, celebrating events such as solstices, equinoxes, and harvests. These celebrations are opportunities for community building, where individuals come together to honor the gods, share food, and partake in the rhythms of the natural world. Engaging in these seasonal rituals not only strengthens communal bonds but also reinforces the connection to nature. By aligning spiritual practices with the environment, practitioners can cultivate a deeper understanding of their place within the universe, creating a harmonious balance between the sacred and the mundane.

The incorporation of nature into spiritual practice is also evident in the use of Norse runes, which are often associated with natural elements and cycles. Each rune carries its own meaning, often reflecting aspects of the natural world, such as fertility, growth, or protection. Practitioners can use these symbols for divination or to guide their spiritual journeys, drawing on the wisdom embedded in nature. This approach highlights the importance of understanding the environment as a source of guidance and insight, encouraging a reverence for the world around us.

Finally, the modern resurgence of Norse paganism often intersects with contemporary environmental movements. As adherents seek to reconstruct historical beliefs, there is a growing awareness of the need to protect and preserve the natural world. This blend of spirituality and environmental activism reflects a commitment to honoring the earth, reminiscent of ancient practices. By fostering a deeper connection to nature, modern practitioners can engage with their spiritual heritage while also contributing to the well-being of the planet, ensuring that the wisdom of the past informs a sustainable future.

## Sustainable Practices in Norse Beliefs

Sustainable practices within Norse beliefs are deeply rooted in the interconnectedness of nature and spirituality. In Norse mythology, the cosmos is often viewed as a web of relationships between various beings, including gods, giants, and the natural world. This worldview encourages an understanding of humans as part of the environment rather than separate from it. The reverence for the land, waters, and all living creatures is evident in ancient texts, where deities like Freyr, associated with fertility and prosperity, underscore the importance of agriculture and the stewardship of the earth. Modern practitioners can draw inspiration from these beliefs to cultivate a harmonious relationship with nature, promoting sustainability in their daily lives.

Agricultural practices in the Viking Age illustrate the importance of sustainability in Norse culture. The Norse people relied heavily on farming and animal husbandry, adapting their methods to the climate and topography of their regions. They practiced crop rotation, selective breeding, and the use of natural fertilizers, reflecting a deep understanding of ecological balance. This traditional knowledge can inform contemporary sustainable agriculture, emphasizing techniques that respect the land and its resources. Reconstructing these practices today not only honors the legacy of our ancestors but also aligns with modern ecological principles that advocate for organic and regenerative farming.

Rituals and ceremonies in Norse paganism also emphasize sustainability. Seasonal festivals, such as Álfablót or Midsummer, celebrate the cycles of nature and the bounty of the earth. These gatherings often involve offerings to the land and spirits, reinforcing the idea of reciprocity between humans and nature. Participants express gratitude for the harvest and seek blessings for future growth, highlighting a commitment to preserving the environment. By integrating similar rituals into contemporary practices, modern Norse pagans can foster community awareness of ecological issues and promote actions that protect the earth.

Norse runes serve as another vehicle for expressing sustainable practices. The runes, viewed not just as letters but as symbols imbued with meaning, can be used in divination and magical workings to invoke protection for the environment. For instance, the rune Bjarkan, associated with growth and renewal, can be employed in rituals aimed at healing the earth or encouraging sustainable practices within a community. By utilizing these ancient symbols, practitioners can connect their spiritual work with tangible efforts that contribute to ecological well-being.

The tension between reconstructionist and eclectic forms of Norse paganism presents an opportunity to explore sustainability from multiple perspectives. Reconstructionists often emphasize historical accuracy, drawing from archaeological and literary sources to inform their practices, while eclectic practitioners may incorporate diverse influences and modern ideals. Both approaches can converge on the principle of sustainability, fostering a shared commitment to environmental stewardship that resonates with the core values of Norse beliefs. By building inclusive communities that respect both historical traditions and innovative practices, modern Norse pagans can create a robust framework for living sustainably in today's world.

# Environmental Ethics in Norse Paganism

Environmental ethics in Norse paganism arise from a profound reverence for nature, which is woven into the very fabric of its mythology and rituals. Central to this belief system is the understanding that the natural world is imbued with spirit and significance. The Norse deities, such as Freyr, who governs fertility and prosperity, are intrinsically linked to the land, waterways, and agricultural cycles. This connection fosters a sense of stewardship over the environment, emphasizing the importance of maintaining balance and harmony with the earth. For modern practitioners, this ancient worldview encourages a respectful relationship with nature, advocating for sustainable practices that honor the interconnectedness of all life.

The concept of land, or "landvættir," plays a critical role in Norse paganism, highlighting the belief that each region has its own protective spirits. These land spirits are often seen as guardians of the environment, and honoring them is essential for maintaining the health of the land. Rituals and offerings to these spirits, such as leaving food or creating sacred spaces, serve to acknowledge their presence and seek their favor. In this context, environmental ethics are not just about conservation; they also involve engaging actively with the spirit of the land, recognizing that every action has repercussions on the broader ecosystem.

Norse mythology also offers rich narratives that speak to the consequences of environmental neglect. Stories of Ragnarok, the end of the world, illustrate the chaotic disruption that follows when balance is lost. This myth serves as a cautionary tale for modern seekers, urging them to consider the long-term effects of their actions on the environment. By reflecting on such narratives, practitioners can draw parallels to contemporary issues like climate change, deforestation, and pollution, reinforcing the ethical imperative to protect the earth as a living entity deserving of respect and care.

Reconstructionist Norse pagans emphasize historical sources and archaeological findings to ground their practices in authenticity. This approach often includes studying the environmental practices of ancient Norse societies, such as their sustainable farming techniques and their relationships with local ecosystems. By integrating these historical insights into modern practice, reconstructionists advocate for a return to more sustainable living. This commitment to environmental ethics not only honors ancestral wisdom but also addresses the pressing ecological challenges faced today, creating a bridge between past and present.

In contrast, eclectic Norse paganism may incorporate a variety of beliefs and practices from different traditions, which can sometimes lead to a more individualistic view of environmental ethics. While this approach allows for personal expression, it may lack the cohesive focus on stewardship found in reconstructionist practices. Nonetheless, many eclectic practitioners also find inspiration in Norse mythology and the natural world, crafting their own rituals and ethics that align with their values. Ultimately, whether through reconstructionist or eclectic lenses, the core tenet of respecting and protecting the environment remains a vital aspect of Norse paganism, reflecting a deep-seated belief that humanity is but one part of a larger, sacred web of life.

# Chapter 6: Reconstructionist vs. Eclectic Norse Paganism

## Defining Reconstructionism

Reconstructionism in the context of Norse paganism refers to the practice of reviving and reconstructing ancient Norse spiritual traditions based on historical, archaeological, and textual evidence. This approach distinguishes itself from eclectic practices by prioritizing authenticity, striving to adhere closely to the beliefs and rituals of pre-Christian Norse societies. Reconstructionists seek to understand the cultural and spiritual frameworks of the time, emphasizing the importance of historical accuracy in their practices. This often involves a deep dive into various sources, including the Eddas, sagas, and archaeological findings, that provide insights into the religious and social lives of the Norse people.

The importance of historical sources in reconstructionism cannot be overstated. Texts such as the Poetic Edda and the Prose Edda are foundational, offering narratives of the gods, creation myths, and heroic tales that inform modern practices. Additionally, archaeological discoveries, such as burial sites, rune stones, and artifacts, provide tangible connections to the past. These findings help reconstructionists decipher how ancient Norse people viewed their deities, celebrated seasonal festivals, and performed rituals. However, it is crucial to approach these sources critically, as they were often written centuries after the events they describe and may reflect the biases of their authors.

Norse runes and their meanings also play a significant role in reconstructionist practices. Runes were not just an alphabet; they held spiritual significance and were often used in rituals and divination. Reconstructionists study the meanings and uses of runes, seeking to incorporate them into their spiritual practices in ways that resonate with ancient traditions. This may involve using runes for divinatory purposes, crafting talismans, or incorporating them into rituals to invoke the energies associated with specific symbols. By doing so, practitioners aim to create a more authentic connection to the past while grounding their modern practices in historical reality.

In examining the relationship between Norse paganism and the environment, reconstructionists often reflect on the ancient Norse worldview, which emphasized a deep connection to nature. The Norse understood themselves as part of a larger ecological system, and this perspective informs contemporary practices that advocate for environmental stewardship and respect for the natural world. Rituals may involve honoring the land, the spirits of nature, and the cycles of the seasons, aligning modern spirituality with ancient reverence for the Earth. This ecological awareness is increasingly relevant in today's world, where many seek to reconnect with nature in meaningful ways.

Finally, community building and gatherings are essential aspects of reconstructionist Norse paganism. These gatherings foster a sense of belonging and shared purpose among practitioners, allowing them to engage in traditional rituals that reflect their understanding of ancient practices. Events may include seasonal festivals, blot (sacrificial offerings), and sumbel (a ritual toasting ceremony) that recreate the communal aspects of Norse spirituality. By coming together, reconstructionists not only celebrate their heritage but also strengthen their connections to one another and to the land that nourishes them, creating a vibrant community that honors the past while navigating the complexities of modern life.

## Eclectic Approaches and Their Appeal

Eclectic approaches to Norse paganism have gained popularity among modern seekers who wish to blend traditional practices with personal beliefs and contemporary values. Unlike strict reconstructionism, which focuses on adhering closely to historical sources and ancient customs, eclecticism allows for a more flexible interpretation of Norse spirituality. This adaptability appeals to many individuals who are navigating their spiritual journeys and seeking to incorporate elements from various traditions, making Norse paganism more accessible and relevant to their lives today.

One of the primary attractions of eclectic Norse paganism is the freedom it offers practitioners to explore a wide range of beliefs and practices. This approach encourages the incorporation of diverse spiritual tools, such as tarot, astrology, and even elements from other pagan traditions, fostering a more personalized practice. Eclectic practitioners often draw inspiration from Norse mythology and its deities, integrating these figures into their rituals and ceremonies while also allowing for interpretations that resonate with their unique experiences. This blending of influences creates a rich, multifaceted spiritual landscape that can be both deeply meaningful and creatively fulfilling.

The appeal of eclectic approaches also extends to community building and gatherings. Many modern Norse pagans find that eclecticism fosters a sense of inclusivity within their communities, as individuals from various backgrounds and belief systems come together to celebrate their shared interests. This diversity can lead to innovative rituals and ceremonies that honor both traditional Norse practices and contemporary values, such as environmental stewardship and social justice. As a result, eclectic gatherings often become vibrant spaces for learning, growth, and collaboration, enriching the spiritual experiences of all participants.

Eclecticism can also serve as a bridge between historical sources and modern interpretations of Norse beliefs. While reconstructionist practices emphasize fidelity to ancient texts and archaeological findings, eclectic approaches encourage seekers to engage with these sources critically and creatively. This engagement allows for a dynamic dialogue between the past and the present, where practitioners can adapt ancient knowledge to address contemporary issues, such as climate change and community resilience. By reinterpreting historical practices through a modern lens, eclectic Norse pagans can cultivate a spirituality that feels relevant and impactful in today's world.

Ultimately, the appeal of eclectic approaches lies in their ability to honor the essence of Norse paganism while also allowing for personal exploration and growth. For many, this journey is not just about adopting a set of beliefs but about forging a spiritual path that resonates with their individual experiences and values. By embracing the eclectic nature of their practice, modern seekers can create a meaningful connection to the rich tapestry of Norse mythology, rituals, and philosophies, ensuring that these ancient traditions continue to thrive and evolve in the modern age.

## Finding a Personal Path

Finding a personal path within Norse paganism requires introspection and a willingness to explore the rich tapestry of beliefs, rituals, and deities that form the foundation of this ancient spiritual practice. Each seeker must embark on a journey that resonates with their own experiences, values, and understanding of the world. The key to this personal path lies in recognizing that Norse paganism is not a one-size-fits-all tradition; rather, it is as diverse and varied as the individuals who practice it. By examining historical sources, engaging with modern interpretations, and allowing personal experiences to shape beliefs, one can create a meaningful spiritual practice that honors the past while reflecting contemporary realities.

Norse mythology offers a wealth of stories and symbols that can guide seekers in their spiritual exploration. The tales of gods like Odin, Thor, and Freyja provide insights into the nature of existence, human behavior, and the interconnectedness of all life. Engaging with these myths can be done through reading, storytelling, or even creative expression. Additionally, understanding the roles of various deities can help individuals identify which aspects resonate most with them, allowing for a more personalized approach to worship and reverence. This connection can lead to the development of unique rituals and ceremonies that honor the deities and the natural world, fostering a deeper relationship with both the divine and the environment.

The practice of divination, particularly through the use of Norse runes, is another avenue for seekers to find their personal path. Runes, steeped in history and symbolism, serve not only as tools for communication but also as mediums for guidance and insight. By learning the meanings and interpretations of the runes, individuals can incorporate them into their spiritual practices, whether through daily readings, meditation, or ceremonial use. This personal engagement with the runes can enhance one's understanding of self and the universe, offering clarity and direction in the pursuit of spiritual goals.

In addition to individual practices, community building plays a crucial role in the journey of a modern Norse pagan. Connecting with like-minded individuals can provide support, inspiration, and shared experiences that enrich one's spiritual path. Participating in gatherings, whether formal like blóts and sumbels or informal meetups, allows for the exchange of ideas, rituals, and personal stories. These interactions can foster a sense of belonging and shared purpose, while also enabling individuals to learn from the diverse practices and beliefs of others. Balancing personal beliefs with communal activities can create a harmonious blend that honors both the individual journey and the collective experience.

Ultimately, finding a personal path in Norse paganism is an ongoing process of discovery and adaptation. It involves a commitment to learning from historical sources while engaging with modern interpretations and practices. As seekers navigate this path, they should remain open to new ideas and experiences, allowing their understanding of Norse spirituality to evolve. This journey is not merely about adhering to tradition but about reconstructing a meaningful spiritual framework that reflects one's values, beliefs, and relationship with the world. Through this dynamic process, individuals can forge a personal connection to the past that informs their present and guides their future.

# Chapter 7: Historical Sources of Norse Beliefs

## Primary Texts: Eddas and Sagas

The Eddas and sagas serve as foundational texts in the study of Norse mythology and the spiritual practices of Norse paganism. The Poetic Edda and the Prose Edda, composed in the 13th century, are particularly crucial for understanding the pantheon of Norse deities, cosmology, and the underlying themes that permeate Norse thought. The Poetic Edda, a collection of Old Norse poems, presents a wealth of mythological narratives and heroic tales that inform practitioners about the qualities and stories of gods such as Odin, Thor, and Freyja. These texts are not merely historical artifacts; they are living sources that continue to inspire modern seekers in their spiritual journeys.

In addition to the Eddas, the sagas offer a narrative tapestry of Norse life, values, and beliefs. The Icelandic sagas, composed between the 12th and 14th centuries, recount the lives of legendary figures and their adventures, providing insight into the cultural and social fabric of Viking society. These stories convey important lessons about honor, kinship, and the relationship between humans and the natural world. For contemporary practitioners, the sagas highlight the significance of community, storytelling, and the connection to ancestral roots, which are essential components of Norse pagan practices.

The narratives found in these texts also provide valuable context for rituals and ceremonies within Norse paganism. Many modern practitioners draw upon the themes and symbols found in the Eddas and sagas to inform their own rituals, whether they involve seasonal celebrations, rites of passage, or personal devotion. The rich imagery and archetypes present in these stories can help individuals create meaningful rituals that resonate with the values and beliefs of their ancestors. This connection to the past is a vital aspect of reconstructionist Norse paganism, where practitioners seek to honor ancient traditions while adapting them to contemporary contexts.

Moreover, the Eddas and sagas are instrumental in understanding Norse runes and their meanings. Runes, as a form of writing and divination, are deeply rooted in the lore found within these texts. The futhark, or runic alphabet, carries significant symbolism that is intertwined with the myths and stories of the gods. Modern seekers often use runes for spiritual guidance, drawing on the wisdom of the past to navigate their present. The relationship between runes and the narratives of the Eddas and sagas allows practitioners to engage with the spiritual and mystical dimensions of their beliefs more fully.

Finally, the influence of the Eddas and sagas extends into popular culture, where these ancient stories continue to resonate with new audiences. Films, literature, and art frequently draw from Norse mythology, sparking interest and curiosity about the ancient beliefs and practices. This cultural revival can foster community building among those interested in Norse paganism, as individuals come together to explore these texts and their relevance in modern life. By engaging with the Eddas and sagas, practitioners not only deepen their understanding of their spiritual heritage but also participate in a broader dialogue about identity, tradition, and the environment in which they live.

# Archaeological Evidence

Archaeological evidence plays a crucial role in understanding Norse paganism and its many facets. Excavations across Scandinavia have unearthed a wealth of materials, from burial mounds to sacred sites, which provide insight into the beliefs, rituals, and daily lives of the Norse people. These findings include altars, sacrificial artifacts, and remnants of feasting, all of which illustrate the interconnectedness of their spiritual practices and community life. By examining these artifacts, modern seekers can gain a clearer picture of how past societies engaged with their deities and the natural world around them.

One of the most significant archaeological discoveries related to Norse paganism is the site of Uppsala in Sweden, which is believed to have been a central hub for worship during the Viking Age. Historical accounts describe a grand temple at Uppsala where rituals were conducted in honor of the gods, particularly Odin, Thor, and Frey. Excavations have revealed not only the remains of structures that may have served religious purposes but also offerings of various animals, suggesting the importance of sacrifice in their practices. Such sites are invaluable to understanding the theological frameworks that underpinned Norse spirituality and the communal aspects of worship.

The findings from burial sites also provide essential insights into Norse beliefs about the afterlife. The practice of ship burials, as seen in locations like Oseberg and Gokstad, indicates a strong connection between their maritime culture and their spiritual worldview. The grave goods found alongside the deceased—ranging from weapons to household items—reflect the Norse belief in a continuation of life after death. This practice underscores the idea that the material world was intimately linked to the spiritual, influencing how modern practitioners view their own rituals and relationships with the divine.

Runes, another significant aspect of Norse culture, have also been illuminated through archaeological discovery. Inscriptions found on stones, weapons, and personal items reveal the use of runes not only as a means of communication but also as a form of magical practice. The meanings attributed to runes, such as protection and divination, highlight their importance in rituals and everyday life. These findings enrich the understanding of how contemporary Norse pagans might incorporate runes into their spiritual practices, emphasizing their historical significance and continued relevance.

Lastly, the study of archaeological evidence invites discussion on the differences between reconstructionist and eclectic approaches to Norse paganism. While reconstructionists seek to adhere closely to historical practices and beliefs, eclectic practitioners may draw from a broader range of influences. The artifacts and sites uncovered can inform both paths, helping seekers navigate their spiritual journeys while remaining rooted in the rich tapestry of Norse heritage. By analyzing these materials, individuals can engage with the past in a meaningful way, allowing history to inform their contemporary expressions of faith and community.

## Folklore and Oral Traditions

Folklore and oral traditions form the bedrock of Norse paganism, providing a rich tapestry of stories and beliefs that have been passed down through generations. These narratives encompass not only the exploits of the gods and goddesses but also the everyday lives of the Norse people. The sagas, poems, and legends offer insights into the values, ethics, and spiritual practices of a culture deeply connected to its environment and the forces of nature. Oral traditions serve as a means of preserving and conveying the wisdom of ancestors, allowing contemporary seekers to engage with the past in meaningful ways.

The significance of oral traditions is particularly evident in the preservation of the Norse pantheon and its associated myths. Stories of deities such as Odin, Thor, and Freyja encapsulate teachings about honor, bravery, and the interconnectedness of life. These tales often illustrate moral lessons and the consequences of one's actions, reinforcing the importance of living harmoniously within one's community and the natural world. By engaging with these stories, modern practitioners can draw parallels between ancient beliefs and present-day values, fostering a deeper understanding of their spiritual path.

Moreover, folklore serves as a cultural touchstone, linking individuals to their heritage and fostering a sense of identity. Through shared narratives, communities can come together to celebrate rituals that honor these traditions. Whether through seasonal festivals, ceremonies marking life milestones, or gatherings that reinforce communal bonds, the act of storytelling remains central to the practice of Norse paganism. These events not only honor the past but also create space for modern interpretations that resonate with contemporary values and concerns, highlighting the adaptability of Norse traditions.

In addition to religious practices, oral traditions encompass a wealth of knowledge about the natural world. Many Norse myths and folktales emphasize the importance of the environment, illustrating humanity's relationship with nature and the necessity of living sustainably. This connection is particularly relevant today, as modern seekers can draw inspiration from these teachings to address contemporary ecological challenges. By understanding the historical context of these stories, practitioners can cultivate a deeper appreciation for the earth and its cycles, reinforcing their commitment to environmental stewardship.

Finally, the role of folklore in shaping community dynamics cannot be overstated. Oral traditions often serve as a foundation for community building, providing a shared narrative that unites individuals with a common purpose. The stories and rituals associated with Norse paganism create opportunities for bonding and collaboration, whether through educational gatherings, workshops on Norse runes, or discussions about the nuances of reconstructionist versus eclectic practices. By engaging with folklore and oral traditions, modern seekers not only honor their ancestors but also contribute to the ongoing evolution of Norse paganism, ensuring its relevance and vitality for future generations.

# Chapter 8: Norse Paganism in Popular Culture

## Influence of Norse Mythology in Modern Media

Norse mythology has significantly influenced modern media, permeating various forms of entertainment and art that resonate with audiences both familiar and unfamiliar with its rich narratives. Films, television series, and literature have embraced the gods, heroes, and mythic tales of the Norse pantheon, often reimagining these ancient stories to fit contemporary themes and values. This trend not only serves to entertain but also to educate modern audiences about the complexities of Norse beliefs and practices, bridging the gap between ancient traditions and modern interpretations.

In cinema, films such as the Marvel Cinematic Universe's Thor series have popularized Norse deities like Thor and Loki, introducing them to a global audience. These portrayals often diverge from traditional depictions, focusing on dynamic character arcs and moral dilemmas that reflect current societal issues. While the films may incorporate elements of the original myths, they also highlight the characters' struggles, ambitions, and relationships, making them accessible and relatable to viewers. This blending of myth with modern storytelling techniques has sparked interest in the original tales and encouraged discussions about their meanings and relevance today.

Television series have followed suit, with shows like Vikings and The Last Kingdom offering a dramatized glimpse into the lives of Norse warriors and their interactions with the mythological world. These series often draw upon historical sources to create rich narratives, intertwining real events with mythological elements. This approach not only entertains but also fosters a deeper appreciation for the cultural and spiritual practices of the Norse people. By incorporating rituals, ceremonies, and the significance of runes, these shows invite viewers to explore the spiritual dimensions of Norse paganism, even if indirectly.

Literature has also seen a resurgence of interest in Norse mythology, with authors like Neil Gaiman and Rick Riordan crafting contemporary retellings that resonate with younger audiences. These works often strip away the archaic language and complex structures of ancient texts, presenting the myths in an engaging and digestible format. Such adaptations play a vital role in educating readers about Norse gods, goddesses, and their associated stories, while also inviting them to ponder the underlying themes of fate, honor, and the interconnectedness of life and death in Norse thought.

The incorporation of Norse mythology into modern media serves a dual purpose: it entertains while simultaneously educating and inspiring. As these narratives permeate popular culture, they create opportunities for individuals to explore Norse paganism and its practices more deeply. This influence encourages community building and gatherings among those interested in reconstructing these ancient beliefs, enhancing the understanding of rituals, spiritual practices, and the environment as perceived by the Norse people. By examining the past through the lens of contemporary media, seekers are empowered to reconnect with their heritage and explore the relevance of these ancient beliefs in the modern world.

# Representation of Norse Paganism in Literature and Film

The representation of Norse Paganism in literature and film has evolved considerably over the years, reflecting both historical interpretations and modern adaptations of ancient beliefs. Early literary works, such as the Icelandic sagas and Eddas, provided a rich tapestry of Norse mythology, detailing the lives of gods, heroes, and mythical creatures. These texts not only preserved the narratives of the past but also served as a foundation for later artistic expressions. In contemporary literature, authors often draw inspiration from these ancient sources, reinterpreting the myths to explore themes of identity, spirituality, and the connection to nature, which are central to Norse Paganism.

In film, Norse Paganism has become increasingly prevalent, often portrayed through epic narratives that emphasize the grandeur of Viking culture and mythology. Movies like "Thor" and "The 13th Warrior" have brought Norse deities and heroic tales to mainstream audiences, albeit with a blend of modern sensibilities and cinematic embellishments. While these films can sometimes prioritize entertainment over accuracy, they have played a significant role in sparking interest in Norse mythology, prompting viewers to seek deeper understanding and exploration of the original texts and beliefs. This representation often highlights the valor and complexities of Viking life, touching on their spiritual practices and the importance of community.

Moreover, the portrayal of Norse Paganism in popular culture has led to a resurgence of interest in ancient rituals and ceremonies. Many modern practitioners of Norse Paganism, especially in Reconstructionist circles, utilize these representations as a springboard to educate others about authentic practices. By dissecting the artistic liberties taken in films and novels, seekers can better understand the core values of Norse spirituality, such as the reverence for nature and the significance of rites of passage. This engagement with popular culture can also facilitate community building, as groups gather to discuss interpretations and celebrate shared interests.

The use of Norse runes in literature and film further enhances the connection to ancient belief systems. Runes, which hold specific meanings and historical significance, often appear as symbols of power or wisdom in various narratives. Their depiction can serve both as a mystical element and a practical tool for character development, grounding the story in authentic Norse traditions. As modern seekers explore these representations, they can reflect on the deeper meanings behind the runes and their applications in spiritual practices, divination, and personal growth within the framework of Norse Paganism.

In summary, the representation of Norse Paganism in literature and film serves as a bridge between ancient beliefs and modern interpretations. While it may not always reflect historical accuracy, it has undeniably contributed to a greater awareness and appreciation of Norse mythology and spiritual practices. As adults engage with these narratives, they are encouraged to delve deeper into the historical sources and community practices of Norse Paganism, fostering a richer understanding of their spiritual heritage and the relevance it holds in contemporary life.

## The Impact of Pop Culture on Modern Practices

The intersection of pop culture and Norse paganism has become increasingly prominent in recent years, influencing modern practices and perceptions of this ancient belief system. With the rise of various forms of media, including films, television series, literature, and video games, Norse mythology and its deities have captured the imagination of a wide audience. This newfound interest has led not only to a revival of traditional practices but also to the emergence of eclectic interpretations that blend historical elements with contemporary themes. As a result, modern practitioners may encounter a mixture of authentic traditions and creative embellishments that shape their spiritual journeys.

One of the most significant impacts of pop culture on Norse paganism is the way it has democratized access to information about Norse mythology and practices. Previously, knowledge was often confined to scholarly texts and specific communities. However, popular media has made these ancient stories and rituals more accessible to the general public. This has fostered a greater appreciation for the complexities of Norse beliefs, allowing individuals to explore the lore of deities like Odin, Thor, and Freyja in a more engaging manner. As a result, many seekers are inspired to delve deeper into historical sources, seeking to distinguish between the romanticized versions presented in media and the authentic teachings of their ancestors.

Viking rituals and ceremonies have also undergone a transformation due to the influence of popular culture. While traditional practices are rooted in historical context, modern interpretations often incorporate elements from various sources, leading to a diverse range of communal gatherings and celebrations. For instance, festivals celebrating the summer solstice or Yule may blend ancient customs with contemporary music, art, and even cosplay. This fusion can enhance the sense of community among practitioners, as individuals come together to celebrate shared interests while honoring their spiritual heritage. However, this blending raises questions about authenticity and the importance of maintaining a connection to historical traditions.

Norse runes, with their rich symbolism and historical significance, have found a place in both spiritual practices and pop culture. Many modern practitioners utilize runes for divination and personal insight, drawing on their meanings as a way to connect with the wisdom of the past. Popular culture has further popularized runes, often depicting them in mystical contexts that may or may not align with their traditional uses. This phenomenon can lead to a broader understanding of runes but may also dilute their meanings, creating potential misunderstandings among those who wish to incorporate them into their spiritual practices. It is essential for seekers to approach these symbols with respect and a desire to understand their historical and cultural significance.

The impact of pop culture on Norse paganism also extends to environmental awareness and activism. As contemporary society grapples with ecological crises, many practitioners are drawing parallels between ancient Norse beliefs and modern environmental movements. Popular media often emphasizes the connection between nature and Norse spirituality, highlighting the reverence for the land, animals, and natural cycles present in historical practices. This alignment has inspired a new generation of Norse pagans to engage in eco-friendly initiatives, encouraging community building around shared values of sustainability and stewardship. In this way, pop culture not only revitalizes interest in Norse traditions but also inspires meaningful action in the modern world.

# Chapter 9: Spiritual Practices and Divination in Norse Paganism

## Daily Spiritual Practices

Daily spiritual practices in Norse Paganism serve as a foundation for connecting with the divine, nature, and the self. Engaging in these rituals can help practitioners cultivate a deeper understanding of their beliefs, fostering a sense of community and continuity with the past. The essence of these practices lies in their flexibility, allowing individuals to tailor them according to personal needs while remaining rooted in historical traditions. This subchapter explores various daily practices that can enrich the spiritual lives of modern seekers.

One common daily practice is the offering of gratitude to the deities and spirits. This can be done through simple acts such as lighting a candle, saying a few words of thanks, or placing small offerings like food, drink, or natural items on an altar or sacred space. The focus here is on sincerity rather than grandeur; even a moment of reflection or a shared meal with loved ones can be a powerful way to honor the gods and ancestors. Such acts promote mindfulness and appreciation for the gifts of life, reinforcing the connection between the spiritual and the material worlds.

In addition to offerings, practitioners may incorporate the use of runes into their daily routines. Runes, as ancient symbols imbued with meaning and power, can serve as tools for divination, reflection, and guidance. A common practice is to draw a rune each day, contemplating its significance and how it might relate to personal experiences or challenges. This not only enhances one's understanding of the runes themselves but also encourages a deeper engagement with the mysteries of existence. By regularly invoking the wisdom of these symbols, practitioners can cultivate a stronger relationship with their spiritual path.

Nature plays a crucial role in Norse spirituality, and daily practices often include connecting with the environment. This can involve spending time outdoors, observing the changing seasons, or performing rituals that honor the land and its spirits. Such practices reinforce the belief in the interconnectedness of all living things and the importance of stewardship over the earth. Engaging with nature can be as simple as taking a walk in the woods, tending to a garden, or performing a small ritual in a natural setting, allowing practitioners to feel grounded and attuned to the rhythms of the world around them.

Finally, community building is an essential aspect of daily spiritual practices in Norse Paganism. While many practices can be performed in solitude, seeking out fellow practitioners for gatherings or shared rituals can deepen one's spiritual journey. Whether through online forums, local meet-ups, or more formal gatherings, sharing experiences and knowledge can enrich individual practices and foster a sense of belonging. As modern seekers navigate their spiritual paths, embracing both individual and communal aspects of Norse Paganism can create a balanced approach to daily spiritual practices, ensuring that the traditions of the past continue to thrive in contemporary contexts.

## Divination Methods: Seidr and Other Techniques

Divination holds a significant place within Norse paganism, offering practitioners a means to connect with the spiritual realm and seek guidance from the deities and the natural world. Among various divination methods, Seidr stands out as a prominent technique, deeply rooted in historical practices and often associated with the goddess Freyja and the god Odin. Seidr is not merely a form of fortune-telling; it is a complex ritual involving trance states, the invocation of spirits, and the weaving of fate. Practitioners, known as seidhkona or seidhkonn, engage with the cosmos to uncover hidden knowledge, heal, and influence the course of events.

In addition to Seidr, Norse paganism encompasses various other divination techniques. One of the most well-known methods is the use of runes, which are both an alphabet and a system of divination. Each rune carries specific meanings and associations with natural forces and deities. Practitioners often cast runes onto a surface or draw them from a bag while focusing on a question or intention. The resulting configuration serves as a guide, revealing insights into the present situation and potential outcomes. Runes can also be used in combination with other elements, such as stones or symbols, to enrich the divination experience and deepen the connection to the Norse worldview.

Another technique found in Norse tradition is the practice of casting lots, which involves using objects like stones or sticks marked with symbols or runes. This method is similar to dice divination and is often used in communal settings, fostering a sense of shared experience among participants. The act of casting lots can be accompanied by prayers or invocations to the gods, emphasizing the communal aspect of seeking divine guidance. This method not only highlights the importance of community in Norse paganism but also reflects the belief that fate is influenced by both individual actions and collective intentions.

Dream interpretation also plays a role in Norse divination practices, as dreams were seen as a medium through which the gods and ancestors could communicate with the living. Norse mythology contains numerous accounts of prophetic dreams guiding heroes and influencing events. Modern practitioners often keep dream journals to track recurring symbols or themes, interpreting them in light of their personal experiences and spiritual journeys. This practice encourages a deeper introspection and understanding of one's life path, integrating the wisdom of the past with contemporary insights.

As Norse paganism continues to evolve, the exploration of divination methods like Seidr and runic practices invites both reconstructionists and eclectic practitioners to engage with the past while adapting these techniques to suit modern contexts. The study of historical sources, alongside personal experiences, allows for the development of a rich tapestry of spiritual practices that honor the traditions of the Norse while also embracing contemporary perspectives. This dynamic interplay between history and modernity cultivates a vibrant community where individuals can come together, share insights, and deepen their spiritual practices through divination and collective gatherings.

## Personal Spiritual Development

Personal spiritual development within Norse paganism requires a deep engagement with its historical roots, deities, and practices. The journey begins with an understanding of Norse mythology, which is rich with narratives that offer insights into the human experience and the natural world. By immersing oneself in these myths, individuals can cultivate a personal connection to the gods and goddesses, drawing inspiration from their stories to guide their own spiritual paths. This connection is not merely intellectual; it is intended to be lived out through rituals, prayers, and the honoring of nature, which plays a central role in Norse belief systems.

To engage in personal spiritual development, seekers often explore the various deities of the Norse pantheon, each embodying unique attributes and lessons. For instance, Odin, the Allfather, represents wisdom, war, and poetry, while Freyja embodies love, fertility, and beauty. By invoking these deities in personal practice, individuals can seek guidance and support in their daily lives. Rituals and offerings can be tailored to honor specific gods and goddesses, creating a personal relationship that fosters spiritual growth. Furthermore, understanding the attributes of these deities allows for a more profound engagement with the rituals and ceremonies that are integral to Norse paganism.

The use of runes in Norse spirituality further enhances personal development. Runes are not only an alphabet but also carry deep symbolic meanings and serve as tools for divination and meditation. Individuals can learn to interpret runes for guidance, using them to reflect on personal challenges and aspirations. This practice encourages introspection and self-discovery, allowing practitioners to align their internal landscapes with the wisdom of the cosmos. By

integrating runes into their spiritual routines, seekers can create a personalized framework for understanding their life experiences through the lens of Norse cosmology.

Community plays an essential role in personal spiritual development within Norse paganism. Engaging with others who share similar beliefs fosters a sense of belonging and collective growth. Participation in gatherings, rituals, and celebrations provides opportunities for learning, sharing experiences, and strengthening bonds with fellow practitioners. These communal activities can enhance individual understanding of Norse traditions, offering diverse perspectives and practices that enrich one's spiritual journey. Building a network of like-minded individuals can also provide support and encouragement, which is vital for sustained spiritual exploration.

Lastly, the relationship between Norse paganism and the environment cannot be overlooked in personal spiritual development. The reverence for nature found in Norse traditions encourages individuals to cultivate a sense of stewardship towards the earth. Engaging with nature through rituals, seasonal celebrations, and personal reflection can deepen one's spiritual practice. This connection not only honors the ancient beliefs but also promotes awareness and responsibility towards the environment, aligning personal growth with the health of the planet. In this way, personal spiritual development in Norse paganism becomes a holistic journey that intertwines the self, the divine, and the natural world.

# Chapter 10: Community Building and Gatherings in Norse Paganism

## The Importance of Community

The concept of community holds significant importance within Norse paganism, serving as a foundational element for both spiritual practice and cultural continuity. In the context of Norse mythology, the gods themselves often embody communal values, as seen in the gatherings of the Aesir at Asgard, where they share knowledge, celebrate victories, and address challenges. This ancient framework reflects a deep understanding that individual spiritual journeys are enriched through collective experiences, making community a vital aspect for modern practitioners seeking connection and support in their beliefs.

Community provides a space for sharing knowledge and practices that are essential for the reconstruction of Norse paganism. In a time when historical sources may be fragmented or interpreted in various ways, gathering with others enables practitioners to exchange insights and perspectives on rituals, deities, and texts. These discussions can lead to a more nuanced understanding of Norse beliefs, allowing individuals to navigate the complexities of reconstructionist versus eclectic approaches. By coming together, practitioners can honor both historical accuracy and personal resonance, fostering a sense of belonging and mutual growth.

Furthermore, community plays a crucial role in the practice of rituals and ceremonies, which are often enhanced by shared participation. Group gatherings for seasonal festivals, rites of passage, or honoring the gods can create powerful collective energy that amplifies individual intentions. This communal aspect of ritual not only strengthens individual connections to the divine but also reinforces the social bonds among participants. Engaging in these shared experiences nurtures a sense of identity and purpose, vital for those committed to living out their beliefs in a modern context.

In addition to spiritual practices, community ties directly into the environmental values inherent in Norse paganism. Many practitioners emphasize a deep respect for nature, often viewing the land as sacred and integral to their spiritual practice. By participating in community initiatives focused on environmental stewardship, practitioners can embody the principles of their beliefs while working together to protect the natural world. This not only aligns with the teachings of the gods and goddesses regarding harmony with nature but also promotes a collective responsibility that transcends individual actions.

Ultimately, the importance of community in Norse paganism extends beyond mere social interaction; it is a vital component of spiritual practice, cultural preservation, and environmental stewardship. By fostering connections with others who share similar beliefs, practitioners can enhance their understanding, deepen their rituals, and actively contribute to the world around them. As modern seekers navigate their paths, embracing the communal aspect of Norse paganism can lead to richer, more fulfilling spiritual journeys that honor both the past and the present.

## Organizing Gatherings and Festivals

Organizing gatherings and festivals within the framework of Norse Paganism is a significant way to foster community and deepen one's spiritual practice. These events provide opportunities for individuals to come together, share knowledge, and participate in rituals that honor the gods, the land, and each other. Whether held in a public park, a private home, or a sacred natural site, these gatherings often reflect the core values of Norse Paganism, emphasizing connection, reciprocity, and reverence for the past.

When planning a gathering, it is essential to consider the purpose and theme of the event. Common themes may include seasonal festivals, such as Yule or Midsummer, which align with the cycles of nature and the agricultural calendar. Each festival can incorporate traditional elements such as feasting, storytelling, and rituals dedicated to specific deities or natural forces. By aligning the gathering with these cycles, participants can engage in practices that resonate deeply with Norse cosmology and encourage active participation in the community's spiritual life.

Logistics play a crucial role in the success of any gathering. Organizers should consider the size of the group, the location, and the necessary resources, including food, materials for rituals, and any ceremonial items. Creating an inviting atmosphere is also important; this can be achieved through decorations that reflect Norse aesthetics or the use of natural elements like stones, plants, and candles. Communication with participants about what to bring, expected conduct, and any specific rituals planned will help ensure everyone feels included and prepared for the experience.

Incorporating educational elements into gatherings can significantly enhance their value. Workshops, discussions, and presentations on topics such as Norse mythology, runes, or historical practices can deepen participants' understanding of their spiritual heritage. Inviting knowledgeable speakers or experienced practitioners to share their insights can foster a richer dialogue within the community and encourage members to explore their own paths more fully. This emphasis on education aligns well with the reconstructionist approach to Norse Paganism, which seeks to base practices and beliefs on historical sources and traditional knowledge.

Ultimately, the act of gathering is a celebration of collective identity and shared beliefs. It allows practitioners to reinforce their connections to one another, the gods, and the natural world. Festivals and gatherings serve not only as religious observances but also as vital opportunities for community building, creating a supportive environment where individuals can explore their spirituality and strengthen ties with others who share their values. By engaging in these communal practices, modern seekers of Norse Paganism can cultivate a vibrant and cohesive community that honors their ancestral traditions while adapting them to contemporary life.

## Online Communities and Resources

Online communities and resources have become indispensable for individuals exploring Norse paganism, offering diverse avenues for learning and connection. These digital platforms serve as hubs for practitioners, scholars, and enthusiasts to share insights, ask questions, and engage in discussions about various aspects of Norse mythology, rituals, and spiritual practices. Social media groups, forums, and dedicated websites provide a wealth of information ranging from historical sources of Norse beliefs to contemporary interpretations of Viking rituals. The accessibility of these resources allows seekers to delve into the rich tapestry of Norse culture no matter where they are located.

One of the most significant advantages of online communities is their ability to foster connections among individuals with shared interests. Many practitioners find solace in virtual spaces where they can discuss their experiences with Norse deities, share personal rituals, and seek guidance on spiritual practices. These interactions often transcend geographical barriers, enabling people from different backgrounds to contribute to a collective understanding of Norse paganism. Furthermore, community gatherings organized through online platforms can lead to in-person events, enhancing the sense of belonging among practitioners.

In addition to facilitating connections, online resources offer a plethora of educational materials. Websites dedicated to Norse mythology and pagan practices often include articles, videos, and podcasts that cover a wide range of topics, such as the meanings of Norse runes, the significance of various deities, and the nuances between reconstructionist and eclectic approaches to the faith. Such resources empower seekers to engage with the material at their own pace, allowing for a more personalized journey through the complexities of Norse pagan practices.

Engaging with online communities also encourages critical thinking and informed discussions about the environmental aspects of Norse paganism. Many modern practitioners emphasize the importance of nature and sustainability, drawing parallels between ancient beliefs and contemporary environmental concerns. Through shared resources and collaborative projects, online communities can raise awareness about ecological issues, fostering a sense of stewardship tied to the spiritual beliefs that honor the earth and its cycles.

Ultimately, the integration of online communities and resources into the exploration of Norse paganism reflects a dynamic and evolving practice. As seekers navigate the complexities of their spiritual journeys, these digital platforms not only provide valuable information but also facilitate meaningful connections and discussions that enrich their understanding of Norse traditions. By actively participating in these communities, individuals can contribute to the ongoing reconstruction of Norse paganism, ensuring its relevance and vitality in the modern world.

# Sacred Seasons: Celebrating the Festivals of Asatru

## Chapter 1: Introduction to Asatru

### Overview of Asatru

Asatru, a modern revival of ancient Norse paganism, emphasizes a deep connection with nature, the cosmos, and the ancestral traditions of the Norse people. Rooted in the pre-Christian beliefs of Scandinavia, Asatru celebrates the divine through the worship of the Aesir and Vanir, two groups of gods central to Norse mythology. This faith encourages practitioners to honor their ancestors, engage in seasonal festivals, and participate in rituals that enhance personal and communal bonds. The modern interpretation of Asatru blends historical practices with contemporary values, creating a dynamic spiritual path that resonates with individuals seeking to connect with their heritage and the natural world.

Seasonal festivals play a significant role in Asatru, serving as communal gatherings that mark important times of the year. These celebrations, such as Yule, Ostara, and Midsummer, are rooted in the cycles of nature and reflect the agricultural traditions of the Norse people. Each festival is imbued with specific rituals and customs that honor the gods, the land, and the changing seasons. During these gatherings, participants may engage in feasting, storytelling, and the sharing of blessings, thereby reinforcing community ties and fostering a sense of belonging. The significance of these festivals lies not only in their historical roots but also in their capacity to provide a framework for spiritual growth and reflection in the modern world.

Norse mythology heavily influences Asatru rituals, providing a rich tapestry of narratives, symbols, and archetypes that practitioners draw upon for spiritual insight and guidance. The stories of gods such as Odin, Thor, and Freyja offer valuable lessons about bravery, wisdom, and fertility, which practitioners incorporate into their daily lives and spiritual practices. The myths serve as a foundation for understanding the natural world and one's place within it, encouraging adherents to seek harmony with the forces of nature and the divine. Asatru rituals often invoke these myths, allowing participants to connect with the archetypal energies represented by the gods and goddesses, thus deepening their spiritual experience.

The practice of honoring ancestors is a cornerstone of Asatru, reflecting the belief that the past informs the present and shapes the future. Ancestors are revered not only for their biological connection but also for the wisdom and strength they impart to their descendants. Rituals that honor ancestors may include offerings, prayers, and the creation of personal altars that serve as sacred spaces for remembrance and reflection. This practice fosters a sense of continuity and belonging, reminding practitioners that they are part of a larger lineage that transcends time. By acknowledging their ancestors, Asatru practitioners cultivate a deeper understanding of their identity and purpose within the cosmos.

Magic and healing play integral roles in Asatru, with various practices designed to invoke protection, well-being, and spiritual insight. This includes the use of runes, which are not only a form of writing but also serve as powerful symbols in magical workings. Spells and invocations may be performed to seek guidance or to provide healing for oneself or others, drawing upon the natural energies present in the world. Offerings and sacrifices, while interpreted in modern contexts, remain a way to express gratitude and forge connections with the divine. By engaging in these practices, Asatru practitioners create a living tradition that acknowledges the sacredness of existence and the interconnectedness of all life.

## Historical Origins and Development

The historical origins of Asatru can be traced back to the ancient Norse and Germanic peoples, whose polytheistic beliefs centered around a pantheon of gods and goddesses. This faith system was deeply intertwined with the natural world, reflecting the seasonal cycles that governed agricultural practices and daily life. Key deities such as Odin, Thor, and Freyja played significant roles in these ancient cultures, embodying various aspects of life and nature. The rituals and celebrations that emerged from these traditions were not merely religious observances; they were essential to the community's identity, providing a framework for understanding their place in the cosmos and fostering a sense of belonging.

As Asatru evolved, it incorporated various cultural influences and regional variations. The Viking Age, marked by exploration and expansion, facilitated the exchange of ideas and practices across Scandinavia and beyond. This period saw the adaptation of rituals as communities interacted with other belief systems, including Christianity. The gradual Christianization of the Norse peoples led to a syncretism where some pagan traditions were preserved and reinterpreted within a new religious context. Despite these changes, many foundational elements of Asatru—such as honoring ancestors and celebrating seasonal festivals—remained intact, highlighting the resilience of these ancient beliefs.

The modern revival of Asatru in the 20th century was fueled by a growing interest in pre-Christian European spirituality and a desire for cultural heritage among individuals of Nordic descent. Groups began to form, creating contemporary interpretations of ancient practices while maintaining a focus on community, nature, and ancestry. This revival was not without challenges, as practitioners sought to differentiate their beliefs from neo-pagan movements that did not align with traditional Norse practices. The establishment of organizations and the publication of texts dedicated to Asatru played pivotal roles in formalizing its doctrines and rituals, fostering a renewed sense of identity and purpose among its adherents.

Today, Asatru is characterized by a diverse range of practices that reflect both historical roots and modern interpretations. Seasonal festivals, such as Yule and Midsummer, continue to hold significant importance, serving as times for community gatherings, feasting, and honoring deities and ancestors. Rituals often incorporate elements such as offerings, prayers, and the use of runes, which connect practitioners to the wisdom of their ancestors. Furthermore, the emphasis on personal altars and sacred spaces allows individuals to cultivate their spiritual practices, fostering a deep connection to both the divine and the natural world.

Asatru's development is a testament to the enduring power of tradition and community in shaping religious identity. The integration of ancient rituals with contemporary practices illustrates how the faith can adapt to modern society while remaining rooted in its historical origins. This dynamic interplay not only honors the past but also invites new generations to engage with their heritage, ensuring that the sacred seasons and the celebrations of Asatru continue to thrive in a rapidly changing world.

## Key Concepts and Beliefs

Key concepts and beliefs in Asatru encompass a rich tapestry of traditions, rituals, and values that are deeply rooted in Norse mythology and the natural world. Central to these beliefs is the reverence for the Aesir and Vanir, the two main pantheons of gods and goddesses in Norse mythology. Followers of Asatru engage in rituals and celebrations that honor these deities, recognizing their influence in the natural cycles of life and the changing seasons. This connection to the divine is not only a matter of worship but also a means of understanding the world and one's place within it.

Seasonal festivals play a significant role in Asatru, marking the passage of time and the rhythms of nature. Each festival, such as Yule, Ostara, and Midsummer, is imbued with specific meanings and practices that reflect the themes of renewal, fertility, and gratitude. These celebrations often involve communal gatherings, feasting, and various forms of ritualistic observance that reinforce the bonds between the community and the natural world. Through these festivals, practitioners express their connection to the cycles of life, fostering a sense of belonging and continuity with their ancestors.

The role of ancestors in Asatru practices cannot be overstated. Ancestors are honored through various means, including the practice of sumbel, a ritual toast that acknowledges their presence and influence in the lives of the living. This connection to the past serves to strengthen the community and individual identities, as practitioners draw wisdom and guidance from their forebears. Ancestor veneration reflects the belief that the past is an integral part of the present, and that honoring those who came before enriches the spiritual journey of each individual.

Magic and the use of runes hold a significant place in Asatru, serving as tools for both personal empowerment and communal rituals. Runes, as ancient symbols, are believed to carry specific meanings and energies that can be harnessed for various purposes, including healing, protection, and divination. Practitioners may create personal altars and sacred spaces to facilitate their magical workings, allowing for a focused environment where intentions can be set and energies directed. The integration of magic into everyday life reflects the belief that the spiritual and physical realms are interconnected, and that individuals have the capacity to influence their circumstances through conscious practice.

Finally, prayers and invocations to the Aesir and Vanir are a vital aspect of Asatru spirituality, providing a means of communication with the divine. These sacred words serve to express gratitude, seek guidance, or request assistance in times of need. The act of invoking the gods and goddesses is often accompanied by specific rituals that enhance the efficacy of the prayers, reinforcing the bond between the practitioner and the divine. As Asatru continues to evolve in contemporary society, these key concepts and beliefs remain central to the practice, allowing for a dynamic and meaningful expression of spirituality that honors both tradition and personal experience.

# Chapter 2: The Wheel of the Year in Asatru

## Overview of Seasonal Festivals

Seasonal festivals in Asatru serve as vital touchpoints connecting practitioners to the cycles of nature and the rhythms of life. These celebrations are deeply rooted in Norse mythology and agricultural practices, reflecting the changing seasons and the associated deities. Each festival marks a significant moment in the solar year, such as the solstices and equinoxes, as well as traditional agricultural milestones like planting and harvest times. This cyclical observance not only honors the deities and spirits of the land but also reinforces the community's bond with nature and each other, creating a sacred space for collective worship and reflection.

The significance of these festivals extends beyond mere observance; they are immersive experiences that integrate rituals, magic, and prayers. Each celebration is typically accompanied by specific rites that may include offerings to the Aesir and Vanir, songs, and communal feasts. These practices are designed to invoke blessings for the coming season, ensuring fertility, prosperity, and protection from misfortune. The rituals often incorporate elements of divination and ancestral veneration, allowing practitioners to seek guidance and blessings from their forebears while honoring their legacy within the natural order.

Norse mythology plays a critical role in shaping the narratives and practices associated with seasonal festivals. Deities such as Freyja, god of fertility and love, and Thor, protector of the harvest, are central figures in the celebrations. Their stories provide context for the rituals performed, connecting the material world to the divine. As practitioners engage in these festivities, they not only celebrate the changing seasons but also reaffirm their cultural heritage and spiritual identity, drawing strength from the myths that have endured through generations.

The role of ancestors in Asatru practices is particularly emphasized during seasonal festivals. These occasions provide an opportunity to honor and remember those who have come before, inviting their presence and guidance into the rituals. Offerings, such as mead or food, are often made to ancestors, illustrating a recognition of their ongoing influence in the lives of the living. This ancestral connection fosters a sense of continuity and belonging, reinforcing the idea that past, present, and future are intertwined within the sacred cycles of existence.

Seasonal festivals also facilitate the exploration of healing and protection spells, which are integral to the practices of Asatru. These spells, often performed in conjunction with the festivals, serve to safeguard individuals and the community as a whole, aligning with the natural energies of the season. The use of runes in these magical practices enhances the potency of the spells, allowing practitioners to tap into ancient wisdom and power. Asatru's seasonal festivals thus embody a holistic approach to spirituality, weaving together elements of ritual, mythology, ancestor reverence, and magic into a rich tapestry that resonates with both the individual and the community.

## Importance of Cycles in Nature

Cycles in nature play a pivotal role in the Asatru faith, reflecting the interconnectedness of all life and the divine rhythms that govern existence. In Norse mythology, the cyclical patterns of the seasons are not merely physical phenomena but are imbued with spiritual significance. Each season embodies distinct energies and themes that influence rituals and celebrations, providing a framework for understanding the world and our place within it. The changing of the seasons serves as a reminder of the eternal cycles of birth, growth, decay, and renewal, echoing the life experiences of individuals and communities alike.

Spring, as the season of rebirth, is celebrated with rituals that honor fertility, growth, and the awakening of the earth. Festivals such as Ostara highlight the importance of planting seeds, both literally in the soil and metaphorically in one's life. This time is often associated with the deities of fertility and renewal, showcasing the deep connections between the Asatru faith and the natural world. The rites performed during this season foster a sense of hope and potential, encouraging practitioners to reflect on their aspirations and the new beginnings that lie ahead.

Summer, characterized by abundance and vitality, emphasizes celebration and gratitude. The festivals during this season are marked by communal gatherings, offerings to the gods, and rituals that honor the sun's life-giving energy. This period invites practitioners to revel in the fruits of their labor and to cultivate relationships with their ancestors, acknowledging their influence on current blessings. Such acts of remembrance and gratitude foster a sense of continuity and belonging, reinforcing the importance of community and shared heritage within the Asatru tradition.

As autumn approaches, the focus shifts to introspection and preparation for the coming winter. Festivals such as Frövi and Álfablót allow practitioners to honor the cycle of life and death, recognizing the inevitability of change and the wisdom that comes with it. This season encourages reflection on past experiences, the lessons learned, and the importance of ancestral ties. The rituals during this time often involve offerings and invocations to the Aesir and Vanir, reinforcing the belief that the spirits of the past guide the present and future.

Winter, often viewed as a time of dormancy, holds its own significance in the cycle of nature. It is during this season that many Asatru practitioners engage in rituals that emphasize protection, healing, and the warmth of community. The long nights provide an opportunity for introspection, divination practices, and the crafting of personal altars that honor the sacred spaces within the home. The end of winter marks the beginning of a new cycle, culminating in the celebrations of spring, thus illustrating that even in darkness, the promise of light and renewal persists. Each season, with its unique gifts and challenges, underscores the importance of cycles in nature, enriching the spiritual path of those who walk the Asatru way.

# The Significance of the Solstices and Equinoxes

The solstices and equinoxes hold profound significance within the Asatru faith, marking pivotal moments in the natural cycle that influences both the physical and spiritual realms. These seasonal transitions align closely with the rhythms of nature, providing a framework for ritual practices and community gatherings. Each event symbolizes a turning point, inviting practitioners to reflect on the interconnectedness of life, death, and rebirth, as well as the vital energies that flow through the world. By honoring these celestial events, Asatru followers deepen their connection to the ancestors and the divine, reinforcing their commitment to living in harmony with the natural world.

The Winter Solstice, or Yule, heralds the return of light as the days begin to lengthen. This celebration is a time for introspection, renewal, and the acknowledgment of the darkness that has passed. Rituals during Yule often involve lighting candles or fires, symbolizing the rekindling of hope and warmth. Offerings to the Aesir and Vanir during this time are common, expressing gratitude for the blessings of the past year and requesting guidance for the year to come. Additionally, the stories of Norse mythology surrounding the rebirth of the sun god, Baldr, resonate strongly with practitioners, embodying themes of sacrifice and renewal that permeate Asatru practices.

The Summer Solstice, or Midsummer, serves as a celebration of abundance and vitality. This event marks the height of the sun's power, a time when nature is in full bloom and the Earth is rich with life. Rituals often focus on gratitude for the harvest and the sun's life-giving energy, with offerings made to both the Aesir and the spirits of the land. The importance of community is particularly emphasized during Midsummer, as gatherings and feasts bring people together to honor their shared heritage, strengthen bonds, and participate in traditional games and activities. Such communal celebrations foster a sense of belonging and continuity, reinforcing the collective identity of the Asatru community.

The equinoxes, both Spring and Autumn, represent balance and transition. Ostara, the Spring Equinox, symbolizes rebirth, fertility, and the awakening of the Earth after the long winter months. This festival is an opportunity for practitioners to engage in rituals that celebrate new beginnings, planting seeds both literally and metaphorically. Autumn Equinox, or Harvest Home, serves as a time of reflection and gratitude for the fruits of the year's labor, acknowledging the cycle of life and death. Both equinoxes encourage practitioners to honor the ancestors, recognizing their guidance and influence in the cycles of life, as well as the importance of maintaining balance within oneself and the community.

Incorporating the significance of solstices and equinoxes into Asatru practice not only enriches individual spiritual journeys but also strengthens communal ties. These celestial events serve as reminders of the continuous cycles of nature, urging practitioners to live in accordance with the rhythms of the Earth. By celebrating these moments through rituals, prayers, and offerings, Asatru followers affirm their connection to their ancestors, the land, and the divine. Ultimately, the observance of solstices and equinoxes embodies the core tenets of Asatru—respect for nature, reverence for the past, and a commitment to living harmoniously in the present.

# Chapter 3: Yule: Celebrating the Winter Solstice

## Rituals and Traditions of Yule

Rituals and traditions of Yule hold significant importance within the Asatru faith, encapsulating the essence of the winter solstice and the rebirth of the sun. Celebrated around December 21st, Yule marks a time of reflection, renewal, and the honoring of both the Aesir and Vanir. Central to Yule rituals is the Yule log, traditionally an oak log that is burned to symbolize warmth, light, and the returning sun. As it burns, practitioners may gather to share stories, invoke blessings, and express gratitude for the past year while setting intentions for the coming one. This act of communal fire not only serves to drive away the darkness but also reinforces bonds within the community, reminiscent of ancient gatherings around hearths.

Another key tradition of Yule involves the creation and decoration of a Yule tree, often an evergreen, symbolizing eternal life and resilience. Participants may adorn the tree with offerings of food, natural elements, and handmade ornaments that reflect personal wishes or ancestral connections. This practice ties back to ancient Norse customs where trees were seen as sacred, embodying the presence of deities and the spirit of nature. During the Yule feast, practitioners often share a meal that includes seasonal foods, invoking the ancestors with toasts and prayers, thereby integrating the past with the present.

Incorporating magic and prayers during Yule rituals enhances the spiritual experience. Many Asatru practitioners engage in specific spells aimed at protection and prosperity for the coming year. These spells can involve the use of runes, which are believed to carry powerful energies and meanings. The Elder Futhark runes might be inscribed on candles or spoken aloud during rituals to invoke their protective attributes. Prayers directed to the Aesir and Vanir, particularly to deities associated with fertility, prosperity, and the sun, create a dialog with the divine, seeking blessings and guidance.

Divination practices also play a vital role during Yule, as practitioners may seek insight into the upcoming year through various methods such as rune casting or tarot. This period of introspection allows individuals to connect with their intuition and the wisdom of their ancestors. Additionally, personal altars are often refreshed and adorned with seasonal symbols, incorporating elements such as holly, mistletoe, and representations of the gods, thereby creating sacred spaces for contemplation and connection.

As contemporary society evolves, so too do the interpretations of Yule rituals within the Asatru community. While many adhere to traditional practices, others innovate by integrating modern elements, reflecting the diversity of beliefs and the importance of personal expression in spirituality. This adaptability not only honors the rich heritage of Norse mythology but also fosters a sense of belonging and relevance for modern practitioners. Ultimately, the rituals and traditions of Yule serve as a profound reminder of the cyclical nature of life, the enduring strength of community, and the ever-present light that emerges from the darkness.

## Symbolism of Light and Darkness

In Asatru, the symbolism of light and darkness plays a crucial role in understanding the cyclical nature of existence and the balance between opposing forces. Light often represents knowledge, purity, and the divine, embodying the qualities of the Aesir, particularly deities such as Baldr, who is associated with goodness and brightness. This symbolism is reflected in seasonal festivals, such as Midwinter and Yule, where the return of the sun is celebrated as a triumph over the darkness of winter. Rituals during these times often include lighting candles or bonfires, signifying hope, renewal, and the reawakening of life as the days gradually lengthen.

Conversely, darkness is not merely the absence of light but a vital component of the Asatru belief system. It embodies mystery, introspection, and the unknown, serving as a reminder of the natural cycles of life and death. The figure of Hel, the goddess of the underworld, represents the darker aspects of existence, including the inevitability of death and the importance of honoring ancestors. Festivals like Þorrablót, which take place in the midst of winter, bring attention to the darker months, emphasizing the need for community strength and resilience in facing the challenges posed by nature.

The interplay between light and darkness is also evident in rituals and magic within the Asatru faith. Practitioners often invoke these dualities when performing spells for healing and protection, acknowledging that both aspects are necessary for a balanced life. For instance, healing spells might incorporate elements of light to symbolize health and vitality, while protection spells may call upon the darkness to shield against harmful influences. This duality encourages practitioners to embrace all facets of existence, rather than shying away from the darker elements that contribute to the wholeness of the self.

Seasonal festivals further highlight this dynamic, allowing practitioners to honor both light and darkness through various offerings and sacrifices. During the summer solstice, for example, offerings may be made to the sun gods to ensure a bountiful harvest, celebrating the peak of light. In contrast, during the winter solstice, sacrifices may be made to the spirits of the land and ancestors, acknowledging their guidance and support as the community navigates the darker months. These practices foster a deeper connection to the natural world and its cycles, reinforcing the importance of balance in both ritual and daily life.

Ultimately, the symbolism of light and darkness in Asatru serves as a powerful reminder of the interconnectedness of all things. It encourages a holistic understanding of the human experience, where joy and sorrow coexist, and where each season brings unique opportunities for growth and reflection. By embracing these dualities, practitioners can cultivate a richer spiritual life, honoring not only the brightness of the sun but also the lessons found in the shadows, creating a more profound connection to their ancestors, the land, and the divine.

# Community Celebrations

Community celebrations within Asatru serve as a vital expression of shared beliefs, cultural heritage, and communal bonds. These gatherings typically coincide with seasonal festivals, marking the changes in nature and honoring the deities associated with each time of year. Celebrations such as Yule, Ostara, and Midsummer not only reflect the rhythms of the natural world but also reinforce the values and teachings found within Norse mythology. As participants come together, they engage in rituals that connect them to their ancestors, fortifying the communal spirit and promoting the importance of lineage and heritage in their practice.

Rituals performed during these celebrations often include prayers and invocations to the Aesir and Vanir, the two main groups of deities in Norse mythology. These ceremonies typically incorporate offerings, such as mead, food, or crafted items, which symbolize gratitude and respect toward the gods. The act of giving is seen as a means of building reciprocal relationships with the divine, fostering an environment where blessings and guidance can flow both ways. Participants may also employ runes in their rituals, invoking their magical properties to enhance the spiritual significance of the event.

Seasonal festivals in Asatru are deeply rooted in the cycles of life, death, and rebirth found within nature. Each festival not only marks a transition in the seasons but also reflects the agricultural practices and livelihoods of the Norse ancestors. For example, the celebration of Midsummer is a time of abundance, symbolizing the height of the growing season, while the observance of Yule heralds the return of the sun after the winter solstice. Community members often engage in storytelling, singing, and feasting, reinforcing the bonds of kinship and shared identity that are central to Asatru.

The role of ancestors is paramount during these gatherings, as honoring them is a key aspect of Asatru practice. Many celebrations include rituals that acknowledge the contributions and sacrifices of those who came before. This connection to ancestry not only provides a sense of continuity but also serves as a source of guidance and protection for contemporary practitioners. By invoking the spirits of their forebears, community members seek wisdom and strength in their personal and collective journeys, drawing upon the rich tapestry of their heritage.

Healing and protection spells may also form an integral part of community celebrations, addressing the spiritual and emotional needs of participants. These spells often involve collective intention-setting and the creation of sacred spaces where individuals can feel safe and supported. Through the power of shared belief and communal energy, participants can harness the magical aspects of their faith, promoting healing not only for themselves but also for the wider community. Such practices embody the essence of Asatru, where the interplay of ritual, magic, and communal celebration creates a dynamic and living tradition.

# Chapter 4: Ostara: Welcoming Spring

## Fertility Rites and Renewal

Fertility rites and renewal hold a significant place within the Asatru tradition, reflecting the deep connection between the natural world and the spiritual practices of practitioners. These rites often align with seasonal festivals, particularly those in spring, when the earth awakens from winter slumber, symbolizing rebirth, growth, and the flourishing of life. Rituals involving fertility celebrate not only the vitality of the earth but also the human experience of creation, procreation, and the interconnectedness of all living beings. Asatru practitioners honor both the Aesir and Vanir, the two families of gods that embody these themes, particularly focusing on the Vanir, who are closely associated with fertility, wealth, and prosperity.

Central to these rites is the invocation of deities such as Freyja and Freyr, whose domains encompass love, fertility, and the bountiful harvest. During rituals, offerings may be made to these gods to seek their blessings for fertile crops and healthy families. These offerings can take many forms, including food, drink, or crafted items, symbolizing gratitude and respect for the gifts of the earth. Additionally, practitioners may engage in communal feasts, where the sharing of food becomes a symbolic act of unity and a celebration of life, reinforcing the bonds among community members and the reverence for the natural cycles that sustain them.

Incorporating Norse mythology into these practices, stories of gods and goddesses provide a framework for understanding the significance of fertility and renewal. Myths surrounding the changing seasons, such as the tale of Baldur's death and resurrection, illustrate the cycle of life, death, and rebirth that permeates both the natural world and human existence. These narratives not only serve to educate practitioners about their spiritual heritage but also inspire the rituals that honor these cycles. By retelling these myths during gatherings, practitioners reinforce their cultural identity and the values that underpin their belief system.

The role of ancestors in fertility rites is also paramount, as honoring those who came before serves to strengthen the connection between generations. Many Asatru rituals incorporate acts of remembrance, such as lighting candles or creating altars adorned with family heirlooms and photos. This practice acknowledges the contributions of ancestors to the present, fostering a sense of continuity and respect for the lineage that shapes individual identities. By invoking the names of ancestors during fertility ceremonies, practitioners create a bridge between the past and the present, emphasizing the importance of family and heritage in the cycle of renewal.

As society evolves, so too do the interpretations of these ancient rituals. Modern Asatru practitioners might incorporate contemporary elements into their fertility rites, blending traditional practices with personal beliefs and modern understandings of ecology and community. The use of runes, for example, can enhance the sacredness of these rituals by inviting specific energies and intentions related to fertility and growth. Whether through divination practices or personal invocations, each practitioner can tailor their approach to reflect their unique spiritual journey while remaining rooted in the rich tapestry of Asatru traditions. Ultimately, fertility rites and renewal are a celebration of life's continuity, a testament to the enduring power of nature, community, and the divine.

# Connecting with Nature

Connecting with nature is a central theme in Asatru, reflecting the belief that the natural world is imbued with spiritual significance. The changing seasons serve as a backdrop for rituals and celebrations, allowing practitioners to align themselves with the rhythms of the earth. Each season offers unique opportunities to engage with the land, the elements, and the cycles of life and death, fostering a deeper connection with the divine. Celebrating these natural cycles not only honors the gods and goddesses but also enriches the spiritual lives of practitioners by reinforcing their bond with the environment.

In Asatru, the festivals are often timed to coincide with seasonal changes, such as the solstices and equinoxes. These moments mark pivotal points in the calendar, symbolizing rebirth, growth, harvest, and rest. For instance, Yule, which occurs during the winter solstice, highlights the return of the sun and the promise of longer days ahead. Rituals during this time often include the lighting of candles and the sharing of food, emphasizing warmth and community. Similarly, Ostara celebrates spring's arrival, focusing on fertility and renewal, encouraging practitioners to reflect on personal growth alongside the flourishing of nature.

The influence of Norse mythology plays a vital role in the connection with nature within Asatru. Many myths feature gods and goddesses personifying natural elements, such as Njord, the god of the sea and winds, or Freyja, the goddess of love and fertility. These stories serve as reminders of the sacredness of the natural world and the interconnectedness of all beings. By invoking these deities in rituals, practitioners not only pay homage to their ancestors but also acknowledge the vital forces that govern the earth, cultivating a sense of respect and responsibility toward the environment.

Ritual practices often include offerings and sacrifices that reflect a commitment to nature. Modern interpretations of these traditions have evolved to emphasize sustainability and ethical practices. Instead of animal sacrifices, practitioners may offer seasonal foods, flowers, or crafted items, which honor the gods while respecting the earth's resources. This shift highlights the importance of stewardship in Asatru, fostering a relationship with the land that is both reverent and responsible. Engaging with nature in this way encourages practitioners to reflect on their impact on the environment and to take active steps toward its preservation.

As practitioners cultivate personal altars and sacred spaces, they often incorporate natural elements to enhance their spiritual practice. Integrating stones, plants, and water into these spaces fosters a tangible connection to the earth and serves as a reminder of the sacredness of the natural world. These altars can be places of meditation, prayer, and reflection, where individuals can honor the changing seasons and the deities associated with them. By nurturing this connection with nature, Asatru practitioners deepen their spiritual experience, recognizing that their faith is not only rooted in ancient traditions but also in an ongoing relationship with the world around them.

## Celebrating Growth and New Beginnings

Celebrating growth and new beginnings is a vital aspect of the Asatru faith, resonating deeply with the cycles of nature and the mythology that informs our practices. In Asatru, the changing seasons are symbolic of life's continuous journey, reflecting the birth, death, and rebirth inherent in both nature and the human experience. Festivals such as Ostara and Midsummer mark significant moments of renewal, where communities come together to honor the fertility of the earth and the promise of new life. These occasions serve as a reminder of the interconnectedness of all beings and the potential for transformation inherent in each cycle.

During these seasonal festivals, rituals often center around offerings to the Aesir and Vanir, the deities embodying various aspects of growth and prosperity. Participants may create altars adorned with seasonal flowers, grains, and symbols representing fertility and vitality. These offerings are not just acts of devotion; they represent a commitment to nurturing the earth and embracing the changes that come with each season. By invoking the blessings of the gods and goddesses, practitioners seek to align their personal growth with the natural world, recognizing that the divine flows through all aspects of life.

The influence of Norse mythology is ever-present in the practices surrounding growth and new beginnings. Stories of gods like Freyja, who presides over fertility and abundance, inspire rituals aimed at invoking personal transformation and community flourishing. Asatru practitioners often draw on these myths to craft prayers and invocations that resonate with their unique experiences, allowing individuals to connect deeply with the divine forces that govern their lives. The retelling of these ancient tales during gatherings fosters a sense of continuity and shared purpose, reinforcing the belief that personal growth is part of a larger cosmic narrative.

Additionally, the role of ancestors plays a significant part in celebrating growth and new beginnings. Rituals honoring those who have come before us remind practitioners of the legacies of strength, resilience, and wisdom that shape their identities. By acknowledging the contributions of their forebears, individuals can draw inspiration and guidance, fostering a sense of responsibility to carry forward the values and lessons learned. This connection to ancestry not only enriches personal growth but also reinforces community bonds, creating a support network for those embarking on new ventures.

Finally, the integration of healing and protection spells into these celebrations underscores the Asatru commitment to personal and communal well-being. As practitioners engage with the energies of the season, they may incorporate runes into their rituals, using them as tools for divination and guidance. This magical aspect of the faith empowers individuals to set intentions for the future, whether it be for personal development, community projects, or environmental stewardship. By combining rituals, offerings, and ancestral honors, Asatru practitioners celebrate growth and new beginnings in a holistic manner, ensuring that their spiritual practices remain vibrant and relevant in the contemporary world.

# Chapter 5: Midsummer: The Height of Summer

## Fire Festivals and Their Significance

Fire festivals hold a prominent place within the Asatru tradition, serving as a conduit for connection between the earthly realm and the divine. These festivals often coincide with significant seasonal transitions, symbolizing renewal and transformation. In Norse mythology, fire is not just a physical element but also a potent symbol of life, warmth, and the power of the gods. Celebrating fire festivals provides practitioners with an opportunity to engage in rituals that honor both the Aesir and Vanir, reinforcing the community's bonds and reaffirming their spiritual beliefs.

The significance of fire in these festivals extends beyond mere celebration; it embodies the dual nature of destruction and creation. In Asatru, fire represents both the forge that shapes new beginnings and the flames that consume the old. This duality mirrors the cycles of nature, where decay leads to regeneration. Rituals during fire festivals often include offerings and sacrifices, invoking blessings for fertility, protection, and prosperity. Participants may gather around bonfires, sharing stories and songs that highlight ancestral wisdom while invoking the presence of their gods and the spirits of the land.

Ancestors play a crucial role in the fire festivals, as these events often serve as a time to honor those who have come before. The act of lighting a fire can be seen as a bridge connecting the living with their ancestors. Rituals may include offerings of food, drink, or symbolic items, all intended to invite the spirits of the ancestors to partake in the festivities. This practice fosters a sense of continuity and belonging, as the community acknowledges its roots and the guidance of those who have passed. It reinforces the importance of lineage in shaping individual and communal identities within Asatru.

Magic and prayers are also integral aspects of fire festivals, with practitioners often incorporating elements of divination and protection spells into their celebrations. The flames are seen as a source of insight, illuminating the path ahead and dispelling darkness. Participants may write their intentions or wishes on pieces of paper, casting them into the fire as an offering to the gods, symbolizing the release of their desires into the universe. This act is accompanied by invocations that call upon the Aesir and Vanir, seeking their favor and guidance in the coming season.

In contemporary society, the evolution of fire festivals within Asatru reflects a blend of ancient traditions and modern interpretations. While the core elements of these celebrations remain rooted in Norse mythology, contemporary practitioners often adapt rituals to fit their personal beliefs and community needs. This adaptability allows fire festivals to remain relevant, fostering a sense of unity and shared purpose among practitioners. Ultimately, fire festivals serve as a reminder of the sacred cycles of life and the enduring connection between the natural world, the divine, and the ancestors, enriching the spiritual landscape of Asatru.

## Celebrating Abundance

Celebrating abundance within the Asatru tradition is a profound acknowledgment of the gifts that nature and the divine bestow upon us. This celebration is not merely a reflection of material wealth but an appreciation of all forms of abundance, including health, community, wisdom, and spiritual growth. The seasonal festivals serve as pivotal moments for practitioners to express gratitude and recognize the interconnectedness of life. By gathering at these times, practitioners reaffirm their ties to the land, the cycles of nature, and the ancestral spirits that guide them.

The significance of abundance is deeply rooted in Norse mythology, where deities such as Freyr, the god of fertility and prosperity, exemplify the blessings that come from the earth. Celebrations often incorporate rituals that honor these deities, invoking their presence to enhance the community's fortunes. These rituals may include offerings of food, drink, and crafted items, which symbolize the fruits of the earth and the labor of the people. In doing so, practitioners not only seek to attract abundance but also to recognize their role as stewards of the land and custodians of its gifts.

In Asatru, the role of ancestors is paramount during celebrations of abundance. Ancestors are seen as the bridge between the living and the divine, and honoring them is a way to receive their guidance and blessings. During seasonal festivals, it is customary to set aside a portion of offerings for the ancestors, creating a space within the celebration for remembrance and gratitude. This practice reinforces familial bonds and fosters a sense of continuity, reminding practitioners that they are part of a larger narrative that transcends generations.

The observance of abundance is also closely tied to the practice of magic within Asatru. Healing and protection spells are often woven into the fabric of these celebrations, aimed at enhancing the well-being of the community and safeguarding against misfortune. Runes, symbols imbued with ancient wisdom, are frequently employed in these rituals, serving as conduits for intention and manifestation. The act of inscribing runes on offerings or personal altars during these festivals amplifies the energy of abundance, aligning the individual's desires with the greater flow of universal prosperity.

Ultimately, celebrating abundance in Asatru serves as a reminder of the delicate balance between giving and receiving. It encourages practitioners to cultivate a mindset of gratitude while also acknowledging the importance of sharing their blessings with others. As modern interpretations of these rituals continue to evolve, the core values of community, reciprocity, and reverence for nature remain steadfast. By embracing the spirit of abundance, Asatru practitioners not only enrich their own lives but also contribute to the collective well-being of their communities and the world at large.

## Honoring the Sun

Honoring the Sun is a central theme in Asatru, deeply interwoven with the seasonal festivals that celebrate the cycles of nature and the deities associated with them. The sun, often personified in Norse mythology through the goddess Sól, represents not only the physical light and warmth that sustain life but also the spiritual illumination that guides practitioners on their path. Rituals dedicated to honoring the sun are typically held at solstices and equinoxes, marking pivotal points in the agricultural calendar. These celebrations serve as a reminder of the sun's vital role in the health and well-being of both the land and its people.

One of the most significant solar festivals in Asatru is the Summer Solstice, or Midsummer, which symbolizes the peak of the sun's power. This festival involves various rituals such as bonfires, feasting, and the sharing of stories that honor the sun's vitality. Participants often gather to invoke blessings for growth, fertility, and prosperity, recognizing the sun's essential contribution to the bountiful harvests that follow. In rituals, offerings may be made to Sól in the form of herbs, flowers, and mead, reflecting gratitude for the sun's life-giving energy.

The Winter Solstice, or Yule, presents a contrasting yet equally important opportunity to honor the sun's return as days begin to lengthen once more. This festival celebrates the rebirth of the sun and the promise of new beginnings. As practitioners light candles and decorate their personal altars, they invoke the warmth of the sun to dispel the darkness of winter. The Yule log, burned in many modern celebrations, symbolizes both the sun and the hope for its return. Through these rituals, participants reaffirm their connection to the cycles of nature and the divine forces that govern them.

In addition to these seasonal celebrations, honoring the sun can be incorporated into everyday practices in Asatru. Sun salutations and invocations are common, often performed at dawn to greet the new day. These practices serve to align practitioners with the rhythms of the earth and the cosmos, fostering a deeper connection to the divine. The use of runes, particularly those associated with solar energies, enhances these rituals, allowing practitioners to draw upon ancient wisdom and invoke protection and blessings from the Aesir and Vanir.

The role of ancestors in honoring the sun is also significant, as many Asatru practitioners look to their forebears for guidance and inspiration. Ancestral veneration often includes invoking the wisdom of those who have come before, seeking their blessings in seasonal rituals. Through this connection, individuals not only honor their heritage but also establish a sense of continuity within their spiritual practice. By embracing the sun's cycle through festivals, daily rituals, and ancestral invocations, Asatru practitioners create a vibrant tapestry of reverence that celebrates the interplay between nature, divinity, and the community.

# Chapter 6: Harvest: The Autumn Equinox

## Gratitude and Thanksgiving

Gratitude and Thanksgiving hold a profound significance within the Asatru faith, serving as essential components of both personal and communal rituals. These practices are deeply rooted in the Norse tradition, where acknowledging the gifts of the gods, nature, and ancestors fosters a sense of interconnectedness among all beings. Celebrating gratitude allows practitioners to reflect on the abundance present in their lives, reinforcing the importance of reciprocity in their relationship with the divine and the natural world. This acknowledgment acts as a bridge between the spiritual and physical realms, fostering respect and appreciation for the blessings received.

The act of giving thanks often manifests during seasonal festivals, which are integral to Asatru practices. These celebrations, aligned with the cycles of nature, provide structured opportunities to express gratitude for the harvest, the changing seasons, and the presence of deities in everyday life. For instance, during the autumn festival of Sigrblot, practitioners express thanks for the bountiful harvest and seek blessings for the upcoming winter. Rituals during these festivals may include communal feasts, offerings, and prayers, emphasizing the collective nature of gratitude within the Asatru community.

Incorporating elements of Norse mythology enhances the understanding of gratitude in Asatru. Stories of the Aesir and Vanir gods often illustrate themes of reciprocity, where acts of giving are met with blessings in return. For example, the tale of Odin's sacrifice for wisdom reminds practitioners of the importance of giving thanks for knowledge and insight gained through life experiences. By invoking these myths in rituals and prayers, Asatru adherents can deepen their connection to ancestral traditions and reflect on the values of gratitude embedded within their cultural heritage.

Furthermore, the role of ancestors is pivotal in the practice of gratitude and thanksgiving. Ancestor veneration is a fundamental aspect of Asatru, where practitioners honor their forebears through offerings and remembrances. This practice not only acknowledges the sacrifices made by previous generations but also reinforces the idea that gratitude extends beyond the present moment, bridging the past with the future. By recognizing the contributions of ancestors, contemporary practitioners can cultivate a profound sense of belonging and continuity, fostering a communal spirit that honors both lineage and legacy.

Finally, the expression of gratitude in Asatru can also take the form of offerings and sacrifices, which have evolved in modern interpretations. While traditional practices may have included the offering of livestock or other material goods, contemporary adherents often opt for symbolic gestures, such as creating personal altars adorned with meaningful objects. These spaces serve as focal points for gratitude, where individuals can engage in prayer, reflection, and intention-setting. The act of giving thanks, whether through ritual or personal practice, remains a vital expression of faith in Asatru, reinforcing the sacred relationship between the divine, the natural world, and the community.

# Preparing for the Winter Months

Preparing for the winter months in Asatru is a time steeped in tradition and reflection, aligning with the natural cycles of the earth and the rhythms of the Norse gods. As the days shorten and the chill sets in, practitioners are encouraged to honor the changing season through various rituals and preparations that emphasize resilience and the importance of community. This period serves as an opportunity to connect with ancestors, seeking their guidance and wisdom as the community prepares for the darker months ahead. Ancestors play a vital role in Asatru, and winter rituals often include offerings and prayers that strengthen these bonds, allowing practitioners to draw on the strength of their lineage.

Central to the winter preparations is the celebration of Yule, a festival that marks the rebirth of the sun and the return of longer days. Activities may include decorating personal altars with symbols of the season, such as evergreen boughs representing eternal life, and lighting candles to symbolize hope and warmth. The ritual of lighting the Yule log, often adorned with runes, can be a powerful act of intention, where practitioners invoke blessings for the coming year. Through these actions, individuals not only honor the gods, particularly the Aesir and Vanir, but also engage in magic that reflects the importance of light amidst darkness.

Asatru practitioners are encouraged to create sacred spaces within their homes to foster a sense of peace and connection. Personal altars can be prepared with seasonal offerings, including food, drink, and crafted items, which serve as both tribute and a means of inviting divine presence into their lives. These altars can be adorned with symbols of protection and healing, such as runes that resonate with the energies of the season. By nurturing these spaces, practitioners cultivate a sanctuary for their spiritual practices, allowing for deeper meditative experiences and opportunities for prayer and invocation.

The winter months also present an ideal time for divination practices, which allow individuals to gain insight into the coming year and the challenges they may face. Techniques such as casting runes or using tarot cards can help practitioners tap into the energies of the season, providing clarity and guidance. The reflective nature of winter encourages a deeper internal exploration, inviting practitioners to consider their goals and intentions for the new year. This period of introspection is enriched by the wisdom of the ancestors, who are often called upon for support in navigating the uncertainties ahead.

Finally, it is important to emphasize the role of communal gatherings during the winter months. These gatherings not only reinforce social bonds but also serve as collective celebrations of the season's magic. Rituals performed together, such as feasting, storytelling, and sharing blessings, foster a sense of unity and shared purpose. By coming together, practitioners can share their individual experiences and insights, enriching the collective wisdom of the community. In this way, the winter months become a sacred time of preparation, reflection, and connection, embodying the enduring spirit of Asatru.

## Ancestor Honoring Rituals

Ancestor Honoring Rituals hold a significant place within the Asatru faith, serving as a bridge between the living and the deceased. These rituals are not merely acts of remembrance; they are profound expressions of respect, gratitude, and recognition of the contributions that ancestors have made to the lives of their descendants. In Asatru, ancestors are viewed as vital participants in the spiritual journey of their descendants, providing guidance, wisdom, and protection. This connection to the past is celebrated through various seasonal festivals, where the lineage and heritage of individuals are honored and acknowledged.

One of the most prominent times for ancestor honoring is during the festival of Disablót, which typically takes place in midwinter. This ritual is dedicated to the Disir, the female spirits associated with fertility, fate, and ancestral influence. During Disablót, offerings are made to the ancestors, including food, drink, and symbolic items that represent the family's lineage and achievements. Participants may gather in a sacred space, creating an atmosphere that invites the presence of the ancestors. The ritual often includes storytelling, where family histories and ancestral deeds are recounted, reinforcing the bond between the living and the departed.

In addition to seasonal festivals, everyday ancestor honoring practices are essential within Asatru. Personal altars can be created to celebrate and acknowledge ancestors, adorned with photographs, heirlooms, and offerings. These sacred spaces serve as focal points for prayer and reflection, allowing practitioners to connect with their lineage on a deeper level. Runes may be incorporated into these altars, inscribing names or symbols that embody the qualities and virtues of the ancestors being honored. This practice not only fosters a sense of continuity but also reinforces the belief that the wisdom of the past is accessible and relevant to contemporary life.

Magic and prayers directed toward ancestors often form an integral part of these rituals. Invocations may be recited to invite the presence of the deceased during ceremonies, creating a sacred dialogue between the living and the spirit world. These prayers not only express reverence but may also seek guidance, healing, and protection from ancestral spirits. The belief in the potency of these communications is rooted in Norse mythology, where the ancestors are seen as guardians and guides, often capable of influencing the fates of their descendants. This intergenerational exchange is a cornerstone of Asatru spirituality, emphasizing the importance of ancestral wisdom in navigating life's challenges.

As society continues to evolve, the practice of honoring ancestors remains a vital aspect of Asatru. Modern interpretations of these rituals often blend traditional elements with contemporary practices, allowing for personal expression and adaptation. This evolution reflects the dynamic nature of the faith, where the past is honored while embracing the present. By engaging in ancestor honoring rituals, Asatru practitioners not only celebrate their heritage but also cultivate a sense of belonging and identity that transcends time, continuing the legacy of their forebears in a meaningful way.

# Chapter 7: The Role of Ancestors in Asatru Practices

## Ancestral Veneration

Ancestral veneration in Asatru is a fundamental practice that underscores the importance of honoring those who have come before us. This connection to our ancestors is not merely a tribute to our lineage; it is a vital aspect of spiritual identity that reinforces community ties and fosters a sense of belonging. In this tradition, ancestors are seen as guiding spirits who can influence our lives, offering wisdom and protection. Celebrating their memories through rituals and offerings provides a means to establish a dialogue with the past, ensuring that their stories and lessons are not forgotten.

Rituals dedicated to ancestral veneration often take place during significant seasonal festivals, such as Disablót, which occurs in the winter months. This festival is specifically aimed at honoring the Disir, or female spirits of fate and ancestry. During Disablót, practitioners may gather to share stories about their forebears, light candles, and set aside offerings of mead, food, or crafted items that symbolize the connection to their lineage. These rituals serve not only as a means of remembrance but also as a way to invoke the strength and guidance of ancestors in the present, creating a bridge between past and present.

The influence of Norse mythology on ancestral veneration is notable, as many deities are considered ancestors themselves. Figures such as Odin and Freyja are not only revered as powerful gods but also as archetypal ancestors whose qualities and narratives resonate deeply within the Asatru community. Rituals may include invocations to these deities, asking for their blessings in honoring family lineage and seeking wisdom from them. This intertwining of mythology and ancestral worship enriches the spiritual experience, reinforcing the significance of ancestral connections through the lens of Norse cosmology.

In modern Asatru practice, the approach to offerings and sacrifices has evolved while maintaining a respectful acknowledgment of tradition. Contemporary practitioners often interpret offerings as symbolic gestures rather than literal sacrifices. This can include setting up an altar with photos of ancestors, personal belongings, or written messages expressing gratitude and reverence. Such practices allow individuals to create sacred spaces where they can meditate on their family history and seek guidance, fostering a deeper understanding of their roots and the responsibilities that come with them.

Ultimately, ancestral veneration serves as a powerful reminder of the interconnectedness of life across generations. By incorporating elements of ritual, myth, and personal reflection, practitioners of Asatru can cultivate a rich spiritual relationship with their ancestors. This reverence not only honors the past but also empowers individuals to navigate their present lives with the wisdom and strength inherited from those who have walked before them. In this way, the practice of honoring ancestors becomes a living tradition, continually shaping the identity and spiritual path of the Asatru community.

## Rituals for Connecting with Ancestors

Rituals for connecting with ancestors hold a vital place in Asatru, emphasizing the importance of lineage and the wisdom passed down through generations. These rituals serve as a bridge between the living and the deceased, allowing practitioners to honor their heritage and seek guidance from those who have come before. The practice of remembering ancestors is rooted in the belief that they continue to influence the lives of their descendants, providing both protection and inspiration. Engaging in these rituals fosters a deeper understanding of one's identity and a profound connection to the past.

One common ritual involves the creation of an ancestral altar, a sacred space where offerings can be made to honor those who have passed. This altar typically includes photographs, heirlooms, and other items that represent the ancestors. Seasonal festivals, such as Samhain, are particularly significant for these practices, as they coincide with times when the veil between the worlds is believed to be thinner. During these festivals, practitioners may light candles, recite prayers, and offer food or drink to their ancestors, inviting their presence and acknowledging their continued role in the family's spiritual life.

Another important aspect of connecting with ancestors is the practice of storytelling. Sharing tales of ancestors' lives, accomplishments, and struggles not only preserves family history but also instills values and lessons for future generations. This oral tradition is a powerful way to keep the memory of ancestors alive, reinforcing the bonds between the living and the dead. Rituals that incorporate storytelling can take place during family gatherings or community events, allowing for collective remembrance and celebration of shared heritage.

In addition to altars and storytelling, practitioners often utilize runes in their rituals to connect with ancestral wisdom. Runes, as symbols of divination and magic, can be carved or drawn to invoke specific ancestors or request their guidance. By focusing on the meanings associated with each rune, practitioners can channel the knowledge and protection of their forebears. This practice not only enhances the connection to the past but also serves as a means of seeking clarity and direction in contemporary life.

Ultimately, rituals for connecting with ancestors serve to strengthen the ties between individuals and their heritage, fostering a sense of belonging and continuity. As practitioners engage in these sacred acts, they not only honor their lineage but also invite the wisdom of their ancestors into their lives. This connection enriches their spiritual journey, grounding them in the traditions of Asatru while encouraging personal growth and insight, reinforcing the significance of ancestry in the ongoing practice of this faith.

# The Importance of Family Heritage

Family heritage plays a crucial role in the Asatru faith, serving as a vital link between individuals and their ancestral roots. In Asatru, the reverence for ancestors is not merely a practice but a foundational principle that informs rituals, celebrations, and personal identity. By honoring family heritage, practitioners connect with the strength and wisdom of their forebears, fostering a sense of belonging and continuity. This connection is especially significant during seasonal festivals, where ancestral stories and traditions are woven into the fabric of communal celebrations, reinforcing ties to both family and the broader Asatru community.

The understanding of family heritage in Asatru extends beyond mere genealogy; it encompasses the values, beliefs, and practices passed down through generations. These elements shape individual and collective identities, influencing how practitioners engage with rituals and the divine. In many Asatru practices, the ancestors are invoked during ceremonies, highlighting their enduring presence and the guidance they offer. By acknowledging and integrating the lessons of the past, adherents not only honor their lineage but also empower themselves to navigate the complexities of contemporary life while remaining grounded in traditional wisdom.

Rituals that emphasize family heritage often include offerings and sacrifices dedicated to ancestors, creating a reciprocal relationship that fosters protection and guidance. Such practices serve to reinforce the communal aspect of Asatru, as individuals gather to share in these sacred moments, strengthening bonds with both their ancestors and one another. Modern interpretations of these rituals vary, yet the core intention remains the same: to honor those who came before and to seek their blessings. This communal aspect enhances the significance of seasonal festivals, where shared heritage becomes a source of inspiration and strength for current and future generations.

The influence of Norse mythology on Asatru rituals cannot be overstated, as many practices are steeped in the stories and lessons conveyed through ancient texts. Family heritage is often reflected in the myths, with figures such as Odin and Freyja embodying traits and values that resonate with the ideals of family, honor, and legacy. By engaging with these mythological narratives, practitioners can deepen their understanding of their own heritage, drawing parallels between the epic tales of gods and the lived experiences of their ancestors. This connection to mythology enriches the practice of Asatru, providing a framework through which individuals can explore their identities and spiritual paths.

In conclusion, the importance of family heritage within the Asatru faith is multifaceted, encompassing both individual and communal dimensions. It fosters a deep connection to the past, informs contemporary practices, and enriches the spiritual lives of adherents. As practitioners engage with their heritage through rituals, offerings, and the stories of their ancestors, they not only honor those who have come before but also lay a foundation for future generations. This ongoing dialogue between the past and the present ensures that the essence of Asatru remains vibrant and relevant, allowing its teachings to resonate through time and inspire a profound sense of belonging and purpose within the community.

# Chapter 8: Healing and Protection Spells in Asatru

## Overview of Spellwork

In Asatru, spellwork is a fundamental aspect that intertwines with the faith's rituals, seasonal festivals, and the reverence for the natural world. Spellwork within this tradition encompasses a variety of practices aimed at harnessing the energies of nature and the divine. It includes not only the casting of spells but also the use of rituals, prayers, and invocations to connect with the Aesir and Vanir, the deities of the Norse pantheon. This connection is essential for practitioners seeking to align their intentions with the cyclical rhythms of nature, reflecting the belief that each season holds unique energies that can be invoked for specific purposes.

The significance of seasonal festivals cannot be overstated when considering spellwork. Each festival, from Yule to Midsummer, embodies distinct themes and energies that practitioners can utilize in their spellcraft. For example, the winter solstice, a time of rebirth and renewal, offers opportunities for spells focused on protection and hope for the coming year. Conversely, the summer solstice is a time for growth and abundance, making it ideal for spells that promote fertility and prosperity. By aligning spellwork with these seasonal energies, practitioners can enhance the efficacy of their magic, fostering a deeper connection to the cycles of life and the natural world.

Norse mythology plays a crucial role in shaping the practice of spellwork in Asatru. The stories of the gods and goddesses provide a rich tapestry of symbols and archetypes that inform the intentions behind spells. The use of runes, for instance, is a significant aspect of Asatru magic, as these ancient symbols are believed to embody powerful energies and meanings. Practitioners often incorporate runes into their spellwork, whether through carving them into objects, using them in divination, or invoking their energies in rituals. This integration of mythological elements reinforces the connection between the practitioner, their ancestors, and the divine, creating a dynamic interplay of intention and spiritual power.

The role of ancestors in Asatru practices also extends to spellwork, emphasizing the importance of honoring familial connections and heritage. Ancestral spirits are believed to offer guidance and protection, and many practitioners invoke their ancestors in spells and rituals. This connection can be particularly powerful during seasonal festivals, where honoring the past becomes a communal experience. Spells for healing, protection, and prosperity are often performed with a focus on ancestral lineage, creating a bridge between past and present that strengthens the practitioner's resolve and intention.

In contemporary society, the evolution of Asatru rituals has led to modern interpretations of traditional spellwork. While the core principles remain rooted in ancient practices, practitioners are encouraged to adapt and personalize their magic to resonate with their unique experiences and beliefs. This evolution reflects a broader understanding of spirituality, where healing and protection spells are not only about the specific outcomes but also about the process of self-discovery and empowerment. By embracing both traditional and contemporary approaches, Asatru practitioners can cultivate a rich, vibrant practice of spellwork that honors their heritage while remaining relevant to their lives today.

# Common Healing Practices

Healing practices within Asatru are deeply rooted in the Norse tradition, emphasizing a holistic approach that integrates body, mind, and spirit. The connection to nature plays a vital role in these practices, as the changing seasons are believed to influence health and well-being. Many Asatru practitioners turn to the natural world for remedies, utilizing herbs, plants, and other resources that are seasonally available. This seasonal awareness not only enhances the efficacy of healing but also aligns the individual with the rhythms of the earth, reinforcing the belief that health is a reflection of one's relationship with the environment.

One prevalent method of healing involves the use of runes, which carry unique energies and meanings. Runes can be drawn or carved for specific healing intentions, such as physical ailments or emotional distress. Practitioners may create rune stones or bind runes into amulets as a form of protective magic. This practice emphasizes intention and the belief that the energy imbued in the runes can aid in the healing process. The act of crafting these runes can also be a meditative exercise, fostering a deeper connection to the spiritual and natural worlds.

Another significant aspect of healing in Asatru is the invocation of the deities, particularly the Aesir and Vanir, who are associated with various aspects of health and wellness. Prayers and invocations are often directed towards specific gods and goddesses, such as Eir, the goddess of healing, seeking their assistance in times of need. Community gatherings, such as sumbels, frequently include blessings and prayers for health, allowing participants to collectively channel their intentions for healing towards individuals or the community as a whole. This communal aspect reinforces the belief that healing is not only an individual journey but a shared responsibility.

The role of ancestors in Asatru also intertwines with healing practices. Ancestor veneration not only honors those who have come before but also seeks their guidance and support in times of illness or distress. Many practitioners engage in rituals or create altars dedicated to their ancestors, where they can offer prayers and requests for healing. This connection to lineage is believed to provide strength and resilience, as practitioners draw upon the wisdom and experiences of those who have faced similar challenges in life.

Lastly, the incorporation of seasonal festivals into healing practices highlights the cyclical nature of life. Festivals such as Midsummer and Yule provide opportunities for rituals that celebrate renewal and restoration. During these times, practitioners may perform specific healing rites that align with the seasonal energies, such as purification rituals in spring or protective rites in winter. By engaging in these practices, individuals not only seek personal healing but also contribute to the collective well-being of their communities, reinforcing the interconnectedness of all life within the Asatru belief system.

## Protective Rituals and Charms

Protective rituals and charms hold significant importance within Asatru, serving as a means to invoke safety and well-being for individuals and communities alike. These practices often draw from ancient Norse traditions, incorporating elements that resonate with the belief in a world filled with unseen forces, both benevolent and malevolent. Rituals designed for protection typically involve the invocation of deities, ancestors, and natural elements, aiming to create a shield against negativity and harm. Understanding these rituals enhances the overall appreciation of Asatru, particularly during seasonal festivals when the veil between the worlds is perceived to be thinner, allowing for more potent connections to spiritual forces.

The use of specific charms, such as protective amulets and talismans, is woven into the fabric of Asatru practices. These items are often inscribed with runes, each carrying its own vibrational energy and meaning. Runes like Algiz, associated with protection, and Tiwaz, symbolizing honor and courage, are commonly incorporated into charms that practitioners wear or keep in sacred spaces. Such charms serve to not only provide a sense of security but also to remind individuals of their inherent strength and the support of the cosmos. Understanding the significance of these symbols deepens the connection to the spiritual world and reinforces the values of Asatru.

Seasonal festivals play a crucial role in the performance of protective rituals. Events such as Yule, Ostara, and Midsummer offer unique opportunities for practitioners to gather and engage in communal rituals that emphasize protection and healing. During these celebrations, offerings are made to the Aesir and Vanir, as well as to ancestors, seeking their blessings and guidance. These gatherings foster a sense of unity and shared purpose, reinforcing the community's commitment to safeguarding one another. The collective energy generated during these festivals amplifies the effectiveness of protective charms and spells, making them more resonant.

The role of ancestors in protective rituals cannot be overstated. Ancestors are viewed as guardians who provide wisdom and protection to their descendants. Invocations during rituals often include calls to the ancestors, seeking their intervention in times of need. Practices such as ancestor altars or offerings of food and drink are common ways to honor these familial spirits, creating a bridge between the past and present. This connection is vital in Asatru, as it acknowledges the lineage and the support system that exists beyond the physical realm, enhancing the protective aspect of the rituals performed.

In contemporary Asatru practice, the evolution of protective rituals reflects a blend of traditional beliefs and modern interpretations. Many practitioners adapt ancient methods to suit their personal spiritual journeys, often incorporating elements from diverse sources. This flexibility allows for the incorporation of new ideas while maintaining a respect for the foundational principles of Asatru. Through the exploration of protective rituals and charms, individuals are empowered to create their own sacred spaces, fostering a deeper connection to their spirituality and the natural world. The ongoing practice and innovation in this area ensure that protective measures remain relevant and effective in safeguarding the community and its members.

# Chapter 9: Offerings and Sacrifices: Modern Interpretations

## Historical Context of Offerings

The practice of offerings within the Asatru faith is deeply rooted in the historical context of Norse and Germanic traditions. Ancient societies honored their gods and spirits through various forms of offerings, which were often made to ensure favor, protection, and prosperity. These offerings, known as "blót," were significant rituals performed during seasonal festivals, agricultural cycles, and important life events. The historical significance of these practices reflects a profound understanding of the interconnectedness between humans, nature, and the divine, establishing a foundation for contemporary Asatru practices.

In ancient times, offerings could take many forms, including the sacrifice of animals, the pouring of mead, or the dedication of crafted goods. Each offering was imbued with intention, serving as a means to communicate with the gods, the spirits of the land, and the ancestors. The practice varied by region and community, reflecting local customs and the specific deities being honored. This diversity within offerings illustrates the adaptability of the Asatru faith and its ability to incorporate various elements of local culture while remaining anchored in shared mythological roots.

The influence of Norse mythology on offerings is evident in the narratives surrounding the gods and their interactions with humanity. Myths often depict gods receiving offerings as a means of maintaining cosmic balance and favoring human endeavors. For instance, the story of Odin hanging from Yggdrasil underscores the importance of sacrifice in gaining wisdom and insight. Such tales reinforce the belief that offerings are not merely acts of devotion but integral components of a reciprocal relationship between the divine and the earthly realms, shaping the moral and spiritual framework of the Asatru faith.

In contemporary Asatru practices, the historical context of offerings has evolved, reflecting modern values while still honoring traditional roots. Many practitioners today reinterpret these ancient rituals to fit contemporary lifestyles, focusing on symbolic offerings that resonate with personal beliefs and experiences. This adaptation may include offerings of food, crafted items, or even acts of service, emphasizing the intent behind the offering rather than the literal sacrifice. The modern interpretation seeks to create a meaningful connection with the divine while fostering a sense of community and shared purpose.

The role of offerings in Asatru extends beyond appeasing deities; they are also acts of remembrance and connection to ancestors. By honoring those who came before, practitioners acknowledge the lineage that shapes their identity and beliefs. This dual purpose of offerings—both as a means of devotion and as a bridge to the past—highlights the enduring relevance of historical practices within the modern Asatru community. As such, offerings remain a vital aspect of ritual life, allowing practitioners to engage with their heritage while navigating the complexities of contemporary spirituality.

## Contemporary Practices

Contemporary practices in Asatru reflect a vibrant tapestry of ancient traditions interwoven with modern interpretations, allowing practitioners to connect deeply with their spiritual heritage. Rituals, viewed through the lens of contemporary life, often incorporate elements that resonate with current values while honoring the foundational beliefs of the faith. Seasonal festivals, such as Yule and Midsummer, remain cornerstones of practice, emphasizing the cyclical nature of life and the importance of community gatherings. These celebrations provide a framework for rituals that honor the cycles of nature, fostering a sense of belonging and continuity among practitioners.

Norse mythology continues to significantly influence the rituals and practices within Asatru, serving as a wellspring of inspiration for contemporary ceremonies. Modern practitioners often draw upon the rich narratives of the Aesir and Vanir gods, intertwining these mythological stories with their rituals to deepen their spiritual experiences. The tales of gods like Odin, Freyja, and Thor are not only recited but are also integrated into the fabric of contemporary rites, allowing adherents to engage with these archetypes in meaningful ways. This connection to mythology enriches the spiritual landscape, encouraging practitioners to explore the lessons and moral teachings embedded within these ancient tales.

The role of ancestors is a vital aspect of contemporary Asatru practice, emphasizing the importance of honoring those who came before. Rituals often include offerings and invocations aimed at acknowledging ancestral spirits, creating a bridge between past and present. By incorporating ancestor veneration into their practices, individuals foster a sense of continuity and identity, reinforcing the belief that the wisdom of the past can guide them in their current lives. This reverence for lineage is often expressed through personal altars and sacred spaces, where practitioners create environments that honor their heritage and facilitate connection with their forebears.

Healing and protection spells have also found renewed relevance in modern Asatru, as practitioners seek to address contemporary challenges while maintaining a connection to traditional practices. These spells, often accompanied by prayers and invocations to the Aesir and Vanir, serve as tools for personal empowerment and community well-being. The use of runes in Asatru magic provides an additional layer of depth, allowing practitioners to harness the symbolic meanings of these ancient characters for both divination and spellwork. This blending of historical practices with present-day needs encourages a dynamic approach to spirituality, wherein practitioners adapt ancient wisdom to serve contemporary purposes.

Finally, the evolution of Asatru rituals in contemporary society reflects a growing understanding of the importance of inclusivity and personal expression within the faith. As practitioners engage with diverse backgrounds and experiences, rituals are increasingly personalized, allowing individuals to incorporate their unique stories into the broader narrative of Asatru. This adaptability not only honors the ancient roots of the faith but also ensures its relevance in a rapidly changing world. By embracing contemporary practices, the Asatru community continues to thrive, celebrating its rich heritage while fostering a spirit of innovation and growth.

## Ethics and Intentions in Offerings

Ethics and intentions play a crucial role in the practice of offerings within Asatru, reflecting the deep respect practitioners have for the deities, ancestors, and the natural world. Offerings, whether they are material goods, acts of service, or personal sacrifices, are not merely transactional gestures; they embody a sacred relationship between the worshipper and the divine. The intention behind each offering speaks volumes about the practitioner's reverence and understanding of the interconnectedness of all things, emphasizing that ethical considerations are paramount in these rituals.

In Asatru, the act of offering is often accompanied by a clear intention that aligns with the values of reciprocity and mutual respect. Practitioners are encouraged to reflect on their motivations and the potential impact of their offerings, ensuring that they come from a place of genuine gratitude and sincerity. This ethical framework fosters a deeper connection to the deities and the ancestral spirits, reinforcing the belief that intentions shape the energy of the offerings and the nature of the blessings received in return.

Moreover, the concept of balance is central to ethical offerings. Asatru teaches that what one gives may return in unexpected ways, highlighting the importance of maintaining harmony in the relationship between the individual and the divine. This principle extends beyond personal gain, urging practitioners to consider the broader implications of their offerings on the community and the environment. Ethical mindfulness prompts individuals to choose offerings that are sustainable, respectful of nature, and beneficial to the collective well-being of their kin and kindred spirits.

The evolution of modern interpretations of offerings also necessitates a reevaluation of ethical standards. Contemporary practitioners may draw from diverse sources and experiences, leading to a rich tapestry of rituals that honor tradition while adapting to current realities. This adaptability calls for a conscientious approach to ethics in offerings, where practitioners critically assess the cultural, social, and environmental impact of their choices. Engaging in dialogue within the community about these practices can enhance understanding and foster a shared commitment to ethical offerings.

Finally, the role of community in shaping the ethics of offerings cannot be overstated. Asatru encourages collective participation in rituals, which amplifies the significance of intentions and the power of offerings. Through shared experiences, practitioners can develop a communal understanding of what constitutes ethical behavior in their offerings, fostering a supportive environment where intentions are openly discussed and refined. By prioritizing ethics and intentions, Asatru practitioners can ensure that their offerings resonate deeply within both the spiritual and physical realms, enriching their faith and the world around them.

# Chapter 10: The Use of Runes in Asatru Magic

## Introduction to Runes

Runes, the ancient symbols of the Norse and Germanic peoples, hold a significant place in Asatru practice, serving as both a tool for divination and a means of connecting with the spiritual world. Each rune is imbued with its own unique meaning and power, reflecting various aspects of life, nature, and the cosmos. The use of runes in Asatru is not merely a matter of historical interest; they are actively employed in rituals and magic, allowing practitioners to tap into the energies they represent. Understanding the runes, their origins, and their applications is essential for anyone wishing to deepen their engagement with the Asatru faith.

Historically, runes were carved into wood, stone, or metal, often used for practical purposes such as marking territory or commemorating events. However, their significance transcended mere communication. Each rune bears a connection to the gods, the cosmos, and the forces of nature, serving as a bridge between the physical and spiritual realms. The Elder Futhark, the oldest known runic alphabet, consists of 24 characters, each holding a wealth of symbolism and lore. For practitioners of Asatru, these symbols are more than just letters; they are a means of invoking the power of the universe to aid in personal growth, healing, and protection.

In Asatru rituals, runes are often incorporated into offerings and sacrifices, embodying the intent of the practitioner. They can be drawn in the air, inscribed on altar items, or even utilized in the crafting of talismans. This integration of runes into worship highlights their role as conduits for spiritual energy. By invoking the meanings associated with specific runes during ceremonies, practitioners can enhance the efficacy of their prayers and intentions. This practice fosters a deeper connection to the deities, particularly the Aesir and Vanir, who are believed to respond to the vibrations and energies that runes represent.

The practice of rune divination is another essential aspect of Asatru, allowing practitioners to seek guidance and insight from the spiritual realm. Runes can be cast or drawn from a bag, with each symbol providing a unique message or reflection on the querent's situation. This method of divination aligns with the belief in the interconnectedness of all things, as well as the influence of the ancestors and the natural world on human affairs. Engaging with runes in this way not only aids in personal introspection but also honors the traditions of Norse mythology, reinforcing the cultural heritage of Asatru.

As the Asatru community evolves, so too does the understanding and application of runes within rituals and personal practices. Modern practitioners may adapt traditional uses to fit contemporary lifestyles while remaining rooted in the core beliefs of the faith. Whether used for personal empowerment, healing, or as part of a communal celebration, runes continue to be a vital element of Asatru. Their enduring presence in rituals, magic, and prayers reflects both the ancient wisdom of the Norse traditions and the dynamic, living nature of the Asatru faith today.

# Rune Casting and Divination

Rune casting is an ancient practice deeply rooted in Norse mythology and the Asatru faith, serving as a powerful tool for divination and insight. Runes, often seen as symbols of magical energy, were traditionally inscribed on stones, wood, or metal and were believed to carry specific meanings and vibrations. In the context of Asatru, rune casting is not merely a method of fortune-telling; it is a sacred practice that connects practitioners to their ancestors, the Aesir and Vanir, and the natural world, allowing them to seek guidance and clarity in their lives amid the changing seasons.

The process of rune casting typically involves selecting a set of runes, often carved from natural materials, and using them to answer questions or provide insight into a situation. Practitioners may cast the runes in a spread or layout, with each rune's position and orientation offering unique interpretations. The meaning of each rune is informed not only by its traditional associations but also by the context of the question posed and the intuition of the caster. This personalized approach creates a dynamic interaction between the caster, the runes, and the energies at play, fostering a deeper understanding of one's circumstances and the potential paths forward.

In Asatru, rune casting is often integrated into seasonal festivals and rituals, reflecting the belief that the cycles of nature influence human experiences. During significant times of the year, such as Yule or Midsummer, rune casting can serve as a means of reflection and intention-setting, aligning personal goals with the energies of the season. This practice reinforces the interconnectedness of all living things and highlights the importance of being attuned to the natural world. By engaging with runes during these sacred times, practitioners can enhance their spiritual awareness and cultivate a deeper relationship with the divine.

Moreover, the use of runes in divination is not limited to personal insight; it can also be a communal activity that strengthens bonds within the Asatru community. Group rune casting sessions can facilitate collective decision-making, healing, and shared wisdom, allowing participants to draw on the strengths and perspectives of the group. Such practices underscore the communal aspect of Asatru, where the wisdom of ancestors and the divine is accessible to all, fostering a sense of unity and shared purpose in navigating life's challenges.

Ultimately, rune casting and divination within Asatru embody a holistic approach to spirituality, integrating the wisdom of the past with the realities of the present. As practitioners engage with this ancient form of magic, they honor their heritage while also adapting the practice to fit contemporary life. This evolution ensures that rune casting remains a vibrant and relevant aspect of Asatru, offering insights and connections that resonate deeply within the hearts of its followers, guiding them through the sacred seasons and the journey of life.

## Incorporating Runes in Rituals

Runes hold a profound significance in the Asatru faith, serving as both a means of communication with the divine and a tool for magical practice. Each rune, with its own unique symbolism and energy, can be seamlessly integrated into rituals to enhance their intention and effectiveness. When practitioners incorporate runes into their ceremonies, they connect with the ancient wisdom of the Norse tradition, inviting the power of the Aesir and Vanir into their sacred spaces. This melding of language and ritual not only deepens spiritual engagement but also fosters a greater understanding of the cosmos and one's place within it.

To effectively incorporate runes into rituals, one must first familiarize themselves with the Elder Futhark, the oldest known runic alphabet, which consists of 24 characters. Each rune embodies specific qualities and attributes that can be invoked during rituals. For example, the rune Fehu, representing wealth and prosperity, might be utilized in a rite aimed at manifesting abundance, while the rune Wunjo, symbolizing joy and harmony, could enhance a gathering focused on community and celebration. By selecting runes that resonate with the intent of the ritual, practitioners can channel focused energy that aligns with their spiritual goals.

In a practical sense, runes can be inscribed on various materials such as wood, stone, or metal, creating physical representations that can be used during rituals. These runic symbols can be placed on altars, worn as talismans, or drawn in the air with the intention of invoking their energy. Additionally, practitioners may choose to create a rune circle, where each rune is laid out in a specific pattern, allowing participants to walk within the circle to absorb their energies. This tactile engagement with runes enhances the ritual experience, creating a multi-sensory connection to the divine.

The invocation of runes also plays a significant role in prayers and invocations to the deities. By weaving runic symbols into spoken or written prayers, practitioners can amplify their intentions and create a sacred dialogue with the gods. This practice not only honors the ancient traditions but also personalizes the connection, as individuals can craft unique invocations that resonate with their own experiences and aspirations. Such prayers may include requests for guidance, protection, or blessings, making the use of runes a dynamic aspect of devotional practice.

Ultimately, incorporating runes into rituals enriches the spiritual landscape of Asatru, bridging the past with the present. As practitioners engage with these ancient symbols, they not only honor their ancestors but also contribute to the ongoing evolution of Asatru rituals in contemporary society. The practice of using runes fosters a deeper connection to the natural world, the ancestral spirits, and the divine, making each ritual a transformative experience that resonates on multiple levels. Through the thoughtful integration of runes, Asatru practitioners can create meaningful and powerful ceremonies that reflect their beliefs and intentions.

# Chapter 11: Prayers and Invocations to the Aesir and Vanir

## Understanding the Aesir and Vanir

Understanding the Aesir and Vanir is fundamental to grasping the rich tapestry of Asatru belief and practice. The Aesir and Vanir are two distinct groups of deities within Norse mythology, each embodying unique attributes, roles, and functions. The Aesir, often associated with power, war, and governance, include prominent figures such as Odin, Thor, and Frigg. In contrast, the Vanir, linked to fertility, prosperity, and nature, feature deities like Njord, Frey, and Freyja. This duality reflects a broader theme in Asatru, where balance between different forces is essential for harmony within both the individual and the community.

The historical narrative of the Aesir and Vanir also includes a significant conflict, known as the Aesir-Vanir War, which ultimately led to their reconciliation. This mythological event symbolizes the necessity of cooperation despite differences and highlights the importance of establishing peace and understanding. In contemporary Asatru practice, this story serves as a reminder of the value of unity and collaboration among diverse groups within the faith, encouraging practitioners to embrace various aspects of spirituality and community life.

Rituals and invocations to both the Aesir and Vanir are integral to Asatru practices, particularly during seasonal festivals. Celebrations such as Yule and Midsummer often honor these deities, acknowledging their influence over different aspects of life. Prayers and offerings made during these times are not merely symbolic; they are seen as vital connections to the divine. The Aesir may be invoked for strength, protection, and guidance, while the Vanir are called upon for blessings of fertility and abundance. The dual invocation acknowledges the necessity of harnessing both power and prosperity in personal and communal endeavors.

The role of ancestors in Asatru also intersects with the worship of the Aesir and Vanir. Ancestors are revered as protectors and guides, and their connection to the deities enhances the spiritual lineage within the faith. By honoring both the Aesir and Vanir, practitioners acknowledge their heritage and the wisdom passed down through generations. This recognition fosters a sense of belonging and continuity, reinforcing the importance of community bonds and ancestral ties in the practice of Asatru.

In the context of modern spirituality, understanding the Aesir and Vanir enables Asatru practitioners to develop a more nuanced approach to their rituals and beliefs. As contemporary society evolves, so too does the interpretation of these ancient figures. The integration of various practices, such as healing spells, offerings, and the use of runes, enriches the connection to these divine forces. By exploring the complexities of the Aesir and Vanir, adherents can cultivate a deeper understanding of their faith, allowing for a more meaningful engagement with the sacred traditions that shape their seasonal celebrations and daily practices.

## Traditional Prayers and Their Purposes

Traditional prayers in Asatru serve as a vital means of communication between practitioners and the divine, specifically the Aesir and Vanir, the two main families of gods in Norse mythology. These prayers are not merely words recited during rituals; they are heartfelt invocations that establish a connection to the divine and the spiritual realm. Each prayer is imbued with intention, aiming to honor the gods, seek guidance, express gratitude, or request assistance for various aspects of life. Understanding the purposes behind these prayers enriches the practice of Asatru, allowing adherents to engage more deeply with their faith.

One of the primary purposes of traditional prayers in Asatru is to honor and show reverence to the deities. This is often achieved through invocations that may include the names of specific gods and goddesses associated with particular aspects of life. For instance, a prayer to Freyja may be directed towards matters of love and fertility, whereas a prayer to Odin might focus on wisdom and guidance in times of uncertainty. These prayers serve as a reminder of the presence of the divine in everyday life and the importance of acknowledging the forces that shape one's existence.

Another significant purpose of traditional prayers is to seek blessings and protection. Asatru practitioners often recite prayers during important life events such as births, marriages, and other rites of passage. By invoking divine favor, practitioners believe they can create a sacred space that invites positive energies and wards off negative influences. These prayers can be personal or communal, often taking place during seasonal festivals where larger gatherings allow for a collective invocation of blessings from the gods.

Prayers in Asatru also serve as a means of connecting with ancestors, reflecting the deeply rooted belief in the importance of lineage and heritage. Many prayers include references to forebears, seeking their wisdom and guidance while honoring their memory. This connection to the past helps to strengthen the communal bonds within the Asatru community, emphasizing the idea that the spiritual legacy of ancestors continues to influence the lives of descendants. Recognizing the role of ancestors through prayer reinforces the cyclical nature of life and the ongoing relationship between the living and the dead.

Finally, traditional prayers function as a tool for personal reflection and spiritual growth. Through the act of praying, practitioners can articulate their hopes, fears, and desires, fostering a deeper understanding of themselves and their place within the cosmos. This introspective aspect of prayer allows individuals to cultivate mindfulness, grounding them in their beliefs and values. In this manner, traditional prayers become not just a means of communication with the divine, but also a vital practice for self-discovery and empowerment within the sacred seasons of Asatru.

## Customizing Invocations for Personal Use

Customizing invocations for personal use is a vital aspect of deepening one's spiritual practice within Asatru. While traditional prayers and invocations hold significant value, personalizing them can enhance one's connection to the divine and create a more intimate experience. Each individual's relationship with the Aesir and Vanir, as well as their ancestors, is unique, and tailoring invocations allows practitioners to express their own beliefs, emotions, and intentions. This customization can range from modifying existing texts to creating entirely new invocations that resonate with personal experiences and aspirations.

When crafting personalized invocations, it is essential to consider the underlying principles and themes found in Norse mythology. Drawing inspiration from the attributes of specific deities can shape the tone and focus of the invocation. For example, invoking Odin might emphasize wisdom and guidance, while a prayer to Freyja could center on love and fertility. By aligning the invocation with these mythological elements, practitioners can ensure that their personalized prayers remain rooted in the rich tapestry of Asatru beliefs, fostering a sense of continuity with the past while expressing contemporary needs.

Another important aspect of customization involves the incorporation of personal experiences and ancestral connections. Asatru emphasizes the significance of ancestry and family heritage, and invocations can reflect this by honoring one's forebears. Individuals can include stories, lessons, or qualities from their ancestors that they wish to invoke, creating a bridge between past and present. This practice not only strengthens the invocation but also reinforces the importance of lineage and the guidance that can be drawn from those who have come before.

The format of an invocation can also be adapted to suit personal preferences. Some may prefer a more formal structure, echoing traditional forms, while others might find free verse or spontaneous expressions more authentic. The inclusion of physical elements, such as the use of runes, can further enhance the power of the invocation. Runes can be integrated into the text or used as symbols during the ritual, adding layers of meaning and intention. This adaptability allows practitioners to engage with their spirituality in a manner that feels both comfortable and profound.

Finally, the setting in which invocations are performed plays a crucial role in their effectiveness. Personal altars and sacred spaces can be tailored to reflect individual beliefs and aesthetics. Whether through the arrangement of natural elements, the inclusion of personal tokens, or the use of specific symbols, the environment can amplify the intent behind the invocation. Creating a dedicated space for these practices invites a sense of sacredness and focus, fostering an atmosphere conducive to spiritual connection. By customizing invocations in these ways, practitioners can cultivate a deeply personal and enriching Asatru experience that honors both individual identity and the collective heritage of the faith.

# Chapter 12: Divination Practices within the Asatru Community

## Overview of Divination Methods

Divination has been an integral part of many spiritual practices throughout history, and within Asatru, it serves as a means of seeking guidance from the divine and understanding the influences of the natural world. Various methods of divination have been employed by practitioners, often drawing upon the rich tapestry of Norse mythology and the cultural heritage of the ancestors. Through these practices, individuals strive to connect with the Aesir and Vanir, the gods and goddesses of the Norse pantheon, as well as their own personal ancestral spirits. The significance of divination extends beyond mere fortune-telling; it is a way to engage in a dialogue with the cosmos and to access deeper insights into one's life and the world around them.

One of the most recognized methods of divination in Asatru is rune casting. Runes, which are characters from ancient Germanic alphabets, were not only used for writing but were also imbued with magical properties. Each rune carries specific meanings and symbolism, allowing practitioners to interpret their messages in a context relevant to their queries. The process typically involves selecting runes either randomly or through a more structured approach, such as drawing from a bag or laying them out in a spread. As practitioners engage with the runes, they often invoke the wisdom of the gods, seeking clarity and direction in their lives.

Another method of divination that holds significance within the Asatru community is the use of ogham, an ancient Celtic tree alphabet. While not Norse in origin, ogham has found a place in some Asatru practices due to its connection with nature and the spiritual attributes assigned to various trees. Diviners can use ogham sticks or cards, interpreting the symbols based on their correspondences with trees and their associated meanings. This method emphasizes a deep connection to the earth and the cycles of nature, aligning perfectly with the seasonal festivals celebrated in Asatru.

Scrying, or the practice of gazing into reflective surfaces such as water, crystals, or mirrors, is another form of divination utilized by some Asatru practitioners. This method allows individuals to enter a meditative state, fostering an intuitive connection to the divine. The images and visions that arise during scrying are interpreted as messages from the spiritual realm. It serves as a reminder of the importance of stillness and receptivity in the pursuit of knowledge, encouraging practitioners to trust their instincts and inner wisdom.

Finally, the practice of casting lots, often using objects like stones or coins, provides yet another avenue for divination within Asatru. This method reflects the ancient traditions of chance and fate, where the outcomes are believed to be influenced by the will of the gods. Each object used in the casting may hold specific meanings, and the results are interpreted according to the context of the inquiry. This approach highlights the interplay between free will and destiny, a recurring theme within Norse mythology and Asatru practices. Through these diverse methods of divination, practitioners can deepen their spiritual journey, gaining insights that guide their decisions and enhance their connection to the divine.

## Tarot, Runes, and Other Tools

Tarot, runes, and other divination tools serve as significant instruments in the practice of Asatru, allowing adherents to connect with the spiritual realm, gain insight into their lives, and enhance their rituals. Tarot cards, often associated with mysticism and fortune-telling, can also be adapted to resonate with Norse mythology and the values of Asatru. Each card can be interpreted through the lens of the gods, goddesses, and mythological stories, providing a deeper understanding of one's path and the energies surrounding seasonal festivals. By incorporating the symbolism of the Major and Minor Arcana, practitioners can create a bridge between the contemporary world and ancient traditions, fostering a unique approach to divination that honors both the past and the present.

Runes hold a particularly esteemed place in Asatru, as they are not only an alphabet but also a system of symbols imbued with spiritual significance. Each rune is believed to carry its own unique energy and meaning, rooted in the Old Norse language and mythology. Practitioners often use runes for divination, inscribing them on wood, stone, or other materials to create rune stones or casting them in various layouts for guidance. This practice connects individuals to the wisdom of the ancestors, allowing for a personal interpretation of the runes that speaks to their own experiences. Runes are also integrated into rituals, creating a sacred space for invoking the Aesir and Vanir, thereby enhancing the spiritual potency of offerings and prayers.

The use of these tools extends beyond mere divination; they are often incorporated into rituals for healing and protection. In Asatru, the act of seeking guidance through tarot or runes can be a form of magic, aligning the practitioner's intentions with the energies of the universe. Healing spells may be crafted using specific runes that symbolize health and well-being, while tarot readings can reveal areas in need of focus and healing. This approach reinforces the belief that the mind, body, and spirit are interconnected, and by utilizing these tools, practitioners can foster a holistic sense of wellness that resonates with the cycles of nature and the changing seasons.

Personal altars and sacred spaces often feature tarot decks, rune stones, and other tools, serving as focal points for meditation and reflection. By creating a dedicated environment, practitioners can cultivate a deeper relationship with the divine and their ancestral heritage. These spaces can be adorned with symbols and offerings that reflect the individual's journey, providing a tangible connection to the spiritual realm. The act of engaging with these divination tools within a sacred space not only enhances personal practice but also invites the presence of the gods and goddesses, enriching seasonal celebrations such as Yule or Midsummer with profound spiritual significance.

In contemporary society, the evolution of Asatru rituals continues to embrace the use of tarot, runes, and other divination practices, allowing for a dynamic and personalized spiritual experience. As practitioners seek to honor their heritage while navigating modern challenges, these tools provide a means of connecting with the ancient wisdom of the Norse tradition. By weaving together the threads of mythology, ancestral reverence, and personal intent, tarot and runes become vital components of Asatru practice, fostering a deeper understanding of the self and the universe. This integration not only enriches individual journeys but also strengthens the communal ties within the Asatru community, celebrating the sacred seasons and the ever-evolving nature of spiritual practice.

## Importance of Intuition in Divination

Intuition plays a crucial role in the practice of divination within the Asatru faith, serving as a bridge between the practitioner and the spiritual realm. As individuals engage with the mysteries of the universe through rituals and tools such as runes, tarot, or other divination methods, it is their intuition that often guides them towards meaningful insights. The practice of divination is not merely about interpreting symbols or signs; it is an active engagement that relies heavily on the intuitive faculties of the practitioner. This connection allows one to tap into deeper layers of understanding, often revealing truths that may not be immediately apparent.

In the context of Asatru, intuition acts as a form of inner wisdom influenced by one's experiences, emotions, and spiritual journey. This wisdom is particularly important during seasonal festivals, where the energies of nature are believed to be heightened. Practitioners often find that their intuitive insights align with the themes of the festivals, whether they are celebrating the rebirth of spring or the introspection of winter. By listening to their intuition, individuals can align their divination practices with the rhythms of the sacred seasons, enhancing both personal and communal rituals.

Moreover, the role of ancestors in Asatru practices emphasizes the importance of intuition in divination. Many practitioners believe that the spirits of their ancestors provide guidance through intuitive nudges or feelings. When engaged in divination, the ability to connect with these ancestral energies can reveal insights that resonate with the individual's personal history and the collective wisdom of their lineage. This ancestral connection not only enriches the divination experience but also deepens the sense of responsibility practitioners feel towards honoring their heritage.

As practitioners explore various divination methods, the interplay between intuition and the tools used becomes evident. For instance, when utilizing runes, it is often the intuitive interpretation of the symbols that yields the most profound insights. Runes are not just letters or symbols; they carry energetic vibrations that resonate with the intuitive mind. A practitioner who trusts their intuition can discern messages that may not be explicitly stated in the runic meanings, thus creating a more personalized and relevant experience. This highlights the transformative nature of divination, where intuition becomes a key player in unlocking hidden knowledge.

Ultimately, the importance of intuition in divination within Asatru cannot be overstated. It serves as both a guiding force and a source of personal empowerment, allowing individuals to navigate their spiritual journeys with clarity and purpose. By fostering a deeper connection with their intuition, practitioners can enhance their understanding of the divine and their place within the cosmos. In a world that often prioritizes rationality over instinct, embracing intuition in divination practices encourages a holistic approach to spirituality, one that honors the sacred interplay between the seen and unseen realms.

# Chapter 13: Personal Altars and Sacred Spaces in Asatru

## Creating a Personal Altar

Creating a personal altar is a deeply meaningful practice within Asatru, serving as a physical manifestation of one's spiritual beliefs and connection to the divine. This sacred space allows practitioners to focus their intentions, honor the gods and goddesses, and connect with their ancestors. When designing a personal altar, it is essential to consider the elements that resonate most with one's spiritual journey, as this space should reflect individual beliefs and the personal significance of various symbols, offerings, and rituals.

The location of the altar holds great importance. It should be situated in a quiet, comfortable area where one can meditate, pray, or perform rituals without distractions. Many choose to set up their altars in a dedicated room or a specific corner of a living space that feels sacred. This area should ideally receive natural light and be easily accessible for regular use. The choice of location can enhance the spiritual energy of the altar, allowing for a deeper connection during rituals and meditative practices.

When selecting items for the altar, practitioners often incorporate symbols that represent their personal beliefs, the gods and goddesses they honor, and elements of Norse mythology. Common items include statues or figurines of deities, runes, candles, crystals, and natural elements such as stones, flowers, or herbs. Each item should hold significance, whether it is a token of gratitude, a representation of a specific intention, or a means of invoking particular energies. Incorporating items that honor ancestors can also strengthen the connection to one's heritage and lineage, making the altar a space of remembrance and respect.

Offerings play a central role in Asatru practices and can be an integral part of altar activities. These offerings may include food, drink, or other items that are meaningful to the practitioner and their deities. It is essential to treat these offerings with reverence, acknowledging the reciprocal relationship between the practitioner and the divine. Seasonal festivals provide an excellent opportunity to refresh the altar with new offerings that align with the energies and themes of the time, fostering a deeper connection to the cycles of nature and the sacred rhythms of life.

Maintaining the personal altar is a dynamic process that evolves with the practitioner's spiritual journey. Regularly cleansing the space, rearranging items, and updating offerings can help keep the altar vibrant and meaningful. As practitioners engage in rituals, prayers, and spells, the altar can become a focal point for healing, protection, and magic. This sacred space not only serves as a personal sanctuary but also as a testament to the practitioner's commitment to their faith, honoring the past while embracing the present and future within the rich tapestry of Asatru.

## Significance of Sacred Spaces

Sacred spaces hold profound significance within the Asatru faith, serving as conduits for spiritual connection and communal gathering. These spaces, whether natural or constructed, are imbued with intention and reverence, allowing practitioners to engage with the divine and the ancestral spirits. In Asatru, the sacredness of a space is often marked by the presence of natural elements such as trees, stones, and water, which are believed to be manifestations of the divine. This connection to nature reinforces the belief that the world is alive with spiritual energy, making every sacred space a unique reflection of the cosmos and its inherent rhythms.

The role of personal altars within these sacred spaces cannot be overstated. Each altar serves as a focal point for individual devotion, allowing practitioners to create a microcosm of their beliefs and intentions. By adorning altars with symbols such as runes, offerings, and images of deities, practitioners cultivate a space that resonates with their spiritual aspirations. These personal sanctuaries become places for reflection, prayer, and ritual, fostering a deep sense of connection to the divine forces of the Aesir and Vanir. The act of tending to an altar is not merely a ritualistic practice; it is an expression of one's commitment to the Asatru faith and its cultural heritage.

Community gatherings in sacred spaces further highlight the importance of these locations within the Asatru tradition. Seasonal festivals, held in nature or designated sacred sites, bring together practitioners to honor the cycles of the year and the deities associated with them. These gatherings emphasize the interconnectedness of individuals and the community, reinforcing the idea that spirituality is enriched through shared experiences. The rituals performed during these festivals, from blóts to sumbels, are steeped in tradition and serve to strengthen bonds among participants, fostering a sense of belonging and collective identity.

Moreover, sacred spaces in Asatru also act as venues for ancestral veneration. The practice of honoring ancestors is central to Asatru beliefs, and sacred sites provide the perfect environment for this essential aspect of worship. By creating spaces that acknowledge the contributions and spirits of those who came before, practitioners invite the wisdom and guidance of their ancestors into their lives. This act of remembrance not only reinforces cultural identity but also allows individuals to seek protection and guidance through the trials of modern life, drawing strength from the lineage that shapes their existence.

Lastly, the evolution of sacred spaces in contemporary Asatru reflects broader changes within society. As practitioners adapt their rituals and practices to modern contexts, the understanding of sacredness expands to include urban environments and personal homes. This adaptability demonstrates the resilience of Asatru as a living tradition, allowing for the integration of contemporary experiences while remaining rooted in ancient wisdom. The significance of sacred spaces, therefore, transcends physical boundaries, embodying the ever-evolving relationship between the individual, the community, and the sacred.

## Maintaining and Honoring Your Space

Maintaining and honoring your sacred space is an essential aspect of practicing Asatru, as it fosters a deep connection to the divine and the natural world. A personal altar or sacred space serves as a physical manifestation of one's faith, a place where rituals, offerings, and prayers can be performed to honor the Aesir and Vanir, the ancestors, and the spirits of nature. This space is not merely a backdrop for rituals; it is a dynamic environment that reflects the practitioner's beliefs, intentions, and seasonal changes. Incorporating natural elements such as stones, plants, and water can enhance this connection, reminding practitioners of their ties to the earth and the cycles of life.

The significance of maintaining a clean and organized sacred space cannot be overstated. Just as one would care for a garden, tending to an altar requires regular attention and intention. This involves clearing away any debris, refreshing offerings, and ensuring that the objects present resonate with the current season or the specific ritual being observed. For example, during the height of summer, bright flowers and fresh herbs could be incorporated, while autumn may invite the use of leaves, pinecones, and other seasonal elements. This attentiveness not only honors the space but also serves as a meditative practice, grounding the individual and preparing them for deeper spiritual work.

Honoring your space also includes the act of making offerings and sacrifices, which is a vital part of Asatru practice. These offerings can range from food and drink to crafted items or natural materials, all meant to express gratitude and respect to the divine and ancestral spirits. Modern interpretations of offerings can adapt to individual circumstances, allowing practitioners to creatively engage with their faith. It is important to view these offerings not as transactions, but as genuine expressions of reverence and love that strengthen the bonds between the practitioner and the spiritual realms.

In addition to physical upkeep, the energy of the sacred space must be nurtured. This can be achieved through rituals of purification, such as smudging with herbs or using water blessed with intentions. Invocations and prayers can also be performed to invite positive energies and dispel any negativity. Seasonal festivals in Asatru provide excellent opportunities to refresh the sacred space, aligning it with the changing energies of the year. By acknowledging and celebrating these shifts, practitioners can cultivate a living relationship with their space, ensuring it remains a vibrant center for spiritual practice.

Finally, the personal nature of a sacred space allows for individual expression and growth within the Asatru faith. Each practitioner may incorporate unique symbols, runes, and artifacts that resonate personally or historically, thereby creating a space that feels authentic and empowering. As practitioners evolve in their spiritual journey, so too should their sacred spaces. This ongoing evolution reflects the dynamic nature of Asatru itself, which honors tradition while embracing personal interpretations and modern practices. By maintaining and honoring their sacred space, individuals reinforce their commitment to their faith and cultivate a deeper understanding of the interconnectedness of all life.

# Chapter 14: The Evolution of Asatru Rituals in Contemporary Society

## Modern Adaptations of Traditional Rituals

Modern adaptations of traditional rituals within Asatru reflect a dynamic interplay between ancient practices and contemporary values. As adherents of Asatru seek to honor their ancestors and the natural cycles of the seasons, they often reinterpret traditional ceremonies to resonate more deeply with their current experiences and societal changes. This evolution is particularly evident in how community gatherings and individual observances are structured, allowing for inclusivity and personal expression while remaining rooted in Norse heritage.

Seasonal festivals play a crucial role in these adaptations, embodying both celebration and reverence for nature's rhythms. Events like Yule and Midsummer, once marked by specific agricultural and solar cycles, have seen modern interpretations that emphasize community bonding, environmental awareness, and personal reflection. Rituals may now include communal feasts, storytelling, and workshops that promote sustainability and local traditions, thereby bridging the past with present-day concerns about ecological responsibility.

The role of ancestors remains central to Asatru practices, yet the approach to honoring them has transformed. While traditional offerings may have included animal sacrifices or physical gifts, contemporary practitioners often focus on symbolic gestures and acts of remembrance. This shift allows for a broader participation, encouraging individuals to create personal altars that incorporate family heirlooms, photographs, and written tributes, fostering a deeper connection to lineage and history without the need for more archaic practices that may not resonate with modern sensibilities.

Healing and protection spells within Asatru also illustrate a modern adaptation of traditional magic. While historical texts may outline specific incantations or rituals, today's practitioners often personalize these spells to address contemporary issues such as mental health, personal safety, and community well-being. This evolution not only validates individual experiences but also integrates modern psychological insights with ancient wisdom, creating a holistic approach to well-being that respects both the past and present.

Lastly, the use of runes has adapted to reflect the changing landscape of Asatru practice. Where runes were once primarily used for divination and magical purposes, they are now frequently incorporated into art, crafts, and personal affirmations. This creative engagement with runes allows practitioners to connect with their cultural heritage while expressing their personal journeys. As Asatru continues to evolve, these modern adaptations of traditional rituals exemplify the faith's resilience and relevance in a contemporary context, ensuring that ancient practices remain vibrant and meaningful.

# Influences of Global Spiritual Practices

Global spiritual practices have played a significant role in shaping and enriching the Asatru faith, allowing it to adapt and resonate with contemporary practitioners while remaining rooted in its ancient traditions. As Asatru draws from Norse mythology and cultural heritage, its rituals, magic, and prayers are often influenced by the spiritual practices of various cultures around the world. This interaction fosters a deeper understanding of the divine and encourages a more inclusive approach to spirituality, recognizing the interconnectedness of different belief systems.

Seasonal festivals in Asatru, such as Yule and Midsummer, are not just celebrations of nature's cycles but also reflect the influence of global spiritual practices that emphasize the importance of seasonal changes. Many cultures have festivals that honor the solstices and equinoxes, acknowledging the earth's rhythms and their impact on human life. By integrating elements from these diverse traditions, Asatru practitioners can enhance their celebrations, making them more vibrant and meaningful. This blending of practices highlights a shared human experience, fostering unity among different spiritual paths.

Norse mythology's rich tapestry of gods, goddesses, and mythical beings serves as a foundation for Asatru rituals, but this mythological framework is often enriched by insights from global spiritual traditions. The stories of creation, heroism, and transformation found in various mythologies resonate with Asatru's narratives, enabling practitioners to draw parallels and deepen their understanding of their own beliefs. This cross-cultural exploration can illuminate the universal themes of life, death, and rebirth, which are central to many spiritual practices around the world, thus enhancing the depth of Asatru rituals.

The role of ancestors is paramount in Asatru, reflecting a common theme found in numerous spiritual traditions globally. Ancestor veneration is a practice that transcends cultures, emphasizing respect for those who came before and recognizing their influence on the present. By incorporating global practices of honoring ancestors, Asatru can develop a more profound appreciation for lineage and heritage. This practice not only strengthens familial bonds but also connects practitioners with a broader spiritual legacy, allowing for the healing and protection spells that draw on ancestral wisdom to become more potent and meaningful.

Finally, the evolution of Asatru rituals in contemporary society is marked by an increasing openness to integrating diverse spiritual influences. As practitioners seek personal altars and sacred spaces that resonate with their individual beliefs, they are also inspired by global spiritual practices that emphasize intention and connection to the divine. The incorporation of runes, prayers, and invocations from various traditions into personal and communal practices illustrates a dynamic interplay of spirituality. This evolution reflects a broader trend within modern spirituality, where the blending of practices not only enriches individual experiences but also fosters a sense of community among diverse practitioners, unified by a shared reverence for the sacred.

## The Future of Asatru Festivals and Rituals

The future of Asatru festivals and rituals is poised for significant evolution, driven by contemporary societal changes and a resurgence of interest in ancestral traditions. As more individuals seek spiritual and communal connections, Asatru practitioners are likely to adapt their rituals to resonate with modern values while still honoring ancient practices. This balancing act will involve a careful consideration of how seasonal festivals, such as Yule and Ostara, can reflect not only traditional Norse cosmology but also the diverse realities of today's practitioners.

The integration of technology into Asatru practices is one area ripe for development. Virtual gatherings and online ceremonies have gained traction, especially in the wake of global disruptions that limited physical congregations. This digital shift allows for an expanded reach, enabling practitioners from across the globe to participate in rituals that might have previously been confined to local communities. The future may see hybrid festivals that blend in-person celebrations with virtual components, thereby fostering a more inclusive environment while maintaining the integrity of traditional customs.

Furthermore, the role of community and individual agency in Asatru rituals is likely to evolve as well. As practitioners seek to personalize their spiritual experiences, we may witness a rise in individualized offerings and prayers that reflect personal circumstances and contemporary issues. The emphasis on personal altars and sacred spaces will continue to grow, allowing individuals to create meaningful connections with the divine that resonate with their unique life experiences. This shift towards personalization can deepen the spiritual significance of rituals and foster a sense of ownership over one's practice.

The understanding of ancestral influence in Asatru will also play a crucial role in shaping future rituals. As communities increasingly value inclusivity, there may be a broader interpretation of ancestry that embraces diverse backgrounds. This expanded view can enrich rituals by incorporating a wider array of traditions and honoring various cultural heritages. The acknowledgment of ancestors as vital participants in contemporary practices may lead to more intricate and varied forms of offerings, enhancing the depth of connection practitioners feel with their forebears.

Finally, the continued exploration of mystical elements such as runes and divination will be integral to the evolution of Asatru rituals. As practitioners delve deeper into these ancient practices, new interpretations and applications will emerge, potentially leading to innovative approaches to magic and spiritual insight. This exploration can create a dynamic interplay between tradition and modernity, allowing Asatru to remain relevant and vital in an ever-changing world. As the community navigates these transformations, the essence of Asatru—rooted in respect for nature, reverence for ancestors, and connection to the divine—will likely continue to guide its rituals and festivals into the future.

# Chapter 15: Conclusion: Embracing Sacred Seasons

## Reflection on Personal Practice

In the journey of embracing Asatru, the act of reflection on personal practice serves as a vital component for growth and understanding. Engaging deeply with the rituals, magic, and prayers inherent in Asatru can foster a greater connection to the sacred cycles of nature and the divine. This personal exploration allows individuals to assess how these practices resonate with their own experiences and beliefs, creating a personalized pathway that honors both tradition and individual spirituality. By reflecting on these elements, practitioners can uncover the layers of meaning embedded within their rituals, enhancing the significance of seasonal festivals and their role in the Asatru faith.

The seasonal festivals in Asatru are rich with historical significance and cultural relevance. Taking time to reflect on how these festivals align with one's personal life can deepen appreciation for the rhythms of nature and the cycles of existence. Each festival, whether it celebrates the rebirth of spring or the introspection of winter, invites practitioners to mark time in ways that honor both personal and communal experiences. This reflection can ignite a sense of belonging within the wider Asatru community, as individuals recognize their place within the tapestry of past and present, connecting their personal journeys to the larger narrative of Norse mythology and its teachings.

The influence of Norse mythology on Asatru rituals is profound and multifaceted. Reflecting on personal practice allows individuals to examine how these ancient stories and deities resonate in their daily lives. Engaging with myths can provide insights into personal challenges and aspirations, making them more than just tales of gods and heroes. As practitioners explore their relationships with the Aesir and Vanir, they may find that these connections inspire them to incorporate mythological themes into their rituals, fostering a sense of continuity and relevance in contemporary practice.

The role of ancestors in Asatru practices is another area ripe for reflection. Ancestral veneration is a cornerstone of the faith, and reflecting on one's lineage can deepen the understanding of personal identity and spiritual heritage. By honoring ancestors through rituals and offerings, practitioners can tap into the wisdom and strength of those who came before them. This practice not only enriches individual spirituality but also reinforces the communal bonds within the Asatru community, as shared ancestry becomes a source of unity and support.

Finally, the exploration of healing and protection spells, offerings and sacrifices, and the use of runes in Asatru magic invites practitioners to reflect on their intentions and the outcomes of their practices. Each spell or ritual can be seen as a conversation with the divine, where personal desires and needs are articulated. Through reflection, individuals can assess the effectiveness of their spiritual engagements, adjusting their practices to align more closely with their evolving understanding of the sacred. This ongoing process of reflection not only enhances personal practice but also contributes to the broader evolution of Asatru rituals in contemporary society, ensuring that they remain vibrant and relevant in the lives of modern practitioners.

## Building Community through Festivals

Festivals play a pivotal role in the Asatru community, serving as vibrant expressions of culture, spirituality, and communal bonding. These gatherings provide opportunities for individuals to connect with their heritage, honoring the cycles of nature and the deities that govern them. Each festival is steeped in tradition, often incorporating rituals that have been passed down through generations. By participating in these events, practitioners not only celebrate their beliefs but also strengthen the ties that bind them to their ancestors and fellow community members.

During seasonal festivals, the Asatru community comes together to mark significant points in the annual cycle, such as solstices, equinoxes, and harvest times. These celebrations are not merely social gatherings; they are opportunities for collective prayer, offering, and ritual that honor the Aesir and Vanir. The significance of these festivals extends beyond individual spirituality, as they foster a sense of unity and shared purpose among practitioners. This communal aspect amplifies the power of the rituals performed, creating a space where collective intentions can manifest more strongly than when practiced in solitude.

The influence of Norse mythology is deeply woven into the fabric of these festivals. Myths of gods and goddesses, heroes and giants, provide the thematic backdrop for the rituals and celebrations held during these times. Storytelling becomes an integral part of the festival experience, allowing participants to engage with their mythology actively. Reenactments of legendary tales, along with songs and poetry, breathe life into ancient stories, ensuring that the lessons and values of the past resonate with contemporary practitioners. This connection to myth not only enriches the festival experience but also serves as a reminder of the values that guide the community.

The festivals also serve as a space for personal reflection and healing, where community members can seek support from one another. Offerings and sacrifices made during these gatherings can take on modern interpretations, reflecting the evolving nature of Asatru practices. Participants may choose to offer not only physical items but also acts of kindness, shared resources, or commitments to personal growth. This spirit of giving reinforces the bonds of community and emphasizes the importance of collective well-being, encouraging individuals to support one another in their spiritual journeys.

In addition to the communal and mythological aspects, the festivals provide opportunities for personal exploration of Asatru's rich practices, including divination and the use of runes. These elements can be incorporated into festival activities, allowing individuals to engage with their spirituality in a communal setting. Personal altars and sacred spaces may be established during these gatherings, inviting attendees to reflect on their individual paths while remaining connected to the larger community. Ultimately, the act of building community through festivals not only nurtures relationships among practitioners but also strengthens the overall foundation of the Asatru faith, ensuring its vitality for future generations.

# The Ongoing Journey of Asatru

The ongoing journey of Asatru reflects the dynamic and evolving nature of this ancient faith as it adapts to contemporary society while remaining rooted in its rich traditions. Asatru practitioners today engage in a vibrant revival of Norse paganism, emphasizing seasonal festivals that honor the cycles of nature and the deities of the Aesir and Vanir. These celebrations, such as Yule, Ostara, and Midsummer, are not merely commemorative but serve as vital expressions of community and spirituality. They provide a structure for rituals and gatherings that allow practitioners to connect with their ancestors, the land, and each other, reinforcing the communal bonds that have characterized Asatru throughout history.

The significance of rituals in Asatru extends beyond mere observance; they are seen as acts of magic that engage the spiritual realms. Rituals, often accompanied by prayers and invocations, create a sacred space where practitioners can interact with the divine. The influence of Norse mythology is palpable in these practices, as stories of gods, goddesses, and mythical beings inform the themes and elements of seasonal celebrations. By invoking the names of deities and performing symbolic acts, practitioners tap into the ancient wisdom of their forebears, ensuring that the teachings of the past continue to resonate in modern contexts.

Ancestors hold a revered position within Asatru, serving as guides and protectors in the ongoing journey of the faith. Honoring the dead through ancestor veneration is a common practice, allowing practitioners to forge a connection with their lineage and heritage. Ritual offerings, such as food, drink, or crafted items, are made to honor these ancestors, reflecting a deep respect for their contributions to the living community. This practice not only enhances the sense of identity among practitioners but also reinforces the continuity of tradition, as stories and lessons from ancestors are passed down through generations.

The modern interpretations of offerings and sacrifices have also evolved, adapting to contemporary ethics and lifestyles. While traditional sacrifices may have included animal offerings, today's practitioners often focus on symbolic gestures that resonate with their values and beliefs. This shift allows for a more inclusive practice that can accommodate a diverse range of participants while still honoring the essence of Asatru. Additionally, the use of runes in magical practices remains a vital aspect of Asatru, as these ancient symbols are employed for divination, protection, and personal empowerment, bridging the gap between the past and the present.

Asatru's ongoing journey is marked by a commitment to personal and communal spiritual growth. The establishment of personal altars and sacred spaces has become increasingly popular among practitioners, providing a focal point for meditation, prayer, and ritual work. These spaces serve as reminders of the sacredness of life and the interconnectedness of all beings. Furthermore, the exploration of divination practices within the community encourages individuals to seek guidance from the spiritual realm, fostering a deeper understanding of their own paths. As Asatru continues to evolve, it remains a testament to the resilience of ancient traditions and the enduring power of faith in the modern world.

# The Allfather and His Kin: A Comprehensive Guide to Odin, Thor, and Freyja

## Chapter 1: Introduction to Norse Mythology

### Overview of the Norse Pantheon

The Norse pantheon is a rich tapestry of deities, each embodying various aspects of life, nature, and the cosmos. Central to this pantheon are the Aesir and the Vanir, two tribes of gods who represent different elements of existence. The Aesir, including major figures such as Odin, Thor, and Frigg, are often associated with war, governance, and the pursuit of knowledge. In contrast, the Vanir are linked to fertility, prosperity, and nature, showcasing the complexity of the Norse belief system. Understanding these divine figures provides insight into the values and priorities of the Norse people, reflecting their understanding of the world around them.

Odin, often referred to as the Allfather, stands as the most prominent figure within the Norse pantheon. He is the god of wisdom, war, and death, embodying the pursuit of knowledge through sacrifice and introspection. His quest for understanding is exemplified in his willingness to sacrifice his eye for wisdom, symbolizing the lengths to which he will go to gain insight. Thor, the thunder god, represents strength, protection, and the defense of both gods and humans against chaos, often personified by the giants. His hammer, Mjölnir, is a powerful symbol of his might and his role as a protector of the realm, highlighting the importance of bravery and loyalty in Norse culture. Freyja, the goddess of love, fertility, and battle, embodies the duality of femininity in Norse mythology, showcasing both nurturing and warrior qualities.

The role of goddesses within Norse mythology is significant, as they are not merely passive figures but active participants in the cosmic order. Goddesses such as Frigg, Freyja, and Skadi wield considerable influence, guiding the fates of both gods and mortals. They represent various aspects of life, from love and fertility to vengeance and war, illustrating the multifaceted nature of femininity in Norse belief. This emphasis on powerful female figures reflects a cultural appreciation for the balance of masculine and feminine energies, revealing a society that recognized the importance of both in maintaining harmony and order.

Beyond the major deities, the Norse pantheon is populated by lesser-known figures who play crucial roles in the myths and the lives of the gods. Deities such as Njord, the god of the sea and winds, and Tyr, the god of war and justice, contribute to the overall narrative of the pantheon, often stepping into the limelight during significant events. Additionally, the Norns, the personifications of fate, influence the lives of gods and mortals alike, weaving the threads of destiny that bind the cosmos. Their presence underscores the interconnectedness of the pantheon and the intricate web of relationships that define Norse mythology.

The Nine Realms serve as the backdrop for the interactions of gods and other beings, each realm embodying different aspects of existence and spirituality. From Asgard, the home of the Aesir, to Hel, the realm of the dead, these domains reflect the complexity of Norse cosmology. The relationship between gods and giants further complicates the pantheon, as these beings often represent chaos and challenge to divine order. Myths and legends featuring these deities illustrate not only their attributes and powers but also the moral lessons and cultural narratives that have persisted through the ages. The ongoing influence of Norse gods in contemporary culture speaks to their timeless relevance, reminding us of the enduring nature of these ancient stories.

## Importance of Mythology in Ancient Scandinavia

The importance of mythology in ancient Scandinavia cannot be overstated, as it served as a foundational framework for understanding the world and the human experience. The Norse pantheon was not merely a collection of gods and goddesses; it was a complex system of beliefs that explained natural phenomena, human behavior, and societal norms. Through myths, the ancient Scandinavians articulated their values, fears, and aspirations, allowing them to navigate the uncertainties of life. This rich tapestry of stories offered insights into the nature of existence, the cosmos, and the intricate relationships between gods, humans, and the forces of nature.

Central to this mythology are the major gods, including Odin, Thor, and Freyja, each embodying distinct attributes and responsibilities that resonated deeply with the people. Odin, the Allfather, represented wisdom, war, and poetry, while Thor, the thunder god, symbolized strength and protection against chaos. Freyja, the goddess of love and fertility, embodied beauty and the power of the feminine. These deities were not just figures of worship but also archetypes that reflected the societal roles and ideals of ancient Scandinavians. Their narratives provided a moral compass and guidance for personal conduct, establishing a connection between the divine and the everyday lives of the people.

The role of goddesses in Norse mythology is particularly significant, as they wielded considerable power and influence. Beyond Freyja, other goddesses, such as Frigg and Hel, played crucial roles in shaping the Norse understanding of fate, love, and death. These female figures often acted as mediators between realms, embodying the complexities of existence and the dualities of life and death. The reverence for these goddesses highlights the recognition of feminine strength within a predominantly patriarchal society, providing women with powerful symbols of agency and autonomy. Their stories often explored themes of sacrifice, resilience, and the interconnectedness of all beings, underscoring the importance of balance in the universe.

Additionally, the myths surrounding the lesser-known deities and beings, such as the Norns and the giants, reveal the multifaceted nature of the Norse belief system. The Norns, who governed fate, represented the inevitability of destiny and the intricate web of life that intertwined gods and mortals alike. The giants, often viewed as adversaries of the gods, played a vital role in the cosmology, embodying the chaotic forces of nature that the gods sought to control. The dynamic interplay between these figures illustrated the complexities of existence, emphasizing that creation and destruction coexist in a perpetual cycle. This understanding fostered a sense of humility and respect for the natural world, encouraging a harmonious relationship with the environment.

In conclusion, mythology in ancient Scandinavia was a crucial aspect of cultural identity, offering profound insights into the human experience. The narratives surrounding the major gods, goddesses, and other divine figures provided a framework for understanding life's challenges, the nature of fate, and the afterlife. These stories continue to resonate today, as they influence contemporary culture and inspire modern interpretations of the Norse gods. The enduring legacy of these myths serves as a reminder of the importance of storytelling in shaping beliefs, values, and the collective consciousness of society.

# Chapter 2: The Major Gods: An Overview of Odin, Thor, and Freyja

## Odin: The Allfather and God of Wisdom

Odin, known as the Allfather, stands at the pinnacle of the Norse pantheon, embodying the complexities of wisdom, knowledge, and power. Revered not only as the chief deity but also as a multifaceted figure, Odin's dominion spans various realms, including war, poetry, and the dead. His relentless pursuit of wisdom is legendary, culminating in his infamous sacrifice of an eye at Mimir's well to gain profound insight into the cosmos. This act symbolizes the lengths to which he would go to acquire knowledge, establishing him as a central figure in discussions about divine wisdom and its implications in Norse belief systems.

As the god of wisdom, Odin is often depicted as a seeker of truth, traversing the nine realms in search of enlightenment. His quests frequently involve interactions with other deities and beings, showcasing his role as a mediator and a teacher. The concept of wisdom in Norse mythology is not merely intellectual; it encompasses practical knowledge, foresight, and the ability to navigate the complexities of fate. Odin's endeavors to understand the Norns, the weavers of destiny, illustrate his recognition of fate's inescapable grip on both gods and mortals. This relationship between wisdom and fate is a recurring theme in Norse narratives, highlighting Odin's unique position in shaping the understanding of human existence.

Odin's influence extends beyond wisdom; he is also a god of war, signifying the duality of his nature. While he embodies the ideals of knowledge and strategy, he is equally associated with the chaos and brutality of battle. His prowess in warfare is often depicted through stories of his chosen warriors, the Einherjar, who reside in Valhalla, preparing for the final confrontation at Ragnarok. This duality complicates the perception of Odin as a benevolent deity, as he embodies both the nurturing aspects of wisdom and the destructive forces of conflict. Such complexity makes him a compelling figure in the examination of the moral and ethical dimensions of power within the Norse pantheon.

In addition to his roles as a god of wisdom and war, Odin is integral to the Norse understanding of poetry and inspiration. He is often credited with the gift of poetic language, which he famously obtained through a treacherous quest involving the mead of poetry. This association with creativity ties Odin to broader themes of communication and cultural identity, emphasizing the significance of storytelling and myth-making in Norse society. Through his connection to poetry, he serves as a bridge between the divine and human experiences, underscoring the importance of narrative in shaping communal values and beliefs.

Odin's complex character and multifaceted roles invite deeper exploration of his relationships with other gods and goddesses in the Norse pantheon, particularly in contrast to figures like Thor and Freyja. While Thor represents strength and protection, and Freyja embodies love and fertility, Odin's wisdom often places him in a more ambiguous moral landscape. This interplay among the deities enriches the Norse mythological framework, inviting religious leaders and scholars alike to consider the implications of divine wisdom, power, and the human condition within the context of their beliefs and practices. Odin remains a pivotal figure, not just in ancient narratives but also in contemporary interpretations of Norse mythology, influencing modern culture and spiritual expressions.

## Thor: The God of Thunder and Protection

Thor, known as the God of Thunder, occupies a central role in Norse mythology as a protector of both gods and humans. His immense strength and bravery are often highlighted in various myths, which depict him as a warrior battling giants and other malevolent forces that threaten the realms. Thor wields Mjölnir, the enchanted hammer that symbolizes both his martial prowess and the protective aspects of his character. This iconic weapon not only serves as a tool for destruction but also as a means of blessing, as it is used in sacred rituals to consecrate marriages and other important events. Through these narratives, Thor emerges as a figure of resilience and power, embodying the ideals of protection and defense against chaos.

In the complex hierarchy of the Norse pantheon, Thor's relationship with his father, Odin, is particularly significant. While Odin represents wisdom, knowledge, and the more enigmatic aspects of existence, Thor stands for physical strength and valor. This distinction is often reflected in the myths where Thor's straightforward, sometimes brash demeanor contrasts with Odin's cunning and strategic thinking. Together, they represent a balance of intellect and might, showcasing the diverse qualities revered in Norse culture. Thor's role as a protector is not just limited to physical combat; he also symbolizes the safeguarding of order and civilization against the destructive forces of chaos, often embodied by the giants.

Thor's presence is felt across the Nine Realms, where he often journeys to confront threats and restore balance. His adventures take him to realms such as Jotunheim, the land of the giants, where he encounters formidable foes that test his strength and resolve. These encounters serve as allegories for the struggles between order and chaos, a recurring theme in Norse mythology. Additionally, Thor's frequent travels highlight the interconnectedness of the realms, emphasizing the importance of cooperation among the gods to maintain peace. His protective nature extends beyond mere physical battles, as he also engages in activities that promote the welfare of humanity, showcasing a nuanced understanding of leadership and responsibility.

The symbolism associated with Thor extends to various artifacts that represent his strength and protective qualities. Mjölnir is perhaps the most famous, but other symbols such as the belt of strength, Megingjörð, and his iron gloves further emphasize his role as a guardian. These items are not merely weapons; they embody Thor's dedication to safeguarding both the divine and mortal realms. In contemporary interpretations, Thor's symbols have transcended their mythological origins, appearing in popular culture and serving as representations of courage and protection. This enduring legacy illustrates how the values associated with Thor resonate with modern audiences, reflecting a timeless admiration for those who stand against adversity.

Thor's narrative also intersects with the concept of fate, particularly in relation to the Norns, the three goddesses who weave the fates of gods and mortals. While Thor embodies strength and action, the Norns represent the inevitability of fate, reminding the gods that their power has limits. This dynamic adds depth to Thor's character, as he navigates his role within a framework governed by forces beyond his control. Additionally, the giants, often portrayed as his adversaries, serve to highlight the complexities of these relationships, as they are both threats and integral components of the mythological landscape. Ultimately, Thor's legacy as the God of Thunder and Protection underscores the significance of strength, resilience, and the ever-present struggle between order and chaos in Norse mythology.

## Freyja: The Goddess of Love, War, and Fertility

Freyja, one of the most prominent goddesses in the Norse pantheon, embodies the complex interplay between love, war, and fertility. As a member of the Vanir, the fertility gods, she represents not only the nurturing aspects of life but also the fierce and often tumultuous nature of human relationships. Freyja's duality is evident in her roles as a goddess who incites passion and desire, while simultaneously commanding respect and fear on the battlefield. This intricate balance makes her an essential figure in understanding the multifaceted nature of Norse spirituality and the human experience.

As the goddess of love, Freyja is often associated with beauty, attraction, and the bonds of romance. She possesses a magical necklace known as Brísingamen, which symbolizes her allure and desirability. Freyja's influence over love and passion is not merely about romantic relationships; it extends to the deep connections formed in friendships and familial ties. In many myths, she is portrayed as a figure who guides lovers together, reflecting the Norse belief in the power of fate and the interconnectedness of all beings. This aspect of her character highlights the significance of love as a driving force in the lives of both gods and mortals.

In her role as a goddess of war, Freyja takes on a more aggressive and commanding presence. She is known to lead the Valkyries, the warrior maidens who choose those who may die and those who may live in battles. Freyja's association with warfare connects her to the notions of honor and valor, as well as the harsh realities of conflict. Her dual nature as both a nurturer and a warrior illustrates the Norse understanding that love and war are often intertwined, reflecting the complexities of human emotions and societal dynamics. This aspect of her character serves as a reminder that strength can manifest in various forms, including the ability to love fiercely.

Freyja's connection to fertility further enriches her character and significance within the pantheon. As a goddess of fertility, she governs not only the growth of crops and the health of livestock but also the blessings of childbirth and family. Her influence extends to the prosperity of the land and the continuation of life, making her a vital figure for both individuals and communities seeking abundance. The reverence for Freyja in this aspect underscores the importance of agriculture and family in Norse society, where survival often depended on the fertility of the earth and the strength of familial bonds.

In exploring Freyja's multifaceted roles, it becomes evident that she is a powerful symbol of the complexities inherent in existence. Her ability to navigate the realms of love, war, and fertility speaks to the Norse understanding of life as a delicate balance between opposing forces. Freyja's presence in mythology serves as a reminder of the intricate relationships between these elements and how they shape the human experience. By studying her character, we gain insight into the values and beliefs of the Norse people, offering a deeper appreciation for the pantheon of gods that continues to resonate in contemporary culture.

# Chapter 3: The Role of Goddesses in Norse Mythology: Power and Influence

## The Significance of Female Deities

The significance of female deities in Norse mythology extends far beyond mere representation; they embody essential aspects of life, death, and the cosmos. While the major gods like Odin and Thor often dominate discussions of the pantheon, goddesses such as Freyja, Frigg, and Hel play pivotal roles in shaping the narratives and spiritual landscape of the Norse belief system. Their powers and responsibilities reflect a complex interplay of fertility, war, wisdom, and the afterlife, highlighting their integral position alongside their male counterparts. By examining these female deities, one gains insight into the multifaceted nature of the divine and the cultural values that inform Norse spirituality.

Freyja, one of the most prominent goddesses, epitomizes the duality of love and war. As the goddess of fertility, she oversees matters of love and sexuality, but she also commands a fierce warrior aspect, leading the Valkyries to choose those who may enter Valhalla. This dual nature not only positions Freyja as a nurturing force but also as a powerful figure who embodies the complexities of human experience. Similarly, Frigg, Odin's wife, represents wisdom and foresight, often associated with domesticity and the protection of family. Her role emphasizes the importance of familial bonds and the maternal aspect of the divine, which balances the often tumultuous, aggressive nature of the male gods.

Furthermore, Hel, the goddess of the underworld, offers a unique perspective on death and the afterlife in Norse cosmology. As the ruler of Helheim, she governs those who do not die gloriously in battle, providing a necessary counterbalance to the valorization of warrior death in Valhalla. Hel's domain challenges the notion of honor associated with death in combat, reminding believers of the inevitability of mortality and the diverse paths of the afterlife. This nuanced portrayal of death and the afterlife underlines the significance of female deities in addressing themes that resonate deeply with human existence.

The roles of these goddesses illuminate the broader cultural understanding of femininity and power within Norse society. Unlike many patriarchal systems that often marginalize female figures, Norse mythology celebrates the strength and agency of its goddesses. They are not merely supportive figures; they wield considerable influence and control over various realms, from love and fertility to fate and the afterlife. This recognition of female power in the pantheon reflects a cultural appreciation for balance and the acknowledgment of both masculine and feminine traits as essential components of the universe.

In conclusion, the significance of female deities in Norse mythology cannot be understated. Their multifaceted roles provide a deeper understanding of the spiritual and moral frameworks within which the Norse people operated. By examining the lives and influences of these powerful goddesses, one appreciates the intricate tapestry of beliefs that shaped Norse culture and continues to resonate in contemporary interpretations of mythology. As discussions about the Norse pantheon evolve, acknowledging the contributions and significance of female deities remains essential for a comprehensive understanding of these ancient beliefs.

## Major Goddesses Beyond Freyja

In addition to Freyja, the Norse pantheon is rich with powerful goddesses, each embodying unique aspects of life, nature, and the cosmos. One of the most significant figures is Frigg, Odin's wife, who represents motherhood, marriage, and the domestic sphere. She is often associated with foresight and wisdom, possessing knowledge of fate that even Odin respects. Frigg's role extends beyond the domestic; she is a protector of the family and the home, and her influence is felt in the everyday lives of the Norse people. As a goddess of fertility and love, her presence is vital in rituals and customs surrounding marriage and childbirth.

Another prominent goddess is Hel, the ruler of the realm that bears her name, where souls of those who did not die in battle reside. Hel embodies the duality of life and death, representing not only the inevitability of mortality but also the importance of honoring ancestors. Her domain is often misunderstood; while she presides over the dead, she also offers a space for reflection and connection with the past. Hel's character challenges the often glorified perception of the afterlife in Norse beliefs, reminding followers of the significance of the cycles of life and the respect owed to those who have passed.

Skadi, the goddess of winter and hunting, further diversifies the roles of women in Norse mythology. Initially a giantess, her union with the Aesir gods symbolizes the blending of different realms and the importance of collaboration between the gods and giants. Skadi's fierce independence and affinity for the wilderness highlight the Norse appreciation for strength and resilience. As a protector of the forest and its creatures, she also embodies the spirit of survival and the harsh realities of nature, serving as a reminder of the balance between humanity and the natural world.

Sif, known for her beautiful golden hair, is associated with the earth and fertility. While she may not possess the same level of complexity as some other goddesses, her role is crucial in the myths surrounding Thor, her husband. Sif represents the nurturing aspects of nature, as well as the agricultural cycle and the blessings it brings to the people. Her character embodies the themes of loyalty and domesticity, and her stories often serve as a backdrop to the heroic tales of Thor, reinforcing the interconnectedness of gods and their families in Norse culture.

Lastly, the Norns, often considered a collective of female figures rather than individual goddesses, hold significant influence in the realm of fate. They are the weavers of destiny, determining the fates of gods and men alike. This trio of sisters, named Urd (past), Verdandi (present), and Skuld (future), underscores the belief in an intricate web of interconnected lives and experiences. Their role emphasizes the importance of time and choice, illustrating how the gods themselves are subject to the same forces that govern humanity. Together, these major goddesses and figures provide a deeper understanding of the female divine in Norse mythology, showcasing the richness and complexity of the pantheon beyond Freyja.

# Chapter 4: Lesser-Known Norse Deities: The Hidden Figures of the Pantheon

## Njord: The God of the Sea and Wealth

Njord, a prominent figure in Norse mythology, embodies the duality of the sea's bounty and the wealth it can bring. As the god of the sea, Njord holds dominion over all marine resources, making him a crucial deity for seafarers, fishermen, and those who relied on the ocean for sustenance and trade. His influence extends beyond mere navigation and fishing; he is also associated with prosperity and the material wealth derived from the sea. In this capacity, Njord represents the interconnectedness of nature and human life, illustrating how the gifts of the ocean can lead to both abundance and challenges.

In the Norse pantheon, Njord is often associated with the Vanir, a group of gods connected to fertility, prosperity, and the natural world. This affiliation highlights the significance of Njord not only as a god of wealth but also as a deity who fosters harmony with nature. The Vanir's eventual alliance with the Aesir, the other primary group of gods that include Odin and Thor, signifies the blending of different aspects of Norse spirituality and the recognition of Njord's essential role within this framework. His presence in the pantheon underscores the importance of balance between human endeavor and the natural environment.

Njord's family ties further enrich his mythological narrative. He is the father of the twin deities Frey and Freyja, who embody fertility and love, respectively. These relationships illustrate a broader theme in Norse mythology: the interplay between wealth, love, and fertility. Njord's children extend his legacy, influencing various aspects of life and spirituality within the Norse cosmology. Moreover, the tales surrounding Njord and his family often explore the complexities of desire, sacrifice, and the pursuit of happiness, reflecting the human condition in a mythological context.

Njord's worship was particularly significant among coastal communities, where sailors would invoke his blessings for safe voyages and bountiful catches. Rituals dedicated to him often involved offerings cast into the sea, symbolizing a deep reverence for the ocean and its unpredictable nature. These practices reveal how Njord was perceived not just as a distant deity but as an integral part of daily life, where his favor was sought to ensure prosperity and protection. The connection between Njord and the sea serves as a reminder of the vital relationship between humanity and the natural world, emphasizing respect and gratitude.

In modern interpretations of Norse mythology, Njord continues to resonate with contemporary themes of environmental stewardship and the significance of marine resources. As discussions surrounding sustainability and the health of our oceans intensify, Njord's role as the god of the sea and wealth can inspire a renewed appreciation for the natural world. By examining Njord's characteristics and influence, individuals can draw parallels between ancient beliefs and current challenges, fostering a deeper understanding of how mythology can inform modern values and practices regarding nature and wealth.

## Baldr: The God of Light and Purity

Baldr, often regarded as the embodiment of light and purity within the Norse pantheon, holds a significant position among the deities. As the son of Odin and Frigg, he is celebrated for his beauty, wisdom, and benevolence. His luminous presence is a beacon of hope and goodness, representing the ideal of harmony in a world often beset by chaos. Baldr's nature is intertwined with themes of innocence and righteousness, making him a figure of immense importance in Norse mythology. His death, a pivotal event in the myths, serves as a profound reminder of the fragility of life and the inevitability of fate.

The stories surrounding Baldr reveal much about his character and the values attributed to him by the ancient Norse. One of the most notable tales is his invulnerability, granted through a vow made by all things in creation to never harm him, except for the mistletoe, which was overlooked. This oversight ultimately leads to his tragic demise at the hands of his blind brother, Höðr, manipulated by Loki. This narrative illustrates the complexities of fate and the interconnectedness of the gods, as even those deemed pure and invincible can fall victim to unforeseen circumstances. Baldr's death not only signifies the loss of light in the Norse cosmos but also sets the stage for future events in the mythology, particularly the prophesied Ragnarok.

Baldr's influence extends beyond his tragic story, as he is often associated with themes of resurrection and renewal. In some interpretations, his death does not mark the end, but rather a cycle of rebirth, highlighting the Norse belief in the cyclical nature of existence. Following Ragnarok, it is foretold that Baldr will return, signifying a restoration of balance and purity to the world. This belief resonates with the overarching themes in Norse mythology regarding the duality of creation and destruction, life and death, and the enduring hope for renewal in the face of adversity.

In examining Baldr's role within the broader context of Norse mythology, it is essential to consider his relationships with other gods and goddesses. His mother, Frigg, embodies protective motherhood and foresight, while his father, Odin, represents wisdom and sacrifice. These connections underscore the importance of familial bonds and the interplay of power dynamics among the gods. Furthermore, Baldr's interactions with figures such as Loki reveal how even the most virtuous can be affected by betrayal and malice, demonstrating the complexity of moral choices in the pantheon.

Baldr's legacy continues to resonate in modern interpretations of Norse mythology, influencing contemporary culture and spirituality. His story has been adapted in various forms, symbolizing hope and the enduring light that can emerge from darkness. In religious contexts, Baldr represents ideals of purity and moral integrity, serving as a guiding figure for those seeking to embody these virtues. As adults and religious leaders explore the depths of Norse mythology, Baldr stands as a testament to the enduring power of light, love, and the resilience of the human spirit amidst challenges.

## Loki: The Trickster God

Loki, often referred to as the Trickster God within the Norse pantheon, embodies a complex and multifaceted character that challenges the traditional notions of divinity. Unlike the other major gods such as Odin, Thor, and Freyja, who are typically associated with wisdom, strength, and fertility respectively, Loki's role is that of a disruptor. He is known for his cunning intelligence and unpredictable nature, which allows him to navigate between the realms of gods and giants. This duality not only makes him a fascinating figure but also illustrates the intricate relationships within Norse mythology, where the boundaries between friend and foe are often blurred.

Loki's origins as the son of the giants Fárbauti and Laufey place him in a unique position within the pantheon. While he is a blood brother to Odin, his actions frequently lead to chaos and strife, particularly evident in tales such as the death of Baldr. Loki's ability to shapeshift and manipulate situations makes him a vital catalyst for many myths, often instigating conflict but also providing solutions, albeit through unconventional means. His existence raises questions about morality and the nature of good and evil, as his trickery serves both to aid the gods and to thwart them, ultimately revealing the complexities of divine relationships.

The role of Loki extends beyond mere chaos; he is an essential figure in the balance of the cosmos. His actions often highlight the theme of fate, particularly in relation to the Norns, the three female entities that control destiny. Loki's involvement in events such as Ragnarök, the prophesied end of the world, underscores his integral part in the cyclical nature of creation and destruction. As a figure who bridges the gap between different realms and beings, Loki represents the unpredictable forces that shape existence, reminding us that order and chaos are often intertwined.

Moreover, Loki's connection to the other gods illustrates the dynamic interplay between deities and their roles within the larger narrative of Norse mythology. His interactions with Thor, particularly during their joint adventures, highlight both camaraderie and tension. Loki's ability to provoke and challenge his fellow gods often results in significant transformations, pushing them to grow, adapt, and confront their own limitations. This dynamic serves as a reflection of the human experience, where relationships can be both a source of strength and conflict.

In modern interpretations, Loki's legacy continues to resonate, influencing contemporary culture through literature, film, and art. His character embodies the spirit of rebellion and the questioning of authority, appealing to those who seek to understand the complexities of identity and morality. As society grapples with themes of truth, deception, and the nature of justice, Loki remains a potent symbol of the trickster archetype, reminding us that even within the divine, the lines between hero and villain can be astonishingly thin. This enduring relevance highlights not just Loki's role in ancient myths, but also his capacity to inspire ongoing dialogue about the human condition.

# Chapter 5: The Nine Realms: The Domains of the Norse Gods

## Asgard: Home of the Aesir

Asgard, the celestial stronghold of the Aesir, occupies a central role in Norse cosmology, serving as the residence of the principal gods, including Odin, Thor, and Freyja. This realm is depicted as a majestic fortress, often imagined as a place of grand halls and magnificent structures, symbolizing the power and authority of its divine inhabitants. Asgard is not merely a physical location; it represents the ideals of heroism, governance, and the spiritual aspirations of the Norse people. The gods of Asgard, each with their unique attributes and responsibilities, govern various aspects of life and the cosmos, embodying the complexities of human existence and the natural world.

Odin, the Allfather, stands at the pinnacle of Asgard's hierarchy, revered for his wisdom, knowledge, and mastery of war. He is the god of poetry, prophecy, and the dead, guiding the souls of warriors to Valhalla, where they prepare for the final battle during Ragnarök. Thor, his son, is the protector of mankind, wielding the mighty Mjölnir to safeguard Asgard and Midgard from the threats posed by giants and other malevolent forces. Freyja, the goddess of love, fertility, and war, embodies the duality of femininity, possessing both nurturing qualities and formidable power. Together, these deities illustrate the balance of strength and compassion inherent in the Norse worldview.

The structure of Asgard is complemented by its connection to the Nine Realms, with pathways such as Bifröst, the rainbow bridge, linking it to other worlds. This connection emphasizes the interdependence of the realms and the gods' role in maintaining cosmic order. Each realm, from the icy expanse of Niflheim to the fiery depths of Muspelheim, reflects aspects of existence that the gods must navigate and influence. The Aesir's responsibilities extend beyond their own realm, as they actively engage with the giants and other beings to uphold the delicate balance of creation and destruction.

The role of goddesses in Asgard and the broader Norse pantheon cannot be overstated. While Odin, Thor, and other male deities dominate many narratives, goddesses like Freyja and Frigg wield significant power and influence. They are not merely consorts or figures of beauty; they are integral to the pantheon, guiding fate and nurturing life. The Norns, who govern the destinies of gods and men alike, further illustrate the intertwined nature of gender and power within Norse mythology, as they weave the fates that shape the cosmos.

In exploring Asgard as the home of the Aesir, one must acknowledge its profound symbolic significance. It serves as a reflection of the Norse understanding of divinity, authority, and the human condition. The myths and legends surrounding Asgard reveal insights into the values of the Norse people, emphasizing themes of bravery, honor, and the ever-present struggle against chaos. As contemporary society continues to draw inspiration from these ancient tales, the legacy of Asgard and its inhabitants endures, reminding us of the enduring nature of myth and the gods who inhabit our collective imagination.

## Midgard: The Realm of Humanity

Midgard, often referred to as the realm of humanity, occupies a central place in the Norse cosmology as one of the Nine Realms connecting the mortal world to the divine. In Norse mythology, Midgard is depicted as a flat land encircled by a vast ocean, with the great serpent Jörmungandr dwelling within its depths. This realm serves as the battleground for human existence, where individuals navigate the complexities of life, struggle against forces of chaos, and seek to fulfill their destinies. Midgard's creation is intrinsically linked to the gods, particularly Odin, who played a pivotal role in shaping the world from the remnants of the slain giant Ymir. This initial act of creation set the stage for humanity's place within the grand narrative of Norse mythology.

The inhabitants of Midgard are viewed as the children of the gods, with Odin being particularly significant in their formation. He and his brothers, Vili and Vé, bestowed humanity with essential gifts such as breath, consciousness, and the ability to reason. These attributes not only distinguished humans from other beings but also set the foundation for moral and ethical behavior within Midgard. The relationship between the gods and humanity is characterized by mutual respect and interdependence, with mortals often seeking the favor of the gods through rituals and offerings, thereby forging a spiritual connection that transcends the physical realm.

In Midgard, the influence of the three major gods—Odin, Thor, and Freyja—is profoundly felt. Odin represents wisdom and knowledge, often guiding humanity through dreams and visions. Thor, the god of thunder, embodies strength and protection, safeguarding Midgard from giants and other malevolent forces. Freyja, the goddess of love and fertility, plays a crucial role in the emotional and communal aspects of human existence, symbolizing the importance of relationships and the natural world. Together, these deities shape the moral framework and cultural practices of the people, providing them with both guidance and inspiration.

The role of goddesses in Midgard is particularly significant, as they often embody the duality of life and death, creation and destruction. Goddesses such as Frigg and Skadi illustrate the multifaceted nature of femininity in Norse mythology, showcasing power, influence, and the capacity for nurturing. This complexity invites reflection on the importance of divine feminine energy within human society. The stories that arise from these goddesses provide essential lessons on resilience, adaptability, and the interconnectedness of all beings within the cosmos.

As humanity navigates the challenges of existence in Midgard, they are influenced by the concept of fate, governed by the Norns—three powerful beings who weave the threads of destiny. The intricate relationship between fate and free will is a central theme in Norse thought, with individuals seeking to understand their place within the tapestry of life. Midgard serves not only as a physical realm but also as a spiritual arena where humans confront their fates, aspire to live honorably, and ultimately seek a connection with the divine. In this intricate dance between gods and mortals, Midgard remains a vital element of the Norse worldview, encapsulating the essence of human experience amidst the grandeur of the cosmos.

## Other Realms: Vanaheim, Alfheim, Jotunheim, Niflheim, Muspelheim, and Hel

Vanaheim, one of the Nine Realms in Norse cosmology, is traditionally associated with the Vanir, a group of gods known for their connection to fertility, prosperity, and the natural world. Unlike the Aesir, who are exemplified by figures like Odin and Thor, the Vanir embody a different ethos, one that emphasizes harmony with nature and the cycles of life. This realm is often depicted as a lush, verdant land, rich in natural resources and teeming with life. The gods of Vanaheim, such as Njord, Freyr, and Freyja, play crucial roles in agricultural fertility and wealth, reflecting the ancient Norse people's dependence on nature for sustenance and survival.

Alfheim, the realm of the Light Elves, is another significant domain within the Norse cosmological framework. Light Elves are often associated with beauty, light, and purity, serving as guardians of nature and its bounty. Freyja, a prominent goddess of love and beauty, is said to have a strong connection to this realm, highlighting the intertwined nature of love, fertility, and the natural world in Norse belief. Alfheim also represents the more ethereal aspects of existence, where the boundaries between the divine and the mortal blur, indicating a profound respect for the interconnectedness of all living beings.

In contrast, Jotunheim is the realm of the giants, or Jotnar, who serve as both adversaries and allies to the Aesir. This realm is characterized by its harsh landscapes, including mountains and forests, reflecting the giants' wild and untamed nature. The Jotnar, often seen as embodiments of chaos and the primal forces of nature, play a crucial role in Norse mythology, challenging the gods and influencing the world in ways both destructive and creative. The relationship between the Aesir and the Jotnar is complex, involving conflict and cooperation, and underscores the balance of order and chaos in the cosmos.

Niflheim and Muspelheim represent the two extremes of the Norse universe, with Niflheim embodying cold, fog, and ice, while Muspelheim is characterized by fire and heat. Niflheim is often associated with death and the afterlife, serving as a realm of darkness and mist where the dead dwell. In stark contrast, Muspelheim is home to fire giants and symbolizes creation and destruction, illustrating the duality inherent in existence. The interaction between these realms has profound implications in Norse mythology, particularly in the context of Ragnarok, the prophesied end of the world, where the clash between these elemental forces culminates in chaos and renewal.

Hel, the realm presided over by the goddess Hel, serves as the final destination for those who do not die a heroic death. Unlike the more celebrated afterlife in Valhalla, Hel represents a more neutral and somber aspect of existence. Hel, the daughter of Loki, governs this realm with a focus on balance and acceptance of fate. The understanding of Hel's domain reflects a nuanced perspective on death and the afterlife in Norse culture, acknowledging the inevitability of mortality and the diverse experiences of the dead. Each of these realms—Vanaheim, Alfheim, Jotunheim, Niflheim, Muspelheim, and Hel—contributes to a rich tapestry of beliefs that explore the complexities of existence, the nature of divinity, and the intricate relationships between gods, giants, and mortals.

# Chapter 6: The Concept of Fate: Norns and Their Influence on the Gods

## Understanding the Norns

The Norns are central figures in Norse mythology, often depicted as the weavers of fate who govern the destinies of gods and mortals alike. Traditionally, they are described as three female beings named Urd, Verdandi, and Skuld, each representing different aspects of time: the past, the present, and the future. This triadic structure illustrates the intertwined nature of time, suggesting that understanding one's fate requires a comprehension of all temporal dimensions. The Norns reside near the well of Urd, beneath the roots of Yggdrasil, the World Tree, signifying their connection to the fundamental structure of the cosmos and the intricate web of life.

The influence of the Norns extends beyond mere fate; they actively shape the lives of individuals and the course of events in the cosmos. Their actions are not arbitrary but are instead reflective of a deeper understanding of the interrelationship between actions and consequences. In this sense, the Norns embody the moral fabric of the universe, reminding both gods and mortals that every decision carries weight and significance. This moral dimension highlights the importance of individual agency within the framework of fate, suggesting that while the Norns may weave the tapestry of life, the threads of that tapestry are spun from the choices made by each being.

In the context of the major gods, the Norns serve as a crucial counterbalance to the power wielded by deities such as Odin, Thor, and Freyja. While these gods are often portrayed as ambitious and seeking to influence the world in their favor, the Norns remind them—and all beings—that ultimate control rests not in divine will but in the natural order of fate. Odin, in particular, has a complicated relationship with the Norns; as the seeker of knowledge and wisdom, he frequently attempts to unravel the mysteries of fate, often at great cost. This tension between divine aspiration and the immutable nature of destiny underscores the complexity of the relationships among the gods and their understanding of their roles in the universe.

The Norns also play a vital role in the afterlife, influencing the fates of souls as they transition from the mortal realm to the realms of the dead. Their decisions affect who is chosen to enter Valhalla, the hall of the slain, or Hel, the realm of the dead. This aspect of their influence emphasizes the importance of living a life of honor and bravery, as one's fate is not solely determined by the gods but also by the judgment of the Norns. Their presence in these critical moments of life and death reinforces their status as arbiters of fate, holding the power to determine the eternal destinies of individuals based on the totality of their actions.

Understanding the Norns provides a more nuanced view of Norse mythology, illustrating the intricate balance between fate and free will. They are not merely passive figures in the background; rather, they are active participants in the cosmic order, shaping the lives of all beings. Their role serves as a reminder of the interconnectedness of all things, urging both gods and mortals to recognize the significance of their choices. In this way, the Norns embody the rich tapestry of Norse belief, where fate is not a predetermined path but a complex interplay of time, action, and consequence.

## The Role of Fate in Norse Mythology

In Norse mythology, the concept of fate is intricately woven into the fabric of existence, influencing not only the lives of mortals but also the deities themselves. Central to this notion are the Norns, powerful female figures who govern the destinies of all beings. These three sisters— Urd, Verdandi, and Skuld—represent the past, present, and future respectively, emphasizing the inevitability of fate in the Norse worldview. Their presence in the mythological narratives serves as a reminder that while the gods possess immense power, they are still bound by the threads of fate that the Norns weave.

The role of fate manifests significantly in the stories of major gods such as Odin, Thor, and Freyja. Odin, often seen as the seeker of wisdom and knowledge, is acutely aware of the limitations imposed by fate. His relentless quest for understanding includes seeking out the Norns to glean insights into the future, illustrating his desire to manipulate or at least comprehend his own fate. Thor, the embodiment of strength and protection, confronts his destined battles with giants, showcasing the intertwining of courage and inevitability. Freyja, associated with love and war, navigates her own fate while influencing others, highlighting the complex interplay between personal agency and predetermined outcomes.

Fate's influence extends beyond the major gods to encompass the entire pantheon, including the lesser-known deities. These figures often find themselves caught in the currents of fate, their stories interlaced with the destinies dictated by the Norns. This dynamic illustrates that even the lesser deities, who might appear insignificant in comparison to their more prominent counterparts, play crucial roles in the grand tapestry of existence. Their fates are no less important, and their interactions with the major gods often reflect the broader themes of destiny and its challenges.

The Nine Realms, the domains presided over by different gods, further emphasize the role of fate in Norse cosmology. Each realm is imbued with its own destiny, shaped by the actions and choices of the beings that inhabit it. The gods' interactions within these realms often revolve around the acceptance or defiance of fate, leading to rich narratives that explore the consequences of such endeavors. This rich mythology serves as a canvas for examining the balance between free will and fate, a theme that resonates deeply with contemporary discussions on destiny and personal agency.

As Norse mythology continues to influence modern culture, the concept of fate remains a pertinent topic. It invites exploration into how contemporary interpretations of the gods reflect ongoing struggles with destiny and the desire for control over one's life. The stories of Odin, Thor, Freyja, and their kin serve as both ancient wisdom and timeless reflections on the human condition, prompting adults and religious leaders alike to engage with the complexities of fate in a nuanced manner. By understanding these narratives, one can better appreciate the moral and philosophical questions they pose, fostering a deeper connection to the rich heritage of Norse mythology.

# Chapter 7: The Afterlife in Norse Beliefs: Gods and Their Roles in Valhalla and Hel

### Valhalla: The Hall of the Slain

Valhalla, known as the Hall of the Slain, stands as one of the most revered realms in Norse mythology. It is a majestic hall located in Asgard, ruled over by Odin, the Allfather. This grand hall serves as the final resting place for those warriors who have died valiantly in battle, chosen by the Valkyries, the warrior maidens who serve Odin. Valhalla is not merely a place of rest; it is a realm where the chosen warriors, or Einherjar, prepare for the ultimate battle during Ragnarök, the prophesied end of the world. The hall itself is depicted as a vast and glorious space, adorned with shields and spears, reflecting the valor and glory of its inhabitants.

In Valhalla, the Einherjar engage in daily battles, honing their skills and camaraderie in preparation for the climactic conflicts to come. Each evening, they feast abundantly, with the meat of the divine boar Sæhrímnir, which is restored each day, symbolizing the eternal vitality of the warriors. The hall is also characterized by its endless supply of mead, served by the horned goats that roam the grounds, ensuring that the warriors never lack for sustenance. This eternal cycle of battle and feasting illustrates a crucial aspect of Norse belief: the intertwining of life, death, and rebirth, and the honor associated with dying in combat.

Odin's choice of Valhalla as the destination for slain warriors underscores his role as a god of war and wisdom. Unlike Hel, the realm of the dead ruled by the goddess Hel, which receives those who die of sickness or old age, Valhalla is reserved for those who have demonstrated exceptional bravery. This dichotomy reflects the Norse understanding of honor and valor, where a noble death in battle is seen as a path to glory in the afterlife. It also highlights Odin's role as a deity who values strength and sacrifice, further emphasizing the warrior ethos deeply embedded in Norse culture.

The concept of Valhalla also serves to reinforce the idea of fate, a central theme in Norse belief systems. The Norns, who weave the fates of gods and men alike, play a significant role in determining who will fall in battle and be chosen for Valhalla. This intricate web of fate not only influences the lives of the warriors but also reflects the broader cosmic order that governs the Nine Realms. Within this framework, Valhalla is not just a place of reward but also a critical component of the cyclical nature of existence, where the end leads to new beginnings.

In contemporary interpretations, Valhalla continues to resonate with themes of honor, sacrifice, and the warrior spirit. Its imagery and concepts have permeated modern culture, inspiring various forms of art, literature, and popular media. As religious leaders and adults explore these themes, they may find valuable lessons within the narratives of Valhalla, particularly regarding the ideals of courage and the significance of one's choices in life and death. The Hall of the Slain stands as a powerful symbol of the enduring legacy of Norse mythology, inviting reflection on the values that shape our understanding of bravery and the afterlife.

## Hel: The Realm of the Dead

Hel, in Norse mythology, is the realm designated for the dead, a significant counterpart to the more celebrated Valhalla, where warriors who died in battle are revered. Governed by the goddess Hel, the daughter of Loki, this domain serves as a final resting place for those who did not die a heroic death. Unlike Valhalla, which embodies honor and valor, Hel represents a more somber aspect of the afterlife, where souls find solace or stagnation, reflecting the varied beliefs surrounding death and the afterlife in Norse culture.

The nature of Hel is multifaceted, characterized by its cold and dark environment, which contrasts sharply with the glory of Valhalla. It is often depicted as a vast and dreary landscape, a place devoid of the warmth and camaraderie found among the warriors in Odin's hall. Souls residing in Hel are those who perished from illness, old age, or misfortune, emphasizing the Norse understanding of death as a natural part of life rather than a punishment or reward. This perspective highlights the importance of living honorably in life, as one's fate in the afterlife reflects their earthly experiences.

Hel, as a goddess, embodies the complexities of life and death. She is often portrayed as a figure who is half alive and half dead, symbolizing the duality inherent in mortality. This duality extends to her role as both a caretaker and a ruler of the deceased, managing the souls that enter her realm and determining their experiences therein. As a protector of the dead, her presence ensures that all souls receive their due place, illustrating the Norse belief in the balance of existence—where every life, no matter how it ends, is accounted for.

The significance of Hel within the broader context of the Norse pantheon cannot be overstated. While Odin and Thor are often celebrated for their heroic exploits and attributes, Hel represents the inevitability of death and the respect that must be afforded to it. This aspect of the Norse belief system acknowledges that not all lives end in glory; some are quiet, and their stories deserve recognition. The reverence for Hel and her realm encourages reflection on the nature of existence and the acceptance of mortality, making her a vital figure in the pantheon.

As modern interpretations of Norse mythology continue to emerge, Hel's role is increasingly recognized and explored. Her complex character and realm resonate with contemporary themes of life, death, and the human experience. This exploration allows for a deeper understanding of not only Norse mythology but also the universal questions surrounding our own mortality and what lies beyond. Through Hel, the ancient Norse beliefs are woven into the fabric of modern culture, reminding us of the timeless connection between life and the afterlife.

# Chapter 8: The Giants and Their Relationship with the Norse Gods

## The Jotnar: Nature of the Giants

The Jotnar, often referred to as giants, occupy a significant and complex role within Norse mythology. These beings, hailing from Jotunheim, are not merely adversaries to the gods; they embody the primal forces of nature and chaos that challenge the order established by the Aesir and Vanir. The Jotnar are diverse in their characteristics and abilities, ranging from elemental giants to those possessing vast knowledge and cunning. They symbolize the untamed aspects of the world, representing both the destructive and creative forces that coexist in nature.

The relationship between the gods and the Jotnar is intricate, marked by conflict, alliances, and intermarriage. Many prominent figures in the Norse pantheon have familial ties to the giants, illustrating a more profound connection that transcends mere opposition. For instance, Loki, one of the most enigmatic deities, is the blood brother of Odin and, intriguingly, a Jotnar himself. This connection blurs the lines between good and evil, suggesting that the giants are not solely the embodiments of chaos but also integral to the cosmic balance. Such relationships invite a deeper exploration of how the gods interact with the forces that oppose them.

Myths recount numerous tales of interactions between the gods and the giants, highlighting both conflict and collaboration. One notable story involves the construction of Asgard's walls, where the gods enlist the help of a Jotun under the condition that he receives the sun, the moon, and the goddess Freyja as payment. This tale underscores the cunning nature of the giants, often portrayed as shrewd negotiators who can outsmart the gods. Through these narratives, the giants serve as a mirror to the gods, reflecting their vulnerabilities and the constant struggle for power and dominion over the cosmos.

The depiction of the Jotnar extends beyond mere antagonism; they also represent essential aspects of existence, such as fertility, the earth, and the cyclical nature of life and death. Many giants are associated with various natural phenomena, emphasizing their role as guardians of the wild and the unpredictable elements of the world. This duality invites reflection on humanity's relationship with nature itself, as the giants remind us of the inherent chaos and unpredictability that pervades life, urging respect and reverence for the forces beyond human control.

In contemporary interpretations, the Jotnar continue to captivate the imagination, serving as symbols of resistance against oppression and the celebration of nature's raw power. Their stories resonate with modern audiences, reflecting ongoing struggles between civilization and the natural world. As religious leaders and adults explore these ancient narratives, they can draw parallels to present-day challenges, fostering a deeper understanding of the balance between order and chaos, and the vital role that the giants play in the broader tapestry of Norse mythology.

## Conflicts and Alliances Between Gods and Giants

Conflicts between gods and giants are a central theme in Norse mythology, reflecting the perpetual struggle between order and chaos. The giants, or Jotnar, represent primordial forces often at odds with the structured and civilized world the gods aim to maintain. This antagonism is vividly illustrated in numerous myths, where giants seek to disrupt the harmony established by the Aesir, the principal group of gods that includes Odin, Thor, and Freyja. These conflicts are not merely physical but also ideological, embodying the tension between creation and destruction, wisdom and ignorance, fostering a rich narrative landscape that defines the Norse cosmology.

Odin, the Allfather, often engages with giants in pursuit of wisdom and power, reflecting his dual nature as a god of war and knowledge. His quest for knowledge frequently leads him into the realms of the giants, where he contemplates the intricate balance between the two races. A notable example is his interaction with Mimir, a wise giant whose well provides knowledge at a price. Odin's sacrifice of an eye for a drink from Mimir's well symbolizes the lengths to which the gods will go to secure wisdom and maintain their supremacy over chaos, showcasing the importance of intelligence in overcoming brute strength.

Thor, the thunder god, represents the embodiment of physical strength and valor in these conflicts. His legendary battles against giants, such as the Midgard Serpent and the giant Hrungnir, illustrate the ongoing struggle to protect the realms of men and gods from the chaos giants embody. Thor's hammer, Mjolnir, serves not just as a weapon but as a symbol of protection and order, reinforcing the notion that the gods, through their strength and courage, are tasked with upholding the balance of the universe against the ever-present threat of giant forces. His victories against giants are celebrated in tales that underscore the importance of bravery and resilience in the face of overwhelming odds.

The alliances between gods and giants, although less frequent, reveal an intriguing facet of Norse relationships. Instances of intermarriage, such as Odin's union with the giantess Grid, illustrate a complex dynamic where cooperation and conflict coexist. Such alliances often occur out of necessity or strategic advantage, underscoring the idea that the boundaries between gods and giants are not always rigid. These relationships can lead to the birth of powerful offspring, like the god Víðarr, who plays a crucial role in avenging Odin during Ragnarök, exemplifying how the blending of divine and giant blood can produce figures pivotal to the Norse mythos.

The narrative of gods and giants reflects broader themes in Norse mythology, including the cyclical nature of conflict and resolution. The ongoing battles serve as allegories for the human experience, illustrating the struggles between opposing forces within oneself and society. The giants, often seen as antagonists, also embody certain truths and raw powers that the gods must confront to thrive. Ultimately, the conflicts and alliances between gods and giants provide a rich tapestry of stories that contribute to our understanding of the Norse pantheon, revealing the intricate relationships that define their existence and influence the overarching narrative of fate, power, and the eternal struggle for balance in the cosmos.

# Chapter 9: Symbols and Artifacts: What the Gods Used and Represented

## Mjolnir: Thor's Hammer

Mjolnir, the hammer of Thor, stands as one of the most iconic symbols in Norse mythology, embodying not just the might of the god of thunder but also the complex interplay of power, responsibility, and divine protection. Crafted by the dwarven brothers Sindri and Brokkr, Mjolnir is unique not only for its formidable strength but also for its magical properties, including the ability to return to Thor's hand after being thrown. This artifact serves as a tool of both destruction and creation, allowing Thor to defend Asgard and Midgard from the forces of chaos, particularly the giants, who often threaten the stability of the realms.

In addition to its physical prowess, Mjolnir symbolizes the sanctification of space and the power of fertility. Thor is often called upon to bless weddings and births, and Mjolnir's role in these rituals underscores its significance as a tool for ensuring harmony and prosperity. The hammer's association with fertility highlights the duality of Thor's character; while he is a fierce warrior, he is also a protector of the family and the agricultural bounty essential to the Norse way of life. Thus, Mjolnir becomes a bridge between the realms of battle and domesticity, reinforcing Thor's multifaceted role within the pantheon.

The myths surrounding Mjolnir are rich and varied, showcasing its importance in numerous tales. One of the most famous stories involves the theft of the hammer by the giant Thrym, who demands the goddess Freyja as his bride in exchange for its return. This narrative not only illustrates the hammer's value but also emphasizes the interconnectedness of the gods and their reliance on one another in times of crisis. It is through their collective strength and cunning that Thor retrieves Mjolnir, reinforcing themes of loyalty and bravery among the gods. This tale, like many others, reveals the moral undertones of Norse mythology, where valor and wit are celebrated.

Mjolnir's significance extends beyond the myths into modern interpretations and cultural symbols. Today, the hammer is often embraced by various communities, including those who seek to reconnect with Norse heritage and values. Its image can be found in jewelry, tattoos, and various forms of art, representing strength and protection. This resurgence in interest highlights the ongoing relevance of Norse mythology and its figures, as people seek to draw inspiration from the past to navigate contemporary challenges. The hammer, therefore, serves as a reminder of the enduring legacy of Thor and the values he represents.

In the broader context of the Norse pantheon, Mjolnir encapsulates the relationship between the gods and their responsibilities toward humanity and the cosmos. As the protector of both Asgard and Midgard, Thor's hammer symbolizes the balance between order and chaos, a theme that resonates deeply within Norse beliefs. The presence of Mjolnir in rituals, stories, and modern culture underscores the importance of Thor's role as a guardian, illustrating how ancient symbols can continue to inform and inspire new generations. Through Mjolnir, we glimpse the intricate tapestry of Norse mythology and the enduring power of its symbols.

# Gungnir: Odin's Spear

Gungnir, the legendary spear of Odin, is a symbol of power and authority within the Norse pantheon. Crafted by the dwarven brothers Brokkr and Sindri, Gungnir was imbued with magical properties that ensured it would never miss its target. Its name, which means "the swaying one," reflects the spear's ability to penetrate the very fabric of existence, embodying the concept of destiny that permeates Norse mythology. As Odin's weapon, Gungnir is not merely a tool for warfare; it represents the Allfather's dominion over fate and his role as a harbinger of both death and victory.

In many tales, Gungnir is more than just a spear; it is a potent symbol of authority and the interconnectedness of the cosmos. Odin, as the god of wisdom, war, and death, wields Gungnir to enforce his will, whether in the heat of battle or in the pursuit of knowledge. The spear is also linked to the Norns, the three fates who weave the destinies of gods and men alike. By invoking Gungnir, Odin asserts his influence over the threads of fate, blurring the lines between chance and inevitability. This relationship underscores the belief that the gods, while powerful, are still subject to the overarching tapestry of fate crafted by these primordial beings.

The significance of Gungnir extends beyond its immediate martial applications. It embodies the duality of creation and destruction, reflecting Odin's complex nature as both a nurturing father and a fierce warrior. In battle, Gungnir is said to ensure victory for those deemed worthy, simultaneously marking the end for those who oppose Odin. This duality is a recurring theme in Norse mythology, where the gods do not exist solely to protect humanity but also to maintain the delicate balance between order and chaos. Gungnir, therefore, serves as a reminder of the gods' multifaceted roles in the Norse worldview.

Moreover, Gungnir has become emblematic of Odin's wisdom and strategic foresight. In various myths, he uses the spear to guide his decisions and to impart wisdom to his followers. The act of throwing Gungnir into the fray of battle is symbolic of Odin's faith in fate and his willingness to embrace the unknown. This act of casting the spear can be seen as a ritualistic acknowledgment of the forces at play in the universe, suggesting that even gods are not immune to the complexities of destiny. The spear's presence in key narratives illustrates the intertwined nature of conflict, wisdom, and fate that defines the Norse mythological tradition.

In contemporary interpretations, Gungnir continues to resonate within modern culture as a symbol of power and authority. Its influence is seen in literature, film, and art, where it often represents the struggle between good and evil, order and chaos. As interest in Norse mythology grows, Gungnir serves as a focal point for discussions about the nature of power, the responsibilities of leadership, and the complexities of fate. In examining Gungnir and its implications, individuals and religious leaders can gain deeper insights into the values and beliefs that shaped the Norse understanding of the divine, ultimately enriching their exploration of the pantheon and its enduring legacy.

## Other Significant Symbols

In the rich tapestry of Norse mythology, numerous symbols serve to encapsulate the beliefs and values of the culture surrounding the pantheon of gods. Beyond the well-known representations of Odin, Thor, and Freyja, other significant symbols emerge, each carrying profound meanings that enhance our understanding of the gods and their influence on the world. These symbols often reflect the attributes, powers, and relationships of the deities, while also illustrating the interconnectedness of the realms they govern.

One of the most potent symbols in this context is Yggdrasil, the World Tree, which connects the Nine Realms and serves as a cosmic axis. Yggdrasil is not merely a tree; it is a living embodiment of the universe and the relationships among its inhabitants. Its roots reach deep into the underworld, while its branches extend to Asgard, the realm of the gods. This symbol captures the essence of Norse cosmology, emphasizing the importance of balance and the interdependence of all beings, from gods to giants to humans. Understanding Yggdrasil helps to illuminate the complex relationships that exist within the pantheon and the significance of fate and destiny, as illustrated by the Norns who weave the fates of gods and mortals alike.

Another prominent symbol associated with the Norse gods is Mjölnir, Thor's hammer, which represents not only his immense strength but also his role as a protector of both gods and humans. Mjölnir is a multifaceted symbol; it signifies protection, blessing, and the power to create and destroy. This duality reflects Thor's essential nature as both a warrior and a guardian. The hammer's significance extends into rituals, where it is used in blessings and weddings, reinforcing the connection between divine power and human life. Mjölnir stands as a testament to Thor's importance within the pantheon and his enduring legacy in contemporary culture, where it continues to symbolize strength and protection.

The Valknut, a symbol consisting of three interlocked triangles, is often associated with Odin and serves as a representation of the transition between life and death. This symbol appears in various archaeological finds, particularly in burial contexts, suggesting its role in funerary practices and beliefs surrounding the afterlife. The Valknut encapsulates the complex themes of fate, sacrifice, and the cyclical nature of existence, central to Norse belief systems. It illustrates Odin's dominion over death and the afterlife, particularly in relation to Valhalla, where warriors are honored and prepared for the ultimate battle at Ragnarok. The Valknut reinforces the idea that the gods are deeply intertwined with the human experience, particularly concerning mortality and the afterlife.

Additionally, the symbol of the Ouroboros, often depicted as a serpent or dragon eating its own tail, signifies the cyclical nature of existence and the interconnectedness of all things. While not exclusively Norse, it resonates deeply within the mythology as it speaks to themes of renewal, destruction, and the eternal cycle of life, death, and rebirth. The Ouroboros reflects the belief in the inevitability of change and the continuous flow of time, which is a recurring theme in Norse myths. Through this symbol, one can explore the relationship between the gods and the giants, as well as their shared fate in the grand scheme of the cosmos, ultimately leading to the apocalyptic events of Ragnarok.

In conclusion, the exploration of these significant symbols within Norse mythology enhances our understanding of the relationships and dynamics among the gods, their domains, and their influence on the mortal realm. Symbols like Yggdrasil, Mjölnir, the Valknut, and the Ouroboros provide insights into the values, beliefs, and complexities of the Norse pantheon. They serve as keys to unlocking the deeper meanings of myths and legends, illustrating the enduring power of these symbols in both ancient and modern interpretations of Norse culture.

# Chapter 10: Myths and Legends: Key Stories Featuring the Norse Gods

## Creation Myths

Creation myths in Norse mythology provide foundational narratives that illustrate the origins of the world and the gods who govern it. Central to these myths is the primordial void known as Ginnungagap, which existed before the creation of the universe. From this emptiness emerged the first beings, including the giant Ymir, whose body would later be used by Odin and his brothers to shape the world. This initial chaos reflects the duality present in Norse cosmology, where creation and destruction are often intertwined, setting the stage for the complex interactions among the gods, giants, and other entities in the Norse pantheon.

The narrative of Ymir's death marks a significant moment in the creation myths. His body was dismembered by Odin and his brothers, Vili and Vé, to form the earth, sky, and seas. This act symbolizes the transformation of chaos into order, a theme prevalent in many mythologies. The blood of Ymir became the oceans, his flesh the land, and his skull the sky. Such vivid imagery not only emphasizes the physical formation of the world but also highlights the role of the Aesir gods as creators and maintainers of cosmic balance. Their actions demonstrate the importance of sacrifice and the interconnectedness of life and death in Norse belief systems.

In addition to the creation of the physical world, these myths also introduce the concept of the Nine Realms, each governed by different gods and mythical beings. As the realms unfold, they reveal a rich tapestry of relationships between gods, giants, and other creatures. Midgard, the realm of humans, is intricately linked to Asgard, the home of the Aesir, and Jotunheim, the land of the giants. The myths illustrate how these realms interact, often in conflict, showcasing the dynamic nature of the universe as seen through the eyes of the Norse people. Each realm, with its unique characteristics and inhabitants, reflects the values and beliefs of the society that created these stories.

The role of the goddesses in these creation myths cannot be overlooked. Figures such as Frigg and Freyja embody fertility, love, and war, illustrating the multifaceted nature of femininity in Norse cosmology. They not only play crucial roles in the lives of the gods but also influence the fates of mortals. The existence of powerful goddesses ensures a balance in the pantheon, demonstrating that creation and nurturing are as vital as destruction and conflict. Their presence serves as a reminder that the divine is not solely masculine, but encompasses a spectrum of powers and influences that shape the world.

Ultimately, the creation myths of Norse mythology encapsulate the complexity of existence as understood by the Norse people. They explore themes of sacrifice, duality, and interconnectedness, reflecting the belief that the cosmos is a living entity comprised of various forces and realms. The stories of Odin, Thor, and Freyja, along with lesser-known deities, weave together a narrative that emphasizes the importance of understanding one's place within the universe. These myths continue to resonate today, offering insights into the spiritual and cultural heritage of the Norse tradition and shaping modern interpretations of myth and divinity.

## Tales of Heroism and Tragedy

Tales of heroism and tragedy weave through the fabric of Norse mythology, illuminating the complexities of the gods and their interactions with both mortals and the cosmos. Central to these narratives are figures like Odin, Thor, and Freyja, each representing different facets of strength, wisdom, and sacrifice. Odin, the Allfather, embodies the pursuit of knowledge at any cost, often leading him into perilous situations. His sacrifice of an eye for wisdom and his self-hanging on Yggdrasil highlight the lengths to which he will go, illustrating a profound understanding of the intertwining of fate and personal choice. These stories serve not only to entertain but to impart moral lessons about the nature of sacrifice and the pursuit of greater truths.

Thor, the thunder god, is another pivotal figure in tales of heroism. His adventures are filled with acts of bravery, strength, and a touch of humility, particularly evident in his encounters with giants and monsters. The myth of Thor's journey to retrieve his stolen hammer, Mjölnir, showcases not only physical prowess but also the importance of camaraderie and loyalty. His relationship with Loki, often characterized by a blend of conflict and cooperation, underscores the idea that heroism can coexist with personal flaws and vulnerabilities. Through these narratives, Thor emerges as a relatable figure, embodying the struggles and triumphs faced by individuals in their own quests for honor and protection of their kin.

Freyja, the goddess of love and war, adds another layer to the narratives of heroism and tragedy within the Norse pantheon. Her tales often reflect the duality of desire and duty, as she navigates the complexities of her role in both the realms of gods and humans. The story of her search for her missing husband, Óðr, reveals her determination and the emotional toll of love intertwined with loss. Freyja's ability to command the Valkyries, choosing those who may enter Valhalla, emphasizes her influence over life, death, and the afterlife. These stories illustrate the powerful position of goddesses in Norse mythology, challenging the often male-dominated narratives and highlighting their critical roles in shaping the destinies of both gods and mortals.

The tales of heroism and tragedy also extend to lesser-known deities and figures within the Norse pantheon, whose contributions are often overshadowed by the major gods. These hidden figures, such as Njord and Skadi, represent vital aspects of the natural world and human experience. Their stories reveal the intricate relationships between gods and giants, the struggles against fate, and the balance between chaos and order. The tragic fates of certain characters, such as the doomed Baldr, serve as poignant reminders of the inevitability of death and the fragility of life, reinforcing the belief that even the mightiest can fall. This interplay of heroism and tragedy reflects the broader themes present in the Norse worldview, where victory often comes at a steep price.

Ultimately, the tales of heroism and tragedy in Norse mythology resonate deeply within contemporary culture. Modern interpretations of these myths often draw parallels to contemporary struggles, highlighting timeless themes of sacrifice, loyalty, and the quest for meaning in a chaotic world. As adults and religious leaders engage with these narratives, they find rich material for reflection on human nature, the complexities of fate, and the enduring power of stories to shape beliefs and values. Through the lens of these ancient tales, the Norse pantheon continues to inspire and provoke thought, reminding us of the enduring relevance of myth in understanding the human condition.

## The Ragnarok Prophecy

The Ragnarok prophecy stands as one of the most significant and foreboding elements within Norse mythology, encapsulating the cyclical nature of time and destiny. According to ancient texts, Ragnarok signifies not just an apocalyptic event but a series of transformative occurrences that lead to the death of several major gods, including Odin, Thor, and Freyja. This prophecy illustrates the inevitability of change, highlighting both the vulnerability of the gods and the resilience of the cosmos, as it ultimately leads to rebirth and renewal. The tales surrounding Ragnarok serve as a reminder of the fragile balance between order and chaos, and the ever-present influence of fate as dictated by the Norns.

At the heart of the Ragnarok narrative is the confrontation between the gods and the giants, an event that signifies the ultimate clash of good versus evil within the Norse cosmology. The giants, often seen as embodiments of chaos and destruction, challenge the established order maintained by the gods. This conflict reveals the complex relationships between these two groups, as well as the notion that even the most powerful deities cannot escape their fated ends. The prophecy foretells numerous battles, including the infamous encounter between Thor and the Midgard Serpent, Jörmungandr, emphasizing the heroic yet tragic nature of these mythic figures.

The role of the goddesses during Ragnarok is particularly notable, as figures like Freyja and Frigg embody both strength and sorrow. While the male gods engage in fierce battles, the goddesses are often depicted as guardians of the home and the afterlife. Freyja, in particular, is associated with the afterlife realm of Folkvangr, where she receives half of those who die in battle. This duality of nurturing and warrior spirit among the goddesses highlights their essential roles in both life and death, further enriching the tapestry of Norse beliefs regarding fate and the cyclical nature of existence.

The aftermath of Ragnarok is equally crucial, as it introduces the concept of rebirth in the Norse worldview. The surviving gods, such as Vidar and Vali, are destined to rebuild and restore balance to the world, signifying a new beginning. This renewal aspect illustrates the transformative power of destruction, where the end of one era paves the way for another. The cyclical theme resonates deeply within Norse culture, reinforcing the belief that endings are not merely conclusions but rather transitions to new beginnings, echoing the eternal dance of life and death.

Understanding the Ragnarok prophecy provides valuable insight into the broader themes of Norse mythology, including the significance of fate, the interplay between gods and giants, and the vital role of goddesses. As religious leaders and adults explore these narratives, they can appreciate the profound lessons embedded within them. These stories challenge modern perspectives on mortality and existence, urging a reflection on the interconnectedness of all beings and the acceptance of fate as an intrinsic part of life's journey. The echoes of Ragnarok continue to resonate, reminding us of the timeless truths that shape our understanding of the world and our place within it.

# Chapter 11: Modern Interpretations: How Norse Gods Influence Contemporary Culture

## Norse Mythology in Literature and Film

Norse mythology has significantly influenced literature and film, manifesting in various forms that explore the rich narratives surrounding its deities and the cosmos they inhabit. The tales of Odin, Thor, and Freyja, along with the intricate relationships between gods, goddesses, and the myriad beings of the Norse pantheon, provide fertile ground for storytelling. Contemporary authors and filmmakers often draw from the ancient texts, such as the Poetic Edda and the Prose Edda, to create compelling narratives that resonate with modern audiences, infusing age-old themes of heroism, fate, and the struggle between good and chaos into their works.

In literature, the impact of Norse mythology is evident in both classic and modern texts. Writers like J.R.R. Tolkien were influenced by these mythic tales, incorporating elements of Norse cosmology and character archetypes into their own fictional worlds. The heroic journey of Thor, with his unwavering strength and moral fortitude, continues to inspire new retellings, while Freyja's dual role as a goddess of love and war presents a complex figure that challenges traditional gender roles. These narratives often reflect contemporary societal values, allowing readers to connect with the ancient myths on a deeper level.

Film adaptations have further popularized Norse mythology, with franchises like Marvel bringing iconic characters to life on the big screen. The portrayal of Thor as a modern superhero has broadened the audience's understanding of Norse mythology, albeit with a contemporary twist. While these adaptations may prioritize entertainment, they also introduce viewers to fundamental aspects of the Norse pantheon, such as the significance of Mjolnir, Thor's hammer, as a symbol of protection and power. This blend of myth and modernity fosters a renewed interest in the original stories and encourages further exploration of their meanings.

The thematic richness of Norse mythology allows for diverse interpretations across various media. The exploration of fate, as embodied by the Norns, can be seen in works that grapple with the complexities of destiny and free will. This concept resonates with audiences, prompting reflections on personal agency within the framework of predetermined paths. The duality of life and death, illustrated through beliefs in Valhalla and Hel, raises questions about morality and the afterlife, themes that continue to captivate writers and filmmakers alike.

As Norse mythology continues to permeate literature and film, it serves as a bridge connecting ancient beliefs with contemporary culture. This ongoing dialogue not only preserves the stories of Odin, Thor, and Freyja but also reinterprets them for new generations. The enduring appeal of these myths lies in their ability to address timeless human experiences, allowing both adults and religious leaders to engage with the complexities of morality, identity, and the divine in ways that are relevant in today's world.

## The Revival of Norse Paganism

The revival of Norse paganism in recent decades reflects a growing interest in ancient belief systems and their relevance in modern society. This movement, often referred to as Heathenry or Ásatrú, has attracted individuals seeking spiritual fulfillment, cultural identity, and a connection to their ancestral roots. Many adherents are drawn to the rich tapestry of myths and legends surrounding the Norse pantheon, which includes prominent deities such as Odin, Thor, and Freyja, each embodying distinct aspects of life, nature, and human experience. This resurgence has prompted a re-examination of the roles these gods play, not only in historical context but also in contemporary practices and beliefs.

Odin, the Allfather, stands at the center of this revival, representing wisdom, war, and poetry. His multifaceted nature resonates with those seeking guidance in a complex world. Thor, the god of thunder, symbolizes strength and protection, appealing to individuals who value resilience and courage in the face of adversity. Freyja, revered for her associations with love, fertility, and war, embodies the power of femininity and the importance of balance in life. The recognition of these major gods facilitates a deeper understanding of how their attributes can inform personal and communal practices within modern Norse paganism.

The role of goddesses in Norse mythology has gained particular attention in the revival movement. Figures like Freyja and Frigg illustrate the significant influence of female deities in a pantheon traditionally dominated by male gods. This shift encourages the exploration of gender dynamics within Norse beliefs, prompting discussions about the power and agency of women in both ancient and contemporary contexts. As practitioners engage with these narratives, they often find empowerment and inspiration, leading to a more inclusive interpretation of Norse spirituality that honors the contributions of both gods and goddesses.

In addition to the well-known deities, lesser-known figures in the Norse pantheon are gaining recognition. Deities such as Njord, the god of the sea and wealth, and his children, Freyr and Freyja, represent aspects of nature and human experience that resonate with modern environmental and social concerns. This broader understanding of the pantheon emphasizes the interconnectedness of all beings and the importance of honoring both the prominent and hidden figures within the mythology. As practitioners explore these relationships, they cultivate a more holistic approach to their spiritual practices, fostering a sense of community and shared responsibility.

The revival of Norse paganism also emphasizes the significance of the Nine Realms and the complex interactions between gods, giants, and other beings. This understanding allows practitioners to contextualize their beliefs within a cosmological framework that encompasses the entire universe. By engaging with the myths and legends that illustrate these connections, individuals are encouraged to draw parallels to their lives, fostering a deeper appreciation for the ancient wisdom that continues to inform contemporary culture. As Norse paganism evolves, it not only reconnects individuals with their heritage but also invites a broader audience to explore the depth and richness of this ancient belief system.

## Influence on Popular Culture and Media

The influence of Norse mythology on popular culture and media is profound and multifaceted, shaping narratives, characters, and themes across various forms of artistic expression. The modern portrayal of figures such as Odin, Thor, and Freyja has transcended ancient texts, entering the realms of cinema, literature, and video games. This resurgence of interest in the Norse pantheon has not only provided a new lens through which to view these deities but has also fostered a deeper understanding of their attributes, relationships, and cultural significance within a contemporary context. As such, the stories of these gods continue to resonate, inspiring creators and audiences alike.

In literature, the revival of Norse mythology has resulted in a plethora of novels and series that delve into the lives and adventures of the gods and their kin. Authors like Neil Gaiman and Rick Riordan have played pivotal roles in this trend, weaving these ancient tales into modern narratives that appeal to both young adults and mature readers. By reinterpreting the myths, these writers shed light on the complexities of the characters, emphasizing their flaws, virtues, and the moral dilemmas they face. This literary exploration contributes to a richer understanding of the Norse gods, inviting readers to engage with themes of power, sacrifice, and fate.

The cinematic landscape has also been significantly impacted by the Norse pantheon, particularly through franchises such as Marvel, which has reimagined Thor and Loki as central figures in a broader superhero narrative. These adaptations often simplify the original myths for entertainment purposes, yet they succeed in introducing the gods to a global audience. The interplay between heroism and villainy, as portrayed in these films, reflects the intricate relationships found within the mythos, highlighting the ongoing relevance of these ancient stories in contemporary storytelling. Furthermore, the visual representation of these gods has sparked interest in their traditional depictions, encouraging viewers to explore the original lore.

In addition to literature and film, video games have emerged as a dynamic medium for exploring Norse mythology. Titles such as God of War and Assassin's Creed Valhalla allow players to immerse themselves in the Nine Realms, interacting with deities and experiencing mythological narratives firsthand. These games not only entertain but also serve as gateways to understanding the complexities of Norse beliefs, including the significance of fate, the role of the Norns, and the duality of life and death. As players navigate these worlds, they encounter the rich tapestry of Norse culture, fostering a deeper appreciation for its intricacies.

The interplay between Norse mythology and popular culture reflects a broader trend of revisiting ancient beliefs and narratives in a modern context. As society seeks to understand its roots and the stories that have shaped human experience, the gods of the Norse pantheon offer compelling archetypes that resonate across time. Their influence extends beyond mere representation; it challenges audiences to grapple with timeless questions of existence, morality, and the nature of power. Through this ongoing dialogue, the legacy of Odin, Thor, Freyja, and their kin continues to thrive, ensuring that their stories endure in the collective consciousness.

# Beyond the Void: Ginnungagap and the Birth of the Cosmos

## Chapter 1: Introduction to Ginnungagap

### The Concept of the Void

The concept of the void, or Ginnungagap, is central to the Norse creation myth, serving as the primordial emptiness that existed before the formation of the universe. This vast expanse is not merely an absence of matter but is imbued with potential and significance, representing a state of nothingness that is both empty and full of possibilities. In the Norse cosmology, Ginnungagap lies between the realms of Niflheim, a land of ice and mist, and Muspelheim, a realm of fire and heat. The interaction of these two opposing forces within the void initiates the creation of the cosmos, illustrating the inherent duality that characterizes Norse mythology.

As the void begins to fill with the chaotic energies of Niflheim and Muspelheim, it gives rise to the first beings in existence, including the frost giants, or Jotunn. These giants symbolize the untamed and wild aspects of nature, embodying the chaos that exists in the universe. In the creation narrative, the frost giants are essential players, as they represent the primal forces that must be balanced by the gods. Their emergence from Ginnungagap signifies not only the birth of life but also the ongoing struggle between order and chaos, a theme that resonates throughout Norse mythology.

Yggdrasil, the world tree, plays a pivotal role in connecting the various realms of existence and serving as a bridge between the divine and the mortal. This immense ash tree arises from the void, symbolizing the interconnectedness of all things and providing a structure within which the cosmos can unfold. Yggdrasil acts as a stabilizing force amid the chaos, reinforcing the idea that even from the void, life can emerge and flourish. The tree's roots extend into the realms of the gods, giants, and humans, illustrating the intricate relationships that bind these disparate entities together within the fabric of existence.

The symbolism of blood and sacrifice further enriches the narrative surrounding Ginnungagap and creation. The gods, particularly Odin, engage in acts of sacrifice to gain wisdom and power, highlighting the importance of offering something of value to bring forth new life. This theme resonates throughout various creation myths, allowing for a comparative analysis between Norse tales and those from other cultures. Such sacrificial elements underscore the idea that creation often arises from destruction, a notion that is prevalent in many mythological traditions.

Artistic representations of the Norse creation myth have evolved over time, reflecting the enduring legacy of these ancient stories within Viking culture and society. From intricate carvings on runestones to vivid illustrations in modern literature, the imagery surrounding Ginnungagap and its implications continues to inspire artists and writers alike. Additionally, the feminine figures within the creation myth, such as the earth goddess and the personification of fertility, play crucial roles in the narrative, highlighting the importance of balance in the cosmos. Through these representations, the concept of the void transcends its initial state of emptiness, transforming into a fertile ground for creativity, growth, and the ongoing interplay of existence.

## Overview of Norse Creation Myths

The Norse creation myths present a rich tapestry of cosmic events, figures, and symbols that offer insight into the beliefs and values of ancient Norse culture. Central to these myths is the concept of Ginnungagap, the primordial void that existed before the world was formed. From this emptiness emerged the first beings: the frost giants, whose existence and actions played a crucial role in shaping the cosmos. The myths describe a world born from chaos, where the interactions between elemental forces led to the creation of land, sea, and life, illustrating the Norse view of a universe in constant flux and conflict.

Yggdrasil, the World Tree, stands as a pivotal symbol in Norse cosmology. This immense ash tree connects the nine realms, serving as a bridge between the divine and the mortal. The roots of Yggdrasil delve into the depths of the underworld, while its branches stretch into the heavens, embodying the interconnectedness of all existence. The tree not only represents the structure of the universe but also the cyclical nature of life and death, emphasizing the importance of balance within creation. As various beings inhabit its realms, Yggdrasil becomes a living metaphor for the complexities of existence and the relationships between gods, giants, and humans.

The frost giants, or Jotnar, are significant figures in Norse creation myths, often portrayed as adversaries to the gods. Their role in the creation narrative is multifaceted, as they are both destructive and creative forces. The giants symbolize the chaos that must be confronted for order to emerge. The myth of the first being, Ymir, whose body was used to create the world, illustrates this duality. From his flesh came the earth, from his blood the seas, and from his bones the mountains. This interplay between order and chaos highlights the Norse belief that creation is not a singular act but a continuous struggle that shapes the universe.

Modern literature has drawn extensively from Norse creation myths, influencing various genres and storytelling traditions. The themes of conflict, sacrifice, and the interplay of divine and mortal realms resonate in contemporary works, reflecting a fascination with the primal narratives that shaped early human thought. Authors often reinterpret these myths, exploring the complex relationships between characters and their environments, and addressing timeless questions about existence, morality, and the nature of the cosmos. This enduring legacy demonstrates the relevance of Norse mythology in understanding both historical and modern narratives.

The symbolism of blood and sacrifice in the creation story is profound, underscoring the idea that life emerges from death and destruction. The act of creating the world from Ymir's remains signifies a necessary transformation, where sacrifice fuels the birth of new existence. This theme is echoed in many cultures' creation narratives, revealing a common understanding of the interconnectedness of life and death. Additionally, the relationship between gods and humans in these myths emphasizes a symbiotic connection, where divine beings shape human destiny while remaining dependent on human worship and reverence. Through these narratives, the Norse creation myths offer not just a glimpse into the cosmos's origins but also a reflection of the values and beliefs that defined a civilization.

# Chapter 2: The Birth of the Cosmos

## From Ginnungagap to Creation

The Norse creation myth begins in the primordial void known as Ginnungagap, a vast, empty chasm that existed before the formation of the cosmos. This void is a fundamental concept in Norse cosmology, representing both the absence of matter and the potential for creation. It is situated between two contrasting realms: Muspelheim, the land of fire, and Niflheim, the realm of ice. The interaction between the heat of Muspelheim and the cold of Niflheim leads to the emergence of life and matter, illustrating the duality inherent in Norse cosmological beliefs. This interplay not only sets the stage for creation but also symbolizes the balance between opposing forces that is central to the Norse understanding of the universe.

From the melting ice of Niflheim, the first being, Ymir, emerges, marking the beginning of creation. Ymir is a frost giant whose body becomes the foundation of the world. The giants, often seen as chaotic forces in Norse mythology, play a crucial role in the creation narrative. Their existence highlights the tension between order and chaos, a recurring theme in Norse stories. The gods, particularly Odin and his brothers Vili and Vé, eventually slay Ymir, using his body to form the earth, sky, and oceans. This act of creation underscores the significance of sacrifice, as the gods must destroy to create. The blood of Ymir floods the void, forming the seas, while his bones become mountains, illustrating the intricate relationship between destruction and creation.

Yggdrasil, the World Tree, further embodies the interconnectedness of all life in Norse mythology. It serves as the axis mundi, connecting the nine realms and providing a structure to the cosmos. Yggdrasil is not only a symbol of life but also of death and rebirth, as it nurtures all beings and absorbs their essence. The tree's roots reach into various realms, including Helheim, the realm of the dead, emphasizing the cyclical nature of existence. The significance of Yggdrasil in the creation myth underscores the importance of continuity and the interdependence of all elements within the universe. Its presence reflects the Norse belief in a holistic cosmos where every entity has its place and purpose.

The influence of the Norse creation myth extends beyond ancient texts, inspiring modern literature and art. Writers like J.R.R. Tolkien drew upon these mythological themes to craft rich, immersive worlds, showcasing the lasting impact of Norse storytelling. The symbolism of blood and sacrifice resonates within these narratives, echoing the Norse belief that creation often arises from loss. Artistic representations of the creation myth, ranging from ancient carvings to contemporary illustrations, further demonstrate how these stories continue to capture the imagination. Such works not only preserve the myth but also encourage reflection on the deeper meanings behind creation, existence, and the human condition.

In comparing the Norse creation myth to other cultural narratives, one can identify both unique elements and shared themes among various traditions. The concept of a primordial void exists in many mythologies, suggesting a universal human inquiry into existence and beginnings. The roles of divine beings and their relationships with humanity also emerge as a common thread. Feminine figures in the Norse myth, such as the goddess Nótt and the earth goddess Jörð, play significant roles in the creation narrative, highlighting the importance of gender in these stories. The Norse creation myth serves not only as a tale of origins but also as a reflection of societal values, the roles of gods and giants, and the intricate tapestry of life within the cosmos.

## The Role of Fire and Ice

In Norse cosmology, the interplay between fire and ice serves as a fundamental narrative device that catalyzes the creation of the universe. This duality is embodied in the primordial void known as Ginnungagap, which lies between the realms of Muspelheim, the land of fire, and Niflheim, the land of ice. As these two opposing forces converge, they create a dynamic tension that leads to the birth of the first beings and the subsequent formation of the cosmos. The melting ice from Niflheim interacts with the heat of Muspelheim, producing the first life forms, including Ymir, the frost giant, who becomes central to the Norse creation narrative. This dichotomy of fire and ice symbolizes not just physical elements but also represents the balance of chaos and order inherent in the universe.

Yggdrasil, the World Tree, stands as a crucial element in Norse cosmology, linking the various realms and serving as a symbol of interconnectedness. Its roots extend into both Niflheim and Muspelheim, drawing from the life-giving properties of water and the warmth of fire. As creation unfolds, Yggdrasil nurtures the beings that emerge from the chaos, including gods, giants, and humans. The tree represents the cyclical nature of life, death, and rebirth, mirroring the ongoing conflict between the elemental forces of fire and ice. The stability provided by Yggdrasil contrasts with the volatility of its surroundings, emphasizing the necessity of balance in the creation narrative.

The frost giants, or Jotnar, play an essential role in the Norse creation myth, embodying the chaotic and destructive aspects of nature. They are not merely antagonists to the gods; rather, they represent the primal forces that must be acknowledged and respected within the cosmos. As Ymir is slain by the gods Odin, Vili, and Ve, the ingredients of the world are derived from his body, symbolizing the transformation of chaos into order. This act of sacrifice introduces a critical theme within the myth: the necessity of blood and destruction for the emergence of life and civilization. The giants, therefore, are integral to understanding the dual nature of creation, illustrating how chaos gives rise to new forms of existence.

Comparative analysis of the Norse creation myth with other traditions reveals intriguing similarities and differences, particularly regarding the roles of elemental forces in shaping the universe. Many cultures feature a primordial void or chaos from which creation emerges, often through the interaction of opposing forces. However, the specific elements of fire and ice in

Norse mythology highlight a unique perspective on the balance of nature. While in other myths, such as those from Mesopotamia or India, creation often involves divine beings exerting power over chaos, the Norse narrative incorporates these elemental forces as integral participants in the creation process, suggesting a more egalitarian relationship between gods and the cosmos.

Artistic representations of the Norse creation myth have evolved through history, capturing the complex themes of conflict, sacrifice, and transformation. From ancient carvings to modern interpretations, artists have depicted the dramatic moments of Ymir's death and the birth of the cosmos in various forms. These representations often reflect societal values and beliefs, illustrating how the myth has influenced Viking culture and society. The presence of feminine figures within the narrative, such as the goddess Nott and the personification of Earth, further enriches the myth, emphasizing the significance of feminine roles in creation and the ongoing relationship between gods and humanity. This artistic legacy continues to inspire contemporary literature and art, highlighting the enduring impact of the Norse creation myth in modern cultural expressions.

# Chapter 3: Yggdrasil: The World Tree

## Structure of Yggdrasil

Yggdrasil, often referred to as the World Tree, serves as the central axis of Norse cosmology, bridging the various realms of existence in a complex and interconnected structure. This immense ash tree not only symbolizes the interconnectedness of all beings but also represents the cyclical nature of life, death, and rebirth. Its roots delve deep into the primordial void of Ginnungagap, intertwining with various realms such as Asgard, home of the gods; Midgard, the realm of humans; and Niflheim, a land of ice and mist. Each of these worlds is linked to Yggdrasil, emphasizing the tree's role as a cosmic connector that sustains the universe.

The structure of Yggdrasil is described through its roots and branches, which stretch across the universe. The three primary roots extend into different realms, each nourishing the tree in unique ways. One root reaches into the well of Mimir, where wisdom and knowledge are found, while another delves into Niflheim, drawing from the waters of the primordial void. The third root connects to Helheim, the realm of the dead. This triadic structure not only highlights the importance of balance within the cosmos but also reflects the Norse belief in the necessity of contrasting elements such as life and death, light and darkness, and creation and destruction.

The significance of frost giants, or Jotnar, in the context of Yggdrasil and Norse creation is paramount. These beings represent chaos and primordial forces that challenge the order established by the gods. Their existence is intricately linked to the creation narrative, as it is from their blood that the earth was formed. The ongoing tension between the gods and the frost giants underscores a central theme in Norse mythology: the struggle to maintain balance and order against the forces of chaos. Yggdrasil itself, with its roots entwined in various realms, symbolizes the constant negotiation between these opposing forces.

Modern literature has drawn heavily from the motifs and themes presented in the Norse creation myth, particularly through the lens of Yggdrasil. Writers and creators have explored the symbolic meanings of the World Tree, often using it as a metaphor for life's interconnectedness and the cyclical nature of existence. The influence of Yggdrasil can be seen in various genres, from fantasy literature to graphic novels, where it serves as a powerful symbol of growth, renewal, and the enduring human spirit against adversity. This enduring legacy demonstrates how ancient myths can be reimagined to resonate with contemporary audiences, illustrating their timeless relevance.

Artistic representations of Yggdrasil throughout history have further cemented its significance in Viking culture and society. Whether depicted in intricate wood carvings, tapestries, or modern interpretations, the imagery of the World Tree encapsulates the essence of Norse mythology. These representations often highlight the relationships between gods, humans, and nature, emphasizing the importance of sacrifice and interconnectedness. Feminine figures in the creation narrative, such as the goddess Nott, who personifies night, and other crucial deities, enhance the understanding of Yggdrasil's role as a life-giving force. In this way, Yggdrasil stands not only as a central figure in the Norse creation myth but also as a profound symbol of the relationships that bind all realms together.

## Yggdrasil in Norse Cosmology

Yggdrasil, the World Tree, occupies a central position in Norse cosmology, acting as a cosmic axis that connects the various realms of existence. This immense ash tree is more than just a physical entity; it symbolizes life, growth, and the interconnectedness of all beings within the Norse universe. Yggdrasil spans the nine realms, including Asgard, the home of the gods; Midgard, the realm of humans; and Hel, the domain of the dead. Its roots and branches weave through the fabric of reality, illustrating the Norse understanding of a universe that is both complex and harmonious, where every realm plays a vital role in the grand tapestry of existence.

The significance of Yggdrasil is further emphasized by its interaction with various creatures and entities that inhabit it. The tree is home to a variety of beings, including the wise eagle perched at its top, the serpent Nidhogg gnawing at its roots, and the squirrel Ratatoskr, who scurries up and down the trunk, delivering messages between the eagle and Nidhogg. Each of these figures symbolizes different aspects of existence, such as wisdom, decay, and communication, thereby reinforcing the idea that all elements of the cosmos are interconnected. The presence of these beings around Yggdrasil enhances its role as a central point of knowledge and power, making it a vital element in the Norse creation narrative.

The frost giants, known as Jotunn, hold a significant place in the creation myth as well. They represent chaos and the primordial forces that existed before the formation of the cosmos. According to the myth, the first beings emerged from the interaction between the cold, dark void of Ginnungagap and the heat of Muspelheim. Ymir, the first frost giant, was born from this primordial chaos. His body, after being slain by the gods Odin, Vili, and Ve, became the material for the world itself. This act of creation through sacrifice emphasizes the duality of existence in Norse mythology, where life arises from death and chaos gives birth to order.

The influence of the Norse creation myth, particularly that of Yggdrasil and the frost giants, resonates in modern literature and art, serving as a rich source of inspiration for contemporary writers and artists. The themes of sacrifice, creation from chaos, and the interconnectedness of life are echoed in various works, from fantasy epics to philosophical discourses. These narratives often draw parallels between the Norse mythology and other creation myths across cultures, highlighting common motifs such as the cosmic tree or the chaotic void from which order emerges. This comparative analysis not only enriches our understanding of the Norse myth but also invites dialogue about the universal themes of existence.

Yggdrasil's depiction in art and literature throughout history reflects its enduring significance in Viking culture and society. The tree is often portrayed as a symbol of life and resilience, embodying the Norse belief in the cyclical nature of existence. Additionally, feminine figures within the creation myth, such as the goddess Frigg, play crucial roles in nurturing and sustaining life. Their presence signifies the importance of balance between masculine and feminine energies in the creation narrative, further illustrating the multifaceted nature of Yggdrasil and its role in the cosmos. As a symbol of interconnectedness, Yggdrasil continues to inspire explorations of creation, existence, and the relationship between humanity and the divine in both ancient and modern contexts.

# Chapter 4: The Frost Giants and Creation

## Origins of the Frost Giants

The origins of the Frost Giants in Norse mythology are deeply rooted in the primordial chaos that existed before the creation of the cosmos. According to the myth, the universe began in Ginnungagap, the vast emptiness that lay between the realms of Niflheim and Muspelheim. Niflheim, the realm of ice and cold, gave birth to the Frost Giants, known as Jotnar, who emerged from the icy rivers that flowed from the well of Hvergelmir. This stark contrast between the frigid environment of Niflheim and the fiery landscape of Muspelheim played a crucial role in shaping the identity of the Frost Giants as beings of immense power and chaos, representing the untamed forces of nature that were integral to the Norse creation narrative.

The Frost Giants are significant in the context of creation as they embody the raw, unrefined aspects of existence. Their emergence from the elemental void signifies the chaotic potential that precedes order and structure. As the first beings to populate the cosmos, the Frost Giants were not merely antagonists to the gods; rather, they represented the primal elements that the gods would later seek to harness and control. In this way, they serve as a necessary counterbalance to the divine order established by Odin and his fellow gods, illustrating the duality of creation where chaos and order coexist, reflecting a fundamental truth found in various other creation myths around the world.

Yggdrasil, the World Tree, plays a pivotal role in connecting the realms of existence, including the lands of the Frost Giants. This immense ash tree symbolizes the interconnectedness of all beings and realms, serving as a bridge between the gods, humans, and the giants. The roots of Yggdrasil delve deep into the realms of Niflheim, highlighting the importance of the Frost Giants in the broader cosmological framework. As guardians of the primordial forces, the Frost Giants are intricately linked to the fate of the cosmos, embodying the idea that creation is not a singular event but rather an ongoing process influenced by the interplay of diverse forces, including those represented by the giants.

The significance of the Frost Giants extends beyond their role in creation; they have also influenced modern literature and artistic interpretations of the Norse creation myth. Their portrayal as formidable beings often reflects the struggle between civilization and the wildness of nature. Contemporary works draw from the rich tapestry of Norse mythology, presenting the Frost Giants as complex characters that challenge the gods, echoing themes of rebellion and the inherent conflict between humanity and the natural world. This evolution in representation highlights a growing appreciation for the multifaceted nature of these beings, allowing for a deeper exploration of the themes of chaos, creation, and the human condition.

The symbolism of blood and sacrifice is another critical aspect of the Frost Giants' narrative. When Odin and his brothers, Vili and Ve, created the world from the body of the slain Frost Giant Ymir, they established a foundation of sacrifice that resonates throughout the Norse creation myth. This act of creation through destruction underscores the belief that order often arises from chaos and that life itself is born from death. The relationship between the gods and the giants encapsulates the complexity of existence, where creation is inextricably linked to destruction, and where the blood of the Frost Giants serves as the very essence of the world. This intricate dance between life and death continues to echo in the cultural and artistic expressions of the Viking Age and beyond, revealing the enduring impact of these ancient narratives.

## Their Role in the Creation Narrative

In the Norse creation narrative, the frost giants, or Jotnar, play a pivotal role in the formation of the cosmos. Emerging from the icy realm of Niflheim, these beings symbolize the chaotic and primordial forces that existed before the ordered world took shape. Their relationship with the gods, particularly Odin and his brothers Vili and Ve, is central to the creation process. The giants represent both a threat and a necessary component in the cosmos, as their existence highlights the duality of chaos and order, a theme that resonates throughout Norse mythology.

Yggdrasil, the World Tree, serves as a crucial axis in Norse cosmology, connecting the various realms of existence. This immense tree symbolizes life, growth, and interconnectedness, standing at the center of the universe. Its roots delve into the realms of the dead and the living, while its branches extend to the heavens. The presence of Yggdrasil in the creation narrative underscores its significance as a mediator between the different forces at play, including the frost giants and the gods. The tree embodies the cyclical nature of life, where destruction and creation coexist, affirming the necessity of balance in the cosmos.

The act of creation itself is steeped in symbolism, particularly the themes of blood and sacrifice. According to the myth, the first humans were fashioned from the remains of Ymir, the primordial giant. This act conveys the idea that life emerges from death, a concept that is echoed in various creation myths worldwide. The blood of Ymir not only serves as the material foundation for the world but also highlights the interconnectedness of all beings. In Norse thought, this sacrifice is not merely a loss but a transformative act that brings forth life, reinforcing the cyclical nature of existence.

The influence of the Norse creation myth extends beyond its own cultural context, echoing through modern literature and popular media. Writers and creators draw upon these ancient stories to explore themes of existence, morality, and the human condition. The juxtaposition of gods and giants, the interplay of chaos and order, and the significance of sacrifice resonate with contemporary audiences, allowing for a rich tapestry of interpretations that bridge ancient and modern narratives. This enduring legacy showcases the myth's relevance and adaptability in addressing timeless questions of existence and identity.

A comparative analysis of the Norse creation myth with other cultural narratives reveals both unique and shared themes. While many creation myths highlight a divine being crafting the universe from nothing, the Norse narrative emphasizes the role of primordial chaos and the necessity of conflict in bringing forth order. This distinction reflects a broader understanding of the universe as a realm of dynamic forces. Furthermore, the feminine figures in Norse mythology, such as the goddess Frigg and the earth goddess Jord, play significant roles in the creation narrative. Their presence underscores the importance of femininity in the cosmos, illustrating that creation is not solely a male endeavor but a collaborative force that encompasses both genders, enriching the narrative fabric of Norse mythology.

# Chapter 5: The Influence on Modern Literature

## Norse Myths in Contemporary Fiction

Norse myths have permeated contemporary fiction, influencing both the themes and narratives found in various modern works. The Norse creation myth, with its vivid imagery and complex characters, serves as a rich source for authors seeking to explore themes of existence, power, and the interplay of chaos and order. As writers draw from the well of myth, they reinterpret the foundational tales, introducing elements like Yggdrasil, the World Tree, which symbolizes interconnectedness and the cyclical nature of life. This deep-rooted connection to Norse cosmology allows modern fiction to resonate with age-old questions about humanity's place in the universe.

Yggdrasil plays a central role in contemporary adaptations of Norse mythology, often depicted as a living embodiment of the cosmos itself. Authors utilize this symbolism to create expansive worlds that mirror the intricate connections present in the original myths. By exploring the various realms connected by Yggdrasil, modern narratives can delve into the relationships between gods, humans, and other beings, illuminating the complexities of existence and the moral dilemmas faced by characters. This exploration often serves to highlight the significance of interdependence, echoing the ancient belief that all life is interconnected through the great tree.

The frost giants, or Jotunn, also find their way into modern fiction, representing chaos and the primal forces of nature. These formidable beings are often portrayed as antagonistic, yet their role in creation cannot be overlooked. In Norse mythology, they embody the raw power of the cosmos, essential for the birth of the world and its inhabitants. Contemporary authors frequently use frost giants to challenge protagonists, serving as a metaphor for the internal and external struggles faced in the quest for identity and purpose. This duality enriches narratives, allowing for a deeper exploration of conflict and resolution.

The influence of the Norse creation myth extends beyond mere character archetypes; it shapes narrative structures and thematic explorations across genres. Writers draw parallels between Norse cosmology and other creation myths, creating a tapestry of stories that reflect universal themes of sacrifice, transformation, and the quest for understanding. By comparing these myths, contemporary fiction often highlights the unique aspects of Norse beliefs, such as the symbolism of blood and sacrifice, which are central to the creation narrative. This comparison not only enriches the modern interpretation of Norse myths but also fosters a broader appreciation for the diverse ways cultures express their understanding of existence.

Artistic representations of the Norse creation myth throughout history further inform contemporary fiction, providing visual and thematic inspiration for modern creators. The feminine figures within these myths, such as the earth goddess Jord and the wise goddess Frigg, exemplify the crucial roles women play in the creation narrative. Recent literary works have begun to explore these characters in greater depth, challenging traditional narratives and offering fresh perspectives on femininity, power, and agency within the context of creation. This re-examination not only honors the original myths but also reflects modern society's evolving understanding of gender and its significance in storytelling.

## Adaptations and Retellings

Adaptations and retellings of Norse creation myths, particularly the tale of Ginnungagap, have taken various forms throughout history, reflecting both the cultural context of their creators and the evolving interpretations of the cosmos. The original narrative, which describes the primordial void and the birth of the universe, has inspired countless adaptations in literature, art, and popular culture. These retellings often emphasize different aspects of the myth, from the grandeur of Yggdrasil, the World Tree, to the complex relationships between gods, giants, and humans, highlighting the fluidity of myth within societal frameworks.

Yggdrasil, as a central figure in Norse cosmology, serves as a bridge between various realms and has been depicted in numerous adaptations. In modern literature, authors often use Yggdrasil to symbolize interconnectedness and the cyclical nature of life and death. This interpretation draws parallels to other creation myths, where trees or plants often represent fertility and the genesis of life. The significance of Yggdrasil extends beyond mere symbolism; it embodies the Norse understanding of existence, where all beings are interwoven in a web of fate, a theme that resonates with contemporary audiences seeking deeper connections to their own narratives.

The frost giants, or Jotnar, play a crucial role in the creation story, often depicted as antagonists to the gods. Their portrayal varies across adaptations, with some emphasizing their brute strength and chaotic nature, while others explore their complexity and potential for creation. This duality reflects the broader theme of conflict in many creation myths, where chaos often precedes order. In literary retellings, frost giants have been reimagined as tragic figures, adding layers to their roles in the cosmic drama and inviting readers to reconsider notions of good and evil.

The influence of the Norse creation myth on modern literature is profound, as contemporary authors integrate elements of these ancient tales into their works. From fantasy novels to graphic novels, the motifs of Ginnungagap, Yggdrasil, and the interactions between gods and humans resonate with current themes of identity, power, and morality. Comparative analyses of Norse creation myths with other cultural narratives reveal similarities and differences that enrich our understanding of human storytelling. Such explorations illuminate how foundational myths shape societal values and collective identities, allowing for a deeper appreciation of the human experience across cultures.

Artistic representations of the Norse creation myth have evolved alongside its retellings, capturing the imagination of artists throughout history. From the intricate wood carvings of the Viking Age to contemporary digital art, these interpretations often highlight the themes of blood, sacrifice, and the void. The symbolism of blood in the creation story speaks to the interconnectedness of life and death, a motif that has permeated artistic expressions. Feminine figures within the myth, such as the goddess of the earth, often receive renewed focus in modern adaptations, reflecting a growing recognition of their vital roles. These artistic interpretations not only preserve the myth but also adapt it to resonate with contemporary audiences, ensuring the enduring relevance of Norse cosmology in today's cultural landscape.

# Chapter 6: Comparative Analysis of Creation Myths

## Norse vs. Greek Mythology

Norse and Greek mythologies present two distinct yet fascinating frameworks for understanding the cosmos and humanity's place within it. While both traditions offer rich narratives about creation, gods, and the universe, they diverge significantly in their themes, characters, and cosmological structures. The Norse creation myth, rooted in the concept of Ginnungagap, emphasizes a primordial void from which the universe emerges, contrasting sharply with the Greek narrative that often begins with the chaotic void of Chaos. This fundamental difference sets the tone for how each culture perceives the relationship between deities, humans, and the cosmos.

In Norse cosmology, the world is structured around Yggdrasil, the World Tree, which connects the nine realms and serves as a symbol of life, death, and rebirth. Yggdrasil is not just a tree but a central axis that represents the interconnectedness of all beings in Norse belief. In contrast, Greek mythology often lacks such a central structural symbol, relying instead on a pantheon of gods, each governing different aspects of life and nature. The Greeks focused on the individual deities' relationships and conflicts, while the Norse tradition emphasizes the cyclical nature of existence and the interconnectedness of all realms through Yggdrasil.

The role of frost giants in the Norse creation narrative stands in stark contrast to the Titans of Greek mythology. Frost giants, or Jotunn, represent the chaotic forces of nature that challenge the gods, embodying the harshness and unpredictability of the natural world. This reflects a belief in a universe where creation is a continuous struggle between order and chaos, a theme less pronounced in Greek myths where Titans, though formidable, often serve as mere antagonists to the Olympian gods. The significance of sacrifice is also more pronounced in Norse mythology, where the blood of Ymir, the primordial being, is integral to the creation of the world, symbolizing the idea that creation often arises from destruction and loss.

Modern literature has drawn extensively from both Norse and Greek myths, but the influence of Norse creation narratives has grown in recent years, particularly in fantasy genres. Works ranging from J.R.R. Tolkien's Middle-earth to contemporary graphic novels explore themes of interconnectedness, sacrifice, and the cyclical nature of existence that resonate with Norse mythology. The artistic representations of these myths throughout history, from Viking Age carvings to modern cinematic portrayals, highlight the enduring appeal of these narratives and their ability to evoke deeper philosophical questions about existence and humanity's role in the cosmos.

Feminine figures in Norse mythology, such as the goddess Frigg and the earth goddess Jord, play essential roles in the creation myth and reflect the society's view of femininity. These deities are often associated with fertility, wisdom, and the nurturing aspects of life, suggesting a more balanced approach to gender roles in the Norse mythological framework compared to the predominantly male-dominated Greek pantheon. The relationship between gods and humans in both traditions further underscores these differences; in Norse myths, there is often a sense of mutual dependence and respect, whereas Greek mythology frequently illustrates a more hierarchical and sometimes adversarial dynamic. Through these comparative lenses, one can appreciate the unique contributions of both mythological traditions to our understanding of creation and existence.

## Connections with Other Cultural Myths

The Norse creation myth, particularly as articulated through the narrative of Ginnungagap, shares intriguing parallels with various other cultural myths around the world. Many ancient cultures describe a primordial void or chaos from which the cosmos emerges, reflecting a universal human attempt to comprehend existence and creation. In Mesopotamian mythology, for example, the chaotic waters of Tiamat serve as a precursor to the creation of the world, echoing the concept of Ginnungagap as the initial emptiness that precedes the birth of the cosmos. This resonance highlights a shared understanding across civilizations regarding the chaotic potentiality that exists before order and form are established.

Central to the Norse creation narrative is Yggdrasil, the World Tree, which functions as a cosmic axis connecting different realms. This motif of a central tree or axis mundi appears in various mythologies, indicating a symbolic representation of the universe's interconnectedness. In Hindu cosmology, the World Tree is represented by the Ashvattha, signifying a similar intertwining of life and the cosmos. Both cultures use the tree as a metaphor for life, death, and rebirth, suggesting a deeper philosophical inquiry into existence and the relationships between different planes of reality.

The significance of frost giants in Norse creation myths also finds parallels in other mythological traditions, where primordial beings often play critical roles in shaping the world. The frost giants are not merely antagonists but are integral to the creative process, as their existence and actions contribute to the formation of the cosmos. This duality can be seen in Greek mythology as well, where Titans embody both chaos and creation, demonstrating that the forces of disorder can lead to the emergence of order and civilization. Such narratives prompt a reflection on the complexity of creation, where destruction and creation coexist in a continuous cycle.

Symbolism surrounding blood and sacrifice in Norse mythology also resonates with other traditions. The act of Odin sacrificing himself on Yggdrasil to gain wisdom reflects a theme of self-sacrifice found in many creation myths. In Christianity, the sacrifice of Jesus holds a similar weight, emphasizing themes of redemption and the necessity of sacrifice for the greater good. This notion of blood as a life force links various cultural narratives, suggesting that the act of giving up one's life or essence is a powerful catalyst for creation and transformation.

Finally, the relationship between gods and humans in creation narratives often reveals cultural values and societal structures. In Norse mythology, the gods engage directly with humans, shaping their destiny and imparting knowledge, similar to the interactions seen in other mythologies like the Greek pantheon. This dynamic fosters a sense of connection between the divine and the mortal, suggesting that humanity is not merely an afterthought in creation but an active participant in the cosmic narrative. Artistic representations throughout history have celebrated these relationships, capturing the essence of creation myths and their impact on cultural identity, demonstrating that these stories are not only foundational to mythic traditions but also pivotal in shaping societal norms and values.

# Chapter 7: Symbolism of Blood and Sacrifice

## The Importance of Blood in Creation

The concept of blood holds profound significance in the Norse creation myth, particularly when examining the primordial events that unfolded after the emergence of the cosmos from Ginnungagap, the void. In this mythological narrative, blood symbolizes life, sacrifice, and transformation. The act of creation is intricately tied to the shedding of blood, most notably in the story of Odin and his brothers, Vili and Vé, who slay the first being, Ymir, a frost giant. From Ymir's flesh, the earth is formed, his bones become mountains, and his blood fills the oceans. This violent act of sacrifice is not merely a means to an end; it represents a necessary disruption of chaos, enabling the birth of order and life.

Furthermore, the blood of Ymir serves as a powerful metaphor for the interconnectedness of all beings within the Norse cosmology. The process of creation, while brutal, illustrates the cyclical nature of life and death. Ymir's remains provide the materials for the world, suggesting that creation arises from destruction. In this way, the blood of the frost giant is not just a source of life but also a representation of the sacrifices that underpin existence. This theme resonates throughout Norse mythology, where the tension between creation and destruction is a constant motif, highlighting the duality inherent in the cosmos.

The symbolism of blood extends beyond the physical realm into the relationships between gods and humans. In Norse mythology, the gods often engage in acts of sacrifice to maintain harmony and balance within the universe. Odin himself is a prime example, as he sacrifices his eye for wisdom and hangs from Yggdrasil, the World Tree, to gain knowledge of the runes. These acts of sacrifice emphasize the importance of blood as a conduit for divine power and wisdom. In this context, the blood of the gods is intertwined with the fate of humanity, suggesting that human existence is intrinsically linked to the sacrifices made by the divine.

The influence of the Norse creation myth, particularly its themes of blood and sacrifice, can be observed in modern literature and artistic representations. Contemporary authors often draw inspiration from these ancient narratives, weaving elements of Norse mythology into their works to explore themes of existence, identity, and the human condition. The visceral nature of blood in the creation story resonates with readers, evoking a sense of the primal forces that shape our world. Artists, too, have depicted these myths, capturing the dramatic and often violent imagery associated with creation, thereby keeping the stories alive in cultural memory.

In examining the role of feminine figures in the Norse creation myth, one can also discern the importance of blood as a symbol of life and continuity. Figures such as the Earth goddess, Jörð, and the giantess, Gunnlod, play vital roles in the narrative, contributing to the creation and sustenance of life. Their connections to blood highlight the essential balance between male and female forces in the universe. Thus, the significance of blood in the Norse creation myth is multifaceted, serving as a reminder of the sacrifices inherent in the act of creation and the ongoing relationship between the divine and the mortal realms.

## Sacrificial Themes in Norse Myth

Sacrificial themes play a significant role in Norse mythology, particularly in the creation narrative that unfolds within the vast cosmic landscape. Central to this narrative is the primordial void, Ginnungagap, which serves as a canvas for the emergence of existence. It is from this void that the first beings materialize, establishing a foundation for the complex interplay of life and death that characterizes Norse cosmology. The act of sacrifice is woven into the very fabric of creation, as gods and beings alike confront the necessity of offering something profound to engender new forms of existence.

One of the most striking examples of sacrifice in the Norse mythological framework is the story of Ymir, the frost giant, whose death marks the transition from chaos to order. Ymir's body is dismembered by Odin and his brothers, a gruesome act that paradoxically gives rise to the world. His flesh becomes the earth, his blood the seas, and his bones the mountains. This theme of life emerging from death underscores the cyclical nature of existence in Norse thought, where creation is inextricably linked to destruction. Such sacrifices are not merely acts of violence but are imbued with a deeper significance that reflects the harsh realities of survival in a world shaped by constant change.

The symbolism of blood within this creation story further emphasizes the importance of sacrifice. In Norse culture, blood was not only seen as the essence of life but also a potent symbol of connectivity among beings. The act of blood sacrifice often served to forge bonds between gods, giants, and humans, illustrating how interdependence is a crucial element of existence. This notion resonates through various aspects of Norse society, influencing rituals, art, and even the interpersonal relationships of its people, who understood that survival often required a willingness to give of oneself.

Additionally, the relationship between gods and humans in the context of sacrifice reveals a reciprocal dynamic. The gods, through their sacrifices, establish the world and its inhabitants, while humans, in turn, engage in acts of devotion and offering to the divine. This interplay is reflective of broader themes found in comparative mythology, where sacrifices often serve as a means of maintaining harmony within the cosmos. The Norse creation myth illustrates how the act of giving is central to both divine purpose and human existence, creating an ongoing cycle of reverence and reciprocity.

Artistic representations of these sacrificial themes in Norse mythology have left a lasting impact on Viking culture and society. From intricate carvings to epic poetry, the narratives of sacrifice resonate through historical artifacts, influencing the values and beliefs of the Norse people. The feminine figures within these myths, such as the goddesses who embody fertility and fate, also partake in the sacrificial themes, highlighting the multifaceted roles that women play in the creation and sustenance of life. As such, sacrificial themes in Norse mythology not only inform the creation narrative but also shape cultural identity, underscoring the enduring relevance of these ancient stories in contemporary literature and art.

# Chapter 8: Interpretation of Ginnungagap

## Philosophical Perspectives

Philosophical perspectives on the Norse creation myth offer profound insights into the nature of existence, the cosmos, and the relationship between beings. Central to this exploration is the concept of Ginnungagap, the primordial void that existed before creation. This empty chasm symbolizes not only the absence of form but also the potential for all existence. In many philosophical traditions, the void serves as a metaphor for the unknown, representing both fear and possibility. In Norse mythology, Ginnungagap is where elemental forces converge, leading to the birth of the cosmos. This duality of creation from emptiness reflects broader philosophical themes concerning existence, nonexistence, and the cyclical nature of life and death.

Yggdrasil, the World Tree, plays a vital role in Norse cosmology, acting as the axis mundi that connects various realms. Philosophically, Yggdrasil can be seen as a symbol of interconnectedness, representing the unity of life and the intricate web of relationships among the gods, humans, and other beings. Its roots delve into the depths of Hel and its branches stretch into the heavens, embodying the duality of life and death, and the continuous flow of existence. This tree not only serves as a physical structure within the myth but also invites contemplation on the nature of reality itself, urging us to consider how all aspects of life are intertwined and how actions resonate throughout the cosmos.

The frost giants, often viewed as antagonists in the creation narrative, embody chaos and destruction but also serve a critical role in the creative process. Their existence raises philosophical questions about the nature of conflict and resolution in the formation of reality. The tension between the gods and the giants illustrates the balance of order and chaos, suggesting that creation is not a straightforward process but rather a dance of opposing forces. This interplay invites reflection on the necessity of struggle in the pursuit of creation and growth, a theme echoed in many cultural narratives where the emergence of life is contingent upon confrontation with chaos.

Comparative analyses of creation myths across cultures reveal intriguing similarities and differences that deepen our understanding of the Norse narrative. While many myths feature a void or chaos preceding creation, the manner in which deities interact with these elements varies widely. In Norse mythology, the gods' relationship with the frost giants contrasts sharply with other traditions where creation might emerge from a single divine act. This diversity prompts philosophical inquiry into the nature of divinity and agency in creation, challenging us to consider how different cultures perceive the roles of gods, humans, and the forces of nature in shaping the universe.

The symbolism of blood and sacrifice permeates the Norse creation story, particularly in the narrative of Odin and the primordial being Ymir. This theme of sacrifice can be philosophically interpreted as a necessary component of creation, emphasizing the idea that new life often emerges from loss. The act of creating the world from Ymir's body serves as a powerful metaphor for transformation and renewal. Additionally, the feminine figures within the myth, such as the earth goddess, contribute to this narrative by embodying fertility and nurturing, thus expanding the philosophical discourse on gender roles and the balance of masculine and feminine energies in the creative process. Together, these elements invite a deeper contemplation of the interconnectedness of life, the significance of sacrifice, and the roles of gender in the mythological landscape.

## Ginnungagap in Modern Thought

Ginnungagap, the primordial void in Norse mythology, has garnered considerable interest in modern thought, particularly as scholars and enthusiasts explore its implications for understanding creation narratives across cultures. In the context of the Norse creation myth, Ginnungagap represents the vast, empty space that existed before the cosmos took form. This void is not merely a backdrop but is instrumental in the narrative of creation, setting the stage for the emergence of Yggdrasil, the World Tree, and the subsequent interactions among deities, giants, and humans. Modern interpretations often draw parallels between Ginnungagap and concepts of the void found in other philosophical and mythological traditions, suggesting a universal intrigue with emptiness and potentiality.

The role of Yggdrasil in Norse cosmology further enriches the understanding of Ginnungagap. As the central axis of the universe, Yggdrasil connects the realms of gods, giants, and humans, illustrating the dynamic interplay between order and chaos. Modern thinkers have used Yggdrasil as a metaphor for interconnectedness and the cyclical nature of life, echoing themes found in various creation myths worldwide. This perspective invites a comparative analysis of how different cultures visualize the interrelation of existence, often highlighting the significance of a central structure that bridges disparate realms.

Frost giants, known as the Jotnar, add another layer to the narrative of creation originating from Ginnungagap. They represent chaos and primal forces, challenging the order established by the gods. In contemporary discourse, these figures are often examined through the lens of conflict between civilization and nature, mirroring modern concerns about environmental degradation and the struggle against chaotic elements in society. The presence of frost giants in the creation myth prompts a discussion on the balance between creation and destruction, inviting reflections on the nature of existence and the dualities that shape human experience.

The influence of the Norse creation myth, particularly the role of Ginnungagap, extends into modern literature and popular culture. Writers and creators have drawn from this rich tapestry of mythology to explore themes of origin, identity, and the human condition. The void serves as a powerful symbol of uncertainty and potential, resonating with contemporary existential inquiries. By weaving elements of the Norse mythos into their narratives, modern authors engage with timeless questions about the nature of reality, the divine, and the place of humanity within the cosmic framework.

Lastly, the symbolism of blood and sacrifice in the Norse creation myth, particularly the death of Ymir, highlights the intricate relationship between gods and humans. This notion of sacrifice as a necessary component of creation reflects broader themes present in various mythological traditions, emphasizing the idea that life often emerges from death. Modern interpretations of these themes have given rise to discussions about the ethical implications of sacrifice and the human condition's inherent struggles. Furthermore, feminine figures in the Norse creation myth, though often overshadowed by their male counterparts, also play critical roles, challenging traditional narratives and inviting a reevaluation of gender dynamics in creation stories. This exploration enriches the discourse surrounding Ginnungagap, emphasizing its relevance in understanding both ancient and modern perspectives on existence and creation.

# Chapter 9: Gods and Humans in Creation

## Divine Relationships

Divine relationships in Norse cosmology provide a complex web of interactions that shape the universe's creation and subsequent existence. Central to this cosmology is Yggdrasil, the World Tree, which symbolizes the interconnectedness of all beings and realms. Its roots delve into the depths of the underworld, while its branches stretch into the heavens, creating a space where gods, giants, and humans interact. It acts as a bridge between different worlds, facilitating communication and relationships among the divine entities. The health of Yggdrasil reflects the harmony of the cosmos, emphasizing the significance of these divine relationships in maintaining the balance of existence.

The frost giants, or Jotnar, play a crucial role in the creation narrative, representing chaos and the primordial forces of nature. Their existence challenges the order established by the gods, particularly Odin and his brothers, who symbolize civilization and structure. The tension between these two groups is foundational to the Norse mythos, as it encapsulates the struggle between creation and destruction. This antagonism is not merely adversarial; it reflects the necessary balance in the cosmos, where divine relationships often oscillate between conflict and cooperation. The frost giants, despite their chaotic nature, contribute to the richness of the narrative, underscoring the idea that creation is a dynamic process, fraught with contradictions.

The Norse creation myth has profoundly influenced modern literature, inspiring countless interpretations and adaptations across various media. Writers and artists have drawn from the rich tapestry of divine relationships, often exploring themes of sacrifice, power struggles, and the interconnectedness of life. The myth's elements, such as the interplay between gods and humans, resonate with contemporary audiences, reflecting ongoing human concerns about identity, existence, and our place in the universe. Authors like J.R.R. Tolkien and Neil Gaiman have incorporated Norse motifs into their works, illustrating how these ancient stories continue to shape modern narratives and cultural expressions.

Blood and sacrifice hold significant symbolism within the creation story, particularly in the relationship between gods and humans. The act of creation itself is steeped in sacrifice—Odin sacrifices his eye for wisdom, while the first humans, Ask and Embla, are formed from the divine essence of the gods. This connection emphasizes the idea that life is intertwined with loss and transformation. The act of giving and the necessity of sacrifice establish a bond between the divine and mortals, suggesting that the gods are not distant deities but integral participants in the human experience. Such relationships elevate the notion of existence, portraying it as a sacred interplay between the mortal and the divine.

Feminine figures in the Norse creation myth also play a pivotal role in shaping divine relationships. Goddesses like Frigg and Freyja embody qualities of fertility, wisdom, and warfare, representing the multifaceted nature of femininity within the cosmos. Their interactions with male gods and giants demonstrate a dynamic where femininity is not merely passive but actively influences creation and order. The presence of these powerful female figures enriches the mythology, indicating that divine relationships are not solely defined by masculine power but are equally informed by feminine strength and agency. This duality reflects a more comprehensive understanding of the cosmos, where all entities, regardless of gender, contribute to the ongoing narrative of existence.

## Human Origin and Purpose

In Norse cosmology, the concept of human origin is intricately woven into a tapestry of creation that reflects the interplay between chaos and order. Central to this narrative is the primordial void known as Ginnungagap, which existed before the formation of the universe. From this emptiness emerged the first elements of existence, shaped by the contrasting realms of fire and ice. The frost giants, particularly Ymir, play a pivotal role in this mythos, as they are not just mere figures of chaos but also the progenitors of the first beings. Ymir's body became the material from which the world was constructed, illustrating a profound connection between destruction and creation, a theme that resonates throughout Norse mythology.

Yggdrasil, the World Tree, serves as a vital axis in this cosmic framework, linking the various realms of existence. This immense ash tree not only connects the worlds of gods, giants, and humans but also symbolizes the interconnectedness of all life. Its roots delve into the depths of the underworld, while its branches stretch into the heavens, embodying the unity of creation. The presence of Yggdrasil in the creation narrative reveals the Norse understanding of human existence as part of a larger cosmic order. Humans, created from the remnants of Ymir, are thus intrinsically linked to both the divine and the chaotic forces that shaped their world, emphasizing the significance of their purpose within this grand design.

The relationship between gods and humans is further illuminated through the act of creation itself, where the gods Odin, Vili, and Vé breathed life into the first humans, Ask and Embla. This act of divine intervention underscores the notion of humanity as a blend of divine essence and earthly matter. Within this context, the symbolism of blood and sacrifice emerges as a critical theme. The creation of humans from Ymir's blood signifies a deep connection to the cycles of life and death, where sacrifice is not merely an act of offering but a transformative process that fuels the continuity of existence. This idea resonates across various creation myths, highlighting the shared motif of life emerging from death, a concept that permeates both Norse and other cultural narratives.

The significance of the Norse creation myth extends beyond its historical context, influencing modern literature and artistic representations. Writers and artists have drawn inspiration from these ancient tales, exploring themes of creation, chaos, and the human experience. The duality of the frost giants and the gods in the creation narrative serves as a rich source for contemporary interpretations, reflecting ongoing struggles between opposing forces within human society. Furthermore, the feminine figures in Norse mythology, such as the goddess Frigg and the earth goddess Jörð, illustrate the essential roles women play in creation and sustenance, challenging traditional gender narratives and enriching the mythological landscape.

Ultimately, the Norse creation myth encapsulates a complex understanding of human origin and purpose, woven into the very fabric of the cosmos. By examining the relationships between gods, giants, and humans within this narrative, we gain insights into the values and beliefs of Viking culture and society. The interplay of order and chaos, life and death, and the divine connection to humanity reveals a rich philosophical framework that continues to resonate today. As we delve into these ancient stories, we uncover timeless truths about existence, reminding us that the quest for understanding our origins is as relevant now as it was in the time of the gods.

# Chapter 10: Artistic Representations

## Historical Artwork and Artifacts

The historical artwork and artifacts related to the Norse creation myth provide invaluable insights into how ancient cultures conceptualized their origins and the cosmos. Among the most significant artifacts are carvings and runestones that depict Yggdrasil, the World Tree, which is central to Norse cosmology. These artistic representations often illustrate the interconnectedness of the nine realms, emphasizing Yggdrasil's role as the axis mundi that holds the universe together. Such artworks reveal not only the aesthetic values of the Norse people but also their deep philosophical understandings of life, death, and rebirth, as seen through the cyclical nature of the myth.

Frost giants, or Jotunn, are pivotal figures in the Norse creation narrative, often represented in various artistic forms. Their depictions help to highlight the duality of chaos and order in the cosmos. For instance, artifacts portraying the battle between the gods and frost giants illustrate the tension that exists in creation, symbolizing the struggle for balance within the universe. These artworks serve as a reminder of the ongoing conflict between these primordial beings and the gods, further emphasizing the significance of sacrifice, as the gods frequently faced peril to establish order.

The influence of the Norse creation myth on modern literature is evident in various artistic expressions, from fantasy novels to graphic illustrations. Many contemporary authors draw upon the rich tapestry of Norse mythology, infusing their narratives with themes of creation, destruction, and the cyclical nature of existence. Artistic interpretations of these myths often reflect modern understandings of heroism and sacrifice, echoing the ancient stories while adapting them to current societal issues. This blending of past and present highlights the enduring legacy of Norse mythology in shaping contemporary storytelling.

Comparative analyses of Norse and other creation myths reveal common motifs, such as the void, sacrifice, and the emergence of life from chaos. Artifacts from different cultures often depict similar themes, showcasing humanity's universal quest to explain existence. In Norse mythology, Ginnungagap, the primordial void, is essential in understanding the creation of the cosmos. Artistic representations of this void often juxtapose emptiness with the richness of life that follows, creating a dialogue between absence and presence that resonates across various cultures' creation narratives.

Lastly, the portrayal of feminine figures within the Norse creation myth deserves special attention, as these characters often embody crucial aspects of creation and life. Art and artifacts that highlight figures such as Durin's wife, who is less frequently acknowledged, challenge traditional narratives and showcase the significance of feminine influence in the birth of the cosmos. These representations underscore the complexities of gender roles within Norse mythology, emphasizing that both divine and mortal women played integral roles in shaping the world. Through these artistic lenses, one can appreciate the multifaceted nature of creation and the diverse voices that contribute to the rich tapestry of Norse cosmological narratives.

## Modern Interpretations in Art

Modern interpretations of the Norse creation myth have evolved significantly, influenced by contemporary artistic movements and an increased interest in mythological themes. Artists today often draw inspiration from the rich tapestry of Norse cosmology, particularly focusing on the primordial void, Ginnungagap, and the critical role of Yggdrasil, the World Tree. These interpretations serve not only as a means of artistic expression but also as a lens through which we can examine the enduring relevance of ancient narratives in a modern context. By reinterpreting these mythological elements, artists contribute to a dialogue that bridges the past and present, allowing audiences to explore the complexities of creation and existence.

The significance of frost giants in the creation narrative is another focal point for modern artists. Traditionally seen as chaotic and formidable forces, frost giants embody the primal aspects of creation and destruction. Contemporary interpretations often reframe these beings, exploring themes of duality and the necessary balance between order and chaos. Artists utilize various mediums, from sculpture to digital art, to challenge preconceived notions about these giants, illustrating their integral role in the cosmos. This approach not only revitalizes the myth but also prompts discussions about the nature of antagonism and harmony in our own lives.

The Norse creation myth's influence on modern literature cannot be understated, as many contemporary writers weave elements from these ancient stories into their narratives. This literary resurgence often reflects a broader fascination with myth as a tool for exploring identity, morality, and the human condition. Themes such as sacrifice and the symbolism of blood resonate across genres, prompting authors to delve deeper into the implications of these motifs. The relationship between gods and humans, depicted in the myth, is reexamined in modern contexts, inviting readers to reflect on their own connections to the divine and the natural world.

In addition to literature, the comparative analysis of creation myths from different cultures highlights shared themes and distinctive elements that enrich our understanding of human storytelling. Modern artists and scholars alike engage with these comparisons, often creating works that juxtapose Norse myths with other traditions. This cross-cultural exploration reveals universal concerns about existence, creation, and the cosmos, allowing for a deeper appreciation of the narratives that shape our worldviews. By situating the Norse creation myth within a broader mythological framework, artists illuminate the ways in which these stories inform and reflect societal values.

The feminine figures within the Norse creation myth also present fertile ground for modern artistic interpretation. Figures such as the goddess Nótt and the personification of Earth, Jord, challenge traditional gender roles and highlight the significance of femininity in creation. Contemporary artworks that center on these characters advocate for a reevaluation of women's roles in myth and society. By emphasizing the contributions of these feminine figures, modern interpretations not only celebrate their importance but also encourage a discussion about the representation of women in mythology and how these narratives can inspire modern feminist ideals.

# Chapter 11: Norse Creation Myth and Viking Culture

## Impact on Society and Values

The Norse creation myth, particularly as articulated through the narrative of Ginnungagap and the creation of Yggdrasil, has profound implications on societal values and cultural narratives in both ancient and contemporary contexts. At the core of this myth is the interplay between chaos and order, embodied by the void, Ginnungagap, which serves as the primordial space from which all existence springs. This duality resonates deeply with human experiences of creation, destruction, and rebirth, reflecting a worldview that acknowledges the necessity of balance between opposing forces. As societies evolve, these myths continue to shape philosophical discussions about existence, morality, and the nature of reality.

Yggdrasil, the World Tree, stands as a pivotal symbol within Norse cosmology, representing interconnectedness and the cyclical nature of life. Its branches reach into various realms, illustrating the relationship between different aspects of existence and the importance of community. In modern society, Yggdrasil's representation of unity and interdependence resonates with contemporary values that emphasize social cohesion and environmental stewardship. The notion that all beings are interconnected reflects an increasingly prevalent awareness of global issues, encouraging societies to foster values that promote harmony and mutual respect across diverse cultures and ecosystems.

The frost giants, as formidable entities in the creation narrative, embody the chaotic forces that challenge the gods and the established order. Their role signifies the struggle against adversity and the necessity for resilience and strength in the face of challenges. This theme has relevance in today's society, where individuals and communities often confront overwhelming obstacles. The narrative encourages a reflection on the virtues of courage and perseverance, urging modern individuals to embrace their inner strength and confront the giants of their own lives, whether they be personal, societal, or environmental.

The influence of the Norse creation myth extends into modern literature and art, where its rich symbolism and archetypes continue to inspire contemporary creators. The themes of sacrifice, rebirth, and the struggle for identity resonate in various forms of storytelling, reflecting the timeless human experience. By examining how these myths have been interpreted and reimagined in modern narratives, we can better understand their impact on current societal values, particularly regarding themes of heroism, sacrifice, and the quest for meaning in an increasingly complex world.

Feminine figures within the Norse creation myth also contribute significantly to societal values, challenging traditional gender roles and emphasizing the importance of balance between masculine and feminine energies. Figures such as the goddess Nótt and the Earth goddess represent essential aspects of creation and nurturing, suggesting a more nuanced understanding of power and influence. Their presence in the narrative invites contemporary society to re-evaluate gender dynamics and recognize the vital contributions of all individuals, regardless of gender, in the ongoing story of creation and existence. This acknowledgment fosters a more inclusive perspective that aligns with modern values of equality and diversity.

## Reflections in Viking Practices

Reflections on Viking practices reveal a rich tapestry woven from the threads of their creation myths, particularly as they relate to the cosmic void of Ginnungagap, the primordial state from which existence emerged. This void represents not only the absence of matter but also the potential for creation, serving as a backdrop against which the actions of the gods and the emergence of the world unfold. In Viking society, this understanding of creation influenced their worldview, informing their rituals, societal structures, and interactions with nature and the divine.

Central to Norse cosmology is Yggdrasil, the World Tree, which embodies the interconnectedness of all realms. Vikings saw Yggdrasil as a symbol of life, growth, and the cyclical nature of existence. Its roots and branches extended into various realms, connecting gods, giants, and humans in a complex web of relationships. This tree not only served as a physical representation of the cosmos but also as a spiritual guide in Viking practices, where rituals often acknowledged their place within this grand design, reinforcing their connection to the divine and the natural world.

The frost giants, or Jotnar, play a significant role in the Norse creation narrative, symbolizing chaos and the primordial forces that the gods must contend with. Their existence reflects the duality present in Norse mythology, where creation is often born from conflict. The Vikings understood the necessity of sacrifice and struggle in the process of creation, leading to the belief that harmony arises from the balance between opposing forces. This perspective permeated their cultural practices, emphasizing the importance of strength, resilience, and the acceptance of the harsh realities of life.

The Norse creation myth has left an indelible mark on modern literature, influencing countless authors and artists who draw upon its themes of creation, destruction, and rebirth. The narrative's archetypes resonate deeply within contemporary storytelling, often reflecting humanity's ongoing quest to understand its origins and the forces that shape existence. The way in which Viking myths are reinterpreted in modern contexts reveals a lasting fascination with these ancient stories, demonstrating their relevance in exploring themes of identity, spirituality, and the human condition.

In examining the roles of feminine figures within the Norse creation myth, one finds a nuanced portrayal of power and agency. Goddesses such as Frigg and Skadi illustrate the significant contributions of women in the cosmic order, challenging the perception of a solely male-dominated narrative. Their presence underscores the importance of balance between masculine and feminine energies in creation, further enriching the Viking understanding of the universe. This recognition of feminine influence in their cosmological narrative reflects broader themes of equality and respect for diverse roles within society, echoing the complexity of human relationships and the divine in Viking practices.

# Chapter 12: Feminine Figures in Creation Myths

### The Role of Goddesses

The role of goddesses in the Norse creation myth is a multifaceted aspect of the narrative that highlights the significance of feminine figures in shaping the cosmos and influencing divine and mortal realms. Central to this mythological structure is the goddess Frigg, often associated with fertility, motherhood, and domesticity. As the wife of Odin, she embodies the nurturing aspects of the divine, fostering life and stability in a world that is constantly teetering on the edge of chaos. Frigg's role extends beyond mere motherhood; she is a powerful seer, possessing knowledge of fate that influences the lives of gods and humans alike. Her presence underscores the notion that femininity in Norse mythology is not simply passive but is integral to the balance and continuity of existence.

Another pivotal goddess is Freyja, who represents love, beauty, and war, embodying the duality of creation and destruction. Freyja's association with the Vanir, a group of deities connected to fertility and prosperity, further emphasizes the connection between the feminine and the natural world. Her character challenges traditional gender roles, showcasing a figure who not only influences romantic and domestic realms but also participates in the martial aspects of existence. Freyja's ability to traverse the realms of the living and the dead through her connection with the afterlife (specifically, her role in selecting the slain for her hall, Folkvangr) illustrates the goddess as a bridge between worlds, signifying the interconnectedness of all beings in the cosmos.

In addition to Frigg and Freyja, the goddess Hel plays a crucial role in the Norse cosmology, governing the realm of the dead. Hel's domain is not merely a place of despair but serves as a vital aspect of life and death, reflecting the cyclical nature of existence. Her presence in the creation narrative signifies the acceptance of mortality as a crucial component of the cosmic order. While often depicted in a negative light, Hel's role challenges simplistic interpretations of good and evil, inviting a deeper exploration of how life and death coalesce in Norse mythology. This nuanced portrayal of feminine figures enriches the understanding of creation, suggesting that goddesses are not only creators but also caretakers of the cycle of life.

The impact of these goddesses extends beyond the mythological texts into the broader cultural landscape, influencing artistic representations and modern literature. The enduring legacy of goddesses like Frigg and Freyja can be seen in contemporary depictions of strong female characters in fantasy literature and media, drawing upon the archetypes established in Norse myth. Their stories resonate with themes of empowerment, sacrifice, and the intricate interplay between creation and destruction, making them relevant in today's narratives. This connection highlights the timeless nature of these stories, revealing how the role of goddesses in the Norse creation myth continues to inspire and shape the portrayal of women in various cultural expressions.

In summary, the role of goddesses in Norse creation mythology serves as a testament to the complexity and richness of feminine influences within the cosmos. Through figures like Frigg, Freyja, and Hel, the narratives explore themes of nurturing, strength, and the acceptance of mortality, emphasizing the importance of these divine women in the overall framework of existence. Their enduring significance in both ancient and modern contexts illustrates how these mythological figures have shaped cultural perceptions of femininity, identity, and the interconnectedness of life, death, and creation. As we delve deeper into the Norse creation myth, the contributions of these goddesses reveal profound truths about the nature of existence itself.

## Women in Norse Creation Narratives

In Norse creation narratives, women often occupy pivotal yet nuanced roles that reflect the complex interplay of gender dynamics within the broader mythos. While the male gods such as Odin and his brothers are prominently featured in the creation of the world from the body of the slain giant Ymir, feminine figures also emerge as crucial contributors to the cosmic order. The female figures, though sometimes overshadowed by their male counterparts, serve as essential agents of life, wisdom, and continuity, embodying the very essence of creation and nurturing in a cosmos that is otherwise marked by chaos and destruction.

Among the most significant feminine figures in these narratives is the earth goddess, known as Jörð, who represents the physical world and is often associated with fertility and sustenance. Her role is emblematic of the nurturing aspects of femininity that counterbalance the violent and destructive tendencies of the male gods. Jörð's relationship with Odin, who is both her lover and a creator, underscores the themes of partnership and collaboration in the act of creation. This dynamic reflects a worldview in which the feminine is not merely passive but actively engaged in shaping the cosmos, emphasizing the importance of balance between masculine and feminine principles.

Another notable figure is the goddess Freyja, who embodies love, war, and fertility, and whose influence extends beyond mere representation to include themes of sacrifice and transformation. Freyja's association with the fallen warriors and her role in guiding souls to the afterlife highlight the dualities present in Norse thought—life and death, creation and destruction. Her presence in the creation narratives serves as a reminder of the interconnectedness of these themes, suggesting that female power is integral to the cyclical nature of existence. This complexity invites a deeper exploration of how feminine energies contribute to the overarching narrative of creation and the maintenance of order in the cosmos.

The frost giants, often portrayed as antagonists in the creation myths, also provide an interesting backdrop against which feminine figures operate. In many accounts, the giants represent chaos and the primordial forces that must be subdued for order to emerge. However, it is worth noting that female giants, such as the giantess Angerboda, also play significant roles in these stories. Their interactions with the gods often highlight the tension between creation and destruction, illustrating that feminine figures are not solely nurturing but can also embody the chaos that challenges the established order. This duality complicates the perception of femininity in Norse mythology, revealing a spectrum of characteristics that reflect both the nurturing and destructive aspects of the universe.

In summary, the roles of women in Norse creation narratives are multifaceted and deeply intertwined with the themes of life, death, and the ongoing struggle for balance in the cosmos. Through figures like Jörð and Freyja, the narratives illustrate how feminine energies contribute vital forces to the process of creation while simultaneously engaging with the chaos represented by the frost giants. This exploration of femininity within Norse mythology not only enriches our understanding of these ancient stories but also invites contemporary audiences to reflect on the enduring significance of feminine archetypes in the ongoing narrative of humanity's relationship with the cosmos.

# Chapter 13: Conclusion

## Summary of Key Themes

The Norse creation myth encapsulates a rich tapestry of themes that explore the origins of the cosmos, the role of deities, and the intricate relationships between gods and humans. At the heart of this narrative lies the primordial void known as Ginnungagap, which serves as the essential backdrop for creation. This void, described as a space of infinite potential, allows for the emergence of life and form. The contrasting elements of fire from Muspelheim and the icy realms of Niflheim converge within Ginnungagap, resulting in the birth of the first beings, including the frost giants and the gods. This foundational theme highlights the duality of creation, where chaos and order coexist, setting the stage for the unfolding of the cosmos.

Yggdrasil, the immense world tree, stands as a central pillar in Norse cosmology, symbolizing the interconnectedness of all realms. Its branches reach into the heavens, while its roots delve deep into the underworld, embodying the cyclical nature of life and death. As a representation of the universe, Yggdrasil illustrates the importance of balance and harmony among the various realms inhabited by gods, giants, and humans. The tree also serves as a meeting point for these beings, emphasizing the relationships and interactions that define existence in Norse mythology. The depiction of Yggdrasil reflects the broader theme of interconnectedness, suggesting that every action has consequences that resonate throughout the cosmos.

Frost giants, or Jotnar, play a critical role in creation, embodying the chaotic forces that challenge the order imposed by the gods. Their existence is integral to understanding the complexities of creation, as these giants are not merely antagonists but also essential components of the cosmic balance. The interaction between gods and frost giants illustrates the theme of conflict and cooperation in the creation narrative, where struggles lead to growth and transformation. This duality resonates with the notion of sacrifice, particularly through the figure of Ymir, whose body was used to form the world. The symbolism of blood and sacrifice underscores the interconnectedness of creation, suggesting that life emerges from destruction and that the cosmos is built on the remnants of primordial beings.

The influence of the Norse creation myth extends beyond its ancient origins, permeating modern literature and artistic representations. Authors and artists have drawn inspiration from these myths, reinterpreting themes of creation, chaos, and the human experience in their works. The Norse mythos resonates with contemporary audiences, reflecting universal themes of existence and identity. Comparative analyses of Norse creation narratives with other cultural myths reveal both unique elements and shared motifs, highlighting the common human quest for understanding the cosmos and our place within it. This interplay of ancient and modern perspectives enriches our appreciation of the Norse myth and its lasting impact on storytelling.

Feminine figures in the Norse creation myth also deserve attention, as they embody essential qualities often overlooked in traditional narratives. Figures such as Embla, the first woman created from the earth, represent the nurturing aspects of creation, emphasizing the theme of fertility and life-giving forces. Their roles challenge the often male-dominated narratives of creation, suggesting a more nuanced understanding of gender dynamics within the cosmos. This exploration of feminine archetypes contributes to a broader interpretation of the Norse myth, highlighting the significance of balance between masculine and feminine energies in the ongoing cycle of creation. The interplay of these themes offers a comprehensive view of the Norse creation myth and its relevance to both ancient and modern contexts.

## The Legacy of Norse Creation Myths

The legacy of Norse creation myths is deeply interwoven with the cultural and spiritual fabric of Scandinavian societies, reflecting a worldview that emphasizes the interconnectedness of all beings. Central to this narrative is Ginnungagap, the primordial void that existed before creation, which serves as a backdrop for the emergence of the cosmos. From this emptiness, the first beings emerged, illustrating the Norse belief in creation as a dynamic process arising from chaos. The narrative of how the world came into being not only highlights the significance of the void but also establishes a foundation for understanding the relationship between the divine and the mortal realms.

Yggdrasil, the World Tree, occupies a pivotal role in Norse cosmology, symbolizing the axis mundi that connects the nine realms of existence. This immense ash tree is not merely a physical structure; it embodies the interdependency of life forms, where gods, giants, and humans coexist and interact. The branches of Yggdrasil reach into the heavens, while its roots delve into the underworld, illustrating the cyclical nature of life and death. This imagery reinforces the idea that creation is a continuous process, with Yggdrasil serving as a reminder of the balance between opposing forces, such as order and chaos, life and death.

The frost giants, or jötunn, play a significant role in the Norse creation myth, representing the elemental chaos from which the world was formed. Their existence underscores the belief that creation arises from conflict and opposition. The slaying of Ymir, the first frost giant, by Odin and his brothers, serves as a metaphor for the triumph of order over chaos. The blood of Ymir becomes the oceans, his flesh the land, and his bones the mountains, illustrating the transformation of chaos into a structured cosmos. This act of creation through violence and sacrifice resonates throughout the myth, reflecting the harsh realities of the Viking worldview and the belief that life is often born out of struggle.

The Norse creation myth has exerted a considerable influence on modern literature, inspiring countless authors and artists over the centuries. Themes of creation, destruction, and rebirth resonate with contemporary audiences, as they explore the complexities of existence and the human condition. Writers such as J.R.R. Tolkien drew upon Norse mythology to craft their own worlds, integrating elements like Yggdrasil and the giants into their narratives. The archetypes present in Norse myths continue to provide a rich tapestry for storytelling, offering insights into the human experience that transcend time and culture.

In examining the legacy of Norse creation myths, one cannot overlook the feminine figures that play crucial roles within these narratives. Characters such as the goddess Freyja and the primordial giantess Angerboda highlight the importance of femininity in the creation process. Their contributions underscore the balance of power between male and female forces, suggesting that creation is not solely a masculine endeavor. This duality is mirrored in the broader context of creation myths from around the world, where feminine figures often embody fertility and nurturing, contrasting with the destructive aspects associated with male figures. The interplay of these dynamics enriches the Norse creation myth, offering a nuanced understanding of the origins of the cosmos and the relationships that define it.

# Realms of Wonder: Exploring Norse Mythology

## Chapter 1: The Major Norse Myths Simplified

### Creation Myths and the Birth of the World

Creation myths serve as the foundation for understanding the cosmos in Norse mythology, illustrating how the world emerged from chaos and the interactions of divine beings. At the heart of these myths is the primordial void known as Ginnungagap, a vast emptiness that existed before creation. From this void, two realms emerged: Muspelheim, a land of fire, and Niflheim, a realm of ice. The meeting of these two opposing forces in Ginnungagap led to the birth of Ymir, the first being, whose body would eventually give rise to the world as we know it. This narrative highlights the Norse belief in the cyclical nature of creation and destruction, suggesting that the universe is constantly evolving.

Ymir's significance extends beyond being merely the first being; he is also the progenitor of the giants, a race often in conflict with the gods. As Ymir slept, other beings emerged from his sweat, including the first man and woman, Ask and Embla, created by the gods Odin, Vili, and Vé. This act of creation not only emphasizes the gods' role in shaping humanity but also illustrates the interconnectedness of all beings in Norse mythology. The narrative shows how the gods sought to bring order to the chaos represented by Ymir and his offspring, setting the stage for the ongoing struggle between order and chaos that defines many Norse myths.

The death of Ymir is as crucial to the creation story as his birth. After he was slain by Odin and his brothers, the gods used his body to form the world. His flesh became the land, his blood the seas, and his bones the mountains. This transformation of Ymir's body into the physical world underscores a key theme in Norse mythology: the idea that life and death are intrinsically linked. The gods' actions in using Ymir's remains to create the world illustrate a profound respect for the cycle of life, suggesting that from death comes new beginnings.

The creation myths also introduce the Nine Realms, a complex structure that reflects the diversity of existence within Norse cosmology. Each realm, from Asgard, home of the gods, to Midgard, the realm of humans, plays a unique role in the overarching narrative of creation and the relationships between beings. These realms are not isolated; they are interconnected, allowing for interactions among gods, giants, elves, and dwarves. This interdependence highlights the importance of balance within the universe, a theme that resonates throughout Norse mythology and serves as a reminder of the delicate nature of existence.

Understanding the creation myths is essential for grasping the broader themes present in Norse mythology, including fate, love, and conflict. These stories not only explain the origins of the world and its inhabitants but also set the stage for the adventures and trials faced by gods and mortals alike. The interplay of creation and destruction, the significance of sacrifice, and the quest for knowledge form the backbone of many tales, inviting young adults to explore the rich tapestry of Norse legends. Through these myths, readers can discover timeless lessons about humanity, destiny, and the enduring power of storytelling.

## The Aesir and the Vanir: Two Clans of Gods

The Aesir and the Vanir represent two distinct clans of gods in Norse mythology, each embodying unique attributes and characteristics. The Aesir, known for their association with power and war, include prominent figures such as Odin, the wise Allfather, and Thor, the thunderous protector of humanity. They reside in Asgard, one of the nine realms, and are often depicted as warriors engaged in the defense of their domain against various threats, including giants and other malevolent beings. Their stories are filled with epic battles and profound wisdom, highlighting themes of strength, honor, and sacrifice.

In contrast, the Vanir are connected to fertility, prosperity, and nature. This clan includes gods like Njord, the god of the sea and winds, and his children, Freyr and Freyja, who represent love, beauty, and abundance. The Vanir inhabit the realm of Vanaheim, where they focus on the bounties of the earth and the cycles of life. Their narratives often emphasize harmony with nature and the gifts it provides, making them central figures in myths that celebrate agricultural festivals and the changing seasons.

The relationship between the Aesir and the Vanir is complex, marked by a significant conflict that ultimately led to a truce and an exchange of hostages. This conflict exemplifies the struggle between different values and approaches to existence. The Aesir's martial prowess clashed with the Vanir's emphasis on fertility and peace, leading to a series of battles that highlighted their differences. However, the resolution of their conflict illustrates the importance of cooperation and understanding, as both clans recognized the value of each other's strengths.

As part of their reconciliation, the two clans merged some of their attributes, leading to hybrid myths and characters that embody elements of both groups. For instance, Freyja, a Vanir goddess, becomes a key figure among the Aesir, known for her beauty and martial skills. This blending of attributes enriches Norse mythology, demonstrating how collaboration can yield new insights and strengths. The stories of their interactions offer valuable lessons about unity, acceptance, and the power of diversity.

Understanding the Aesir and the Vanir is crucial for anyone exploring the depths of Norse mythology. Their tales resonate with modern themes of conflict resolution and the importance of embracing different perspectives. As young adults delve into these myths, they can appreciate how the gods reflect human traits and struggles, making their stories timeless and relevant. The adventures of Odin, Thor, and the other deities provide not only entertainment but also insights into the complexities of relationships, fate, and the natural world, encouraging readers to reflect on their own lives and the lessons learned from these ancient tales

## The End of Days: Ragnarok Explained

Ragnarok, often referred to as the "Twilight of the Gods," is a cataclysmic event in Norse mythology that signifies the end of the world as we know it. This epic saga unfolds in a series of battles, natural disasters, and the ultimate destruction of the cosmos, leading to the death of many key figures, including Odin, Thor, and Loki. The mythology surrounding Ragnarok is not just a narrative of doom; it encapsulates themes of fate, sacrifice, and rebirth, reminding us of the cyclical nature of existence. Young adults exploring these stories will find that Ragnarok is a rich tapestry of conflict, moral lessons, and the inevitable passage of time.

The events leading up to Ragnarok begin with a series of signs and omens. The world experiences a harsh winter, known as Fimbulwinter, which lasts for three successive seasons without a summer. This winter heralds chaos, as brother turns against brother, and moral decay sweeps through the land. The breaking of bonds and the rise of treachery set the stage for the final battle. The once-peaceful realms are plunged into strife and confusion, illustrating the Norse belief in the fragility of human relationships and the ever-present potential for conflict. Young adults can reflect on the relevance of these themes in their own lives, where loyalty and betrayal often walk a fine line.

As the story unfolds, the gods prepare for the impending doom. Odin, the Allfather, seeks wisdom and counsel from the past, while Thor readies his hammer, Mjölnir, for battle against the giants. Loki, the trickster god, plays a crucial role, embodying chaos and unpredictability. His actions lead to the betrayal of the gods and the unleashing of monstrous creatures like Fenrir, the wolf, and Jörmungandr, the Midgard Serpent. The characters in this myth reflect various aspects of human nature, with young adults encouraged to consider how these traits manifest in their own lives and relationships.

The climactic battle of Ragnarok is marked by fierce confrontations and the inevitable fall of the gods. Odin faces Fenrir, while Thor battles the serpent, each combat representing the struggle between order and chaos. As the gods fall, the world is engulfed in flames and floods, leading to its destruction. However, this destruction is not the end; it paves the way for rebirth. The surviving gods and two human beings, Lif and Lifthrasir, will repopulate the world, symbolizing hope and renewal. This cycle of death and rebirth underscores the Norse belief in fate and the idea that endings bring forth new beginnings.

In the aftermath of Ragnarok, a new world emerges, lush and vibrant, where the remaining gods reunite and peace is restored. This resolution highlights the importance of resilience and the enduring spirit of life, reaffirming that even in the face of devastation, there is potential for regeneration. Young adults are encouraged to contemplate the lessons of Ragnarok, recognizing that challenges and endings are often precursors to new opportunities. The myths of Ragnarok serve not only as a thrilling narrative but also as a profound reflection on the human experience, emphasizing the ongoing journey of growth, transformation, and the hope that follows even the darkest times.

# Chapter 2: The Adventures of Odin: Tales of the Allfather

## Odin's Quest for Wisdom

Odin's quest for wisdom is one of the most profound narratives in Norse mythology, illustrating the lengths to which the Allfather would go to acquire knowledge. Unlike many other deities who might take wisdom for granted, Odin understood that true understanding required sacrifice. This theme of sacrifice is central to his journey, as he willingly gave up one of his eyes in exchange for a drink from the well of Mimir, a source of immense wisdom. This act not only reflects the value placed on knowledge but also sets the tone for Odin's character as a relentless seeker of truth, often at great personal cost.

As Odin traveled through the Nine Realms, his quest took him to various beings of great wisdom, including the wise giant Mimir and the seeress who could glimpse into the threads of fate. These encounters reveal Odin's desire to understand both the present and the future, as well as the forces that shape destiny. His interactions with these figures highlight the Norse belief that wisdom is often intertwined with the understanding of fate and the unpredictable nature of existence. This connection emphasizes a recurring theme in Norse mythology, where knowledge can illuminate one's path but may also bring burdens and challenges.

One of the most significant aspects of Odin's quest is his willingness to embrace the unknown. He hung himself from the World Tree, Yggdrasil, for nine days and nights, pierced by his own spear, in a ritual of self-sacrifice. This experience granted him the knowledge of the runes, symbols that held the power to manipulate reality itself. This act exemplifies the idea that wisdom often comes through trials and tribulations, a lesson that resonates deeply in the human experience. Young adults navigating their own quests for identity and understanding can find inspiration in Odin's willingness to endure suffering for the sake of enlightenment.

Odin's quest also serves as a reminder of the importance of humility. Even as the Allfather, he recognized that no single being could possess all knowledge. His constant quest for wisdom reveals his respect for the insights of others, from gods to mortals. This humility is essential in the pursuit of wisdom; it encourages open-mindedness and a willingness to learn from diverse perspectives. Through Odin's journey, young readers can appreciate the value of collaboration and learning from those around them, particularly in an age where information is abundant yet often superficial.

Ultimately, Odin's quest for wisdom is not just about acquiring knowledge but also about understanding the complexities of existence. His adventures illustrate that wisdom encompasses not only facts and data but also emotional intelligence, moral dilemmas, and the intricacies of relationships. Young adults can glean from Odin's tales that the quest for wisdom is a lifelong journey, filled with challenges and revelations. By engaging with these stories, readers are invited to reflect on their own paths, encouraging them to seek knowledge while recognizing the importance of empathy and connection in their lives.

# The Sacrifice of Odin: Hanging on Yggdrasil

The story of Odin hanging on Yggdrasil, the World Tree, is one of the most profound and significant myths in Norse mythology, illustrating the themes of sacrifice and wisdom. According to the myth, Odin, the Allfather and chief god, sought deeper knowledge and understanding of the runes, which held the power to influence fate, magic, and life itself. To attain this wisdom, he was willing to undergo a harrowing trial, famously sacrificing himself by hanging for nine long nights on the branches of Yggdrasil. This act of self-sacrifice highlights Odin's commitment to knowledge and serves as a powerful reminder of the lengths one must go to in pursuit of wisdom.

While suspended from the tree, Odin faced immense pain and suffering. He was pierced by his own spear and denied the comfort of food and water. This period of hanging was not merely a physical ordeal but also a spiritual journey. Odin's experience symbolizes the transformative power of sacrifice; through his suffering, he gained insight into the mysteries of the universe. This myth serves as an essential lesson for young adults about the importance of perseverance and the idea that true growth often comes from overcoming significant challenges.

The imagery of Yggdrasil itself is crucial to understanding this myth. As the axis mundi connecting the nine realms of Norse cosmology, Yggdrasil represents the interconnectedness of all things. Odin's choice to sacrifice himself on this sacred tree emphasizes the belief that knowledge and wisdom come at a cost. By hanging on Yggdrasil, Odin not only sought personal enlightenment but also aimed to benefit all of creation. This act reinforces the idea that wisdom is not just for oneself but is a gift meant to be shared with others.

The runes, which Odin ultimately discovered during his trial, are central to numerous Norse myths and are often associated with fate and magic. They signify the power of language and the importance of communication in shaping reality. Odin's mastery of the runes allowed him to influence events, heal, and even commune with the dead. This aspect of the myth speaks to young adults navigating their own paths in life, suggesting that the knowledge we seek can empower us to make choices that affect not only our lives but also the lives of those around us.

Odin's sacrifice on Yggdrasil has left a lasting legacy in Norse mythology and continues to resonate in modern adaptations of these ancient tales. Whether in literature, film, or games, the themes of sacrifice, wisdom, and the pursuit of knowledge remain relevant. The story serves as a reminder that the journey towards understanding often involves trials and tribulations, but the rewards can be profound. As young adults explore these timeless narratives, they can draw inspiration from Odin's experience, realizing that their own quests for knowledge and purpose may also require courage and sacrifice.

# Odin and the Battle for Valhalla

In the sprawling tapestry of Norse mythology, few figures loom as large as Odin, the Allfather. His quest for knowledge and power is central to the myths surrounding Valhalla, the majestic hall where fallen warriors gather. Valhalla is not just a grand abode; it represents the ultimate reward for those who have fought bravely in battle. Odin, driven by a desire to assemble the mightiest warriors for the coming Ragnarok, is constantly at odds with the forces that threaten to disrupt the delicate balance of the cosmos. His strategic maneuvers and sacrifices highlight the depth of his character and the high stakes involved in the battle for Valhalla.

Odin's pursuit of warriors is facilitated by the Valkyries, fierce maidens tasked with choosing those who will die and those who will live in battle. These warrior maidens are not merely Odin's servants; they embody the spirit of valor and fate, guiding the chosen souls to Valhalla. The Valkyries, each with their own unique attributes and stories, are essential to the narrative of Odin's recruitment. Their interactions with both mortals and the gods underscore the intertwining of fate and free will, a theme prevalent throughout Norse mythology. As they traverse the battlefields, they not only decide the fates of warriors but also remind us of the harsh realities of war and honor.

The significance of Valhalla extends beyond its role as a resting place for warriors. Within its golden halls, the chosen warriors, known as the Einherjar, prepare for the ultimate battle against the forces of chaos during Ragnarok. This preparation involves daily combat training and feasting, which solidifies the warriors' bonds and fortifies their resolve. Odin's leadership and wisdom play a crucial role in this environment. He instills the values of bravery and loyalty in the Einherjar, ensuring they are ready to face the inevitable doom that awaits them. This aspect of Valhalla illustrates the Norse belief in the importance of community and camaraderie in the face of adversity.

Odin's journey to fortify Valhalla is fraught with challenges, including encounters with other gods and mythical beings. His willingness to sacrifice his own eye for wisdom, as well as his relentless quest for knowledge, are emblematic of his character. These sacrifices are not merely personal; they resonate with the theme of leadership in Norse tales, where the sacrifices of a leader are essential for the greater good. Odin's struggles and triumphs reflect the complexities of power and responsibility, shedding light on the nature of heroism in Norse culture. The tales of his battles, both physical and mental, provide valuable lessons on resilience and determination.

Ultimately, the battle for Valhalla is a microcosm of the larger conflicts within Norse mythology, where destiny, honor, and sacrifice intertwine. As Odin gathers warriors and prepares for Ragnarok, he embodies the ideals of bravery and wisdom. The stories surrounding this battle serve not only to entertain but also to impart crucial lessons about the human experience—about courage in the face of insurmountable odds, the bonds of friendship forged in battle, and the acceptance of fate. For young adults exploring these myths, Odin's journey offers both inspiration and a profound understanding of the themes that resonate throughout Norse mythology, making it a compelling chapter in the vast narrative of the Realms of Wonder.

# Chapter 3: Thor's Journey: Simplifying the Thunder God's Tales

## Thor and the Jotun: Battles Against Giants

Thor, the mighty god of thunder, is most renowned for his fierce battles against the Jotun, the giants who inhabit the vast and often chaotic realm of Jotunheim. These colossal beings are not just mere antagonists in Thor's adventures; they embody the primal forces of nature and chaos that threaten the order of the cosmos. In Norse mythology, the conflict between gods and giants symbolizes the ongoing struggle between order and chaos, making Thor's confrontations with them significant both in terms of narrative and thematic depth.

One of the most famous tales of Thor's battles against the giants is found in the myth of Utgard-Loki. In this story, Thor and his companions, including Loki, venture into the realm of the giants, where they encounter the cunning giant Utgard-Loki. To demonstrate their strength and wit, Thor faces a series of seemingly impossible challenges, each designed to test his abilities. These trials reveal not only the might of Thor but also the cleverness of the giants, who often employ trickery and deception. This duality of strength and cunning is a recurring theme in Norse mythology, highlighting that brute force is not always the solution to every problem.

Another notable encounter occurs in the tale of Thor's journey to retrieve his stolen hammer, Mjölnir. The giant Thrym steals the hammer, intending to use it for his own nefarious purposes. Disguised as the goddess Freyja, Thor infiltrates the giants' realm to reclaim his weapon. This story showcases not just Thor's physical prowess but also his ability to adapt and strategize in the face of overwhelming odds. It emphasizes the importance of resourcefulness and wit, traits that resonate with young adults facing their own challenges and obstacles in life.

The battles between Thor and the Jotun also serve as a reflection of deeper philosophical ideas within Norse mythology. The giants often represent the untamed aspects of nature and the chaos inherent in life. Thor's victories over them can be interpreted as a metaphor for humanity's struggle against disorder and the challenges posed by the natural world. Each clash embodies the idea that while chaos is a part of existence, it can be confronted and managed, a lesson that resonates with the trials of young adulthood.

In contemporary culture, Thor's battles with the giants have been adapted and reimagined in various media, from comic books to films. These adaptations often emphasize the action and adventure of Thor's encounters, making the ancient myths accessible to a modern audience. However, the core themes of bravery, resilience, and the eternal struggle against chaos remain relevant, inviting young adults to explore the rich tapestry of Norse mythology and its lessons on facing life's challenges head-on. Through these narratives, the legendary battles of Thor and the Jotun continue to inspire and entertain, bridging the ancient and the modern.

# The Quest for the Hammer: Mjolnir's Origins

The quest for Mjolnir, the legendary hammer of Thor, is a captivating tale rooted in Norse mythology that underscores the interplay of creation and conflict. Mjolnir, known for its incredible power and ability to return to Thor after being thrown, was not merely a weapon; it embodied the essence of protection and order in the cosmos. The origins of this iconic artifact can be traced back to the masterful dwarven craftsmen, Sindri and Brokkr, who forged it under extraordinary circumstances that highlight the themes of rivalry and ingenuity prevalent in Norse tales.

According to the myth, the story begins with Loki, the trickster god, who, in a moment of mischief, cut off the hair of Sif, Thor's wife. To appease Thor's wrath and avoid dire consequences, Loki promised to replace Sif's hair with something even more beautiful. This promise led him to the dwarves, renowned for their unparalleled skill in crafting magical items. Loki's journey to the realm of the dwarves not only set the stage for the creation of Mjolnir but also exemplified the intricate ties between gods and the powerful beings of the underground world.

The competition between Sindri and Brokkr resulted in the forging of Mjolnir. The two dwarves wagered with Loki, who served as a catalyst for the creation of remarkable treasures. While Sindri worked the bellows, Brokkr forged Mjolnir, but the hammer's handle turned out shorter than intended due to Loki's interference. Despite this flaw, Mjolnir emerged as a symbol of strength and resilience, destined to play a crucial role in the battles between gods and giants. The hammer's creation reflects the duality of fate and free will, emphasizing how even mistakes can lead to significant outcomes in the vast tapestry of Norse mythology.

Mjolnir's significance extends beyond its physical might; it embodies the ideals of sacrifice and responsibility. Thor, as the god of thunder, wielded Mjolnir to protect the realms from chaos, particularly from the giants who threatened the order of the cosmos. The hammer became an essential tool in his heroic quests, showcasing the importance of wielding power with purpose. Through Thor's adventures, young adults can glean valuable lessons about bravery, the weight of duty, and the consequences of one's actions, themes that resonate deeply in both ancient and modern narratives.

In the broader context of Norse mythology, Mjolnir serves as a reminder of the intricate relationships between gods, giants, and the elements of fate. The hammer's legacy continues to inspire adaptations in contemporary media, reinforcing its status as a cultural icon. As young adults explore these myths, they encounter not only the thrilling adventures of Thor and his companions but also the deeper philosophical questions regarding destiny, loyalty, and the nature of heroism. The quest for Mjolnir stands as a testament to the enduring power of storytelling, inviting readers to reflect on their own journeys and the challenges they may face along the way.

## Thor's Role in Protecting Asgard

In Norse mythology, Thor stands as a central figure in the protection of Asgard, the realm of the gods. Known for his immense strength and bravery, Thor is the son of Odin and the Earth goddess, Jord. His primary weapon, Mjölnir, the legendary hammer, not only symbolizes his power but also serves as a tool of defense against the many threats that loom over Asgard. From frost giants to monstrous serpents, Thor consistently rises to the occasion, embodying the spirit of a protector who values honor and loyalty above all.

Thor's role in safeguarding Asgard is often highlighted in the tales of his battles against giants, who frequently attempted to invade the realm. These giants, representing chaos and destruction, posed a significant threat to the order established by the gods. In various myths, Thor's confrontations with these formidable foes showcase his unwavering determination and combat skills. His encounters are not just mere acts of violence; they are symbolic of the struggle between order and chaos, illustrating the importance of maintaining balance in the cosmos.

Moreover, Thor's protective nature extends beyond physical battles. He is also a guardian of the Aesir, the principal pantheon of Norse gods. Through his actions, Thor demonstrates the importance of camaraderie and teamwork, often embarking on adventures with his fellow gods, such as Loki and Sif. These journeys not only strengthen their bonds but also emphasize the value of unity in the face of adversity. In one notable story, Thor and Loki venture into the realm of the giants, where they confront various challenges that test their skills and friendship, ultimately reinforcing the idea that collaboration is key to overcoming obstacles.

In addition to his martial prowess, Thor's character embodies the virtues of bravery and resilience, qualities that resonate deeply with young adults navigating their own challenges. His willingness to confront danger head-on serves as an inspiration, encouraging individuals to face their fears and protect those they care about. Thor's adventures are filled with lessons about accountability, courage, and the significance of standing up for what is right, making him a relatable and motivational figure in the realm of mythology.

Through his actions and the myths surrounding him, Thor's role in protecting Asgard highlights the intricate interplay between heroism and responsibility. His stories are not just ancient tales; they continue to inspire modern interpretations in literature and media, reminding us of the timeless values that transcend generations. As young adults explore these narratives, they can draw parallels to their own lives, understanding that the essence of Thor's character lies in the commitment to safeguarding not only one's realm but also the relationships and values that define our existence.

# Chapter 4: The Trickster God: Loki's Myths and Their Lessons

## Loki's Origins and His Role Among the Gods

Loki, one of the most intriguing figures in Norse mythology, presents a complex character that captivates both young and old. Unlike the noble gods such as Odin and Thor, Loki's origins are shrouded in ambiguity. He is often described as a Jötunn, a giant, yet he holds a unique position among the Aesir, the principal pantheon of Norse gods. This duality is significant; it reflects the idea that he embodies both chaos and order. His birth story varies across sources, but a common thread is that he is the son of the giant Fárbauti and the goddess Laufey, which already sets the stage for his unpredictable nature.

As a child of giants, Loki's relationship with the Aesir is fraught with tension. He is known for his cunning and trickery, often using his wit to navigate the complexities of divine politics. His role among the gods is multifaceted; he is both a companion to the gods and a source of strife. Loki's ability to shift allegiances and manipulate situations makes him an essential character in many myths. He assists the gods in their quests, providing solutions to challenges, yet his actions often lead to unforeseen consequences, highlighting the dual nature of his character.

One of the most significant stories involving Loki is the tale of the theft of Idunn's apples, which grant the gods eternal youth. In this myth, Loki's cunning is put to the test as he is compelled to rescue Idunn from the clutches of the giant Thiassi. His actions ultimately save the gods from aging, reinforcing his role as a trickster who can be both a savior and a disruptor. This duality prompts a deeper examination of the nature of good and evil in Norse mythology, suggesting that even the most chaotic figures can serve a vital purpose in the grand tapestry of existence.

Loki's most notorious act, however, is his role in the death of Baldr, the beloved god of light. This event marks a significant turning point in Norse mythology, as it sets off a chain reaction leading to Ragnarok, the end of the world. Loki's betrayal is a poignant reminder of the themes of love and betrayal that permeate Norse legends. His actions not only affect the gods but also resonate with the concept of fate, illustrating how individual choices contribute to the unfolding of destiny. This story serves as a cautionary tale about the consequences of betrayal and the unpredictable nature of loyalty.

Ultimately, Loki's character embodies the complexities of human nature and the intricate relationships among the gods. His origins as a giant and his subsequent rise among the Aesir challenge the notion of belonging and identity. In exploring Loki's myths, young adults can glean valuable lessons about the balance of chaos and order, the impact of betrayal, and the importance of understanding one's role within a larger narrative. Through Loki's adventures and misadventures, the rich tapestry of Norse mythology comes to life, offering insights that remain relevant in today's world.

# The Trickster's Deceits: Key Tales of Loki

Loki, the enigmatic trickster of Norse mythology, stands as one of the most multifaceted figures among the pantheon of gods. His stories are woven with threads of cunning, chaos, and complexity, making him a character of both admiration and disdain. The tales of Loki reveal not only his mischievous nature but also the underlying themes of fate, love, and betrayal that resonate throughout Norse mythology. By examining key episodes from his life, we gain insight into the duality of his character and the lessons embedded within his adventures.

One of the most famous stories involving Loki is the tale of his involvement in the death of Baldr, the beloved god. Baldr was cherished by all, and his death marked a significant turning point in the myths. Loki's jealousy and manipulation led him to craft a plan that ultimately resulted in Baldr's demise. This act not only showcases Loki's deceitful nature but also highlights the themes of betrayal and the consequences of envy. The death of Baldr sets off a chain of events that culminates in Ragnarok, the end of the world, demonstrating how one trickster's actions can have far-reaching implications.

Another significant tale is the story of Loki's transformation into a female horse and his subsequent encounter with the stallion Svaðilfari. In this myth, Loki shapeshifts to give birth to Sleipnir, Odin's eight-legged horse. This story reflects the fluidity of identity and challenges traditional gender roles within the context of Norse culture. It also emphasizes Loki's ability to navigate between worlds, as he effortlessly shifts from one form to another. The tale serves as a reminder of the complexity of existence and the unexpected ways in which fate can unfold.

Loki's relationship with the other gods often oscillates between camaraderie and animosity. In the tale of the building of Asgard's walls, Loki initially aids the gods by devising a clever plan to attract the help of the giant builder. However, when the giant demands the goddess Freyja as payment, Loki's trickery turns against him. This narrative encapsulates the themes of love, sacrifice, and the balance of power among the gods. It also illustrates how Loki's deceptions can backfire, leading to unforeseen consequences that affect not only him but the entire divine community.

Ultimately, Loki's tales serve as a reflection of the human condition, encapsulating the duality of our nature—our capacity for both creation and destruction. His stories remind us that deception can lead to both humorous outcomes and tragic consequences. As readers delve into the complexities of Loki's character, they are prompted to consider the intricate web of relationships, fate, and morality that defines the Norse mythological cosmos. Through Loki's adventures, we learn that the trickster's deceits, while entertaining, carry profound lessons about the nature of existence and the choices we make.

## Lessons Learned from Loki's Actions

Loki, the trickster god of Norse mythology, embodies a complex character whose actions provide valuable lessons applicable to modern life. His cunning and unpredictable nature often lead to chaos, yet they also highlight the importance of adaptability and intelligence in overcoming challenges. Young adults can glean insights from Loki's stories, particularly in understanding the duality of one's nature and the consequences that arise from choices. His escapades remind us that while cleverness can be a powerful tool, it can just as easily spiral into mischief with lasting repercussions.

One significant lesson from Loki's actions is the concept of consequences. Loki's deceit often leads to dire outcomes, not only for himself but for others as well. This underscores the importance of considering how our actions affect those around us. In a world where decisions can have far-reaching implications, learning to assess the potential fallout from our choices is crucial. Loki teaches us that even the most seemingly harmless trick can lead to unexpected fallout, emphasizing the need for responsibility and foresight.

Additionally, Loki's ability to adapt and transform highlights the significance of flexibility in one's approach to life. Whether through shapeshifting or outsmarting his opponents, Loki demonstrates that sometimes the best way to confront a challenge is to embrace change. For young adults navigating the complexities of adulthood, this lesson is particularly relevant. Life rarely goes according to plan, and those who can pivot and adjust their strategies are often the ones who succeed. Loki's story encourages us to be resourceful and open-minded in the face of adversity.

Moreover, the relationships Loki engages in reveal the intricacies of trust and betrayal. His actions often lead to broken alliances and fractured friendships, showcasing the impact of betrayal on personal relationships. Young adults can learn from these dynamics, recognizing the importance of loyalty and the fragility of trust. By understanding the consequences of betrayal, individuals can strive to build more meaningful connections based on honesty and integrity, avoiding the pitfalls that Loki so frequently encounters.

In summary, the lessons gleaned from Loki's actions serve as a guide for young adults as they navigate their own journeys. From understanding the weight of consequences to embracing adaptability and valuing trust, Loki's tales resonate with timeless truths. By reflecting on his experiences, individuals can cultivate a deeper comprehension of their own choices and relationships, paving the way for a more enlightened and intentional approach to life.

# Chapter 5: The Nine Realms: A Guide to Norse Mythological Worlds

## Asgard: Home of the Aesir

Asgard, the majestic home of the Aesir gods, stands as a central realm in Norse mythology, symbolizing power, bravery, and the divine order of the universe. It is often depicted as a breathtaking fortress floating high above the earth, accessible only by the shimmering Bifrost, the rainbow bridge that connects it to Midgard, the realm of humans. In this realm, the Aesir gods, including Odin, Thor, and Frigg, reside, each playing a crucial role in the intricate tapestry of Norse myths. The grandeur of Asgard not only reflects the strength of the gods but also sets the stage for countless adventures, battles, and lessons that resonate through time.

The architecture of Asgard is characterized by its impressive halls and imposing structures, including Valhalla, the hall of the slain warriors. Here, the bravest souls who died in battle are welcomed by Odin and the Valkyries, who serve as divine choosers of those worthy of a place among the gods. Valhalla is not merely a resting place; it is a realm of eternal feasting and preparation for the final battle, Ragnarok. This idea of Valhalla highlights the Norse reverence for bravery and valor, demonstrating that a noble death in battle is celebrated and rewarded, shaping the cultural identity of the Norse people.

In Asgard, the gods engage in various activities that showcase their personalities and relationships. Odin, the Allfather, is often found seeking wisdom, even at great personal cost, while Thor, the thunder god, embodies strength and courage, often embarking on adventures to protect the realms from giants and other threats. Loki, the trickster god, adds a layer of complexity with his cunning and unpredictable nature, reminding us that not all tales in Asgard are about heroism; some reveal the consequences of deception and betrayal. These interactions not only entertain but also impart important moral lessons, reflecting the complexities of human nature.

The landscape of Asgard is rich with symbolism and lore. From the sacred grove of Yggdrasil, the World Tree that connects all realms, to the various halls that house other gods and beings, every aspect is steeped in meaning. The presence of mythical creatures, such as the majestic eagle that resides atop Yggdrasil, further enriches this world, showcasing the interconnectedness of all beings in Norse mythology. Asgard serves as a reminder that the divine and the mortal are intertwined, with each realm influencing the other in profound ways.

Understanding Asgard is essential for grasping the broader themes of Norse mythology. It represents not only the pinnacle of divine power but also the struggles and triumphs of the gods who inhabit it. Through the adventures and relationships of its deities, Asgard offers young adults insights into courage, loyalty, and the complexities of fate. As new generations explore these ancient tales, the allure of Asgard continues to captivate, reminding us that the lessons of the past remain relevant in our modern lives.

# Midgard: The Realm of Humans

Midgard, in Norse mythology, is the realm that embodies the world of humans. It is one of the Nine Realms and is situated at the center of the cosmos, connected to Asgard, the home of the gods, by the Bifrost, a shimmering rainbow bridge. The name Midgard translates to "middle earth," reflecting its position between the divine and the chaotic realms. This realm is not just a physical space; it serves as the stage for countless tales of human bravery, love, and struggle against the backdrop of the grand cosmic order embodied by the Norse gods.

The landscape of Midgard is diverse, ranging from lush forests and rolling hills to icy mountains and deep fjords. It is populated by various tribes and communities, each with its own unique customs and traditions. The Norse people saw themselves as part of a larger mythological narrative, one where their actions could influence their fate and that of the world around them. This belief is particularly evident in their reverence for the gods, who they viewed as both protectors and overseers of Midgard. The everyday lives of humans were intertwined with the divine, as they sought favor and guidance from deities like Odin, Thor, and Freyja.

Humanity's connection to the divine is most vividly illustrated through the heroic sagas and myths that emerged from this realm. Tales of Odin's wisdom and Thor's strength resonate deeply within Midgard, inspiring individuals to embody these virtues in their own lives. The adventures of Thor, for instance, often involve him battling giants and monsters, symbolizing the human struggle against overwhelming odds. These stories served not only as entertainment but also as moral lessons, teaching young adults about courage, loyalty, and the importance of standing up for what is right.

Midgard is also a place where love and betrayal play pivotal roles in shaping the destinies of its inhabitants. The romantic myths, such as those involving gods and mortals, highlight the complexities of relationships, the pain of loss, and the joy of love. Characters like Freyja, the goddess of love, embody these themes, showing that even among the gods, emotions can lead to both beautiful and tragic outcomes. These narratives encourage young adults to reflect on their own experiences with love and relationships, drawing parallels between their lives and the timeless tales of the gods.

Fate is another crucial aspect of life in Midgard, where the concept of wyrd, or destiny, governs the lives of all beings. The Norns, powerful figures who weave the threads of fate, remind humans that their choices matter. While the gods have their own destinies, so too do the inhabitants of Midgard, who must navigate their paths with wisdom and courage. Understanding this interplay between fate and free will can empower young adults to take control of their own stories, recognizing the impact of their actions while remaining aware of the larger forces at play in their lives.

# Hel and the Underworld: The Realm of the Dead

Hel, the enigmatic ruler of the underworld in Norse mythology, presides over a realm known as Helheim. This domain is often depicted as a cold and gloomy place, distinct from the fiery depths of other mythological underworlds. In Helheim, the souls of those who did not die a heroic death, such as those who succumbed to illness or old age, find their eternal resting place. Unlike the honored warriors who ascend to Valhalla, the inhabitants of Helheim exist in a state of shadow, reflecting their unremarkable exits from the world of the living.

The goddess Hel, daughter of Loki and the giantess Angerboda, embodies the duality of life and death. Unlike many depictions of death in various mythologies, Hel is not an evil figure but rather a necessary part of the cosmic balance. Her appearance, half alive and half decayed, symbolizes the inevitability of death and the importance of accepting one's fate. This unique representation challenges the traditional views of death as something to be feared, suggesting instead that it is merely another phase in existence.

The journey to Helheim is portrayed as a daunting one. Souls must cross the river Gjöll, guarded by the fearsome being Garmr, before entering Hel's domain. This river serves as a boundary, separating the living from the dead. The journey emphasizes the theme of transition, highlighting the Norse belief in an afterlife where the dead continue to exist, albeit in a different form. This notion reinforces the idea that life does not end abruptly but continues in a different realm, allowing for the exploration of themes such as memory, legacy, and the impact of one's actions during their lifetime.

In the broader context of Norse mythology, Hel and her realm serve as a counterbalance to the glory of Valhalla and the heroic ideals associated with it. This dichotomy encourages reflection on the variety of human experiences and the importance of recognizing every individual's story, regardless of how they meet their end. The tales of Hel remind us that not all lives are defined by heroic deeds; some are marked by quiet endurance and the struggle against everyday challenges, which deserve acknowledgment and respect.

Hel's role within the tapestry of Norse mythology invites young adults to contemplate their own lives and the legacies they wish to create. By understanding the significance of Hel and Helheim, readers can appreciate the complexities of existence and the ways in which different narratives coexist within the mythological framework. Through her, Norse mythology offers profound insights into themes of mortality, acceptance, and the continuum of life and death, urging young adults to embrace their journeys, irrespective of the paths they may take.

# Chapter 6: Mythical Creatures in Norse Tales: Giants, Elves, and Dwarves

## The Jotnar: Giants and Their Role

The Jotnar, often referred to as giants in Norse mythology, occupy a significant and complex role within the mythic landscape. They are primarily associated with chaos and the primordial elements of the universe. This duality makes them both adversaries and essential components of the cosmos, as they embody the raw forces of nature that the gods must constantly contend with. The Jotnar are not merely antagonists; they represent the untamed aspects of existence, challenging the order that the gods strive to maintain.

In the Norse cosmology, the Jotnar hail from Jotunheim, one of the Nine Realms. This land is characterized by its rugged mountains, vast forests, and an overall wildness that reflects the giants' nature. Unlike the gods, who are often depicted as wise and orderly, the giants are raw, powerful, and unpredictable. This contrast highlights the balance between creation and destruction in the universe. Notably, some giants possess remarkable wisdom and knowledge, suggesting that their role extends beyond mere brute force.

The relationships between the giants and the gods are intricate and often tumultuous. Many of the tales reflect a deep interconnection, with giants such as Loki, who, despite his trickster nature, is considered part of the Aesir due to his blood brotherhood with Odin. This relationship illustrates how the boundaries between gods and giants can blur, creating a rich tapestry of alliances, betrayals, and conflicts. The giants often challenge the gods, leading to epic battles that emphasize the themes of fate and destiny, central to Norse belief.

The stories of the Jotnar are also filled with lessons about humility and the acceptance of one's place in the world. For instance, in the tale of Thor's encounter with the giant Skrymir, the thunder god learns that strength alone does not guarantee victory. The giants, while often seen as adversaries, provide crucial lessons about the importance of wisdom, strategy, and the acceptance of one's limitations. These narratives encourage young adults to reflect on the complexities of their own challenges and the importance of understanding their own strengths and weaknesses.

In modern adaptations of Norse mythology, the Jotnar continue to captivate audiences, appearing in various forms across literature, film, and video games. Their portrayal often emphasizes their formidable nature, yet it is essential to recognize the depth and nuance of these characters. As young adults explore these stories, they can appreciate the Jotnar not just as giants to be conquered, but as vital players in the grand narrative of existence, reminding us that chaos and order coexist in an ever-shifting balance.

## Elves: Light and Dark

Elves in Norse mythology are fascinating beings often categorized into two distinct types: the light elves and the dark elves. Light elves, or "Ljósálfar," are associated with beauty, purity, and the light of the heavens. They are believed to inhabit Álfheimr, one of the Nine Realms, where they bask in the glow of the sun. The light elves are considered benevolent, often aiding gods and humans alike in their quests for knowledge and strength. Their ethereal beauty and grace are reflected in their role as guardians of nature and inspiration for art, music, and poetry, making them integral to the cultural tapestry of Norse legends.

In contrast, dark elves, known as "Dökkálfar," dwell in the depths of the earth. Unlike their light counterparts, dark elves are often depicted as sinister and mischievous, embodying the more chaotic aspects of nature. They are skilled in the arts of magic and craft, sometimes associated with the creation of powerful artifacts. Stories recount how they can be both allies and adversaries, depending on the circumstances and their whims. The duality of light and dark within elven nature reflects broader themes in Norse mythology, where the balance between good and evil continually shapes the narrative landscape.

The interactions between light and dark elves are not confined to mere tales of conflict. They often serve as metaphors for the struggles between light and dark within the human experience. Young adults navigating their own journeys can find parallels in these myths, as they explore the complexities of identity, morality, and the choices that define them. Just as the gods and mortals grapple with the influence of both light and dark elves, individuals must navigate their own paths, learning from the lessons these ancient stories present.

Elves also play a crucial role in the larger mythological framework, often interacting with key figures such as Odin and Thor. The tales of their involvement highlight the interconnectedness of all beings within the Norse cosmos. Light elves are frequently depicted as bestowers of gifts and wisdom, while dark elves might pose challenges that test the resolve and character of heroes. This dynamic enriches the narratives, making them not only entertaining but also profound explorations of the human condition.

In modern adaptations of Norse mythology, the portrayal of elves continues to evolve, capturing the imaginations of young adults through films, literature, and games. These representations often emphasize the enchantment and mystery of elves, while also acknowledging their darker aspects. As audiences engage with these stories, they are invited to reflect on the dualities present in their own lives. The exploration of elves, both light and dark, serves as a reminder that within every individual lies the potential for both brilliance and shadow, shaping the ongoing saga of existence in the realms of wonder.

# Dwarves: Master Craftsmen of Mythology

Dwarves hold a prominent place in Norse mythology, often celebrated as master craftsmen whose skills are unparalleled. These beings, known for their short stature and rugged appearance, possess a deep connection to the earth and its treasures. In the myths, dwarves are depicted as the creators of some of the most powerful artifacts in the cosmos, including Thor's hammer, Mjölnir, and Odin's spear, Gungnir. Their exceptional craftsmanship is not merely a matter of physical ability; it reflects a profound understanding of the materials they work with, allowing them to imbue their creations with magical properties.

The origins of dwarves can be traced back to the ancient texts, particularly the Prose Edda and the Poetic Edda, where they are often referred to as "Svartálfar" or "dark elves." This can lead to confusion, as they are distinct from the more ethereal and light-filled elves. Dwarves are closely associated with mining and metallurgy, residing in the underground realms of Nidavellir and Svartalfheim. Their homes are filled with the sounds of hammers striking anvils, as they tirelessly craft weapons, jewelry, and tools, all while harnessing the power of the earth's minerals. This industrious nature highlights their role as essential figures within the mythological economy.

The dwarves' craftsmanship is not only functional but also deeply symbolic. Each artifact they create serves a purpose that often intertwines with the fate of gods and men alike. For instance, the creation of Mjölnir was not just a gift to Thor; it symbolizes protection and the maintenance of order against chaos. Similarly, the dwarves crafted the golden hair of Sif, Thor's wife, which represents beauty and fertility. Through these creations, dwarves illustrate the interconnectedness of various elements in Norse mythology, showcasing how craftsmanship can influence the very fabric of existence.

Dwarves also embody themes of fate and destiny in Norse mythology. Their creations often serve as catalysts for significant events, reflecting the belief that destiny is shaped by actions and choices. For example, the story of the cursed ring, Andvaranaut, demonstrates how the dwarves' work can have unforeseen consequences, leading to greed and tragedy. This narrative reveals the moral lessons embedded in their craftsmanship, reminding us that while skill and artistry are to be admired, they can also carry heavy burdens.

In modern adaptations of Norse mythology, the legacy of dwarves continues to resonate. Their portrayal in films, literature, and games often emphasizes their role as skilled artisans and guardians of ancient knowledge. As young adults explore these myths, they can appreciate the dwarves not just as characters in stories, but as vital contributors to the complexities of the Norse mythological landscape. By understanding the significance of dwarves, readers can gain insight into the craftsmanship, morality, and interconnectedness that define the myths of this ancient culture.

# Chapter 7: The Role of Fate: Understanding Norse Concepts of Destiny

## Norns: The Fates of Norse Mythology

In Norse mythology, the Norns occupy a unique position, embodying the very essence of fate and destiny. They are often depicted as three powerful female figures who weave the threads of life for every being in the cosmos. Their names—Urd, Verdandi, and Skuld—represent the past, present, and future, respectively. This triad of fate illustrates the interconnectedness of time and the inevitability of destiny, reminding us that every action has consequences that ripple through existence. The Norns reside at the base of Yggdrasil, the World Tree, where they draw water from the Well of Urd to nurture its roots, symbolizing the nurturing of life and the influence of fate on the living world.

The Norns not only weave the destinies of gods and humans but also play a crucial role in the overall narrative of Norse mythology. Their actions can be seen as both benevolent and malevolent, reflecting the complex nature of fate itself. While they grant some individuals great power and success, they also impose limits and inevitable endings. This duality of the Norns emphasizes the idea that destiny is not entirely predetermined; instead, it is shaped by choices and circumstances, making the pursuit of knowledge and understanding vital for those who seek to navigate their fates.

In many tales, the Norns interact with prominent figures, including the gods. One notable story involves a confrontation between Odin and the Norns, where the Allfather seeks knowledge of the future. This encounter highlights the tension between seeking wisdom and the acceptance of fate, as Odin learns that some truths are better left undiscovered. The Norns remind us that while one can strive for greatness, there are aspects of life that remain beyond control, encapsulating the Norse view that fate is a powerful force that governs existence.

The influence of the Norns extends beyond mythological tales into contemporary discussions about destiny and free will. Young adults exploring these themes can find resonance in the concept that their choices matter, even when faced with overwhelming odds. The Norns serve as a metaphor for the struggles individuals face in understanding their paths in life. By acknowledging the interplay between fate and personal agency, young readers can gain insight into their own journeys, recognizing that while some elements may be predetermined, they still have the power to shape their stories.

Finally, the Norns invite reflection on the broader implications of fate within the Norse cosmos. Their presence in various myths serves as a reminder that every being is part of a larger tapestry, interconnected with others through destiny. This interconnectedness is also mirrored in the diverse realms of Norse mythology, where gods, giants, and mortals interact in a dance of fate. By embracing the lessons of the Norns, young adults can cultivate a deeper appreciation for their own lives and the rich narratives that shape them, ultimately inspiring a sense of wonder and curiosity about their role in the grand story of existence.

# The Weaving of Fate: Concepts of Destiny

In Norse mythology, the concept of fate is intricately woven into the fabric of existence, influencing the lives of gods and mortals alike. Central to this idea are the Norns, three powerful beings who govern the destinies of all creatures. Urd, Verdandi, and Skuld represent the past, present, and future, respectively. They reside at the base of Yggdrasil, the World Tree, where they spin the threads of fate for every individual. This imagery highlights the belief that life is a tapestry, with each thread contributing to the greater picture, illustrating that while fate is predetermined, individuals still play a role in shaping their paths.

The intertwining of fate and free will is a persistent theme in Norse stories. Characters like Odin often grapple with their destinies, seeking knowledge and power yet facing the inescapable nature of their fates. For instance, Odin sacrifices an eye for wisdom, a choice that reflects the tension between agency and destiny. This duality invites reflection among young adults as they navigate their own lives, balancing decisions with the understanding that some aspects of existence are beyond control. The myths serve as a reminder that while one can strive for greatness, certain outcomes may still be written in the stars.

Thor, the thunder god, also embodies the concept of destiny through his adventures. His journey often pits him against formidable foes, yet he approaches each challenge with courage, suggesting that fate can be confronted. This idea resonates with young adults who may feel overwhelmed by their futures. Thor's trials exemplify the importance of resilience and bravery in the face of uncertainty. By facing his fate head-on, he inspires individuals to take charge of their lives and confront challenges, transforming destiny into an ally rather than a foe.

Loki, the trickster god, adds a layer of complexity to the understanding of fate in Norse mythology. His actions often disrupt the natural order, leading to unforeseen consequences that affect the gods and the cosmos alike. Loki's antics highlight the unpredictability of fate, suggesting that even those who believe they can manipulate their destinies may find themselves ensnared by their choices. This serves as a cautionary tale for young adults, emphasizing the importance of understanding the ripple effects of one's actions and the potential for unintended outcomes.

Ultimately, the Norse perspective on fate encourages contemplation about the balance between destiny and personal agency. Myths from this rich tradition invite young adults to reflect on their own lives, recognizing that while fate may guide their journey, they possess the power to influence their paths. The tales of Odin, Thor, and Loki provide valuable lessons on navigating the complexities of existence, urging individuals to embrace their unique stories while understanding the interconnectedness of all beings within the tapestry of fate.

## Free Will vs. Fate in Norse Beliefs

In Norse mythology, the tension between free will and fate is a central theme that significantly influences the lives of gods and mortals alike. The concept of fate, known as "wyrd," suggests that certain events are predestined and unavoidable. The Norns, three female figures who spin the threads of destiny, govern this aspect of Norse belief. They weave the fates of all beings, ensuring that some outcomes are predetermined, which raises questions about the extent to which individuals can exercise free will within a framework of established destiny.

Despite the overarching influence of fate, many Norse myths highlight the power of individual agency. Characters like Odin and Thor often make choices that reflect their desires and ambitions, suggesting that while fate may lay out a path, the journey along that path is shaped by personal decisions. Odin's relentless pursuit of knowledge, even at great personal cost, exemplifies the struggle against fate. His journey teaches that even when faced with dire prophecies, one's choices can significantly impact the course of events.

The duality of free will and fate is particularly evident in the story of Ragnarok, the prophesied end of the world. Here, despite knowing that a great battle will lead to the death of many gods, characters like Thor confront their fates head-on. This epic narrative illustrates a profound acceptance of destiny while simultaneously embracing the courage to fight against it. The inevitability of Ragnarok does not negate the heroism displayed in the actions leading up to it, emphasizing that even in a world governed by fate, the choices made in the face of doom are what define one's legacy.

Moreover, the interplay between love and betrayal in Norse myths often encapsulates this conflict. For instance, the relationship between Loki and the other gods reveals how personal choices can lead to tragic outcomes, challenging the idea that fate is entirely predetermined. Loki's actions, driven by jealousy and cunning, lead to significant consequences, suggesting that individuals possess the power to alter their fates through their decisions. This complexity encourages young adults to reflect on their own lives, considering how their choices can shape their paths, even when faced with seemingly insurmountable challenges.

Ultimately, the Norse belief system presents a nuanced perspective on free will and fate. It teaches that while certain aspects of life may be predetermined, individuals still wield the power to make choices that can influence their journey. This theme resonates with young adults navigating their own paths, encouraging them to embrace both their agency and the mysteries of destiny. Understanding this balance allows for a deeper appreciation of the rich tapestry of Norse mythology, where every choice, no matter how small, contributes to the unfolding of one's personal saga.

# Chapter 8: Love and Betrayal: The Romantic Myths of Norse Legends

## The Love Stories of the Gods

The love stories of the gods in Norse mythology are rich tapestries woven with passion, betrayal, and the complexities of relationships that reflect the human experience. At the heart of these tales is the relationship between the Allfather Odin and Frigg, his wife, who embodies both wisdom and love. Their bond represents a partnership built on mutual respect and understanding, yet it is also marked by the trials that come with their divine responsibilities. Frigg, often seen as a protective figure, uses her foresight to navigate the challenges of love, showcasing the delicate balance between fate and free will that permeates Norse tales.

Another significant love story is that of Frey and Gerd, which illustrates the theme of longing and desire. Frey, the god of fertility and prosperity, falls deeply in love with the giantess Gerd, a union that symbolizes the connection between the realms of gods and giants. Their love story is one of yearning, as Frey is willing to sacrifice his prized sword to win her heart. This act emphasizes the lengths to which one might go for love, highlighting the interplay between sacrifice and reward in relationships. The tale also serves as a reminder that love can bridge the divide between opposing forces.

Loki, the trickster god, adds a unique twist to the narrative of love in Norse mythology. His relationships, especially with the goddess Sigyn, reveal the darker side of love—betrayal and loyalty. Loki's cunning nature often leads him into trouble, and his interactions with the other gods frequently put his loved ones at risk. Sigyn's unwavering devotion to Loki, especially during his punishment, illustrates a love that endures despite adversity. This contrast between Loki's chaotic nature and Sigyn's steadfastness provides valuable lessons about love's complexities and the sacrifices that come with it.

The tales of the Valkyries also contribute to the theme of love in Norse mythology. These warrior maidens, who choose those who may die and those who may live in battle, are often depicted in their relationships with mortal heroes. The love stories involving Valkyries highlight themes of honor, bravery, and the bonds formed in the heat of conflict. Their romances often transcend mortal limitations, as they navigate the expectations placed upon them as both warriors and lovers. This duality reflects the intricate nature of love, where duty and desire must often find a compromise.

In understanding the love stories of the gods, we gain insight into the broader themes of Norse mythology—fate, sacrifice, and the dualities of existence. These narratives not only entertain but also serve to teach valuable lessons about the nature of love, the challenges it presents, and the resilience required to maintain it. As young adults explore these myths, they can draw parallels between the gods' experiences and their own, recognizing that love, in all its forms, is a powerful force that shapes destinies across the realms of existence.

## Betrayals and Their Consequences

Betrayals in Norse mythology often carry significant weight, affecting not only the individuals involved but the very fabric of the realms themselves. These betrayals can arise from a variety of motives, including jealousy, ambition, and revenge, and they frequently lead to dire consequences. One of the most notorious examples is Loki's betrayal of the gods. Initially a companion to Odin and Thor, Loki's cunning and deceptive nature eventually led him to assist the giants against the gods. This pivotal act set off a chain of events that culminated in Ragnarök, the cataclysmic battle that would bring about the end of the world as the gods knew it.

The consequences of betrayal in these myths are not limited to the immediate fallout; they often extend to larger themes of fate and destiny. In Norse belief, fate is seen as a force that intertwines the actions of gods and mortals alike. Loki's treachery illustrates how one individual's choices can disrupt the cosmic order. After his betrayal, Loki is punished severely, reflecting the belief that actions have consequences that resonate through time and space, impacting not just the betrayer but also those who are betrayed and the world around them.

Another significant betrayal occurs in the tale of Sigurd and the treachery of the Valkyrie Brynhild. Sigurd, a hero renowned for his strength, becomes entangled in a web of love and deceit when he unwittingly breaks an oath made to Brynhild. This betrayal leads to tragic outcomes, including the destruction of relationships and the loss of life. The story serves as a cautionary tale about the fragility of trust and the devastating effects that betrayal can have on even the strongest bonds, emphasizing that even heroes are not immune to the consequences of their choices.

Betrayals also manifest in the relationships among gods and their interactions with mortals. The story of Freyja and the theft of her necklace, Brísingamen, by the trickster Loki highlights how trust can be manipulated. Freyja's reliance on Loki ultimately leads to a series of events that not only affect her but also the balance of power among the gods. This myth illustrates the precarious nature of alliances and the potential for betrayal to alter the course of relationships, showcasing how even the divine are not free from the repercussions of deceit.

Ultimately, the theme of betrayal in Norse mythology serves as a reflection on human nature and the complexities of relationships. It reveals that betrayals, whether born of malice or misunderstanding, often lead to irreversible consequences. The tales remind young adults that the choices they make, particularly in matters of trust and loyalty, can have far-reaching implications, echoing the lessons of the past in their own lives. These stories convey the importance of integrity and the understanding that betrayal can shatter not only individual lives but also the very foundations of society.

# Lessons on Love from Norse Myths

Norse mythology is rich with tales that delve into the complexities of love, showcasing both its beauty and its potential for betrayal. Through the stories of gods, giants, and mortals, we learn that love is often intertwined with fate, sacrifice, and the struggles of life. The relationships depicted in these myths serve as powerful reminders of the multifaceted nature of human emotions, teaching us valuable lessons that resonate even in today's world.

One of the most compelling narratives involves the love between Odin and Frigg, the Allfather and his queen. Their bond exemplifies loyalty and mutual respect, highlighting the importance of partnership in overcoming challenges. Despite the trials they face, including Odin's relentless pursuit of wisdom, their love remains a guiding force. This tale encourages young adults to appreciate the significance of commitment and understanding in their own relationships, emphasizing that true love often demands compromise and patience.

In contrast, the story of Sigurd and Brynhild offers a poignant lesson on the darker side of love. Their passionate romance is marred by deception and betrayal, illustrating how trust can be easily shattered. Loki's role in manipulating their fates serves as a reminder that love can be vulnerable to external influences and the choices of others. This narrative urges young adults to be vigilant about the trust they place in their relationships and to recognize the potential consequences of betrayal.

Moreover, the tale of Freyja, the goddess of love and fertility, showcases the power of love as a catalyst for personal growth and transformation. Freyja's relentless quest for her lost husband, Óðr, emphasizes the lengths one might go to for love. Her journey reveals that love can inspire resilience and bravery, pushing individuals to confront their fears and challenges. This encourages young adults to embrace love as a motivating force, driving them to pursue their passions and connections with vigor.

Ultimately, Norse myths provide a profound exploration of love's complexities, blending joy with sorrow, unity with discord. These stories reflect the realities of human relationships, reminding young adults that love is not just an emotion but a journey filled with lessons. By engaging with these ancient tales, they can glean insights that help navigate their own experiences with love, ensuring that they approach their relationships with wisdom, empathy, and courage.

# Chapter 9: The Valkyries: Warrior Maidens of Norse Mythology

## Who Are the Valkyries?

The Valkyries are among the most captivating figures in Norse mythology, embodying the dualities of war and fate. These warrior maidens, often depicted as fierce and beautiful, serve Odin, the Allfather, guiding the souls of slain warriors to Valhalla, the great hall of the slain. The term "Valkyrie" itself translates to "chooser of the slain," reflecting their vital role in selecting those worthy of a glorious afterlife. The Valkyries not only honor the bravery of warriors but also underscore the Norse belief in destiny, as they operate within the framework of fate, determining who will live and who will die in battle.

In the myths, Valkyries are often portrayed riding winged horses, adorned in armor, and wielding weapons. They appear on the battlefield as ethereal figures, inspiring fear and admiration. Their presence is a reminder of the thin line between life and death, as they escort the souls of the brave to Valhalla, where these warriors prepare for Ragnarok, the end of the world. Valkyries are not merely passive figures; they actively participate in the fate of warriors, showcasing their significance in the broader narrative of Norse mythology.

Each Valkyrie possesses unique characteristics and names, often reflecting their individual roles and attributes. Some are known for their beauty, while others are recognized for their martial prowess. Notable Valkyries include Brynhildr and Sigrdrifa, each with her own story and legends. These tales illustrate the complexities of their characters, revealing that they are not just instruments of fate but also beings capable of deep emotions, love, and even betrayal. Their intricate relationships with mortals and gods alike add layers to their mythological significance.

The Valkyries also embody themes of honor and valor, essential elements in Norse culture. By selecting the bravest warriors for Valhalla, they reinforce the cultural ideals of courage and loyalty. This aspect of their role speaks to the importance placed on honor in battle, a central tenet in Norse society. The warriors chosen by the Valkyries are not only celebrated in life but are destined to partake in the grandest of battles in the afterlife, highlighting the belief that valor is rewarded, even beyond death.

In modern media, the Valkyries have been adapted and reimagined in various forms, from literature to film. Their portrayal often emphasizes their warrior spirit and independence, resonating with contemporary themes of empowerment. These adaptations continue to draw from the rich tapestry of their mythological origins while exploring new dimensions of their characters. The Valkyries remain a symbol of strength and resilience, capturing the imagination of young adults and inviting them to delve deeper into the enchanting world of Norse mythology.

# The Role of Valkyries in Battle

The Valkyries hold a distinctive place in Norse mythology as divine warrior maidens who serve Odin, the Allfather. Their primary role is to choose those who will die in battle and those who will live. This selection process is not arbitrary; it is guided by their keen judgment and understanding of valor and fate. The Valkyries are often depicted as fierce and beautiful, embodying both the grace of warriors and the wisdom of the gods. By determining the outcome of battles, they actively influence the fate of warriors and the course of history, making them crucial figures in the mythological narratives of the Norse realm.

In the heat of battle, Valkyries are said to swoop down, clad in armor and wielding weapons, to survey the conflict. Their presence is both awe-inspiring and fearsome, as they possess the ability to shift the tide of war. According to various myths, they are often depicted riding swift horses through the skies, their armor glinting like stars. This imagery emphasizes their otherworldly nature and the supernatural power they wield. The choice of the fallen is not merely about death; it is a sacred duty that leads the chosen warriors, known as the Einherjar, to Valhalla, Odin's grand hall, where they prepare for the final battle of Ragnarok.

The Valkyries also symbolize the connection between life and death. They are not just harbingers of doom; they are also guides for the souls of the brave. In Valhalla, the Einherjar engage in endless feasting and combat, training for the ultimate showdown during Ragnarok. The Valkyries serve as their caretakers, ensuring that these warriors are honored and revered. This reflects a broader theme in Norse mythology, where death is viewed not as an end, but as a transformation into a new existence. The Valkyries, therefore, play a pivotal role in this cycle of life, death, and rebirth.

Beyond their battlefield duties, Valkyries are often depicted in stories as having complex relationships with the heroes they choose. Some tales explore romantic entanglements between Valkyries and mortal warriors, highlighting themes of love, loyalty, and sacrifice. These relationships can lead to dramatic consequences, both for the Valkyries and the chosen warriors. Such narratives serve to enrich the mythology surrounding these figures, illustrating that even divine beings are not immune to the trials of love and personal conflict.

In modern media, the Valkyries have been embraced as symbols of female strength and empowerment, resonating with contemporary audiences. Their portrayal has evolved, reflecting changing societal views about women in mythology and beyond. From comic books to films, the Valkyries continue to inspire new interpretations, showcasing their enduring legacy in popular culture. As we explore the role of Valkyries in battle, it becomes evident that they embody not only the fierce spirit of the warrior but also the intricate tapestry of fate, love, and destiny that defines Norse mythology.

## Valkyries and the Afterlife: Choosing the Fallen

Valkyries, often depicted as fierce warrior maidens, play a crucial role in Norse mythology, particularly in their connection to the afterlife. Their name, which translates to "choosers of the slain," reflects their responsibility in selecting those who would die in battle and those who would be taken to Valhalla, the grand hall of the slain ruled by Odin. This task is not merely about choosing the fallen but is deeply intertwined with concepts of honor, bravery, and fate. The Valkyries embody the ideals of warrior culture, demonstrating the respect accorded to those who fought valiantly, making their selection process a significant aspect of Norse beliefs about life, death, and the afterlife.

In the mythological narratives, the Valkyries are often depicted riding through the skies, clad in armor and wielding weapons. Their presence on the battlefield signals both a blessing and a harbinger of death. To the warriors, the sight of a Valkyrie could inspire courage as they fought, knowing that their deeds might earn them a place in Valhalla. This connection to the afterlife underscores the Norse perception of life as a series of trials where honor and bravery could lead to eternal glory. The Valkyries, therefore, are not just agents of death; they are mediators of fate, ensuring that only the most deserving warriors are chosen for a posthumous reward.

The selection process of the Valkyries is marked by their discerning nature. They evaluate the courage and skill of the fighters, deciding who is worthy of honor in death. This notion reflects a broader theme in Norse mythology, where fate plays a pivotal role in the lives of individuals. The Valkyries are often seen as instruments of the Norns, the three fate goddesses who weave the destinies of all beings. This interconnection highlights the inevitability of fate in Norse belief systems, as even the Valkyries are bound to the decisions that have already been set in motion by the Norns.

The concept of Valhalla, where the chosen warriors reside, is integral to understanding the afterlife in Norse mythology. Here, the fallen warriors engage in endless feasting and fighting, preparing for Ragnarok, the end of the world. The Valkyries serve these warriors in Valhalla, further reinforcing their role as both selectors and caretakers of the honored dead. This afterlife is not merely a reward but a continuation of the warrior's journey, where they can demonstrate their valor in a different realm. The Valkyries, therefore, symbolize the transition from the mortal realm to a place where bravery is eternally celebrated.

In modern interpretations, the Valkyries have transcended their mythological origins, appearing in various forms of media and popular culture, often embodying traits of strength, independence, and fierce loyalty. Their legacy continues to inspire interpretations of female empowerment and heroism. As young adults explore these stories, they can appreciate how the Valkyries reflect both the complexities of Norse culture and the timeless themes of choice and consequence that resonate through the ages. Understanding the Valkyries' role in the afterlife enriches the appreciation of Norse mythology, revealing deeper insights into the values and beliefs that shaped the legendary tales of the past.

# Chapter 10: Norse Myths in Modern Media: Adaptations and Influences

## Norse Mythology in Literature

Norse mythology has significantly influenced literature throughout the ages, serving as a rich source of inspiration for countless authors. From ancient texts like the Poetic Edda and the Prose Edda to modern interpretations in novels, films, and graphic novels, the stories of gods, giants, and mythical creatures have captivated readers and provided fertile ground for exploring themes of heroism, fate, and the human condition. These tales not only entertain but also offer profound insights into the values and beliefs of the Norse culture, making them relevant to contemporary audiences.

One of the most prominent figures in Norse mythology is Odin, the Allfather, whose adventures have been retold in various forms. His quest for knowledge and wisdom often leads him into conflict with other gods and creatures, showcasing both his strength and vulnerability. In literature, Odin's character serves as a complex symbol of leadership and sacrifice, reflecting the struggles of modern heroes who seek to balance power with morality. Authors have taken inspiration from Odin's tales, crafting narratives that delve into the intricacies of his character and the lessons he imparts about seeking knowledge and the price it may demand.

Thor, the god of thunder, is another iconic figure whose exploits resonate with audiences today. His journeys are filled with action, humor, and camaraderie, making them appealing to young adults who enjoy tales of adventure and bravery. Literature featuring Thor often highlights themes of friendship and loyalty, as seen in his relationships with the other gods and his battles against giants. Contemporary adaptations frequently reinterpret these stories, placing Thor in modern contexts while preserving the essence of his character and the moral lessons inherent in his adventures.

Loki, the trickster god, adds a layer of complexity to Norse myths, embodying themes of chaos and transformation. His stories are rich with moral ambiguity, challenging readers to consider the nature of good and evil. In literature, Loki's cunning and unpredictable behavior serve as a reflection of the human experience, prompting questions about identity, loyalty, and the consequences of one's actions. Writers often use Loki as a catalyst for conflict, driving the narrative forward while also encouraging readers to explore deeper philosophical questions about fate and free will.

The vast tapestry of Norse mythology also encompasses a variety of mythical creatures, realms, and unique concepts like the Valkyries and the role of fate. These elements enrich literary works, allowing authors to weave together intricate plots that explore themes of love, betrayal, destiny, and the struggle between good and evil. Modern adaptations often draw connections between these ancient myths and contemporary issues, making them relatable to today's readers. By presenting Norse mythology in a fresh light, literature continues to celebrate and reinterpret these timeless tales, ensuring their place in the hearts and minds of young adults.

## Film and Television Adaptations

Film and television adaptations of Norse mythology have gained immense popularity in recent years, bringing ancient tales to a modern audience. These adaptations often simplify complex narratives to make them accessible and engaging for young adults. By focusing on key figures such as Odin, Thor, and Loki, filmmakers and showrunners highlight the core themes of heroism, betrayal, and the struggle between fate and free will, drawing viewers into the rich tapestry of Norse myths.

One of the most prominent adaptations is the Marvel Cinematic Universe's portrayal of Thor and Loki, characters that have transcended their mythological roots to become global icons. The films depict Thor as a mighty warrior and protector, while Loki, the trickster god, embodies both charm and chaos. This duality captivates audiences and encourages them to explore the original myths, where both characters have much deeper and more nuanced stories. The films effectively introduce viewers to the concept of the Nine Realms, setting the stage for further exploration of Norse worlds and their inhabitants.

Another noteworthy adaptation is the television series "Vikings," which, while not strictly adhering to the mythological narratives, infuses Norse mythology into its storytelling. The series weaves historical figures with mythological elements, exploring themes of fate and destiny as characters navigate their lives in a world governed by the Norse pantheon. By incorporating mythical references and characters, "Vikings" creates a rich backdrop that resonates with young adults who appreciate both history and mythology, sparking interest in the original tales.

Animated films and series also play a significant role in popularizing Norse mythology among younger audiences. Productions like "How to Train Your Dragon," while primarily focused on dragons and adventure, draw inspiration from Norse culture and aesthetics. These adaptations not only entertain but also introduce elements of Norse myths, such as the concepts of bravery and the bond between humans and mythical creatures, encouraging a deeper understanding of the source material among young viewers.

As Norse mythology continues to inspire modern media, young adults are presented with a unique opportunity to explore these ancient stories in new formats. Adaptations serve as gateways, inviting audiences to delve into the complexities of love, betrayal, and the intricate relationships between gods and mortals. Through these narratives, young adults can engage with the timeless lessons found within Norse mythology, fostering a deeper appreciation for the realms of wonder that have captivated humanity for centuries.

## The Impact of Norse Myths on Popular Culture

The influence of Norse myths on popular culture is profound and far-reaching, weaving its way into various forms of media, literature, and art. From ancient tales of gods and heroes to contemporary adaptations, these myths have intrigued and inspired generations. Young adults today encounter Norse mythology not only in textbooks but also through movies, television shows, video games, and graphic novels. This cultural permeation reflects a growing fascination with the narrative complexities and moral lessons inherent in these ancient stories.

In films and television, Norse mythology has been reimagined and revived in exciting ways. The Marvel Cinematic Universe, for instance, has popularized characters like Thor and Loki, presenting them with modern twists while maintaining connections to their mythological roots. This portrayal has introduced a new audience to the adventures of Odin and the dynamics of the Norse pantheon, illustrating themes of heroism, sacrifice, and the struggle between order and chaos. These adaptations often simplify complex tales for younger viewers, making the myths accessible while sparking interest in the original narratives.

Literature has also embraced Norse mythology, with authors drawing from ancient texts to create engaging stories for young adults. Novels often feature the heroic journeys of figures like Thor, exploring their character development and the moral dilemmas they face. The romantic myths, including tales of love and betrayal, provide rich material for writers seeking to delve into themes of passion and conflict. These narratives resonate with young readers, reflecting their own experiences with relationships and personal growth, making the ancient myths relevant in today's context.

Video games have emerged as a powerful medium for exploring Norse mythology, allowing players to immerse themselves in the Nine Realms. Games like God of War and Assassin's Creed Valhalla offer interactive experiences where players can encounter mythical creatures, battle gods, and explore the significance of fate and destiny. These gaming experiences not only entertain but also educate players about the foundational elements of Norse mythology, encouraging them to engage with the stories on a deeper level. The blending of action and lore captivates young adults, fostering a new appreciation for these ancient tales.

The resurgence of interest in Norse mythology in popular culture underscores a broader trend of exploring ancient belief systems and their relevance in contemporary society. Through various adaptations and creative expressions, young adults are invited to reflect on timeless themes such as heroism, morality, and the complexities of human relationships. As they navigate their own journeys in a rapidly changing world, the lessons learned from the adventures of Odin, the cunning of Loki, and the valor of the Valkyries resonate more than ever, ensuring that these ancient myths continue to inspire and influence future generations.

# Heimdall's Watch: Guardian of the Nine Realms

## Chapter 1: Introduction to Heimdall

### The Significance of Heimdall in Norse Mythology

Heimdall, often referred to as the watchman of the gods, holds a significant place in Norse mythology. As the guardian of the Bifrost, the rainbow bridge connecting Asgard to Midgard, Heimdall is tasked with overseeing the passage between realms. His role is not just one of vigilance; he embodies the qualities of foresight and protection. His keen senses allow him to detect even the faintest disturbances, making him an essential figure in safeguarding the gods from external threats. This vigilance reflects the broader theme of guardianship prevalent throughout Norse myths, where protection of the realms is paramount.

Central to Heimdall's significance is his lineage and origins. According to the myths, he is the son of nine giantesses, which endows him with unique attributes that are both divine and earthly. This extraordinary parentage signifies his connection to various realms, further enhancing his role as a mediator between gods and humans. The duality of his nature allows him to traverse different worlds, making him an indispensable figure in the narrative of creation and the ongoing struggle against chaos. His birth is often seen as a pivotal moment in the cosmic order, symbolizing the emergence of light and clarity amidst the darkness.

Heimdall's role extends beyond mere observation; he actively participates in the fate of the cosmos, especially during Ragnarok, the prophesied end of the world. In this climactic battle, he faces off against Loki, his sworn enemy, highlighting the themes of conflict and resolution inherent in Norse mythology. This confrontation is not just a personal rivalry; it represents the struggle between order and chaos, a central theme in the Norse worldview. Heimdall's courageous stand at Ragnarok emphasizes his importance in the cosmic balance, illustrating how guardianship comes with the weight of responsibility and sacrifice.

Moreover, Heimdall's attributes contribute to his significance in creation myths. His ability to hear grass grow and see for hundreds of miles underscores his role as a perceptive observer of the world. This heightened awareness grants him the authority to guide and protect the realms from potential dangers. In many narratives, he is depicted as a bridge between the divine and the mortal, ensuring that the lines of communication remain open. His vigilance serves as a reminder to humanity of the importance of awareness and preparedness in the face of life's uncertainties.

In essence, Heimdall represents the values of vigilance, protection, and balance within Norse mythology. His multifaceted character not only enriches the creation myths but also serves as a symbol of the interconnectedness of all realms. As the guardian of the Bifrost, he plays a crucial role in maintaining the harmony of the cosmos. This significance is not merely historical; it resonates with contemporary themes of guardianship and responsibility, making Heimdall a timeless figure in the exploration of myth and meaning.

## Overview of the Nine Realms

The Nine Realms in Norse mythology represent a complex and interconnected cosmology, each realm serving a distinct purpose and embodying unique characteristics. At the heart of this intricate structure lies Yggdrasil, the World Tree, which binds the realms together and provides a connection between the divine, the mortal, and the monstrous. The realms are divided into three primary categories: the realms of the gods, the realms of the giants, and the realms of humanity, with each realm playing a significant role in the larger narrative of creation and existence.

Asgard, the realm of the Aesir gods, is a place of grandeur and power where deities like Odin, Thor, and Frigg reside. This realm is often depicted as a majestic fortress, surrounded by fortified walls and accessible only through the Bifrost, the rainbow bridge that Heimdall guards. Asgard is not just a home for the gods; it is also a center of governance and decision-making, with the Well of Mimir providing wisdom and insights that guide the actions of the Aesir. The significance of Asgard is profound, as it represents the ideals of order, strength, and the protection of the cosmos from chaos.

In stark contrast to Asgard is Jotunheim, the realm of the giants. This land is characterized by rugged mountains, dense forests, and a wild, untamed nature that reflects the chaotic essence of its inhabitants. The giants, or Jotnar, embody the forces of chaos and destruction, often clashing with the gods in a perpetual struggle for balance. The tension between Asgard and Jotunheim highlights the ongoing conflict between order and chaos, a theme central to Norse mythology. It is in this realm that many of the myths unfold, showcasing the giants' interactions with gods, heroes, and humanity.

Midgard, the realm of humans, serves as the bridge between the divine and the earthly. It is connected to Asgard by the Bifrost and is often depicted as a circular land surrounded by the vast oceans. Midgard is inhabited by humans who are shaped by their experiences and interactions with the gods and other beings from the Nine Realms. The struggles and triumphs of humanity are central to many Norse myths, as they highlight the importance of courage, loyalty, and honor. Heimdall's role as the guardian of Midgard is crucial, as he watches over the realm, ensuring the safety of its inhabitants and standing ready to defend against any threats that may arise.

The remaining realms, including Vanaheim, Alfheim, Svartalfheim, Niflheim, and Muspelheim, add further depth to the Norse cosmology. Each of these realms contributes to the rich tapestry of myths that explore themes of creation, destruction, and the cyclical nature of existence. Vanaheim, home to the Vanir gods, represents fertility and prosperity, while Alfheim is inhabited by light elves, symbolizing beauty and grace. Svartalfheim, the realm of dwarves, is renowned for craftsmanship and innovation, whereas Niflheim and Muspelheim embody the extremes of cold and heat, respectively. Together, these realms illustrate the diverse and multifaceted nature of the universe in Norse mythology, highlighting Heimdall's critical role as the guardian who oversees the balance between them all.

# Chapter 2: The Creation of the Nine Realms

### The Cosmic Egg and the Birth of the World

The concept of the Cosmic Egg is a significant element in various creation myths, including those found in Norse mythology. This primordial egg symbolizes the potential for life and existence contained within a singular entity. According to some interpretations of Norse myths, the Cosmic Egg is said to have floated in the vast void of Ginnungagap, the great emptiness that existed before the creation of the world. From this egg, the first beings emerged, setting the stage for the formation of the Nine Realms and the intricate tapestry of life that would follow.

In the beginning, the Cosmic Egg was nourished by the contrasting forces of ice from Niflheim and the heat from Muspelheim. The interaction of these two elements created a fertile environment where the first being, Ymir, was born. Ymir, the primordial giant, represents chaos and the raw, untamed energies of creation. His presence marked the beginning of the world's physical form. As the story unfolds, Ymir's body becomes the very foundation of the earth, illustrating how creation often arises from chaos and destruction.

Heimdall, the vigilant guardian of the Bifrost Bridge, plays a crucial role in this narrative. While he is not directly involved in the initial creation, his significance lies in the protection and maintenance of the worlds that arise from Ymir's sacrifice. Heimdall, known for his keen sight and hearing, embodies the watchful spirit that ensures the stability of the realms. His presence is a reminder that, even in a world born from chaos, there exists a force dedicated to order and protection.

The birth of the world from the Cosmic Egg and Ymir's sacrifice also introduces the concept of interconnectedness in Norse cosmology. Each realm, from Asgard to Midgard, is intricately linked, forming a complex web of relationships and dependencies. Heimdall's role as a guardian emphasizes the importance of each realm's harmony, suggesting that the cosmic balance must be preserved to maintain existence. This theme resonates with young adults, encouraging them to consider their own roles in the larger tapestry of life and the importance of guardianship in their communities.

In conclusion, the Cosmic Egg and the birth of the world highlight the dynamic interplay between chaos and order in Norse creation myths. Heimdall stands as a symbol of vigilance in a universe that emerged from tumultuous beginnings. As young adults explore these themes, they are invited to reflect on their own responsibilities within their worlds, recognizing that like Heimdall, they too can be guardians of their own realms, fostering balance and harmony in the face of life's challenges.

## The Role of Ymir and the Formation of the Realms

In Norse mythology, Ymir plays a pivotal role in the creation of the cosmos. Known as the first being, Ymir was a primordial giant who emerged from the collision of heat and cold in the void of Ginnungagap. His body was formed from the melting ice of Niflheim and the fiery sparks from Muspelheim. As the progenitor of the giants, Ymir's existence was closely tied to the creation of the realms that would eventually shape the universe. His blood, bones, and flesh became the very fabric of the worlds that followed, illustrating the interconnectedness of life and death in Norse belief.

Ymir's demise marked a significant turning point in the creation process. After he was slain by Odin and his brothers, Vili and Ve, his body was transformed into the world as we know it. The giants, who descended from Ymir, were both creators and adversaries in the unfolding drama of existence. The brothers used Ymir's flesh to form the earth, his blood to create the oceans, and his bones to shape the mountains. This act not only established the physical realms but also set the stage for the ongoing struggle between the gods and the giants, underscoring the duality of creation and destruction in Norse mythology.

Furthermore, the formation of the realms was not merely a physical act but also a symbolic one. The nine realms—Asgard, Midgard, Vanaheim, and others—represent different aspects of existence and the diverse experiences of beings within them. Asgard, home to the Aesir gods, symbolizes order and civilization, while Midgard, the realm of humans, reflects the balance between the divine and the mundane. The other realms, such as Helheim and Jotunheim, showcase the complexities of life, including death, chaos, and the untamed forces of nature that stemmed from Ymir's legacy.

Heimdall, the watchman of the gods, has a crucial role in safeguarding these realms. As the guardian of Bifrost, the bridge connecting Asgard to Midgard, he ensures that the balance between the realms is maintained. His vigilance is essential in the ongoing conflict between the gods and the giants, stemming from Ymir's descendants. Heimdall's keen eyesight and acute hearing enable him to detect any threats that arise, embodying the idea that vigilance is a necessary component of harmony in the universe.

In conclusion, Ymir's significance in Norse creation myths cannot be overstated. His existence and ultimate sacrifice laid the groundwork for the formation of the nine realms, intertwining themes of life, death, and the eternal struggle between order and chaos. Heimdall's protective role further emphasizes the importance of guardianship and balance within this intricate web of existence. Through understanding the relationship between Ymir and the realms, one gains deeper insight into the rich tapestry of Norse mythology and the lessons it imparts about the universe and our place within it.

## The Aesir and Vanir: The Divine Families

The Aesir and Vanir represent two distinct but interconnected divine families in Norse mythology, each embodying unique qualities and characteristics. The Aesir are often seen as the primary gods, associated with power, war, and governance. Key figures in this pantheon include

Odin, the chief god, and his sons Thor and Balder, each contributing to the mythic narratives that shape the cosmos. The Aesir reside in Asgard, a majestic realm connected to Midgard, the world of humans. Their stories often explore themes of wisdom, bravery, and the quest for knowledge, reflecting the values of the Norse people.

In contrast, the Vanir are linked to fertility, prosperity, and nature. This group of deities includes figures like Njord, the god of the sea and wealth, and his children Freyr and Freyja, who are associated with love and abundance. The Vanir are often portrayed as more harmonious and connected to the earth, emphasizing the importance of the natural world in Norse cosmology. Their home, Vanaheim, is a realm that symbolizes the bounty of nature and the seasonal cycles that dictate life on Midgard.

The relationship between the Aesir and Vanir is complex, marked by both conflict and cooperation. This dynamic is famously illustrated in the Aesir-Vanir War, a significant event that arose from misunderstandings and differing values. Initially, the two families fought fiercely, each seeking to assert their dominance. However, this conflict ultimately led to a peace treaty, resulting in the exchange of hostages, which included the Vanir sending Njord and his children to live among the Aesir. This exchange symbolizes the blending of their distinct qualities, leading to a richer understanding of the divine.

Heimdall, a key figure in this narrative, serves as a bridge between these two divine families. As the guardian of the Bifrost, the rainbow bridge connecting the realms, Heimdall embodies vigilance and foresight. His role extends beyond mere protection; he is also a symbol of unity, emphasizing the need for coexistence between the Aesir and Vanir. By watching over the realms, Heimdall ensures that the lessons learned from their conflicts and collaborations are preserved, providing guidance for both gods and mortals.

The interaction between the Aesir and Vanir highlights the importance of understanding different perspectives and finding harmony in diversity. Their stories remind us that even powerful beings face challenges in their relationships, and that cooperation can lead to greater strength. Through Heimdall's watchful eye, young adults can learn about the significance of unity and respect for nature, values that resonate not only in myth but also in the world today. The tales of these divine families serve as enduring lessons about the balance between strength and harmony, making them relevant to contemporary discussions on coexistence and understanding.

# Chapter 3: Heimdall's Origins

### The Birth of Heimdall

The birth of Heimdall is an essential element within Norse creation myths, showcasing his unique origins and the significance he holds in the cosmic order. According to the lore, Heimdall, often referred to as the watchman of the gods, was born from nine mothers, each representing a different aspect of the sea. This unusual parentage not only highlights his divine nature but also establishes his role as a bridge between various realms. The nine mothers, who are sometimes interpreted as personifications of the waves, symbolize the interconnectedness of nature and the divine, emphasizing that Heimdall is a guardian crafted from both the mortal and the mystical.

Heimdall's birth is steeped in mystery, as it is said that he emerged from the depths of the ocean, fully formed and radiant. This miraculous arrival signifies his readiness to take on the responsibilities that would define his existence. As a child of the sea, he embodies qualities of vigilance and clarity, which are critical for his future role as the sentinel of Asgard. His extraordinary hearing and sight are said to have been gifted to him by the very forces of nature from which he was born, making him an ideal protector against the threats looming over the nine realms.

The significance of Heimdall's role transcends mere guardianship; it is a representation of the balance between the realms and the importance of vigilance in maintaining order. His ability to see and hear across vast distances equips him with the tools necessary to monitor any disruption that may arise. This vigilance is not just a physical attribute but also a metaphorical reminder of the necessity for awareness in a world filled with chaos and unpredictability. Heimdall stands as a symbol of hope, ensuring that even in the darkest times, there is someone watching over the realms, ready to act when danger approaches.

In the broader context of Norse mythology, Heimdall's origins reflect the intricate relationships between different beings and realms. His nine mothers, representing the ocean's various facets, underscore the idea that every entity within the cosmos is interconnected. This theme resonates with the Norse belief in fate and the cyclical nature of life, suggesting that Heimdall's existence is part of a greater tapestry woven by the Norns, the goddesses of fate. His birth marks not only the emergence of a guardian but also the unfolding of a narrative that intertwines the destinies of gods, giants, and humans alike.

Ultimately, the birth of Heimdall serves as a foundational myth that encapsulates key themes of vigilance, interconnection, and the guardianship of the cosmos. As young adults explore these stories, they can draw parallels to their own lives, recognizing the importance of being watchful and responsible stewards of their own realms. Heimdall stands as a reminder that everyone has a role to play in maintaining balance and harmony, whether in personal relationships or within the wider community. Understanding Heimdall's origin and purpose deepens the appreciation for the rich tapestry of Norse mythology and its timeless relevance.

## The Seven Mothers: A Unique Lineage

The Seven Mothers represent a unique and powerful lineage within the realm of Norse mythology, each embodying distinct qualities and attributes that contribute to the fabric of creation myths. These figures are not merely maternal archetypes; they are the guardians of life, wisdom, and fate, playing crucial roles in shaping the destinies of gods and mortals alike. In the context of Heimdall's watch over the realms, understanding the influence of the Seven Mothers provides insight into the interconnectedness of beings within the cosmos.

Each of the Seven Mothers possesses unique powers that reflect the various aspects of existence. They are often associated with essential elements such as earth, water, fire, and air, each element corresponding to the different realms they oversee. These mothers are seen as nurturers and protectors, guiding the growth and development of life across the Nine Realms. Their connection to creation myths indicates that they are integral to the cycles of birth and rebirth, illustrating the importance of balance in the universe.

As guardians, the Seven Mothers wield significant influence over the fates of all beings. Their blessings or curses can shape the paths of heroes and villains, impacting the larger narrative of the cosmos. This power serves as a reminder of the delicate interdependence of all life forms, reinforcing the idea that every action has consequences. Heimdall, as the vigilant watcher, plays a vital role in ensuring that the balance maintained by the Seven Mothers is not disrupted, highlighting his importance in the creation and preservation of the Nine Realms.

The stories of the Seven Mothers also emphasize the importance of unity and collaboration. Together, they form a network of support and guidance, each contributing to the overall harmony of their domain. Their interactions with one another and with other deities showcase the necessity of relationships and community in achieving a greater purpose. Heimdall embodies this principle as well, serving as a bridge between the realms and facilitating communication among the gods, further enhancing the cooperative spirit that the Seven Mothers represent.

In exploring the lineage of the Seven Mothers, one uncovers a rich tapestry of lore that underscores their significance in Norse creation myths. Their legacies resonate through time, reminding us that the past is woven into the present and future. As Heimdall stands watch over the Nine Realms, he not only protects the realms from chaos but also honors the profound influence of the Seven Mothers, ensuring that their stories continue to inspire generations to come.

## The Gifts Bestowed Upon Heimdall

Heimdall, the watchman of the gods, is a figure of immense significance in Norse mythology, often regarded for the unique gifts he possesses. These gifts, bestowed upon him by the Aesir, serve not only to enhance his abilities but also to underline his critical role in the pantheon. Among these gifts, his acute senses stand out prominently. Legends recount that Heimdall can hear the grass grow and see for an astounding distance, making him the ultimate sentinel. His extraordinary perception ensures that he remains vigilant against any threats to Asgard, the realm of the gods, and the other Nine Realms.

In addition to his heightened senses, Heimdall is endowed with a powerful horn known as Gjallarhorn. This horn is not merely a musical instrument; it serves as a signal of impending danger. When Heimdall blows Gjallarhorn, it reverberates across the realms, alerting both gods and mortals alike of the chaos that may be approaching. The sound of Gjallarhorn is said to be so loud that it can be heard in the farthest corners of the universe. This gift symbolizes Heimdall's role as a bridge between the divine and mortal worlds, showcasing his capacity to warn and protect.

Another remarkable gift given to Heimdall is his invulnerability. Unlike other gods, who may have weaknesses or vulnerabilities, Heimdall is described as being nearly impossible to defeat in battle. His strength and resilience ensure that he stands firm against any adversaries that threaten the peace of Asgard. This attribute emphasizes his role as a guardian and protector, reinforcing the idea that he is always ready to face challenges head-on. His invulnerability inspires confidence in the other gods, as they know that Heimdall will stand at the front lines when danger approaches.

Heimdall's gifts extend beyond physical abilities; he also possesses a deep understanding of the runes and the wisdom of the cosmos. This knowledge grants him insight into the fate of the worlds and the events that are to unfold. His connection to the runes allows him to perceive the underlying patterns of existence, making him a vital advisor to the gods. This wisdom is crucial as the gods navigate the complexities of their relationships with mortals and the other beings inhabiting the Nine Realms. Heimdall's insight helps maintain balance and harmony among the realms, affirming his importance in the broader tapestry of Norse mythology.

Finally, Heimdall's gifts reflect his unique position as a bridge between different worlds and beings. His role is not only to watch over the realms but also to facilitate communication and understanding among them. With each gift he possesses, Heimdall embodies the qualities of vigilance, strength, knowledge, and connection. These traits are essential in a world where chaos often threatens the delicate balance of existence. Through his gifts, Heimdall stands as a testament to the idea that guardianship is not merely about strength but also about wisdom and the ability to perceive the unseen. As the guardian of the Nine Realms, Heimdall's gifts illuminate his path and the paths of those he protects.

# Chapter 4: The Guardian of Bifrost

### Understanding Bifrost: The Rainbow Bridge

Bifrost, often referred to as the Rainbow Bridge, is a vital element in Norse mythology, serving as the connection between Midgard, the realm of humans, and Asgard, the home of the gods. This shimmering bridge is depicted as a vibrant arc of colors, resembling a rainbow, which symbolizes not only beauty but also the link between different worlds. The significance of Bifrost extends beyond its aesthetic; it represents the passage between the mortal realm and the divine, illustrating the interaction between humans and gods. As a structure forged from fire, water, and air, Bifrost embodies the idea of balance and harmony among the elements.

Heimdall, the ever-watchful guardian of Bifrost, plays a crucial role in maintaining the integrity of this bridge. Known for his keen senses and vigilance, Heimdall is tasked with overseeing the passage across Bifrost. He possesses extraordinary hearing and sight, allowing him to detect even the faintest sounds and the most distant lights. This heightened awareness is essential for his duty, as he must be prepared to warn the gods of any approaching threats, particularly during Ragnarök, the prophesied end of the world. His role as the guardian emphasizes the importance of vigilance and protection in the face of impending danger.

The construction of Bifrost is often attributed to the creativity and craftsmanship of the gods, reflecting their desire to establish a direct connection with humanity. This bridge illustrates the belief that the gods are not distant figures but are actively involved in the lives of mortals. The colors of Bifrost, which include red, blue, and green, may also symbolize the different aspects of life and the universe: passion, tranquility, and growth. In this way, Bifrost serves as a reminder that the divine and the earthly are intertwined, and that the gods are ever-present, watching over their creations.

In various myths, Bifrost serves as a passage for both gods and mortals, emphasizing its dual role in Norse cosmology. It is said that only the bravest and most worthy can traverse the bridge without fear of falling into the abyss. This aspect of Bifrost represents the trials and tribulations individuals must face in their journey through life. The bridge also underscores the idea of destiny, suggesting that every being has a path to follow, and that the gods play a pivotal role in guiding those journeys.

Understanding Bifrost and Heimdall's role as its guardian enriches our appreciation of Norse mythology. Their stories remind us of the connections we share with others, the importance of vigilance, and the interplay between fate and free will. As we explore these myths, we gain insight into the values and beliefs of the Norse people, particularly their views on the divine and the human experience. Through Heimdall's watchful eye over Bifrost, we learn that the journey between realms is not just a physical passage but also a spiritual one, filled with lessons and opportunities for growth.

## Heimdall's Role as the Watcher

Heimdall, known as the Watcher, holds a crucial position in Norse mythology, serving as the guardian of Bifröst, the rainbow bridge that connects the realms of gods and humans. His role is not merely that of a gatekeeper but also of a vigilant sentinel, tasked with observing the movements and actions of all beings across the nine realms. With keen eyesight that allows him to see great distances and acute hearing that enables him to hear the grass grow, Heimdall exemplifies the idea of vigilance and protection. This heightened awareness makes him an essential figure in safeguarding the realms from various threats, including the impending chaos of Ragnarok.

As the Watcher, Heimdall embodies the principles of foresight and preparedness. He is often portrayed as a figure of light and clarity, representing the need for constant vigilance in a world filled with uncertainty. His role extends beyond mere observation; he actively engages in sounding the Gjallarhorn, a powerful horn that signals the arrival of danger. This act is pivotal in alerting the gods to the onset of Ragnarok, thus emphasizing his responsibility in maintaining the balance between order and chaos. Through this, Heimdall highlights the importance of being aware of one's surroundings and the potential consequences of inaction.

Heimdall's lineage further emphasizes his significance in Norse creation myths. Born of nine mothers, each a personification of the sea, his origins underscore the connection between the elemental forces and the duty of guardianship. This unique heritage grants him the ability to traverse the boundaries between realms effortlessly, reinforcing his role as a mediator and protector. The symbolism of water in his birth also suggests a deep-rooted connection to life and purity, which he must uphold as he stands watch over the realms. His lineage reflects the intertwined nature of existence, where every entity plays a role in the cosmic order.

In addition to his duties as the Watcher, Heimdall serves as a bridge between the gods and humanity. His awareness of the happenings in Midgard, the realm of humans, allows him to intervene when necessary. This connection signifies the importance of understanding and cooperation between the divine and mortal worlds. Heimdall's presence in both realms illustrates the idea that the guardianship of the universe is a shared responsibility. His ability to see and hear all reminds us that every action has consequences, urging both gods and humans to act with integrity and foresight.

Ultimately, Heimdall's role as the Watcher encapsulates the themes of vigilance, protection, and interconnectedness that are central to Norse creation myths. Through his unwavering watch over the nine realms, he embodies the qualities necessary to prevent chaos and maintain harmony. His character teaches young adults about the importance of being aware of their surroundings, understanding the implications of their actions, and recognizing the bonds that connect all beings. In a world that often feels tumultuous, Heimdall stands as a symbol of hope and readiness, reminding us of the power of observation and the necessity of guardianship in our own lives.

## The Significance of His Horn, Gjallarhorn

Gjallarhorn, the legendary horn of Heimdall, holds profound significance within Norse mythology, particularly in relation to the creation myths and the role of the gods. As the guardian of the Bifrost, the rainbow bridge connecting the realms, Heimdall is tasked with watching over the cosmos and protecting it from impending threats. Gjallarhorn serves as both a symbol of his vigilance and a tool for communication across the realms. When blown, it emits a sound so powerful that it can be heard in all nine realms, signaling the onset of significant events, including the approach of Ragnarök, the end of the world.

The horn's name itself, Gjallarhorn, translates to "the ringing horn," which reflects its purpose of alerting the gods and inhabitants of the realms to danger. In the context of creation myths, this signifies the transition from calm to chaos. Heimdall, with his acute senses, stands as a central figure responsible for maintaining order. The sound of Gjallarhorn is associated with the awakening of the gods and their preparation for battle, thus reinforcing Heimdall's role as a harbinger of crucial moments in Norse lore.

Moreover, Gjallarhorn embodies the concept of communication in the Norse universe. It connects the divine with the mortal, emphasizing the interconnectedness of all beings. When Heimdall sounds the horn, it serves as a reminder of the impending challenges faced by the gods and humanity alike. This act symbolizes the call to unity among the realms, urging the gods to come together in defense against the forces of chaos. In this way, Gjallarhorn transcends its physical form, becoming a metaphor for the necessity of collaboration and awareness in times of crisis.

The horn's significance extends beyond mere alertness; it also signifies the cyclical nature of time and existence in Norse mythology. The sounding of Gjallarhorn marks not only the approach of Ragnarök but also the rebirth that follows. In this context, Heimdall's role as a guardian is not just to defend but to oversee the continuous cycle of destruction and renewal, reflecting the belief in an eternal, unending cycle of life. This aspect of Gjallarhorn highlights the idea that endings are often necessary for new beginnings, a theme prevalent in many creation myths.

In conclusion, Gjallarhorn is much more than a simple horn; it is a powerful symbol of Heimdall's unwavering vigilance and the interconnectedness of the nine realms. Its significance lies in its ability to herald important events, unite the gods and mortals, and represent the cyclical nature of existence. Through the lens of Gjallarhorn, readers can appreciate the intricate tapestry of Norse mythology and the vital role Heimdall plays in maintaining the balance between order and chaos. Understanding the implications of this legendary horn deepens one's insight into the creation myths and the enduring legacy of the gods in Norse tradition.

# Chapter 5: The Role of Heimdall in the Aesir-Vanir Conflict

## The Prelude to War: Tensions Between the Two Clans

In the ancient world of Norse mythology, the balance between the realms was often threatened by the conflicts between powerful clans. The two most prominent clans, the Aesir and the Vanir, were locked in a struggle for supremacy that would ultimately lead to war. This conflict was rooted in deep-seated differences in their beliefs, values, and approaches to life. As guardians of different aspects of creation, the Aesir represented order and civilization, while the Vanir embodied nature and fertility. Their contrasting philosophies set the stage for a tumultuous relationship that would challenge the stability of the Nine Realms.

Tensions began to escalate when the Vanir, feeling slighted by the Aesir's dominance in matters of governance and power, sought to assert their influence. They believed that their connection to the earth and the cycles of life gave them rightful claim to a more significant role in the creation and sustenance of the realms. The Aesir, perceiving this as a direct challenge to their authority, responded with hostility. Small skirmishes broke out, fueled by misunderstandings and the pride of both clans. Each side believed they were the rightful rulers, leading to a series of confrontations that would only serve to deepen the divide.

The situation grew increasingly precarious when the Aesir captured one of the Vanir's most revered deities, Njord, along with his children, Freyr and Freyja. This act was intended to demonstrate Aesir superiority but backfired spectacularly. Instead of quelling the Vanir's ambitions, it ignited their fury, uniting them in a common cause against their captors. As the Vanir rallied their forces, they began to prepare for a more significant conflict, determined to rescue their kin and restore balance in their favor. The cries for war echoed across the realms, creating an atmosphere thick with anticipation and dread.

In response to the brewing storm, Heimdall, the watchful guardian of the Bifrost Bridge, recognized the looming danger that threatened to engulf both clans. Known for his keen foresight and ability to perceive the threads of fate, Heimdall sought to mediate the rising tensions. He understood that the fallout from a full-scale war could unravel the very fabric of creation. Gathering representatives from both clans, Heimdall urged them to consider the consequences of their actions. His wisdom and insights, however, were met with skepticism, as pride impeded rational discourse.

As the drums of war began to sound louder, the stage was set for a confrontation that would reshape the fate of the Nine Realms. Each clan prepared their warriors and strategized their next moves, unaware that the conflict between them would not only lead to destruction but also pave the way for unforeseen alliances and transformations. The Prelude to War was not just a chapter of aggression; it was a pivotal moment that would reveal the true nature of power, sacrifice, and the interconnectedness of all beings in the cosmos, themes that resonate deeply within the heart of Norse creation myths.

## Heimdall's Involvement in Peace Negotiations

Heimdall, known as the watchman of the gods, plays an intriguing role in the peace negotiations among the realms in Norse mythology. His keen sense of sight and hearing, able to detect the slightest disturbances across vast distances, positions him as an ideal mediator. As tensions rise between the Aesir and the Vanir, two powerful groups of gods, Heimdall's involvement becomes pivotal. He serves not only as a guardian but also as a facilitator, utilizing his unique abilities to gather intelligence and foster understanding between the conflicting parties.

During the initial stages of the conflict, misunderstandings and mistrust fueled animosity between the Aesir and the Vanir. Heimdall recognized that the only path to a lasting peace lay in addressing these misconceptions directly. He took it upon himself to observe both factions closely, listening to grievances and aspirations. By doing so, Heimdall gained insights into the fundamental differences that drove the two groups apart, including their distinct values and approaches to governance. This knowledge would later prove invaluable in his role as a negotiator.

When the time came for formal discussions, Heimdall's presence ensured that both sides felt secure in the process. He established a neutral ground, a sacred space where the Aesir and the Vanir could gather without fear of aggression. His reputation as a fair and impartial figure allowed the parties to engage openly. Heimdall's ability to remain calm under pressure and his commitment to fairness helped reduce the tension in the room, allowing for constructive dialogue rather than heated debates.

As the negotiations unfolded, Heimdall utilized his extensive understanding of the cultures involved to suggest compromises that would satisfy both groups. He proposed the exchange of hostages, a common practice in ancient times, which was aimed at building trust. By suggesting that each side send representatives to the other, Heimdall sought to create bonds that went beyond mere agreements. This strategy not only facilitated the peace process but also laid the groundwork for future cooperation and mutual respect between the realms.

Ultimately, Heimdall's involvement in the peace negotiations was a testament to his role as a guardian and mediator. His dedication to fostering understanding and collaboration among the Aesir and the Vanir exemplifies the importance of communication in resolving conflicts. Through his efforts, not only were the immediate tensions alleviated, but a framework was established for ongoing dialogue, ensuring that the realms would remain interconnected and peaceful for generations to come. Heimdall's legacy as a peacekeeper continues to resonate, reminding us of the power of diplomacy and the value of listening in the face of division.

## The Aftermath and Unity of the Gods

The aftermath of the cataclysmic events that unfolded during the Ragnarok brought forth a new era for the gods of Asgard. As the dust settled and the ashes of the old world began to clear, a sense of unity emerged among the surviving deities. This unprecedented collaboration was essential, as the gods needed to rebuild not only their homes but also their relationships with one another. The trials of Ragnarok had tested their alliances, exposing weaknesses and rivalries that had long simmered beneath the surface. In the wake of destruction, the gods recognized the importance of solidarity, uniting their strengths to create a harmonious existence in the newly reborn realms.

Heimdall, the vigilant guardian of the Bifröst, played a pivotal role in this rebirth. His keen sense of duty and unwavering watchfulness were crucial during the tumultuous times following Ragnarok. As the gods began to emerge from the chaos, Heimdall took it upon himself to ensure their safety and the stability of the realms. He rallied the gods, emphasizing the need for cooperation and mutual respect in their efforts to restore balance. His wisdom and foresight proved invaluable as they navigated the complexities of rebuilding their society while facing the lingering threats from the remnants of their former enemies.

The process of re-establishing unity among the gods was not without challenges. Old grudges and rivalries resurfaced, threatening to undermine their newfound collaboration. However, Heimdall's role as a mediator became increasingly significant. He encouraged the gods to reflect on the lessons learned from their previous conflicts and to focus on their shared objectives. By fostering open communication and understanding, Heimdall helped to bridge the divides that had once separated them, transforming animosity into a collective vision for the future of the Nine Realms.

As the gods worked together, they also recognized the value of their diverse strengths and perspectives. Each deity brought unique abilities and insights to the table, and Heimdall's guidance helped them appreciate the importance of collaboration. The creation of new alliances and partnerships among the gods symbolized a shift away from isolationism toward a more inclusive approach to governance. This newfound unity not only strengthened their resolve but also inspired the inhabitants of the Nine Realms, who witnessed the harmony among the gods and felt encouraged to embrace cooperation in their own communities.

In the end, the aftermath of Ragnarok served as a powerful reminder of the resilience of the gods and the strength found in unity. Heimdall's leadership and unwavering commitment to safeguarding the realms allowed the gods to emerge from the ashes of their past and forge a brighter future together. As they rebuilt their world, they instilled in their followers the importance of working together, regardless of differences, to create a more harmonious existence. The legacy of Heimdall as the guardian of the Nine Realms would forever stand as a testament to the enduring power of unity in the face of adversity.

# Chapter 6: Prophecies and Omens

## The Importance of Prophecy in Norse Culture

In Norse culture, prophecy holds a significant place, shaping both the worldview and the moral framework of its people. The ancient Norse believed that the future was not entirely predetermined, but rather influenced by the actions of gods and mortals alike. This interplay between fate and free will is vividly illustrated in various myths, where prophecies serve as a guiding force, often driving characters to fulfill or defy their foretold destinies. Such narratives highlight the importance of foresight and wisdom in navigating the complexities of life, emphasizing that knowledge of the future can be both a gift and a burden.

One of the most compelling aspects of Norse prophecy is its connection to the concept of fate, represented by the three Norns—Urd, Verdandi, and Skuld—who weave the destinies of individuals. This trio of female figures embodies the past, present, and future, suggesting that understanding one's fate is essential for making informed choices. Within this context, prophecies serve as a critical reminder that while individuals may strive to change their fates, they must also acknowledge the larger cosmic order. This duality encourages a sense of responsibility, as individuals grapple with the consequences of their actions in the grand tapestry of existence.

Heimdall, the watchman of the gods, plays a pivotal role in the transmission of prophecy in Norse mythology. Known for his keen sight and hearing, Heimdall is often depicted as a guardian who stands at the threshold between different realms. His ability to see into the future allows him to anticipate events, particularly the catastrophic battle of Ragnarök. This foresight positions him as a vital figure in the preservation of knowledge and the protection of divine order. By serving as a bridge between the known and the unknown, Heimdall embodies the significance of prophecy as both a warning and a guide for the gods and humanity alike.

The stories of figures like Odin, who often seeks out prophecies to gain wisdom, further illustrate the value placed on foresight in Norse culture. Odin's relentless pursuit of knowledge leads him to sacrifice much, including his own eye, to gain insight into the fates of both gods and men. This theme of sacrifice for knowledge underscores the idea that understanding the future, even at great personal cost, is vital for leaders and warriors. In a world filled with uncertainty, the ability to foresee potential outcomes allows individuals to prepare for challenges and make choices that align with their values and goals.

Ultimately, the importance of prophecy in Norse culture is rooted in its ability to inspire action and foster a sense of purpose. While prophecies may outline a predetermined path, they also empower individuals to confront their destinies head-on. The narratives surrounding Heimdall and other prophetic figures encourage young adults to consider their roles within the larger narrative of existence. By embracing the lessons of prophecy, they can cultivate wisdom, make informed decisions, and actively participate in shaping their own fates, much like the heroes and deities of their ancient lore.

## Heimdall's Prophetic Abilities

Heimdall, the vigilant guardian of the Bifrost Bridge, is not only known for his role as a sentry but also for his remarkable prophetic abilities. In Norse mythology, prophecy plays a crucial role in shaping the destinies of gods and mortals alike. Heimdall possesses a unique insight that allows him to foresee events that will come to pass, making him a vital figure in the lore surrounding the creation myths of the Nine Realms. His foresight is often linked to the concept of fate, which is central to Norse beliefs, where the actions of individuals can be influenced by the knowledge of future events.

One of the key aspects of Heimdall's prophetic abilities is his connection to the Nine Realms. As the guardian of the Bifrost, he oversees the bridge that connects these realms, granting him a vantage point from which he can observe the unfolding of events across the cosmos. This position not only allows him to protect the realms from threats but also to gain insights into the future. His ability to see and hear far beyond the ordinary limits of a mortal makes him a figure of immense power and knowledge. In many stories, he is depicted as being able to hear the grass grow and see for hundreds of miles, further emphasizing his extraordinary senses that contribute to his prophetic skills.

Heimdall's prophecies often serve as warnings to the gods and other beings within the Norse cosmos. For instance, he is known to have foreseen the events of Ragnarök, the cataclysmic battle that will result in the death of many gods and the reshaping of the world. His warnings about the impending doom illustrate the burden of knowledge he carries; while he knows what fate has in store, his role as a guardian compels him to prepare others for the inevitable. This theme of foreknowledge and the moral dilemmas it presents resonates deeply within Norse creation myths, highlighting the tension between fate and free will.

The significance of Heimdall's prophetic abilities can also be understood through his interactions with other gods. He often serves as a mediator, conveying vital information that can alter the course of events. For example, his warnings to Odin and the other gods about threats to the realms demonstrate his role not just as a guardian but as a crucial advisor. These interactions emphasize the collaborative nature of the Norse pantheon, where knowledge and foresight are shared among the gods to navigate the complexities of their existence.

In conclusion, Heimdall's prophetic abilities are intertwined with his identity as the guardian of the Nine Realms. His foresight not only highlights the importance of vigilance and preparation but also raises questions about the nature of fate and destiny. As a character deeply embedded in the Norse creation myths, Heimdall embodies the paradox of knowledge—while he can see the future, he must grapple with the implications of that knowledge. This duality makes him a compelling figure in Norse mythology, as he stands at the intersection of prophecy, protection, and the inexorable flow of fate.

# The Predictions of Ragnarök

The predictions of Ragnarök are a central theme in Norse mythology, marking the end of the world as foretold in ancient texts. This cataclysmic event is characterized by a series of devastating occurrences, including natural disasters, fierce battles, and the death of several major gods. The prophecies surrounding Ragnarök highlight the inevitability of fate and the cyclical nature of existence in Norse cosmology. Understanding these predictions provides crucial insights into the beliefs and values of the Norse people, as well as the role of key figures like Heimdall.

Heimdall, the watchman of the gods, is intricately linked to the events of Ragnarök. Known for his exceptional eyesight and hearing, he stands guard at the Bifröst, the rainbow bridge connecting the realms of gods and humans. As Ragnarök approaches, Heimdall is foretold to blow his horn, Gjallarhorn, signaling the onset of the final battle. This act not only marks the beginning of the end but also underscores Heimdall's pivotal role as a protector of the cosmos. His vigilance is essential, as the forces of chaos, led by the monstrous Fenrir and the fire giant Surtr, threaten to engulf the nine realms.

The predictions outline a series of battles that will unfold during Ragnarök, involving gods like Odin, Thor, and Loki. Heimdall is prophesied to confront Loki in a fierce struggle, emphasizing the personal stakes involved in this cosmic conflict. The clash between these two figures represents the broader themes of loyalty, betrayal, and the inevitable clash between order and chaos. As the guardian of the realms, Heimdall embodies the hope of the gods, standing firm against the tide of destruction that threatens to unravel the fabric of existence.

In the aftermath of Ragnarök, the world is said to be reborn, a theme that resonates deeply in Norse mythology. The predictions suggest that after the destruction, a new and fertile land will emerge, populated by a few surviving gods and righteous humans. This cyclical view of creation and destruction reflects the Norse understanding of life as a series of cycles rather than a linear progression. Heimdall's role in this rebirth is significant, as his actions during the final battle ensure a continuation of life and the promise of renewal.

The predictions of Ragnarök serve as a powerful reminder of the interconnectedness of all beings within Norse mythology. Heimdall's unwavering vigilance and bravery illustrate the importance of guardianship in maintaining balance within the cosmos. As young adults explore these myths, they can draw parallels to their own lives, understanding the significance of standing firm in the face of adversity and embracing the cycles of change. The stories of Ragnarök, with Heimdall at the forefront, encourage a deeper appreciation for the struggles and triumphs that shape the world, both in myth and reality.

# Chapter 7: Heimdall and the Guardianship of the Realms

## His Role in Protecting Midgard

Heimdall, known as the ever-watchful guardian of the Bifröst, plays a crucial role in the protection of Midgard, the realm of humans in Norse mythology. His vigilance and foresight set him apart as a key figure in the pantheon of gods. Born of nine mothers, Heimdall possesses extraordinary abilities, including acute hearing and sight, which enable him to detect threats from great distances. This unique combination of traits positions him as the primary defender against the forces that seek to disrupt the balance of the Nine Realms, particularly Midgard.

As the sentinel of the Bifröst, Heimdall's responsibilities extend beyond mere observation. He is tasked with monitoring all that occurs in the realm of humans and the impending dangers posed by the giants and other malevolent beings. His horn, Gjallarhorn, is not just a tool for communication; it serves as a warning system. When he blows the horn, its sound resonates throughout the Nine Realms, alerting the gods and the inhabitants of Midgard to imminent threats. This proactive approach to guarding the realms underscores his commitment to preserving the safety and integrity of human life.

Heimdall's role also encompasses a deep connection with the inhabitants of Midgard. He is not merely a passive observer; he engages with humanity, offering guidance and protection when necessary. His influence is felt in various aspects of life, from instilling courage in warriors to safeguarding the realms against the forces of chaos. While the gods often intervene directly in human affairs, Heimdall's approach is more subtle, fostering a sense of resilience among the people of Midgard. His presence imbues them with the understanding that they are watched over, providing a sense of security in a world fraught with peril.

The significance of Heimdall's role in protecting Midgard is further emphasized during the events leading to Ragnarök, the prophesied end of the world. As threats escalate, Heimdall's vigilance becomes more critical than ever. He stands ready to defend against the giants and other monstrous beings that emerge from the shadows. His loyalty and bravery are pivotal in the final battles, where he not only protects the realms but also fights alongside other gods. This ultimate confrontation highlights his unwavering dedication to Midgard and the sacrifices he is willing to make for its preservation.

In conclusion, Heimdall's role in protecting Midgard is multifaceted and integral to the fabric of Norse mythology. His watchfulness, proactive defense strategies, and deep connection to humanity illustrate the importance of guardianship in maintaining balance across the Nine Realms. As a protector, he embodies the ideals of vigilance and courage, serving as a symbol of hope for those who dwell in Midgard. Through his actions and sacrifices, Heimdall reinforces the notion that even in the face of overwhelming darkness, there is always a guardian ready to stand watch.

## The Relationship with Humans

Heimdall, known as the watchman of the gods in Norse mythology, occupies a unique position in the pantheon due to his intricate relationship with humanity. As the guardian of the Bifrost, the rainbow bridge connecting the realms, Heimdall serves not only as a protector of the gods but also as a bridge between the divine and the mortal. His role emphasizes the interconnectedness of all beings in the Norse cosmos, highlighting that even the mightiest gods are bound to the fate and actions of humans. This relationship underscores the belief that human deeds can influence the broader tapestry of existence, resonating through the realms.

The significance of Heimdall's connection to humans is rooted in his keen observation and vigilance. With his acute senses, he can hear grass growing and see for hundreds of miles, symbolizing an omnipresent awareness. This ability reflects the idea that the divine is always watching over humanity, suggesting a protective force that is attentive to both the good and the ill deeds of mortals. In this way, Heimdall embodies the moral compass of the universe, urging humans to strive for honor and virtue, as their actions ultimately resonate in the greater scheme of existence.

Moreover, Heimdall's relationship with humans serves as a reminder of the responsibilities that come with free will. In Norse creation myths, the gods often intervene in human affairs, influenced by the choices made by mortals. Heimdall's role as the guardian of the Bifrost reinforces the idea that while humans possess the freedom to act, their decisions carry weight. This connection between human action and divine consequence encourages young adults to reflect on their own choices and the potential impact they may have on the world around them.

In addition to his protective and observant nature, Heimdall also symbolizes the potential for cooperation between gods and humans. While the gods possess great power, they rely on the loyalty and bravery of humans to aid them in times of need. This mutual dependence fosters a sense of community, suggesting that both realms are intertwined in their struggles and triumphs. Through this lens, young adults can appreciate the importance of teamwork and collective effort, emphasizing that collaboration can lead to greater achievements.

Ultimately, Heimdall's relationship with humans in Norse mythology serves as a profound reminder of the interconnectedness of all beings. His vigilant watch over the realms illustrates the balance between divine oversight and human agency, urging individuals to act with purpose and integrity. As young adults navigate their own paths, the lessons drawn from Heimdall's role encourage a deeper understanding of their place in the world, inspiring them to honor the ties that bind them to both the divine and their fellow beings.

## The Defense Against Threats from Giants

The giants, known as Jotnar in Norse mythology, are formidable beings that pose significant threats to the realms of gods and men alike. Their immense size and strength enable them to wreak havoc, challenging the order established by the Aesir and Vanir. In the context of Heimdall, the vigilant guardian of the Bifröst Bridge, the defense against threats from giants becomes a crucial aspect of his role. Heimdall's keen senses and sharp intellect are essential in detecting the approach of these colossal adversaries, allowing the gods to prepare for potential conflicts.

Heimdall's primary defense mechanism against the giants lies in his ability to see and hear across vast distances. He is said to possess eyesight that can pierce the darkest night and hear the grass growing on the earth. This remarkable power enables him to spot approaching giants long before they reach Asgard, giving the gods ample time to strategize and organize their defenses. His vigilance ensures that he can sound the Gjallarhorn, a powerful horn that alerts the gods to impending danger, summoning them to prepare for battle. This element of surprise is critical in thwarting the giants' plans.

In addition to vigilance, Heimdall embodies the virtues of wisdom and foresight. He understands that brute force is not always the answer to the threats posed by giants. Instead, he employs cunning and strategy to outsmart them. The myths often depict Heimdall engaging in clever tactics to divert or outmaneuver giants, illustrating that intelligence can be just as powerful as strength. By using his innate knowledge of the giants' weaknesses and tendencies, Heimdall crafts defensive strategies that minimize conflict while safeguarding the realms.

Collaboration among the gods is another essential aspect of defending against giants. Heimdall possesses the unique ability to unify the Aesir and Vanir by fostering alliances and encouraging teamwork. In times of crisis, he calls upon the strengths of other gods such as Thor, the god of thunder, whose might is legendary, and Freyja, whose magic can influence the outcomes of battles. Together, they form a formidable force against the giants, demonstrating the importance of unity in overcoming great challenges. Through collaboration, Heimdall ensures a multifaceted approach to defense that leverages the unique abilities of each deity.

Ultimately, Heimdall serves not only as a guardian but also as a symbol of resilience and readiness. His commitment to safeguarding the realms reflects the broader themes of protection and vigilance found within Norse mythology. By embodying the principles of alertness, wisdom, and collaboration, he teaches young adults the significance of being prepared for threats, no matter their form. As these lessons resonate, they inspire a generation to confront their own challenges with the same steadfastness that Heimdall displays in the face of the giants, ensuring the continued balance of the Nine Realms.

# Chapter 8: The Final Battle: Ragnarök

## The Events Leading Up to Ragnarök

The events leading up to Ragnarök, the prophesied end of the world in Norse mythology, are intricately woven into the fabric of the cosmos and the lives of the gods. Central to these events is the character of Heimdall, the watchman of the Bifröst, the rainbow bridge connecting Asgard to the other realms. As the guardian, Heimdall possesses keen foresight and awareness of the impending doom that looms over the Nine Realms. His role is crucial, for he is not only tasked with safeguarding the gods but also with preparing them for the cataclysmic battles to come.

One of the primary catalysts for the events leading to Ragnarok is the growing tension between the gods and the giants, particularly the Jotnar. The giants, ancient beings representing chaos and destruction, begin to stir, fueled by the death of the god Baldr, which serves as a significant turning point. Baldr's death, brought about by the treachery of Loki, sets off a chain reaction of grief and vengeance among the gods. Heimdall, with his acute senses, perceives the shifting tides of fate and understands the implications of these events. He prepares himself and his fellow gods for the inevitable confrontation with the forces of chaos.

As the prophecy unfolds, the world experiences a series of ominous signs. The Fimbulwinter, a great winter lasting three years, engulfs the earth, signaling the approach of Ragnarök. This harsh winter leads to widespread despair, turning brother against brother and fostering an environment ripe for conflict. Heimdall, ever vigilant, watches as morality declines and the bonds of kinship are shattered. He recognizes these events as part of the larger tapestry leading to the final battle, reminding the gods to unite and strengthen their resolve against the chaos that threatens their existence.

In addition to the natural disasters and societal breakdown, the role of Loki becomes increasingly significant. After being imprisoned for his role in Baldr's death, Loki breaks free, rallying the giants and other monsters to join him in the assault against the gods. Heimdall knows that Loki's cunning and deceit will play a pivotal role in the unfolding conflict. As the guardian of the Bifröst, Heimdall prepares to sound his horn, Gjallarhorn, to summon the gods when the time comes, ensuring they are ready to face the impending onslaught.

The culmination of these events leads to the climactic battle during Ragnarök, where gods, giants, and various creatures clash in a struggle for dominance over the realms. Heimdall's unwavering vigilance and foresight make him an essential figure in the battle, as he stands ready to defend Asgard and the cosmos. The unfolding of these events highlights Heimdall's importance not just as a guardian, but as a harbinger of fate, demonstrating how his role is intertwined with the very essence of creation myths in Norse tradition. As the Nine Realms brace for the cataclysm, Heimdall embodies the resilience and hope that even in the face of chaos, the legacy of the gods will endure.

# Heimdall's Stand Against Loki

Heimdall, the vigilant guardian of the Bifrost, stood as a bastion of light against the encroaching darkness brought forth by Loki, the trickster god. In Norse mythology, Heimdall is often depicted as the ever-watchful protector, tasked with safeguarding the realms from threats both external and internal. His role becomes particularly crucial when faced with Loki's cunning and deceitful nature. The tension between these two figures symbolizes the struggle between order and chaos, a recurring theme in Norse creation myths.

The conflict between Heimdall and Loki escalates during Ragnarok, the prophesied end of the world. Heimdall, endowed with extraordinary senses and foresight, is acutely aware of Loki's intentions. He knows that Loki, having been bound by the gods for his treachery, will eventually break free and lead an army of giants and monsters against Asgard. Heimdall's unwavering vigilance is not merely a duty but a vital necessity to prepare for this impending doom. His foresight enables him to strategize and rally the other gods, ensuring they remain ready to confront Loki's formidable forces.

Their clash is not simply a physical confrontation but also a battle of wits. Heimdall, representing order, uses his wisdom and insight to anticipate Loki's moves. In contrast, Loki's unpredictable and manipulative nature poses a unique challenge. He employs trickery, attempting to sow discord among the gods and undermine Heimdall's authority. This psychological warfare highlights the complexity of their relationship, as both are essential figures in the cosmic order, yet their motivations often place them at odds with one another.

As the events of Ragnarok unfold, Heimdall and Loki ultimately confront each other at the edge of the Bifrost. This final showdown is not just a fight for survival but a representation of the eternal struggle between good and evil. Heimdall, wielding his horn Gjallarhorn, blows a warning to all realms, signaling the onset of the cataclysmic battle. Their clash is fierce, each embodying the attributes of their respective roles—Heimdall's strength and vigilance against Loki's guile and chaos. This moment encapsulates the culmination of their rivalry, illustrating the deep-rooted themes of conflict inherent in the myths.

In the aftermath of their confrontation, Heimdall and Loki's fates are intertwined in a poignant manner. Both meet their end during Ragnarok, a testament to the inevitability of change and the cyclical nature of existence in Norse cosmology. Heimdall's sacrifice serves as a reminder of the importance of vigilance and duty, while Loki's demise signifies the consequences of chaos and betrayal. Their stand against each other reinforces the notion that even the most formidable forces of good and evil are destined to clash, shaping the narrative of creation and destruction within the Nine Realms.

# The Aftermath of the Battle

The aftermath of the battle marked a significant turning point in the narrative of Heimdall's role within Norse creation myths. As the dust settled and the echoes of clashing weapons faded into silence, the Nine Realms bore witness to the consequences of the conflict. The once vibrant landscapes were now scarred, a poignant reminder of the struggle between light and darkness. In this new reality, the balance of power shifted, and the guardianship of Heimdall took on an even more critical dimension. His vigilance became essential, as threats from the shadows loomed ever closer, seeking to exploit the chaos left in the wake of battle.

Heimdall, known as the ever-watchful guardian of the Bifrost, stood at the precipice of a new era. The destruction wrought by the battle was not merely physical; it also created rifts among the realms. Alliances that once flourished were now strained, and trust was a luxury few could afford. In this delicate landscape, Heimdall's role transformed from mere observer to active protector. As he surveyed the remnants of the battlefield, he understood that his duty was to mend the fractures caused by conflict, to restore harmony among the realms, and to prepare for the inevitable threats that would seek to capitalize on this vulnerability.

The psychological impact on the inhabitants of the Nine Realms was profound. The battle served as a stark reminder of mortality and the fragility of peace. Fear and uncertainty permeated through the lands, creating a sense of urgency for Heimdall. He recognized that the physical scars would heal over time, but the emotional wounds might linger indefinitely. As a guardian, his mission extended beyond mere protection; it encompassed the healing of those affected by the turmoil. Heimdall began to engage with the people of the realms, listening to their fears and hopes, and fostering a collective spirit of resilience.

In the wake of the battle, Heimdall also faced challenges from within. The very essence of his role was questioned by some who believed that the guardianship system had failed to prevent the conflict. This internal dissent required Heimdall to reaffirm his commitment to his duties and to inspire confidence among the beings he protected. He organized gatherings where the leaders of the realms could come together to discuss their grievances and desires for a brighter future. Through these dialogues, Heimdall endeavored to bridge the gaps that had formed and to remind all that unity was the key to overcoming adversity.

Ultimately, the aftermath of the battle served as a crucible for Heimdall, shaping him into an even more formidable guardian. His experiences during this tumultuous time deepened his understanding of the complexities of loyalty, sacrifice, and the weight of responsibility. As he continued to stand sentinel at the Bifrost, he became a symbol of hope and resilience for the Nine Realms. The lessons learned from the conflict would guide his actions in the future, ensuring that he remained a steadfast protector against whatever darkness lay ahead. In this way, the aftermath of the battle not only defined the present but also illuminated the path for the realms' future.

# Chapter 9: Legacy of Heimdall

## Heimdall in Modern Culture

Heimdall, the enigmatic guardian of the Bifröst, has transcended his origins in Norse mythology to become a significant figure in modern culture. With his keen senses and unwavering vigilance, he has captured the imagination of writers, filmmakers, and artists alike. The portrayal of Heimdall in contemporary media often reflects themes of guardianship and the importance of vigilance in a chaotic world. These interpretations not only preserve his mythological roots but also adapt his character for new narratives that resonate with today's audience.

In recent years, Heimdall has appeared in various forms of entertainment, most notably in the Marvel Cinematic Universe. Portrayed by Idris Elba, this modern depiction emphasizes Heimdall's role as a protector, showcasing his extraordinary abilities and his pivotal position at the gateway to Asgard. The films highlight his loyalty and strength, emphasizing the character's commitment to safeguarding the realms from threats. This representation introduces Heimdall to a younger audience, making him a relatable figure who embodies courage, responsibility, and the fight against injustice.

Literature has also embraced Heimdall, with numerous novels and series drawing inspiration from Norse mythology. Authors often weave Heimdall into their narratives as a symbol of resilience and watchfulness. In these stories, he frequently serves as a mentor or guide, helping protagonists navigate their journeys and confront their fears. This modern literary portrayal reinforces the idea that vigilance, much like Heimdall's own watch over the Bifröst, is essential for overcoming obstacles in life.

Video games have further expanded Heimdall's presence in popular culture, allowing players to engage with his character in interactive ways. Games set in mythological worlds often feature Heimdall as a formidable guardian, challenging players to prove their worthiness. This interactive representation not only deepens the connection players have with the character but also encourages them to embody qualities such as bravery and perseverance, mirroring the lessons found in the original myths.

The resurgence of interest in Norse mythology, fueled by various media, has sparked discussions about the relevance of figures like Heimdall in contemporary society. As young adults seek meaningful narratives, Heimdall stands as a symbol of vigilance and protection, reminding them of the importance of being watchful in their own lives. By engaging with Heimdall's character across different platforms, today's youth can explore themes of duty, sacrifice, and the fight against chaos, making ancient myths relevant and inspiring in the modern world.

# The Continued Fascination with Norse Mythology

The fascination with Norse mythology has endured for centuries, captivating audiences with its rich tapestry of gods, giants, and mystical realms. Central to this mythology is Heimdall, the vigilant guardian of Bifrost, the rainbow bridge connecting the realms of gods and mortals. His role in creation myths not only highlights the significance of protection and vigilance but also reflects the values and beliefs of the Norse culture. As young adults explore these ancient tales, they find themes of heroism, sacrifice, and the search for identity that resonate deeply in contemporary society.

Heimdall's character embodies the essence of watchfulness, a trait that is increasingly relevant in today's fast-paced world. As the watchman of the gods, Heimdall possesses keen senses and unparalleled awareness, allowing him to perceive threats even from great distances. This characteristic serves as a metaphor for the importance of being attuned to one's surroundings and the responsibilities that come with guardianship. Young adults may see themselves in Heimdall's role, grappling with their own responsibilities and the need to be vigilant against the challenges they face as they navigate adulthood.

Moreover, Heimdall's involvement in the creation myths underscores the interconnectedness of all beings within Norse cosmology. He is said to have played a crucial role in the events leading to the formation of the world, bridging the gap between gods and humans. This connection emphasizes the idea that every action has consequences, a lesson that resonates with young adults who are beginning to understand the impact of their choices on themselves and others. The exploration of Heimdall's role encourages a deeper appreciation for the complexities of relationships and the importance of community.

The revival of interest in Norse mythology, fueled by literature, films, and video games, illustrates the timeless appeal of these stories. Characters like Heimdall are often reimagined in modern narratives, making ancient myths accessible to new generations. This cultural resurgence allows young adults to engage with these myths in ways that are relevant to their lives today. The blend of ancient wisdom with contemporary storytelling invites readers to reflect on their own experiences while drawing inspiration from the legends of the past.

Ultimately, the continued fascination with Norse mythology, particularly through the lens of Heimdall's role in creation myths, serves as a reminder of the enduring power of stories. They not only provide entertainment but also offer valuable insights into the human experience. As young adults delve into these tales, they can appreciate the rich symbolism and lessons embedded within, fostering a deeper understanding of themselves and their place in the world. Through Heimdall's watchful eyes, they are encouraged to embrace their journeys, face their challenges, and safeguard the connections that bind them to one another and to their own histories.

## Lessons from Heimdall's Story

Heimdall, known as the watchman of the gods, holds a significant role in Norse creation myths that extends beyond his duties as the guardian of Asgard. His story offers valuable lessons about vigilance, the importance of duty, and the interconnectedness of all beings in the cosmos. As a character who possesses extraordinary senses, Heimdall teaches us that awareness and perception are vital in navigating our own lives and the challenges we face. By understanding his vigilance, young adults can learn the importance of being present and attuned to their surroundings, which is crucial in a world filled with distractions.

A key aspect of Heimdall's narrative is his unwavering commitment to his responsibilities. Tasked with guarding the Bifröst, the rainbow bridge connecting the realms, Heimdall exemplifies the value of duty and loyalty. His dedication is not merely about fulfilling a role; it reflects a deeper understanding of the balance between realms and the importance of maintaining order. For young adults, this lesson emphasizes the need to embrace responsibilities, whether in personal relationships, education, or community involvement. By committing to their duties, they contribute to a larger purpose that benefits themselves and those around them.

Heimdall's unique abilities, including his keen sense of hearing and sight, symbolize the importance of awareness and insight in our lives. His capacity to hear grasses grow and see for miles showcases an extraordinary level of perception that can inspire young adults to sharpen their own senses. This awareness is not just about physical senses; it also encompasses emotional and social intelligence. In a rapidly changing world, being attuned to one's environment and the feelings of others can foster stronger connections and better decision-making. Thus, Heimdall's story encourages young adults to cultivate their awareness to navigate life's complexities effectively.

Moreover, Heimdall's role in the cosmic balance highlights the interconnectedness of all beings. His existence is tied to the fate of the gods, giants, and humans alike. This interconnectedness serves as a reminder that individual actions can have far-reaching consequences. Young adults can learn from this lesson by recognizing the impact of their choices on their communities and the environment. By understanding that they are part of a larger tapestry, they can become more conscientious in their actions, striving to ensure that their contributions promote harmony rather than discord.

Finally, Heimdall's story culminates in the events of Ragnarök, where he ultimately faces the giant Loki. This confrontation signifies the inevitability of conflict and change, reminding young adults that challenges are an intrinsic part of life. The lesson here is not about avoiding conflict but rather facing it with courage and resilience. Just as Heimdall stands ready to defend against impending chaos, young adults can draw strength from his example. By embracing challenges and approaching them with determination, they can emerge stronger and more capable, embodying the spirit of a true guardian in their own lives.

# Chapter 10: Conclusion

## Reflections on Guardianship and Duty

Guardianship, as embodied by Heimdall in Norse creation myths, underscores the profound responsibilities he undertakes for the Nine Realms. As the watchman of the gods, Heimdall is tasked with overseeing the Bifröst, the rainbow bridge connecting Midgard to Asgard. This duty involves not only vigilance but also readiness to confront any impending threats. His unique position highlights the necessity of vigilance in safeguarding one's community and loved ones, representing the archetype of a guardian who is always prepared to act in defense of the greater good.

The sense of duty that Heimdall embodies goes beyond mere watchfulness; it signifies a deep commitment to the well-being of the realms. He possesses extraordinary abilities, such as acute hearing and sight, which enable him to detect danger from vast distances. This remarkable perception serves as a metaphor for the importance of awareness in our own lives. In a world filled with distractions, being attentive to our surroundings and the people in our lives is crucial. It encourages young adults to reflect on their roles within their communities and consider how they can embody the spirit of guardianship in their everyday actions.

Heimdall's guardianship also raises questions about sacrifice and personal cost. He is known to have sacrificed his own sense of comfort and peace to fulfill his role. This theme of sacrifice is prevalent in many heroic narratives and serves as a reminder that true guardianship often requires individuals to put the needs of others before their own. The journey of young adults often involves navigating their own responsibilities and finding a balance between personal desires and the obligations they have towards friends, family, and society. By examining Heimdall's choices, readers can gain insight into the complexities of duty and the strength it takes to uphold it.

Moreover, the concept of guardianship in Norse mythology is not limited to physical protection alone; it encompasses the preservation of wisdom and knowledge. Heimdall is also associated with the transmission of vital information between realms. This aspect of his role emphasizes the importance of communication and understanding in any community. Young adults are encouraged to recognize their potential as carriers of knowledge and advocates for truth. By sharing insights and fostering dialogue, they can contribute to a more informed and cohesive society.

Ultimately, reflections on guardianship and duty through the lens of Heimdall's character serve as a call to action for young adults. It is an invitation to consider how they can be vigilant in their own lives, whether that means standing up for what is right, supporting those in need, or simply being present for friends and family. Just as Heimdall stands watch over the Nine Realms, young adults have the power to be guardians in their own right, shaping the future through their choices and actions. Embracing this responsibility can lead to personal growth and a stronger, more resilient community.

# The Enduring Influence of Heimdall in Our Lives

Heimdall, often referred to as the watchman of the gods, holds a unique and enduring influence that resonates deeply in contemporary society. His role in Norse creation myths is multifaceted, reflecting themes of vigilance, protection, and the importance of boundaries. As the guardian of Bifrost, the rainbow bridge connecting the realms of gods and mortals, Heimdall embodies the idea of safeguarding not just physical spaces but also the moral and ethical boundaries that define our interactions. This vigilance serves as a reminder of our responsibilities to ourselves and to others, echoing the importance of mindfulness in our daily lives.

The tales of Heimdall emphasize the significance of communication and awareness. Known for his acute senses, he is said to hear grass growing and see for hundreds of miles, making him a symbol of perception and insight. In an age dominated by technology and rapid information exchange, the lessons drawn from Heimdall's attributes are particularly relevant. Young adults today navigate a complex landscape of social media, where the ability to discern truth from misinformation is crucial. By channeling Heimdall's vigilance, individuals can develop a sharper awareness of their surroundings and the information they consume, promoting a more thoughtful and intentional approach to communication.

Heimdall's role as a guardian also extends to concepts of community and cooperation. In Norse mythology, he watches over the gods and mortals, ensuring that both realms are secure from external threats. This sense of guardianship can inspire young adults to take an active role in their communities, fostering a spirit of cooperation and support. Whether through volunteer work, activism, or simply being a reliable friend, embodying Heimdall's protective nature can lead to a more cohesive society. The idea of standing watch over those we care about can encourage individuals to advocate for justice and equality, reinforcing the bonds that unite us.

Moreover, Heimdall's character reflects the importance of preparation and resilience. The mythological narratives depict him as a figure ready to sound the Gjallarhorn, signaling the onset of Ragnarok, the end of the world as known in Norse myth. This readiness to confront chaos resonates with young adults facing the uncertainties of the modern world. It serves as a powerful metaphor for the necessity of being prepared for challenges, both personal and societal. By adopting a mindset similar to Heimdall's—one of vigilance and readiness—young individuals can better navigate their paths, equipped to confront obstacles with confidence and resilience.

Finally, the enduring influence of Heimdall in our lives can be seen in the values he represents: vigilance, communication, community, and resilience. These principles are not just relics of ancient myth but are essential in shaping a positive future. As young adults reflect on these qualities, they can draw inspiration from Heimdall's legacy, integrating these values into their own lives. By doing so, they not only honor the mythological past but also contribute to a more aware, connected, and resilient society, echoing the timeless lessons of Heimdall across the generations.

# Living the Nine Noble Virtues: A Practical Guide for Everyday Life

## Chapter 1: Introduction to the Nine Noble Virtues

### Definition and Origin

The Nine Noble Virtues are a set of ethical principles rooted in ancient Norse and Germanic traditions, reflecting a code of conduct that emphasizes honor, courage, truth, and integrity. These virtues have been distilled from historical texts, sagas, and the cultural practices of the Norse people, serving as guiding principles for personal development and community cohesion. The virtues include Courage, Truth, Honor, Fidelity, Discipline, Hospitality, Self-Reliance, Industriousness, and Perseverance. Each virtue represents an essential aspect of character that individuals can cultivate to navigate life's challenges effectively.

The origin of the Nine Noble Virtues can be traced back to the early medieval period when the Norse and Germanic tribes established their societal norms. These tribes valued strength, loyalty, and honor, which were crucial for survival in a harsh environment. The virtues were often conveyed through oral traditions and later documented in texts such as the Poetic Edda and the Prose Edda. As these societies evolved, so did the understanding of these virtues, adapting them to fit the changing cultural landscape while maintaining their core essence.

Historically, the Nine Noble Virtues served not only as personal guidelines but also as communal standards that fostered unity and cooperation among tribes. They provided a framework for conflict resolution, emphasizing the importance of honor and truthfulness in interpersonal relationships. These virtues were intrinsically linked to the idea of personal and communal responsibility, where individuals were expected to uphold these values to contribute positively to their communities. As such, the virtues became a means of social cohesion, reinforcing the bonds that held communities together.

In contemporary society, the relevance of the Nine Noble Virtues extends beyond their historical context. They offer practical applications that resonate with modern ethical dilemmas and personal development goals. For adults seeking to enhance their character, the virtues provide a structured approach to self-improvement and ethical decision-making. By embodying these principles, individuals can foster a sense of integrity and purpose in their lives, which can also influence the environment around them, including workplace culture and family dynamics.

Furthermore, the Nine Noble Virtues possess a timeless quality that allows them to be integrated into various aspects of life, including spiritual practices and community building. They encourage individuals to reflect on their values and behaviors, leading to meaningful discussions about ethics and morality. By teaching these virtues to children and incorporating them into everyday interactions, society can nurture a new generation that values honor, courage, and integrity, ensuring that these principles continue to thrive in an ever-changing world.

## Overview of the Nine Noble Virtues

The Nine Noble Virtues are a set of ethical principles that have roots in ancient Norse culture and are often associated with modern Heathenry. These virtues provide a framework for personal conduct and community interaction, emphasizing values that promote individual integrity and social cohesion. The virtues include Courage, Truth, Honor, Fidelity, Discipline, Hospitality, Self-Reliance, Industriousness, and Perseverance. Each virtue serves as a guide for making ethical decisions and fostering a sense of responsibility towards oneself and others.

Courage is the foundation of the Nine Noble Virtues, encouraging individuals to confront challenges and face fears head-on. This virtue is not only about physical bravery but also encompasses moral courage—the strength to uphold one's beliefs and values in the face of adversity. In everyday life, practicing courage can manifest as standing up for what is right, speaking truthfully in difficult situations, or taking risks that lead to personal growth. By embodying courage, individuals inspire others and contribute to a culture of resilience.

Truth, the second virtue, emphasizes the importance of honesty and integrity in all aspects of life. It calls for a commitment to factualness and transparency, promoting trust within relationships and communities. Practicing truth involves not only being honest with oneself but also fostering open communication with others. In a world often clouded by misinformation and deceit, upholding truth cultivates a sense of authenticity, enabling deeper connections between individuals and enhancing collective understanding.

Honor and fidelity further strengthen the moral fabric of society. Honor involves respecting oneself and others, maintaining dignity in actions and decisions. It is about living in accordance with one's values and holding oneself accountable. Fidelity complements this by emphasizing loyalty and commitment, whether to family, friends, or principles. Together, these virtues create a strong foundation for relationships, encouraging individuals to act with respect and loyalty, thereby nurturing trust and stability within communities.

The remaining virtues—discipline, hospitality, self-reliance, industriousness, and perseverance—each offer unique contributions to personal and communal development. Discipline fosters self-control and the ability to focus on long-term goals, while hospitality promotes generosity and the welcoming of others into one's life. Self-reliance encourages independence and confidence, and industriousness values hard work and commitment to excellence. Finally, perseverance highlights the importance of resilience in overcoming obstacles. Collectively, these virtues guide individuals in building meaningful lives, fostering supportive communities, and navigating the complexities of modern existence while remaining connected to their ethical roots.

## Importance in Modern Life

In the context of modern life, the Nine Noble Virtues serve as a guiding compass for ethical behavior and personal development. These virtues—courage, truth, honor, fidelity, discipline, hospitality, industriousness, self-reliance, and perseverance—are timeless principles that can be applied in various aspects of daily living. As society grapples with rapid change, uncertainty, and moral ambiguity, these virtues provide a framework for individuals to navigate challenges and make sound decisions. They encourage self-reflection and foster a sense of responsibility, both to oneself and to the community.

Incorporating the Nine Noble Virtues into daily life enhances personal growth and character development. By actively practicing these virtues, individuals cultivate qualities that enable them to face adversity with resilience and integrity. For example, embracing perseverance can lead to improved problem-solving skills and a greater ability to overcome obstacles. Similarly, the virtue of discipline can help individuals develop routines that promote productivity and well-being. This personal evolution not only benefits individuals but also creates a ripple effect that positively impacts their relationships and broader communities.

Teaching the Nine Noble Virtues to children is crucial for fostering a generation equipped with strong moral foundations. By instilling these virtues early on, parents and educators can guide children in understanding the importance of ethical behavior and community engagement. Practical applications, such as storytelling and role-playing, can effectively communicate these principles in a relatable manner. As children learn to embody these virtues, they are more likely to grow into responsible adults who contribute positively to society, reinforcing the cycle of virtue across generations.

In the workplace, the Nine Noble Virtues can play a significant role in shaping a healthy organizational culture. Companies that prioritize these virtues often see increased employee morale, collaboration, and productivity. For instance, promoting honor and integrity within a workplace fosters trust among team members, while hospitality encourages a supportive and inclusive environment. When organizations adopt these values, they not only enhance their operational effectiveness but also contribute to the personal development of their employees, creating a more cohesive and motivated workforce.

Finally, the relevance of the Nine Noble Virtues extends into modern spiritual practices and community building. Many individuals seek deeper meaning and connection in their lives, and these virtues provide a pathway to achieve that. By incorporating the virtues into spiritual practices, individuals can cultivate a sense of purpose and fulfillment. Furthermore, community initiatives that emphasize these principles can lead to stronger bonds among members, fostering a culture of mutual respect and cooperation. As society continues to evolve, the Nine Noble Virtues remain a vital resource for individuals and communities striving for a more ethical and harmonious existence.

# Chapter 2: The Nine Noble Virtues Simplified

## Courage

Courage stands as a fundamental virtue in the framework of the Nine Noble Virtues, serving as a catalyst for personal growth and resilience. In everyday life, courage manifests not only in grand gestures but also in the small, often overlooked moments where one must choose to confront fear or uncertainty. Whether it is speaking truthfully in difficult conversations, standing up for personal beliefs, or facing the unknown, courage empowers individuals to take action despite the potential for negative outcomes. This virtue encourages a mindset that embraces challenges, reinforcing the idea that true strength often lies in vulnerability.

In practical applications, courage can be integrated into daily routines by setting personal goals that push one beyond their comfort zone. This could include pursuing a new career path, engaging in public speaking, or simply initiating conversations that may lead to uncomfortable yet necessary change. By recognizing and facing fears head-on, individuals not only develop resilience but also inspire those around them to do the same. Courage, thus, becomes a collective force that fosters an environment where others feel empowered to take risks in their own lives.

Teaching courage as part of the Nine Noble Virtues to children is crucial for their development. It is essential to create a safe space where children can express their fears and learn how to confront them. Parents and educators can model courageous behavior, demonstrating how to handle adversity and make ethical decisions. Encouragement to take calculated risks, such as trying out for a team or participating in a debate, helps children understand that failure is a stepping stone to success. Instilling this virtue early on equips the younger generation with the tools needed to face the complexities of life with confidence.

In the context of workplace culture, courage can lead to transformative change. Organizations that foster an environment of openness and bravery encourage employees to share innovative ideas, voice concerns, and challenge the status quo. This culture of courage not only enhances collaboration but also drives progress, as team members feel valued and supported. By integrating courageous practices into the workplace, companies can cultivate a resilient workforce that is better equipped to navigate challenges and seize opportunities.

The relevance of courage extends beyond personal and professional realms into modern spiritual practices. Many spiritual traditions emphasize the importance of courage in the journey toward self-discovery and authenticity. Recognizing and confronting inner fears allows individuals to align more closely with their true selves and values. This alignment fosters a sense of purpose and fulfillment, as individuals act in accordance with their beliefs. Courage, therefore, is not just a virtue to be admired; it is a necessary component of a meaningful life that enriches personal development and community building.

# Truth

Truth stands as a fundamental pillar within the framework of the Nine Noble Virtues, offering a guiding light for personal integrity and ethical conduct. In the pursuit of truth, individuals are encouraged to seek authenticity in their thoughts, words, and actions. This commitment to honesty not only fosters self-awareness but also cultivates trust within relationships and communities. By living truthfully, one aligns with a path that promotes transparency and accountability, creating a foundation for meaningful interactions.

Practicing truth in daily life can manifest in various ways, from honest communication to the courage to confront uncomfortable realities. In interactions with others, truth involves not only stating facts but also being genuine in expressing feelings and intentions. This virtue encourages individuals to listen actively and respond sincerely, which enhances emotional connections and reduces misunderstandings. In personal development, embracing truth can lead to deeper self-reflection, allowing individuals to acknowledge their strengths and weaknesses without the distortion of self-deception.

Teaching the virtue of truth to children is essential for their moral and ethical development. By instilling a value for honesty from a young age, parents and educators can help shape a future generation that prioritizes integrity. This can be achieved through storytelling, where narratives emphasize the importance of truth and the consequences of deceit. Engaging children in discussions about truth can also foster critical thinking skills, enabling them to discern fact from fiction and understand the implications of their choices.

In the workplace, incorporating truth as a core value can significantly enhance organizational culture. When employees feel empowered to express their thoughts and concerns openly, it leads to a more collaborative and innovative environment. Leaders who prioritize transparency in decision-making build trust among their teams, resulting in increased morale and productivity. Moreover, a culture of truth encourages ethical behavior, reducing the likelihood of misconduct and fostering a sense of shared responsibility among colleagues.

The significance of truth extends beyond individual and community contexts, influencing broader societal dynamics. In modern spiritual practices, truth serves as a pathway to enlightenment and understanding, encouraging individuals to seek deeper connections with themselves and others. When truth is upheld as a virtue, it challenges individuals to confront biases and assumptions, promoting a more inclusive and compassionate society. Ultimately, living in alignment with truth not only enhances personal fulfillment but also strengthens the fabric of our communities and the world at large.

## Honor

Honor is a cornerstone of the Nine Noble Virtues, representing a commitment to integrity, respect, and dignity in all interactions. In everyday life, honor manifests in the way individuals conduct themselves, uphold their promises, and treat others with fairness. It is not merely a personal attribute but a societal expectation that fosters trust and cooperation. By embracing honor, individuals contribute to a culture of respect, which is vital for nurturing relationships in both personal and professional settings.

In practical applications, honor can be observed in how one navigates challenges and conflicts. When faced with difficult decisions, honoring commitments and valuing the truth can guide individuals toward ethical resolutions. For example, in a workplace context, an employee who honors their commitments will not only foster goodwill among colleagues but also enhance their own reputation. This creates a ripple effect, encouraging others to adopt similar standards, thereby cultivating an environment where integrity is paramount.

Teaching the virtue of honor to children is essential for their moral development. Instilling a sense of honor in the younger generation involves modeling respectful behavior and emphasizing the importance of keeping one's word. Parents and educators can engage children in discussions about the significance of honesty and fairness, using stories and examples to illustrate how honor shapes character. By integrating honor into their upbringing, children learn to navigate social dynamics with respect and accountability.

Incorporating honor within workplace culture can lead to enhanced collaboration and productivity. Organizations that prioritize honor create an atmosphere where employees feel valued and respected, which in turn boosts morale and reduces conflicts. Practices such as recognizing achievements, maintaining transparency in communication, and encouraging ethical decision-making can all reinforce a culture of honor. This not only benefits individual employees but also drives the overall success of the organization.

The concept of honor extends beyond individual interactions; it plays a vital role in community building and conflict resolution. Communities that uphold honor foster a sense of belonging and mutual respect among members. When conflicts arise, approaching them with honor—by valuing diverse perspectives and seeking equitable solutions—can facilitate healing and reconciliation. By understanding the historical context and evolution of honor within the framework of the Nine Noble Virtues, individuals can appreciate its lasting significance and strive to embody it in both their personal lives and communal engagements.

# Fidelity

Fidelity, one of the Nine Noble Virtues, embodies loyalty, faithfulness, and a steadfast commitment to one's principles, relationships, and responsibilities. In a world where distractions and temptations abound, practicing fidelity becomes essential for personal integrity and the building of trust within communities. This virtue encourages individuals to stay true to their word, uphold commitments, and foster meaningful connections with others. By embodying fidelity, one not only strengthens personal relationships but also enhances the sense of community and collective responsibility.

In practical applications, fidelity can be observed in various aspects of daily life. It manifests in honoring commitments at work, such as meeting deadlines and supporting colleagues. In personal relationships, fidelity requires individuals to maintain trust and loyalty, whether in friendships, family dynamics, or romantic partnerships. This virtue encourages a culture of accountability, where individuals take ownership of their promises and strive to keep their word. By integrating fidelity into daily routines, adults can create an environment that values commitment and reliability, which in turn fosters stronger relationships and community bonds.

Teaching fidelity to children lays a foundation for their moral development. Instilling this virtue early on helps children understand the importance of being true to their commitments and the impact of their actions on others. Parents and educators can model fidelity through their own behaviors, demonstrating consistency in their promises and support. Engaging children in discussions about loyalty, trust, and the consequences of broken commitments reinforces the significance of this virtue. As children learn to appreciate the value of fidelity, they cultivate resilience and accountability, essential traits for their future personal and professional relationships.

In the workplace, incorporating fidelity enhances organizational culture and employee morale. When leaders model fidelity by being transparent and honoring their commitments, they foster an atmosphere of trust and collaboration. Employees are more likely to feel valued and engaged when they witness fidelity in action. This can result in improved teamwork, higher levels of productivity, and reduced conflict. Organizations that prioritize fidelity in their values and practices create a stable environment where individuals are encouraged to work together towards common goals, ultimately contributing to the overall success of the organization.

The role of fidelity extends beyond personal and professional realms; it also plays a crucial part in modern spiritual practices. Many spiritual traditions emphasize the importance of loyalty to one's beliefs and community. Fidelity in this context encourages individuals to engage with their spiritual practices sincerely and consistently, promoting personal growth and development. Moreover, fidelity can serve as a guiding principle in conflict resolution, as individuals committed to this virtue are more likely to seek understanding and compromise rather than division. By recognizing fidelity as a core component of the Nine Noble Virtues, individuals can navigate their lives with integrity, fostering deeper connections and contributing positively to the fabric of society.

# Discipline

Discipline is a cornerstone of personal development and a vital aspect of living the Nine Noble Virtues. In the context of these virtues, discipline manifests as self-control, consistency, and the ability to adhere to one's values even in the face of adversity. It requires a commitment to continuous improvement and the willingness to confront personal weaknesses. By cultivating discipline, individuals can create a strong foundation for practicing other virtues such as courage, truth, and honor. This foundational quality not only enhances personal growth but also contributes to the overall well-being of communities.

In practical applications, discipline serves as a guide for everyday decision-making. For adults navigating the complexities of modern life, establishing routines and setting clear goals can significantly enhance productivity and fulfillment. This involves prioritizing tasks, managing time effectively, and resisting distractions that veer one off course. Discipline in daily life reinforces accountability and encourages individuals to take responsibility for their actions. By committing to disciplined practices, one can align their daily activities with the broader aspirations of living the Nine Noble Virtues.

Teaching discipline to children is equally important, as it lays the groundwork for their character development. Children learn best through modeling behavior, so adults must exemplify discipline in their own lives. Structured environments, clear expectations, and consistent consequences can help instill the value of discipline in young minds. Engaging children in activities that require focus and perseverance, such as sports or arts, can further develop their ability to practice self-discipline. By nurturing this trait, we prepare future generations to embrace the Nine Noble Virtues as guiding principles in their own lives.

Discipline also plays a crucial role in workplace culture. Organizations that foster a disciplined environment often see enhanced collaboration, productivity, and ethical behavior among employees. Implementing systems that promote accountability, such as performance reviews and feedback mechanisms, can encourage individuals to adhere to the values of the Nine Noble Virtues. In this context, discipline is not merely about compliance; it is about cultivating a culture where ethical considerations are prioritized, and employees feel empowered to contribute positively to the organization's mission.

Finally, discipline is essential in modern spiritual practices as well. Many spiritual paths emphasize the importance of routine, meditation, and self-reflection, all of which require a disciplined approach. By integrating discipline into spiritual practice, individuals can deepen their understanding of the Nine Noble Virtues and their significance in everyday life. This disciplined pursuit of personal growth not only enriches one's spiritual journey but also enhances one's ability to navigate challenges with grace and purpose. Ultimately, discipline is a vital thread that weaves through the fabric of the Nine Noble Virtues, guiding individuals towards a life of integrity and fulfillment.

# Hospitality

Hospitality, as one of the nine noble virtues, encompasses more than just the act of welcoming guests into our homes. It is a fundamental expression of generosity, kindness, and respect towards others. In its essence, hospitality signifies a commitment to treating people with dignity and providing comfort, whether they are friends, family, or strangers. This virtue encourages us to create an environment where individuals feel valued and supported, fostering connections that can lead to deeper understanding and community ties.

Practically applying hospitality in daily life can be as simple as being attentive to the needs of those around us. This could involve inviting a neighbor over for coffee, helping a colleague navigate a challenging project, or simply offering a warm smile to someone who seems down. These acts of kindness not only enhance our personal relationships but also contribute positively to the atmosphere in our workplaces and communities. By embodying hospitality, we set a standard that encourages others to reciprocate, creating a ripple effect of goodwill that can transform our interactions.

Teaching the virtue of hospitality to children is equally vital. Instilling this value early on helps cultivate empathy and social responsibility. Children can learn to express hospitality through small gestures, such as sharing toys, including peers in their play, or greeting new classmates with friendliness. These lessons in generosity and kindness lay the groundwork for their future relationships, teaching them the importance of nurturing connections and supporting those in need. As they grow, these early experiences will shape their understanding of community and the role they play within it.

Incorporating hospitality into workplace culture can significantly enhance team dynamics and productivity. When employees feel welcomed and valued, they are more likely to contribute positively and collaborate effectively. Employers can foster a hospitable environment by encouraging open communication, recognizing individual contributions, and creating spaces where employees can connect beyond their work roles. This not only boosts morale but also cultivates a sense of belonging, ultimately leading to a more cohesive and motivated workforce.

The historical context of hospitality reveals its longstanding significance across various cultures and societies. From ancient traditions of welcoming travelers to modern-day practices of inclusivity, the virtue of hospitality has evolved yet remains a cornerstone of ethical behavior. Understanding its roots can deepen our appreciation for the value of hospitality in contemporary life. By recognizing the universal need for connection and support, we can actively promote this virtue, enhancing our personal development and contributing to a more compassionate and understanding world.

## Self-Reliance

Self-reliance is a cornerstone of the Nine Noble Virtues, emphasizing the importance of individual strength and accountability in one's life. This virtue encourages adults to cultivate a sense of independence, fostering the ability to rely on oneself in both thought and action. Self-reliance empowers individuals to make decisions based on their values and beliefs, rather than succumbing to external pressures or societal expectations. In practical applications, it means taking ownership of one's life choices, understanding that personal responsibility is essential for growth and success.

Incorporating self-reliance into daily life can be achieved through various practices that enhance personal autonomy. Setting personal goals, developing new skills, and embracing challenges are all ways to reinforce self-reliance. Adults can practice self-reflection to understand their strengths and weaknesses, allowing them to make informed decisions that align with their true selves. By prioritizing self-reliance, individuals can navigate life's complexities with confidence, reducing reliance on others for validation or direction.

Teaching self-reliance to children is equally vital, as it lays the foundation for their future independence. Parents and educators can encourage children to solve problems on their own and make decisions that reflect their values. This guidance fosters resilience and confidence, equipping children with the tools they need to face life's challenges head-on. By instilling the principles of self-reliance early on, we can cultivate a generation that values personal responsibility and the strength of character necessary to thrive in a complex world.

In the workplace, self-reliance can significantly enhance culture and productivity. When employees take ownership of their roles and responsibilities, they contribute to a more dynamic and engaged work environment. Encouraging self-reliance fosters innovation, as individuals feel empowered to share ideas and solutions without fear of judgment. Organizations can promote this virtue by providing opportunities for professional development and encouraging a culture of accountability, where team members support one another while also taking responsibility for their contributions.

Finally, self-reliance plays a crucial role in modern spiritual practices, where individuals are encouraged to seek their own paths to understanding and fulfillment. By relying on their intuition and experiences, individuals can create a personal relationship with their beliefs. This self-directed approach not only strengthens personal faith but also encourages a deeper connection with the community. Emphasizing self-reliance within spiritual contexts allows individuals to explore their spirituality authentically, fostering a sense of belonging and purpose while remaining true to themselves.

# Industriousness

Industriousness is a cornerstone of the nine noble virtues, embodying the spirit of hard work, diligence, and perseverance. It encourages individuals to approach tasks with dedication and a strong work ethic, recognizing that effort is often the key to success. In practical terms, industriousness is not merely about the quantity of work produced but also the quality and commitment behind that work. By embracing industriousness, individuals cultivate a mindset that values persistence and resilience, essential traits for overcoming challenges and achieving personal and professional goals.

Incorporating industriousness into daily life can be transformative. It begins with setting clear objectives and breaking them down into manageable tasks. This approach not only makes large projects less daunting but also allows for measurable progress. By fostering a routine that prioritizes productivity, one can develop habits that enhance focus and efficiency. For instance, dedicating specific blocks of time to work without distractions can lead to significant accomplishments. This practice also helps in building a sense of discipline, which reinforces one's commitment to industriousness.

Teaching industriousness to children is equally important, as it lays the foundation for their future endeavors. Children learn by example, so demonstrating a strong work ethic in everyday activities can inspire them to adopt similar values. Engaging children in tasks that require effort, whether it's completing homework, participating in sports, or contributing to household responsibilities, can instill a sense of achievement and responsibility. Encouraging them to take pride in their work promotes an understanding of the rewards that come from diligence and perseverance.

In the workplace, industriousness plays a vital role in fostering a culture of productivity and collaboration. Organizations that prioritize hard work and accountability often see increased morale and performance among employees. By recognizing and rewarding industrious behavior, companies can create an environment where individuals feel motivated to contribute their best efforts. Additionally, promoting teamwork and shared goals encourages everyone to pull together, ultimately enhancing the overall success of the organization.

Finally, the value of industriousness extends beyond individual and workplace applications; it is also a significant aspect of community building. By working collectively towards common goals, communities can harness the power of industriousness to achieve meaningful change. Volunteering, participating in local initiatives, and supporting local businesses are all expressions of industriousness that strengthen community ties. When individuals come together with a shared commitment to hard work, they not only enhance their own lives but also contribute to the well-being and growth of the community as a whole.

# Perseverance

Perseverance, as a noble virtue, embodies the strength and determination required to overcome obstacles and persist in the face of adversity. In the context of the Nine Noble Virtues, it serves as a fundamental pillar that supports the pursuit of personal growth and ethical living. This virtue encourages individuals to maintain focus on their goals and values, fostering resilience against challenges that may arise in daily life. Whether in personal endeavors, professional pursuits, or communal responsibilities, the practice of perseverance is essential for achieving meaningful outcomes and realizing one's potential.

Incorporating perseverance into everyday life requires a conscious effort to cultivate a mindset that embraces challenges as opportunities for growth. This involves setting clear, achievable goals and remaining committed to them despite setbacks. Adults can apply this virtue in various aspects of their lives, such as pursuing career advancements, maintaining relationships, or engaging in community service. By recognizing that failures and obstacles are part of the journey, individuals can develop a more robust sense of determination that propels them forward, ultimately leading to greater achievements and fulfillment.

Teaching perseverance to children is equally crucial, as instilling this virtue at a young age sets the foundation for lifelong resilience. Parents and educators can model perseverance by sharing stories of their own challenges and the strategies they employed to overcome them. Encouraging children to tackle difficult tasks and celebrating their efforts, rather than solely their successes, reinforces the importance of persistence. This approach not only nurtures their ability to face challenges but also fosters a growth mindset, equipping them with the tools necessary to navigate future obstacles with confidence.

In the workplace, perseverance plays a vital role in shaping a culture of resilience and innovation. Organizations that encourage employees to embrace challenges and persist in the face of difficulties can foster higher levels of engagement and creativity. Leaders can cultivate this environment by recognizing and rewarding efforts that demonstrate perseverance, regardless of the immediate outcomes. By integrating this virtue into workplace practices, companies can enhance collaboration, problem-solving, and overall performance, contributing to a more dynamic and productive organizational culture.

The value of perseverance transcends individual and professional contexts. It is also a core element in community building and conflict resolution. When individuals within a community demonstrate perseverance, they inspire others to remain committed to shared goals and values, even in challenging circumstances. This collective resilience can lead to stronger bonds and a greater sense of belonging. Furthermore, in conflict resolution, perseverance allows parties to engage in constructive dialogue and work through differences, ultimately leading to solutions that honor the interests of all involved. Thus, perseverance not only enhances personal development but also strengthens the fabric of communities and relationships.

# Chapter 3: Practical Applications of the Nine Noble Virtues in Daily Life

## Integrating Virtues into Daily Routines

Integrating virtues into daily routines is a powerful way to enhance personal development and foster a positive environment in both personal and professional spheres. The nine noble virtues—courage, truth, honor, fidelity, discipline, hospitality, self-reliance, industriousness, and perseverance—provide a framework for ethical living that can be seamlessly incorporated into everyday practices. By consciously choosing to embody these virtues, individuals can not only enrich their own lives but also positively influence those around them, creating a ripple effect within families, workplaces, and communities.

One practical approach to integrating these virtues is through mindful reflection at the beginning or end of each day. Setting aside time to consider how each virtue can be expressed in daily interactions allows individuals to align their actions with their values. For instance, reflecting on opportunities to show hospitality can encourage individuals to extend kindness to neighbors or colleagues. Similarly, contemplating the virtue of perseverance can motivate individuals to push through challenges at work or in personal projects, reinforcing the idea that resilience is key to achieving goals.

Incorporating virtues into daily routines also involves setting specific, actionable goals related to each virtue. For example, a person might aim to demonstrate discipline by establishing a consistent exercise routine or practicing self-reliance by taking on a new project independently. By breaking down each virtue into tangible objectives, individuals can track their progress and celebrate small victories, which reinforces their commitment to living virtuously. This goal-oriented approach makes the virtues more accessible and relatable, particularly for those who may struggle with abstract concepts.

Teaching the nine noble virtues to children is another vital aspect of their integration into daily life. Parents and educators can create opportunities for children to practice these virtues through storytelling, role-playing, and real-life scenarios. For example, discussing the importance of truth can be woven into everyday conversations about honesty in schoolwork or friendships. This not only helps children understand the virtues but also instills a sense of responsibility to embody them in their interactions with others.

Finally, organizations and workplaces can benefit greatly from a culture that emphasizes the nine noble virtues. By fostering an environment where values such as honor, industriousness, and teamwork are prioritized, leaders can cultivate a more engaged and collaborative workforce. Initiatives like team-building exercises centered around these virtues or recognition programs that reward virtuous behavior can reinforce a shared commitment to ethical practices. This not only enhances workplace culture but also contributes to overall community well-being, as employees carry these virtues into their interactions outside of work.

## Decision-Making Based on Virtues

Decision-making based on virtues involves aligning choices with core ethical principles that foster personal integrity and community well-being. The Nine Noble Virtues—Courage, Truth, Honor, Fidelity, Discipline, Hospitality, Self-Reliance, Industriousness, and Perseverance—serve as a robust framework for guiding individuals in their decision-making processes. Each virtue offers a lens through which to evaluate options, ensuring that decisions reflect not only personal values but also contribute positively to the broader community.

Courage, as the first of the Nine Noble Virtues, empowers individuals to confront challenges and make difficult choices. In situations where fear or uncertainty looms, drawing on courage can lead to decisions that reflect authenticity and strength. This is particularly relevant in workplace environments, where leaders must often make tough calls that impact their teams. By prioritizing courage, decision-makers can inspire others to act in alignment with ethical standards, fostering a culture of accountability and resilience.

Truth serves as another critical virtue in decision-making, emphasizing the importance of honesty and transparency. When faced with dilemmas, individuals who prioritize truth are more likely to seek out accurate information and present it candidly, even when it may be uncomfortable. This commitment to truth not only enhances personal credibility but also builds trust within relationships, whether in personal interactions or professional settings. A culture rooted in truth encourages open dialogue and collaborative problem-solving, ultimately leading to better outcomes for all stakeholders involved.

Honor and fidelity are intertwined virtues that emphasize loyalty and respect in decision-making. Upholding honor involves acting in ways that reflect personal and communal values, while fidelity encourages commitment to promises and responsibilities. In practice, decisions that honor relationships—whether familial, professional, or communal—are crucial for maintaining healthy dynamics. When individuals prioritize these virtues, they create environments where trust flourishes, and people feel valued and respected, paving the way for collaborative efforts and collective growth.

Finally, incorporating virtues such as discipline, hospitality, self-reliance, industriousness, and perseverance into the decision-making framework enriches the process by promoting a holistic view of ethics. Each of these virtues contributes to a balanced approach that encourages individuals to consider not only the immediate effects of their choices but also their long-term implications. By integrating these principles into daily life and teaching them to children, adults can cultivate a generation that values ethical decision-making and is equipped to navigate complex moral landscapes with confidence and integrity.

# Building Resilience through Virtues

Building resilience is a critical aspect of navigating the complexities of modern life, and the Nine Noble Virtues provide a strong foundation for this endeavor. Each virtue encapsulates qualities that enhance our ability to adapt and thrive in the face of challenges. By embodying virtues such as courage, truth, and perseverance, individuals can cultivate a mindset that not only withstands adversity but also transforms it into an opportunity for growth. This subchapter explores how integrating these virtues into daily practices fosters resilience and empowers individuals to face life's uncertainties with confidence.

Courage stands as a cornerstone of resilience. It encourages individuals to confront fears and take calculated risks, which are essential in overcoming obstacles. When one embodies courage, they are more likely to step outside their comfort zones, enabling personal and professional growth. In moments of difficulty, drawing on the strength of courage can lead to decisive actions rather than paralysis by fear. This proactive approach not only strengthens individual resolve but also inspires those around them, creating a ripple effect that fosters a resilient community.

Truth is another vital virtue that plays a significant role in building resilience. Embracing truth encourages self-awareness and honesty in one's circumstances and relationships. By acknowledging reality—whether it is personal limitations, challenges at work, or conflicts within communities—individuals can develop effective strategies to address these issues. This clarity fosters resilience as it empowers individuals to make informed decisions and seek solutions rather than succumbing to denial or avoidance. Moreover, a commitment to truth strengthens trust in relationships, creating a supportive environment where resilience can flourish.

Perseverance is essential in the face of setbacks. It embodies the tenacity to push through difficulties and maintain focus on long-term goals. When individuals practice perseverance, they learn that failure is not an endpoint but a stepping stone to success. This mindset is crucial for resilience, as it allows individuals to bounce back from disappointments with renewed determination. By cultivating perseverance through the Nine Noble Virtues, individuals can develop a robust internal framework that encourages them to keep striving, even when the path forward is fraught with challenges.

Integrating the Nine Noble Virtues into everyday life can provide practical applications that enhance resilience. In personal development, for instance, individuals can set goals aligned with these virtues, fostering a holistic approach to growth. In workplace culture, leaders who embody these virtues can create environments that prioritize collaboration and support. Furthermore, teaching these virtues to children instills a sense of resilience early on, equipping future generations with the tools necessary to navigate life's complexities. By fostering a culture anchored in the Nine Noble Virtues, communities can build a collective resilience that empowers individuals and strengthens social bonds.

# Chapter 4: Teaching the Nine Noble Virtues to Children

## Age-Appropriate Methods

Age-appropriate methods for imparting the Nine Noble Virtues ensure that each virtue resonates with different age groups while remaining relevant to the adult audience. Adults often serve as the primary educators and role models for the next generation. Therefore, understanding how to simplify these virtues without diluting their significance is crucial. The goal is to craft a framework that allows individuals to convey profound teachings in a manner that is accessible and engaging for children and young adults.

When teaching the virtues of courage and truth, for example, adults can utilize storytelling as a powerful tool. Stories resonate with children and can illustrate these virtues in action. By sharing tales from literature or personal experiences where courage was essential, adults can highlight the importance of standing up for what is right. Engaging children in discussions about these stories encourages them to reflect on their values and consider how they might apply these virtues in their own lives. This interactive method not only deepens understanding but also fosters critical thinking.

Incorporating role-playing activities is another effective method for teaching the Nine Noble Virtues. Adults can create scenarios that require children to make decisions based on these virtues. For instance, a role-playing exercise might involve a dilemma that tests honesty or generosity. Adults can guide children through these situations, prompting them to think critically about their choices and the consequences of their actions. This hands-on approach allows children to experience the virtues in a tangible way, reinforcing lessons through practice rather than mere explanation.

Furthermore, discussions about the virtues can be woven into everyday conversations. Adults can seize opportunities during daily activities, such as family meals or outings, to introduce concepts like loyalty or hospitality. By framing these discussions around real-life experiences, adults can help children see the relevance of the virtues in their everyday actions. Encouraging children to share their thoughts and experiences related to the virtues not only enhances their understanding but also fosters a sense of community and shared values within families.

Lastly, creating a supportive environment where these virtues are consistently modeled is perhaps the most impactful method of all. Adults must embody the Nine Noble Virtues in their behavior, as children are keen observers and often emulate adult actions. By demonstrating integrity, compassion, and respect in daily interactions, adults provide a living example for children to follow. This method solidifies the teaching of virtues, as children learn not only through words but also through the powerful influence of example. In doing so, adults contribute to a culture that values and practices these virtues, ensuring that they remain alive and relevant in future generations.

## Storytelling as a Teaching Tool

Storytelling serves as a powerful teaching tool, particularly when conveying complex concepts such as the nine noble virtues. Through engaging narratives, individuals can connect emotionally and intellectually to the values being presented. Instead of simply listing virtues or defining them in abstract terms, storytelling allows for the embodiment of these ideals through characters and their experiences. This method not only makes the virtues more relatable but also illustrates their practical applications in everyday life, enabling listeners to envision how they might incorporate these principles into their own actions and decisions.

In the context of teaching the nine noble virtues to children, storytelling can be especially effective. Children often resonate with stories that involve heroes, challenges, and moral dilemmas. By weaving the virtues into tales of adventure, perseverance, and personal growth, educators and parents can instill these values in a manner that is engaging and memorable. For instance, a story about a young character who demonstrates courage in the face of adversity can inspire children to embrace bravery in their own lives. This narrative approach not only fosters understanding but also encourages children to reflect on their own choices and the virtues they wish to embody.

Moreover, storytelling can significantly enhance personal development for adults as well. By exploring narratives that highlight the struggles and triumphs associated with living the nine noble virtues, individuals can gain insights into their own lives. Reflecting on stories where characters exhibit qualities such as honor, fidelity, and wisdom can prompt adults to assess their own behaviors and motivations. This self-reflection can lead to meaningful personal growth, as individuals identify areas for improvement and commit to living more virtuous lives. Stories thus become a mirror, allowing people to see themselves in the experiences of others.

In workplace culture, storytelling can be an effective means of incorporating the nine noble virtues into team dynamics. Leaders can share stories that exemplify collaboration, loyalty, and industriousness, creating a shared understanding of the values that the organization aims to uphold. These narratives can help to foster a sense of belonging and purpose among employees, as they learn about the ideals that guide their collective efforts. Additionally, storytelling can facilitate discussions around ethical decision-making, as employees consider how the virtues apply to real-life scenarios they may encounter in their professional roles.

Finally, storytelling connects individuals to community building and conflict resolution. Through shared narratives, communities can establish common values and foster a sense of unity. When people engage in storytelling that emphasizes virtues such as hospitality and generosity, they are encouraged to practice these values within their communities. In conflict resolution, stories can help individuals understand differing perspectives and promote empathy, allowing for more constructive dialogue. Ultimately, storytelling serves as a bridge, connecting the nine noble virtues to real-world applications and reinforcing the importance of these ideals in fostering strong, ethical communities.

## Encouraging Virtuous Behavior

Encouraging virtuous behavior begins with understanding the foundational principles of the nine noble virtues: courage, truth, honor, fidelity, discipline, hospitality, industriousness, self-reliance, and perseverance. Each of these virtues serves as a guidepost for individuals seeking to navigate their personal and professional lives with integrity and purpose. By emphasizing the importance of these virtues, individuals can cultivate a mindset that not only benefits themselves but also positively influences those around them. This approach fosters an environment where virtuous behavior is recognized, celebrated, and emulated.

Incorporating the nine noble virtues into daily routines can be approached through practical applications. For instance, one can start the day by setting intentions that align with these virtues, such as practicing self-reliance by taking personal responsibility for actions or demonstrating hospitality by offering kindness to others. Small actions, like helping a colleague or being honest in communications, create a ripple effect that encourages a culture of virtue. By making conscious choices rooted in these principles, individuals can reinforce their commitment to virtuous living while inspiring others to do the same.

Teaching the nine noble virtues to children is an essential aspect of fostering a future generation that values integrity and ethical behavior. Parents and educators can introduce these concepts through storytelling, discussions, and real-life examples that illustrate the virtues in action. Engaging children in conversations about courage in the face of fear or the importance of honesty can help them internalize these values. By creating opportunities for children to practice these virtues in safe environments, adults can guide them in understanding how these principles shape character and influence decision-making.

In the workplace, the nine noble virtues can serve as a framework for creating a positive organizational culture. Encouraging employees to embrace virtues such as industriousness and discipline can lead to increased productivity and job satisfaction. Companies can implement programs that recognize and reward virtuous behavior, fostering an atmosphere of collaboration and respect. By aligning corporate values with the nine noble virtues, organizations can cultivate a workforce that not only excels in their roles but also contributes to a more ethical and supportive workplace environment.

The relevance of the nine noble virtues extends beyond personal development and workplace culture; they also play a critical role in modern spiritual practices and community building. Many contemporary spiritual movements emphasize the importance of ethical living, which aligns closely with the virtues outlined in this framework. By incorporating these principles into community initiatives, individuals can strengthen bonds and create a sense of belonging. Moreover, understanding the historical context and evolution of these virtues can enrich personal and collective narratives, providing a deeper appreciation for their significance in fostering a virtuous society.

# Chapter 5: The Nine Noble Virtues and Personal Development

## Self-Reflection and Growth

Self-reflection is a crucial component of personal growth and development, especially when striving to embody the Nine Noble Virtues in everyday life. By taking the time to examine our thoughts, actions, and their impacts on ourselves and others, we can better understand how we align with these virtues. This introspection enables us to identify areas where we excel and aspects that may require improvement. When we consciously reflect on our behaviors and decisions, we cultivate self-awareness, which is essential for meaningful growth.

Incorporating self-reflection into our daily routines can be achieved through various methods. Journaling, for instance, provides a structured way to express thoughts and feelings, allowing individuals to track their progress in living out the virtues. Setting aside quiet time for contemplation can also enhance this process, providing a mental space to evaluate personal challenges and victories. Engaging in discussions with trusted friends or mentors can further facilitate reflection, offering different perspectives that may illuminate blind spots in our understanding of the virtues.

The Nine Noble Virtues offer a framework for evaluating our growth. Each virtue serves as a guidepost, helping us to measure our actions and motivations. For example, when faced with a difficult situation, we can ask ourselves how we can demonstrate courage or integrity. This intentional approach to assessing our decisions against the virtues encourages us to act with purpose and clarity. By recognizing moments where we embody these principles, we strengthen our commitment to them, while also identifying situations where we may have fallen short.

As we engage in self-reflection, it is essential to approach our findings with compassion rather than judgment. Growth often involves making mistakes and learning from them, and self-criticism can hinder progress. By treating ourselves with kindness, we create an environment conducive to growth, where mistakes become opportunities for learning. This mindset not only promotes personal development but also makes it easier to teach these virtues to others, including children, who are often influenced by how adults model behavior.

Ultimately, self-reflection fosters a culture of continuous improvement, both personally and within our communities. As we develop a deeper understanding of ourselves, we become better equipped to share the Nine Noble Virtues with others, whether in family settings, workplaces, or broader social contexts. This collective commitment to reflection and growth can lead to stronger, more resilient communities that prioritize ethical behavior and mutual respect, embodying the essence of the virtues in action.

## Setting Goals Aligned with Virtues

Setting goals that align with virtues is a transformative approach to personal development. By grounding our aspirations in the nine noble virtues, we create a framework that not only guides our actions but also enriches our character. Each virtue—courage, truth, honor, fidelity, discipline, hospitality, self-reliance, industriousness, and perseverance—provides a moral compass that can shape our objectives. By consciously integrating these virtues into our goal-setting process, we ensure that our pursuits resonate with deeper ethical principles, fostering a sense of fulfillment beyond mere achievement.

When establishing goals, it is essential to reflect on how each goal embodies one or more of the nine virtues. For instance, a goal of advancing in one's career can be aligned with industriousness and discipline. This alignment encourages individuals to not only work hard but to do so with integrity and purpose. Similarly, when considering personal relationships, goals centered around hospitality and fidelity can lead to more profound connections with others. By framing our objectives through the lens of virtues, we create a holistic approach that emphasizes not just the outcome but also the journey and the values we uphold along the way.

Incorporating the nine noble virtues into goal-setting can also enhance accountability. When our goals are rooted in virtues, we are more likely to stay committed to them, as they reflect our core beliefs and values. For example, if one of your goals is to volunteer regularly, it embodies the virtue of hospitality and can be a powerful motivator. This intrinsic motivation reinforces our commitment and helps us navigate challenges with resilience. By discussing our goals with others who share similar values, we can cultivate a supportive environment that encourages adherence to these virtues.

Teaching these virtues in the context of goal setting is equally important, especially for families and educators. Introducing children to the concept of aligning their aspirations with virtues can instill a strong ethical foundation early on. This practice not only encourages children to define their goals thoughtfully but also fosters critical thinking about the consequences of their actions. As they grow, they will carry this understanding into adulthood, making decisions that reflect their values and contribute positively to society.

Finally, the integration of the nine noble virtues into workplace culture can significantly enhance organizational effectiveness and employee satisfaction. When employees set goals that reflect virtues such as honor and cooperation, it can lead to more harmonious and productive work environments. Organizations that prioritize these virtues in their culture encourage a collective commitment to ethical practices, which fosters trust and collaboration. By aligning individual and organizational goals with the nine noble virtues, we can create a more engaged and ethically driven workforce, ultimately benefiting both individuals and the community at large.

## Overcoming Challenges with Virtue

Overcoming challenges is an intrinsic part of the human experience, and the Nine Noble Virtues offer a framework to navigate these obstacles effectively. Each virtue—courage, truth, honor, fidelity, discipline, hospitality, industriousness, self-reliance, and perseverance—provides a unique lens through which individuals can confront difficulties. By embodying these virtues, adults can cultivate resilience, enabling them to transform challenges into opportunities for growth and self-improvement. The practice of these virtues not only aids in personal development but also enhances one's ability to inspire and guide others, including children and colleagues.

Courage is often the first step toward overcoming any challenge. It empowers individuals to face fears and uncertainties, whether they arise in personal life, at work, or within the community. By embracing courage, adults can take risks that might otherwise seem daunting. This could mean advocating for oneself in a professional setting, standing up for a friend in need, or confronting personal limitations. The act of being courageous builds confidence and sets a positive example for children, teaching them the importance of facing challenges with bravery.

Truth is another essential virtue that plays a critical role in overcoming challenges. When faced with difficulties, the temptation to evade or distort reality can be strong. However, embracing truth fosters transparency and authenticity, allowing individuals to confront their situations honestly. This virtue encourages open communication, which is vital in both personal and professional relationships. By promoting an environment of truthfulness, adults can help create a culture in which challenges are addressed collaboratively, leading to more effective solutions and a stronger community spirit.

Honor and fidelity are closely intertwined virtues that reinforce commitment and integrity during challenging times. Upholding one's honor involves staying true to personal values and principles, even when faced with adversity. Fidelity, on the other hand, emphasizes loyalty to others, whether family, friends, or colleagues. Together, these virtues help build trust and cohesion within relationships. In workplaces, for example, honoring commitments and being faithful to one's team fosters a supportive environment where challenges can be faced collectively, rather than in isolation.

Finally, the virtues of perseverance and self-reliance serve as powerful tools in overcoming obstacles. Perseverance encourages individuals to maintain effort and determination despite setbacks, reinforcing the idea that resilience is key to success. Self-reliance complements this by instilling a sense of independence and responsibility for one's actions. By cultivating these virtues, adults not only enhance their problem-solving abilities but also set an empowering example for children. This approach instills a belief that challenges can be met with tenacity and personal agency, creating a legacy of strength and virtue in future generations.

# Chapter 6: Incorporating the Nine Noble Virtues in Workplace Culture

## Creating a Virtue-Based Workplace

Creating a virtue-based workplace involves integrating the nine noble virtues into the very fabric of organizational culture. By fostering an environment that emphasizes these virtues, businesses can enhance employee satisfaction, increase productivity, and cultivate a sense of community among staff. The noble virtues—courage, truth, honor, fidelity, discipline, hospitality, self-reliance, industriousness, and perseverance—serve as guiding principles that can shape workplace behavior and decision-making processes. When these virtues are actively promoted, employees are more likely to feel valued and engaged, leading to a more cohesive work environment.

One practical way to implement a virtue-based workplace is through clear communication of the organization's core values, which should align closely with the nine noble virtues. This can be achieved by incorporating these virtues into mission statements, company policies, and performance evaluations. For instance, fostering a culture of honesty requires transparent communication from leadership, while encouraging hospitality can manifest through employee recognition programs that celebrate acts of kindness among colleagues. By embedding these principles within the organizational framework, employees are more likely to embody the virtues in their daily interactions and responsibilities.

Training and professional development programs can further reinforce the importance of the nine noble virtues in the workplace. Workshops and seminars aimed at educating employees about these virtues can provide practical scenarios and role-playing exercises that illustrate their application. For example, training on conflict resolution can emphasize the value of honor and truthfulness, guiding employees toward ethical decision-making during disputes. Additionally, mentorship programs can pair experienced employees with newer staff, allowing for the sharing of wisdom and the cultivation of virtues in a supportive environment.

Leadership plays a vital role in the establishment of a virtue-based workplace. Leaders who exemplify the nine noble virtues set a powerful example for their teams. By demonstrating courage in decision-making, maintaining fidelity to the company's values, and practicing industriousness, leaders inspire employees to adopt similar behaviors. Furthermore, recognizing and rewarding employees who embody these virtues can create a positive feedback loop, encouraging others to aspire to the same standards. This alignment between leadership and employee behavior fosters a strong, virtue-driven culture that can withstand challenges and promote resilience.

In conclusion, creating a virtue-based workplace is not only beneficial for employee morale and organizational health but also essential for long-term success. By actively promoting the nine noble virtues through communication, training, and leadership, organizations can cultivate an environment where individuals feel empowered to thrive, collaborate, and contribute positively. As the workplace evolves, the integration of these timeless virtues will serve as a cornerstone for ethical conduct and personal development, ultimately leading to a more harmonious and productive work environment.

## Leadership and the Nine Noble Virtues

Leadership embodies a multifaceted approach that can greatly benefit from the integration of the Nine Noble Virtues. These virtues—Courage, Truth, Honor, Fidelity, Discipline, Hospitality, Self-Reliance, Industriousness, and Perseverance—serve as guiding principles for leaders seeking to inspire and motivate their teams. By embracing these virtues, leaders not only enhance their moral compass but also create an environment that fosters trust, respect, and collaboration among team members. This alignment with ethical standards encourages a workplace culture where individuals feel valued and empowered to contribute their best efforts.

Courage is an essential virtue for leaders, enabling them to make difficult decisions and face challenges head-on. A leader who exemplifies courage inspires others to act with bravery in their own roles, fostering an atmosphere of resilience. When leaders demonstrate truthfulness, they build credibility and transparency, essential for effective communication. This honesty encourages an open dialogue within the team, allowing for the sharing of ideas and constructive feedback, which are vital for growth and innovation.

Honor and fidelity further enhance a leader's capability to unite their team under shared values and commitments. Leaders who honor their promises and uphold ethical standards set a powerful example for their followers. This commitment to integrity cultivates a sense of loyalty and dedication among team members, creating a cohesive unit that can work together toward common goals. By modeling fidelity, leaders reinforce the importance of accountability, encouraging their teams to also remain true to their commitments.

Discipline and industriousness are virtues that drive productivity and efficiency within teams. A disciplined leader establishes clear expectations and boundaries, promoting a strong work ethic that influences team dynamics positively. When leaders practice industriousness, they demonstrate the value of hard work and perseverance, motivating others to adopt a similar mindset. This collective effort not only enhances individual performance but also contributes to the overall success of the organization.

Finally, hospitality and self-reliance play crucial roles in fostering a supportive and empowering work environment. Leaders who practice hospitality create a welcoming atmosphere that encourages collaboration and open communication. This approach builds strong relationships among team members, enhancing their sense of belonging. Self-reliance, on the other hand, encourages individuals to take initiative and be accountable for their own contributions. By integrating these nine noble virtues into their leadership styles, leaders can cultivate a thriving workplace that prioritizes ethical behavior, personal development, and community building, ultimately leading to enduring success.

## Enhancing Team Dynamics through Virtues

Enhancing team dynamics through virtues involves fostering an environment where the nine noble virtues serve as foundational principles guiding interactions and relationships among team members. Each virtue, from courage to hospitality, can significantly influence how individuals collaborate, resolve conflicts, and build trust within a group. By integrating these virtues into the fabric of a team's culture, organizations can create a more cohesive and productive work environment, ultimately leading to improved outcomes and employee satisfaction.

Courage, one of the nine noble virtues, plays a pivotal role in team dynamics. Encouraging team members to express their ideas and take risks fosters innovation and creativity. When individuals feel empowered to speak up without fear of retribution, the team benefits from a wider range of perspectives. This openness not only enhances problem-solving capabilities but also strengthens relationships as members learn to value and respect differing viewpoints. By cultivating a culture of courage, teams can navigate challenges more effectively and embrace opportunities for growth.

Another virtue that significantly affects team dynamics is loyalty. A loyal team is one where members support each other through challenges and celebrate successes together. This sense of belonging and mutual respect creates a strong foundation for collaboration. When loyalty is prioritized, it fosters a safe space for individuals to share their thoughts and concerns, knowing they have the backing of their peers. Such an environment reduces conflict and enhances morale, leading to a more engaged and motivated workforce.

Compassion is equally essential in enhancing team dynamics. By promoting empathy and understanding among team members, organizations can reduce misunderstandings and build stronger relationships. When team members practice compassion, they are more likely to consider the feelings and perspectives of others, leading to more effective communication and collaboration. This virtue encourages individuals to support one another, particularly during stressful times, thereby creating a more resilient team that can weather challenges together.

Finally, incorporating the virtue of wisdom into team dynamics can lead to more informed decision-making. Wisdom encourages individuals to reflect on their experiences, learn from successes and failures, and apply that knowledge to current situations. By fostering an environment where wisdom is valued, teams can improve their strategic thinking and problem-solving capabilities. This not only enhances productivity but also contributes to a culture of continuous improvement, where learning and growth are prioritized. Ultimately, by embracing the nine noble virtues, teams can enhance their dynamics, leading to a more harmonious and effective workplace.

# Chapter 7: The Nine Noble Virtues in Modern Spiritual Practices

## Spirituality and Ethical Living

Spirituality and ethical living are deeply intertwined, providing a framework through which individuals can navigate the complexities of life while adhering to a moral compass. The Nine Noble Virtues serve as a guiding principle for ethical living, offering a set of ideals that encourage personal integrity, responsibility, and respect for others. By embracing these virtues, individuals can cultivate a spiritual environment that fosters growth and ethical decision-making in both personal and communal contexts. This approach not only enriches one's spiritual life but also enhances the quality of interactions with others, creating a ripple effect of positive change.

At the core of spirituality is the connection between the self and something greater, which can manifest in various forms, including nature, community, or the divine. The Nine Noble Virtues—courage, truth, honor, fidelity, discipline, hospitality, industriousness, self-reliance, and perseverance—embody these spiritual connections by promoting characteristics that elevate ethical living. When individuals practice these virtues, they engage in a form of ethical spirituality that transcends mere belief systems, fostering a sense of belonging and purpose. This is particularly relevant in modern society, where many seek deeper meaning beyond material success.

In practical applications, living out the Nine Noble Virtues can transform daily routines into opportunities for spiritual growth. For instance, integrating hospitality into everyday interactions can enrich relationships and create a supportive community atmosphere. Likewise, practicing self-reliance encourages individuals to trust their instincts and abilities, fostering a sense of autonomy that is spiritually empowering. By consistently applying these virtues, adults can create a life that reflects their values and beliefs, reinforcing their ethical stance in various aspects of life, including family, work, and social interactions.

Teaching the Nine Noble Virtues to children is another vital aspect of promoting ethical living and spirituality. By instilling these values from a young age, parents and educators can cultivate a generation that prioritizes ethical considerations in their decisions and actions. Engaging children in discussions about the virtues and their relevance can help them understand the importance of integrity and compassion in navigating their own lives. This foundational knowledge supports their personal development and enables them to contribute positively to their communities, ultimately fostering a more ethical society.

Furthermore, the Nine Noble Virtues can be seamlessly integrated into workplace culture, enhancing both individual and collective ethical standards. Organizations that embrace these virtues often experience improved collaboration, greater employee satisfaction, and a stronger sense of community. By promoting a workplace environment that values honor, discipline, and industriousness, companies can encourage their employees to engage in ethical practices that align with their spiritual beliefs. This alignment not only benefits the organization but also nurtures a sense of fulfillment among employees, leading to a holistic approach to living that bridges spirituality and ethical living in a meaningful way.

## Rituals and Practices that Embrace Virtues

Rituals and practices that embrace virtues serve as a foundation for embodying the Nine Noble Virtues in everyday life. These rituals, whether individual or communal, provide a structured way to internalize and express values such as courage, truth, honor, and hospitality. By integrating these virtues into daily routines, individuals can cultivate a mindset that prioritizes personal growth and ethical living. Engaging in such practices not only reinforces one's commitment to these principles but also encourages others to reflect on and adopt similar values.

One effective ritual is the daily reflection or journaling practice focused on the Nine Noble Virtues. Each day, an individual can choose one virtue to contemplate, exploring its significance, how it has manifested in their life, and areas for improvement. This practice fosters self-awareness and accountability, allowing for a deeper understanding of how these virtues influence personal behavior and decision-making. Over time, this reflective process can lead to transformative insights and a strengthened commitment to living by these principles.

Community rituals, such as group discussions or workshops centered on the Nine Noble Virtues, can also play a critical role in reinforcing these values. When individuals come together to share experiences and insights related to the virtues, they create a supportive environment that encourages growth and accountability. These gatherings can include storytelling sessions where participants share personal anecdotes that highlight the virtues in action, thus enriching the collective understanding and appreciation of these ethical principles. Engaging in community practices fosters a sense of belonging and shared purpose, further embedding the virtues into the fabric of the group.

Incorporating the Nine Noble Virtues into workplace culture can take the form of regular team-building exercises that emphasize collaboration, respect, and integrity. Rituals such as recognition ceremonies, where employees acknowledge each other's adherence to these virtues, can create a positive atmosphere that promotes ethical behavior. By aligning workplace values with the Nine Noble Virtues, organizations can cultivate a culture of trust and accountability, enhancing overall productivity and employee satisfaction. This approach not only benefits individuals but also strengthens the organization as a whole.

Finally, modern spiritual practices can incorporate the Nine Noble Virtues through meditation, mindfulness, and intention-setting rituals. These practices encourage individuals to visualize embodying the virtues in their lives, promoting a holistic approach to personal development. By focusing on the virtues during meditation or prayer, individuals can deepen their spiritual connection while actively working towards moral improvement. Ultimately, the integration of rituals and practices that embrace the Nine Noble Virtues offers a practical pathway for individuals and communities to live more ethically, fostering a culture of virtue that benefits all aspects of life.

# Community and Spiritual Connection

Community and spiritual connection are integral components of living the Nine Noble Virtues. When individuals commit to these virtues, they not only enhance their personal lives but also contribute to the greater good of their communities. The sense of belonging and shared values that arise from practicing these virtues creates a foundation for strong interpersonal relationships. Through acts of kindness, integrity, and respect, individuals can foster an environment where trust and collaboration flourish, ultimately leading to a richer community life.

Incorporating the Nine Noble Virtues into community practices encourages collective growth and spiritual development. Communities that embrace these virtues often find that they can work together more effectively, resolving conflicts with a focus on understanding and compassion. For example, when honesty and honor are prioritized, individuals feel safe to express their thoughts and feelings, paving the way for open dialogues and collaborative solutions. This not only strengthens community bonds but also promotes a shared spiritual journey, as members support each other in aligning their actions with these noble principles.

Furthermore, the Nine Noble Virtues can serve as a guiding framework in modern spiritual practices. Many individuals seek deeper meaning in their lives while navigating the complexities of contemporary society. By reflecting on virtues such as courage and perseverance, individuals can cultivate resilience and a sense of purpose. This personal growth translates into a more profound connection with others, as individuals who embody these virtues often inspire those around them to pursue their own paths of integrity and ethical living. The community becomes a nurturing ground for spiritual exploration, where members encourage each other to thrive.

Teaching the Nine Noble Virtues to children is another way to instill a sense of community and spiritual connection from an early age. When children learn the importance of virtues like hospitality and generosity, they develop empathy and an understanding of their roles within a larger social fabric. Such education can take place within families, schools, and local organizations, ensuring that the next generation not only values these principles but also actively practices them. As children grow into adults who prioritize community welfare, the cycle of virtue continues, reinforcing a culture that values connection and mutual support.

Lastly, the Nine Noble Virtues play a crucial role in conflict resolution within communities. When disagreements arise, individuals grounded in these virtues approach conflicts with a mindset geared towards understanding and reconciliation. By prioritizing virtues like fairness and loyalty, parties can navigate disputes without resorting to hostility. This creates a culture where differences are respected and resolved through dialogue rather than division. In this way, the virtues not only enhance personal development but also serve as essential tools for building cohesive, spiritually connected communities that thrive on collaboration and mutual respect.

# Chapter 8: Comparison of the Nine Noble Virtues with Other Ethical Systems

## Virtue Ethics Overview

Virtue ethics is a philosophical approach that emphasizes the role of character and virtue in moral philosophy rather than focusing solely on the consequences of actions or adherence to rules. This ethical framework has its roots in ancient philosophical traditions, notably in the works of Aristotle, who argued that the ultimate goal of human life is to achieve eudaimonia, often translated as flourishing or well-being. Central to virtue ethics is the belief that cultivating virtuous traits leads individuals toward a more fulfilling and meaningful life, which aligns harmoniously with the principles of the Nine Noble Virtues.

The Nine Noble Virtues offer a contemporary means to explore virtue ethics in a practical context. Each virtue serves as a guiding principle that fosters personal growth and ethical living. For adults navigating the complexities of modern life, these virtues provide a framework for making decisions that reflect integrity, courage, and responsibility. By internalizing these traits, individuals can cultivate a character that not only benefits themselves but also positively impacts their communities.

Incorporating the Nine Noble Virtues into daily life requires intentional practice and reflection. Adults can apply these virtues in various settings, from personal relationships to professional environments. For example, the virtue of hospitality encourages individuals to create welcoming spaces, fostering connections that enhance community bonds. Similarly, the virtue of wisdom can guide decision-making processes, ensuring that choices are informed and considerate of the broader implications on both personal and communal levels.

Teaching the Nine Noble Virtues to children is another vital aspect of promoting virtue ethics within society. By instilling these values early on, parents and educators can help shape a generation that prioritizes character development alongside academic achievement. Practical applications of virtues in storytelling and literature can engage children's imaginations and provide relatable contexts for understanding these principles, making the virtues more accessible and actionable in their lives.

Finally, the relevance of the Nine Noble Virtues extends beyond individual development; they can also play a pivotal role in workplace culture and community building. Organizations that embrace these virtues foster environments of trust, respect, and collaboration, which are essential for effective teamwork and conflict resolution. By integrating the virtues into workplace ethics and practices, organizations can create a culture that not only drives productivity but also nurtures the moral character of their employees, leading to a more harmonious and ethically grounded society.

## Contrasting with Utilitarianism

Utilitarianism, a consequentialist ethical theory primarily associated with philosophers like Jeremy Bentham and John Stuart Mill, emphasizes the greatest good for the greatest number. This approach evaluates the moral worth of an action based on its outcomes, striving for overall happiness and minimizing suffering. In contrast, the Nine Noble Virtues, rooted in ancient Norse and Viking traditions, prioritize character and personal integrity over the outcomes of specific actions. While utilitarianism seeks to quantify the benefits and harms of actions, the Nine Noble Virtues advocate for a holistic approach centered on virtues such as courage, truth, honor, and fidelity.

The fundamental difference between these ethical frameworks lies in their focus. Utilitarianism is inherently situational, often requiring individuals to make decisions that may compromise personal virtues for the sake of collective well-being. For instance, utilitarian reasoning might justify dishonest behavior if it results in a greater overall benefit. In contrast, the Nine Noble Virtues emphasize the importance of maintaining one's integrity, regardless of the potential outcomes. This approach fosters a sense of personal responsibility and accountability, encouraging individuals to act in accordance with their values even when faced with challenging choices.

Moreover, the Nine Noble Virtues provide a robust framework for personal development that extends beyond mere calculations of pleasure and pain. By cultivating virtues such as bravery and wisdom, individuals can develop strong moral character that guides their actions and decisions. This character-driven approach contrasts sharply with utilitarianism's often transactional nature, which can lead to ethical dilemmas where the end justifies the means. In the realm of personal growth, the Nine Noble Virtues offer a pathway that emphasizes moral clarity and the intrinsic worth of individuals, rather than reducing ethical considerations to mere outcomes.

In workplace culture, the contrast between these ethical systems becomes particularly pronounced. A utilitarian approach may prioritize profit and efficiency, potentially at the expense of employee well-being and ethical practices. Conversely, incorporating the Nine Noble Virtues into a workplace environment fosters a culture of respect, collaboration, and trust. Organizations that prioritize virtues like loyalty and generosity create an atmosphere where employees feel valued not just for their productivity, but for their character and contributions to the collective good. This shift can lead to a more engaged workforce and a healthier organizational culture.

Lastly, in modern spiritual practices, the Nine Noble Virtues serve as guiding principles that encourage individuals to seek meaning and purpose beyond transient outcomes. While utilitarianism may appeal to a desire for tangible results, the Nine Noble Virtues invite a deeper exploration of one's values and the impact of one's character on the world. By embracing these virtues, individuals are encouraged to reflect on their actions within a broader ethical context, fostering a sense of interconnectedness and responsibility that transcends individual desires for success or happiness. This perspective not only enriches personal lives but also contributes to stronger communities grounded in shared values and mutual respect.

## Insights from Other Philosophical Traditions

Exploring the nine noble virtues through the lens of other philosophical traditions offers valuable insights that can enhance our understanding and application of these principles in everyday life. Various ethical systems around the world, from Eastern philosophies like Confucianism and Buddhism to Western traditions such as Stoicism and Virtue Ethics, emphasize values akin to the nine noble virtues. By examining these systems, we can draw parallels and distinctions that enrich our interpretation and practice of these virtues.

For instance, Confucianism places a strong emphasis on virtues such as filial piety, respect, and loyalty. These values resonate with the noble virtues of loyalty and honor, highlighting the importance of community and familial bonds. In practical terms, individuals can incorporate these principles into their daily interactions by fostering respect within their families and communities, thereby nurturing a culture of support and mutual respect. This approach not only strengthens personal relationships but also contributes to a more cohesive society.

Buddhism, with its focus on compassion and mindfulness, aligns closely with the noble virtue of compassion. The practice of empathy in Buddhist teachings encourages individuals to be aware of their actions and their impacts on others. This mindfulness can be applied in various settings, from personal relationships to workplace dynamics. By adopting a compassionate mindset, individuals can improve communication, enhance collaboration, and resolve conflicts more effectively. This practical application of compassion fosters a more harmonious environment, whether at home or in professional settings.

Stoicism, on the other hand, emphasizes virtues such as wisdom and courage, which correspond with the noble virtues of wisdom and bravery. Stoics advocate for resilience in the face of adversity and the pursuit of knowledge as a means of achieving a fulfilling life. This philosophical approach encourages individuals to confront challenges with courage and to seek wisdom through reflective practice. In daily life, this can manifest as a commitment to continuous learning and personal growth, allowing individuals to navigate life's complexities with confidence and clarity.

Incorporating insights from these diverse philosophical traditions into our understanding of the nine noble virtues not only enriches our personal development but also enhances our ability to teach these principles to others, including children. By drawing connections between these ethical systems, we can create a comprehensive framework that supports community building, conflict resolution, and personal growth. Ultimately, understanding the broader philosophical context of the nine noble virtues empowers individuals to live more virtuous lives, fostering a culture of respect, compassion, and resilience in every aspect of life.

# Chapter 9: The Nine Noble Virtues in Literature and Storytelling

## Virtues in Classic Literature

Classic literature serves as a rich repository for exploring virtues, often reflecting the ethical dilemmas and moral quandaries faced by humanity throughout history. Many authors have woven the nine noble virtues—courage, truth, honor, fidelity, discipline, hospitality, self-reliance, industriousness, and perseverance—into their narratives, offering readers profound insights into character development and personal growth. These stories illuminate how these virtues manifest in human behavior and the consequences of their absence, providing timeless lessons that remain relevant in today's society.

In works such as Homer's "The Iliad" and "The Odyssey," characters are often tested by their adherence to virtues such as honor and courage. Achilles embodies the struggle between personal honor and collective responsibility, while Odysseus exemplifies cunning and self-reliance in overcoming trials. These narratives not only showcase these virtues but also emphasize the complexities of human nature. Readers can draw parallels between these ancient struggles and contemporary challenges, prompting introspection about their own lives and the virtues they uphold.

Similarly, Shakespeare's plays frequently delve into themes of fidelity and truth, with characters grappling with loyalty and moral integrity. In "Hamlet," the titular character's quest for truth leads to profound consequences, illustrating the weight of honesty and the often painful journey toward self-discovery. These literary explorations encourage adults to reflect on the importance of truth in their own lives, reinforcing the need for transparency and authenticity in personal and professional relationships.

Moreover, classic literature often serves as a vehicle for teaching virtues to younger generations. Stories like "The Adventures of Tom Sawyer" and "Little Women" offer moral lessons embedded within engaging narratives. These tales can be instrumental in imparting values to children, demonstrating how virtues such as hospitality and industriousness can lead to personal fulfillment and positive community interactions. By engaging with these texts, parents and educators can facilitate discussions about the virtues, helping young readers recognize their significance in real-world scenarios.

Finally, the exploration of virtues in classic literature fosters a sense of community and shared values. As readers engage with these texts, they find common ground in the struggles and triumphs of characters who embody the nine noble virtues. This shared engagement can lead to meaningful conversations about personal and societal ethics, encouraging individuals to cultivate virtues within their own lives and communities. By reflecting on literature's portrayal of noble virtues, adults can better appreciate their role in fostering a more ethical and compassionate society.

# Modern Interpretations of Virtuous Characters

Modern interpretations of virtuous characters have evolved significantly as society grapples with new ethical dilemmas and cultural shifts. While the nine noble virtues—courage, truth, honor, fidelity, discipline, hospitality, industriousness, self-reliance, and perseverance—remain rooted in historical and philosophical traditions, their application in contemporary contexts reflects an ongoing dialogue about morality and character. Today's interpretations often emphasize the adaptability of these virtues in various aspects of life, including personal development, workplace culture, and community building.

In personal development, virtuous characters are increasingly seen as essential to fostering resilience and emotional intelligence. The virtue of courage, for instance, is interpreted not only as physical bravery but also as the willingness to face internal fears and vulnerabilities. This modern understanding encourages individuals to embrace authenticity and vulnerability as pathways to growth. Similarly, the virtue of self-reliance is evolving to highlight the importance of interdependence within communities, suggesting that true self-reliance involves knowing when to seek support while maintaining personal accountability.

The workplace also serves as a fertile ground for the application of the nine noble virtues. Modern interpretations advocate for a culture of honor and fidelity, where trust and loyalty among team members create a positive and productive environment. Employers are increasingly recognizing that when they embody these virtues, they not only enhance employee morale but also drive organizational success. Discipline is redefined in this context as a balance between structure and flexibility, where employees are encouraged to take initiative while adhering to ethical standards and collaborative goals.

In literature and storytelling, virtuous characters continue to resonate with audiences, but they are often depicted through complex narratives that reflect contemporary challenges. Characters embodying these virtues navigate moral ambiguity, demonstrating that the path to virtuous living is rarely straightforward. This complexity allows readers to engage with the virtues on a deeper level, prompting reflection on their own values and choices. The stories serve as vehicles for exploring the relevance of the nine noble virtues in real-life situations, bridging the gap between ancient principles and modern realities.

Community building through the nine noble virtues emphasizes the collective nature of virtuous living. Modern interpretations highlight the role of hospitality and industriousness in creating inclusive environments that foster collaboration and mutual support. By embodying these virtues, individuals contribute to a culture of respect and understanding, essential for resolving conflicts and promoting harmony. As communities increasingly seek to address issues of diversity and inclusion, the nine noble virtues provide a framework for establishing shared values that unite rather than divide, reinforcing the importance of character in fostering a cohesive society.

# Storytelling as a Means of Virtue Education

Storytelling has long been a powerful medium for imparting moral lessons and ethical values. In the context of virtue education, stories serve as a bridge connecting abstract concepts to real-life experiences. The Nine Noble Virtues—courage, truth, honor, fidelity, discipline, hospitality, self-reliance, perseverance, and industriousness—become more accessible when woven into narratives that resonate with our daily lives. Through storytelling, these virtues can be illustrated in ways that engage the imagination, evoke emotions, and inspire action, making them not just theoretical ideals but practical guidelines for behavior.

The effectiveness of storytelling in virtue education lies in its ability to present complex moral dilemmas in relatable scenarios. When characters face challenges that require them to embody virtues, it allows readers or listeners to reflect on their own values and choices. For instance, a tale of perseverance in the face of adversity can encourage individuals to confront their own struggles with resilience. By seeing how characters navigate their trials, audiences can internalize the lessons of virtue and apply them to their personal experiences, fostering a deeper understanding of what it means to live by these ideals.

Furthermore, storytelling can serve as a tool for teaching the Nine Noble Virtues to children. Through engaging narratives, children can learn these values in a manner that is both entertaining and educational. Stories featuring heroic figures or relatable protagonists can instill a sense of right and wrong, illustrating the importance of virtues in forming character. As children identify with characters and their journeys, they are more likely to adopt similar principles in their own lives, laying the groundwork for a morally grounded adulthood.

In the workplace, storytelling can be instrumental in cultivating a culture that embodies the Nine Noble Virtues. By sharing stories that highlight team members who exemplify these virtues, organizations can reinforce desired behaviors and values. For example, a narrative showcasing an employee's industriousness in overcoming obstacles can motivate others to strive for excellence. This approach not only enhances individual development but also fosters a sense of community, as shared stories create a collective identity rooted in virtuous principles.

Finally, storytelling plays a significant role in modern spiritual practices. Many spiritual teachings rely on parables and myths to convey deeper truths about human existence and moral living. By incorporating the Nine Noble Virtues into these narratives, individuals can explore their spiritual journeys while embedding virtue into their everyday lives. This integration of storytelling and virtue education can help individuals navigate their personal growth, enrich their relationships, and contribute positively to their communities, ultimately leading to a more virtuous society.

# Chapter 10: Community Building Through the Nine Noble Virtues

## Fostering a Sense of Belonging

Fostering a sense of belonging is fundamental to the practice of the Nine Noble Virtues, as it strengthens the bonds within communities and enhances individual well-being. Belonging creates an environment where individuals feel accepted, valued, and understood, which is essential for the application of virtues such as loyalty, honor, and hospitality. When people feel they belong, they are more likely to engage actively with their communities and contribute positively to the collective ethos. This sense of belonging can be cultivated through intentional practices that align with the virtues, encouraging individuals to connect with one another on deeper levels.

One practical application of fostering belonging is through the virtue of hospitality. This virtue goes beyond merely welcoming others into our homes; it involves creating spaces where people feel comfortable sharing their thoughts and experiences. By organizing community gatherings, workshops, or even casual meet-ups, individuals can practice hospitality, thereby reinforcing connections among members. These events serve as platforms for sharing stories, celebrating achievements, and addressing challenges, all of which contribute to a more cohesive community. When people come together in such settings, they learn to appreciate their differences and find common ground, enriching the sense of belonging.

The Nine Noble Virtues can also play a crucial role in teaching children about the importance of belonging. By instilling values such as loyalty and courage, parents and educators can help children understand the significance of supporting one another. Activities that promote teamwork and collaboration, such as group projects or community service, enable children to experience the rewards of belonging firsthand. When they learn that their contributions matter and that they are part of something larger, they develop a strong sense of identity and purpose. This foundation fosters resilience and empathy, crucial traits that encourage lifelong connections.

In the workplace, fostering a sense of belonging can enhance organizational culture and employee satisfaction. Incorporating the Nine Noble Virtues, such as integrity and industriousness, into company values encourages a collaborative atmosphere where employees feel respected and valued. Leaders can promote belonging by recognizing individual contributions, encouraging open communication, and creating diverse teams. When employees feel a sense of belonging, they are more motivated to engage with their work, share ideas, and support their colleagues, leading to increased productivity and a positive workplace environment.

Ultimately, fostering a sense of belonging through the Nine Noble Virtues enriches both individual lives and the broader community. As people engage with these virtues, they cultivate relationships built on trust, respect, and shared values. This collective effort not only enhances personal development but also strengthens the fabric of society. By actively promoting belonging in various aspects of life, individuals can create a supportive network that honors the virtues and encourages everyone to thrive.

# Collaborative Projects and Community Service

Collaborative projects and community service embody the essence of the Nine Noble Virtues, serving as a practical application of these principles in real-world scenarios. Engaging in collective efforts not only strengthens community bonds but also fosters personal growth and development. By working together towards a common goal, individuals can put into practice virtues such as loyalty, courage, and generosity, demonstrating their commitment to the greater good. These collaborative endeavors can take various forms, from local clean-up initiatives to larger-scale charity events, each providing an opportunity to reinforce the values that underpin the Nine Noble Virtues.

Participating in community service helps individuals connect with others, transcending personal boundaries and fostering a sense of belonging. This connection is vital in cultivating loyalty, a key virtue. When individuals invest their time and energy in community projects, they build relationships based on shared experiences and mutual goals. This loyalty extends beyond the project itself, creating a network of support that can be invaluable in times of need. Furthermore, the act of serving others can instill a sense of pride and purpose, reinforcing the individual's commitment to living in accordance with the virtues.

Courage is another virtue that finds expression in collaborative projects. Stepping outside one's comfort zone to contribute to community efforts often requires individuals to confront their fears and insecurities. Whether it's leading a team, advocating for a cause, or simply stepping up to volunteer, these actions embody the courage to make a difference. By encouraging adults to engage in these activities, communities foster an environment where individuals feel empowered to take initiative, inspiring others to do the same and creating a ripple effect of positive action.

Additionally, generosity is a virtue that is naturally amplified in collaborative settings. When individuals come together for a common cause, they often share their resources, skills, and time in ways that reflect a deep commitment to the welfare of others. This spirit of giving not only aids in achieving the project's objectives but also nurtures a culture of kindness and support within the community. As people witness the impact of their contributions, they are more likely to continue engaging in acts of generosity, thereby reinforcing the cycle of virtue in their daily lives.

Finally, the integration of the Nine Noble Virtues into collaborative projects can significantly enhance workplace culture. Organizations that encourage team-based initiatives and community service align their mission with the ethical standards represented by these virtues. Such a culture promotes employee engagement, satisfaction, and retention, as individuals feel a sense of purpose in their work. By embracing the principles of the Nine Noble Virtues, workplaces can cultivate an environment where collaboration thrives, ultimately benefiting both the organization and the broader community.

# Virtue-Driven Leadership in Communities

Virtue-driven leadership in communities serves as a foundational pillar for fostering cooperation, trust, and mutual respect among individuals. Leaders who embody the nine noble virtues—courage, truth, honor, fidelity, discipline, hospitality, industriousness, self-reliance, and perseverance—create environments where these values can thrive. By practicing these virtues, leaders inspire others to adopt similar principles, thereby establishing a cultural norm that emphasizes the importance of ethical behavior and communal responsibility. This approach not only enhances individual character but also fortifies the collective spirit of the community.

In practical terms, virtue-driven leadership manifests in various community initiatives and activities. Leaders can organize workshops, discussions, and projects that align with the nine noble virtues, allowing community members to engage actively with these principles. For instance, a community leader might initiate a project focused on hospitality, encouraging neighbors to share meals and stories to strengthen bonds. By cultivating such interactions, leaders demonstrate how virtues can be integrated into everyday life, making them accessible and relevant to all members of the community.

Moreover, teaching the nine noble virtues to children is an essential aspect of virtue-driven leadership. By instilling these values at a young age, leaders can help shape future generations who prioritize ethical decision-making and social responsibility. Community leaders can collaborate with schools and families to create educational programs that incorporate the virtues into curricula, providing children with a solid moral foundation. This proactive approach not only benefits the children but also enhances the overall character of the community as these young individuals grow into responsible adults.

In the workplace, virtue-driven leadership can significantly influence organizational culture. Leaders who embody the nine noble virtues create an environment where employees feel valued and motivated to work towards common goals. This can lead to increased productivity, improved employee morale, and a greater sense of belonging. By promoting virtues such as honesty and industriousness, leaders foster a workplace atmosphere built on trust and collaboration, which ultimately benefits the entire community as businesses thrive and contribute to local development.

Finally, the role of virtue-driven leadership extends to conflict resolution within communities. Leaders who practice the nine noble virtues are better equipped to handle disputes and disagreements in a constructive manner. By emphasizing truth and honor in discussions, leaders can facilitate open dialogue and encourage understanding among conflicting parties. This approach not only helps to resolve issues effectively but also reinforces the importance of virtues in maintaining harmony and unity within the community. In essence, virtue-driven leadership acts as a catalyst for positive change, nurturing a culture that values ethical living and communal well-being.

# Chapter 11: The Role of the Nine Noble Virtues in Conflict Resolution

## Understanding Conflict through Virtues

Understanding conflict is essential for personal growth and community harmony, and the Nine Noble Virtues provide a robust framework for navigating these challenges. Each virtue offers insights into human behavior, guiding individuals toward constructive responses rather than destructive reactions. When individuals embody virtues such as courage, truth, and honor, they cultivate an environment where conflicts can be addressed openly and respectfully. This approach not only mitigates the escalation of disputes but also fosters understanding and empathy among conflicting parties.

Courage, a fundamental virtue, empowers individuals to confront conflicts directly. Rather than avoiding difficult conversations or shying away from uncomfortable truths, courageous individuals engage with issues head-on. This proactive stance can diffuse tensions and open pathways for dialogue. By facing conflicts with a courageous heart, one demonstrates a commitment to resolution and growth. This virtue encourages individuals to advocate for themselves and others, ensuring that all voices are heard in the resolution process.

The virtue of truth plays a critical role in understanding and resolving conflicts. Clear and honest communication is vital in any disagreement, as it lays the groundwork for resolution. When individuals commit to speaking truthfully, they reduce misunderstandings and foster a culture of transparency. Furthermore, the pursuit of truth helps parties involved in a conflict to confront their biases and assumptions, fostering a more nuanced understanding of the situation. By prioritizing truth, individuals can navigate conflicts with integrity and fairness.

Honor also significantly influences how conflicts are approached and resolved. Upholding honor means respecting oneself and others, which is crucial when tensions run high. Individuals who act with honor are more likely to treat others with dignity, even in disagreement. This respect creates a safe space for dialogue, allowing for more constructive exchanges rather than combative interactions. When honor governs behavior, conflicts can transform into opportunities for collaboration and mutual understanding, rather than mere contention.

Incorporating the Nine Noble Virtues into conflict resolution not only benefits individuals but also enhances community dynamics. When groups collectively embrace these virtues, they set a standard for behavior that prioritizes empathy, respect, and collaboration. This shared commitment to virtuous conduct encourages a culture where conflicts are not seen as nuisances but rather as opportunities for growth and connection. As communities learn to navigate disputes through the lens of the Nine Noble Virtues, they become more resilient and cohesive, ultimately leading to a more harmonious existence.

## Practical Strategies for Resolution

Practical strategies for resolution rooted in the Nine Noble Virtues can transform conflicts into opportunities for growth and understanding. By embodying these virtues—courage, truth, honor, fidelity, discipline, hospitality, industriousness, self-reliance, and perseverance—individuals can approach disputes with a mindset that prioritizes resolution over escalation. This approach is not merely theoretical; it is a practical framework that can be applied in various contexts, from personal relationships to workplace dynamics, and even to community interactions.

One effective strategy is to cultivate an atmosphere of open communication. The virtue of truth encourages individuals to express their thoughts and feelings honestly while also listening actively to others. By fostering a space where all parties feel safe to share their perspectives, misunderstandings can be clarified, and deeper connections can be established. This openness paves the way for collaborative problem-solving, allowing individuals to address the root causes of conflicts rather than merely treating the symptoms.

Incorporating the virtue of honor into conflict resolution practices can also be highly beneficial. This involves respecting the dignity of all individuals involved, regardless of the situation's intensity. When parties approach a disagreement with the intent to honor each other's viewpoints, they are more likely to engage in constructive dialogue. The recognition that each person brings valuable insights to the table can shift the focus from confrontation to cooperation, ultimately leading to a more amicable resolution.

Discipline plays a crucial role in maintaining focus during conflict resolution. Emotions can often run high during disagreements, which may lead to impulsive reactions that hinder productive discussions. By practicing discipline, individuals can remain calm and centered, allowing for a more thoughtful and deliberate approach to resolving issues. This virtue encourages individuals to take a step back, assess the situation critically, and respond in a manner that aligns with their values, thereby fostering a more respectful and effective resolution process.

Lastly, the virtue of perseverance is essential when navigating complex conflicts. Not all disputes can be resolved quickly or easily; some may require sustained effort and commitment. Embracing perseverance means being willing to engage in ongoing dialogue and working through challenges together. This dedication not only strengthens relationships but also reinforces the belief that conflicts can lead to deeper understanding and unity. By applying these practical strategies grounded in the Nine Noble Virtues, individuals can transform conflict into a powerful catalyst for personal and communal growth.

# Building Peaceful Relationships

Building peaceful relationships is essential for creating a harmonious environment in both personal and professional settings. The Nine Noble Virtues provide a framework that can enhance interpersonal interactions by promoting values such as honor, truth, and fidelity. These virtues serve as guiding principles that encourage respect and understanding among individuals, fostering a culture of peace. By emphasizing these qualities, individuals can cultivate deeper connections that contribute to both personal fulfillment and community cohesion.

To build peaceful relationships, it is important to practice effective communication, which aligns with the virtue of truth. Honest and open dialogue allows individuals to express their thoughts and feelings without fear of judgment. By actively listening and validating each other's perspectives, conflicts can be resolved more constructively. This approach not only strengthens bonds but also encourages a culture where differences are embraced rather than feared, enhancing mutual respect and understanding.

Another key aspect of building peaceful relationships is the virtue of courage, which empowers individuals to confront issues directly and respectfully. When challenges arise, it takes courage to address them rather than allowing resentment or misunderstandings to fester. By approaching conflicts with a mindset focused on resolution rather than blame, relationships can be fortified. This proactive stance exemplifies how the Nine Noble Virtues can guide individuals in navigating the complexities of human interactions.

Incorporating the virtue of hospitality is equally crucial in building peaceful relationships. Welcoming others into one's space, whether physical or emotional, creates an atmosphere of safety and belonging. Acts of kindness and generosity foster goodwill and open up avenues for deeper connections. When individuals feel valued and cared for, they are more likely to reciprocate, leading to a cycle of positivity that strengthens community ties.

Lastly, the role of patience cannot be overstated in the context of developing peaceful relationships. The virtue of patience encourages individuals to understand that building lasting connections takes time and effort. By practicing patience, one can navigate misunderstandings and conflicts with grace, allowing for growth and healing. This virtue reminds us that relationships are a journey rather than a destination, and through consistent application of the Nine Noble Virtues, individuals can cultivate a more peaceful and harmonious existence.

# Chapter 12: Historical Context and Evolution of the Nine Noble Virtues

## Origins in Ancient Cultures

The concept of virtues has been a fundamental aspect of human civilization, tracing back to the earliest known societies. Ancient cultures, from the Mesopotamians to the Greeks, recognized the importance of moral principles in guiding individual behavior and fostering community cohesion. These early civilizations developed ethical frameworks that emphasized virtues such as courage, wisdom, and justice, setting the stage for later philosophical explorations of morality. The Nine Noble Virtues, which draw inspiration from various historical and cultural sources, reflect a synthesis of these ancient ideals, adapting them to resonate with contemporary life.

In Norse culture, the Nine Noble Virtues emerged as a set of guiding principles for both personal conduct and community interaction. Concepts such as honor, hospitality, and self-reliance were not merely idealistic but were woven into the fabric of everyday life. The sagas and eddas of the Norse people illustrate how these virtues were lived out in their society, emphasizing the significance of loyalty and respect among kin and community members. This historical context reveals an intrinsic understanding of the virtues as essential tools for navigating the complexities of human relationships, thus providing a foundation for modern interpretations and applications.

Similarly, ancient Greek philosophy contributed significantly to the understanding of virtues, particularly through the teachings of Socrates, Plato, and Aristotle. Their discussions on ethical behavior and the pursuit of eudaimonia, or human flourishing, highlighted the importance of cultivating virtues in achieving a good life. The Greeks viewed virtues not as isolated traits but as interconnected qualities that together promote a well-rounded character. This holistic approach to virtues continues to influence how we perceive and apply the Nine Noble Virtues today, encouraging a comprehensive understanding of personal development.

In addition to the Greeks and Norse, other ancient cultures, such as the Chinese and Indian civilizations, developed their own systems of virtues. Confucianism emphasized values like filial piety and benevolence, while Hinduism and Buddhism offered perspectives on compassion and non-violence. These diverse traditions showcase the universal recognition of virtues as essential for societal harmony and personal growth. By examining these various cultural approaches, we can appreciate the shared human experience that transcends geographical and temporal boundaries, affirming the relevance of the Nine Noble Virtues in our daily lives.

The evolution of the Nine Noble Virtues reflects a rich tapestry of historical influences, each contributing to a deeper understanding of what it means to live a virtuous life. As we explore these origins, we uncover not only the roots of our ethical beliefs but also the practical applications of these virtues in contemporary society. Emphasizing the importance of these ancient teachings in modern contexts fosters a sense of continuity and connection, allowing us to draw upon the wisdom of past civilizations while navigating the challenges of the present. Understanding the origins of the Nine Noble Virtues thus provides a solid foundation for integrating these principles into our everyday practices and interactions.

# Evolution through Historical Events

The Nine Noble Virtues, deeply rooted in historical contexts, have evolved through various significant events that shaped their interpretations and applications. Understanding this evolution provides a richer perspective on how these virtues can be integrated into contemporary life. The historical narrative surrounding these virtues showcases their resilience and adaptability, allowing them to remain relevant across generations. This evolution reflects the changing societal norms and challenges faced by communities, offering a framework that can be applied to modern dilemmas.

One of the pivotal events in the history of the Nine Noble Virtues is the Viking Age, during which these virtues were not merely ethical guidelines but also essential components of a warrior culture. During this time, virtues such as courage, truth, and honor were celebrated in sagas and stories that emphasized the importance of bravery in battle and loyalty to one's kin. This cultural emphasis on virtues helped forge strong community bonds, as individuals were encouraged to act in ways that upheld the collective values and traditions. The Viking Age serves as an example of how shared virtues can unify a society and provide a sense of identity amidst external threats.

As history progressed, the influence of Christianity brought about a transformation in the understanding and application of these virtues. The introduction of Christian ideals prompted a blending of values, leading to a reinterpretation of the Nine Noble Virtues within a more compassionate and altruistic framework. This shift often emphasized virtues like generosity and humility, aligning them with the teachings of love and kindness found in Christian doctrine. The dialogue between these two belief systems illustrates the adaptability of the Nine Noble Virtues, allowing them to coexist with emerging ethical philosophies while retaining their fundamental principles.

In more recent history, the resurgence of interest in Norse mythology and pagan practices has sparked renewed discussions around the Nine Noble Virtues. The modern reinterpretation often focuses on personal development and community building, highlighting how these virtues can foster resilience and strength in the face of contemporary challenges. Movements that emphasize self-empowerment and ethical living draw upon the historical significance of these virtues, creating a bridge between ancestral wisdom and modern practices. This revival showcases the enduring nature of the virtues, encouraging individuals to find personal meaning and relevance in ancient teachings.

Finally, examining the historical evolution of the Nine Noble Virtues reveals their potential to contribute to conflict resolution and community cohesion today. The virtues provide a common language and framework for addressing disputes, emphasizing respect and integrity in interpersonal relationships. By understanding the historical contexts from which these virtues emerged, individuals and communities can draw upon their lessons to foster dialogue and collaboration. This perspective not only honors the legacy of the virtues but also empowers individuals to actively engage in creating a more ethical and harmonious society.

## Contemporary Relevance and Adaptation

Contemporary society often grapples with ethical dilemmas and the search for meaning in everyday life. The Nine Noble Virtues, rooted in ancient wisdom, provide a framework that remains relevant in today's fast-paced world. These virtues—Courage, Truth, Honor, Fidelity, Discipline, Hospitality, Self-Reliance, Industry, and Perseverance—offer practical guidelines that can enhance personal development and foster stronger community ties. As adults seek to navigate complex social landscapes, these virtues can serve as a moral compass, guiding behavior and decision-making in a manner that promotes integrity and respect.

In the realm of personal development, the Nine Noble Virtues encourage self-reflection and growth. Each virtue can be viewed as a pillar upon which individuals can build their character. For instance, cultivating Courage can empower individuals to face challenges head-on, while embracing Truth fosters honesty in both personal and professional relationships. By actively integrating these virtues into daily routines, adults can develop a deeper sense of purpose and resilience, ultimately leading to a more fulfilled life. This approach also facilitates a better understanding of oneself and others, enhancing emotional intelligence and interpersonal skills.

The application of the Nine Noble Virtues in workplace culture is particularly significant in an era where corporate ethics are under scrutiny. Organizations that prioritize these virtues can create an environment of trust and collaboration. For example, promoting Industry and Discipline can lead to improved productivity, while emphasizing Honor and Fidelity encourages loyalty among team members. When leaders embody these virtues, they inspire their employees to adopt similar values, fostering a positive corporate culture that attracts talent and enhances employee satisfaction. This alignment not only benefits the organization but also contributes to the overall well-being of its members.

Teaching the Nine Noble Virtues to children is another crucial aspect of their contemporary relevance. By instilling these values at a young age, parents and educators can help shape the ethical foundations of future generations. Interactive storytelling, role-playing, and community involvement are effective methods for imparting these virtues. Children who learn the importance of Hospitality and Cooperation, for instance, are more likely to become empathetic and socially responsible adults. This educational approach not only prepares them for personal challenges but also equips them to contribute positively to society, creating a ripple effect of virtue-driven behavior.

Lastly, the Nine Noble Virtues have a unique place in modern spiritual practices, bridging ancient traditions with contemporary beliefs. Many individuals are seeking deeper connections to their spirituality, and these virtues can serve as guiding principles in their journeys. By aligning personal beliefs with the virtues of Courage and Self-Reliance, individuals can cultivate a sense of empowerment and purpose. Furthermore, exploring the comparison of these virtues with other ethical systems can enrich one's understanding of morality and ethics, showcasing the universal themes that resonate across cultures. Ultimately, the Nine Noble Virtues not only hold historical significance but also possess the adaptability needed to thrive in modern contexts, making them invaluable in today's world.

# Chapter 13: Conclusion and Call to Action

## Reflecting on Personal Virtue Practice

Reflecting on personal virtue practice is essential for anyone seeking to integrate the Nine Noble Virtues into their daily lives. Each virtue serves as a guiding principle, encouraging individuals to cultivate qualities such as courage, truth, honor, fidelity, discipline, hospitality, self-reliance, industriousness, and perseverance. By engaging in a reflective practice, individuals can assess how well they embody these virtues and identify areas in which they can grow. This self-assessment fosters a deeper understanding of one's values and motivations, ultimately leading to greater integrity and authenticity in personal and professional interactions.

Incorporating the Nine Noble Virtues into everyday life requires conscious effort and a commitment to self-improvement. Adults can start by setting specific intentions around each virtue, perhaps selecting one to focus on each week. Journaling about experiences related to the chosen virtue can provide insights into successes and challenges faced during that period. This practice not only enhances self-awareness but also builds a framework for accountability. By documenting these experiences, individuals can track their progress and recognize patterns that may either reinforce or hinder their virtuous conduct.

Teaching the Nine Noble Virtues to children can further reinforce personal practice. Adults can model these virtues in their interactions, demonstrating how they manifest in real-life situations. Engaging children in discussions about the virtues and their importance can help instill a sense of ethical responsibility from a young age. Additionally, storytelling can be a powerful tool for illustrating the virtues; sharing tales that exemplify courage or honor can resonate with children and make the virtues relatable. By fostering an environment where these virtues are celebrated, adults can create a culture of virtue that benefits both personal growth and community cohesion.

The workplace is another arena where reflecting on virtue practice can yield significant benefits. Incorporating the Nine Noble Virtues into workplace culture can enhance collaboration, improve morale, and promote ethical decision-making. Reflecting on how virtues like industriousness and discipline manifest in professional settings encourages employees to align their personal values with organizational goals. Leaders can facilitate discussions about the virtues and encourage team members to share their reflections, fostering a supportive environment where everyone is encouraged to contribute to a culture of integrity and respect.

In conclusion, reflecting on personal virtue practice is a vital step in living the Nine Noble Virtues authentically. Individuals who commit to this process not only enhance their personal development but also positively influence those around them. Whether through teaching children, fostering a virtuous workplace, or engaging in community-building efforts, the impact of embodying these virtues extends beyond the individual. By making the Nine Noble Virtues a foundational aspect of daily life, adults can contribute to a more ethical and harmonious society, enriching their own lives and the lives of others in the process.

## Encouraging Community Involvement

Community involvement is essential for fostering a sense of belonging and shared purpose among individuals. By actively participating in their communities, adults can embody the nine noble virtues, promoting attributes such as courage, truth, and honor. These virtues serve as guiding principles that encourage individuals to engage in meaningful activities that benefit their surroundings. Through volunteer work, local initiatives, or simply supporting neighbors, adults can create a ripple effect that enhances the community's overall well-being.

One of the most effective ways to encourage community involvement is by leading through example. Adults who demonstrate a commitment to the nine noble virtues inspire others to follow suit. For instance, participating in community clean-up days not only promotes environmental stewardship but also embodies the virtue of stewardship itself. By showing dedication to the community's health and aesthetics, individuals can motivate others to take similar action, thus reinforcing the importance of collective effort.

Creating opportunities for participation is another key aspect of fostering community involvement. Organizations and groups can organize events that allow adults to engage with their neighbors, share their skills, and contribute to common goals. Workshops, educational seminars, and social gatherings can provide platforms for individuals to collaborate and learn from one another. When community members feel that their contributions are valued, they are more likely to engage and support initiatives that reflect the nine noble virtues.

Furthermore, recognizing and celebrating community involvement strengthens the bonds between individuals and their communities. Acknowledging the efforts of volunteers or local leaders can instill a sense of pride and ownership among residents. By highlighting stories of courage, generosity, and wisdom within the community, individuals are reminded of the virtues they strive to embody. This recognition not only motivates continued participation but also encourages others to get involved, creating a cycle of positive engagement.

Lastly, integrating the nine noble virtues into community initiatives can provide a framework for conflict resolution and personal development. When community members are equipped with the understanding of these virtues, they can approach challenges with a mindset focused on collaboration and respect. This not only enhances individual growth but also fosters a harmonious community atmosphere. By nurturing a culture rooted in the nine noble virtues, individuals can ensure that their community remains vibrant, resilient, and supportive for all its members.

# Future of the Nine Noble Virtues in Society

The future of the Nine Noble Virtues in society holds significant promise as these principles resonate with contemporary values, offering a framework for ethical living in an increasingly complex world. As individuals seek meaning and guidance in their personal and professional lives, the virtues can serve as a compass, promoting integrity, courage, and honor. With growing awareness of mental health and personal development, these virtues can be integrated into daily practices, encouraging individuals to reflect on their actions and decisions. The rising demand for authenticity in leadership and interpersonal relationships further underscores the relevance of the Nine Noble Virtues in fostering trust and collaboration.

Incorporating the Nine Noble Virtues into educational systems presents an opportunity for holistic development. Teaching children about these virtues can instill a strong moral foundation, equipping them with the skills necessary to navigate challenges and conflicts in life. Schools that emphasize character education can cultivate environments where respect, responsibility, and resilience thrive. By bridging the gap between traditional ethical teachings and modern educational practices, the Nine Noble Virtues can be a cornerstone of curricula, promoting a sense of community and shared values among students.

The workplace is another arena where the Nine Noble Virtues can play a transformative role. As organizations increasingly prioritize corporate social responsibility and employee well-being, integrating these virtues into workplace culture can enhance team dynamics and employee satisfaction. Virtues such as truthfulness and industriousness encourage transparency and hard work, contributing to a culture of accountability and collaboration. Furthermore, a strong ethical foundation can help organizations navigate dilemmas and foster a positive reputation, ultimately leading to sustainable success.

In modern spiritual practices, the Nine Noble Virtues offer a secular yet profound approach to personal growth and ethical living. Many individuals today seek spiritual fulfillment outside traditional religious frameworks, finding resonance in ethical systems that emphasize personal responsibility and communal harmony. By incorporating the virtues into daily spiritual practices, individuals can cultivate mindfulness and intentionality in their lives, creating a deeper connection to themselves and their communities. This alignment of personal values with spiritual growth can lead to a more meaningful and purposeful existence.

Lastly, the Nine Noble Virtues can serve as powerful tools for community building and conflict resolution. In an era marked by division and strife, these virtues encourage dialogue, understanding, and cooperation among diverse groups. By emphasizing shared values such as hospitality and loyalty, communities can foster inclusive environments that celebrate differences while uniting around common goals. The virtues provide a framework for resolving conflicts through respectful communication and empathy, paving the way for collaborative solutions that honor the dignity of all individuals involved. As society evolves, the continued application of the Nine Noble Virtues will undoubtedly shape a more harmonious and ethical future.

# Threads of Destiny: Unraveling the Web of Wyrd in Norse Mythology

## Chapter 1: Introduction to the Web of Wyrd

### Definition and Historical Context

The concept of the web of wyrd, rooted deeply in Norse mythology, serves as a complex tapestry that intertwines fate, destiny, and the choices individuals make throughout their lives. Often symbolized by a web or a series of interconnected threads, wyrd represents a multifaceted understanding of how destiny unfolds. Historically, wyrd was perceived not merely as a predetermined sequence of events but as a dynamic interplay between fate and personal agency. This duality invites exploration into how ancient Norse communities navigated their existence within this framework, acknowledging both the weight of destiny and the importance of individual actions.

In the context of historical interpretations, the web of wyrd has been analyzed through various lenses, including literary, archaeological, and cultural studies. Early sources, such as the Poetic Edda and the Prose Edda, illuminate how the Norse viewed their lives as being woven into a larger cosmic design. Scholars have noted that wyrd was not a singular force but a collective phenomenon shaped by the actions and decisions of countless individuals. This understanding reflects a communal aspect of fate, where personal choices contribute to the broader narrative of existence, resonating with the societal values of the time.

Modern pagan practices often draw from the web of wyrd, integrating its principles into rituals and spiritual beliefs. Practitioners view the web as a symbol of interconnectedness, highlighting the impact of one's actions on the broader tapestry of life. In contemporary paganism, the web serves as a reminder of the responsibility individuals hold in shaping their destinies while remaining cognizant of the influences around them. This symbol has evolved into a powerful motif in various ceremonies, emphasizing the balance between fate and free will and encouraging practitioners to reflect on their life paths within a larger cosmic framework.

Literature and storytelling have long utilized the symbolism of the web of wyrd, weaving it into narratives that explore themes of fate, choice, and consequence. From classic Norse tales to modern fantasy literature, the web serves as a poignant reminder of the interconnectedness of characters and their journeys. Writers often employ this motif to illustrate the complexities of personal agency in the face of destiny, prompting readers to consider how their own lives are influenced by the myriad threads that bind them to others. Such representations enrich the storytelling landscape, inviting deeper engagement with the characters' struggles against or acceptance of their fates.

In the realm of mental health and mindfulness, the web of wyrd offers a unique perspective on coping with life's uncertainties. Understanding one's life as a series of interconnected threads can foster a sense of belonging and purpose, encouraging individuals to engage with their experiences holistically. This perspective aligns with contemporary therapeutic practices that emphasize the importance of narrative and storytelling in personal healing. By recognizing the web of wyrd, individuals may find empowerment in their choices while embracing the unpredictability of life, ultimately reinforcing the idea that, although fate plays a role, personal agency remains a powerful force in shaping one's destiny.

## The Concept of Wyrd in Norse Mythology

The concept of Wyrd in Norse mythology serves as a foundational element in understanding the intricate relationship between fate, free will, and the interconnectedness of all beings. Wyrd, often translated as fate or destiny, is perceived as a web that encompasses the past, present, and future, tying individuals to their actions and choices. In Norse thought, Wyrd is not merely a predetermined path but a dynamic system influenced by individual actions and the collective experiences of a community. This understanding invites a deeper exploration of how the threads of Wyrd weave into the tapestry of life, shaping narratives both ancient and modern.

In historical interpretations, Wyrd has been analyzed through various lenses, revealing its multifaceted nature. Early Norse texts, such as the Poetic Edda and the Prose Edda, illustrate Wyrd as a powerful force that governs the lives of gods and mortals alike. Scholars have debated its implications, with some suggesting that Wyrd represents a deterministic worldview while others argue for a more nuanced understanding that includes the element of choice. This duality highlights the complexity of human existence in Norse culture, where individuals are seen as active participants in their fate rather than mere puppets of destiny.

The influence of Wyrd extends beyond historical contexts into modern pagan practices, where it is often embraced as a guiding principle. Contemporary practitioners draw upon the concept to foster a sense of connection to ancestral traditions and the natural world. Rituals and meditative practices centered around Wyrd encourage individuals to reflect on their life choices and their impact on the web of existence. This modern interpretation emphasizes the importance of mindfulness and intentionality, suggesting that understanding one's Wyrd can lead to a more fulfilling and harmonious life.

Symbolically, the web of Wyrd is rich with imagery that resonates in literature and storytelling. The idea of interconnected threads has inspired countless narratives, where characters navigate their destinies while grappling with the forces of fate. This symbolism often serves as a metaphor for personal growth and transformation, illustrating how each choice influences the larger narrative of life. In contemporary art, representations of the web of Wyrd continue to evolve, reflecting the ongoing relevance of these themes in society. Artists often explore the tension between fate and free will, inviting viewers to ponder their place within the intricate web of existence.

Finally, the interplay of fate and free will within the framework of Wyrd has implications for mental health and mindfulness. Recognizing the threads of Wyrd can encourage individuals to take responsibility for their actions, fostering a sense of agency in their lives. This understanding promotes resilience and adaptability, as individuals learn to navigate the complexities of their circumstances. Furthermore, the comparative analysis of Wyrd with other cultural concepts of fate, such as the Greek Moirai or the Hindu karma, reveals universal themes of interconnectedness and responsibility. In role-playing games and fantasy literature, the web of Wyrd often serves as a narrative device that enriches character development and world-building, connecting players to a broader exploration of destiny and choice.

## The Significance of Threads in Fate

The concept of threads within the framework of fate in Norse mythology is both intricate and profound, reflecting the interconnectedness of all beings and events. In the narrative of Wyrd, each person's life is depicted as a thread woven into a vast tapestry, where the actions of individuals are not isolated but rather part of a larger, cosmic design. This imagery serves to illustrate the belief that fate is not a rigid path but a dynamic interplay of choices, experiences, and consequences. The threads symbolize the delicate balance between predestined events and personal agency, suggesting that while certain outcomes may be preordained, the manner in which individuals navigate their lives contributes to the overall pattern of existence.

Historically, interpretations of the web of Wyrd have varied, with scholars and practitioners examining its implications across different contexts. In the Viking Age, the web was primarily understood as a manifestation of the Norns, the three fate-weaving goddesses who spin, measure, and cut the threads of life. This triad represents the past, present, and future, emphasizing the cyclical nature of time and existence. Modern interpretations, however, have expanded upon these ancient views, incorporating psychological and philosophical dimensions that align the web of Wyrd with contemporary understandings of fate and free will. This evolution of thought showcases the enduring relevance of these ancient symbols in addressing the complexities of human experience.

In modern pagan practices, the web of Wyrd has become a significant motif, embodying the principles of interconnectedness and shared destiny. Rituals often invoke the imagery of weaving, symbolizing the conscious effort to align one's intentions with the broader tapestry of life. Practitioners may reflect on their personal threads and how they intertwine with those of others, fostering a sense of community and collective purpose. This approach not only highlights the importance of individual choices but also reinforces the idea that each person's actions can influence the greater web, promoting a sense of responsibility and mindfulness in everyday life.

The symbolism of the web of Wyrd extends into literature and storytelling, where it serves as a powerful metaphor for the human condition. Authors and creators often draw upon this imagery to explore themes of fate, choice, and the consequences of actions. The web becomes a narrative device that allows for the exploration of characters' struggles against predetermined paths, framing their journeys as a dance between destiny and autonomy. This literary exploration also resonates with audiences, inviting them to reflect on their own lives and the threads they weave within their personal stories.

Artistic representations of the web of Wyrd in contemporary art further illustrate its significance in modern culture. Artists frequently depict the web as a visual metaphor for the complexities of existence, using various mediums to explore the interplay of fate and free will. These works often invite viewers to engage with their own narratives, encouraging introspection and contemplation on how individual threads contribute to the larger tapestry of life. In this way, the web of Wyrd continues to inspire both creativity and mindfulness, serving as a reminder of the intricate connections that bind us all together in the fabric of existence.

# Chapter 2: Historical Interpretations of the Web of Wyrd

## Early Sources and Textual Evidence

The concept of the web of wyrd in Norse mythology is deeply rooted in early sources, primarily derived from texts such as the Poetic Edda and the Prose Edda. These texts, compiled in the 13th century but based on traditions and oral narratives that predate them, serve as foundational sources for understanding the complex interplay of fate and free will within Norse cosmology. The Poetic Edda, a collection of Old Norse poems, presents wyrd as an intricate web that binds individuals to their fates, suggesting that one's actions reverberate through time and ultimately shape their destiny. The Prose Edda, written by Snorri Sturluson, further elucidates these themes and provides a framework for interpreting the significance of wyrd within the context of the gods, heroes, and the overarching narrative of existence.

In addition to the Eddas, sagas and historical accounts from the Viking Age offer textual evidence of how the web of wyrd influenced daily life and societal structures. The sagas often portray characters who actively engage with their fates, illustrating the tension between predetermined paths and personal agency. This duality is evident in the stories of figures such as Sigurd and Gudrun, whose lives are marked by choices that resonate with the concept of wyrd. The sagas serve not only as literary artifacts but also as reflections of the cultural beliefs of the time, where fate was perceived as both a guiding force and a set of constraints within which individuals operated.

Archaeological findings also contribute to our understanding of the web of wyrd, revealing how ancient Norse communities visualized and interpreted this concept. Artifacts such as rune stones, grave goods, and decorative motifs often feature symbols associated with fate, suggesting that the web of wyrd was not merely an abstract idea but a tangible aspect of life. These symbols, frequently found in burial sites, indicate a belief in the interconnectedness of life and death, reinforcing the notion that one's actions have lasting implications that transcend the physical realm. This integration of belief and material culture underscores the significance of wyrd in both the spiritual and practical dimensions of Norse life.

The influence of the web of wyrd extends into modern interpretations and practices, particularly within contemporary paganism. Many modern practitioners draw upon the concept of wyrd to explore themes of personal responsibility and the interconnectedness of all beings. Rituals and practices that honor wyrd often emphasize mindfulness and intentional living, encouraging individuals to recognize their role within the broader tapestry of existence. This revival of interest in wyrd reflects a growing desire to engage with ancient wisdom as a means of navigating the complexities of modern life, fostering a sense of agency amidst the challenges of contemporary existence.

Comparative analysis of the web of wyrd with other cultural concepts of fate reveals both unique characteristics and shared themes across different traditions. For instance, the Greek concept of Moirae or the Fates parallels the notion of wyrd, emphasizing the inescapable nature of destiny while still allowing for human agency. By examining these parallels, one can gain a deeper appreciation for how different cultures interpret the relationship between fate and free will. This exploration not only enriches our understanding of Norse mythology but also highlights the timeless relevance of these themes in literature, storytelling, and even in contemporary artistic expressions, where the web of wyrd continues to inspire creativity and reflection on the human experience.

## Scholarly Perspectives on Wyrd

Scholarly perspectives on wyrd provide a multifaceted understanding of this intricate concept within Norse mythology. At its core, wyrd represents a complex interweaving of fate, destiny, and the personal choices individuals make throughout their lives. Scholars have explored how wyrd serves not only as a guiding force but also as a reflection of societal values and beliefs in a world where the interplay of fate and free will is a central theme. This duality raises questions about the nature of human agency and the extent to which individuals can influence their destinies, a topic that resonates in both historical texts and contemporary discussions.

Historical interpretations of wyrd have evolved significantly, particularly as new archaeological findings and literary analyses emerge. Early texts, such as the Poetic Edda and the Prose Edda, reveal how wyrd was perceived by the Norse, often depicted as a web spun by the Norns. This imagery emphasizes the interconnectedness of all beings and events, suggesting that actions reverberate through time. Scholars have noted that the depiction of wyrd in these texts often reflects the existential struggles faced by the Norse people, providing insight into their worldview and the cultural significance of fate as a guiding principle in their lives.

Modern pagan practices have also drawn heavily on the concept of wyrd, integrating it into rituals and spiritual frameworks. Practitioners often view wyrd as a means of understanding personal destiny and the cyclical nature of life. This contemporary interpretation highlights the adaptability of ancient concepts to modern spiritual practices, allowing individuals to navigate their lives with a sense of purpose and connection to their ancestry. As such, wyrd serves as a bridge between past and present, facilitating a deeper understanding of one's place within the greater tapestry of existence.

The symbolism of the web of wyrd extends beyond mythology and spirituality into the realms of literature and storytelling. Many contemporary authors draw on the motif of the web to explore themes of interconnectedness and the consequences of choices. This literary device serves to illustrate how characters are bound by their fates while also highlighting their struggles against predetermined paths. The web of wyrd thus becomes a powerful metaphor for the human experience, illustrating the delicate balance between fate and free will that defines our narratives.

Artistic representations of wyrd in contemporary art further enrich the dialogue surrounding this concept. Artists often depict the web as a dynamic and evolving entity, using various mediums to express the complexities of fate, choice, and interconnectedness. These visual interpretations invite viewers to engage with the themes of wyrd on a personal level, fostering a dialogue about the role of fate in their own lives. Additionally, the exploration of wyrd in relation to mental health and mindfulness underscores its relevance in contemporary society, as individuals seek to understand their narratives and find meaning within the web of their experiences. Through comparative analyses with other cultural fate concepts, scholars and practitioners can appreciate the universal themes of destiny while recognizing the unique contributions of the Norse understanding of wyrd.

## Evolution of the Concept Through the Ages

The concept of wyrd, often depicted as a web intricately woven with the threads of fate, has undergone significant transformation throughout history. In its earliest interpretations within Norse mythology, wyrd represented a deterministic force guiding the lives of mortals and gods alike. This notion was deeply intertwined with the belief in Norns, the three fates who spun, measured, and cut the threads of human destiny. The understanding of wyrd as a binding force emphasized the inevitability of fate, reflecting a worldview in which individuals were seen as subject to the whims of divine powers, leading to a sense of helplessness in the face of predestined events.

As the Norse worldview evolved, so too did interpretations of wyrd. The Viking Age, with its complex social structures and burgeoning exploration, began to incorporate a more nuanced understanding of fate and free will. Scholars and sagas began to suggest that individuals could influence their wyrd through actions and choices, emphasizing the interplay between fate and personal agency. This shift allowed for a more dynamic relationship with wyrd, where one's character and decisions could alter the course of their destiny. Such evolution in thought parallels the emergence of heroic ideals in sagas, where protagonists often faced their fates with bravery, suggesting a growing belief in the power of human determination.

The influence of wyrd extends beyond ancient narratives into modern pagan practices, where it has been revitalized as a symbol of interconnectedness and personal empowerment. Contemporary practitioners of Norse paganism often embrace the concept of wyrd as a guiding principle in their spiritual journeys. By recognizing the threads of their lives and the choices that weave them, individuals find a sense of agency within the larger tapestry of existence. This modern interpretation encourages mindfulness, as adherents reflect on their actions and their potential to shape future outcomes, fostering a sense of personal responsibility that resonates deeply in today's fast-paced world.

The symbolism of the web of wyrd also finds its place in literature and storytelling, where it serves as a powerful metaphor for the complexities of fate and free will. Authors and playwrights draw on the imagery of weaving to explore themes of destiny, often portraying characters who grapple with the constraints of their fates while seeking to assert their autonomy. This narrative device not only enriches storytelling but also invites readers to reflect on their own lives, considering the interplay of choices and circumstances that shape their paths. As such, the web of wyrd transcends time, continuing to inspire creative expression and philosophical inquiry.

Finally, the contemporary artistic representations of the web of wyrd further illustrate its enduring relevance. Artists across various mediums interpret wyrd through visual motifs, installations, and performances that evoke the intricacies of fate, choice, and interconnectedness. These modern interpretations often invite audiences to engage with their own experiences of destiny and free will, fostering a dialogue about mental health and mindfulness. By contemplating the threads of their own lives and the broader human experience, individuals can find solace in the understanding that while they may be woven into a larger tapestry, they possess the power to influence the design of their own narratives.

# Chapter 3: The Web of Wyrd and Modern Pagan Practices

## Reconstructionist Approaches to Wyrd

Reconstructionist approaches to Wyrd focus on understanding and interpreting the concept through a lens grounded in historical and archaeological evidence. Wyrd, often translated as fate or destiny in Norse mythology, embodies a complex interplay of personal agency and cosmic forces. Scholars emphasize the importance of examining ancient texts, runic inscriptions, and artifacts to reconstruct a more accurate representation of how early Norse societies perceived Wyrd. This historical context allows for a nuanced understanding that goes beyond mere superstition, revealing a worldview that integrated fate with individual choices and societal responsibilities.

In exploring the symbolism of the web of Wyrd, reconstructionists highlight its representation as a complex network that connects individuals to their ancestors, communities, and the cosmos. The imagery of a web suggests not only the interconnectedness of all beings but also the intricate nature of fate, where every action influences the broader tapestry of existence. This perspective can be particularly relevant to modern practitioners of paganism who seek to honor their ancestral roots while navigating contemporary realities. By understanding the web as both a symbol and a framework, individuals can better appreciate their place within this intricate system and cultivate a sense of mindfulness about their choices.

Artistic representations of Wyrd in contemporary mediums also reflect reconstructionist approaches. Artists and writers draw upon historical motifs while infusing their works with modern interpretations, creating a dialogue between past and present. This artistic exploration often serves as a means to engage with themes of fate, free will, and the human experience, resonating with audiences who seek to understand their own narratives. By examining how Wyrd is depicted in literature, visual arts, and performance, one can gain insight into the evolving meanings of fate and agency in contemporary culture.

The role of mental health and mindfulness in relation to the web of Wyrd becomes evident through reconstructionist practices that encourage self-reflection and personal growth. By recognizing the interconnected nature of their experiences, individuals can develop a deeper awareness of how their choices impact both their own lives and those around them. This understanding fosters a sense of responsibility and empowerment, aligning closely with the ancient Norse belief in the significance of individual actions within the broader tapestry of fate. Techniques such as journaling and meditation inspired by Wyrd can aid in processing emotions and fostering resilience, providing tools for navigating modern life's complexities.

Finally, comparative analysis of the web of Wyrd with other cultural concepts of fate reveals both unique attributes and universal themes. Many cultures possess similar ideas of interconnected destinies, suggesting a shared human experience regarding the quest for meaning and understanding in a seemingly chaotic world. By studying these parallels, reconstructionists can enrich their interpretations of Wyrd, situating it within a global context that highlights the interplay between fate and free will. This broader perspective not only enhances the appreciation of Norse mythology but also invites individuals to reflect on their own beliefs and practices regarding destiny, agency, and their place in the universe.

## Rituals and Beliefs Surrounding Fate

Rituals and beliefs surrounding fate in Norse mythology are deeply intertwined with the concept of Wyrd, which represents the intricate web of destiny that governs the lives of gods and mortals alike. In ancient Norse culture, rituals were not merely ceremonial acts but were infused with profound significance, serving as a means to connect individuals with their fates. These rituals often involved offerings to the Norns, the three goddesses who weave the threads of fate, ensuring that individuals acknowledged their place within the larger tapestry of existence. Such acts were believed to influence the course of one's life, inviting the divine to intervene in the unfolding of personal destinies.

One of the most significant rituals was the blót, a sacrificial offering made to the gods and spirits. The blót was a communal event that reinforced social bonds and sought favor from the divine, thereby influencing fate. Participants would gather to share stories and invoke the Norns, seeking guidance and clarity regarding their paths. This collective recognition of fate fostered a sense of belonging and responsibility among individuals, as they understood their lives as part of a larger narrative shaped by divine forces. The act of coming together to honor these rituals also served as a reminder that while fate is predetermined, the choices made within that framework can still bear significant weight.

Beliefs surrounding fate were also reflected in the sagas and eddas, where characters often grappled with their destinies. The notion of inescapable fate was prevalent, yet the literature also portrayed moments of defiance and struggle against predetermined outcomes. This duality sparked a rich dialogue on the nature of free will versus fate, suggesting that while Wyrd lays the groundwork for life's events, individuals still possess agency. This interplay is pivotal in understanding how Norse mythology influences modern pagan practices, where contemporary practitioners often seek to engage with their Wyrd, embracing both the inevitability of fate and the power of choice in their spiritual journeys.

In contemporary artistic representations, the web of Wyrd continues to inspire a plethora of interpretations that echo the ancient beliefs. Artists draw on the symbolism of the web, depicting the complex interconnections among beings and their fates. This artistic exploration not only revitalizes ancient themes but also invites reflection on modern existential concerns. The web serves as a metaphor for mental health, illustrating how individual actions, relationships, and choices weave into the broader fabric of life, influencing personal well-being and mindfulness. By engaging with these themes through art, individuals can confront their own narratives and the impact of their actions within the shared human experience.

The comparative analysis of Wyrd alongside other cultural concepts of fate reveals a rich tapestry of beliefs that resonate through various societies. Similar to the Greek concept of Moirai or the Hindu idea of Karma, the web of Wyrd emphasizes the interconnectedness of all life and the intricate designs of destiny. In role-playing games and fantasy literature, these themes are often explored, allowing players and readers to navigate their own stories within the framework of Wyrd. By embodying characters who confront fate, individuals gain insight into their relationships with destiny and choice, fostering a deeper understanding of their own lives and the universal struggle between fate and free will.

## Influence on Neo-Paganism and Heathen Traditions

Neo-Paganism and Heathen traditions have seen a significant resurgence in recent decades, drawing from ancient practices and beliefs to form contemporary spiritual frameworks. Central to many of these traditions is the concept of the web of wyrd, a complex symbol that embodies the interconnectedness of fate and agency within Norse mythology. This intricate tapestry of life illustrates how individual actions influence not only personal destiny but also the collective fate of communities. As practitioners explore the web of wyrd, they often find themselves reflecting on their own lives, seeing their choices as threads woven into a larger narrative shaped by both divine forces and personal will.

The influence of the web of wyrd on modern pagan practices can be observed in rituals, storytelling, and community gatherings. Many Neo-Pagans incorporate the web of wyrd into their ceremonies, using it as a symbol of interconnectedness and the cyclical nature of existence. This practice reinforces the idea that every action has consequences that extend beyond the individual. Rituals may focus on honoring the past, acknowledging the present, and shaping the future, allowing practitioners to engage with their personal experiences and the broader tapestry of life. This connection to the web of wyrd fosters a sense of responsibility and mindfulness, encouraging individuals to consider how their lives impact the world around them.

Literature and storytelling have also embraced the symbolism of the web of wyrd, as authors draw upon its rich imagery to explore themes of fate, free will, and the human condition. The web serves as a metaphor for the complexity of life, illustrating how seemingly random events are often interconnected. Contemporary narratives often weave elements of Norse mythology into their plots, creating characters who grapple with the implications of their choices against the backdrop of a predetermined fate. This literary device not only captivates readers but also invites them to reflect on their own lives and the intricate patterns of fate that shape their destinies.

Artistic representations of the web of wyrd have emerged across various mediums, from visual art to performance. Contemporary artists frequently employ the web as a motif, exploring themes of connection, identity, and the passage of time. These artistic interpretations can serve as a form of meditation, inviting viewers to contemplate their place within the larger scheme of existence. Through these works, the web of wyrd becomes a canvas for expressing the complexities of the human experience, illustrating how art can be both a personal exploration and a communal reflection on the nature of life and destiny.

Finally, the web of wyrd's relevance extends beyond spiritual and artistic realms, finding a place in discussions about mental health and mindfulness. By encouraging individuals to recognize the interconnectedness of their experiences, the web of wyrd promotes a holistic approach to well-being. This perspective can help individuals navigate challenges by fostering a sense of purpose and belonging. As practitioners of Neo-Paganism and Heathen traditions continue to explore the web of wyrd, they contribute to a growing understanding of how ancient concepts can inform modern lives, bridging the past with the present and shaping a more mindful future.

# Chapter 4: Symbolism of the Web of Wyrd in Literature and Storytelling

## Wyrd in Norse Sagas and Eddas

Wyrd, a central concept in Norse mythology, embodies the intertwining threads of fate and destiny that govern the lives of gods and mortals alike. Within the Norse sagas and Eddas, Wyrd is often depicted as an inexorable force, shaping the destinies of individuals while simultaneously allowing for personal agency. This duality presents a rich tapestry of existential themes, illustrating how characters navigate their fates amidst the constraints imposed by Wyrd. The sagas and Eddas serve as a reflection of the belief in fate's omnipresence, while also hinting at the potential for human intervention within that framework, thus creating a complex interplay between predetermined destiny and the exercise of free will.

The concept of Wyrd is intricately connected to the motifs of weaving and threads, symbolizing the interconnectedness of all beings and events in the cosmos. In texts such as the Poetic Edda and the Prose Edda, Wyrd is often illustrated through the imagery of the Norns, the three female figures who weave the fates of gods and men. This visual representation emphasizes the notion that lives are woven together in a grand, cosmic tapestry, where individual choices contribute to a collective narrative. The sagas frequently explore how these woven fates can be influenced by actions, decisions, and even the desires of individuals, reinforcing the idea that while Wyrd is a guiding force, it does not render human agency obsolete.

In contemporary interpretations, the web of Wyrd has found resonance within modern pagan practices, where individuals seek to understand their place within the interconnected fabric of existence. This revival of interest emphasizes the relevance of Wyrd in personal spiritual journeys, reminding practitioners that their actions and intentions have far-reaching consequences. As such, the web of Wyrd serves not only as a historical concept but also as a living practice, fostering a sense of mindfulness and responsibility in navigating one's path. This perspective challenges adherents to consider their role in the grand design and encourages a reflective approach to life's choices.

Literature and storytelling continue to draw on the symbolism of Wyrd, demonstrating its profound influence on narrative structures and character development. Many contemporary authors integrate the themes of fate and free will into their works, echoing the complexities found in Norse sagas. This literary exploration often reveals the struggle between characters' desires and the weight of destiny, inviting readers to ponder their own lives through the lens of Wyrd. Moreover, role-playing games and fantasy literature frequently utilize the web of Wyrd as a framework for character motivations, plot progression, and moral dilemmas, allowing players to engage with the concept in a dynamic and immersive manner.

As discussions around mental health and mindfulness gain prominence, the web of Wyrd emerges as a metaphor for understanding one's mental state and emotional well-being. By recognizing that individuals are part of a larger interconnected web, there is potential for healing and growth. This perspective encourages a holistic view of existence, where personal struggles can be contextualized within a broader narrative, fostering resilience and a sense of belonging. The comparative analysis of Wyrd with other cultural concepts of fate reveals universal themes of interconnectedness, ultimately illustrating that while paths may diverge, the human experience is bound by shared destinies woven through time and space.

## Modern Literary Interpretations

Modern literary interpretations of the web of wyrd have evolved significantly, reflecting contemporary concerns and interests while staying rooted in the rich tapestry of Norse mythology. Authors today often explore the intricate interplay between fate and free will, drawing parallels between ancient beliefs and modern existential dilemmas. This reinterpretation allows for a nuanced understanding of how individuals navigate their destinies within the broader framework of societal expectations and personal choices, emphasizing that while the threads of wyrd may be woven by external forces, individuals still possess agency within their lives.

In literature, the symbolism of the web of wyrd serves as a powerful motif that resonates with themes of interconnectedness and the cyclical nature of existence. Contemporary writers frequently employ this imagery to illustrate the idea that every action has repercussions, echoing the Norse belief that one's choices weave into the larger fabric of fate. This approach not only enriches character development but also invites readers to consider their own roles in the tapestry of life, fostering a deeper understanding of the consequences that arise from seemingly insignificant decisions.

The influence of the web of wyrd extends beyond literary texts into modern pagan practices, where it serves as a guiding principle for rituals and spiritual exploration. Practitioners often invoke the concept of wyrd to emphasize the importance of living in harmony with one's own fate while acknowledging the interconnectedness of all beings. In this context, the web becomes a source of empowerment, encouraging individuals to embrace their unique paths and cultivate mindfulness as they navigate the complexities of existence. This perspective aligns with contemporary discussions around mental health, where the web of wyrd is seen as a metaphor for resilience and self-discovery.

Artistic representations of the web of wyrd in contemporary art have also flourished, with artists using various mediums to express the intricate relationships between fate, identity, and the cosmos. Through visual storytelling, creators capture the essence of wyrd, inviting viewers to reflect on their own connections to the universe. This artistic exploration often transcends cultural boundaries, leading to comparative analyses with other cultural concepts of fate, such as the Greek Moirai or the Hindu concept of Karma. These comparisons enrich the dialogue surrounding fate and free will, illustrating how different cultures grapple with similar existential themes.

Finally, the web of wyrd has found a unique place within role-playing games and fantasy literature, where it serves as a framework for world-building and character arcs. Game designers and authors incorporate the web as a narrative device, allowing players and readers to engage with the notion of fate in an interactive manner. This not only enhances storytelling but also encourages a deeper understanding of the consequences of choices made within fictional realms. As these interpretations continue to evolve, the web of wyrd remains a vital thread in the ongoing conversation about destiny, agency, and the human experience.

## The Role of Wyrd in Folklore and Myth

The concept of Wyrd in Norse mythology serves as a profound framework for understanding fate, destiny, and the interconnectedness of all beings. Rooted in the ancient belief systems of the Norse, Wyrd represents a web that links past, present, and future, illustrating how choices and actions shape one's path. Folklore and myth surrounding Wyrd often depict it as a tapestry woven by the Norns, the three female figures who govern fate. This imagery emphasizes the complexity of life's narrative, suggesting that while individuals may exert free will, they remain intricately bound to the threads of Wyrd that dictate the outcomes of their choices.

In examining the historical interpretations of Wyrd, one finds that ancient texts and sagas often reflect a tension between determinism and free will. The Norse people viewed life as a series of preordained events influenced by the actions of gods, heroes, and ordinary individuals. This interplay is evident in stories such as that of Sigurd, whose fate is foreshadowed by prophecies yet ultimately shaped by his decisions and moral character. The narratives evoke a sense of inevitability, reinforcing the idea that while Wyrd sets the stage, human agency plays a critical role in how the drama unfolds.

The influence of Wyrd extends beyond ancient texts, permeating modern pagan practices and contemporary spiritual beliefs. In these contexts, Wyrd is often embraced as a guiding principle that encourages practitioners to acknowledge the interconnectedness of their actions and the universe. Rituals and meditative practices frequently draw upon the symbolism of the web of Wyrd, aiming to foster awareness of one's place within this intricate tapestry. Through such engagements, individuals can cultivate a deeper understanding of their personal destinies and the collective fate of their communities.

Literature and storytelling have long employed the symbolism of Wyrd to explore themes of fate and free will. Authors and poets often invoke the web metaphor to illustrate characters' struggles against their predetermined paths, creating rich narratives that resonate with readers. Works ranging from classical epics to modern fantasy literature utilize Wyrd to evoke the tension between individual desires and cosmic order. This literary device not only captivates audiences but also invites them to reflect on their own lives and the forces that shape them, providing a lens through which to examine their relationships with fate.

In contemporary art, the web of Wyrd finds expression in various forms, serving as a powerful symbol for the complexities of human experience. Artists often portray the interwoven threads of Wyrd to convey themes of connection, struggle, and resilience. This artistic representation resonates with modern audiences, particularly in relation to mental health and mindfulness. By visualizing Wyrd, individuals can confront their own narratives, acknowledging the influence of past experiences on their present state and future possibilities. Through this exploration, the web of Wyrd transcends its mythological roots, becoming a tool for personal reflection and growth in the journey of life.

# Chapter 5: Fate and Free Will in the Web of Wyrd

## Philosophical Implications of Wyrd

The concept of Wyrd in Norse mythology embodies a complex intertwining of fate, destiny, and the choices made by individuals. Philosophically, it raises significant questions about determinism and free will. While Wyrd suggests that certain events are preordained, it does not entirely negate the role of individual agency. This duality creates a dynamic interplay where people are both shaped by their circumstances and capable of shaping their own paths. The philosophical implications of Wyrd challenge the binary view of fate versus free will, inviting deeper exploration into how these forces coexist in human experience.

In the historical context, interpretations of Wyrd have evolved, reflecting changing societal beliefs about fate and destiny. Early Norse societies viewed Wyrd as a web, intricately woven with the actions of past generations, presenting a collective experience of fate. This perspective emphasizes communal responsibility and interconnectedness, where individual choices resonate throughout the web of existence. Modern interpretations often draw from these ancient understandings, fostering a renewed appreciation for the collective aspects of fate in contemporary life, particularly in relation to community and shared narratives.

The influence of Wyrd extends into modern pagan practices, where it serves as a guiding principle for those who seek to align their lives with the rhythms of the universe. Practitioners often engage with the web of Wyrd through rituals and meditative practices, emphasizing the importance of intention and mindfulness. This engagement reflects a philosophical stance that recognizes the impact of personal choices while acknowledging the larger cosmic forces at play. By understanding Wyrd as both a guiding force and a canvas for individual action, modern pagans cultivate a sense of empowerment within the framework of fate.

In literature and storytelling, the symbolism of the web of Wyrd manifests in various forms, illustrating the intricate connections between characters, events, and themes. This symbolism often serves as a narrative device that emphasizes the consequences of choices and the inevitable intertwining of lives. Writers draw upon the rich tapestry of Wyrd to explore existential questions, such as the nature of human existence and the search for meaning within the constraints of fate. As a result, the web of Wyrd becomes a profound metaphor for the human condition, resonating with audiences across cultures and epochs.

The philosophical exploration of Wyrd also intersects with contemporary discussions around mental health and mindfulness. Understanding one's life as part of a larger web can foster a sense of belonging and purpose, promoting mental well-being. The recognition that individual actions contribute to a larger narrative encourages individuals to engage thoughtfully with their choices. Additionally, the concept of Wyrd invites reflection on how personal experiences shape one's path, offering a framework for resilience and growth. In a world where individuals often grapple with feelings of isolation, the web of Wyrd serves as a reminder of the interconnected nature of existence, fostering a deeper appreciation for both personal and shared journeys.

## Tension Between Destiny and Choice

The tension between destiny and choice is a central theme in Norse mythology, particularly as embodied in the concept of Wyrd. Wyrd refers not only to fate but also to the interconnectedness of all events in the universe, suggesting a complex web where each thread represents choices made by individuals and the influence of the gods and the cosmos. This duality raises important questions about the extent to which humans are bound by fate or possess the agency to shape their own destinies. The Norse believed that while certain fates were inescapable, individuals still wielded the power to make choices that could alter their paths, creating a dynamic interplay between predestination and free will.

In historical interpretations, the web of Wyrd has often been viewed through the lens of fatalism, where the outcomes of one's life seem predetermined by the gods or the cosmos. However, this perspective can overshadow the nuanced understanding that ancient Norse culture had regarding personal agency. For instance, the heroic tales often depict characters who confront their fates, sometimes successfully altering their trajectories through bravery and cunning. This suggests that while Wyrd may lay out a certain path, it is the choices made along the way that can lead to varying outcomes, emphasizing the importance of individual action within the framework of fate.

Modern pagan practices have drawn inspiration from the web of Wyrd, integrating its principles into rituals and belief systems that honor both fate and free will. Practitioners often invoke Wyrd as a reminder of the interconnectedness of their actions and the broader universe. This acknowledgement of Wyrd serves as a foundation for ethical living, where choices are seen as significant and impactful. Consequently, modern interpretations often emphasize the responsibility individuals hold in shaping their destinies, fostering a sense of empowerment and mindfulness in everyday life.

The symbolism of the web of Wyrd extends into contemporary literature and storytelling, where it manifests as a metaphor for the complex interplay of choice and consequence. Authors frequently utilize this imagery to explore characters' struggles with their destinies, reflecting the timeless human experience of navigating between predetermined paths and the desire for autonomy. Through these narratives, the web of Wyrd becomes a powerful tool for examining the nature of fate, encouraging readers to reflect on their own lives and the choices that define their journeys.

In artistic representations, the web of Wyrd continues to inspire creators across various mediums, from visual art to role-playing games. This symbolism resonates with audiences seeking to understand their place in the universe, offering a framework for exploring themes of fate and free will. By engaging with the web of Wyrd, contemporary artists and storytellers invite their audiences to grapple with the age-old question of how much control we truly have over our destinies, ultimately enriching the ongoing dialogue surrounding the balance of destiny and choice in the human experience.

## Case Studies from Norse Mythology

The concept of the web of wyrd in Norse mythology serves as a rich tapestry that interweaves fate, free will, and the intricate connections between individuals and their destinies. Examining case studies from this mythological framework reveals how the actions of gods and mortals alike contribute to the unfolding of their fates. One prominent example is the tale of Odin and the Norns, the three sisters who weave the fates of gods and men. Their influence underscores the belief that while fate is predetermined, there exists a dynamic interplay with individual choices that can alter the course of events, illustrating the duality of control and destiny.

Another compelling case study is the story of Sigurd and the dragon Fafnir. Sigurd's journey, marked by bravery and treachery, epitomizes the struggle between fate and free will. His choice to pursue Fafnir, driven by the desire for glory and wealth, highlights how personal ambition can lead to significant consequences, both foreseen and unforeseen. This narrative resonates deeply within the context of modern pagan practices, as practitioners often reflect on the delicate balance between accepting one's fate and actively shaping one's path through conscious decisions.

The tale of Loki and his eventual downfall further illustrates the complexities of the web of wyrd. Loki's cunning and manipulative nature, leading to the cataclysmic events of Ragnarok, showcases how one's actions can reverberate through the fabric of fate, affecting not just the individual but the entire cosmos. This case study serves as a cautionary tale in contemporary interpretations of the web of wyrd, emphasizing the importance of accountability and ethical choices. It also offers a lens through which to explore themes of mental health and mindfulness, as individuals grapple with their own inner demons and the repercussions of their actions.

In literature, the web of wyrd has inspired countless interpretations and artistic representations. One notable example is the modern retelling of the Volsunga Saga, which infuses contemporary themes and moral dilemmas within the traditional framework of fate. The symbolism of the web manifests in various forms, from intricate illustrations of the Norns weaving to metaphorical references in poetry and prose. These artistic expressions not only enrich the narrative but also invite audiences to contemplate their own interactions with fate and the essence of their life stories.

Lastly, the influence of the web of wyrd extends into the realm of role-playing games and fantasy literature, where characters navigate the complexities of fate and choice. Game mechanics often reflect the tension between preordained destiny and player agency, allowing individuals to explore the consequences of their actions in a controlled environment. This interactive engagement with the concept of wyrd fosters a deeper understanding of its implications, encouraging players to reflect on their real-life choices and the broader patterns that shape their existence. Through these case studies, the web of wyrd emerges as a multifaceted symbol, bridging ancient beliefs with modern interpretations and practices.

# Chapter 6: Artistic Representations of the Web of Wyrd in Contemporary Art

## Visual Interpretations of Wyrd

Visual interpretations of Wyrd serve as a powerful bridge between ancient Norse mythology and contemporary understanding of fate, destiny, and interconnectedness. The imagery associated with Wyrd often evokes the intricate web, symbolizing how every action and event is interwoven with others, creating a tapestry of life that reflects the complexities of existence. Artists have drawn upon this symbolism to create works that resonate with the themes of fate and personal agency, inviting viewers to contemplate their own place within the vast network of life. These visual representations not only honor the historical interpretations of Wyrd but also explore its relevance in modern contexts, making the ancient concept accessible to contemporary audiences.

In literature and storytelling, the web of Wyrd has inspired countless artistic depictions, from traditional illustrations in Norse sagas to modern graphic novels and paintings. Artists often employ motifs such as the three Norns weaving the fate of gods and men, emphasizing the communal aspect of destiny. The visual narrative invites audiences to reflect on the role of individual choice amidst predetermined paths, encapsulating the duality of fate and free will. This thematic exploration continues to influence not only literature but also visual art, as creators seek to portray the tension between the inevitable and the mutable in human experience.

Contemporary art has embraced Wyrd's symbolism, with many artists interpreting the concept through various mediums, including painting, sculpture, and digital art. Exhibitions often feature works that depict intricate webs, knots, and other interconnected designs, symbolizing the complex relationships between individuals and their environments. These pieces encourage mindfulness and reflection, serving as reminders of the interconnectedness of all beings. By engaging with Wyrd visually, artists contribute to a broader dialogue about mental health, prompting viewers to consider how their lives are interwoven with those of others, fostering a sense of empathy and communal support.

Modern pagan practices have also adopted the web of Wyrd as a central theme in rituals and ceremonies, illustrating the ongoing relevance of Norse mythology in contemporary spirituality. Visual representations in this context often take the form of altarpieces, ritual tools, or tattoos, each imbued with personal significance and connection to the greater web of existence. These artistic expressions facilitate a deeper understanding of Wyrd's teachings, allowing practitioners to navigate their spiritual journeys while honoring their ancestral roots. Such interpretations highlight the fluidity of Wyrd, showcasing its adaptability to the evolving nature of belief systems.

In comparative cultural studies, the web of Wyrd finds parallels with various fate concepts from around the world, such as the Greek Moirai or the Hindu concept of Karma. Artistic interpretations serve as a visual language that transcends cultural boundaries, illustrating shared human concerns about fate and agency. By examining these similarities through art, scholars and enthusiasts alike can appreciate the universal themes that connect different cultures while recognizing the unique attributes of Wyrd. This cross-cultural exploration not only enriches our understanding of fate but also emphasizes the importance of storytelling and visual art in conveying complex philosophical ideas across generations.

## Influence on Modern Art Movements

The concept of the web of wyrd, with its intricate interconnections and threads representing fate, has significantly influenced various modern art movements, particularly those that embrace themes of interconnectedness, fate, and the human experience. Artists, inspired by Norse mythology, have woven elements of the web of wyrd into their works, creating pieces that reflect the complexities of life and the notion that every action reverberates through time and space. This thematic exploration can be seen in movements such as surrealism and abstract expressionism, where artists delve into the unconscious and the chaotic nature of existence, echoing the unpredictable patterns of wyrd.

In contemporary art, the symbolism of the web of wyrd serves as a powerful narrative tool that speaks to the human condition. Artists often utilize visual motifs that resemble webs or interconnected lines to convey ideas about fate, choice, and the myriad influences that shape individual destinies. These representations not only draw from Norse mythology but also resonate with universal themes found in storytelling and literature. By engaging with the web of wyrd, artists create a dialogue between the ancient and the modern, allowing viewers to reflect on their own lives and the unseen forces that guide them.

The exploration of mental health and mindfulness has also seen the web of wyrd emerge as a relevant theme in modern artistic practices. Artists increasingly recognize the importance of understanding one's place within the web of existence, leading to a growing interest in works that promote introspection and self-awareness. Through visual art, performance, and installations, creators encourage audiences to consider how their individual threads are woven into the larger tapestry of life, fostering a sense of connection and emotional resonance. This approach not only nurtures personal growth but also highlights the role of creativity as a means of navigating the complexities of mental health.

Moreover, the web of wyrd has found its way into role-playing games and fantasy literature, where it acts as a narrative device that explores the interplay between fate and free will. Game designers and writers draw on the web's symbolism to create intricate storylines that challenge players and readers to confront their choices and the consequences that arise from them. This aspect of the web of wyrd enriches the gaming experience, making it an engaging metaphor for understanding life's unpredictability and the impact of decisions. As characters navigate through quests and dilemmas, they embody the very essence of the web, reinforcing the idea that every thread matters.

In summary, the influence of the web of wyrd on modern art movements manifests in various forms, from visual arts and literature to gaming. The threads of wyrd serve not only as a source of inspiration but also as a framework for understanding the complexities of fate, choice, and interconnectedness in contemporary society. As artists continue to explore these themes, they invite audiences to reflect on their own lives, encouraging a deeper appreciation of the intricate web that binds all beings. Through this lens, the web of wyrd remains a vital and evolving symbol in the tapestry of modern artistic expression.

## Artists and Their Works

The concept of the web of wyrd in Norse mythology has inspired numerous artists across various mediums, reflecting the intricate interplay of fate, free will, and the human experience. These artists, through their unique interpretations, have sought to capture the essence of wyrd, showcasing its multifaceted nature. From painters to sculptors, each has contributed to a rich tapestry of artistic expression that resonates with both historical interpretations and modern understandings of this ancient concept. Their works serve not only as reflections of personal creativity but also as vessels for cultural and spiritual exploration.

In visual arts, the web of wyrd often manifests through symbolic imagery that evokes the threads of fate woven by the Norns. Artists utilize intricate patterns and motifs to represent the interconnectedness of all beings and the consequences of their actions. For instance, contemporary painters might depict the Norns at their weaving loom, surrounded by vibrant colors that symbolize the various paths of life. This artistic choice not only honors traditional narratives but also invites viewers to reflect on their own life choices and the potential impact of those decisions on their destinies.

Literature has also played a significant role in interpreting the web of wyrd, offering narratives that delve into the themes of fate and free will. Authors often weave the concept into their storytelling, creating characters who grapple with their destinies while navigating the complex web of relationships and events surrounding them. Modern fantasy literature, particularly in role-playing games, borrows heavily from Norse mythology, embedding the web of wyrd into its mechanics and lore. This incorporation allows players to explore the tension between predestined paths and the freedom of choice, mirroring the struggles faced by mythological figures.

In addition to traditional and literary art forms, contemporary artists have begun to explore the web of wyrd in relation to mental health and mindfulness. By engaging with the concept of interconnectedness, these artists create works that encourage self-reflection and awareness of one's place within the larger narrative of life. Installations and interactive pieces invite participants to consider how their actions ripple through the fabric of existence, fostering a deeper understanding of personal and collective fate. This focus on mindfulness not only highlights the relevance of ancient themes but also demonstrates how they can be applied to modern psychological practices.

The comparative analysis of the web of wyrd with other cultural fate concepts further enriches the dialogue among artists and scholars alike. By examining how different traditions interpret fate and free will, artists can draw parallels and contrasts that enhance their work. This cross-cultural exploration often leads to innovative interpretations that blend elements from various mythologies, creating a more inclusive understanding of destiny. As the web of wyrd continues to inspire new generations of artists, its enduring significance is a testament to the universal human quest for meaning in the face of life's uncertainties.

# Chapter 7: The Web of Wyrd in Relation to Mental Health and Mindfulness

## Understanding Wyrd as a Tool for Reflection

Wyrd, a complex concept woven throughout Norse mythology, serves as a profound lens through which individuals can explore their personal narratives and the intricate tapestry of existence. At its core, wyrd represents the intertwining of fate, destiny, and the choices made throughout one's life. By reflecting on the nature of wyrd, individuals can gain insight into how their actions resonate within the larger pattern of their lives, and how historical interpretations of this concept can shape modern understandings of responsibility and consequence.

The historical interpretations of wyrd reveal its multifaceted nature, encompassing not just the inevitability of fate but also the agency individuals possess in navigating their paths. In ancient Norse culture, wyrd was often depicted as a web, symbolizing the interconnectedness of all beings and events. This imagery encourages a reflective practice, prompting individuals to consider how their choices impact not only their own lives but also the broader community and the unfolding narrative of existence. By engaging with these historical contexts, modern readers can appreciate the nuanced understanding of fate as a dynamic interplay of forces rather than a rigidly predetermined outcome.

In contemporary pagan practices, wyrd is often embraced as a guiding principle that encourages mindfulness and self-awareness. Practitioners draw upon the concept to reflect on their life choices and the potential consequences of those actions. This reflective practice fosters a deeper connection to one's own life story, encouraging individuals to acknowledge their past while remaining open to future possibilities. Such engagement with wyrd can serve as a powerful tool for personal growth, as it emphasizes the importance of living consciously and with intention, aligning one's actions with their values and beliefs.

The symbolism of the web of wyrd extends beyond personal reflection, influencing storytelling and literature. Authors and artists utilize this concept to explore themes of fate and free will, often depicting characters who must navigate their wyrd while contending with external forces. This narrative framework invites readers to reflect on their own life choices, considering how personal agency interacts with larger societal or cosmic forces. Through this lens, stories become a mirror for self-exploration, prompting audiences to ponder their roles within the intricate web of life and the stories they weave.

As the web of wyrd finds its place in modern discussions about mental health and mindfulness, it offers a framework for understanding the complexities of human experience. By reflecting on the interconnectedness of thoughts, feelings, and actions, individuals can cultivate a greater sense of awareness and acceptance of their circumstances. This perspective aligns with therapeutic practices that emphasize the importance of recognizing one's agency in shaping personal narratives. Ultimately, engaging with the concept of wyrd fosters a deeper understanding of the self, encouraging individuals to embrace their unique threads within the intricate fabric of existence.

## Wyrd and Acceptance in Mental Health Practices

Wyrd, a fundamental concept in Norse mythology, refers to the interwoven strands of fate that shape individuals' lives and destinies. In mental health practices, this notion of interconnectedness can foster a deeper understanding of personal experiences and the acceptance of circumstances beyond one's control. Embracing the principle of wyrd allows individuals to recognize that while certain aspects of life may be predetermined, there remains an opportunity for agency and choice in how one responds to those events. This duality can be empowering, as it encourages a balance between acceptance and proactive engagement with one's mental health journey.

The acceptance of wyrd in mental health practices aligns well with contemporary therapeutic approaches, such as Acceptance and Commitment Therapy (ACT). ACT emphasizes the importance of accepting one's thoughts and feelings, rather than struggling against them. This resonates with the idea of wyrd, where individuals are encouraged to acknowledge their fate while taking responsibility for their actions within that framework. By integrating practices that promote acceptance of both personal circumstances and mental health challenges, individuals can cultivate resilience and a sense of peace, ultimately leading to improved well-being.

Additionally, the web of wyrd serves as a metaphor for the complexity of mental health, illustrating how various life experiences, relationships, and societal influences are interwoven. This interconnectedness can help individuals understand that their mental health struggles are not isolated but part of a larger tapestry of human experience. By recognizing the shared nature of these struggles, individuals may find solace in community support and collective healing, which are essential components of effective mental health practices.

Furthermore, the symbolism of wyrd in literature and storytelling can offer valuable insights into the human condition. Many narratives reflect themes of fate and free will, allowing individuals to explore their own experiences through the lens of myth. These stories can serve as a therapeutic tool, providing a framework for understanding personal challenges and reinforcing the notion that while fate may play a role in one's life, there is always room for growth and transformation. Engaging with these narratives can inspire hope and resilience, encouraging individuals to navigate their mental health with a sense of purpose.

In conclusion, the integration of wyrd into mental health practices not only fosters acceptance but also emphasizes the importance of personal agency. By embracing the complexities of fate and the interconnectedness of experiences, individuals can develop a holistic understanding of their mental health. This approach aligns with contemporary therapeutic methods and encourages a mindful engagement with life's challenges, ultimately leading to a greater sense of empowerment and well-being. As the threads of wyrd continue to be woven into the fabric of modern mental health practices, they provide a rich tapestry through which individuals can explore their own destinies.

## Mindfulness Techniques Inspired by Wyrd

Mindfulness techniques inspired by the concept of Wyrd offer a unique approach to self-awareness and personal growth by drawing on the intricate web of fate and interconnectedness present in Norse mythology. Wyrd, often depicted as a tapestry woven by the Norns, symbolizes the understanding that our lives are shaped by a combination of fate, choices, and the influence of others. Practicing mindfulness through this lens encourages individuals to acknowledge their role within this web, fostering a deeper connection to themselves and the world around them.

One effective mindfulness technique inspired by Wyrd is visualization. Practitioners can imagine themselves as threads within a vast tapestry, each representing their experiences, choices, and relationships. This mental imagery can help individuals recognize the interdependence of their actions and those of others, enhancing empathy and understanding. By visualizing the tapestry of Wyrd, one can cultivate a sense of belonging and responsibility, leading to a more mindful approach to daily interactions and decision-making.

Another technique involves journaling as a means to explore personal narratives in relation to the web of Wyrd. By reflecting on past experiences and the choices that led to their current situation, individuals can gain insight into how their lives are intertwined with the lives of others. This practice not only fosters self-awareness but also highlights the impact of fate and free will in shaping one's destiny. Journaling can serve as a tool for recognizing patterns, releasing negative emotions, and embracing the concept of growth through the acceptance of one's circumstances.

Mindfulness meditation can also be adapted to incorporate the principles of Wyrd. Practitioners can focus on their breath while contemplating the nature of their existence within the web of fate. This practice encourages individuals to be present in the moment while acknowledging the broader context of their lives. By cultivating a sense of acceptance and gratitude for the interconnectedness of all beings, one can experience a profound sense of peace and clarity, reducing anxiety and fostering resilience in the face of life's challenges.

Finally, engaging in creative expression can serve as a mindfulness technique that honors the symbolism of the web of Wyrd. Whether through art, music, or storytelling, individuals can explore their emotions and experiences in a way that acknowledges the complexity of their existence. This creative process allows for the integration of personal narratives into a larger framework of fate and free will, promoting healing and self-discovery. By embracing the layers of meaning inherent in their experiences, individuals can cultivate a mindful appreciation for the richness of life, ultimately enriching their understanding of Wyrd and its relevance to their journey.

# Chapter 8: Comparative Analysis of the Web of Wyrd and Other Cultural Fate Concepts

## Similarities with Greek Moirai

The concept of fate in Norse mythology, particularly as represented by the web of wyrd, bears striking similarities to the Greek Moirai, also known as the Fates. Both traditions personify fate as an inexorable force, shaping the destinies of gods and mortals alike. In Greek mythology, the Moirai consist of three sisters: Clotho, who spins the thread of life; Lachesis, who measures it; and Atropos, who cuts it when the time comes. Similarly, in Norse belief, the Norns, often identified as Urd, Verdandi, and Skuld, weave the threads of destiny for all beings. This shared imagery of weaving underscores the idea that fate is a complex tapestry, woven together by various forces, reflecting a universal understanding of life's unpredictability.

Both the Moirai and the Norns operate within a framework where fate is predetermined yet intrinsic to the narrative of existence. In both mythologies, while fate is portrayed as a powerful and unchangeable force, there remains an underlying tension between fate and free will. In Norse mythology, individuals can make choices within the bounds of their fate, suggesting a nuanced interplay between predestination and personal agency, much like the Greek understanding where mortals can exert influence over their lives despite the Moirai's overarching authority. This duality invites deeper exploration into the philosophical implications of fate, free will, and the human experience across cultures.

The symbolism of weaving in both traditions serves as a rich metaphor for understanding life's interconnectedness. The act of weaving threads into a coherent fabric illustrates how individual lives and choices contribute to a larger narrative. In contemporary interpretations, this imagery resonates within modern pagan practices, where individuals seek to understand their personal wyrd or fate through rituals and symbolic acts. The Moirai's threads and the Norns' web not only represent fate but also signify the intricate relationships between individuals, their communities, and the cosmos, fostering a sense of belonging and purpose within a broader existential framework.

Artistic representations of the Moirai and Norns further highlight their symbolic roles across different cultures. In literature and contemporary art, these figures are often depicted as powerful yet compassionate, embodying the dual nature of fate as both a guiding force and a source of existential dread. This representation can be seen in various art forms, from classical paintings to modern graphic novels, where the imagery of weaving is used to convey complex narratives about life, death, and the passage of time. Such artistic explorations not only deepen the appreciation of these mythological figures but also encourage reflection on the nature of destiny in our own lives.

The comparative analysis of the web of wyrd and the Moirai opens avenues for understanding fate's role in mental health and mindfulness practices. Engaging with these mythological concepts can provide individuals with insights into their struggles with control and acceptance in the face of life's uncertainties. By recognizing the threads of their own wyrd, individuals may find empowerment in navigating their choices while acknowledging the larger forces at play. This balance between acceptance and action fosters a mindful approach to life, enhancing well-being and resilience in the face of the unpredictable nature of existence, ultimately reminding us that while we may not weave our fates alone, our threads are nonetheless vital to the tapestry of life.

## Parallels in Eastern Philosophies

Eastern philosophies offer rich and diverse perspectives on fate, destiny, and the interconnectedness of all things, which resonate intriguingly with the Norse concept of the web of wyrd. In traditions such as Hinduism and Buddhism, the notions of karma and samsara illustrate the intricate web of cause and effect that governs the lives of individuals. Just as the web of wyrd suggests that every action influences the tapestry of fate, Eastern philosophies emphasize the importance of one's actions and intentions in shaping future experiences. This parallel highlights a shared understanding that our lives are not solely dictated by external forces but are also shaped by personal choices and moral conduct.

In Hindu philosophy, the idea of karma embodies the principle that every action has consequences, weaving a complex narrative of past, present, and future lives. The cyclical nature of existence in samsara aligns closely with the Norse belief in the cyclical patterns of fate and the inevitability of certain events. The concept of dharma, or duty, further parallels the wyrd, as individuals navigate their responsibilities within the larger framework of existence. This interplay of action and consequence underscores a universal truth: that while fate may provide a framework, it is the individual's choices that mold the path ahead.

Buddhism introduces another layer to this discussion through the concept of interdependence, or dependent origination, which posits that all phenomena arise in relation to one another. This mirrors the web of wyrd's emphasis on interconnectedness, suggesting that individual lives are threads woven together, influencing and being influenced by one another. In both frameworks, the interplay of fate and free will is essential; individuals are seen as active participants in shaping their destinies, even within the constraints of a preordained tapestry. This perspective fosters a sense of agency and responsibility, emphasizing that one's actions can reverberate through the web of existence.

The parallels extend to modern interpretations of both Eastern philosophies and the web of wyrd within contemporary practices. In mindfulness and meditation, both traditions encourage individuals to cultivate awareness of their thoughts and actions, recognizing how these contribute to the larger fabric of their lives. This awareness can enhance mental health and well-being, as individuals learn to navigate their fates with intention and clarity. Furthermore, the symbolism inherent in both the web of wyrd and Eastern teachings often finds expression in literature and artistic representations, where stories of fate, choice, and interconnectedness resonate with audiences, bridging cultural divides.

In the realm of fantasy literature and role-playing games, the thematic exploration of fate and free will is prevalent, drawing upon both Norse and Eastern concepts. Characters often grapple with their destinies, navigating the tension between predetermined paths and their desires to forge new ones. This dynamic is reflective of the broader human experience, where individuals seek to understand their place within the intricate tapestry of life. By examining these parallels, we can gain deeper insights into the universal themes of fate, choice, and interconnectedness that transcend cultural boundaries, enriching both our understanding of the web of wyrd and the philosophies that inform our existence.

## Cross-Cultural Perspectives on Fate

Cross-cultural perspectives on fate reveal a rich tapestry of beliefs that resonate across various civilizations, each weaving their unique threads into the concept of destiny. While Norse mythology presents the web of wyrd as a complex interplay of fate and free will, other cultures offer distinct interpretations that enrich our understanding of how fate is perceived and experienced. For instance, in ancient Greek culture, the Moirai, or Fates, were seen as three sisters who controlled the thread of life for every individual, emphasizing a more deterministic view of fate. This contrasts with the Norse perspective, where wyrd suggests a more fluid interaction between predetermined events and individual choices, allowing for a nuanced exploration of personal agency.

In Eastern philosophies, such as Hinduism and Buddhism, the concept of karma introduces a different dimension to fate. Karma emphasizes the moral implications of actions, suggesting that one's current fate is shaped by past deeds. This belief system aligns with the Norse understanding of wyrd, where individuals are not merely passive recipients of fate but active participants in shaping their destinies through choices and actions. The interconnectedness of past, present, and future within both frameworks highlights a shared recognition of the importance of personal responsibility and ethical living in navigating the complexities of fate.

The influence of fate on modern pagan practices also reflects cross-cultural adaptations of the web of wyrd. Many contemporary pagans draw inspiration from various cultural interpretations of fate, integrating elements that resonate with their spiritual beliefs. This synthesis often results in rituals and practices that acknowledge the web of wyrd while incorporating concepts of karma and other fate-related ideologies. Such practices foster a deeper sense of connection to the natural world and a recognition of the interconnectedness of all beings, echoing the themes found in both Norse and Eastern philosophies.

Literature and storytelling serve as powerful mediums for exploring the symbolism of fate across cultures. In Norse sagas, the web of wyrd is intricately woven into the narrative structure, often depicted through motifs of fate that illustrate the struggle between destiny and free will. Similarly, in other cultural narratives, fate can be portrayed as an inevitable force that characters must confront, often leading to profound personal revelations. This thematic exploration not only sheds light on the universal human experience of grappling with fate but also invites readers to reflect on their own lives and the choices that shape their paths.

Artistic representations of the web of wyrd in contemporary art also draw on cross-cultural themes of fate. Modern artists often blend symbols from various traditions, creating works that invite viewers to contemplate the nature of destiny and personal agency. This artistic dialogue between cultures highlights the ongoing relevance of these ancient concepts in contemporary society. Furthermore, the exploration of fate in role-playing games and fantasy literature often mirrors these cross-cultural perspectives, allowing players to engage with the complexities of choice and consequence within richly crafted worlds. Through these various lenses, the web of wyrd emerges as a dynamic, multifaceted concept that continues to inspire and challenge our understanding of fate.

# Chapter 9: The Web of Wyrd in Role-Playing Games and Fantasy Literature

## Integration of Wyrd in Game Mechanics

The integration of Wyrd in game mechanics serves as a compelling framework for exploring the intricate dynamics of fate and choice within both role-playing games (RPGs) and broader fantasy literature. By embedding the concept of Wyrd—representing the interconnectedness of fate, destiny, and personal agency—game designers can create rich narratives that resonate with players on multiple levels. This interplay encourages players to engage deeply with their characters and the world, fostering a sense of immersion that reflects the philosophical underpinnings of Norse mythology. The mechanics surrounding Wyrd can manifest in various ways, from character attributes that reflect a character's fate to narrative branches that evolve based on player decisions.

One effective method of integrating Wyrd into game mechanics is through the implementation of a fate system. This system can allow players to influence their character's destiny through actions and choices, echoing the belief in Wyrd as both a predetermined path and a flexible narrative. For instance, players might accumulate "Wyrd points" based on their actions, which can be spent to alter outcomes, manipulate events, or even invoke powerful abilities. This not only reinforces the theme of personal agency but also invites players to reflect on the consequences of their choices, aligning with the philosophical tension between fate and free will present in Norse mythology.

Additionally, the relationship between characters and Wyrd can be represented through interconnected storylines that reveal how individual actions impact the broader narrative. Games can utilize branching story arcs that lead to multiple endings, illustrating the impact of player decisions on the world around them. This mechanic can enhance the experience of storytelling within the game, as players witness the unfolding of events that stem from their choices, mirroring the interconnected threads of fate depicted in the concept of Wyrd. Such design choices not only enrich the gameplay experience but also encourage players to engage with the narrative at a deeper level.

Artistic representations of Wyrd can also inform the visual and thematic elements of the game. Incorporating symbols and motifs associated with Wyrd, such as the Yggdrasil tree or the Norns, can enhance the game's aesthetic and narrative depth. These elements can serve not only as visual cues but also as integral parts of the gameplay, where players may interact with these symbols to unlock new abilities or insights into their character's fate. This artistic integration reinforces the idea that Wyrd is not merely a backdrop but a living aspect of the game world, actively shaping the experiences and journeys of the players.

Finally, the inclusion of Wyrd in game mechanics can provide opportunities for reflection on mental health and mindfulness. By allowing players to explore the consequences of their choices within a structured environment, games can serve as a tool for understanding personal agency and the nature of fate. Players may find themselves contemplating their own lives and decisions as they navigate the complexities of Wyrd within the game. In this way, the mechanics surrounding Wyrd can transcend mere gameplay, inviting players to engage with larger existential themes that resonate beyond the virtual world, ultimately enriching their personal and collective narratives.

## Impact on World-Building in Fantasy Genres

The concept of the web of wyrd profoundly impacts world-building in fantasy genres, offering a rich tapestry through which authors can explore themes of fate, free will, and interconnectedness. In Norse mythology, wyrd is often depicted as a complex web that binds the fates of individuals, communities, and even gods. This intricate framework allows writers to create worlds where destiny is not merely a backdrop but a driving force that shapes characters' actions and their consequences. By integrating the web of wyrd into their narratives, authors can deepen their plots, develop multidimensional characters, and create settings where the interplay of fate and choice resonates with readers.

Fantasy authors frequently draw upon historical interpretations of the web of wyrd to craft immersive cultures and societies. The varied meanings attached to wyrd across different periods and texts provide a rich source of inspiration for world-building. For example, the portrayal of wyrd in the Old Norse sagas emphasizes not only individual fate but also the collective destiny of clans and tribes. This collective aspect can lead to the creation of societies in fantasy worlds where communal actions and decisions significantly influence the trajectory of their fate, echoing the interconnectedness found in modern interpretations of the web of wyrd.

The influence of the web of wyrd extends into modern pagan practices, where practitioners often embody the principles of interconnectedness and personal responsibility. Fantasy narratives that incorporate these elements can resonate with contemporary audiences, allowing for a deeper exploration of spiritual themes. The portrayal of rituals, beliefs, and moral dilemmas within these worlds can reflect real-world practices, creating a dialogue between fantasy and modern spirituality. By weaving these practices into their worlds, authors can encourage readers to contemplate their own beliefs about fate and agency.

Symbolism plays a crucial role in how the web of wyrd is represented in literature and storytelling. The web often symbolizes the intricate connections between characters and their destinies, creating a visual representation of the narrative's thematic undercurrents. Authors can use this symbolism to enhance their storytelling, employing metaphors and motifs that reinforce the idea that every choice has repercussions. Additionally, the web serves as a reminder of the fragile nature of existence, urging characters and readers alike to consider the weight of their decisions within the broader context of their lives.

Lastly, the role of fate and free will within the web of wyrd presents an engaging tension that many fantasy writers exploit to create compelling narratives. Characters may grapple with preordained paths while seeking to assert their agency, leading to conflicts that drive the plot forward. This dynamic can also be reflected in artistic representations, where contemporary art often depicts the web as a visual metaphor for human experience. The exploration of the web of wyrd in role-playing games and fantasy literature invites players and readers to engage actively with these themes, offering a participatory experience that challenges perceptions of destiny and personal choice, thus enriching the landscape of modern fantasy.

## Case Studies of Notable RPGs and Novels

The exploration of the web of wyrd in notable role-playing games (RPGs) and novels reveals how this ancient Norse concept of fate and interconnectedness resonates within modern storytelling. One prominent example is the RPG "The Elder Scrolls V: Skyrim," which intricately weaves the notion of wyrd into its narrative and gameplay mechanics. Players navigate a world where their choices have significant consequences, echoing the idea that every action reverberates through the fabric of fate. The game's emphasis on destiny, combined with its rich lore surrounding the gods and the threads of human lives, provides a contemporary interpretation of wyrd, inviting players to reflect on their own agency within the larger tapestry of existence.

Another notable case is Neil Gaiman's "Norse Mythology," which retells the stories of gods, giants, and heroes while embedding the concept of wyrd in its narrative structure. Gaiman's portrayal emphasizes the inevitability of fate and the characters' struggles against it, illustrating the tension between free will and destiny. This duality serves as a reminder of the inherent unpredictability of life, a theme that resonates deeply with adult readers. Gaiman's accessible yet profound storytelling allows modern audiences to engage with ancient concepts in a way that feels relevant and relatable, encouraging a deeper understanding of how these ideas shape our interpretations of fate today.

The RPG series "Dark Souls" delves into the darker aspects of the web of wyrd, where the cyclical nature of life, death, and rebirth reflects the Norse understanding of fate. Players confront the consequences of their actions in a world marked by despair and hopelessness, yet it is through this struggle that they find meaning. The game's lore presents a complex interplay between the players' choices and the predetermined paths laid out by the gods, echoing the philosophical inquiries into fate versus free will. This exploration not only captivates players but also prompts them to reflect on their own life choices and the potential for personal agency within the constraints of their circumstances.

In the realm of literature, works like "American Gods" by Neil Gaiman also illustrate the web of wyrd through the interactions of gods and mortals in a modern context. The narrative grapples with the decline of traditional beliefs in the face of contemporary society, highlighting how the threads of fate are influenced by cultural shifts. The characters' journeys often illustrate the struggle against or acceptance of their fates, resonating with themes of identity and belief systems in modern pagan practices. This connection between ancient mythology and contemporary life emphasizes the enduring relevance of the web of wyrd, inviting readers to consider how these ancient ideas manifest in their own beliefs and practices.

Finally, the influence of the web of wyrd extends into contemporary art, where visual representations often explore the interplay of fate and free will. Artists frequently draw on Norse mythology to create works that symbolize the web of wyrd, employing intricate designs to depict the interconnectedness of all beings. These artistic expressions serve as a meditation on the nature of existence, offering viewers a space to reflect on their own lives and the broader human experience. Through these case studies, it becomes clear that the web of wyrd continues to inspire and challenge modern creators, reinforcing its significance in both historical interpretations and contemporary practices.

# Chapter 10: Conclusion and Future Perspectives

## The Continuing Relevance of Wyrd

The concept of Wyrd in Norse mythology continues to resonate with contemporary audiences, reflecting a complex interplay between fate and free will. This ancient notion, often depicted as a web, encapsulates the idea that individual choices are interwoven with a larger cosmic tapestry. As adults engage with this theme, they navigate an intricate landscape where personal agency meets predetermined destiny. The continuing relevance of Wyrd invites a deeper exploration of how these ancient beliefs inform modern perspectives on life, decision-making, and the interconnectedness of all beings.

Historically, the interpretations of Wyrd have evolved, yet its core significance remains intact. Scholars have traced the origins of the term to Old English and Old Norse texts, where it signifies a force that shapes both individuals and their fates. In examining historical texts, one can observe how Wyrd served as a guiding principle for the Norse people, influencing their understanding of life events, social dynamics, and moral responsibilities. This historical lens enriches contemporary discussions, as many adults find parallels in their own lives, grappling with the balance of fate and free will in a world that often feels predetermined.

The influence of Wyrd extends beyond historical analysis into the realm of modern pagan practices. Many contemporary pagans draw upon the symbolism of the web of Wyrd to navigate their spiritual journeys. Rituals and ceremonies often reflect the interconnectedness of actions and consequences, echoing the ancient wisdom that one's life is a thread in a greater design. Adults engaged in these practices often report a heightened sense of mindfulness and awareness, recognizing how their choices contribute to the broader tapestry of existence. This connection to Wyrd fosters a sense of responsibility and intentionality in their daily lives.

In literature and storytelling, the symbolism of the web of Wyrd serves as a powerful narrative device. Writers and artists incorporate this motif to explore themes of destiny, choice, and the human condition. The complexity of Wyrd allows for rich character development and plot progression, as protagonists wrestle with their fates while asserting their agency. Contemporary narratives in fantasy literature and role-playing games often draw upon this archetype, inviting players and readers to immerse themselves in worlds where the threads of fate can be manipulated, yet remain intricately bound to larger cosmic forces.

Moreover, the relevance of Wyrd extends into the realms of mental health and mindfulness. The acknowledgment of Wyrd encourages individuals to reflect on their life paths, understanding the interplay of fate and personal choices. This awareness can foster resilience and a greater sense of purpose, as individuals recognize that while some aspects of their lives may be influenced by external forces, they still hold the power to shape their own narratives. As adults delve into the web of Wyrd, they may find not only a framework for understanding their experiences but also a pathway to greater emotional well-being and self-awareness.

## Future Research Directions

Future research directions in the exploration of the web of wyrd in Norse mythology could significantly benefit from a more interdisciplinary approach. Scholars from fields such as psychology, literature, anthropology, and religious studies can collaborate to provide a holistic understanding of how the web of wyrd influences not only historical interpretations but also contemporary beliefs and practices. By engaging with modern pagan communities, researchers can document how the web of wyrd is integrated into rituals and belief systems, thereby enriching both the academic discourse and the lived experiences of practitioners.

Another promising avenue for research lies in the symbolic interpretations of the web of wyrd within literature and storytelling. Analyzing various texts, both ancient and modern, can reveal the evolution of the web's symbolism and its impact on narrative structure. This exploration could extend to examining how contemporary authors draw upon the concept to address themes of fate, free will, and interconnectedness in their works. Such studies could illuminate the ways in which the web of wyrd serves as a narrative device that resonates with modern audiences, fostering a deeper understanding of its relevance across time and culture.

The relationship between the web of wyrd and mental health is an emerging topic that warrants further investigation. Researchers could explore how the concept of interconnectedness, as represented by the web, can inform practices of mindfulness and holistic well-being. By examining the psychological implications of viewing life through the lens of wyrd, studies could reveal how this perspective may aid individuals in navigating challenges related to agency and destiny. Furthermore, the therapeutic potential of incorporating the web of wyrd into mental health practices could provide valuable insights for both practitioners and clients.

Comparative analysis of the web of wyrd with other cultural concepts of fate opens another rich field for inquiry. By contrasting the Norse understanding of fate with Greek, Hindu, and indigenous beliefs, scholars can uncover universal themes as well as unique cultural nuances. This comparative framework could not only enhance our understanding of the web of wyrd but also contribute to broader discussions about the nature of fate, choice, and destiny in human experience. Such research can foster cross-cultural dialogues that highlight the interconnectedness of human beliefs and narratives.

Finally, the influence of the web of wyrd on contemporary artistic representations, including visual arts and role-playing games, presents a vibrant area for exploration. Researchers could examine how artists and game designers utilize the concept to convey themes of fate and interconnectedness, as well as to engage audiences in interactive storytelling. Analyzing these artistic expressions can reveal how the web of wyrd continues to inspire creativity and innovation, shaping modern interpretations of ancient themes. By understanding these contemporary applications, scholars can trace the ongoing legacy of the web of wyrd and its enduring impact on culture and society.

## The Legacy of Wyrd in Modern Culture

The legacy of Wyrd in modern culture manifests in various ways, resonating through literature, art, and spirituality. As a concept deeply rooted in Norse mythology, Wyrd signifies the interconnectedness of fate, actions, and consequences. This notion of an intricate web of destiny has found its way into contemporary storytelling, where authors explore themes of fate versus free will, often drawing parallels to the Wyrd. In modern literature, narratives frequently depict characters grappling with their destinies, echoing the ancient belief that one's actions weave into the greater tapestry of existence. This exploration serves not only as entertainment but also as a reflection on the human condition and the choices that define our lives.

The influence of Wyrd extends into modern pagan practices, where it has become a symbol of spiritual interconnectedness and responsibility. Many contemporary practitioners of Heathenry and other pagan traditions incorporate the concept of Wyrd into their rituals and beliefs, viewing it as a guiding principle that emphasizes the importance of living in harmony with one's environment and community. This revival of interest in Wyrd reflects a broader trend toward understanding and integrating ancient wisdom into modern spiritual frameworks, offering individuals a sense of purpose and connection in an increasingly fragmented world.

Artistic representations of Wyrd have emerged in various forms, from visual art to performance, capturing the essence of this complex concept. Contemporary artists often interpret the web of Wyrd through symbolic imagery, illustrating the entanglement of fate and choice. These artistic expressions invite viewers to reflect on their own lives and the threads that connect them to others. Furthermore, the rise of digital art and media has allowed for innovative interpretations of Wyrd, blending traditional motifs with modern techniques, thus expanding the reach and relevance of this ancient symbol in today's society.

In the realm of mental health and mindfulness, the web of Wyrd offers a framework for understanding personal experiences and the interconnectedness of thoughts and actions. Therapists and mindfulness practitioners sometimes draw upon the concept of Wyrd to encourage individuals to recognize the consequences of their choices and the impact of their lives on the larger community. This perspective fosters a sense of agency and responsibility, helping individuals navigate their paths with awareness and intention. By acknowledging the web of connections that shape their experiences, people can cultivate a deeper understanding of themselves and their roles in the world.

Finally, Wyrd has significantly influenced modern role-playing games and fantasy literature, where it serves as a foundational concept for world-building and character development. Game designers and writers often incorporate themes of fate and destiny into their narratives, allowing players to explore the ramifications of their choices within richly woven storylines. This interactive engagement with Wyrd not only enriches the gaming experience but also invites players to consider the broader implications of their decisions, paralleling the ancient understanding of Wyrd as both a guiding force and a reflection of personal agency. Through these various avenues, the legacy of Wyrd continues to thrive, inviting new generations to engage with its profound and timeless wisdom.

# Wisdom Through Sacrifice: Odin's Journey to Enlightenment

## Chapter 1: The Quest for Wisdom

### The Origins of Odin

The figure of Odin in Norse mythology is steeped in profound symbolism and rich narrative, with his origins closely tied to the theme of sacrifice for the pursuit of wisdom. As the chief deity of the Aesir, Odin's journey begins not with an assertion of power, but with an earnest quest for knowledge. His desire for enlightenment drives him to make significant sacrifices, including the loss of an eye, which he willingly gives up in exchange for a sip from the Well of Mimir. This act not only signifies the value he places on wisdom but also illustrates the lengths to which he is willing to go to attain it. The very essence of his character is encapsulated in this duality of sacrifice and knowledge, establishing a foundational myth that resonates throughout Norse culture.

The symbolism of Odin's sacrifices extends beyond the mere act of giving; it reflects a deeper understanding of the interconnectedness of knowledge and power. In Norse thought, wisdom does not come without cost, and Odin's journey serves as a reminder that enlightenment is often accompanied by trials and tribulations. His sacrifice of an eye represents a willingness to see beyond the superficial and to embrace the complexities of existence. This willingness to endure loss for the sake of greater insight mirrors the universal theme found in many cultures, where sacrifice is a prerequisite for gaining profound truths. The narrative encourages modern seekers to recognize that the pursuit of wisdom often demands personal sacrifice, be it time, comfort, or even relationships.

Odin's quest for wisdom is not unique to Norse mythology; it parallels the experiences found in various mythologies around the world. Many cultures tell stories of deities or heroes who undergo trials for enlightenment, highlighting a shared understanding that knowledge is not freely given but earned through sacrifice. The archetype of the wise figure who suffers for greater insight can be seen in multiple traditions, illustrating a common human experience. This comparative analysis reveals a profound psychological insight: the act of sacrifice often leads to personal transformation, suggesting that the struggle itself is integral to the process of becoming wise.

The significance of the Well of Mimir in Odin's journey cannot be overstated. This mythical well is not just a source of wisdom; it symbolizes the depths of knowledge that one must dive into to achieve true understanding. By sacrificing his eye, Odin gains access to the well's wisdom, which empowers him in his role as the Allfather. This act highlights the notion that the pursuit of knowledge often requires one to confront uncomfortable truths about oneself and the world. The well serves as a metaphor for the depths of the psyche, where seekers must be willing to explore their innermost fears and desires in order to achieve enlightenment.

Odin's relationship with runes further illustrates the connection between sacrifice and wisdom. The runes, seen as symbols imbued with knowledge, were revealed to him only after he hung for nine nights on the world tree, Yggdrasil, pierced by his own spear. This act of self-sacrifice emphasizes that wisdom is not merely acquired but earned through profound experiences and personal trials. In contemporary spirituality, Odin's narrative continues to resonate, encouraging individuals to embrace their own sacrifices as paths to self-discovery and enlightenment. His journey serves as an enduring lesson: true wisdom often demands the courage to face one's own limitations and the willingness to sacrifice for a greater understanding of the self and the universe.

## The Nature of Wisdom in Norse Mythology

The nature of wisdom in Norse mythology is intricately tied to the figure of Odin, the Allfather, who embodies the pursuit of knowledge through sacrifice. In Norse narratives, wisdom is not merely an abstract quality; it is a profound understanding of the cosmos, human existence, and the interplay of fate. Odin's quest for wisdom is marked by significant sacrifices, most notably the loss of his eye at the Well of Mimir, where he sought to gain insight into the mysteries of life and death. This act exemplifies the deeper principle that wisdom often comes at a high price, a theme that resonates throughout various mythologies.

Odin's sacrifice serves as a powerful symbol within Norse mythology, illustrating the lengths to which one must go to attain enlightenment. By relinquishing his eye, Odin shows that true wisdom is often accompanied by personal loss and transformation. This act of giving up something valuable signifies a willingness to undergo suffering for the greater good of understanding. Such symbolism encourages modern seekers to contemplate the nature of their own sacrifices in the pursuit of knowledge, suggesting that growth often stems from overcoming adversity and letting go of attachments.

The role of sacrifice in the pursuit of knowledge is a recurring theme across cultures, highlighting a universal truth about the human experience. From the ancient Greeks to indigenous cultures, stories abound of figures who endure trials and tribulations to gain wisdom. Odin's journey reflects this motif, as he not only sacrifices his eye but also engages in other trials, such as hanging from Yggdrasil for nine nights to discover the runes. This pattern reinforces the idea that wisdom is not easily attained; it requires dedication, perseverance, and often the courage to confront one's own limitations.

Central to Odin's quest for wisdom is the significance of the Well of Mimir, which symbolizes the depths of knowledge and the necessity of sacrifice to access it. The well is portrayed as a source of wisdom, guarded by Mimir, who represents the ancient knowledge of the world. By drinking its waters, Odin gains insights that are crucial to his role as a god of war and poetry, blending the martial and the mystical. This duality underscores the multifaceted nature of wisdom, suggesting that it encompasses both the practical and the philosophical, vital for navigating the complexities of life.

Odin's relationship with the runes further exemplifies the connection between sacrifice and wisdom. The runes are not just symbols; they carry profound meanings and insights that Odin unlocks through his trials. The psychological implications of such sacrifices for enlightenment reveal a deep understanding of self-discovery and personal growth. In contemporary spirituality, Odin's journey remains relevant, encouraging individuals to seek their own paths of wisdom through introspection, sacrifice, and the courage to confront the unknown. In this way, the legacy of Odin continues to inspire modern seekers in their quest for enlightenment, emphasizing that the pursuit of wisdom is both a personal and collective journey.

# Chapter 2: The Sacrifice at Yggdrasil

## The Tree of Life and Knowledge

The Tree of Life and Knowledge stands as a profound symbol in Norse mythology, representing the interconnectedness of all beings and the pursuit of wisdom. At its core is Yggdrasil, the World Tree, which connects the nine realms of existence. Odin's sacrifice at this sacred tree epitomizes the lengths to which one must go to attain true knowledge. By hanging himself from Yggdrasil for nine long nights, he sought not only to understand the mysteries of the universe but also to gain insight into the runes, the symbols of knowledge and power. This act of self-sacrifice highlights the belief that enlightenment often requires profound personal cost.

The symbolism of Odin's sacrifice resonates deeply within the framework of sacrifice in various cultures. Throughout history, numerous traditions have held that true wisdom is achieved through suffering and loss. From the ancient Greeks to indigenous practices across the globe, the notion that one must give up something valuable to gain deeper understanding is a recurring theme. In Norse tradition, Odin's willingness to endure pain and isolation at the roots of Yggdrasil serves as a reminder of the transformative power of sacrifice, reinforcing the idea that enlightenment is often born from hardship.

Odin's quest for wisdom provides modern seekers with valuable lessons. In a world that often prioritizes convenience and instant gratification, his story encourages individuals to engage in introspection and embrace the challenges that come with the pursuit of knowledge. It suggests that growth and understanding are not merely acquired through passive learning, but through active participation in one's journey, often requiring sacrifices of time, comfort, or preconceived notions. This perspective can empower contemporary seekers to approach their own quests for wisdom with a renewed sense of commitment and resilience.

The significance of the Well of Mimir, where Odin sought knowledge through sacrifice, further emphasizes the connection between wisdom and self-denial. Mimir's Well is a source of immense knowledge, guarded by Mimir, who represents the wisdom of ages. By sacrificing an eye to drink from the well, Odin illustrates the idea that true insight often comes at the expense of something fundamental. This narrative serves to remind seekers that the journey towards enlightenment is fraught with choices that demand introspection and determination, positioning sacrifice as a crucial element in the search for deeper truths.

Odin's relationship with runes encapsulates the essence of wisdom in Norse mythology. The runes, imbued with power and meaning, symbolize not just knowledge, but the mysteries of existence itself. By sacrificing for this understanding, Odin became a master of the runes, thus linking sacrifice directly to the attainment of wisdom. In turn, the impact of his sacrifice rippled through Viking culture, shaping their beliefs and practices. The psychological implications of such sacrifices suggest a complex relationship between suffering, identity, and enlightenment, offering insights for contemporary spirituality and self-discovery. Odin's journey stands as a testament to the enduring nature of sacrifice in the quest for knowledge, urging modern seekers to reflect on the value of their own sacrifices in the pursuit of wisdom.

## The Nine Nights of Sacrifice

The Nine Nights of Sacrifice is a pivotal event in Norse mythology that encapsulates Odin's relentless pursuit of wisdom. This profound journey begins when Odin, the Allfather, sacrifices himself to gain a deeper understanding of the mysteries of existence. He hangs from the branches of Yggdrasil, the World Tree, for nine nights, pierced by his own spear. This act of self-sacrifice symbolizes the lengths one must go to attain true knowledge and enlightenment. It serves as a powerful reminder that wisdom often demands a steep price, echoing the universal theme that to gain something valuable, one must be willing to relinquish something of significance.

The symbolism inherent in Odin's sacrifice resonates deeply within the context of Norse mythology and extends beyond into a broader cultural narrative. The act of hanging from Yggdrasil is not merely a physical ordeal; it represents a metaphysical endeavor to transcend ordinary understanding. The nine nights signify a transformative period, where Odin confronts the depths of suffering and isolation. Through this experience, he gains access to the runes, which are imbued with cosmic knowledge and power. Odin's journey reflects the notion that enlightenment often springs from confronting one's fears and enduring trials, a theme that is prevalent across various cultural narratives throughout history.

Sacrifice as a means to acquire knowledge is a recurring theme across many cultures. From ancient Greek philosophers who engaged in self-denial to Eastern traditions that emphasize detachment and humility, the act of sacrificing personal comfort for greater understanding is a universal principle. Odin's experience can be likened to these traditions, illustrating that the pursuit of wisdom is rarely comfortable or easy. The Nine Nights of Sacrifice exemplifies how personal sacrifice can lead to profound insights, urging modern seekers to reflect on what they are willing to give up in their quest for knowledge and self-discovery.

The significance of the Well of Mimir in Odin's journey underscores the vital connection between sacrifice and wisdom. Mimir's well is a source of profound knowledge, but accessing its waters requires a sacrifice—Odin trades one of his eyes for a drink. This act reinforces the idea that wisdom often comes at a cost, a theme echoed in various mythologies where deities or heroes must give up something precious to gain deeper insight. In contemporary spirituality, this concept invites individuals to consider the sacrifices they must make in their own lives, whether it be time, comfort, or ego, in pursuit of enlightenment and self-realization.

The impact of Odin's sacrifice extends beyond mythological tales; it profoundly shaped Viking culture and beliefs. The lessons derived from Odin's journey resonate within the Viking ethos, emphasizing courage, resilience, and the value of wisdom. In modern contexts, the psychological implications of such sacrifices highlight the transformative power of enduring hardship for personal growth. Odin's wisdom serves as a guiding force for contemporary seekers, encouraging them to embrace their own journeys of sacrifice as a pathway to enlightenment. Through this lens, the Nine Nights of Sacrifice becomes not just a mythological account but a timeless narrative that speaks to the human condition and the eternal quest for understanding.

# Chapter 3: The Well of Mimir

## The Significance of the Well

The significance of the Well of Mimir in Odin's journey cannot be overstated, as it represents the profound depths of knowledge and understanding that one must seek in the pursuit of enlightenment. This well, located beneath one of the roots of Yggdrasil, the World Tree, is a source of wisdom that has been revered in Norse mythology. When Odin sacrificed his eye to gain access to the well, he demonstrated that acquiring true knowledge often requires immense personal sacrifice. This act not only reflects the value placed on wisdom in Norse culture but also serves as a powerful symbol of the lengths to which individuals must go to achieve deeper understanding.

Odin's quest for wisdom through the Well of Mimir also highlights a broader theme found in many cultures: the necessity of sacrifice for the sake of enlightenment. Throughout history, various myths and legends depict figures who undergo trials or make significant sacrifices to attain knowledge. Whether it be Prometheus stealing fire for humanity or the sacrifices made by figures in other mythologies, these narratives emphasize that wisdom is not freely given; it is earned through struggle and loss. In this way, Odin's story resonates with universal human experiences, encouraging modern seekers to reflect on the sacrifices they might need to make in their own quests for understanding.

In the context of Viking culture, Odin's sacrifice had profound implications. The act of giving one's eye in exchange for wisdom was not merely a personal endeavor but a communal lesson on the importance of knowledge and foresight. The Vikings revered Odin as a god of wisdom, and his actions informed their own values and beliefs. The significance of this sacrifice is mirrored in their understanding of fate and the importance of making informed choices. As they navigated their own lives, the story of Odin served as a reminder that wisdom often comes at a cost, reinforcing the idea that the pursuit of knowledge is a noble and essential endeavor.

The relationship between Odin and the runes further amplifies the significance of the Well of Mimir. Upon drinking from the well, Odin gained insight into the runes, which represented not only language but also the mysteries of the universe. This connection illustrates that wisdom is multidimensional, encompassing practical knowledge as well as spiritual insight. For contemporary seekers, this intertwining of sacrifice and the acquisition of wisdom through symbols like runes offers a pathway to self-discovery and personal growth. It invites individuals to explore their own symbols and practices that may lead to enlightenment.

Ultimately, the psychological implications of sacrifice in the pursuit of wisdom are profound. Odin's willingness to give up a part of himself for greater understanding serves as a metaphor for the internal sacrifices individuals often face in their own journeys. It challenges us to consider what we are willing to let go of in our pursuit of knowledge and self-awareness. In modern spirituality, the lessons gleaned from Odin's sacrifice resonate deeply, inviting individuals to engage with their own sacrifices, whether they be emotional, social, or spiritual, as vital steps toward achieving enlightenment and cultivating a richer understanding of themselves and the world around them.

## The Price of Wisdom

The price of wisdom, as illustrated through Odin's journey, serves as a poignant reminder of the sacrifices necessary for profound understanding and enlightenment. In Norse mythology, Odin's pursuit of wisdom is not merely a desire for knowledge but a quest for deeper truths about existence, fate, and the cosmos. His willingness to sacrifice an eye at the Well of Mimir symbolizes the profound cost of enlightenment. This act reflects the notion that true wisdom often demands personal sacrifice, resonating with the idea that gaining insight frequently requires letting go of something precious.

The symbolism of Odin's sacrifice extends beyond the mere act of losing an eye. It embodies the essence of seeking knowledge despite the price one must pay. In many cultures, the theme of sacrifice for enlightenment recurs, illustrating a universal truth that the pursuit of wisdom often involves significant personal loss or hardship. From the mythological tales of other cultures to philosophical teachings of ancient scholars, the idea remains consistent: attaining wisdom is fraught with challenges that test one's resolve and commitment to understanding the greater mysteries of life.

Odin's quest for wisdom offers valuable lessons for modern seekers, highlighting the importance of perseverance and courage in the face of adversity. His journey encourages individuals today to embrace their own sacrifices, whether they be time, comfort, or conventional beliefs, in the pursuit of deeper knowledge. This pursuit often requires stepping outside of one's comfort zone and confronting the unknown. By reflecting on Odin's experiences, contemporary seekers can find inspiration to embark on their own paths of enlightenment, understanding that the journey is as significant as the wisdom gained.

The Well of Mimir, a central element in Odin's quest, serves as a powerful symbol of the depths of knowledge and the sacrifices required to access it. In Norse mythology, this well is associated with wisdom and understanding, suggesting that profound insights are often hidden beneath the surface and accessible only through significant personal sacrifice. The water from this well, which Odin drinks to gain insight, represents the transformative power of wisdom and the necessity of paying a price to obtain it. This theme resonates in various mythologies, where sacred wells or sources of knowledge often demand respect and sacrifice from those who seek their gifts.

The impact of Odin's sacrifices on Viking culture and beliefs highlights the broader psychological implications of sacrifice for enlightenment. The Vikings revered Odin not just as a god of war but as the ultimate seeker of wisdom, embodying the belief that knowledge and power come at a cost. This perception influenced their values, shaping a culture that esteemed courage, sacrifice, and the relentless pursuit of knowledge. In contemporary spirituality, Odin's narrative continues to inspire individuals seeking self-discovery and enlightenment, reinforcing the idea that wisdom often arises from the willingness to endure challenges and make sacrifices along the way.

# Chapter 4: Symbolism of Sacrifice in Norse Mythology

## Blood and Offerings

In Norse mythology, the theme of sacrifice is pivotal to understanding Odin's relentless pursuit of wisdom. The god's most notable sacrifice is his own eye, willingly offered to Mimir in exchange for a drink from the Well of Mimir, which is renowned for its profound knowledge. This act of self-mutilation is laden with symbolism, representing the lengths one must go to attain true understanding. It signifies that enlightenment often demands a personal cost, a theme echoed in various cultural narratives where sacrifice is intertwined with the quest for knowledge and enlightenment.

The symbolism of Odin's sacrifice extends beyond the physical loss of his eye. It embodies the idea that wisdom is not easily gained; it requires individuals to confront their limitations and make significant sacrifices. This notion resonates across cultures, where figures like Prometheus in Greek mythology and Gautama Buddha in Eastern traditions similarly endure suffering or loss for the sake of enlightenment. In each tale, the underlying message remains consistent: the pursuit of knowledge often necessitates a departure from comfort, security, and even parts of oneself.

Central to Odin's journey is the Well of Mimir, a mystical source of wisdom that reinforces the significance of sacrifice in the acquisition of knowledge. The well is not merely a reservoir of information; it represents a transformative experience. To gain insight, Odin had to engage in a profound exchange that altered his very essence, emphasizing the transformative power that knowledge holds. This encounter illustrates that true wisdom is not passive; it demands active participation and often comes at a high price, teaching modern seekers that personal growth frequently involves confronting uncomfortable truths.

The impact of Odin's sacrifice rippled through Viking culture, shaping their beliefs and practices. The Norse viewed sacrifice as a necessary part of life, both in a religious context and in the pursuit of personal goals. This cultural acceptance of sacrifice reflects a broader psychological understanding of its implications. The act of giving up something valuable can lead to a deeper sense of purpose and connection to the greater universe, fostering resilience and determination among individuals. In contemporary spirituality, this concept remains relevant, as many seek to understand their own sacrifices as a pathway to enlightenment and self-discovery.

Odin's relationship with runes further illustrates the connection between sacrifice and wisdom. The runes, believed to hold mystical knowledge, were revealed to Odin only after he hung for nine nights on Yggdrasil, the World Tree, pierced by his spear. This act of self-sacrifice for the sake of understanding the runes reinforces the idea that knowledge is often cloaked in trials and tribulations. In the modern context, Odin's journey serves as a powerful reminder that the pursuit of wisdom is inherently linked to the willingness to sacrifice, inviting individuals to reflect on their own journeys and the costs that accompany their quest for enlightenment.

## The Cycle of Life and Death

The cycle of life and death is a central theme in Norse mythology, particularly in the narrative of Odin, the Allfather, whose sacrifices illuminate the profound relationship between knowledge and existence. Odin's quest for wisdom epitomizes the transformative power of sacrifice, illustrating that the acquisition of deep understanding often demands a personal cost. This cycle is not merely a linear progression; rather, it is a recurring theme woven into the fabric of existence, where each end serves as a precursor to a new beginning. Through his sacrifices, Odin embodies the notion that wisdom is not freely given but earned through trials that transcend the physical realm.

In Norse mythology, the symbolism of Odin's sacrifice is rich and multifaceted. His willingness to hang from the Yggdrasil tree for nine nights, pierced by his own spear, signifies an initiation into a higher state of consciousness. This act reflects the cyclical nature of life and death, as the pain endured leads to profound insights, including the discovery of the runes, which symbolize knowledge and the mysteries of the universe. Thus, Odin's sacrifice becomes a powerful metaphor for the journey of enlightenment, where the shedding of old selves is necessary to birth new understanding. This symbolism resonates across cultures, suggesting that the path to enlightenment often mirrors the cyclical process of death and rebirth.

Exploring the role of sacrifice in the pursuit of knowledge across various cultures reveals striking parallels to Odin's journey. Many traditions emphasize that true wisdom is often accompanied by suffering or loss. For instance, the hero's journey in numerous mythologies frequently involves trials that test and ultimately transform the seeker. This universal theme highlights the idea that enlightenment is not merely an intellectual endeavor but rather a profound metamorphosis that requires one to confront the depths of despair and emerge renewed. The psychological implications of such sacrifices extend to modern seekers, who may find themselves grappling with the challenges and costs associated with personal growth and self-discovery.

The Well of Mimir, a significant element in Odin's quest for wisdom, is emblematic of the sacrifices made in the name of knowledge. By sacrificing an eye, Odin gains access to the well's profound insights, reinforcing the idea that wisdom often requires the relinquishment of something precious. This act serves as a reminder that the quest for understanding is intrinsically linked to the cycles of loss and gain, mirroring the natural world. The well's waters symbolize the depths of knowledge that can only be accessed through sacrifice, illustrating that wisdom is often hidden beneath layers of experience and suffering.

Odin's influence on Viking culture and beliefs further underscores the importance of sacrifice in the pursuit of wisdom. His stories instilled a sense of resilience and the understanding that life's challenges are not to be feared but embraced as opportunities for growth. In contemporary spirituality, the lessons from Odin's journey resonate with those seeking self-discovery. The acknowledgment of sacrifice as a vital component of the quest for enlightenment encourages individuals to confront their fears and limitations, ultimately leading to a deeper understanding of themselves and the world. Thus, the cycle of life and death, as embodied in Odin's sacrifices, continues to offer valuable insights for modern seekers navigating the complexities of existence.

# Chapter 5: The Role of Sacrifice in the Pursuit of Knowledge Across Cultures

## Comparative Sacrifices in Global Mythologies

Comparative sacrifices across global mythologies reveal profound insights into the universal quest for knowledge and understanding. In Norse mythology, Odin's sacrificial act of hanging from Yggdrasil, the World Tree, for nine days and nights is emblematic of the lengths to which he was willing to go to attain wisdom. This act mirrors similar themes found in various cultures, where deities and heroes often endure trials or make significant sacrifices to gain insights that elevate their understanding of existence. In many traditions, these sacrifices not only serve as initiation rites but also as gateways to deeper truths that transcend mere mortal experience.

The symbolism of Odin's sacrifice is rich and multifaceted. The act of self-sacrifice highlights the theme of death and rebirth, a common motif in mythologies worldwide. For instance, in Greek mythology, Prometheus defies the gods to bring fire to humanity, suffering greatly as a consequence. Both figures illustrate the belief that enlightenment often comes at a great cost. These sacrifices also signify a transformation, as the knowledge gained through suffering leads to greater responsibility and a deeper connection to the cosmos. Odin's willingness to endure pain for wisdom illustrates a critical lesson: that true understanding often requires us to confront our limitations and fears.

The role of sacrifice in the pursuit of knowledge is a recurring theme in many cultures. For example, in Hinduism, the story of the creation of the universe involves the sacrifice of the cosmic being Purusha, whose body is transformed into the world. Similarly, in Christianity, the sacrifice of Jesus serves as a profound symbol of love and redemption, underscoring the belief that through suffering, one can achieve spiritual enlightenment and connection to the divine. These narratives reflect a collective awareness that the path to wisdom is fraught with challenges and that sacrifices, whether they be physical, emotional, or spiritual, are often necessary to attain higher truths.

Odin's quest for wisdom offers valuable lessons for modern seekers. In an age where the pursuit of knowledge is often linked to material gain or intellectual achievement, the Norse god's example invites a reevaluation of what it means to be wise. It suggests that true wisdom requires introspection, sacrifice, and a willingness to embrace discomfort. Contemporary spirituality often emphasizes personal growth through trials, echoing the sacrificial themes found in Odin's journey. By understanding the depth of these sacrifices, individuals can cultivate resilience and a deeper appreciation for their own paths toward enlightenment.

The significance of the Well of Mimir in Odin's journey further illustrates the importance of sacrifice in the pursuit of wisdom. This well, containing the waters of knowledge, represents the ultimate reward for those who are willing to make profound sacrifices. Odin sacrifices one of his eyes to gain a drink from the well, symbolizing the idea that insight often requires us to give up a part of ourselves. This theme resonates across various mythologies, where the act of sacrificing something valuable leads to greater insight or understanding. Such narratives underscore the psychological implications of sacrifice, suggesting that the journey toward enlightenment is a transformative process that reshapes both the individual and their understanding of the world.

## Lessons from Ancient Practices

The ancient practices surrounding sacrifice serve as a foundational element in understanding Odin's journey toward enlightenment. In Norse mythology, Odin's willingness to sacrifice his eye for a sip from the Well of Mimir exemplifies the profound lengths to which seekers of wisdom must go. This act symbolizes the idea that true knowledge often comes at a significant personal cost. The concept of sacrificing something of great value in exchange for deeper understanding resonates across various cultures, highlighting a universal truth about the pursuit of enlightenment. Whether it is the offering of material possessions, time, or even aspects of one's identity, the act of sacrifice remains a powerful theme in the quest for knowledge.

In examining the symbolism of Odin's sacrifice, it becomes clear that it represents more than mere loss. The act itself is a transformative journey, suggesting that wisdom is not merely acquired, but forged through experience and hardship. The eye, a symbol of perception and insight, reflects the necessity of relinquishing a part of oneself to gain a greater vision of the world. This notion parallels the experiences of many cultures where similar sacrifices are made, revealing a common thread in the human condition: the need to confront and overcome obstacles to achieve deeper understanding. The sacrifices made by figures in mythology often serve as allegories for the challenges faced by individuals in their own quests for knowledge.

Odin's quest for wisdom offers critical lessons for modern seekers. In a world filled with distractions and superficial engagements, the ancient practice of sacrifice can remind us of the importance of commitment and focus in our own journeys. Many contemporary spiritual paths emphasize the need for personal sacrifice as a means of achieving greater clarity and purpose. By drawing from Odin's example, individuals can explore what they may need to relinquish—be it time spent on trivial pursuits, unhealthy relationships, or unexamined beliefs—in order to cultivate a more profound understanding of themselves and their place in the world.

The Well of Mimir stands as a significant symbol in Odin's journey, representing the depths of wisdom that can be accessed through sacrifice. Mimir's wisdom is not just knowledge, but a deeper understanding of existence, fate, and the interconnectedness of all things. This well serves as a metaphor for the sources of insight that require dedication and the willingness to confront difficult truths. In various cultures, similar wells or sacred sites are revered as places of transformation that demand respect and personal commitment. The act of seeking knowledge from these sources often requires a relinquishing of ignorance or preconceived notions, echoing Odin's sacrifices.

Finally, the psychological implications of sacrifice in the pursuit of enlightenment reveal the complexities of human consciousness. Sacrifice can lead to a profound inner transformation, as the act itself forces individuals to confront their fears, desires, and motivations. This aligns with contemporary spiritual practices that emphasize the necessity of self-examination and the courage to change. The legacy of Odin's wisdom continues to impact modern spiritual seekers, encouraging a deeper exploration of what it means to sacrifice for enlightenment. By applying these ancient lessons to contemporary life, individuals can find pathways to wisdom that resonate with the timeless struggles of the human spirit.

# Chapter 6: Odin's Relationship with Runes

## The Creation of Runes

The creation of runes is intricately tied to Odin's profound sacrifice, a pivotal moment that underscores the depth of his quest for wisdom. In Norse mythology, Odin hung for nine long nights on Yggdrasil, the World Tree, pierced by his own spear. This act of self-sacrifice is not merely a display of strength but rather a profound commitment to seeking knowledge. Through this ordeal, he endured suffering and isolation, which ultimately led to his revelation of the runes—symbols that encapsulate the essence of the cosmos, the mysteries of existence, and the pathways to enlightenment. Each rune embodies a specific concept, energy, or force, reflecting the interconnectedness of all things in the universe.

The symbolism of the runes extends beyond their practical applications in divination or magic; they represent the very fabric of wisdom itself. Each character is steeped in meaning, serving as a bridge between the physical and spiritual realms. For Odin, the runes were not just tools but sacred symbols that conveyed deep insights into the nature of reality. The act of inscribing or invoking them was a form of reverence to the knowledge they held. In this context, the creation of runes becomes a powerful metaphor for the transformative journey of self-discovery— emphasizing that true wisdom often demands personal sacrifice and introspection.

Odin's quest for wisdom resonates with the wider theme of sacrifice across various cultures. Many traditions emphasize that profound insight and enlightenment often come at a cost. This notion is echoed in the stories of other mythological figures who, through trials and tribulations, gain extraordinary knowledge. The common thread among these narratives is the idea that enlightenment requires sacrifice, whether it be through physical pain, emotional turmoil, or the relinquishing of ignorance. By examining these parallels, one can appreciate how the act of sacrificing for knowledge is a universal motif that transcends cultural boundaries, inviting modern seekers to reflect on their own journeys.

The significance of the Well of Mimir further enriches the understanding of Odin's relationship with wisdom and sacrifice. It is said that Odin sacrificed an eye to gain access to this well, which contained the waters of wisdom and knowledge. This act of giving up a part of himself underlines the concept that enlightenment often involves relinquishing something valuable. The Well of Mimir serves as a symbol of the depths of understanding one can achieve when willing to pay the price. Thus, Odin's sacrifices are not mere tales of heroism; they embody essential lessons for contemporary seekers who aspire to attain deeper insight into their lives and the world around them.

In examining the psychological implications of Odin's sacrifices, one can discern the transformative power of suffering in the pursuit of enlightenment. The act of sacrificing for knowledge fosters resilience and encourages individuals to confront the darker aspects of their psyche. In modern spirituality, Odin's journey serves as a reminder that wisdom often emerges from struggle and self-reflection. As individuals navigate their paths toward self-discovery, the creation of runes stands as a testament to the enduring relevance of Odin's legacy. The runes, rich with meaning and history, continue to inspire seekers today, inviting them to explore the depths of their own sacrifices in the quest for wisdom.

## Runes as Tools of Wisdom

Runes, as tools of wisdom in Norse mythology, are deeply intertwined with Odin's relentless quest for knowledge. Odin's sacrifice of himself—hanging for nine nights on Yggdrasil, the World Tree—was not merely a test of endurance but a profound act of surrender to the mysteries of existence. This sacrifice was pivotal in granting him insight into the runes, which are more than mere letters; they are symbols imbued with meaning and power. Each rune represents a facet of life, offering guidance and understanding to those who seek to decode their wisdom. In this context, they become instruments that facilitate a deeper connection to the cosmos and the self.

The symbolism of Odin's sacrifice is multilayered, reflecting the universal theme of seeking knowledge through suffering. In many cultures, the idea that enlightenment often comes at a price is echoed in various mythologies. The act of sacrifice serves as a bridge between the mortal and the divine, suggesting that true wisdom is attained not through ease but through trials and tribulations. This notion resonates across different cultural narratives, where figures must endure hardship to gain profound insights. Odin's willingness to face death to unlock the secrets of the runes exemplifies this archetype, emphasizing that the pursuit of wisdom is a journey that demands both courage and commitment.

Central to Odin's journey is the Well of Mimir, a fount of wisdom that he sacrifices to access. This well, guarded by the wise Mimir, represents the depths of knowledge that lie beyond the surface of everyday experience. By sacrificing one of his eyes, Odin demonstrates the idea that insight often requires the relinquishing of something valuable. The well is a metaphor for the deep inner work required to attain wisdom; it invites seekers to confront their limitations and make sacrifices that may initially seem daunting. The lessons gleaned from Odin's experience resonate with modern seekers who strive for enlightenment, reminding them that true understanding often necessitates personal sacrifice.

Odin's relationship with runes extends beyond their symbolic meanings; it represents a tangible connection to the universe's mysteries. Each rune embodies specific energies and lessons, acting as a roadmap for those navigating the complexities of life. In contemporary spirituality, the practice of rune casting has emerged as a means of self-discovery and guidance. The wisdom encoded within the runes encourages individuals to explore their inner landscapes, prompting them to confront their fears, desires, and aspirations. This exploration is not unlike Odin's own journey, where he learned that wisdom is a dynamic interplay between knowledge and experience.

The impact of Odin's sacrifice on Viking culture and beliefs is profound, as it established a framework for understanding the relationship between sacrifice and enlightenment. Viking society revered wisdom, and Odin became a central figure embodying the ideal of a seeker who embraced hardship to gain insight. This cultural narrative underscores the psychological implications of sacrifice in the pursuit of enlightenment, suggesting that individuals grow through their struggles. By embracing the lessons of Odin and the wisdom of the runes, modern seekers can navigate their paths with a deeper awareness of the transformative power of sacrifice, ultimately leading to a more profound understanding of themselves and the world around them.

# Chapter 7: Lessons for Modern Seekers

## Sacrifice in Personal Growth

Sacrifice in personal growth is a theme intricately woven into the fabric of Odin's narrative, reflecting the profound impact of self-giving on the quest for enlightenment. In Norse mythology, Odin's decision to hang himself from Yggdrasil, the World Tree, for nine days and nights is emblematic of the lengths one must go to attain true wisdom. This act of self-sacrifice serves not only as a personal trial but also as a universal lesson about the necessity of enduring hardship and relinquishing comfort for the sake of knowledge and understanding. Such sacrifices are essential in transcending limitations and unlocking deeper insights into oneself and the world.

The symbolism of Odin's sacrifice is multifaceted, resonating with the notion that wisdom often comes at a steep price. His offering of an eye in exchange for a drink from the Well of Mimir underscores the belief that gaining profound knowledge requires a willingness to lose a part of oneself. This reflects a common thread in various cultures, where sacrifices—be they material, emotional, or physical—are seen as a prerequisite for accessing higher truths. The act of giving up something valuable is not merely a loss but a transformative experience that can lead to personal growth and enlightenment.

Across cultures, the role of sacrifice in the pursuit of knowledge manifests in diverse forms. Many mythologies and spiritual traditions emphasize that enlightenment is not easily attained; it often demands a surrender of ego, desires, and sometimes, even life itself. The stories of sages, heroes, and deities reveal that personal growth frequently requires facing fears, enduring suffering, and making choices that challenge the status quo. In this way, Odin's journey serves as a mirror for modern seekers, illustrating that the path to wisdom is fraught with trials that ultimately strengthen the spirit and broaden one's understanding of existence.

The Well of Mimir stands as a powerful symbol in Odin's quest for wisdom, representing the depths of knowledge that can only be accessed through sacrifice. By risking his own well-being, Odin demonstrates that growth often lies in the willingness to confront the unknown. The water from the well offers not just wisdom, but also the clarity that comes from understanding one's place in the cosmos. This quest for knowledge is mirrored in contemporary spiritual practices, where individuals are encouraged to explore their own depths, often through challenging experiences that compel them to reevaluate their beliefs and motivations.

The psychological implications of sacrifice for enlightenment are significant, suggesting that personal growth is inherently linked to the willingness to endure discomfort. Odin's sacrifices resonate with anyone striving for self-discovery, as they highlight the importance of resilience and courage in the face of adversity. As modern seekers navigate their own journeys, they are reminded that true wisdom often requires relinquishing the familiar and embracing the transformative power of sacrifice. In this light, Odin's narrative continues to inspire individuals in their pursuit of enlightenment, illustrating that the path to wisdom is both a personal and collective endeavor, rooted in the age-old understanding that sacrifice is an essential component of growth.

## Embodying Odin's Wisdom Today

Embodying Odin's wisdom today requires an understanding of the profound sacrifices he made in the pursuit of knowledge. Odin, the Allfather of Norse mythology, is renowned for his relentless quest for wisdom, which led him to sacrifice his eye at Mimir's Well. This act symbolizes the lengths one must go to attain true understanding. By giving up something of great personal value, Odin teaches us that the pursuit of knowledge often demands significant personal sacrifice, a lesson that resonates with individuals seeking enlightenment in modern life.

The symbolism of Odin's sacrifice extends beyond mere physical loss; it represents a deeper spiritual journey that encourages self-reflection and transformation. In various cultures, the concept of sacrifice is intertwined with the quest for wisdom. From the ancient Greeks to the indigenous tribes of the Americas, many narratives illustrate that knowledge often comes at a cost. Embracing this idea can inspire contemporary seekers to recognize that personal growth may require letting go of comfort, ego, or outdated beliefs in favor of deeper truths.

Odin's quest for wisdom offers valuable lessons for modern seekers. His willingness to embrace discomfort and endure trials serves as a guide for those navigating their own paths to enlightenment. Today, individuals can embody this wisdom by actively seeking experiences that challenge their perspectives and push them beyond their limits. This might involve engaging in difficult conversations, pursuing new educational opportunities, or facing fears that have long held them back. By doing so, one can cultivate resilience and a richer understanding of themselves and the world around them.

The significance of Mimir's Well in Odin's journey cannot be understated. It symbolizes the profound depths of knowledge that lie beyond superficial understanding. In seeking counsel from Mimir, Odin illustrates that wisdom is often found in the willingness to ask for help and to learn from others. This cooperative aspect of learning is essential in today's interconnected world, where collaboration and shared knowledge can lead to greater insights. By acknowledging the value of community and mentorship, individuals can enhance their own journeys toward wisdom.

Finally, the psychological implications of sacrifice for enlightenment are profound. Engaging with Odin's narrative encourages adults to reflect on their own experiences with sacrifice, whether in relationships, career pursuits, or personal growth. Embracing the notion that enlightenment may require relinquishing certain comforts can lead to a more fulfilling life. By embodying Odin's wisdom, individuals can navigate their paths with a sense of purpose, recognizing that the pursuit of knowledge is not merely an intellectual endeavor but a transformative journey that shapes one's very essence.

# Chapter 8: The Impact of Odin's Sacrifice on Viking Culture

## Beliefs and Practices Influenced by Odin

Beliefs and practices influenced by Odin are deeply woven into the fabric of Norse mythology and the cultural heritage of the Viking Age. Central to these beliefs is the understanding of sacrifice as a necessary path to wisdom. Odin, the Allfather, embodies the archetype of the seeker who willingly endures great trials to gain knowledge. His self-sacrifice, notably hanging from Yggdrasil for nine nights, signifies the profound connection between suffering and enlightenment. This act is not merely a mythological tale but serves as a guiding principle for those who seek wisdom through their own personal challenges.

The symbolism of Odin's sacrifice resonates in various cultural narratives where enlightenment is achieved through sacrifice. Across many mythologies, deities undergo similar trials, reflecting a universal truth: knowledge often demands a price. For instance, the ancient Greeks revered figures like Prometheus, who suffered for the benefit of humanity. Similarly, Odin's choice to give up an eye to drink from the Well of Mimir underscores the idea that true insight often requires making significant sacrifices. This theme transcends cultures, revealing a common understanding that wisdom is not easily obtained and often involves personal loss or hardship.

In contemporary spirituality, Odin's quest for wisdom provides valuable lessons for modern seekers. The practice of self-reflection, meditation, and the acceptance of life's challenges can be seen as modern equivalents of Odin's trials. The act of seeking knowledge today may not involve literal sacrifice, but it demands a commitment to personal growth and transformation. Individuals are encouraged to confront their fears, embrace vulnerability, and engage with their shadows, echoing Odin's journey. This transformative process can lead to deeper insights and a richer understanding of oneself and the world.

The Well of Mimir serves as a significant symbol in Odin's journey, representing the depths of wisdom that can be accessed through sacrifice. Mimir, the guardian of the well, embodies the knowledge that comes from experience and the understanding of the cosmos. By sacrificing part of himself, Odin gains access to profound truths that shape his understanding of existence. This narrative emphasizes the importance of seeking wisdom outside oneself and acknowledges that enlightenment often requires guidance from those who have traversed the path before us. The well symbolizes not only the quest for knowledge but also the interconnectedness of all beings who seek to understand their place in the universe.

Odin's influence on Viking culture is evident in the reverence for knowledge, skill, and the practice of runes as tools of wisdom. Runes, believed to be gifts from Odin, represent the intersection of language, magic, and insight. Their use in divination and communication highlights the belief that words carry power and that understanding the deeper meanings behind symbols is vital for personal and communal growth. The psychological implications of such beliefs suggest that the act of sacrifice, whether physical or metaphorical, can catalyze significant personal transformations. In this way, Odin's legacy continues to inspire those on the path of self-discovery, encouraging the embrace of challenges as a means to unlock the wisdom that lies within.

## Legacy of Sacrifice in Viking Society

The legacy of sacrifice in Viking society is intricately woven into the fabric of their beliefs and practices, serving as a testament to the profound impact that the concept of sacrifice had on their understanding of wisdom and knowledge. Central to this legacy is the figure of Odin, the Allfather, who exemplified the highest ideals of sacrifice in pursuit of enlightenment. His willingness to hang for nine nights on the World Tree, Yggdrasil, in exchange for the knowledge of the runes symbolizes a broader cultural understanding that wisdom often comes at a great personal cost. This narrative not only reflects Odin's journey but also embodies the values held by the Norse people, where the pursuit of higher understanding was seen as a noble and worthy endeavor.

The symbolism of Odin's sacrifice resonates deeply with the Viking ethos, where selflessness and the willingness to endure hardship were heralded as virtues. Sacrifice was not merely an act of giving up something valuable; it was perceived as a transformative process that elevated one's status. The Vikings believed that true knowledge and wisdom were attained through trials and tribulations, much like Odin's own experiences. This view fosters a societal framework where learning and growth are intrinsically linked to the acceptance of sacrifice, thus reinforcing the idea that wisdom is not an easy gift but rather a hard-won prize.

The role of sacrifice in the pursuit of knowledge is a theme that transcends Norse mythology, appearing in various cultures throughout history. From the ancient Greeks to Eastern philosophies, the notion that profound insights often require significant personal sacrifice is a universal truth. This comparative perspective emphasizes that the journey towards enlightenment is not confined to a singular narrative but is a shared human experience. For modern seekers, understanding this theme can provide a deeper appreciation for their own struggles in the quest for knowledge and self-discovery, echoing the sacrifices made by figures like Odin and the wisdom they ultimately gained.

Odin's quest for wisdom through sacrifice also underscores the significance of the Well of Mimir, a source of knowledge that he accessed after sacrificing an eye. This act highlights the physical manifestation of sacrifice in the quest for enlightenment, reinforcing the idea that some knowledge requires a steep price. The Well itself represents a reservoir of ancient wisdom, reminding us that the pursuit of understanding often involves navigating the depths of personal loss and transformation. The psychological implications of such sacrifices reveal a complex relationship between suffering and enlightenment, suggesting that the path to greater awareness is often fraught with challenges that shape one's character and insight.

The impact of Odin's sacrifice on Viking culture and beliefs is evident in their spiritual practices and societal values. The reverence for wisdom and the acceptance of sacrifice as a necessary precursor to knowledge shaped the Viking worldview, influencing their decisions in both daily life and warfare. In contemporary spirituality, Odin's legacy continues to resonate, encouraging individuals to embrace their own journeys toward wisdom, often through personal trials. By recognizing the significance of sacrifice in their own lives, modern seekers can find inspiration in Odin's story, understanding that the pursuit of enlightenment remains a noble and transformative endeavor that can yield profound rewards.

# Chapter 9: Psychological Implications of Sacrifice for Enlightenment

## The Psychology of Letting Go

The psychology of letting go is intricately woven into the fabric of Odin's narrative, illustrating how the act of relinquishing what is familiar can pave the way for profound growth and enlightenment. Odin's sacrifices, particularly his self-immolation on Yggdrasil, the World Tree, exemplify the necessity of surrendering one's current state to gain deeper insights. This act of letting go is reflective of a broader psychological principle: to embrace transformation, one must often sever ties with past identities, beliefs, and comforts. Odin's willingness to endure suffering in exchange for knowledge underscores the psychological struggle that many face when confronted with the need to abandon the familiar in pursuit of a greater truth.

In Norse mythology, the symbolism of Odin's sacrifice resonates with the fundamental human experience of loss and the subsequent quest for meaning. By sacrificing his eye at the Well of Mimir, Odin embodies the idea that wisdom often comes at a significant cost. This act serves as a powerful metaphor for the sacrifices individuals make in their own lives, whether it is through the loss of time, relationships, or security in the pursuit of enlightenment. This psychological journey reveals how the act of letting go can lead to a more profound understanding of oneself and the world, highlighting the transformative power of sacrifice as a catalyst for personal growth.

Across cultures, the role of sacrifice in the pursuit of knowledge is a recurring theme that transcends mythology. From ancient rituals to modern spiritual practices, the willingness to let go of the old self for the sake of acquiring wisdom is a universal tenet. The psychological implications of this act are significant; they challenge individuals to confront their fears and attachments. Just as Odin's quest required him to endure pain and isolation, so too must modern seekers navigate their own psychological barriers. This process often involves grappling with the discomfort of change, suggesting that growth frequently necessitates a conscious decision to relinquish the past.

The significance of the Well of Mimir in Odin's journey serves as a poignant reminder of the deep wells of knowledge that often lie just beyond the threshold of sacrifice. In the context of psychological development, this well symbolizes the depths of the unconscious mind, where true wisdom resides. To access this knowledge, individuals must be willing to confront their inner demons and let go of superficial understandings. Odin's relationship with the runes further illustrates this connection, as they represent the hidden truths that can only be unveiled through the trials of sacrifice and introspection. The psychological journey of unlocking these symbols mirrors the path of self-discovery that many adults embark upon in their quest for meaning.

Ultimately, the impact of Odin's sacrifice on Viking culture reflects a collective understanding of the necessity of letting go for the sake of enlightenment. As a revered figure, Odin's actions underscore a cultural acknowledgment of the psychological complexities surrounding sacrifice and knowledge. In contemporary spirituality, Odin's wisdom continues to resonate, encouraging individuals to embrace the challenges of letting go as a means of self-discovery. This enduring narrative not only highlights the sacrifices made in pursuit of wisdom but also serves as an invitation for modern seekers to explore their own psychological landscapes, fostering a deeper connection with the transformative power of surrender.

## Sacrifice as a Path to Self-Discovery

Odin's journey in Norse mythology is emblematic of the profound connection between sacrifice and the pursuit of wisdom. His willingness to hang from the World Tree, Yggdrasil, for nine days and nights is a powerful testament to the lengths one must go to attain knowledge. This act of self-sacrifice not only illustrates Odin's dedication but also serves as a catalyst for personal transformation. By willingly enduring pain and isolation, he transcended his limitations, ultimately gaining insight into the mysteries of existence. This narrative reinforces the idea that sacrifice is often a necessary step toward self-discovery, compelling individuals to confront their fears and embrace vulnerability.

The symbolism of Odin's sacrifice resonates deeply within both Norse mythology and the broader human experience. In sacrificing his eye at the Well of Mimir, Odin illustrates the notion that true wisdom comes at a cost. This well, representing knowledge and insight, is a reminder that to gain deep understanding, one often must give up something of great value. Across various cultures, similar themes emerge: the idea that enlightenment frequently requires relinquishing comfort or security. Whether through mythological stories or personal experiences, the act of sacrifice becomes a transformative process that leads to profound self-awareness and growth.

Odin's quest for wisdom offers valuable lessons for modern seekers. In a world that frequently prioritizes instant gratification, Odin's journey encourages a deeper exploration of the self. It challenges individuals to reflect on what they are willing to sacrifice in their own lives to achieve personal and spiritual growth. This introspection fosters a richer understanding of one's motivations and aspirations, creating a pathway toward self-discovery. By embracing sacrifice, individuals can cultivate resilience and fortitude, qualities essential for navigating life's challenges and evolving into their authentic selves.

The significance of the Well of Mimir in Odin's journey further underscores the relationship between sacrifice and knowledge. This mythical well is not just a source of wisdom but also a symbol of the profound interconnectedness of all knowledge. Odin's sacrifice to access its waters illustrates that understanding is rarely without effort; it highlights the importance of seeking wisdom actively. In contemporary spirituality, this narrative serves as a reminder that individuals must often endure trials and tribulations to uncover deeper truths about themselves and the universe, reinforcing the timeless notion that knowledge is intertwined with sacrifice.

The psychological implications of sacrifice for enlightenment reveal a critical aspect of Odin's wisdom. Engaging in acts of sacrifice can lead to greater self-awareness, allowing individuals to confront their inner demons and acknowledge their limitations. This process can ultimately foster a sense of empowerment and purpose, as one learns to navigate the complexities of life through the lens of sacrifice. Odin's teachings, reflected in the modern pursuit of self-discovery, highlight the transformative potential of embracing sacrifice as a pathway to enlightenment, encouraging individuals to delve deeper into their psyche and emerge with newfound clarity and strength.

# Chapter 10: Odin's Wisdom in Contemporary Spirituality

## Modern Interpretations of Norse Wisdom

Modern interpretations of Norse wisdom often revolve around the profound sacrifices made by figures like Odin, whose quest for knowledge remains relevant in contemporary thought. Odin's self-sacrifice, where he hung from Yggdrasil for nine nights, exemplifies the idea that true wisdom often comes at a cost. This notion resonates across various cultures, where the pursuit of knowledge frequently demands personal sacrifice. In a world where instant gratification is the norm, Odin's journey serves as a reminder that deeper understanding and enlightenment require dedication and a willingness to confront hardships.

The symbolism of Odin's sacrifice is rich and multifaceted. By sacrificing himself to gain the wisdom of the runes, Odin not only achieved personal enlightenment but also became a symbol of the transformative power of sacrifice. This act reflects a broader theme in mythology, where divine figures often endure trials to obtain knowledge that benefits their people. Odin's experience invites modern seekers to consider what they might be willing to give up in their own lives to achieve greater understanding, urging them to reflect on the often overlooked value of patience and perseverance in personal growth.

The role of sacrifice in the pursuit of knowledge is not unique to Norse mythology; it appears in various cultural narratives around the world. Many traditions emphasize the necessity of sacrifice as a means of unlocking deeper truths. Whether through the trials of heroes in Greek mythology or the ascetic practices in Eastern philosophies, the theme is consistent: knowledge is often found on the other side of hardship. This comparative approach highlights a universal truth about the human experience—the pursuit of wisdom is fraught with challenges that require sacrifices, whether they be time, comfort, or even relationships.

Odin's quest for wisdom offers valuable lessons for modern seekers navigating a complex and often overwhelming world. His journey illustrates the importance of embracing discomfort as a catalyst for growth. In an age dominated by information overload, the ability to discern valuable knowledge from trivial distractions is crucial. Odin's story encourages individuals to engage in introspective practices, such as meditation or self-reflection, in order to cultivate a deeper understanding of themselves and their place in the world. This modern application of Norse wisdom emphasizes that enlightenment is not merely about acquiring knowledge, but about transforming oneself through the process.

The significance of the Well of Mimir in Odin's pursuit of wisdom further underscores the importance of seeking knowledge. This mythical well, known for its profound insights, symbolizes the depths of understanding that are accessible through sacrifice. In today's context, the Well of Mimir can be seen as a metaphor for the various sources of wisdom available to us, whether they be from ancient texts, mentors, or personal experiences. As contemporary spirituality increasingly focuses on self-discovery, the lessons drawn from Odin's journey remind us that the path to enlightenment is a deeply personal one, requiring us to confront our own limitations and embrace the sacrifices that lead to profound insights.

## The Relevance of Odin's Teachings Today

Odin's teachings continue to resonate with contemporary seekers of wisdom, reflecting timeless themes of sacrifice and enlightenment. At the core of Norse mythology lies Odin's profound commitment to acquiring knowledge, exemplified by his willingness to sacrifice his eye for a drink from the Well of Mimir. This act serves as a powerful reminder of the lengths one must go to gain true understanding. In today's fast-paced world, where instant gratification often overshadows deeper pursuits, Odin's sacrifices encourage individuals to reflect on what they are willing to give up in their quest for knowledge and self-discovery.

The symbolism of Odin's sacrifice extends beyond personal enlightenment; it reflects a broader cultural understanding of the importance of sacrifice in the pursuit of knowledge. Across various cultures, sacrificial acts have been integral to spiritual and intellectual growth. Whether through rites, rituals, or personal sacrifices, the notion that wisdom often comes at a cost is a universal theme. Odin's journey exemplifies this principle, reminding modern seekers that true growth often requires stepping outside of one's comfort zone and facing the unknown.

Odin's quest for wisdom offers valuable lessons for today's individuals navigating their paths. His relentless pursuit serves as an inspiration for those seeking to deepen their understanding of the world and themselves. In contemporary spirituality, Odin can be viewed as a guide, encouraging the integration of knowledge and experience. The lessons derived from his journey highlight the necessity of resilience, open-mindedness, and the willingness to embrace challenges in the ongoing quest for enlightenment.

The Well of Mimir stands as a significant symbol in Odin's journey, representing the depths of wisdom that can be accessed through sacrifice. This well embodies the idea that profound knowledge often lies beneath the surface, requiring effort and commitment to uncover. In modern contexts, the metaphor of the well can inspire individuals to delve deeper into their own lives, seeking wisdom that may not be readily apparent. By recognizing the importance of persistence in the pursuit of knowledge, individuals can cultivate a more profound understanding of their own experiences.

The impact of Odin's sacrifice on Viking culture underscores the relevance of his teachings in shaping collective beliefs and values. The act of sacrificing for wisdom not only influenced individual seekers but also fostered a cultural ethos that valued knowledge, courage, and sacrifice. As contemporary society grapples with its own challenges and uncertainties, the principles embodied by Odin's journey remain significant. They encourage a reevaluation of the relationship between sacrifice and enlightenment, prompting individuals to consider how their own sacrifices can lead to personal growth and a greater understanding of the world around them.

# Odin's Call: Invoking the Allfather Through Prayer and Offerings

## Chapter 1: Introduction to Norse Spirituality

### Understanding the Norse Pantheon

The Norse pantheon is a complex and rich tapestry of deities, each embodying different aspects of life, nature, and human experience. At its center stands Odin, the Allfather, known for his wisdom, battle prowess, and deep connection to the mysteries of existence. Alongside Odin are other prominent gods and goddesses, such as Thor, the god of thunder and protector of humanity, and Freyja, the goddess of love, fertility, and war. Understanding these deities and their relationships with one another is crucial for those looking to engage in prayer and rituals. Each god and goddess serves a unique purpose and represents various elements of life that practitioners can invoke in their daily spiritual practices.

Odin, as the chief of the Aesir, presides over knowledge, poetry, and the fate of warriors. His quest for wisdom often involved sacrifice, including the famous act of hanging from Yggdrasil, the World Tree, to gain insight into the runes. This narrative underscores the importance of sacrifice and commitment in the practice of Norse spirituality. Rituals dedicated to Odin can involve offerings of mead, poetry, or symbolic items that represent wisdom and knowledge. As practitioners seek to connect with the Allfather, they must reflect on their intentions and the qualities they wish to embody, making their prayers a profound personal journey.

Thor, with his hammer Mjölnir, represents strength and protection. He is often called upon for aid in times of trouble and is revered for his role as a guardian of both gods and humans. His festivals, such as Midsummer and Midwinter, provide opportunities for communal celebrations, where offerings can be made to invoke his blessings. Rituals associated with Thor often include elements of nature, such as fire and stone, symbolizing strength and endurance. When praying to Thor, practitioners might focus on themes of protection, courage, and resilience, drawing on the vigor that the god embodies.

Freyja stands as a powerful figure in the realm of love and fertility. She is also associated with war and death, reflecting the duality of existence within Norse beliefs. Her connection to the Vanir, a group of fertility gods, highlights the blending of different aspects of life and spirituality. Those invoking Freyja in prayer often seek assistance in matters of love, family, and fertility. Rituals may include offerings of flowers, jewelry, or personal tokens that resonate with themes of beauty and connection. Engaging with Freyja encourages practitioners to explore their desires and relationships, fostering a deeper understanding of love in all its forms.

To fully embrace the Norse pantheon in prayer and ritual, practitioners should also consider the role of their ancestors and the importance of creating sacred spaces. Ancestors hold a significant place in Norse spirituality, as they are believed to provide guidance and protection. Incorporating ancestor veneration into one's practice can enrich the connection to the gods. Creating a designated sacred space for worship, adorned with symbols and offerings relevant to the deities being honored, enhances the spiritual experience. By understanding the Norse pantheon and its intricacies, individuals can develop a more meaningful and personalized practice, invoking the gods with intention and reverence.

## The Significance of Prayer in Norse Traditions

The significance of prayer in Norse traditions is deeply rooted in the relationship between mortals and the divine. In these ancient practices, prayer serves not only as a means of communication but as a vital expression of one's intentions, desires, and reverence for the gods. Unlike the more formalized prayer structures found in some other religious traditions, Norse prayer is often spontaneous and personal, allowing practitioners to connect with the deities on an intimate level. This direct communion emphasizes the importance of individual sincerity and authenticity in the act of supplication or gratitude.

Daily prayer rituals hold a special place in Norse spirituality, forming a bridge between the mundane and the sacred. Practitioners often incorporate simple prayers into their daily routines, whether it be during morning rituals or at mealtime. These informal prayers can invoke gods like Odin for wisdom, Freyja for love, or Thor for protection, reflecting the diverse needs of the community and the individual. Such daily practices reinforce a sense of connection and continuity with the divine, grounding practitioners in their heritage while fostering a daily awareness of the spiritual realm.

Seasonal celebrations in Norse traditions also play a significant role in prayer practices. Festivals like Yule, Midsummer, and the harvest celebrations provide opportunities for communal prayer, where offerings are made to the gods to ensure blessings for the coming seasons. These rituals often involve specific prayers that reflect the themes of the season, such as gratitude for the harvest or hopes for fertility and abundance. By aligning prayers with the natural cycles, practitioners not only honor the gods but also acknowledge their dependence on the rhythms of nature, reinforcing a sense of community and shared purpose among participants.

Invoking Odin, in particular, is a practice steeped in rich tradition and varied techniques. Many practitioners seek to invoke Odin through specific prayers that call upon his wisdom and guidance. This might involve offerings of mead or poetry, acknowledging his association with knowledge and inspiration. By engaging with Odin in this manner, worshippers tap into a legacy of wisdom that transcends time, inviting the Allfather into their lives to assist in personal growth and understanding. Techniques may vary, but the underlying principle remains the same: a heartfelt desire to connect with a deity whose traits resonate deeply with the practitioner.

The role of ancestors in Norse prayer practices cannot be overlooked. In many traditions, honoring ancestors is considered essential, as they are believed to influence the lives of their descendants. Prayers directed towards ancestors often serve to seek guidance, protection, or blessings, creating a vital link between the past and the present. This aspect of prayer emphasizes the importance of lineage and memory, allowing individuals to draw strength from those who came before them. By creating sacred spaces for these prayers, practitioners enhance their spiritual practices, cultivating an environment that is conducive to reflection, invocation, and connection with both the divine and their ancestral heritage.

## The Role of Offerings in Worship

The act of offering holds a significant place in Norse worship, serving as both a form of communication with the divine and a means of establishing a reciprocal relationship with the gods. Offerings can take many forms, ranging from food and drink to handcrafted items, each chosen to reflect the worshiper's intentions and desires. In the context of invoking Odin, offerings are particularly important as they symbolize respect, devotion, and the acknowledgment of the Allfather's wisdom and power. Through offerings, practitioners seek to honor Odin while also inviting his presence and guidance into their lives.

In Norse tradition, the offerings made during worship are not merely gifts; they are expressions of gratitude and requests for favor. The types of offerings can vary widely depending on the season, the specific deity being honored, and the personal needs of the worshiper. For Odin, offerings might include mead, bread, or even symbolic items that represent knowledge and sacrifice, such as runestones or weapons. These offerings serve as a tangible connection to the spiritual realm, reinforcing the belief that the gods are intimately involved in the affairs of humans and that they respond to sincere gestures of devotion.

Seasonal celebrations in Norse culture also play a crucial role in the practice of offerings. Festivals such as Yule, Midsummer, and the autumn harvest are often marked by communal rituals that include the presentation of offerings to the gods. These occasions serve not only to honor the deities but also to strengthen community ties among practitioners. By gathering to share in rituals that include offerings, individuals reinforce their shared beliefs and values, fostering a collective identity rooted in Norse spirituality. Such celebrations enhance the experience of worship, creating a sense of continuity with ancestral practices and a deeper connection to the natural cycles of life.

The significance of offerings extends beyond mere material gifts; they also embody the broader concepts of sacrifice and reciprocity in Norse spirituality. Worshipers believe that by giving something of value, they demonstrate their commitment to the gods and, in return, receive blessings and protection. This exchange is particularly vital when invoking Odin, who is associated with wisdom, war, and death. The act of offering is seen as a way to align oneself with Odin's attributes, inviting his insight and strength into one's life. Through this dynamic, offerings become a powerful tool for personal transformation and spiritual growth.

Furthermore, the practice of making offerings is deeply intertwined with the concept of ancestor reverence in Norse traditions. Ancestors are often invoked during worship, and offerings can be made in their honor, creating a bridge between the past and present. This practice not only acknowledges the influence of forebears on contemporary lives but also reinforces the continuity of cultural and spiritual heritage. By incorporating offerings into their prayer practices, worshipers cultivate a sacred space that honors both the gods and their ancestors, enriching their spiritual journey and fostering a sense of belonging within the larger tapestry of Norse mythology.

# Chapter 2: How to Pray to the Norse Gods

## The Basics of Norse Prayer

The basics of Norse prayer revolve around a deep understanding of the relationship between the worshiper and the deities. In Norse mythology, prayer is not merely a request for favors but a means of establishing a connection with the divine. Worshipers often begin by acknowledging the gods and goddesses, particularly Odin, the Allfather, as well as other deities like Freyja and Thor, depending on their specific needs or intentions. This acknowledgment is essential in setting the stage for a genuine and respectful exchange, as it demonstrates reverence and understanding of the powers at play.

Daily prayer rituals can vary significantly among individuals, but they often include offerings and invocations tailored to the practitioner's personal needs. Many people choose to create a small altar in their homes, where they can light candles, place runes, or offer food and drink. These offerings serve as tokens of gratitude and respect, establishing a reciprocal relationship with the divine. Daily prayers might include simple expressions of thanks, requests for guidance, or reflections on personal challenges, allowing practitioners to weave spirituality into their everyday lives.

Seasonal celebrations play a crucial role in Norse prayer practices, as they align with the cycles of nature and the changing seasons. Major festivals such as Yule, Midsummer, and harvest celebrations provide opportunities for collective worship and communal prayers. During these events, specific rituals are performed that honor the gods and invoke their blessings for the coming season. Participants may recite traditional prayers, share stories of the gods, and engage in communal feasting, reinforcing their connection to the Norse pantheon and the rhythms of the earth.

Invoking Odin specifically requires a focused approach, given his complex nature as the god of wisdom, war, and death. Techniques may include meditation, chanting, or the use of specific symbols associated with him, such as the Valknut or the spear Gungnir. Offerings to Odin can range from mead to poetic verses, which align with his love for knowledge and artistry. Practitioners often seek Odin's guidance during times of uncertainty or when facing significant life decisions, embodying the belief that divine wisdom can illuminate their paths.

In addition to individual prayers, the role of ancestors in Norse spirituality cannot be overlooked. Ancestor veneration is a fundamental aspect of Norse prayer practices, where individuals honor their forebears for their guidance and protection. This can be done through specific prayers or rituals that invite the presence of ancestors into the sacred space. By combining these elements with modern spirituality, practitioners can create a holistic approach to their prayers that honors both the ancient traditions and their contemporary experiences, fostering a deeper connection to their heritage and the divine.

## Crafting Personal Prayers

Crafting personal prayers is an intimate and reflective process that deepens one's connection to the Norse gods, particularly Odin. Personal prayers allow practitioners to articulate their desires, fears, and gratitude in a way that resonates with their individual experiences and spiritual journey. When crafting these prayers, it is essential to consider the specific attributes and domains of the deities you wish to invoke. For instance, if you are seeking wisdom or guidance, focusing on Odin's role as the Allfather and seeker of knowledge can enhance the potency of your prayer.

Begin by setting a sacred space that reflects your intentions. This space can be adorned with symbols relevant to your practice, such as runes, candles, or images of the gods. Creating an atmosphere that feels sacred can help center your thoughts and emotions. Once you are in a conducive environment, take a moment to ground yourself through meditation or deep breathing. This practice can help clear your mind and open your heart, allowing for a more authentic expression of your intentions in your prayer.

When writing your prayer, consider using a format that feels comfortable for you. This could be a structured approach, such as beginning with an invocation, followed by your request or offering, and concluding with gratitude. Alternatively, you may prefer a more freeform style, where you allow your thoughts and feelings to flow naturally. Remember that the language you use should feel genuine and resonate with your personal beliefs. Whether you choose to employ Old Norse phrases or modern vernacular, the sincerity behind your words is what truly matters.

Incorporate seasonal elements into your prayers to align with the cycles of nature and the Norse calendar. Each season brings unique energies and opportunities for growth, reflection, and celebration. For example, during the winter solstice, you might focus on themes of rebirth and renewal, invoking Odin's wisdom to guide you through the dark months ahead. Conversely, in spring, you may wish to express gratitude for new beginnings and seek blessings for fertility and love, perhaps calling upon Freyja for assistance in matters of the heart.

Finally, remember that personal prayers are not only about asking for guidance or assistance; they also serve as a medium for expressing gratitude and honoring the Norse deities and your ancestors. Acknowledging their presence and influence in your life fosters a deeper connection to your spiritual heritage. As you continue to craft and refine your personal prayers, you will find that this practice not only enhances your communication with the gods but also enriches your understanding of yourself and your place within the tapestry of existence.

# Rituals and Intentions in Prayer

Rituals and intentions serve as the backbone of prayer within Norse spirituality, providing structure and focus to the act of communion with the gods. When invoking Odin, the Allfather, practitioners often engage in specific rituals that enhance their connection to the divine. These rituals may vary from simple daily prayers to elaborate seasonal celebrations, but they all share the common goal of aligning the worshipper's intentions with those of the deities. By carefully selecting rituals that resonate with their personal beliefs and needs, individuals can create a more profound and meaningful prayer experience.

Intentions in prayer are crucial, as they set the stage for what is being sought from the gods. When addressing Odin, practitioners might focus on intentions related to wisdom, knowledge, or guidance, reflecting the attributes commonly associated with the Allfather. It is essential that these intentions be clear and sincere, as the energy behind them is believed to influence the outcome of the prayer. By stating intentions aloud or writing them down, worshippers can solidify their desires, allowing for a more focused and directed appeal to the divine.

Incorporating seasonal celebrations into prayer can enrich the spiritual experience and deepen one's connection to the cycles of nature and the Norse deities. Each season brings unique opportunities for reflection and gratitude, encouraging practitioners to align their prayers with the rhythms of the earth. For instance, during Yule, prayers may center around themes of rebirth and renewal, while during Midsummer, they might focus on abundance and vitality. By tailoring prayers to the seasons, worshippers honor the natural world and its influence on their spiritual lives.

The act of creating sacred spaces for prayer is another vital aspect of Norse worship. These spaces can be simple altars adorned with offerings, symbols, and items that resonate with the deities being invoked. When preparing a sacred space, practitioners should consider the significance of each item, as every element contributes to the overall intention of the prayer. This conscious curation of the space not only elevates the prayer experience but also serves as a physical manifestation of the worshipper's devotion and respect for the gods.

Lastly, integrating modern spiritual practices with traditional Norse prayers can create a unique and personalized approach to worship. Many people find that blending elements from various spiritual paths enriches their connection to the divine while allowing for a more inclusive practice. This fusion can include contemporary visualization techniques, meditation, or even the use of modern symbols alongside ancient Norse iconography. By embracing both the old and the new, practitioners can cultivate a dynamic spiritual practice that honors the traditions of their ancestors while remaining relevant to their current lives.

# Chapter 3: Daily Prayer Rituals for Norse Deities

## Morning Prayers to the Gods

Morning prayers to the gods serve as a vital practice within Norse spirituality, setting the tone for the day and fostering a deeper connection to the divine. Starting the day with intention and reverence can enhance one's relationship with the gods, particularly Odin, who is often considered the Allfather and the source of wisdom and guidance. Morning prayers can include invocations, expressions of gratitude, and requests for protection and guidance, allowing practitioners to align their energies with the forces of the universe and the specific deities they seek to honor.

When engaging in morning prayers, it is beneficial to create a sacred space. This can be as simple as a designated area in your home adorned with symbols associated with the Norse gods, such as runes, images, or offerings of natural elements like stones and flowers. Lighting a candle or burning incense can serve as a physical representation of the light of the gods entering your space. The act of creating this environment not only prepares the mind for prayer but also invites the presence of the divine into your daily life.

The structure of a morning prayer can vary among practitioners, but it often begins with an acknowledgment of the gods and ancestors. Invoking Odin may involve reciting a specific prayer or mantra that highlights his attributes, such as wisdom and protection. Following this invocation, practitioners may express gratitude for the blessings they have received and seek guidance for the challenges ahead. This moment of reflection can cultivate a sense of mindfulness, grounding individuals in the present while connecting them to the broader tapestry of Norse mythology.

In addition to personal prayers, incorporating elements that celebrate the changing seasons can enrich morning rituals. Norse traditions emphasize the cyclical nature of life, and aligning prayers with seasonal festivals allows practitioners to honor the gods in context. For instance, during the spring equinox, prayers to Freyja can focus on themes of love and fertility, while in winter, offerings may be made to Odin for protection and guidance during the darker months. This practice not only strengthens the connection to the divine but also deepens the understanding of the natural world and its rhythms.

Finally, morning prayers can serve as a form of divination and introspection. By incorporating tools such as runes or tarot cards, practitioners can seek clarity on personal issues or decisions. This not only provides direction but also reinforces the belief that the gods are active participants in the lives of their followers. Ultimately, morning prayers to the Norse gods are a powerful practice that fosters a daily connection to the divine, encourages gratitude, and promotes a holistic understanding of one's place within the universe.

## Evening Reflections and Gratitude

Evening reflections serve as a crucial time within Norse spiritual practices, allowing practitioners to connect with the divine and express gratitude for the day's experiences. This time of day, when the sun sets and darkness begins to envelop the world, creates a natural atmosphere for contemplation. It is during these quiet moments that individuals can turn their thoughts inward, reflecting on the lessons learned, the challenges faced, and the blessings received throughout the day. This practice not only fosters a deeper connection with the Norse gods, particularly Odin, but also encourages personal growth and self-awareness.

Gratitude is a powerful sentiment in Norse spirituality, where acknowledging the gifts and lessons from the gods and ancestors is essential. Practitioners might start their evening prayers by offering thanks to Odin for his wisdom and guidance. Expressing appreciation for the small victories and the protection offered during the day can open pathways for further blessings. A simple yet profound prayer, acknowledging the abundance in one's life, can be a gateway to receiving more from the divine. This gratitude can also extend to the ancestors, honoring their role in shaping one's path and acknowledging the sacrifices they made.

Creating a sacred space for evening reflections can enhance the experience, allowing individuals to immerse themselves in the ritual. This space might include symbols associated with the Norse gods, such as runes or images of Odin and Freyja, along with natural elements like stones or candles that represent the earth and fire. Lighting a candle can symbolize the illumination of the mind and spirit, creating a warm and inviting environment conducive to prayer and meditation. This practice can be further enriched by the use of specific offerings, such as mead or bread, which can be placed on an altar as a gesture of gratitude and respect.

As part of the evening ritual, practitioners can also engage in divination practices, seeking guidance for the days ahead. Techniques such as casting runes or consulting with tarot cards can provide insights into personal situations and help clarify intentions. This reflective practice not only allows for deeper communication with the divine but also aids in understanding the interconnectedness of one's life with the broader tapestry of fate. The insights gained can then be integrated into the following day's actions, creating a continuous cycle of reflection and gratitude.

Ultimately, evening reflections and gratitude form a vital component of daily prayer rituals in Norse spirituality. By cultivating a practice that honors the gods, ancestors, and the natural world, individuals can establish a profound connection with their heritage. This nightly ritual not only fosters personal growth but also strengthens the bonds with the divine, creating a sense of purpose and direction. Through these reflections, one can navigate life's challenges with the wisdom of the Allfather and the support of their spiritual community.

## Incorporating Daily Offerings

Incorporating daily offerings into your spiritual practice can enhance your connection to the Norse gods, particularly Odin, while fostering a sense of discipline and intention in your daily life. Daily offerings serve as a reminder of your devotion and help create a sacred space in which you can communicate with the divine. These offerings can take various forms, from simple acts of gratitude to more elaborate rituals, depending on your personal beliefs and circumstances. The key is consistency; making offerings a part of your daily routine can deepen your spiritual journey and strengthen your relationship with the gods.

To begin incorporating daily offerings, consider the elements that resonate most with you. Offerings can include food, beverages, or symbolic items that hold significance in Norse mythology. Odin, for instance, is often associated with wisdom and war, so offerings of mead or bread can be particularly meaningful. You might also consider dedicating a small altar space in your home where you can place these offerings, allowing for a dedicated area that invites the presence of the Allfather and other deities you wish to honor.

When preparing your daily offerings, approach the act with mindfulness and intention. Take a moment to ground yourself before making your offering. This can involve a brief meditation or simply focusing on your breath. As you present your offering, express your intentions clearly, whether you seek wisdom, protection, or guidance. Speaking your prayers aloud can amplify their energy, creating a more profound connection with the divine. Odin is known for his affinity for spoken word, so articulating your thoughts and desires can be a powerful way to invoke his presence.

In addition to physical offerings, consider incorporating daily prayers that align with the themes of your offerings. Each day can be dedicated to a specific aspect of life or a particular deity, allowing you to explore various facets of Norse spirituality. For instance, if you choose to offer food, pair it with a prayer for abundance or gratitude. Seasonal celebrations can also provide inspiration for your daily offerings, as they often reflect the rhythms of nature and the cycles of life. By connecting your daily acts with these broader themes, you enrich your spiritual practice and create a sense of continuity within the Norse tradition.

Finally, remember that the act of giving is reciprocal in nature. As you offer to the gods, be open to receiving their guidance and blessings in return. Trust that the energy you invest in your daily offerings will manifest in different ways throughout your life. This ongoing dialogue with the divine not only strengthens your personal practice but also aligns you with the ancient traditions of the Norse people, who understood the importance of reciprocity in their relationship with the gods. Incorporating daily offerings into your routine is a step toward honoring the sacred and inviting the presence of the Norse deities into your everyday life.

# Chapter 4: Seasonal Celebrations and Their Prayers

## The Wheel of the Year in Norse Tradition

The Wheel of the Year in Norse tradition draws upon the cyclical nature of life, reflecting the changing seasons and their significance in the spiritual practices of the Norse people. This framework, while not as rigidly defined as in some other pagan traditions, is nonetheless vital for understanding how ancient Norse cultures honored their gods and the natural world. The year is marked by key festivals, each tied to specific deities, agricultural cycles, and mythological events that resonate with the rhythms of life and death, growth and decay.

The eight significant festivals, or "blóts," are integral to this wheel, including Yule, Ostara, Midsummer, and the autumnal harvests. Each celebration serves as a reminder of the interconnectedness of all things and provides an opportunity for devotees to invoke the blessings of the gods. For instance, Yule, celebrated during the winter solstice, marks the rebirth of the sun and is a time for reflection, feasting, and honoring family ancestors. Prayers during this time often focus on renewal, warmth, and protection through the long winter months.

As the seasons progress, the festivals encourage practitioners to align their prayers and offerings with the energies and themes of each time. Ostara, heralding spring, is dedicated to fertility and growth, invoking deities like Freyja and Freyr. Rituals often include planting seeds, both literal and metaphorical, as symbols of new beginnings and hope. This is an ideal time for prayers that seek love, fertility, and abundance, allowing individuals to connect deeply with the earth and its rhythms.

Midsummer, or Litha, celebrates the peak of the sun's power, emphasizing joy, abundance, and community. Rituals may involve bonfires, a symbol of the sun's strength, along with offerings to the gods for protection and prosperity. Prayers during this time often express gratitude for the bounty of nature and ask for continued blessings. This seasonal celebration reinforces the importance of community and the shared experience of divine connection, allowing for collective invocations that resonate through the ages.

The cycle concludes with autumn celebrations, such as Samhain, when the veil between worlds is believed to be thinnest. This time is dedicated to honoring ancestors and the departed, fostering a sense of continuity and remembrance. Rituals may include lighting candles in honor of those who have passed, along with prayers for guidance and protection. The Wheel of the Year, therefore, not only serves as a calendar for worship but also as a profound reminder of life's cyclical nature, inviting practitioners to engage with the divine in a deeply meaningful way throughout the year.

# Celebrating Yule: Prayers for Renewal

Celebrating Yule holds a special significance within Norse traditions, marking the winter solstice and the return of light as the days begin to lengthen. This time is not just a celebration of the season but also a period for reflection, renewal, and connection with the divine. As practitioners gather to honor the gods, particularly Odin, the Allfather, they do so with prayers that invoke blessings, protection, and guidance for the coming year. Emphasizing the themes of rebirth and hope, Yule prayers serve as a bridge between the past and the future, fostering a deeper relationship with the Norse deities.

During Yule, the act of prayer becomes a communal experience, often accompanied by rituals that enhance the spiritual atmosphere. Setting up a sacred space with symbols of the season—such as evergreens, candles, and offerings—creates an environment conducive to divine communication. Participants may begin their prayers by expressing gratitude for the blessings of the past year, acknowledging the hardships faced, and seeking the strength to overcome future challenges. This act of recognition is vital, as it aligns the heart and mind with the cycles of nature and the divine will of the gods.

Prayers for renewal during Yule can take various forms, from structured invocations to spontaneous expressions of gratitude and hope. Many practitioners incorporate traditional verses that honor Odin, calling upon his wisdom and guidance. Invoking his name, participants may recite prayers that seek not only personal renewal but also communal strength, emphasizing the interconnectedness of all life. These prayers often include requests for protection from the harshness of winter and for the warmth of love and light to fill their homes and hearts in the coming months.

In addition to prayer, offerings play a crucial role during Yule celebrations. These offerings can range from food and drink to crafted items symbolizing the season's bounty. By presenting these gifts to the gods, practitioners acknowledge the reciprocal nature of their relationship with the divine. The act of giving reinforces the intentions set forth in prayer, enhancing the likelihood of manifesting desired outcomes. As the offerings are made, participants often recite specific blessings that resonate with the themes of abundance, protection, and renewal, creating a powerful synergy between intention and action.

As Yule comes to a close, the focus shifts toward integrating the insights gained through prayer and ritual into everyday life. This is a time for setting intentions and making resolutions that align with the values of courage, wisdom, and community embodied by Odin. Reflecting upon the prayers offered, individuals are encouraged to carry the spirit of Yule into their daily practices, ensuring that the renewal experienced during this sacred season remains a guiding force throughout the year. By embracing both the ancient and modern aspects of these traditions, practitioners foster a deeper connection to their heritage while finding personal significance in the timeless cycle of renewal.

# Spring Equinox Celebrations: Fertility and Growth

The Spring Equinox, a powerful moment of balance between light and darkness, marks a time of renewal and the awakening of nature. In Norse tradition, this period is deeply intertwined with themes of fertility and growth. Celebrations during this equinox honor the gods and goddesses who preside over these vital aspects of life, particularly Freyja, who embodies love, beauty, and fertility. For practitioners, engaging in rituals and prayers during this time serves as a way to connect with these deities and invite their blessings into one's life.

To celebrate the Spring Equinox, practitioners often create sacred spaces adorned with symbols of fertility and growth. This can include flowers, seeds, and images of Freyja or other fertility deities. Setting up an altar with offerings such as honey, eggs, or grains can invoke the energy of abundance. These items symbolize the sustenance and prosperity that come with the warmer months. It is essential to prepare this space with intention, focusing on the desires for growth not only in the physical world but also in personal development and relationships.

Prayers offered during the Spring Equinox can take various forms, from simple spoken words to elaborate rituals. A common practice is to recite prayers that express gratitude for the past winter and hopes for the forthcoming season. These prayers can be directed toward Freyja, asking for her guidance in matters of love and fertility, or to Odin, seeking wisdom and protection as new ventures begin. Incorporating elements of divination, such as casting runes or drawing cards, can further enhance the connection with the divine and provide insight into the paths ahead.

In addition to individual practices, community gatherings are a vital aspect of Spring Equinox celebrations. These events often include feasting, music, and storytelling, reinforcing the ties between individuals and their shared heritage. Participants can engage in group prayers and rituals, amplifying their intentions through collective energy. The communal aspect of these celebrations not only honors the gods but also strengthens bonds among participants, fostering a sense of unity and support as everyone embarks on their personal journeys of growth.

Finally, as practitioners reflect on the themes of fertility and growth inherent in the Spring Equinox, it is crucial to consider the role of ancestors in these celebrations. Honoring the wisdom and guidance of those who came before can provide a deeper understanding of one's purpose and connection to the land. Prayers can be offered to ancestors, asking for their blessings and support in the coming season. By acknowledging the past while embracing the potential of the future, practitioners can cultivate a rich spiritual practice that honors the cycles of nature and the divine forces at play in their lives.

# Midsummer Rituals: Honor and Abundance

Midsummer, known as Litha in some traditions, is a time of celebration and reflection in Norse culture. It marks the height of summer, a period when the days are longest and nature is in full bloom. This season is not merely about revelry; it is a sacred opportunity to honor the gods and express gratitude for the abundance of life. The rituals associated with Midsummer focus on invoking blessings, fertility, and protection, making it a pivotal time for those who wish to deepen their connection with the Norse deities.

One of the central practices during Midsummer is the creation of offerings to the gods. These offerings can take many forms, including food, drink, flowers, and handmade crafts. The act of giving is rooted in the belief that the gods favor those who show appreciation for their blessings. As you prepare your offerings, consider what symbolizes abundance and gratitude in your life. This could be fresh fruits, herbs, or items that represent personal achievements over the past year. Place these offerings on a sacred altar or a natural setting, allowing the energy of the season to infuse them with intention.

In addition to offerings, Midsummer rituals often include prayers and invocations directed towards specific deities. Odin, as the Allfather, embodies wisdom and protection, making him a significant figure to invoke during this time. A simple yet profound prayer can be crafted to express your desires for guidance and strength in the coming months. Freyja, goddess of love and fertility, is also honored during this season. Prayers directed to her may focus on themes of personal relationships, abundance, and the nurturing aspects of life. Combining these prayers with elements like fire or water can enhance their potency, as both are powerful symbols of transformation and renewal.

Communal celebrations are another integral aspect of Midsummer traditions. Gathering with like-minded individuals to share in the festivities can amplify the energy of your rituals. Consider organizing a feast that includes seasonal foods, and invite participants to share their own offerings and prayers. This collective energy fosters a sense of community and strengthens the bonds between participants, creating a sacred space for worship and gratitude. Additionally, storytelling and sharing personal experiences can deepen the connection with the deities, as it allows for a more intimate understanding of their influence in your lives.

Finally, the role of ancestors in Midsummer rituals cannot be overlooked. Many traditions emphasize honoring those who have come before us, acknowledging their contributions to our lives. Setting up a small altar with photographs or mementos of ancestors can create a space for reflection and remembrance. Offering prayers for their guidance and protection can enhance your spiritual practice, connecting you to the wisdom of your lineage. As you engage in these Midsummer rituals, remember that the essence of this season is not only about celebrating abundance but also about fostering a deeper relationship with the gods, your ancestors, and the natural world around you.

## Autumn Harvest: Gratitude and Reflection

As autumn descends upon the earth, it brings with it not just a change in scenery, but an opportunity for deep reflection and gratitude. The season's palette, filled with vibrant reds, oranges, and yellows, serves as a reminder of the cyclical nature of life and the importance of acknowledging the fruits of our labor. In Norse tradition, this period aligns with the harvest, a time when communities would come together to celebrate the bounty bestowed upon them by the gods. It is crucial to take a moment during this season to express gratitude to Odin, the Allfather, who presides over the harvest and the wisdom it brings.

Embracing the spirit of autumn involves creating rituals that honor the abundance of the earth and the lessons learned throughout the year. Setting aside time for prayer and reflection can deepen one's connection to the divine. A simple yet meaningful ritual might include gathering offerings such as grains, fruits, or handmade crafts that symbolize the season's yield. These offerings can be placed on a sacred altar, accompanied by prayers that express gratitude for the blessings received and acknowledgment of the challenges faced. Such acts not only honor Odin but also reinforce the bond between the practitioner and the natural world.

The act of reflection during the autumn harvest provides an opportunity to evaluate personal growth and intentions. As the leaves fall, so too can we let go of what no longer serves us. This is a time to meditate on the past months, recognizing achievements and struggles alike. By invoking Odin during this process, one can seek guidance and wisdom. Prayers for clarity can be articulated, asking for insight into the lessons learned and the strength to embrace new beginnings as winter approaches. This practice aligns with the Norse belief in the cyclical nature of existence, where endings lead to new possibilities.

Additionally, the transition into autumn invites a focus on ancestral connections and the wisdom they impart. The Norse held their ancestors in high regard, believing that the spirits of those who came before us could offer guidance and protection. Creating a sacred space for prayer that includes photographs, heirlooms, or other memorabilia can enhance this connection. As you offer prayers of gratitude for the guidance and support received from ancestors, invoke their spirits to be present in your rituals. This can deepen one's sense of belonging and reinforce the idea that we are part of a larger tapestry woven through time.

In conclusion, the autumn harvest season serves as a pivotal time for gratitude and reflection within Norse spiritual practices. By engaging in rituals that honor the earth's bounty and the wisdom of the Allfather, practitioners can cultivate a profound sense of connection with both the divine and their ancestral lineage. As you enter this season, consider the ways you can express gratitude and reflect on your journey, allowing the essence of autumn to enrich your spiritual life and prepare you for the transformative months ahead.

# Chapter 5: Invoking Odin: Techniques and Offerings

## Understanding Odin's Role in Norse Mythology

Odin, often referred to as the Allfather, occupies a central position in Norse mythology, embodying a complex interplay of wisdom, war, and death. His multifaceted nature is reflected in his many names, such as Woden and Hangatyr, each representing different aspects of his character and dominion. As the chief of the Aesir gods, he is associated with knowledge, poetry, and the runes, which further emphasizes his role as a seeker of truth. Understanding Odin's role is crucial for those wishing to invoke him in prayer and offerings, as it allows for a deeper connection to the rich tapestry of Norse spiritual practices.

Odin's pursuit of wisdom is legendary, often leading him to make great sacrifices. The most notable of these is his sacrifice of an eye at Mimir's Well, which granted him unparalleled knowledge. This act illustrates the importance of sacrifice in Norse spirituality, a theme that resonates through various rituals and prayers. When invoking Odin, it is essential to recognize that he values the earnestness of the seeker. Those who approach him should be prepared to dedicate their time and effort to understanding the deeper meanings of their desires and the wisdom they seek.

In addition to wisdom, Odin's association with war and death plays a significant role in his mythology. He is depicted as a god who selects the slain to join him in Valhalla, a majestic hall where warriors prepare for Ragnarok, the end of the world. This aspect of Odin emphasizes the importance of valor and honor in life and death. For practitioners, invoking Odin can serve as a powerful reminder of the virtues of courage and the acceptance of fate. Prayers offered for protection or guidance in times of conflict can be directed towards him, seeking his support in navigating life's challenges.

Seasonal celebrations in Norse culture, such as Yule and Midsummer, often include rituals dedicated to Odin. These festivities provide an opportunity to reflect on his role as a deity who oversees the cycles of life and death. During these times, practitioners can engage in specific prayers and offerings that resonate with Odin's attributes. By aligning one's spiritual practice with the natural rhythms of the seasons, followers can create a more profound connection with Odin, inviting his presence and influence into their lives during these significant times.

Understanding Odin's role in Norse mythology also involves recognizing the importance of community and ancestry in prayer practices. Odin is often seen as a bridge between the living and the dead, guiding souls to their rightful place in the afterlife. By honoring one's ancestors and integrating their wisdom into daily prayer rituals, practitioners can invoke Odin's guidance in fostering a sense of belonging and continuity. Creating sacred spaces and incorporating Norse symbols can enrich these practices, allowing individuals to deepen their relationship with Odin and the broader pantheon of Norse deities.

## Techniques for Invoking Odin

To effectively invoke Odin, understanding the foundational techniques and rituals is essential. One of the primary methods involves creating a sacred space. This space should be quiet and free from distractions, allowing for focused contemplation and connection with the Allfather. You can enhance this environment by incorporating symbols associated with Odin, such as the raven, the spear, or the Valknut. Lighting candles or incense can also help create an atmosphere conducive to prayer, inviting divine presence and attention.

Another significant technique is the use of offerings. Odin, known for his wisdom and sacrifice, appreciates gestures that reflect gratitude and reverence. Offerings can include mead, bread, or even simple tokens like feathers or stones that hold personal significance. When presenting these offerings, it is vital to express your intentions clearly, stating what you seek from Odin, whether it be guidance, knowledge, or protection. This act of giving creates a reciprocal relationship, inviting the deity's influence into your life.

In addition to creating a sacred space and making offerings, vocal invocations and prayers play a crucial role in connecting with Odin. You may choose to recite traditional prayers found in historical texts or compose your own, articulating your thoughts and feelings. The power of spoken word can be amplified by using runes or other Norse symbols during the invocation. Chanting can also be an effective technique, as it helps to elevate your energy and focus your intentions, thereby making your call to Odin more potent.

Seasonal celebrations can also serve as significant moments for invoking Odin. The cyclical nature of the seasons aligns with Norse mythology, providing a natural rhythm for prayer and reflection. For instance, during Yule, a time of rebirth and renewal, you might focus on themes of wisdom and transformation. Incorporating specific seasonal rituals, such as lighting a Yule log or sharing stories of Odin's journeys, can deepen your connection and enhance the experience of invocation.

Finally, integrating personal experiences and reflections into your practice can create a more profound connection with Odin. Keeping a journal to document your prayers, experiences, and any signs or messages you receive can help in understanding the dynamics of your relationship with the deity. This practice not only serves as a record but also fosters a deeper spiritual awareness, allowing you to recognize the influence of Odin in your everyday life. By embracing these techniques, you can cultivate a meaningful and enriching practice of invoking the Allfather.

## Offerings Suitable for Odin

Offerings suitable for Odin are steeped in tradition and reflect the multifaceted nature of the Allfather himself. As the god of wisdom, war, and death, Odin appreciates offerings that resonate with these aspects of his character. Common offerings include mead, which symbolizes the gift of inspiration and is often associated with poetry and knowledge. By presenting mead during rituals, devotees honor Odin's connection to the poetic arts and the pursuit of wisdom. Additionally, bread, particularly rye bread, can serve as an offering, representing nourishment and the sustenance of life that Odin provides to his followers.

Another significant offering to Odin is the sacrifice of a wooden item, particularly from an ash tree. The ash tree is sacred to Odin, as it is believed that the first man and woman were created from its branches. By carving a small token or creating a wooden representation of something significant to your prayers, you can give this to Odin as a gesture of respect and devotion. These wooden offerings not only symbolize a connection to the earth but also demonstrate a willingness to engage in the sacred relationship between the worshiper and the divine.

In times of seeking guidance or wisdom, a thoughtful offering might include a collection of personal thoughts or questions written on parchment. Presenting these to Odin during a ritual or prayer can be an effective way to invoke his insight and clarity. This practice reflects the Norse tradition of communicating directly with the gods, where the act of writing becomes an offering in itself. It is essential to approach this with sincerity, as the intention behind the offering is as critical as the offering itself.

Seasonal celebrations also provide a unique opportunity to honor Odin through offerings that align with the changing cycles of nature. During the winter solstice, for instance, offerings of food, drink, and crafted items can be laid at an outdoor altar or in a sacred space. This practice not only acknowledges Odin's role as a deity associated with the darker months but also reinforces the connection to family and community, echoing the values that Odin embodies. Rituals during these times may include storytelling and sharing wisdom, further enhancing the spiritual experience.

Lastly, incorporating symbols of Odin such as the raven, wolf, or the Valknut into your offerings can deepen the act of devotion. These symbols carry profound meanings and represent aspects of Odin's power and presence. By including them in your rituals—whether through crafted items, drawn symbols, or simply acknowledging their significance during prayer—you create a more profound connection to Odin. This holistic approach to offerings not only honors the Allfather but also enriches your own spiritual journey, aligning your intentions with the ancient practices of Norse worship.

# Chapter 6: Prayers for Protection from Norse Mythology

## Invoking the Aesir for Safety

Invoking the Aesir for safety is a practice rooted deeply in Norse tradition, where the gods, particularly Odin, Thor, and Freyja, are seen as protectors against chaos and danger. This subchapter explores the significance of these deities in safeguarding our lives and how one can effectively call upon them through prayer and offerings. In times of uncertainty or peril, many practitioners find solace in connecting with the Aesir, believing that these divine forces can provide not only physical protection but also emotional and spiritual security.

To begin invoking the Aesir, it is essential to establish a sacred space that honors their presence. This can be achieved by creating an altar adorned with symbols associated with the gods, such as Thor's hammer for protection or Freyja's necklace for love and fertility. Including offerings like bread, mead, or flowers can enhance the connection, demonstrating respect and gratitude towards these powerful entities. Lighting candles or incense can further elevate the energy of the space, creating an inviting atmosphere for divine communication.

Prayer is a personal yet structured way to invoke the Aesir for safety. A simple yet profound approach is to recite a prayer that calls upon Odin, the Allfather, asking for wisdom and guidance in navigating life's challenges. A prayer may focus on specific fears or threats, articulating your needs clearly while invoking the strength and support of the gods. Additionally, incorporating elements of traditional Norse poetry or alliteration can deepen the resonance of the prayer, making it more impactful and memorable.

Seasonal celebrations also play a vital role in invoking the Aesir. These festivals, such as Yule or Midsummer, are ideal times to engage in communal or solitary rituals aimed at safety and protection. During these times, the energy of the Aesir is believed to be particularly potent, allowing for a more profound connection. Participating in traditional practices, such as feasting, storytelling, and making offerings, can create a sense of unity with the divine and with the community, reinforcing the safety net provided by the gods.

Lastly, integrating divination practices, such as runes or tarot, can complement the invocation of the Aesir for safety. These tools can offer insight and clarity regarding personal safety concerns or decisions that require divine guidance. After invoking the Aesir through prayer, drawing runes can reveal messages or warnings from the gods, helping practitioners navigate their paths with care and wisdom. By combining these prayer practices with seasonal celebrations and divination, individuals can cultivate a robust spiritual framework that invokes the protective powers of the Aesir in their daily lives.

## Protective Symbols and Their Meanings

Protective symbols play a significant role in Norse spirituality, offering both physical and metaphysical safeguards to practitioners. These symbols, often derived from ancient runes and mythological motifs, encapsulate the essence of Norse beliefs and serve as powerful tools for invoking protection from malevolent forces. Among the most recognized symbols is the Ægishjalmur, or Helm of Awe, which is believed to instill fear in one's enemies while granting the wearer invincibility. This symbol can be drawn or carved onto personal items, altars, or even the skin to create a shield of spiritual protection during rituals or daily life.

Another vital protective symbol is the Valknut, associated with the god Odin himself. Comprising three interlocked triangles, the Valknut represents the transition between life and death, and is often linked to the idea of protection for warriors and those journeying into the unknown. Wearing this symbol or placing it in sacred spaces can help to honor Odin's guidance, fostering a connection to the Allfather while offering reassurance during times of uncertainty. Incorporating the Valknut into prayer rituals can amplify intentions for safety and courage, making it a powerful addition to any protective practice.

The Mjölnir, or Thor's Hammer, is perhaps one of the most iconic symbols in Norse mythology. It signifies strength and protection, particularly against chaos and evil. Traditionally, Mjölnir amulets were worn by both men and women, serving as a physical reminder of Thor's safeguarding presence. In prayer rituals, invoking Thor alongside this symbol can enhance the protective qualities of one's offerings. Many practitioners create altars adorned with Mjölnir to channel its might, especially during times of vulnerability or when facing challenges that require fortitude.

The use of these symbols is not merely decorative; they embody deep spiritual meanings and serve as focal points during prayer. When practitioners incorporate protective symbols into their daily routines or seasonal celebrations, they reinforce their intentions for safety and connection with the divine. For example, during Midwinter celebrations, invoking the Helm of Awe alongside offerings to Odin can create a powerful atmosphere of protection against the darkness of winter. This merging of symbolism and ritual enhances the spiritual experience, allowing for a more profound connection to the Norse deities.

In modern practice, these protective symbols can also be adapted to fit contemporary spiritual frameworks. Combining traditional Norse symbols with modern interpretations allows practitioners to create personalized rituals that resonate with their individual beliefs. Whether through meditation, visualization, or physical representation, the protective symbols of Norse mythology serve as vital tools for fostering security and resilience. By understanding and utilizing these symbols, practitioners can enhance their spiritual journeys and deepen their connection to the rich tapestry of Norse tradition.

# Rituals for Personal and Home Protection

Rituals for personal and home protection hold a significant place in Norse spiritual practices, offering a means to invoke the divine for safety and security. These rituals often draw upon the powerful energies of the gods, particularly Odin, who embodies wisdom and protection. Engaging in these practices can create a sacred space that nurtures both physical and spiritual well-being. To start, it is essential to prepare the environment, ensuring that it is clean and free from distractions. This preparation serves as a symbolic act of inviting the divine presence into one's home.

One effective ritual for personal protection involves the creation of a protective charm or talisman. This can be a simple object, such as a piece of wood or stone, that resonates with the individual's energy. Before crafting the charm, practitioners should meditate on their intentions, focusing on the specific type of protection they seek—be it emotional, physical, or spiritual. Once the charm is created, it can be anointed with oil or inscribed with symbols that represent protection, such as the Valknut or a bind rune. The charm should then be charged with energy through prayer, calling upon Odin or other deities, asking for their guidance and safeguarding.

In addition to personal charms, rituals for home protection can include the use of salt, a substance revered in many cultures for its purifying properties. Sprinkling salt at the thresholds of doors and windows is a traditional practice believed to create a barrier against negative energies. This act can be accompanied by a specific incantation or prayer, invoking Odin's protective qualities. As the salt is placed, practitioners should visualize a shield forming around their home, repelling any harmful influences and inviting only positive energy into their space.

Seasonal celebrations also provide a unique opportunity to reinforce protection rituals. Events like Yule, which marks the return of the light after the darkest days of winter, can be particularly potent for invoking blessings of safety. During such gatherings, participants can light candles or a bonfire, symbolizing the light overcoming darkness. This communal energy enhances the protective intentions and can include collective prayers or offerings to Odin, asking for guidance and strength for the coming year.

Finally, integrating ancestral remembrance into protection rituals can deepen the connection to one's heritage and spiritual lineage. Ancestors often serve as protectors, guiding their descendants in times of need. Setting up a small altar dedicated to ancestors, with photographs or personal items, allows for a space to honor their memory. During protection rituals, invoking the names of ancestors alongside Odin can create a powerful synergy, calling upon both divine and ancestral support. This holistic approach not only fosters a sense of safety but also reinforces the importance of community, lineage, and the sacred connections that bind us all.

# Chapter 7: Divination and Prayer Practices in Norse Traditions

## Understanding Divination in Norse Culture

Divination in Norse culture encompasses various practices aimed at seeking guidance, understanding the will of the gods, and predicting future events. Rooted in a rich tradition, it reflects the Norse belief in fate and the interconnectedness of all beings. Central to this practice is the concept of wyrd, which signifies the web of fate woven by the Norns, the three female figures who control destiny. Norse divination often involves rituals that invoke the gods and seek their insight, emphasizing the importance of establishing a connection with the divine.

One of the most recognized forms of divination in Norse traditions is the use of runes. The runic alphabet, consisting of symbols imbued with magical significance, was not only a means of communication but also a tool for divination. Practitioners would cast runes, seeking answers to specific questions by interpreting the symbols that fell face up. Each rune carries its unique meaning, and understanding these meanings is crucial for effective divination. This practice, known as rune casting, allows individuals to tap into the wisdom of the gods, drawing on their guidance in personal matters and broader life challenges.

Another method of divination is the use of seidr, a form of magic associated with the goddess Freyja and practiced by shamans known as völvas. Seidr involves entering altered states of consciousness to gain insight and communicate with the spiritual realm. This practice often includes chanting, drumming, and other ritualistic elements that help practitioners connect with the divine. Through seidr, individuals can seek answers about their personal lives, community affairs, or even the fate of their people, reinforcing the idea that divination serves both personal and collective purposes in Norse society.

The role of the gods and ancestors in Norse divination cannot be overstated. Invoking Odin, the Allfather, is particularly significant, as he is the god of wisdom, knowledge, and prophecy. Practitioners often offer prayers and sacrifices to Odin before engaging in divinatory practices, seeking his favor and insight. Similarly, honoring ancestors during divination rituals serves to strengthen the connection between the living and the dead, emphasizing the belief that those who came before us continue to influence our lives. This ancestral connection reinforces the idea that divination is not merely a personal endeavor but a communal one, linking individuals to their heritage.

Understanding divination in Norse culture thus requires an appreciation for its multifaceted nature and the spiritual framework within which it operates. Whether through rune casting, seidr, or invoking the gods, these practices reflect a deep-seated belief in the interconnectedness of fate, divinity, and humanity. As individuals engage in these rituals, they not only seek guidance for themselves but also participate in a broader spiritual dialogue that has persisted through centuries. In this way, divination serves as a vital component of Norse spirituality, enriching the practices of prayer and offering in the quest for understanding and connection with the divine.

# Techniques for Rune Casting

Rune casting is an ancient practice deeply rooted in Norse tradition, utilized as a means of divination and communication with the divine. To effectively engage in rune casting, practitioners often begin by creating a sacred space that invites the energies of the gods and ancestors. This space can be as simple as a designated area in the home or as elaborate as an outdoor altar adorned with natural elements. The intention behind this practice is to foster an environment that is conducive to spiritual connection, allowing for focused meditation and the invocation of Odin's wisdom.

Preparation is key in rune casting, and it typically involves cleansing the runes and the casting area. This can be achieved through various methods, such as smudging with sage or passing the runes through the smoke of incense. Following this, practitioners should take a moment to ground themselves, perhaps through breathing exercises or visualization techniques. Grounding helps to center the mind and spirit, making it easier to receive guidance from the runes. It is also beneficial to set a clear intention for the reading, whether seeking insight into a specific question or guidance on a broader life path.

When it comes to the actual casting of runes, there are several techniques that can be employed. One common method is the "three rune spread," where three runes are drawn to represent the past, present, and future. This technique allows for a comprehensive view of the situation at hand, offering insights from different temporal perspectives. Another technique is the "single rune draw," which can serve as a daily affirmation or guidance point. This method is particularly useful for those looking to incorporate rune casting into their daily prayer rituals, providing a quick yet meaningful connection to the divine.

Interpreting the runes is a significant aspect of the casting process. Each rune carries its own symbolism and meaning, often deeply connected to Norse mythology and the qualities of the gods. Practitioners should familiarize themselves with these meanings, as well as the context of their question or intention. It is also recommended to keep a rune journal, where one can document the castings, interpretations, and any insights received during the process. This practice not only aids in deepening understanding but also helps to track personal growth and the evolution of one's spiritual journey.

Finally, closing the casting session is an essential step that is often overlooked. After interpreting the runes, practitioners should take time to express gratitude to Odin and any other deities involved in the process. This can be done through a simple prayer or offering, acknowledging the guidance received. Completing the session with a grounding ritual, such as eating a small meal or spending time in nature, helps to integrate the insights into daily life. By following these techniques for rune casting, practitioners can enhance their spiritual practices, fostering a deeper connection with the Norse gods and the wisdom they offer.

## Incorporating Prayer into Divination Practices

Incorporating prayer into divination practices can enrich the experience for those seeking deeper insights and guidance from the Norse gods. The act of divination itself is a sacred ritual, often used to gain clarity on questions or situations in life, and when combined with prayer, it creates a powerful conduit for communication with the divine. Prayers can serve not only as a means of invocation but also as a way to establish intention, inviting the gods into the divinatory process and fostering a sense of connection with the spiritual realm.

Before engaging in any divination practice, it is essential to prepare both the physical space and the mental state. Creating a sacred environment can involve cleansing the area, lighting candles, or setting up a small altar with symbols of the Norse deities. As part of this preparation, practitioners may choose to recite a prayer dedicated to Odin or other relevant deities, asking for guidance, protection, and wisdom. This initial prayer sets the tone for the session and aligns the practitioner's energy with the divine, inviting the gods to lend their insight to the unfolding process.

During the divination itself, prayers can be woven into the practice at various stages. For example, before casting runes or drawing tarot cards, one might offer a prayer expressing gratitude for the opportunity to seek knowledge and clarity. This can include specific requests for insight into a particular issue or a general plea for understanding. By doing so, practitioners not only honor the gods but also remain open to receiving messages that may come through during the divination. This approach helps to create a dialogue between the practitioner and the divine, allowing for a more interactive and meaningful experience.

After completing the divination session, it is equally important to conclude with prayer. A closing prayer can serve multiple purposes: thanking the deities for their guidance, reflecting on the messages received, and asking for continued support in integrating the insights gained into daily life. This practice of gratitude reinforces the connection established during the session and acknowledges the role of the divine in personal growth. It can also be a moment to offer blessings upon oneself and loved ones, further extending the reach of the divine influence.

Incorporating prayer into divination is not just about seeking answers; it is about building a relationship with the Norse gods and understanding their presence in one's life. By fostering this connection through intentional prayer, practitioners can enhance their divinatory practices, making them more profound and spiritually enriching. As individuals navigate their journeys, these sacred interactions can provide them with the wisdom and support needed to move forward with confidence and clarity, guided by the ancient traditions of the Norse pantheon.

# Chapter 8: Communicating with Freyja: Love and Fertility Prayers

## The Significance of Freyja in Norse Mythology

Freyja holds a prominent place in Norse mythology, symbolizing love, fertility, and war. As one of the most revered deities in the pantheon, her significance extends beyond mere attributes; she embodies the complexities of life, including passion, beauty, and the harsh realities of conflict. Freyja is often depicted riding a chariot pulled by two cats, a reflection of her connection to both the domestic and the wild, showcasing her dual nature as a nurturing figure and a fierce warrior. This duality resonates deeply within the practices of those who invoke her, as they seek not only blessings of love and fertility but also strength and courage in facing life's adversities.

In prayer rituals and offerings to Freyja, practitioners often focus on themes of personal transformation and empowerment. By engaging with her, individuals can explore their own desires and motivations, channeling her energy to manifest love in their lives or to enhance their personal relationships. Freyja's association with fertility also extends to creative endeavors, encouraging worshippers to seek inspiration and passion in their artistic pursuits. Rituals may involve the use of flowers, honey, or sacred herbs, which are symbolic of her nurturing aspects, aiming to invoke her blessings for growth and abundance in various life aspects.

Freyja's significance is further underscored by her role in the afterlife, where she receives half of those who die in battle in her hall, Folkvangr. This aspect of her character connects her to themes of valor and honor, making her an essential figure for warriors and those seeking protection. Invoking Freyja in prayers for protection can be particularly powerful, as she is believed to watch over her devotees, ensuring their safety in both physical and emotional realms. Incorporating her name into protective rituals can provide a sense of security, as followers align themselves with her formidable spirit.

Seasonal celebrations in Norse tradition often honor Freyja, particularly during the time of spring and fertility festivals. These occasions provide a vibrant backdrop for individuals to express gratitude for her gifts while seeking her guidance in new beginnings. Rituals may include communal gatherings, feasting, and storytelling, creating a shared space for reflection and celebration of life's cycles. As practitioners engage in these seasonal practices, they deepen their connection to Freyja, reinforcing the importance of community in spiritual endeavors.

Ultimately, Freyja's significance in Norse mythology extends far beyond her immediate attributes. She represents the interconnectedness of love, war, and personal empowerment, making her a multifaceted figure in the spiritual lives of her devotees. By establishing a relationship with Freyja through prayer, offerings, and ritual, individuals can tap into her wisdom and strength, fostering a deeper understanding of their own journeys. In this way, invoking Freyja becomes not just an act of devotion but a pathway to self-discovery and transformation in the context of Norse spirituality.

## Prayers for Love and Relationships

In the realm of Norse spirituality, love and relationships are often intertwined with the divine energies of the gods and goddesses. Among these deities, Freyja stands out as the goddess of love, beauty, and fertility. Invoking her through prayer can help individuals cultivate deeper connections, enhance romantic bonds, and foster harmonious relationships. Freyja's influence is believed to attract love and strengthen existing partnerships, making her a central figure in rituals aimed at nurturing personal connections. By honoring her through specific prayers and offerings, devotees can create an atmosphere conducive to love and emotional fulfillment.

To begin the practice of praying for love and relationships, one might set up a small altar dedicated to Freyja. This sacred space can be adorned with symbols associated with her, such as roses, amber, or images of cats, which are sacred to her. Lighting candles and placing offerings like honey or mead can enhance the connection to her energy. As part of the ritual, practitioners can recite prayers that express their desires for love, whether seeking a new partner or deepening an existing bond. These prayers should be heartfelt, reflecting genuine intentions and desires, allowing the energy of the words to resonate with the divine.

In invoking Freyja, it is important to incorporate seasonal celebrations that align with her essence. The festival of Blótmál, which honors the gods and celebrates the harvest, provides an excellent opportunity to focus on love and relationships. During this time, prayers can be offered that express gratitude for current relationships and ask for blessings in love. Combining the themes of gratitude and intention aligns one's personal desires with the rhythms of nature, creating a powerful synergy that can amplify the effectiveness of the prayers.

Additionally, communication plays a crucial role in nurturing relationships. Incorporating prayers for open and honest communication can help bridge gaps between partners. These prayers can be spoken during quiet moments of reflection or included in daily rituals, emphasizing the need for understanding and empathy. By asking for guidance from Freyja, individuals can receive the strength to express their feelings and the wisdom to listen deeply to their partners, fostering a nurturing environment for love to flourish.

Finally, connecting with ancestors can further enhance the practice of seeking love and nurturing relationships. Ancestors often hold wisdom and insights that can guide current generations in their pursuits. By honoring them in conjunction with prayers to Freyja, individuals can create a lineage of love that transcends time. This practice not only strengthens the bond with one's ancestry but also invites the collective energy of love to support present relationships. In this way, the prayers become a conduit for both divine and ancestral energy, enriching the journey of love and connection.

# Rituals for Fertility and Abundance

Rituals for fertility and abundance hold a significant place in Norse traditions, often intertwined with the reverence for deities such as Freyja and Odin. These practices are designed to invoke the blessings of these gods, fostering a connection to the earth's cycles and the divine forces that govern prosperity. Engaging in these rituals can create a profound sense of community and personal empowerment, allowing practitioners to align their intentions with the natural world and its rhythms.

A common practice involves creating a sacred space dedicated to the deities associated with fertility. This space can be adorned with symbols such as the Yggdrasill tree or offerings of fruits, grains, and flowers, which are believed to attract the positive energies of abundance. Lighting candles and incense can help purify the area, inviting the presence of the gods. As part of the ritual, practitioners may recite prayers or invocations, expressing their desires for fertility and prosperity, while also acknowledging the interconnectedness of life and the importance of gratitude for what they already possess.

Seasonal celebrations, particularly those tied to the harvest, offer additional opportunities to engage in rituals for fertility and abundance. The festival of Freyfaxi, for instance, honors Freyja and her association with fertility. During this time, offerings of the first fruits of the harvest are made, accompanied by prayers that ask for continued blessings on the land and its people. These rituals serve not only to honor the gods but also to strengthen community bonds through shared intentions and collective gratitude.

Incorporating divination practices into fertility rituals can also enhance their effectiveness. Runes or tarot cards can be utilized to gain insight into one's path toward abundance. Practitioners may cast runes while focusing on their intentions for fertility, seeking guidance on how to align their actions with the blessings they wish to invoke. This process not only deepens the spiritual practice but also encourages reflection on personal desires and the steps necessary to achieve them.

Finally, the role of ancestors in these rituals should not be overlooked. Invoking ancestral spirits can provide additional strength and wisdom, as they are believed to guide and protect their descendants. Creating an ancestor altar and including offerings of food, drink, or personal items can create a powerful connection to the past. During the rituals, practitioners might share stories of their ancestors, acknowledging their contributions and seeking their blessings in the journey toward fertility and abundance. Through these combined practices, individuals can cultivate a rich spiritual life that honors both the ancient traditions and their personal aspirations.

# Chapter 9: The Role of Ancestors in Norse Prayer Practices

## Honoring Ancestors: A Norse Tradition

Honoring ancestors is a significant aspect of Norse tradition, deeply woven into the fabric of spirituality and daily life. In Norse culture, the ancestors are not merely remnants of the past; they represent a living connection to the divine and the continuity of wisdom. This reverence for the ancestors is reflected in various rituals and practices aimed at acknowledging their influences and seeking their guidance. Through these acts of remembrance, individuals forge a link that transcends time, reinforcing the belief that the past shapes the present and future.

The practice of honoring ancestors typically involves creating a sacred space in the home or outdoors, where offerings can be made. This space might include items that represent the ancestors, such as photographs, heirlooms, or symbols of their lives. In these areas, practitioners may place offerings like food, drink, or small tokens crafted from natural materials. Such offerings serve not only as gifts but also as expressions of gratitude and respect. By inviting the presence of the ancestors into this sacred space, individuals create an atmosphere conducive to reflection, communication, and spiritual connection.

Ritual practices vary throughout the seasons, echoing the cycles of nature and the rhythms of life. During significant times of the year, such as the autumn equinox or the winter solstice, special ceremonies are held to honor those who have passed. These gatherings often include storytelling, where the lives and deeds of ancestors are recounted, reinforcing their legacies and imparting lessons to the living. The act of remembering in this communal context strengthens familial bonds and fosters a collective identity rooted in shared history and values.

In invoking the ancestors, practitioners may also incorporate specific prayers and invocations tailored to individual needs or circumstances. These prayers can serve various purposes, from seeking guidance in personal matters to requesting protection during challenging times. When invoking the ancestors, it is essential to approach them with sincerity, humility, and respect, recognizing their wisdom and the unique insights they can provide. Such practices not only enhance the spiritual experience but also foster a deeper understanding of one's heritage and identity.

Ultimately, honoring ancestors is more than a mere ritual; it is a profound expression of gratitude and respect. In the Norse tradition, this practice embodies the belief that the ancestors remain influential in the lives of their descendants. By engaging in these rituals, individuals connect with a broader spiritual lineage, enriching their own lives while ensuring that the legacies of those who came before them continue to resonate through time. This connection serves as a powerful reminder of the importance of family, memory, and the enduring nature of the human spirit.

# Ancestor Worship and Communication

Ancestor worship holds a significant place in Norse spirituality, serving as a bridge between the living and the departed. In Norse tradition, ancestors are revered not merely as relics of the past but as active participants in the lives of their descendants. This relationship emphasizes the importance of remembrance and respect, which can manifest through various rituals and offerings. Incorporating ancestor worship into daily practices not only enriches one's spiritual life but also strengthens familial bonds and honors the legacy of those who came before.

To communicate effectively with ancestors, one must create a sacred space that invites their presence. This can be achieved by establishing an altar adorned with personal items, photographs, or symbols that represent your lineage. Lighting candles and offering food or mead can serve as gestures of respect and invitation for your ancestors to join you in your practices. It is essential to approach this interaction with a mindset of humility and reverence, recognizing that ancestors often offer guidance, wisdom, and protection to their living kin.

Daily rituals can be simple yet profound. A morning or evening prayer can include a moment of silence to honor the ancestors, followed by spoken words that express gratitude for their sacrifices and teachings. Additionally, invoking specific ancestors whose traits or experiences resonate with your current life situations can provide focused support. These rituals can vary, from a brief acknowledgment to elaborate ceremonies that incorporate offerings and storytelling, which serve to keep the memory of ancestors alive within the family narrative.

Seasonal celebrations also present meaningful opportunities to connect with ancestors. Events such as the autumnal harvest or winter solstice often included honoring those who had passed, reflecting the cyclical nature of life and death in Norse belief. These gatherings can be enhanced with traditional foods, songs, and shared memories, creating a communal atmosphere that unites the living with the spirit of the ancestors. Engaging in these practices reinforces a sense of continuity and belonging, reminding participants of their place within a larger lineage.

Incorporating ancestor worship into the broader context of Norse spiritual practices fosters a richer experience when invoking the gods. Whether through prayer, offerings, or seasonal celebrations, the connection to ancestors adds depth to the relationship with deities like Odin and Freyja. By acknowledging and communicating with those who have come before, practitioners not only honor their heritage but also invite the wisdom and protection that comes from a well-tended ancestral bond, ultimately enriching their spiritual journey and enhancing their daily lives.

# Rituals for Connecting with Ancestral Spirits

Rituals for connecting with ancestral spirits are a vital aspect of Norse spirituality, acknowledging the profound influence that ancestors have on the living. These rituals serve as a bridge between the past and the present, allowing individuals to honor their lineage, seek guidance, and cultivate a deeper understanding of their roots. In the Norse tradition, ancestors are revered as wise beings who can offer insights and support. Engaging with them through specific rituals not only strengthens familial bonds but also enriches one's spiritual practice.

One effective ritual for connecting with ancestral spirits involves creating a dedicated space for remembrance and communication. This sacred area can be adorned with photographs, heirlooms, or items that belonged to ancestors, alongside symbols significant in Norse mythology, such as runes or the Yggdrasil tree. Lighting candles and burning incense can enhance the atmosphere, promoting a sense of reverence. It is essential to enter this space with a clear intention, focusing on the specific ancestors you wish to connect with, inviting their presence and wisdom into your ritual.

Another powerful practice is the offering of food and drink, which is rooted in the belief that ancestors appreciate tangible gifts. Preparing a meal that was traditionally enjoyed by your ancestors or presenting a favorite beverage can serve as a heartfelt gesture of gratitude. Place these offerings on an altar or dedicated space, and take a moment to speak aloud your intentions or prayers, expressing your desire for connection and guidance. This act of sharing sustains the relationship between the living and the dead, honoring the contributions of those who came before.

Divination is also a compelling practice to engage with ancestral spirits. Techniques such as rune casting or using tarot cards can be employed to seek messages from the past. Before the divination session, take time to meditate and invite your ancestors into the process. As you draw the runes or cards, remain open to the insights that arise, recognizing that your ancestors may communicate through symbols or intuitive feelings. Recording these messages in a journal can help in tracking patterns and understanding the ancestral guidance received over time.

Seasonal celebrations provide another opportunity to connect with ancestral spirits, particularly during festivals such as Samhain or Midwinter. Incorporating specific rituals that honor ancestors during these times can deepen the spiritual experience. This may include storytelling, where you recount family histories or anecdotes about ancestors, reinforcing their presence in your life. By integrating these rituals into your spiritual practice, you not only honor your ancestors but also weave their wisdom into the fabric of your daily existence, enriching both your life and your connection to the Norse spiritual tradition.

# Chapter 10: Creating Sacred Spaces for Norse Worship

## Designing an Altar for Norse Deities

Designing an altar for Norse deities is an essential practice for those seeking to deepen their connection with the gods and goddesses of the Norse pantheon. An altar serves as a focal point for prayer, offerings, and meditation, creating a sacred space that invites the presence of the divine. To begin, consider the materials and elements that resonate with the Norse tradition. Natural materials such as wood, stone, and metal reflect the earth's elements and the craftsmanship valued by the ancient Norse. These materials can be used to create a sturdy base for the altar, which should ideally be elevated and distinct from other spaces within the home.

When arranging the altar, select symbols and items that represent the deities you wish to honor. For Odin, you might include a representation of his ravens, Huginn and Muninn, along with a spear or a representation of the runes. Freyja's altar could feature items associated with love and fertility, such as flowers, crystals, or a small figurine. Seasonal elements can also be incorporated, reflecting the changing tides of nature and the cycles of life that are central to Norse beliefs. Incorporating these symbols not only enhances the aesthetic of the altar but also serves as a reminder of the attributes and stories associated with each deity.

In addition to physical representations, the altar should be adorned with offerings that are meaningful and respectful. These can range from simple offerings like bread, mead, or herbs to more elaborate gifts reflective of the changing seasons or personal intentions. Seasonal celebrations, like Yule or Midsummer, provide excellent opportunities to refresh the offerings and incorporate more elaborate rituals. Each offering should be made with intention and gratitude, as these acts of devotion foster a deeper bond with the deities.

Lighting is another crucial aspect of altar design. Candles, representing light and warmth, not only enhance the atmosphere but also symbolize the connection between the physical and spiritual realms. Different colors can be used to align with specific intentions; for example, blue for wisdom when invoking Odin or green for growth when honoring Freyja. Incorporating incense or essential oils can also elevate the experience, as the aromas create an inviting ambiance and signify the purification of the space.

Finally, it is essential to maintain the altar regularly, ensuring it remains clean and the offerings are refreshed. This practice not only shows respect to the deities but also reinforces the commitment to the spiritual path. Regularly engaging with the altar through prayer, meditation, or ritual solidifies it as a sacred space in your life. By thoughtfully designing and maintaining an altar for Norse deities, practitioners can create a powerful conduit for communication, devotion, and spiritual growth, connecting deeply with the rich heritage of Norse mythology.

## Elements of a Sacred Space

A sacred space is an essential component for engaging with the divine, particularly in Norse spirituality. These spaces serve as a physical and metaphysical bridge between the practitioner and the gods, providing an environment conducive to prayer, meditation, and ritual. To create a sacred space for invoking Odin or other Norse deities, one must consider several key elements that foster a sense of connection and reverence. Each element plays a vital role in establishing an atmosphere that honors the traditions and intentions of the practices involved.

The first element is location. Choosing a space that resonates with personal significance enhances the connection to the divine. This could be an outdoor area surrounded by nature, reflecting the beauty of the Nine Realms, or a corner of a room dedicated to spiritual activities. The location should be free from distractions and infused with tranquility, allowing for deep focus during rituals and prayers. Incorporating natural elements such as stones, plants, or water can further enrich the ambiance, reminding practitioners of the earth's sacredness and the divine presence within it.

Another critical aspect is the use of altars. An altar serves as a focal point for offerings, prayers, and symbols that represent the divine. It can be as simple or elaborate as desired, adorned with items that hold personal significance or traditional Norse symbols. Incorporating images or statues of Odin, Freyja, and other deities, as well as objects like runestones, candles, or incense, creates a tangible connection to the divine. This space should be regularly maintained and refreshed, reflecting the ongoing relationship between the practitioner and the gods.

Ritual tools are also vital in creating a sacred space. Items such as ceremonial knives, drinking horns, and offerings of food or drink not only enhance the aesthetic of the altar but also serve practical purposes during rituals. Each tool should be treated with respect and intention, often consecrated through prayers or rituals to invoke their sacredness. The presence of these tools can help in signaling the transition from the mundane to the sacred, marking the space as one reserved for divine interaction.

Lastly, intention is perhaps the most powerful element in establishing a sacred space. The practitioner's mindset and purpose for engaging in prayer or ritual significantly influence the energy of the space. Setting clear intentions before beginning any practice helps to align the practitioner's focus with the goals of their worship. Whether seeking guidance, protection, or connection with ancestors, articulating these intentions creates a powerful resonance that invites the divine into the sacred space. By cultivating these elements—location, altar, ritual tools, and intention—practitioners can create a nurturing environment that honors the Norse gods and enhances their spiritual practices.

# Maintaining and Cleansing Your Sacred Space

Maintaining and cleansing your sacred space is essential for anyone invoking the Norse gods, particularly Odin. A sacred space is not merely a physical area; it is an energetic sanctuary where you can connect with the divine. This space should reflect your personal relationship with the Norse deities, serving as a focal point for your prayers, offerings, and rituals. Regular maintenance and cleansing of this space ensure that it remains a vibrant environment conducive to spiritual practice.

To begin with, it is vital to regularly declutter your sacred space. Clutter can create stagnant energy, making it difficult to connect with the divine. Dedicate time to remove any unnecessary items that do not serve your spiritual practice. This may include old offerings, debris, or items that no longer resonate with your intentions. Instead, consider incorporating symbols and artifacts that hold spiritual significance, such as runes, images of the gods, or natural elements that evoke the spirit of the Nordic landscape.

Cleansing your sacred space can be achieved through various techniques, each with its own merits. One powerful method is the use of smoke from herbs, such as sage or juniper, which can purify the energy of the space. As you waft the smoke around the area, visualize it clearing away any negativity or stagnant energy, creating an open and inviting environment for your prayers. Additionally, sound cleansing—using bells, singing bowls, or even your voice—can be effective in shifting the energy and enhancing the vibrational frequency of your sacred area.

Another important aspect is the seasonal cleansing and re-dedication of your space. The Norse calendar is rich with seasonal celebrations that align with the cycles of nature, such as the solstices and equinoxes. Use these occasions as opportunities to refresh your sacred space, reflecting the changing energies of the seasons. For example, during the winter solstice, you might incorporate evergreen branches to symbolize rebirth, while in spring, fresh flowers could represent renewal. This practice not only honors the cyclical nature of the world but also deepens your connection with the divine through the changing energies of the year.

Finally, the energy you bring into your sacred space plays a crucial role in its maintenance. Approach your rituals with intention, mindfulness, and respect for the deities you are invoking. Regularly spend time in this space, expressing gratitude, and making offerings that are meaningful to you. This not only strengthens your bond with the gods but also helps keep the energy alive and dynamic. By maintaining and cleansing your sacred space, you create an environment that is welcoming for divine communication, enriching your spiritual practice and enhancing your connection with Odin and the other Norse gods.

# Chapter 11: Norse Prayer Symbols and Their Meanings

## Common Symbols in Norse Spirituality

Symbols play a crucial role in Norse spirituality, acting as conduits for divine energy and as focal points for prayer and meditation. One of the most recognized symbols is the Valknut, which consists of three interlocked triangles. This symbol is often associated with Odin and represents the connection between life, death, and the afterlife. The Valknut serves as a reminder of the cyclical nature of existence and encourages practitioners to reflect on their own mortality and the legacy they leave behind. It is commonly used in rituals dedicated to honoring the dead and invoking Odin's guidance in matters of fate and destiny.

Another significant symbol is the Yggdrasil, the World Tree, which connects the nine realms of Norse cosmology. Yggdrasil represents the interconnectedness of all life and the importance of balance within the universe. When praying to the Norse gods, individuals may visualize Yggdrasil as a way to ground their intentions and seek harmony in their lives. This symbol is particularly effective during seasonal celebrations, where it can be integrated into rituals that honor the cycles of nature and the changing seasons. The presence of Yggdrasil in these practices reminds practitioners of their place within the larger tapestry of existence.

The Mjölnir, or Thor's hammer, is another powerful symbol associated with protection and strength. Often worn as an amulet, Mjölnir serves as a talisman to ward off negative energies and ensure safety in one's endeavors. When invoking Thor, practitioners may hold or visualize Mjölnir while reciting prayers for protection or during rituals aimed at overcoming obstacles. The hammer symbolizes not only physical strength but also the power of resilience in the face of adversity. Its use in daily prayer rituals can reinforce the idea of seeking divine support in personal challenges.

The Helm of Awe, or Ægishjálmur, is a symbol of protection and invincibility. Traditionally, it was believed that wearing this symbol would instill fear in one's enemies and provide the bearer with unmatched strength. In contemporary practices, individuals may use the Helm of Awe in their spiritual work to invoke courage and fortitude. This symbol can be incorporated into rituals aimed at overcoming fear or initiating significant life changes. By visualizing or drawing the Helm of Awe during prayer, practitioners can connect with the fierce protective energies it embodies.

Lastly, the runes hold immense significance in Norse spirituality, serving as both a system of writing and a means of divination. Each rune carries its own unique energy and meaning, making them essential tools for communication with the divine. When crafting prayers or intentions, practitioners may choose specific runes to enhance their spiritual work. For example, the rune Fehu, symbolizing wealth and abundance, can be invoked during prayers for prosperity, while the rune Gebo, representing partnership and gifts, may be used in rituals focused on love and relationships. Understanding the meanings of these symbols allows individuals to deepen their connection to the Norse deities and enrich their spiritual practices.

# The Importance of Symbolism in Prayer

The use of symbolism in prayer serves as a crucial bridge between the physical world and the spiritual realm, especially within the context of Norse traditions. Symbolism enriches the act of prayer, providing deeper layers of meaning and connection to the divine. For practitioners invoking the Allfather Odin, symbols like the Valknut, Yggdrasil, and runes serve not only as visual representations of their beliefs but also as conduits for their intentions and emotions. Each symbol encapsulates stories and qualities associated with the gods, enhancing the spiritual experience and allowing practitioners to align their thoughts with the virtues of the deities they seek to honor.

Incorporating specific symbols into daily prayer rituals can amplify the practitioner's focus and intention. For instance, using the Valknut, which represents the transition between life and death, can be particularly powerful when praying for protection or guidance from Odin. This symbol can help remind the practitioner of the interconnectedness of all things, reinforcing the idea that their prayers are part of a larger cosmic framework. By integrating these symbols into their rituals, individuals can create a more immersive experience that resonates with the ancient traditions while fostering a personal connection to the divine.

Seasonal celebrations within Norse tradition are rich with symbolism that enhances the significance of the prayers offered during these times. Each season brings with it specific symbols that align with agricultural cycles, nature's rhythms, and the lore of the gods. For example, during Yule, symbols of rebirth and light can be invoked to celebrate the return of the sun. Each symbol serves as a reminder of the cyclical nature of life and the importance of honoring the deities through prayer and offerings. Therefore, understanding and utilizing these symbols during seasonal rituals can deepen one's connection to both the gods and the natural world.

The act of invoking Odin, in particular, is steeped in symbolic meaning. Practitioners may incorporate runes, which are not only letters but also carry magical significance, into their prayers to call upon specific energies and qualities associated with the Allfather. Each rune can embody different aspects of wisdom, war, and knowledge, allowing individuals to tailor their prayers to their specific needs. This intentionality in prayer, coupled with the use of symbols, creates a more profound engagement with the divine, making the act of communication more dynamic and effective.

Finally, the role of ancestors in Norse prayer practices cannot be overlooked when discussing symbolism. Ancestors often serve as symbols of continuity and strength, connecting the present with the past. When invoking the importance of ancestry in prayer, symbols representing familial bonds, such as the family tree or specific ancestral runes, can be powerful tools. They remind practitioners of their heritage and the guidance offered by those who came before them. By embracing these symbols within their prayers, individuals can honor their lineage while simultaneously seeking wisdom and protection from both their ancestors and the Norse gods.

## Incorporating Symbols into Personal Practice

Incorporating symbols into personal practice can significantly enhance one's connection to the Norse gods, particularly Odin. Symbols serve as powerful tools that encapsulate meaning, intention, and the essence of the deities being invoked. By integrating symbols into daily rituals and prayer practices, practitioners can create a more profound spiritual experience. The use of symbols allows individuals to focus their intentions, drawing upon the rich tapestry of Norse mythology and tradition while fostering a deeper understanding of their own spiritual journey.

One of the most prominent symbols associated with Odin is the Valknut, a symbol consisting of three interlocking triangles. This emblem is often linked to Odin's role as a god of the slain and is a powerful reminder of the cycle of life and death. When incorporating the Valknut into personal practice, one might choose to create an altar space where this symbol is prominently displayed. During prayer, practitioners can meditate on the meaning of the Valknut, contemplating themes of sacrifice, transition, and the connection to the spiritual realm. This focus can help deepen the practitioner's connection to Odin and the mysteries he embodies.

Another significant symbol is the Yggdrasil, the World Tree, which represents the interconnectedness of all things in the Norse cosmology. By incorporating Yggdrasil into personal rituals, individuals can reflect on their place within the universe and the importance of balance in their lives. This can be done by visualizing the tree during meditation, using Yggdrasil imagery in prayer offerings, or even drawing the symbol in sacred spaces. Such practices encourage mindfulness of the cyclical nature of existence and the importance of harmony with the natural world, key elements in Norse spirituality.

Runes also play a crucial role in Norse symbolism and can be incorporated into personal practices in various ways. Each rune carries its own unique meaning and energy, making them ideal for divination, protection, and intention-setting. Practitioners might consider creating a set of runes that resonate with them, using them in ritual to enhance their prayers or to seek guidance from Odin and other deities. By casting runes before prayer or during seasonal celebrations, individuals can tap into the ancient wisdom of the runes, enriching their spiritual experience and fostering a deeper connection with the divine.

Finally, the act of combining symbols with offerings can further amplify the power of one's prayers. Whether it be dedicating a specific item, such as a carved figure or a crafted talisman, to a deity or incorporating natural elements like stones or herbs that represent different symbols, these offerings can become conduits for communication with the gods. By infusing these symbols with personal meaning and intention, practitioners can create a sacred dialogue with Odin and other Norse deities, ultimately enhancing their overall spiritual practice and reinforcing their commitment to honoring these ancient traditions.

# Chapter 12: Combining Norse Prayers with Modern Spirituality

## Integrating Norse Practices into Contemporary Life

Integrating Norse practices into contemporary life requires a thoughtful approach that respects the ancient traditions while allowing for personal expression and adaptation. The first step in this integration involves understanding the foundational beliefs of Norse spirituality, particularly the significance of the gods, ancestors, and nature. By familiarizing oneself with the myths and rituals, individuals can create a meaningful framework for their spiritual practices. Engaging with texts that explore the lore, such as the Poetic and Prose Edda, provides context and inspiration for incorporating these ancient teachings into daily life.

Daily prayer rituals can be woven seamlessly into modern routines, serving as moments of reflection and connection with the divine. Setting aside time each morning or evening for prayer allows individuals to invoke the Norse gods, such as Odin or Freyja, seeking guidance, protection, and inspiration. Simple offerings, whether it be a candle, a small bowl of water, or herbs, can enhance these rituals, creating a tangible connection to the spiritual realm. As one develops a personal prayer practice, it is essential to remain open to the nuances that emerge, allowing the experience to evolve over time.

Seasonal celebrations rooted in Norse traditions, such as Yule, Ostara, or Midsummer, provide excellent opportunities for communal gatherings and personal reflection. These festivals often honor the cycles of nature and the changing seasons, aligning one's spiritual practice with the rhythms of the Earth. Incorporating specific prayers and rituals associated with these celebrations fosters a deeper connection to the cycles of life and the ancestors who came before. Crafting unique traditions and ceremonies that resonate with personal beliefs can help revive these ancient practices in a contemporary context.

Divination practices, such as rune casting or scrying, can serve as powerful tools for communication with the divine and for gaining insight into personal challenges. Integrating these techniques into daily life not only enhances spiritual awareness but also encourages a proactive approach to problem-solving. Setting aside time for divination, perhaps during the new moon or full moon, allows for a reflective process that can guide decision-making. By incorporating these methods into prayer practices, individuals can cultivate a dynamic dialogue with the gods and their own inner wisdom.

Creating sacred spaces for worship enables individuals to establish a physical manifestation of their spiritual journey. This space can be as simple as a dedicated altar adorned with symbols of Norse mythology, such as Mjölnir or runes, or a more elaborate setup that includes natural elements like stones, plants, and water. The act of designing and maintaining this space fosters a sense of reverence and commitment to the practices being integrated into daily life. By combining ancient symbols and rituals with modern spirituality, individuals can develop a rich, personal practice that honors both their heritage and their contemporary existence.

## Finding Balance Between Tradition and Modernity

Finding balance between tradition and modernity is essential for those seeking to incorporate Norse spirituality into their daily lives. As contemporary practitioners of Norse traditions navigate the rich tapestry of ancient beliefs, they often find themselves at a crossroads, where the rituals and practices of the past can feel at odds with the realities of modern life. Understanding how to blend these two worlds allows for a more authentic and meaningful spiritual experience, ensuring that the wisdom of the ancestors continues to resonate in today's context.

One key to achieving this balance lies in the recognition that tradition is not static but rather a living, evolving practice. The Norse gods and goddesses were deeply connected to the natural world and the lives of their followers, adapting to the changing needs of their worshippers. By honoring the core principles of Norse spirituality—such as respect for nature, the importance of community, and the acknowledgment of the cycles of life—modern practitioners can create rituals that reflect their current realities while still paying homage to the past. This approach encourages creativity and personal expression, allowing individuals to tailor their practices in a way that feels authentic to them.

Incorporating modern elements into traditional rituals can also enhance their relevance and accessibility. For example, daily prayer rituals can be adapted to fit into busy schedules, making it easier for individuals to connect with the divine on a regular basis. Utilizing technology, such as prayer apps or online communities, can foster a sense of connection and support among practitioners. Seasonal celebrations can be infused with contemporary themes, drawing parallels between ancient customs and modern values, thereby enriching the spiritual experience and making it more relatable to a wider audience.

Moreover, prayer practices rooted in Norse mythology can serve as powerful tools for addressing contemporary issues. Prayers for protection, love, and fertility can be personalized to reflect modern struggles, allowing for a deeper connection to the divine. Communication with deities like Odin and Freyja can be approached through a lens that embraces both ancient wisdom and modern understanding, providing a holistic approach to spirituality that acknowledges the complexities of life today. By invoking these deities in ways that resonate with current experiences, practitioners can forge a stronger bond with the divine.

Ultimately, finding balance between tradition and modernity in Norse spirituality is about honoring the past while embracing the present. It involves a commitment to both learning about ancient practices and adapting them to fit into the contemporary world. This harmonious blend not only enriches individual spiritual journeys but also revitalizes Norse traditions, ensuring they remain relevant and powerful sources of guidance for future generations. By navigating this delicate balance, practitioners can cultivate a vibrant, dynamic spiritual life that honors their heritage while thriving in the modern age.

# Creating a Personalized Spiritual Practice

Creating a personalized spiritual practice is essential for anyone seeking a deeper connection with the Norse gods, particularly Odin. A tailored approach allows individuals to engage authentically with their beliefs and traditions. Start by reflecting on your personal relationship with Odin and the qualities you wish to invoke, such as wisdom, courage, and protection. Consider how these traits manifest in your daily life and spiritual aspirations. This introspection lays the groundwork for a practice that resonates with who you are and your unique spiritual journey.

Daily prayer rituals can be a cornerstone of your personalized practice. Establish a routine that fits your lifestyle, whether it involves morning invocations to set your intentions for the day or evening reflections to express gratitude. Choose specific prayers that align with your goals, such as those seeking guidance from Odin or protection from challenges. Incorporating elements from Norse mythology, like the use of runes or symbols, can enhance these rituals, making them more meaningful and impactful. Consistency is key, as regular engagement helps deepen your connection with the divine.

Seasonal celebrations also offer opportunities to enrich your spiritual practice. The Norse calendar is filled with festivals that honor various deities and natural cycles. Take time to learn about these celebrations, such as Yule or Midsummer, and how they relate to Odin and other gods. Create rituals that reflect the essence of these seasons, incorporating specific prayers and offerings that acknowledge the changing energies. This alignment with nature's rhythms not only honors the gods but also fosters a sense of community and continuity in your spiritual practice.

Invoking Odin through specific techniques and offerings can further personalize your spiritual journey. Research various methods, such as meditation, visualization, or trance work, to find what resonates with you. Offerings can vary from simple tokens like mead or bread to more elaborate altars dedicated to Odin. The act of giving is a powerful way to establish a reciprocal relationship with the Allfather. Document your experiences and feelings during these practices to observe how your connection evolves over time, allowing you to refine your approach as needed.

Finally, consider the role of ancestors in your spiritual practice. Norse traditions place significant emphasis on honoring those who came before us, recognizing that their wisdom and experiences can guide us. Create a space for ancestor veneration within your practice, perhaps through dedicated prayers or an altar featuring ancestral symbols. This connection can enhance your spiritual journey, providing a sense of belonging and continuity. By weaving these elements into your personalized practice, you cultivate a deeper understanding of your place within the Norse spiritual landscape and the broader universe.

# From Odin to Today: Tracing the Asatru Revival

## Chapter 1: The Roots of Norse Paganism

### Historical Context of Norse Beliefs

The historical context of Norse beliefs is essential for understanding the foundations of the Asatru revival. Rooted in the ancient pagan practices of the Norse people, these beliefs were intricately tied to their environment, social structures, and daily lives. Norse mythology, with its pantheon of gods like Odin, Thor, and Freyja, served not only as a religious framework but also as a narrative that explained the world around them. These myths encapsulated a rich tapestry of values, including honor, bravery, and the interconnectedness of life and death. As Christianity spread throughout Scandinavia, many of these beliefs were suppressed or transformed, leading to a syncretic blend of old and new traditions.

The transition from ancient Norse paganism to modern Asatru can be traced through historical texts, archaeological findings, and the evolving cultural landscape. During the Viking Age, Norse beliefs were dynamic, adapting to the influences of neighboring cultures while retaining core elements. The decline of Norse paganism was marked by the Christianization of Scandinavia in the 10th and 11th centuries. However, remnants of Norse spirituality persisted in folklore and customs, which would later inspire the Asatru revival in the 20th century. Modern practitioners draw upon these historical roots, seeking to reconnect with the spiritual heritage of their ancestors through reconstructionist approaches that emphasize authenticity and historical accuracy.

Reconstructionist approaches to Norse paganism are characterized by a commitment to studying ancient texts, archaeological evidence, and ethnographic research to inform contemporary practices. This scholarly effort aims to breathe life into the ancient traditions while adapting them to modern contexts. Rituals and celebrations, such as Blóts and Sumbels, are carefully reconstructed to honor the gods and ancestors, fostering a sense of community among practitioners. The revival of these rituals not only serves a spiritual purpose but also acts as a means of cultural preservation, allowing modern devotees to experience a tangible connection to their heritage.

Ancestor worship holds a significant place in both Norse paganism and Asatru, reflecting the belief in the continuing presence and influence of those who have passed on. This practice emphasizes respect for lineage and the reverence of one's forebears, encouraging individuals to acknowledge their roots and the wisdom of past generations. Through offerings, prayers, and storytelling, practitioners honor their ancestors, fostering a deep sense of identity and belonging. This focus on ancestry contributes to a broader understanding of spiritual continuity and the intergenerational transmission of beliefs, reinforcing the idea that the past is an integral part of the present.

The impact of Viking history on modern Norse spirituality is profound, influencing not only the revival of Asatru but also shaping cultural perceptions of the Norse people. The Vikings' exploratory spirit, martial prowess, and rich mythology have captivated contemporary imagination, leading to romanticized views of Norse culture. This fascination, however, is paired with a critical examination of historical narratives, prompting modern practitioners to engage with the complexities of their Viking heritage. Furthermore, themes such as gender roles and the feminine divine are explored within the framework of Asatru, challenging traditional narratives and embracing a more inclusive spirituality. As environmentalism and nature worship gain prominence in modern spiritual practices, the ancient Norse reverence for the natural world also finds renewed expression, connecting past beliefs with contemporary values.

## Key Deities and Myths

The pantheon of Norse deities serves as a cornerstone of both ancient Norse paganism and the modern Asatru faith. Key figures such as Odin, Thor, and Freyja hold significant places in the mythology and rituals that shape contemporary practices. Odin, the Allfather, embodies wisdom and the quest for knowledge, often associated with the pursuit of runic understanding. His multifaceted nature allows for varied interpretations, making him a pivotal figure in the spiritual journeys of modern practitioners. Thor, representing strength and protection, is celebrated not only for his warrior attributes but also for his role in ensuring the prosperity of the land and its people. Freyja, the goddess of love, fertility, and war, brings a feminine perspective to the divine landscape, emphasizing the importance of both nurturing and empowerment within the faith.

Myths surrounding these deities create a rich tapestry that informs the principles of Asatru today. Stories such as the creation of the world from the body of the slain giant Ymir or the prophecy of Ragnarok, the end of the world, highlight themes of cyclical renewal and transformation that resonate with modern practitioners. These narratives not only provide a moral framework but also establish a connection to the natural world, reflecting the belief in the interdependence of all beings. The continuation of these myths within contemporary rituals allows adherents to engage with their heritage while adapting to current values, creating a dynamic bridge between the past and present.

Reconstructionist approaches to Norse paganism emphasize the importance of historical accuracy in reviving ancient practices. This involves meticulous research into historical texts, archaeological findings, and cultural customs from the Viking Age. Many Asatru communities strive to honor the traditions of their ancestors while also recognizing the necessity for evolution in practice. This balance between authenticity and modern relevance fosters a spiritual environment that respects the past while addressing contemporary concerns, such as environmentalism and gender equality. Furthermore, rituals and celebrations, deeply rooted in these historical narratives, serve both as a means of connecting with the divine and as community-building experiences.

Ancestor worship is a fundamental aspect of Norse paganism that continues to play a vital role in Asatru practice. By honoring ancestors, practitioners maintain a connection to their lineage and heritage, recognizing the influence of those who came before them. This aspect of worship often involves rituals that include offerings, storytelling, and the sharing of family history, reinforcing the belief that ancestors continue to guide and protect their descendants. The reverence for lineage not only strengthens community bonds but also encourages individuals to reflect on their personal journeys and the interconnectedness of all life.

The impact of Viking history on modern Norse spirituality is evident in the revival of symbols, practices, and beliefs that were significant in the Viking Age. The resurgence of interest in the Viking way of life has inspired contemporary adherents to explore their roots and incorporate elements such as runes, nature worship, and gender dynamics into their spiritual practices. Asatru practitioners today often seek to create a faith that honors the past while fostering inclusivity and environmental consciousness. This evolution of Norse deities and their significance demonstrates how ancient beliefs can adapt and thrive within modern contexts, ensuring that the legacy of Norse mythology continues to inspire and guide future generations.

## The Role of Nature in Norse Spirituality

The role of nature in Norse spirituality is fundamental, deeply woven into the fabric of both ancient beliefs and modern Asatru practices. In Norse cosmology, the world is perceived as a living entity, imbued with spirit and significance. The natural elements—mountains, rivers, forests, and the sea—are not merely physical landscapes; they are sacred spaces that hold power and meaning. This intrinsic connection to the natural world reflects a worldview where humans coexist with the land, animals, and the elements, recognizing that each aspect of nature carries its own spirit or essence.

In the historical context of Norse paganism, nature was revered as a source of sustenance and spiritual guidance. The ancient Norse people celebrated natural cycles through their agricultural practices, aligning their rituals with the seasons. Festivals such as Yule and Midsummer were not only agricultural markers but also times to honor the deities connected to fertility and growth, such as Freyja and Njord. These celebrations reinforced a communal bond with the earth and acknowledged the reciprocal relationship between humans and nature, a principle that continues to resonate in contemporary Asatru.

Modern Asatru practitioners often draw upon these ancient concepts, emphasizing the importance of environmental stewardship and nature worship. Many adherents engage in rituals that honor the land, such as blóts (sacrificial offerings) to local spirits or landvættir, acknowledging the guardians of specific places. This practice highlights a commitment to respecting and protecting the environment, reflecting a broader trend within contemporary paganism that embraces ecological awareness. Asatru encourages its followers to engage with their surroundings, fostering a sense of responsibility toward the natural world.

The relationship with nature in Norse spirituality also extends to a deep appreciation for the cycles of life and death. The reverence for ancestors is intertwined with the land, as many believe that ancestral spirits inhabit the earth and continue to influence the living. This connection creates a holistic view of existence, where the past, present, and future coexist in the natural world. Rituals often involve honoring these ancestors through offerings or by visiting sacred sites, reinforcing the idea that the land is a repository of collective memory and spiritual heritage.

In summary, the role of nature in Norse spirituality serves as a bridge linking ancient practices with modern Asatru beliefs. This connection fosters a sense of community and responsibility towards the environment while honoring ancestral ties. As contemporary practitioners navigate their spiritual paths, they continue to draw inspiration from the natural world, ensuring that the essence of Norse spirituality remains vibrant and relevant in today's ecological landscape.

# Chapter 2: The Asatru Revival

## Origins of the Asatru Movement

The Asatru movement, a modern revival of ancient Norse paganism, traces its origins back to the late 19th and early 20th centuries. This period saw a growing interest in folklore, mythology, and the romantic ideals of pre-Christian Northern European cultures. Influenced by the rise of nationalism and a renewed appreciation for indigenous traditions, scholars and enthusiasts began to explore the rich tapestry of Norse mythology. Figures such as the Icelandic poet and nationalist Jónas Hallgrímsson, along with the folklorist and historian Guðbrandur Vigfússon, played pivotal roles in bringing attention to Norse heritage, setting the stage for a spiritual awakening that would evolve into the Asatru faith.

The early 20th century marked a significant turning point for the Asatru movement, as various groups sought to reconstruct and revitalize ancient Norse religious practices. The incorporation of scholarly research into Norse texts, such as the Poetic Edda and the Prose Edda, provided a foundation for contemporary practitioners. This reconstructionist approach emphasized understanding the historical context of rituals and beliefs, allowing modern Asatru followers to connect deeply with their ancestral roots. During this time, the movement began to gain traction, culminating in the formation of various Asatru organizations that sought to create a cohesive community around shared beliefs and practices.

As the Asatru movement evolved, rituals and celebrations became central to its identity. Drawing from ancient customs, contemporary practitioners celebrate seasonal festivals such as Yule, Ostara, and Midsummer, which honor the cycles of nature and the gods. These celebrations often include feasts, toasts, and the sharing of stories that reinforce a sense of community and continuity with the past. Additionally, modern rituals frequently incorporate elements of ancestor worship, reflecting the importance of honoring lineage and heritage. This practice is deeply rooted in Norse paganism, where the veneration of ancestors plays a crucial role in spiritual life, reinforcing connections between the past and present.

The Viking Age, with its rich history of exploration, conquest, and cultural exchange, has significantly impacted the modern Norse spiritual landscape. The image of the Viking warrior, often romanticized in contemporary culture, has shaped perceptions of Norse spirituality and its values. Asatru practitioners draw inspiration from the Viking ethos, embodying principles such as bravery, honor, and respect for the natural world. This historical context not only enriches the spiritual practices of Asatru but also fosters a sense of identity and belonging among its followers, who see themselves as part of a long lineage of Norse heritage.

In recent years, Asatru has increasingly embraced contemporary issues such as environmentalism and gender roles. Many practitioners advocate for a deep respect for nature, aligning their beliefs with ecological principles and sustainability. This modern interpretation of Norse spirituality emphasizes the interconnectedness of all life and the importance of preserving the natural world. Furthermore, the role of the feminine divine has gained prominence, with many Asatru followers recognizing the significance of goddesses and female figures within the Norse pantheon. As these themes continue to evolve, the Asatru movement reflects a dynamic interplay between ancient beliefs and modern values, creating a rich tapestry that resonates with contemporary seekers of spirituality.

## Early Practitioners and Influences

Early practitioners of Norse paganism laid the groundwork for what would eventually evolve into modern Asatru, a faith that seeks to revive and reconstruct the ancient beliefs and practices of the Norse people. These early practitioners were often individuals who felt a deep connection to their ancestral roots, drawn by a desire to reconnect with the mythology and spirituality of the Viking Age. They sought to explore the ancient texts, artifacts, and oral traditions that had been passed down through generations, aiming to create a living, breathing expression of Norse spirituality that resonated with contemporary values and experiences.

Influences from a range of sources played a critical role in shaping the early revival of Norse paganism. Scholars, historians, and enthusiasts contributed to a growing body of literature that examined the historical and cultural contexts of the Norse gods, myths, and rituals. The works of figures such as Jakob Grimm and later, the folklorist and mythologist Joseph Campbell, provided frameworks for understanding the significance of mythology in human experience. These early influences also included a resurgence of interest in folklore, which helped to bridge the gap between the ancient practices and modern interpretations, allowing for a more nuanced understanding of the Norse spiritual landscape.

Reconstructionist approaches became a hallmark of early Asatru practitioners, who sought to create a faith that was both authentic to its historical roots and relevant to the modern world. This involved careful study of primary sources such as the Poetic Edda and the Prose Edda, as well as archaeological findings. Practitioners aimed to reconstruct rituals and celebrations that honored the traditional festivals of the Norse calendar, such as Yule and Midsummer, while also adapting them to fit contemporary lifestyles. This blend of the old and the new allowed for a dynamic practice that respected historical integrity while embracing the evolving nature of spirituality.

Rituals and celebrations within contemporary Asatru reflect this blend of historical practices and modern sensibilities. Many Asatru practitioners engage in blóts, or sacrifices, to honor the gods and spirits, and sumbels, a communal ritual of toasting to deities, ancestors, and personal intentions. These rituals are often accompanied by offerings of mead or food, which symbolize the connection between the human and divine realms. The emphasis on community and personal experience in these rituals fosters a sense of belonging and shared purpose among practitioners, reinforcing the importance of cultural heritage while inviting individual expression.

The role of ancestor worship is a significant aspect of Asatru that draws directly from Norse pagan traditions. Early practitioners recognized the importance of honoring one's ancestors, viewing them as guiding spirits who continue to influence the lives of their descendants. This ancestral connection is often celebrated through rituals that invoke the memory and presence of loved ones, emphasizing the continuity of lineage and shared identity. Asatru practitioners today embrace this aspect of their faith, integrating it into their personal practices and communal gatherings, thus ensuring that the legacy of their ancestors remains alive and relevant in a modern context.

## Legal Recognition and Community Building

Legal recognition of Asatru and similar religious practices has evolved significantly over the past few decades, reflecting a broader societal acceptance of diverse spiritual paths. In many countries, Asatru practitioners have sought formal acknowledgment as a legitimate faith, which has led to increased visibility and the establishment of legal frameworks that support their religious rights. This recognition often involves navigating complex legal systems, including the registration of organizations, the right to perform ceremonies, and the ability to access public lands for rituals. Such legal recognition not only affirms the beliefs of practitioners but also fosters a sense of legitimacy and community within the Asatru movement.

Building a community around Asatru is integral to its modern practice, as followers often seek connection with others who share their beliefs. Community-building initiatives can take many forms, including local gatherings, online forums, and larger events like festivals. These gatherings provide opportunities for education, ritual, and fellowship, enabling individuals to deepen their understanding of Norse mythology and its contemporary applications. The communal aspect is crucial, as it creates a supportive environment where practitioners can explore their spirituality, share experiences, and celebrate shared values.

Historically, Norse paganism was deeply intertwined with the social structures of its time, and contemporary Asatru often mirrors this by emphasizing collective identity and shared traditions. The reconstructionist approach to Norse paganism highlights the importance of historical accuracy, while also allowing for adaptation to modern contexts. This balance between honoring ancient practices and addressing contemporary issues is vital in fostering a dynamic and vibrant community. Through rituals and celebrations rooted in Norse tradition, practitioners can engage with their heritage in meaningful ways that resonate with current societal values.

Rituals and celebrations play a crucial role in reinforcing community ties and promoting a shared spiritual identity. Events such as blóts and sumbels serve not only as religious observances but also as communal gatherings that strengthen bonds among participants. These rituals often incorporate elements of ancestor worship, reflecting a core belief in the importance of lineage and heritage within Asatru. By honoring ancestors, practitioners recognize their place within a larger narrative, fostering a sense of continuity and connection to the past while simultaneously cultivating a vibrant present.

As Asatru continues to evolve, it increasingly addresses modern concerns such as environmentalism and gender roles, further enriching its community fabric. The integration of nature worship reflects a growing awareness of ecological issues and the need to respect the Earth, drawing parallels with ancient Norse reverence for the natural world. Additionally, discussions surrounding gender roles and the feminine divine highlight the inclusivity and adaptability of contemporary Asatru practices. By actively engaging with these themes, the Asatru community not only honors its historical roots but also positions itself as a relevant and progressive spiritual path for modern individuals seeking meaning and connection.

# Chapter 3: Historical Influence of Norse Mythology

## Myths in Modern Culture

Myths play a significant role in shaping modern culture, particularly in the revival of Asatru, a contemporary manifestation of Norse paganism. These myths, deeply rooted in ancient storytelling, provide a rich tapestry that informs the beliefs, practices, and values of modern Asatru practitioners. The narratives of gods like Odin, Thor, and Freyja not only serve as spiritual archetypes but also as symbols that resonate with the contemporary quest for identity and meaning. The revival of these myths reflects a desire to reconnect with ancestral traditions while adapting them to the challenges and realities of modern life.

The historical influence of Norse mythology on modern Asatru practices is evident in various rituals and celebrations that mirror ancient customs. For instance, the observance of Yule during the winter solstice connects practitioners with the cyclical nature of life, celebrating rebirth and renewal. Similarly, the blóts, or sacrificial offerings, remain a central feature of Asatru, allowing individuals to honor the gods and spirits of their ancestors. These practices are not merely recreations; they embody a living tradition that evolves while retaining its core values. By integrating these ancient myths into contemporary life, practitioners find relevance and inspiration in the stories of their forebears.

Reconstructionist approaches to Norse paganism emphasize the importance of authenticity and historical accuracy in practice. This perspective seeks to distill the essence of ancient rituals and beliefs, often using archaeological findings and historical texts as guides. However, the challenge lies in interpreting these sources, as much of the ancient Norse worldview is fragmented and open to various interpretations. As modern Asatru practitioners navigate this complex landscape, they often engage in dialogues about what it means to honor tradition while embracing personal and cultural evolution.

Ancestor worship is another critical element that emerges from Norse mythology and is central to Asatru. The reverence for ancestors reflects a deep-seated belief in the continuity of life and the importance of familial bonds. Modern practitioners often create altars or perform rituals to honor their forebears, thereby fostering a sense of connection with their lineage. This practice not only cultivates respect for the past but also serves as a reminder of the lessons learned from previous generations, reinforcing the idea that the past is a vital part of one's identity.

Gender roles and the feminine divine are also significant topics in the discourse surrounding modern Asatru. While traditional Norse society often emphasized masculine ideals, contemporary interpretations increasingly recognize the contributions of female deities like Freyja and Skadi. This shift encourages a more inclusive understanding of spirituality that honors the divine feminine alongside the masculine. Furthermore, discussions surrounding environmentalism and nature worship in Asatru highlight a growing awareness of the interconnectedness of all life, urging practitioners to engage with the natural world in a respectful and sustainable manner. Through these explorations, modern Asatru continues to evolve, demonstrating how ancient myths can inform and enrich contemporary spiritual practices.

## Literature and Art Inspired by Norse Themes

Literature and art inspired by Norse themes have played a significant role in shaping the modern understanding and expression of Asatru. From the ancient sagas and Eddas that document the mythology and beliefs of the Norse people to contemporary works that reinterpret these themes, the influence of Norse mythology is profound. Authors such as J.R.R. Tolkien and Neil Gaiman have drawn upon these ancient narratives to create rich, imaginative worlds that resonate with contemporary audiences. Their works not only entertain but also serve as a bridge connecting modern spirituality with historical traditions, allowing readers to explore the complexities of Norse mythology through a modern lens.

In addition to literature, visual art inspired by Norse themes has flourished, reflecting the vibrant imagery and symbolism found in the old Norse texts. Artists have depicted scenes from the myths, such as the battles of the gods, the beauty of the Valkyries, and the mysteries of Yggdrasil, the World Tree. This artistic expression serves both as a homage to the ancient stories and as a means of engaging with them in a contemporary context. Through painting, sculpture, and digital art, creators are able to reinterpret Norse symbols and deities, making them relevant to today's spiritual seekers and ensuring the continuity of these ancient narratives.

The revival of interest in Norse mythology has also prompted a new wave of literature that explores themes of spirituality, ritual, and community within Asatru. Writers within the Asatru community are producing texts that delve into the practical aspects of modern Norse paganism, discussing rituals, celebrations, and the significance of ancestor worship. These writings often emphasize the importance of reconnection with heritage and the natural world, aligning with the values of environmentalism and nature worship that are central to many contemporary practitioners. The integration of ancient beliefs with modern practices encourages a holistic approach to spirituality that honors both the past and the present.

Furthermore, the exploration of gender roles and the feminine divine in Asatru has inspired a wealth of artistic and literary works. Female figures from Norse mythology, such as Freyja and Frigg, have been re-examined and celebrated, leading to a reimagining of their roles within the spiritual landscape. This examination not only empowers women within the Asatru community but also enriches the broader discourse on gender and spirituality, making room for diverse expressions of the divine. Literary portrayals and artistic representations of these deities challenge traditional narratives and invite deeper reflection on the roles of women in both ancient and modern contexts.

Ultimately, the interplay between literature, art, and Norse themes is a dynamic and evolving aspect of the Asatru revival. Through various mediums, practitioners and enthusiasts alike are able to explore the rich tapestry of Norse mythology while fostering a deeper connection to their spiritual heritage. This ongoing conversation between the past and present not only preserves ancient traditions but also inspires new interpretations and practices, ensuring that the essence of Norse spirituality continues to thrive in contemporary society.

## Norse Mythology in Popular Media

Norse mythology has permeated popular media in a variety of forms, from literature to film, art, and video games, significantly influencing contemporary perceptions of Norse paganism and Asatru. The resurgence of interest in Norse mythology can be traced back to the 19th century, but it gained substantial traction in the 21st century with the advent of blockbuster films and television series that depict gods, heroes, and the vibrant worlds of the Norse pantheon. These portrayals often simplify complex narratives and characters but serve to introduce broader audiences to the rich tapestry of Norse beliefs and practices, igniting curiosity about the historical roots of these stories and their modern reinterpretations.

Major films such as the Marvel Cinematic Universe's Thor series have popularized figures like Thor and Loki, embedding them deeply in contemporary culture. While these adaptations take creative liberties, they have sparked interest in the actual mythological texts, encouraging viewers to explore the original sagas and Eddas. This fascination with Norse deities and their narratives has encouraged some individuals to delve into Asatru as a spiritual path, seeking to understand the historical and cultural significance of these figures beyond their cinematic representations. As a result, there is a notable interplay between popular media and the revival of ancient practices, with many enthusiasts seeking to reconcile mythological portrayals with authentic Asatru beliefs.

Video games, too, have embraced Norse mythology, providing immersive experiences that allow players to explore mythical worlds and lore. Titles like God of War and Assassin's Creed Valhalla present players with opportunities to engage with Norse themes, from epic battles with gods to quests for honor and legacy. These interactive formats not only entertain but also educate players about aspects of Norse culture, history, and spirituality. This blend of education and entertainment helps to demystify Norse mythology, making it more accessible to a younger generation that may be seeking spiritual connections in a world dominated by modernity.

The representation of Norse mythology in popular media also intersects with discussions on gender roles and the feminine divine in Asatru. Contemporary adaptations often highlight strong female characters derived from mythological figures, such as the Valkyries or Freyja. This shift toward showcasing the feminine aspect of Norse spirituality has led to a reevaluation of gender roles within Asatru practices, empowering individuals to embrace a more inclusive understanding of the divine. Such portrayals challenge traditional narratives and encourage a broader acceptance of diverse expressions within modern Norse spirituality, resonating with contemporary movements that advocate for gender equality and the recognition of feminine power.

Finally, the environmental themes often present in Norse mythology resonate with the modern emphasis on nature worship and environmentalism within Asatru. Many practitioners today draw inspiration from the deep connections between the Norse gods and the natural world, fostering a sense of stewardship and respect for the earth. Popular media that emphasizes these themes, whether through storytelling or visual art, reinforces the relevance of ancient beliefs in addressing contemporary ecological concerns. This synthesis of mythology and modern values not only reinforces the spiritual practices of Asatru but also encourages a new generation to engage with the natural world through the lens of Norse spirituality, fostering a renewed appreciation for both the past and the environment.

# Chapter 4: Reconstructionist Approaches

## Defining Reconstructionism

Reconstructionism in the context of Norse paganism refers to a scholarly and spiritual approach that seeks to revive and practice the ancient beliefs, rituals, and customs of the Norse peoples. This methodology emphasizes historical accuracy, drawing from archaeological findings, historical texts, and folklore to inform contemporary practices. Reconstructionists aim to create a faithful representation of Norse spirituality by grounding their beliefs in the authentic traditions of the past rather than modern reinterpretations or syncretic practices that may dilute or alter the original meanings.

Central to the reconstructionist approach is the careful study of primary sources, such as the Poetic Edda and Prose Edda, alongside archaeological evidence from Viking Age sites. These texts and artifacts provide insight into the cosmology, mythology, and daily practices of the Norse people. Reconstructionists often focus on the cultural context in which these beliefs were practiced, understanding that Norse spirituality was deeply intertwined with the social, political, and environmental aspects of life during that era. This historical lens allows practitioners to engage with their spirituality in a manner that respects the integrity of the past.

The role of rituals and celebrations in contemporary Asatru is also influenced by reconstructionist principles. Many modern practitioners seek to replicate festivals like Yule, Midsummer, and other seasonal celebrations that were significant to the Norse. These events are not merely historical reenactments but are infused with personal significance and community engagement. Rituals are designed to honor the gods, celebrate the cycles of nature, and strengthen connections within the community, all while being rooted in ancient practices. This approach encourages a sense of belonging and continuity with the past.

Ancestor worship is another vital component of reconstructionist Asatru, reflecting the Norse emphasis on kinship and heritage. Practitioners honor their ancestors through remembrance rituals, altars, and offerings, recognizing the importance of familial connections in shaping identity and spiritual practice. This focus on lineage highlights the belief that ancestral spirits can guide and protect the living, creating a bridge between generations. By integrating ancestor veneration into their spirituality, modern practitioners affirm their roots and foster a deeper connection to their heritage.

Incorporating elements of environmentalism and nature worship is an increasingly relevant aspect of contemporary Asatru, aligning with the Norse reverence for the natural world. Reconstructionists advocate for a relationship with nature that mirrors the ancient Norse respect for the land and its cycles. This perspective not only honors the gods and spirits associated with various natural elements but also promotes stewardship of the earth. As modern challenges such as climate change and ecological degradation come to the forefront, the principles of Norse spirituality provide a framework for advocating for a harmonious relationship with the environment, resonating with both ancient wisdom and contemporary concerns.

## Sources of Historical Knowledge

Sources of historical knowledge play a crucial role in understanding the development and revival of Asatru, the modern practice of Norse paganism. These sources encompass a range of materials, including archaeological findings, historical texts, folklore, and oral traditions, all of which contribute to a comprehensive understanding of ancient Norse beliefs and practices. The study of these sources allows contemporary practitioners to reconstruct their spiritual heritage and find relevance in the ancient traditions that shape their faith today.

Archaeological evidence provides invaluable insights into the everyday lives of the Norse people, revealing details about their rituals, social structures, and spiritual practices. Excavations of burial sites, temples, and settlements have uncovered artifacts such as amulets, tools, and remnants of sacrifices, which help scholars piece together the spiritual and cultural landscape of the Viking Age. These findings not only inform modern Asatru practices but also highlight the significance of nature and the environment in Norse spirituality, a theme that resonates strongly with contemporary practitioners who emphasize environmentalism and nature worship.

Historical texts, such as the Poetic Edda and the Prose Edda, serve as foundational sources of Norse mythology and cosmology. Compiled in the 13th century, these texts preserve the stories of gods, heroes, and the creation of the world, offering a narrative framework that informs modern rituals and celebrations. The Eddas also provide insight into the values and beliefs of the Norse people, including gender roles and the depiction of the feminine divine, which are critical elements in the practice of Asatru today. By interpreting these texts, practitioners can forge connections between ancient wisdom and contemporary spiritual experiences.

Folklore and oral traditions are equally significant in understanding the evolution of Norse spirituality. These stories, passed down through generations, reflect the lived experiences and beliefs of communities over time. They often incorporate elements of ancestor worship, emphasizing the importance of honoring one's lineage, which remains a central tenet of modern Asatru. By engaging with these narratives, practitioners can cultivate a deeper connection to their ancestry and integrate these values into their spiritual practices, thereby enriching their faith.

Asatru's revival is further enhanced by cross-cultural comparisons with other pagan traditions. By examining similarities and differences, practitioners can gain a broader perspective on spirituality and ritual practices, fostering a sense of community among diverse faiths. The exploration of symbols, such as runes, and their interpretations across various cultures can also provide deeper insights into the shared human experience of seeking meaning and connection in the natural world. Ultimately, the diverse sources of historical knowledge not only illuminate the path from ancient Norse paganism to contemporary Asatru but also empower individuals to create a meaningful and relevant practice that honors both their heritage and the present.

## Contemporary Practices Based on Ancient Traditions

Contemporary practices in Asatru reflect a blend of ancient traditions and modern interpretations, illustrating the dynamic nature of this spiritual path as it evolves from its historical roots. The revival of Norse paganism has prompted practitioners to revisit ancient rituals and beliefs, while also adapting them to fit contemporary life. This synthesis shows how the core tenets of Asatru remain relevant today, emphasizing community, nature, and personal connections to the divine, all of which have historical significance in Norse culture.

One of the most prominent influences on modern Asatru practices is the ritualistic framework established by ancient Norse communities. Historical celebrations such as Yule, Midsummer, and Winternights have been revitalized, often incorporating both traditional elements and new practices that align with contemporary values. Rituals now frequently emphasize inclusivity and personal expression, allowing practitioners to create meaningful experiences that resonate with their individual beliefs while honoring the ancestral customs that inform them. This adaptability illustrates a conscious effort to maintain the spirit of Norse traditions while making them accessible and relevant to today's practitioners.

Reconstructionist approaches to Norse paganism play a crucial role in shaping contemporary Asatru. Practitioners often delve into historical texts, archaeological findings, and folklore to inform their spiritual practices. This scholarly engagement fosters a deep respect for the ancient traditions while also allowing room for innovation. Many Asatru practitioners take care to distinguish between what can be historically verified and what is reconstructed or interpreted, ensuring that their practices remain grounded in authenticity while embracing the fluidity of modern spirituality.

Ancestor worship is another significant aspect of contemporary Asatru that draws directly from ancient customs. Honoring one's ancestors not only connects individuals to their heritage but also reinforces the communal aspect of the faith. Rituals such as sumbel, where participants share drinks and toasts in honor of their ancestors, have seen a resurgence in modern practices. This focus on lineage promotes a sense of identity and continuity, bridging the past with the present and allowing individuals to cultivate a deeper understanding of their place within the larger narrative of their ancestry.

The interplay between gender roles and the feminine divine in Asatru also reflects a contemporary reinterpretation of ancient traditions. While Norse mythology features powerful female figures such as the Norns and Freyja, modern practitioners are increasingly emphasizing gender equality and the sacredness of the feminine. This shift not only honors ancient representations of women in Norse culture but also aligns with broader societal movements advocating for gender inclusivity. Asatru today seeks to embrace a holistic view of spirituality that acknowledges the divine in all forms, fostering a more comprehensive understanding of the sacred that resonates with a diverse audience.

# Chapter 5: Rituals and Celebrations

## Major Festivals in Asatru

Major festivals in Asatru serve as vital touchstones for practitioners, blending ancient traditions with modern interpretations. These celebrations are often rooted in the seasonal cycles of nature, reflecting the agricultural calendar that was central to Norse life. Key festivals include Yule, which celebrates the winter solstice, and the coming of longer days. These celebrations are not only a time for feasting and merriment but also for reflection and honoring the gods and ancestors. Through rituals such as the Yule blot, practitioners invoke the blessings of deities like Odin and Frey, ensuring a bountiful year ahead.

Another significant festival is Ostara, linked to the spring equinox, which symbolizes rebirth and renewal. This celebration often includes the honoring of fertility gods and goddesses, mirroring the ancient customs of welcoming the return of life to the earth. Participants may engage in rituals that focus on planting seeds, both literally in gardens and metaphorically in their lives. The themes of growth and vitality resonate deeply within the Asatru community, inspiring rituals that emphasize personal development and connection to the natural world.

Midsummer, celebrated around the summer solstice, marks the height of the sun's power and is often associated with the god Baldr. This festival is characterized by bonfires, feasting, and festivities, representing joy and abundance. In contemporary Asatru, Midsummer serves as an occasion to honor the interconnectedness of all life, with rituals that emphasize gratitude for the earth's gifts. The celebration also provides an opportunity for community bonding, as practitioners come together to share stories, music, and dance, reinforcing social ties and collective identity.

The autumn festival of Harvest, or Freyfaxi, acknowledges the bounty of the earth and is a time for giving thanks. This festival honors Frey, the god of fertility and prosperity, and often includes rituals that focus on the harvest's abundance. Participants express gratitude for the food and resources they have received throughout the year, acknowledging their reliance on the land and ancestral practices. This celebration serves as a reminder of the importance of sustainability and respect for nature, themes that resonate in modern Asatru, where environmental consciousness is increasingly emphasized.

Throughout the Asatru calendar, each festival invites practitioners to reflect on their values, traditions, and the natural world. These celebrations are not merely historical reenactments but dynamic expressions of a living faith. By honoring the cycles of nature and the legacy of their ancestors, modern Asatru practitioners forge a meaningful connection to their heritage. In doing so, they create a vibrant spiritual community that honors the past while adapting to contemporary life, ensuring that the essence of Norse paganism continues to thrive in today's world.

# Daily and Seasonal Rites

Daily and seasonal rites play a pivotal role in both the historical practices of Norse paganism and the modern revival of Asatru. These rituals serve as a connection to the cycles of nature, honoring the rhythms of the Earth and the deities that inhabit the Norse cosmology. Daily rites may include simple acts such as morning offerings to the gods or the ancestors, often involving the lighting of candles or the pouring of mead, while seasonal rites are more elaborate celebrations that mark significant points in the agricultural calendar, such as the solstices, equinoxes, and major festivals like Yule and Midsummer. Through these practices, adherents not only acknowledge the changing seasons but also reinforce their ties to a rich cultural heritage.

The historical influence of Norse mythology on contemporary Asatru practices is evident in the way rituals are constructed and performed. Many modern practitioners draw directly from the Eddas and sagas, interpreting the stories and symbols within them to create meaningful rituals that resonate with their personal experiences and beliefs. For example, the practice of blot, a sacrificial offering to the gods, has its roots in ancient traditions and is adapted today to suit modern sensibilities. Similarly, the concept of sumbel, a ceremonial toast that includes the honoring of gods, ancestors, and community members, remains a central aspect of gatherings, fostering a sense of unity and shared purpose among practitioners.

Reconstructionist approaches to Norse paganism emphasize authenticity and historical accuracy in the revival of these ancient rituals. This involves a meticulous study of historical texts, archaeological findings, and folklore to inform contemporary practices. However, as Asatru evolves, so too does the interpretation of its rites. Many practitioners blend traditional elements with personal significance, creating a dynamic practice that honors the past while being relevant to modern life. This flexibility allows for a diverse range of expressions within the faith, accommodating various cultural influences and individual spiritual journeys.

Ancestor worship holds a significant place in both Norse paganism and modern Asatru, providing a vital link between the past and the present. Rituals honoring ancestors often include offerings, prayers, and storytelling, allowing individuals to connect with their heritage and seek guidance from those who came before them. This practice fosters a deep sense of community and continuity within Asatru, as individuals recognize their place within a larger familial and cultural narrative. The reverence for ancestors can also inspire ethical living and a commitment to the values of one's forebears, reinforcing the importance of lineage and legacy in contemporary spiritual practice.

Asatru's relationship with nature and environmentalism is also reflected in its daily and seasonal rites. The reverence for the land, animals, and natural cycles is integral to the faith, influencing how practitioners engage with their environment. Seasonal celebrations often include rituals that honor the Earth and its bounty, reinforcing a commitment to stewardship and sustainability. This connection to nature resonates with modern environmental movements, positioning Asatru as a path that not only honors ancient traditions but also seeks to address contemporary ecological challenges. Through these daily and seasonal rites, practitioners of Asatru cultivate a profound respect for the world around them, fostering a spirituality that is both rooted in history and responsive to the needs of the present.

# Community Gatherings and Their Significance

Community gatherings play a pivotal role in the Asatru revival, serving as vital spaces for connection, learning, and the practice of shared beliefs. These gatherings, often rooted in both historical traditions and contemporary interpretations, create a sense of belonging among practitioners. By coming together, individuals reinforce their commitment to the Asatru faith while engaging in meaningful rituals that honor their Norse heritage. The act of gathering is not only about socializing; it is a way to strengthen communal ties and foster a collective identity that celebrates the values of kinship, loyalty, and respect for the natural world.

At these events, various rituals and celebrations are conducted, allowing participants to experience the richness of Norse mythology and its relevance in today's society. Seasonal festivals, such as Yule and Midsummer, often involve traditional activities that echo ancient customs, such as feasting, storytelling, and honoring the gods and ancestors. This reenactment of historical practices serves not only as a homage to Norse traditions but also as a means of educating newer members about the significance of these rituals. The celebratory atmosphere encourages individuals to express their spirituality openly, fostering an environment where both personal and communal connections can flourish.

The significance of ancestor worship is particularly emphasized during community gatherings. Asatru practitioners often honor their forebears through rituals that recognize and celebrate the lineage that connects them to their past. This practice underlines the importance of remembering one's roots and acknowledging the influence of ancestors on contemporary lives. By invoking the names and spirits of those who came before, practitioners create a dialogue between the past and the present, reinforcing the idea that their identities are shaped by a rich tapestry of histories and experiences. This connection to ancestry not only enriches individual spirituality but also unites the community in a shared heritage.

Moreover, community gatherings in Asatru reflect the evolving understanding of gender roles and the divine feminine. Many groups are increasingly recognizing the importance of inclusivity, ensuring that both men and women have equal opportunities to participate in rituals and leadership. This shift acknowledges the powerful feminine aspects of the Norse pantheon, such as goddesses like Freyja and Frigg, who embody wisdom, fertility, and war. By exploring these themes during gatherings, communities foster a more holistic understanding of spirituality that embraces diverse expressions of gender and divinity, contributing to a more balanced and inclusive practice.

Finally, the gatherings often serve as platforms for discussions on contemporary issues such as environmentalism and nature worship. Asatru emphasizes a deep respect for the natural world, which resonates strongly with modern concerns about ecological sustainability. By integrating these themes into community events, practitioners address the relevance of their faith in combating contemporary challenges. These discussions not only reinforce the commitment to honor the earth but also inspire collective action within the community, further solidifying the ties that bind practitioners together in a shared mission to protect and cherish the world around them.

# Chapter 6: Ancestor Worship

## The Importance of Ancestors in Norse Belief

The role of ancestors holds significant importance within Norse belief systems, both in historical contexts and in contemporary Asatru practices. Ancestor veneration is deeply rooted in the cultural fabric of the Norse peoples, reflecting a worldview where the past is inextricably linked to the present. This connection emphasizes the continuity of life, whereby the deeds, values, and wisdom of those who came before are seen as guiding forces for their descendants. In Norse mythology, figures such as the god Odin are often depicted as deeply connected to their forebears, showcasing the reverence for ancestral lineage that permeates the tradition.

In the context of Asatru, ancestor worship serves as a foundational practice, often incorporated into rituals and celebrations. Modern practitioners may honor their ancestors through various rites, including offerings at altars, the sharing of stories, and the invocation of ancestral spirits during significant life events. These practices not only foster a sense of identity and belonging but also encourage individuals to reflect on their heritage and the lessons passed down through generations. The ritual of sumbel, for instance, allows participants to toast their ancestors, affirming their presence and influence within the community.

Furthermore, the emphasis on ancestors in Norse belief highlights the importance of personal and familial history. Asatru practitioners often delve into genealogy to connect with their roots, seeking to understand their lineage and the cultural narratives that inform their spiritual practices. This journey into one's ancestry can serve as a source of empowerment, reinforcing the idea that individuals are part of a larger narrative that extends beyond their immediate lives. By acknowledging the sacrifices and achievements of their forebears, modern practitioners can cultivate a sense of gratitude and responsibility towards maintaining their ancestral legacy.

The impact of Viking history on the spiritual practices of contemporary Asatru cannot be overstated. The Viking Age was characterized by a strong emphasis on community and kinship, where the bonds formed through bloodlines were paramount. This historical context continues to resonate today, as Asatru communities often prioritize familial ties and shared ancestry in their gatherings and rituals. Such connections not only enhance communal bonds but also create a rich tapestry of shared experiences and values that are celebrated and honored through various rites.

In conclusion, the importance of ancestors in Norse belief systems is a multifaceted concept that bridges the ancient and the modern. Asatru practitioners today draw from the deep well of ancestral wisdom to guide their spiritual paths. This connection to the past fosters a sense of continuity, communal identity, and personal responsibility, reinforcing the idea that individuals are part of a living tradition. As the Asatru revival continues to flourish, the reverence for ancestors remains a vital aspect, ensuring that the teachings and legacies of those who came before are not only remembered but actively integrated into the spiritual lives of contemporary practitioners.

## Modern Practices of Ancestor Veneration

Modern practices of ancestor veneration within Asatru reflect a deep-rooted tradition that emphasizes the importance of familial connections and reverence for those who have come before. In contemporary Asatru communities, ancestor veneration often takes the form of rituals that honor both known and unknown ancestors, integrating practices from historical Norse paganism with modern interpretations. These rituals may include offerings of food, drink, or personal tokens at altars or gravesites, serving as a tangible connection to the past and a way to express gratitude and respect for the sacrifices made by previous generations.

In many Asatru traditions, the concept of "veneration" goes beyond mere remembrance; it is viewed as an active engagement with the ancestral spirits. This engagement is often facilitated through the use of ancestral altars, where practitioners place photographs, heirlooms, and other items that symbolize their lineage. Celebratory gatherings, such as sumbels, are commonly held to honor ancestors, where participants raise their cups in toasts, recount stories, and share memories, creating a communal space for recognizing the impact of ancestors on their lives. This practice not only strengthens individual identity but also fosters a sense of belonging within the larger community.

The historical influence of Norse mythology plays a significant role in shaping modern ancestor veneration practices. Myths and sagas often highlight the importance of ancestry, with tales of gods and heroes emphasizing the value of lineage and heritage. As practitioners draw upon these narratives, they find inspiration in the relationships between gods and their ancestors, reflecting a broader understanding of how ancestral connections shape personal and communal identities. This intertwining of mythology and personal history enriches the spiritual lives of modern Asatru practitioners, reinforcing the idea that the past is ever-present in their lives.

Reconstructionist approaches to Norse paganism also inform how ancestor veneration is practiced today. Many Asatru groups strive to authentically recreate ancient rituals while adapting them to the contemporary context. This often includes developing new customs that resonate with modern values, such as inclusivity and environmental consciousness, while still honoring traditional beliefs about the importance of ancestors. By blending historical accuracy with modern sensibilities, practitioners create a living tradition that respects its roots while remaining relevant to contemporary life.

In the context of contemporary Asatru, ancestor worship serves not only as a means of spiritual connection but also as a catalyst for personal growth and ethical living. By acknowledging the contributions and struggles of their ancestors, practitioners are encouraged to reflect on their own lives and choices, fostering a sense of responsibility to honor their legacy through actions that reflect their values. This practice of ancestor veneration thus becomes a powerful tool for self-discovery and community cohesion, reinforcing the notion that individuals are part of a larger tapestry woven through time, linking them to both their past and future.

## Connections Between Ancestors and Identity

The relationship between ancestors and identity is a cornerstone of Asatru, deeply rooted in Norse paganism. This connection fosters a sense of belonging that extends beyond the individual, linking practitioners to their forebears and the cultural heritage of the Norse people. In contemporary Asatru, the veneration of ancestors serves as a bridge to the past, allowing individuals to explore their heritage while shaping their personal and communal identities. This practice not only honors the memory of those who came before but also reinforces the values and beliefs that have been passed down through generations, creating a rich tapestry of spiritual and cultural continuity.

Ancestor worship in Norse paganism traditionally involved honoring those who have shaped one's lineage, emphasizing the importance of familial ties and the wisdom inherited from previous generations. Rituals often included offerings, prayers, and storytelling, which served to reinforce the bonds between the living and the dead. In modern Asatru, these practices have evolved but remain central to the faith, with many practitioners incorporating ancestor altars and seasonal celebrations such as Disablót to honor their forebears. These rituals not only acknowledge the contributions of ancestors but also invite their guidance and protection, weaving their presence into the fabric of contemporary spiritual life.

The influence of Viking history cannot be understated in shaping modern Norse spirituality. The Viking Age, characterized by exploration and expansion, forged connections between diverse cultures and created a legacy that continues to resonate today. This history informs the values of courage, honor, and resilience, which are often celebrated within Asatru. Contemporary practitioners draw inspiration from the tales of Viking exploits, finding in them a sense of identity that transcends time. This historical consciousness fosters a collective identity among Asatru practitioners, linking them to a shared narrative that celebrates their Norse ancestry while adapting to the complexities of modern life.

The role of gender in Asatru also reflects the connections between ancestors and identity, as practitioners often seek to redefine traditional roles within the context of their spiritual beliefs. The reverence for female deities, such as Freyja and Frigg, highlights the importance of the feminine divine in Norse mythology. Modern Asatru communities actively engage in discussions around gender roles, embracing a more inclusive approach that honors both masculine and feminine energies. This evolution not only strengthens the identity of practitioners but also aligns with broader movements for gender equality, allowing for a more holistic interpretation of spiritual heritage.

Environmentalism and nature worship are increasingly significant in contemporary Asatru, echoing the deep connections Norse ancestors had with the land. Many Asatru practitioners view the natural world as sacred, advocating for a stewardship that honors the environment as part of their spiritual heritage. This perspective fosters a sense of responsibility to protect the earth, reflecting the values of their ancestors who lived in harmony with nature. By integrating these ecological principles into their practice, modern Asatru practitioners reinforce their identity as custodians of the earth, linking their spiritual beliefs with contemporary environmental challenges, thus continuing the legacy of their ancestors in a meaningful way.

# Chapter 7: Viking History and Spirituality

## The Viking Age and Its Spiritual Landscape

The Viking Age, spanning from approximately 793 to 1066 CE, marked a significant period in the development of Norse spirituality. During this era, the spiritual landscape was deeply intertwined with the natural world, and the Norse gods and goddesses played a central role in the daily lives of the people. The pantheon, including figures like Odin, Thor, and Freyja, not only represented various aspects of life and nature but also embodied the values and ideals of Viking society. This connection to the divine was not merely theoretical; it manifested in rituals, sacrifices, and communal celebrations that honored these deities and sought their favor in both personal and communal endeavors.

The beliefs and practices of the Viking Age have left a lasting imprint on modern Asatru, a contemporary revival of Norse paganism. The emphasis on lore, sagas, and historical texts serves as a foundation for modern practitioners who seek to reconnect with their ancestral heritage. Asatru practitioners often draw upon the Eddas and Sagas to inform their rituals and understanding of the cosmos, creating a spiritual framework that honors the past while addressing contemporary values and concerns. This historical influence is crucial, as it provides a sense of continuity and legitimacy to the practices embraced by modern followers.

Reconstructionist approaches, which focus on reviving ancient practices as authentically as possible, play a vital role in the Asatru revival. These approaches emphasize the importance of historical accuracy and cultural context in shaping contemporary rituals. Practitioners may engage in rites that reflect the seasonal cycles, such as Yule and Midsummer, mirroring the celebrations of their Viking ancestors. By carefully studying archaeological findings, historical texts, and folklore, modern Asatru practitioners strive to create a spiritual practice that resonates with the ancient ways while being relevant to today's world.

Rituals and celebrations within contemporary Asatru often emphasize community, nature, and personal connection to the divine. These gatherings serve not only as spiritual observances but also as opportunities for social bonding and cultural expression. Ancestor worship is a key component, wherein practitioners honor their forebears, recognizing the influence of ancestry on personal identity and spiritual lineage. This focus on the past fosters a sense of belonging and continuity, aligning modern practitioners with the communal values that characterized Viking society.

The Viking Age's impact on modern Norse spirituality extends beyond rituals and celebrations. Gender roles and the feminine divine are increasingly recognized within Asatru, reflecting a broader cultural shift toward inclusivity. The veneration of goddesses such as Freyja and Skadi highlights the importance of feminine power and wisdom in spiritual practice. Additionally, contemporary Asatru often incorporates environmentalism and nature worship, echoing the Vikings' deep respect for the land and its cycles. This modern interpretation not only honors the ancestral connection to nature but also addresses current ecological concerns, demonstrating how the spiritual landscape of the Viking Age continues to evolve and resonate in today's world.

## Historical Figures and Their Influence

The revival of Asatru, a modern manifestation of Norse paganism, has deep roots intertwined with historical figures who significantly shaped its narrative. Figures such as Snorri Sturluson, the 13th-century Icelandic historian, played a pivotal role in preserving Norse myths and legends through his work, the Prose Edda. His writings provided a foundational text for understanding the pantheon of Norse gods, the creation myths, and the heroic sagas that continue to inspire contemporary practitioners. Sturluson's influence is particularly evident in how these ancient tales are interpreted and integrated into modern rituals and celebrations, showcasing the resilience of Norse spirituality through the ages.

Another critical figure is the 19th-century poet and philosopher, W. B. Yeats, who, although not directly a Norse pagan, was influenced by the romantic revival of folklore and mythology during his time. Yeats' work inspired a broader interest in ancient traditions, including Norse mythology, leading to a resurgence of interest in Asatru during the early 20th century. His poetic expressions of the mystical and the divine resonate with modern practitioners who seek to connect with the archetypal elements of Norse spirituality, emphasizing how historical figures can shape the beliefs and practices of future generations.

The role of scholars and activists in the 20th century further propelled the Asatru revival. Figures such as Stephen McNallen, founder of the Asatru Folk Assembly, emphasized the importance of cultural identity and ancestral connections in contemporary practice. His advocacy for a reconstructionist approach to Norse paganism has influenced many modern practitioners to explore their heritage, incorporating traditional rituals and values into their spiritual lives. This emphasis on ancestry and cultural continuity reflects a significant aspect of Asatru, where the past informs the present, and the practices of historical figures provide a template for modern beliefs.

Moreover, the feminist movements of the late 20th century brought attention to the feminine divine within Norse mythology, reshaping the understanding of gender roles in Asatru. Historical figures like the goddess Freyja, associated with love, fertility, and war, have been reinterpreted to empower women within the faith. This shift highlights how contemporary practitioners are not only reclaiming ancient traditions but also redefining them to align with modern values, fostering a more inclusive and balanced spiritual practice that honors both the masculine and feminine aspects of the divine.

Lastly, the influence of environmentalism on modern Asatru practices can be traced back to historical figures who revered nature as sacred. The Viking Age was marked by a profound respect for the natural world, reflected in their rituals and cosmology. Contemporary Asatru practitioners often draw inspiration from this reverence, integrating ecological awareness into their beliefs and practices. Figures like John Michael Greer, who advocate for a deep connection to the land, echo ancient principles of nature worship, demonstrating how the teachings of historical figures continue to resonate in today's spiritual landscape. This intersection of history and modernity illustrates the enduring legacy of Norse spirituality and its capacity for evolution in a changing world.

# Viking Legacy in Contemporary Asatru

The Viking legacy remains a powerful influence in contemporary Asatru, shaping its practices, beliefs, and community dynamics. Asatru, a modern revival of Norse paganism, draws heavily on the historical traditions of the Vikings, intertwining their mythology, rituals, and values into a modern spiritual framework. This revival has seen a resurgence of interest in Viking history, with individuals seeking to connect with their ancestral roots and the rich tapestry of Norse lore. Through this connection, practitioners of Asatru honor the legacy of their forebears while adapting ancient teachings to fit contemporary contexts.

Historically, Norse mythology serves as the backbone of modern Asatru practices. The tales of gods and goddesses like Odin, Thor, and Freyja provide a rich narrative foundation for contemporary rituals and celebrations. Many Asatru practitioners engage in storytelling, drawing from the Eddas and sagas to enrich their understanding of the cosmos and the human experience. This historical influence manifests in various ways, including the incorporation of traditional feasts, seasonal celebrations, and rites of passage that reflect ancient customs while being tailored to suit present-day beliefs and lifestyles.

Reconstructionist approaches to Norse paganism play a critical role in shaping contemporary Asatru. Practitioners often seek to understand the historical context of their faith, striving to reconstruct practices that align with the values and rituals of the Viking Age. This includes not only celebrating the ancient gods but also reviving specific ceremonies such as blóts (sacrificial offerings) and sumbels (ritual toasts). The emphasis on authenticity in these practices underscores a broader commitment to honoring the past while engaging with the present, ensuring that the spiritual lineage remains connected to its roots.

Rituals and celebrations within contemporary Asatru reflect this commitment, as they are designed to foster community and personal connection with the divine. Seasonal festivals, such as Yule and Midsummer, are celebrated with traditional food, songs, and communal gatherings, echoing the Viking traditions of honoring the cycles of nature and the turning of the seasons. These events not only serve as spiritual observances but also as opportunities for community building, allowing practitioners to share their experiences and strengthen their bonds with one another in a shared spiritual journey.

The legacy of the Vikings also influences contemporary Asatru in the realms of ancestor worship and environmentalism. Ancestor veneration is a significant aspect of the faith, as practitioners seek to honor their forebears and acknowledge their contributions to the present. This practice reinforces a sense of identity and belonging, linking individuals to a broader historical narrative. Additionally, modern Asatru often emphasizes a deep respect for nature, reflecting the Vikings' understanding of their environment. This environmental ethos promotes a harmonious relationship with the earth, encouraging sustainable practices and a reverence for the natural world that resonates with contemporary concerns about ecological stewardship.

# Chapter 8: Gender Roles and the Feminine Divine

## Exploration of Gender in Norse Mythology

In Norse mythology, gender roles are intricately woven into the fabric of the narratives, influencing how deities and figures interact with one another and with the human realm. The pantheon features a diverse range of characters, from the powerful and often aggressive male gods like Odin and Thor to formidable female figures such as Freyja and Frigg. These goddesses are not mere consorts or secondary characters; they possess agency, wielding influence over fate, love, and war. This duality presents a complex understanding of gender, challenging modern perceptions of masculinity and femininity.

The portrayal of gender in Norse mythology also reflects the societal structures of the Viking Age. While men were predominantly seen as warriors and providers, women held significant roles that extended beyond the domestic sphere. Historical sources indicate that women could own property, manage households, and even participate in religious rites. Figures such as the Valkyries, who chose the slain in battle, demonstrate the intersection of femininity and power. Their existence highlights a cultural reverence for female strength, suggesting that Norse society recognized a balance between masculine and feminine ideals.

In contemporary Asatru practices, these historical depictions inform the reconstructionist approaches to gender roles within the faith. Many modern practitioners seek to reclaim and reinterpret these ancient narratives, emphasizing the importance of both male and female divine figures. Rituals often incorporate both masculine and feminine energies, encouraging a holistic understanding of spirituality that transcends binary gender norms. This approach fosters inclusivity, allowing individuals to explore their identities within the framework of Norse paganism.

Moreover, the concept of the feminine divine is vital in contemporary Asatru. Goddesses like Freyja symbolize not only love and fertility but also war and death, showcasing the multifaceted nature of femininity. Modern Asatru adherents often celebrate these attributes in their rituals, honoring the balance of both genders in their spiritual practice. This recognition of the divine feminine encourages practitioners to embrace a more comprehensive understanding of their own identities, promoting empowerment through the acknowledgment of strength in vulnerability.

As the Asatru revival continues to grow, the exploration of gender within Norse mythology plays a crucial role in shaping modern beliefs and practices. By examining the historical narratives and their implications for contemporary spirituality, practitioners can forge a path that honors the complexity of gender in both the ancient and modern contexts. This exploration not only enriches individual spiritual journeys but also contributes to a broader dialogue about gender roles in society today, reflecting the enduring influence of Norse mythology on contemporary life.

# The Role of Women in Asatru Practices

The role of women in Asatru practices is a multifaceted subject that reflects historical traditions, contemporary reinterpretations, and the ongoing evolution of gender roles within the faith. Historically, Norse society placed women in significant positions, particularly as practitioners of seidr, a form of magic associated with fate and prophecy. Women, such as the völva or seeress, held respected roles in their communities, often leading rituals and serving as intermediaries between the gods and people. This historical precedent establishes a foundation for women's active participation in modern Asatru, where their contributions are increasingly recognized and celebrated.

In contemporary Asatru, women are reclaiming and redefining their roles, often emphasizing equality and collaboration within the faith. Many Asatru groups now prioritize inclusivity, seeking to dismantle traditional gender stereotypes that may have limited women's participation in spiritual practices. Women engage in rituals, celebrations, and leadership positions, highlighting their importance not only as participants but also as leaders and decision-makers. This shift reflects a broader societal movement towards gender equality and the recognition of diverse expressions of spirituality.

Rituals and celebrations in modern Asatru often embrace the feminine divine, drawing inspiration from Norse mythology. Goddesses such as Freyja and Frigg are celebrated for their strength, wisdom, and nurturing qualities, offering diverse models of femininity. These figures inspire women in Asatru to connect with their own identities and roles within the community. Through rituals that honor these goddesses, practitioners create a space for women's experiences and perspectives to be valued, enriching the spiritual tapestry of Asatru.

Additionally, the practice of ancestor worship in Asatru underscores the significance of maternal lineage and the role of women in familial and ancestral connections. Women are often seen as the bearers of tradition, passing down knowledge, values, and spiritual practices through generations. This emphasis on ancestry allows for a deeper appreciation of women's contributions to cultural heritage, reinforcing the idea that their roles extend beyond the present to shape the future of the faith. Ancestor veneration in Asatru provides a platform for honoring female ancestors alongside male figures, fostering a holistic understanding of lineage.

As Asatru continues to evolve, the recognition of women's roles within the tradition is essential for its growth and relevance. The integration of feminist perspectives within the faith encourages a more inclusive understanding of spirituality, where both men and women can explore their identities and experiences. This ongoing dialogue about gender roles not only honors the historical significance of women in Norse culture but also paves the way for a modern Asatru that embraces diversity and equality, ensuring that all voices are heard and celebrated.

## Feminine Deities and Their Modern Interpretations

Feminine deities in Norse mythology, such as Freyja, Frigg, and Skadi, hold significant roles that reflect the complexity of gender dynamics in ancient Norse society. Freyja, for instance, is not only a goddess of love and beauty but also of war and death, embodying the duality of femininity. Frigg, the wife of Odin, represents wisdom and foresight, often associated with domesticity yet wielding considerable power in her own right. Skadi, the goddess of winter and hunting, illustrates the strength and independence attributed to women in the Norse pantheon. These figures challenge traditional gender roles, emphasizing a multifaceted understanding of femininity that resonates with contemporary discussions on gender identity and empowerment.

In modern interpretations of Asatru, these feminine deities are often reimagined to align with current values of gender equality and empowerment. Practitioners may invoke Freyja not just as a goddess of romantic love but as a symbol of personal strength and autonomy in their own lives. Rituals celebrating these deities can provide a space for women to explore their identities and assert their power, creating a bridge between ancient beliefs and contemporary feminist movements. By celebrating the attributes of these goddesses, modern practitioners can reclaim narratives that highlight female strength and resilience, fostering a deeper connection to their spiritual roots.

Furthermore, the role of feminine deities in Asatru is increasingly embraced in the context of communal rituals and celebrations. Festivals dedicated to specific goddesses, such as Freyja's feast, encourage gatherings that honor the feminine divine while promoting community bonding. These events often serve as platforms for discussing gender roles within Asatru and broader societal contexts, allowing participants to share personal experiences and insights. The communal aspect of these rituals reinforces the importance of collective identity, where the strength of feminine deities is celebrated alongside the value of sisterhood and solidarity among practitioners.

The reconstructionist approaches to Norse paganism also emphasize the need to interpret the feminine divine in ways that reflect both historical accuracy and contemporary relevance. Scholars and practitioners engage in critical discussions about the portrayal of female deities, examining ancient texts and archaeological findings to understand their original significance. This scholarly work is essential in ensuring that modern practices do not overlook the nuances of these figures, allowing for a more authentic and respectful integration of feminine deities into contemporary Asatru. By grounding their practices in historical context while adapting to modern sensibilities, practitioners can honor the legacy of these goddesses while making them relevant today.

In the broader context of Norse spirituality, the exploration of feminine deities facilitates discussions about gender roles and the balance of power within the Asatru community. As the movement grows, there is a conscious effort to ensure that both masculine and feminine energies are honored equally. This evolution reflects a larger cultural shift towards inclusivity and respect for diverse expressions of identity. By recognizing and revering the feminine divine, modern Asatru practitioners can foster a spiritual environment that values equality and celebrates the richness of both male and female contributions to their beliefs and practices.

# Chapter 9: Environmentalism and Nature Worship

## Nature as a Sacred Element

Nature holds a sacred place in the hearts of those who practice Asatru, reflecting a deep reverence for the natural world that is intrinsic to Norse paganism. This connection to nature is not merely a cultural relic; it is a vital aspect of the faith that has evolved over time. In ancient Norse society, nature was seen as infused with the divine, with every mountain, river, and tree possessing its own spirit or essence. This worldview continues to resonate within modern Asatru practices, where the natural environment is honored as a manifestation of the sacred. The landscapes of Scandinavia, filled with forests, fjords, and rugged mountains, serve as reminders of this profound relationship, inspiring practitioners to engage with the land as a vital aspect of their spiritual journey.

Asatru practitioners today often seek to rekindle this bond with nature through rituals and celebrations that honor the cycles of the earth. Seasonal festivals, such as Yule and Midsummer, are rooted in ancient traditions that recognize the changing seasons and their significance in the cycle of life. These celebrations often involve communal gatherings in natural settings, where participants may share food, chant, and perform rituals that express gratitude for the bounty of the earth. Such practices not only foster a sense of community but also encourage individuals to reflect on their place within the larger tapestry of existence, emphasizing the interconnectedness of all living things.

The reverence for nature within Asatru is also intertwined with a strong commitment to environmentalism. Many modern practitioners view the degradation of the earth as a spiritual crisis, calling upon the teachings of their ancestors to advocate for sustainable practices. This eco-conscious perspective is a direct response to contemporary challenges, emphasizing the need to protect the land and its resources for future generations. The notion of "Earth as sacred" is now a rallying point for many in the Asatru community, as they strive to align their spiritual beliefs with action that honors the planet. This modern interpretation reflects an understanding that caring for nature is inherently a part of the Asatru path, echoing the ancient Norse understanding of the earth's sacredness.

In addition to environmentalism, nature worship in Asatru often includes ancestor veneration, linking the past to the present in a meaningful way. Ancestors are considered integral to the practice, with many rituals acknowledging their presence and influence in the lives of the living. By honoring the spirits of those who came before, practitioners reaffirm their connection to the land and its history. This act of remembrance often takes place outdoors, where the natural world serves as a backdrop for honoring lineage and heritage. Through these practices, individuals not only pay homage to their ancestors but also cultivate a deeper appreciation for the landscape that shaped their forebears' lives.

Ultimately, nature as a sacred element in Asatru encapsulates a holistic view of spirituality that transcends the boundaries of time and culture. It invites practitioners to engage with the world around them in a way that is mindful, respectful, and rooted in ancient wisdom. As modern individuals navigate the complexities of contemporary life, the lessons drawn from Norse paganism offer a pathway to reconnect with the earth and its rhythms. This journey toward understanding the sacredness of nature is not just a revival of past practices; it is an essential aspect of living in harmony with the world, fostering a sense of stewardship that resonates deeply in today's society.

## Contemporary Environmental Practices

Contemporary environmental practices within the Asatru community reflect a deep-rooted connection to nature that is integral to the faith's principles. Asatru, with its historical foundations in Norse paganism, emphasizes the importance of the natural world, viewing it not merely as a backdrop for human activities but as a living entity deserving respect and care. This perspective is influenced by ancient beliefs that recognized the interconnectedness of all beings, prompting modern practitioners to adopt sustainable practices that honor the earth. Initiatives such as community clean-ups, tree planting, and wildlife conservation efforts are becoming increasingly common among Asatru groups, showcasing a commitment to preserving the environment for future generations.

The revival of Norse mythology in contemporary Asatru also inspires a unique approach to environmental stewardship. Many practitioners draw parallels between the myths and the importance of balance within nature. For instance, the myth of Yggdrasil, the World Tree, symbolizes the interconnectedness of all life. This mythical framework encourages adherents to reflect on their actions and their impact on the environment, motivating them to engage in eco-friendly practices. The emphasis on living in harmony with nature is often echoed in rituals that celebrate seasonal changes, reinforcing the idea that humans are part of a larger ecological system.

Rituals and celebrations within contemporary Asatru often incorporate themes of environmental awareness. Festivals such as Midsummer and Winter Solstice not only honor the cycles of nature but also serve as occasions for practitioners to express gratitude for the earth's bounty and to recommit to protecting it. During these celebrations, rituals may include offerings to the land and invocations of spirits associated with nature, reinforcing the belief that the natural world is imbued with spiritual significance. This blend of reverence and action fosters a culture where environmentalism is seen as a sacred duty.

The role of ancestor worship in modern Asatru also intersects with contemporary environmental practices. Many adherents believe that honoring their ancestors involves caring for the land they inhabited and ensuring its health for future generations. This connection to lineage and land fosters a sense of responsibility, encouraging practitioners to engage in sustainable living and to pass down these values to younger generations. As the Asatru community grows, there is an increasing awareness of how ancestral teachings can guide modern efforts to combat environmental challenges.

In conclusion, contemporary environmental practices within the Asatru faith demonstrate a vibrant synthesis of ancient beliefs and modern ecological consciousness. By embracing their historical roots while actively engaging with pressing environmental issues, practitioners of Asatru are forging a path that honors both the past and the future. This commitment to sustainability not only reinforces the spiritual aspects of their faith but also positions the Asatru community as a proactive force in the global movement toward ecological preservation. Through rituals, celebrations, and a deep-seated respect for the earth, Asatru adherents are contributing to a broader narrative of environmentalism that resonates with both their heritage and contemporary values.

## The Connection Between Asatru and Nature Conservation

The connection between Asatru and nature conservation is deeply rooted in the principles of the ancient Norse worldview, which held a profound respect for the natural world. Asatru, as a modern revival of Norse paganism, draws from historical beliefs that emphasize the interconnectedness of all life and the sacredness of the earth. This reverence is reflected in the worship of deities associated with nature, such as Freyja, who embodies fertility and the bounty of the land, and Njord, the god of the sea and winds. By honoring these deities, practitioners of Asatru acknowledge their dependence on nature and its cycles, fostering a sense of responsibility towards environmental stewardship.

In contemporary Asatru practices, rituals and celebrations often include elements that honor the changing seasons, agricultural cycles, and the natural elements. Events like Blóts (sacrificial offerings) and Sumbels (ritual toasts) are commonly held to celebrate seasonal transitions, such as the summer solstice or winter solstice, which align with nature's rhythms. These gatherings serve not only as spiritual observances but also as opportunities to engage with the community in discussions about sustainable practices and conservation efforts. By embedding environmental consciousness into their rituals, Asatru followers are actively participating in the modern movement towards ecological responsibility.

Reconstructionist approaches to Norse paganism further emphasize the significance of nature conservation within Asatru. Many practitioners strive to align their beliefs and practices with historical traditions, which inherently recognize the importance of the environment. This includes understanding Norse mythology as a source of wisdom that encourages respect for the land and its resources. By studying ancient texts and archaeological findings, modern practitioners can glean insights into how their ancestors interacted with the environment, leading to a resurgence of interest in sustainable living practices that mirror those of the past.

The role of ancestor worship in Asatru also plays a crucial part in the connection to nature conservation. Ancestors are often viewed as guides who have a vested interest in the well-being of their descendants and the land they inhabit. This sense of lineage fosters a commitment to preserving the natural world, as practitioners consider the impact of their actions on future generations. By honoring their ancestors through remembrance and rituals, Asatru followers are reminded of their responsibility to protect the earth, thereby linking personal heritage with broader environmental concerns.

Ultimately, the modern Asatru revival reflects a holistic approach to spirituality that intertwines reverence for nature with a commitment to conservation. As practitioners draw from the rich tapestry of Norse mythology and historical practices, they cultivate a contemporary faith that addresses pressing environmental issues. This not only enriches their spiritual lives but also empowers them to take actionable steps towards preserving the planet for future generations, creating a living tradition that honors both the past and the earth itself.

# Chapter 10: Cross-Cultural Comparisons

## Asatru and Other Pagan Traditions

Asatru, a modern revival of ancient Norse paganism, shares many similarities and differences with other pagan traditions, offering a unique perspective on spirituality that resonates with contemporary seekers. At its core, Asatru emphasizes a deep connection to nature, honoring the gods and goddesses of the Norse pantheon, and fostering a sense of community among practitioners. This focus on the natural world aligns with other pagan paths, such as Wicca and Druidry, which also prioritize the cycles of nature and the reverence of deities associated with the earth, water, and sky. Such shared themes create a tapestry of beliefs that highlight the diverse expressions of pagan spirituality.

Historically, Norse mythology has influenced various pagan traditions by introducing archetypes and motifs that transcend cultural boundaries. For instance, the concept of the Great Mother, found in many pagan faiths, can be traced back to figures like Frigg and Freyja in Norse lore. Moreover, the heroic sagas and tales of gods and giants serve as moral and ethical guides, much like the stories found in other spiritual traditions. The interplay of myth and history in Norse paganism enriches the modern Asatru practice, allowing it to draw from a wellspring of ancient wisdom while engaging with contemporary issues.

Reconstructionist approaches to Norse paganism play a significant role in shaping modern Asatru. Practitioners strive to revive and adapt ancient customs, rituals, and beliefs in a way that honors historical accuracy while meeting the needs of today's spiritual seekers. This often involves researching archaeological findings, historical texts, and folklore to create authentic practices. In contrast to eclectic pagan traditions that may borrow freely from various sources, Asatru emphasizes a commitment to its Norse roots, ensuring that rituals and celebrations reflect the rich heritage of the Viking Age.

Rituals and celebrations within contemporary Asatru are deeply rooted in the cycles of nature, reflecting both the agricultural calendar and the spiritual significance of seasonal changes. Festivals such as Yule, Ostara, and Midsummer echo the celebrations found in other pagan traditions, with each event serving as an opportunity for community bonding, honoring the gods, and celebrating the cycles of life and death. Ancestor worship, a key element of Norse paganism, also plays a critical role in these rituals. By honoring their forebears, practitioners foster a sense of continuity and connection that enhances their spiritual journey.

Asatru's emphasis on the feminine divine and gender roles offers a progressive perspective within the context of modern spirituality. While traditional Norse society often reflected patriarchal structures, contemporary Asatru embraces a more egalitarian view, recognizing the importance of female deities and their influence in both myth and practice. This shift parallels movements within other pagan traditions that seek to empower women and promote gender equality. Additionally, the growing focus on environmentalism and nature worship within Asatru reflects broader trends in modern paganism, emphasizing stewardship of the earth and a deep respect for the natural world, thus creating a bridge between ancient beliefs and contemporary values.

## Similarities and Differences in Beliefs

In exploring the similarities and differences in beliefs between historical Norse paganism and contemporary Asatru, it is essential to recognize that both traditions share a deep reverence for nature and the cosmos. Historical Norse pagans celebrated the cycles of the seasons and the natural world, which were intrinsic to their understanding of life and spirituality. This connection to nature remains a cornerstone of modern Asatru, where practitioners often engage in rituals that honor the earth, the elements, and the changing seasons. Both traditions emphasize the importance of community and familial ties, as seen in the way both honor their ancestors and the communal aspects of their celebrations.

Despite these shared values, significant differences exist in the interpretation and practice of these beliefs. Historical Norse paganism was heavily influenced by the cultural and social dynamics of the Viking Age, including the hierarchical structures of society and the warrior ethos. In contrast, contemporary Asatru often incorporates egalitarian principles and a more individualistic approach to spirituality. This shift reflects broader societal changes and a desire for inclusivity and personal expression within the modern practice, allowing for diverse interpretations of deities and rituals that may not have existed in the strictures of the past.

Rituals and celebrations also showcase both similarities and differences. In historical Norse paganism, rituals were often communal, tied to agricultural cycles, and involved sacrifices to gods and spirits. These were performed with specific intent and in accordance with established traditions. Modern Asatru, while still valuing communal rituals such as blóts and sumbels, often emphasizes personal connection and intention. Practitioners may adapt traditional rituals to fit their personal beliefs and circumstances, leading to a more fluid interpretation of what it means to honor the divine and celebrate the cycles of life.

The role of ancestor worship serves as another point of convergence and divergence. In ancient Norse culture, honoring ancestors was crucial for maintaining familial bonds and ensuring the well-being of the household. This practice continues in contemporary Asatru, where many practitioners seek to forge connections with their forebears, often incorporating ancestor veneration into their rituals. However, modern interpretations can vary widely, with some practitioners focusing more on personal spiritual growth and less on the specific customs that defined historical practices, thus reshaping the relationship with ancestors in a contemporary context.

Lastly, the evolution of Norse deities within contemporary spiritual practices reflects both continuity and change. Historical beliefs centered around a pantheon of gods and goddesses, each embodying specific aspects of life and nature. In modern Asatru, while these deities are still revered, their interpretations may be more symbolic or metaphorical, representing ideals such as strength, wisdom, or fertility rather than being seen purely as historical figures. This evolution allows practitioners to engage with the divine in a way that resonates with their personal experiences and contemporary values, reflecting a broader trend in modern spirituality where ancient beliefs are recontextualized to fit current understandings of the world and the self.

## Learning from Other Spiritual Paths

Learning from other spiritual paths can enrich the practice of Asatru and deepen the understanding of its principles. Many practitioners of Asatru find value in exploring various religious and spiritual traditions, drawing parallels and contrasts that can illuminate their own beliefs. This cross-pollination of ideas encourages a broader perspective, allowing practitioners to appreciate the unique aspects of Norse paganism while recognizing the common threads that weave through human spirituality. By examining other paths, Asatru practitioners can better articulate their own beliefs and practices, enhancing their connection to their spiritual heritage.

One significant area of exploration is the emphasis on nature and the environment found in various spiritual traditions. Many indigenous and pagan faiths honor the Earth as sacred, emphasizing a deep reverence for the natural world. This perspective resonates strongly with Asatru, which traditionally celebrates the cycles of nature and the interconnectedness of all living beings. By studying these other traditions, Asatru practitioners can discover practices that promote environmental stewardship and sustainability, aligning their spiritual beliefs with the urgent need for ecological awareness in contemporary society.

Another fruitful avenue for learning lies in the study of ancestor worship. Various cultures across the globe place significant importance on honoring their forebears, recognizing their influence on the present. In Asatru, ancestor veneration is a cornerstone, with rituals aimed at connecting with those who came before. By examining how other spiritual paths incorporate ancestor worship, Asatru practitioners can gain new insights into their rituals, perhaps adopting elements that resonate with their own practices. This can lead to a more profound and personal experience of honoring ancestry, enriching the spiritual journey.

Gender roles and the feminine divine present another area for thoughtful exploration. Asatru has traditionally been male-dominated, but many modern practitioners are actively seeking to incorporate a more balanced view of gender and femininity. By learning from feminist spiritual movements and other pagan traditions that celebrate the divine feminine, Asatru practitioners can expand their understanding of gender dynamics within their faith. This can lead to a more inclusive approach that honors both masculine and feminine energies, fostering a holistic understanding of divinity in the Norse spiritual framework.

Lastly, the use of symbols and sacred texts, such as runes, invites comparison with other spiritual traditions that employ similar tools for divination and spiritual guidance. Runes hold a special place in Norse spirituality, but many cultures utilize symbolic systems to convey spiritual truths. By studying these parallels, Asatru practitioners can deepen their understanding of runes and their significance, exploring how other systems of symbols can enhance their spiritual practice. This exploration encourages a more profound engagement with the mystical aspects of Asatru, connecting the ancient with the contemporary in a meaningful way.

# Chapter 11: The Use of Runes

## Historical Significance of Runes

Runes, the ancient characters used in Germanic languages, hold a profound historical significance that extends far beyond their function as mere writing systems. Originating in the early centuries of the Common Era, runes were first used by the Germanic tribes of Northern Europe, with the Elder Futhark being the oldest known runic alphabet. These symbols were not only tools for communication but also imbued with spiritual meaning and used in various rituals. The connection between runes and Norse mythology is crucial, as many of the symbols are associated with gods and cosmic principles, reflecting the beliefs and values of the societies that crafted them.

In the context of Norse paganism, runes served multiple purposes, including divination, magical practices, and the marking of important events. The practice of runic divination, known as "rune casting," allowed practitioners to seek guidance from the divine or to understand the mysteries of their existence. Each rune was thought to encapsulate specific energies and meanings, linking the user to the spiritual world. This intersection of language, magic, and spirituality illustrates the deep reverence that ancient Norse cultures had for these symbols, cementing their role in both daily life and sacred practices.

As modern Asatru practitioners look to reconstruct and revitalize their spiritual heritage, the use of runes has experienced a significant revival. Contemporary interpretations often focus on the symbolic and metaphysical aspects of runes, blending traditional meanings with modern insights. This reconstructionist approach emphasizes the importance of understanding the historical context of each rune while adapting their use to fit contemporary spiritual practices. For many, runes serve as a bridge between the past and present, allowing individuals to connect with their ancestors and the rich tapestry of Norse mythology.

Rituals and celebrations in modern Asatru frequently incorporate runes, showcasing their enduring relevance. Whether inscribing runes on altars, invoking their meanings during ceremonies, or using them in personal meditation, practitioners integrate these ancient symbols into their spiritual expressions. This ritualistic use not only honors the traditions of the past but also fosters a sense of community among practitioners, as they collectively engage with the symbols that bind them to their cultural roots. The presence of runes in these celebrations emphasizes the continuity of Norse spirituality, reflecting both historical significance and contemporary relevance.

The role of runes in modern Asatru also intersects with broader themes such as ancestor worship and nature reverence. Runes are often seen as a means of connecting with the wisdom of ancestors, as well as the natural world. This connection underscores a central tenet of Asatru: the belief in the cyclical nature of existence and the importance of honoring the past while living in harmony with the present. As practitioners continue to explore and redefine the meanings of runes, they contribute to a living tradition that respects ancient wisdom while embracing the complexities of modern spiritual life.

## Modern Interpretations and Uses

Modern interpretations and uses of Norse mythology and Asatru reflect a dynamic engagement with the past, allowing adherents to connect with historical traditions while adapting them to contemporary life. One of the most significant aspects of this revival is the emphasis on personal spirituality and individual interpretation. Modern practitioners often draw from ancient texts, archaeological discoveries, and folkloric traditions, creating a rich tapestry of beliefs and practices that resonate with today's societal values. This approach acknowledges the historical context of Norse paganism while allowing flexibility for personal experience and understanding, leading to a diverse array of expressions within the Asatru community.

The historical influence of Norse mythology on modern Asatru practices is evident in the rituals and celebrations that have emerged. Many contemporary observances, such as blóts (sacrificial offerings) and sumbels (toasting ceremonies), are rooted in ancient customs but have been adapted to fit modern sensibilities. Celebrations like Yule, which marks the winter solstice, are infused with both traditional elements and new interpretations that emphasize themes of rebirth and renewal. These practices serve not only to honor the gods and ancestors but also to foster community and connection among practitioners, reinforcing the social bonds that are vital to the Asatru experience.

Reconstructionist approaches to Norse paganism play a crucial role in the Asatru revival, as many adherents strive to accurately reflect ancient beliefs while considering the implications of their practices today. This involves a careful study of historical texts, such as the Poetic and Prose Eddas, as well as archaeological evidence to reconstruct rituals and beliefs. However, the reconstructionist approach is not without its challenges, as practitioners grapple with the incomplete nature of the historical record and the need to interpret ancient practices in a way that is meaningful in a modern context. This tension between authenticity and adaptation is a central theme in the ongoing development of Asatru.

Ancestor worship holds a significant place in both Norse paganism and contemporary Asatru. Reverence for ancestors is seen as a bridge between the past and the present, allowing individuals to honor their lineage and draw strength from their heritage. Rituals often include offerings or remembrances of ancestors, reinforcing the belief that the past is an integral part of one's identity. This practice not only deepens the spiritual connection to one's roots but also encourages a sense of responsibility toward future generations, highlighting the cyclical nature of life and the importance of maintaining cultural continuity.

The impact of Viking history on modern Norse spirituality extends beyond just ritual practices; it influences broader themes such as gender roles and environmentalism. Asatru's recognition of the feminine divine, exemplified in goddesses like Freyja and Frigg, invites a reevaluation of gender dynamics within spiritual practices. Additionally, contemporary Asatru often emphasizes a deep connection to nature, reflecting a growing environmental consciousness among practitioners. This focus on nature worship aligns with broader pagan movements, fostering a sense of stewardship and respect for the earth. As the Asatru revival continues to evolve, it remains a vibrant and multifaceted expression of spirituality that bridges ancient traditions with modern values.

## Runes in Divination and Personal Practice

Runes, the ancient symbols of the Norse and other Germanic peoples, hold a significant place in both historical practices and modern interpretations within the Asatru faith. Traditionally, runes were more than mere letters; they were seen as magical symbols imbued with power and meaning. Each rune carries its own set of associations, often linked to aspects of life, nature, and the cosmos. In the context of divination, runes serve as tools for insight, guidance, and reflection, allowing practitioners to connect with their inner selves and the broader universe. This connection is particularly relevant today as many Asatru practitioners seek to integrate historical practices into their personal spiritual journeys.

In contemporary Asatru, the use of runes in divination often mirrors ancient methods while also adapting to modern sensibilities. Practitioners may create their own rune sets, using materials that resonate with them, such as wood, stone, or clay. When casting runes, individuals typically focus on a specific question or intention, allowing the symbols to reveal insights relevant to their lives. This practice not only fosters a deeper understanding of the self but also encourages a connection to ancestral wisdom, as many Asatru practitioners view their use of runes as a way to honor the past while navigating the complexities of modern life.

The historical context of runes is essential for understanding their modern applications. Runes were used for various purposes beyond divination, including inscribing messages, marking territory, and invoking protection. This multifaceted nature of runes informs how they are utilized today. Many Asatru practitioners engage with runes in rituals or celebrations, integrating them into communal gatherings or personal ceremonies. Such practices not only reinforce individual beliefs but also strengthen the communal bonds within the Asatru community, fostering a shared appreciation for the heritage and significance of these symbols.

The role of ancestor worship in Norse paganism and Asatru further enriches the practice of rune divination. By invoking the guidance of ancestors during rune readings, individuals can deepen their spiritual connection and gain perspectives rooted in their lineage. This ancestral focus aligns with the Asatru belief in the importance of honoring those who came before, creating a rich tapestry of spiritual insight that combines personal experience with historical legacy. The act of consulting runes becomes a means of bridging the past and present, allowing practitioners to forge a path that acknowledges their heritage while addressing contemporary challenges.

As the Asatru revival continues to evolve, the application of runes reflects broader themes within the tradition, including environmentalism, gender roles, and the feminine divine. Modern rune practice often embraces an inclusive approach, recognizing the significance of both masculine and feminine energies in the interpretation of symbols. Additionally, the connection to nature and the environment is reinforced through the materials and settings chosen for rune work. As practitioners engage with runes in their personal and communal practices, they contribute to a dynamic living tradition that honors the past while adapting to the needs and values of modern spirituality.

# Chapter 12: The Evolution of Norse Deities

## Changes in the Understanding of Deities

The evolution of the understanding of deities within the context of Norse paganism and its modern counterpart, Asatru, reflects significant cultural shifts and philosophical developments over time. In ancient Norse belief systems, deities were often perceived as powerful, anthropomorphic figures who governed various aspects of life and nature. This view was deeply intertwined with the natural world, where gods like Odin, Thor, and Freyja were invoked for protection, prosperity, and guidance. Their personalities, relationships, and exploits were chronicled in sagas and poems, providing a rich tapestry of narratives that reinforced their importance in daily life and communal identity.

As the Asatru revival gained momentum in the late 20th century, a re-examination of these deities emerged. Modern practitioners began to distance themselves from the purely mythological representations of the past, seeking to understand the deeper meanings behind these ancient figures. This involved not only a scholarly approach to historical texts but also a personal exploration of how these deities resonate with contemporary spiritual practices. Asatru practitioners often emphasize the values and attributes these gods embody, such as wisdom, courage, and fertility, allowing them to serve as moral exemplars rather than distant, unattainable figures.

Reconstructionist approaches within the Asatru community further highlight this shift in understanding. Scholars and practitioners alike strive to create a practice that is both authentic to historical sources and relevant to modern life. This has led to a more nuanced interpretation of deities, viewing them not just as beings to be worshipped, but as archetypal representations of human experiences. This perspective encourages individuals to engage with the gods on a personal level, fostering relationships that reflect both ancient traditions and modern sensibilities.

Rituals and celebrations in contemporary Asatru also demonstrate how the understanding of deities has transformed. While traditional rites may include offerings and invocations, modern practitioners often adapt these practices to resonate with their current lives and values. Festivals such as Yule and Midsummer are imbued with contemporary significance, emphasizing themes of renewal, community, and connection to the earth. This evolution of ritual highlights the dynamic nature of faith, allowing followers to integrate their understanding of the divine into their everyday experiences.

Lastly, the role of ancestor worship within Asatru underscores a deepened connection to heritage and identity. In ancient Norse culture, ancestors were revered as vital components of one's lineage, embodying the wisdom and strength of the past. Today, many Asatru practitioners honor their ancestors as a way to forge a personal bond with their history while also acknowledging the influence of these figures in their spiritual journeys. This practice not only reinforces the understanding of deities as integral to personal and communal identity but also aligns with a broader trend in modern spirituality, where the past is honored as a guide for the present and future.

## Modern Worship Practices

Modern worship practices within Asatru have evolved significantly, reflecting both a return to ancient traditions and a response to contemporary societal values. As practitioners seek to reconnect with their Norse heritage, they often incorporate elements that resonate with modern sensibilities. This fusion of the old and the new manifests in various ways, including the adaptation of rituals, the inclusion of community-oriented practices, and the emphasis on personal spirituality. Understanding these practices requires an exploration of how historical influences shape current expressions of faith.

At the heart of modern Asatru is a commitment to reconstructionist approaches that aim to ground rituals in historical authenticity while allowing for personal interpretation. Practitioners often study ancient texts, archaeological findings, and ethnographic records to reconstruct the beliefs and practices of their Norse ancestors. This scholarly effort is balanced by an acknowledgment that contemporary practitioners live in a vastly different world, necessitating flexible interpretations of tradition. As such, modern Asatru rituals may blend ancient customs with personal significance, creating a dynamic faith that honors the past while embracing the present.

Rituals and celebrations play a crucial role in modern Asatru, serving as expressions of community, identity, and spirituality. Common observances include seasonal festivals that mirror the agricultural cycles and natural rhythms celebrated by the Norse. Events such as Yule, Ostara, and Midsummer are marked by communal gatherings, feasting, and the recitation of traditional lore. These celebrations foster a sense of belonging and continuity among practitioners, reinforcing the connection to both the gods and the land. Asatru rituals often emphasize the importance of intention, encouraging participants to engage deeply with their spiritual practices, whether through offerings, prayers, or meditative reflection.

Ancestor worship is another significant aspect of contemporary Asatru, rooted in the belief that the spirits of the deceased remain present in the lives of their descendants. This practice draws on the Norse cultural reverence for lineage and the importance of familial ties. Modern practitioners honor their ancestors through memorial rituals, storytelling, and the creation of altars dedicated to those who have passed. This connection to ancestry not only strengthens individual identity but also reinforces community bonds, as shared stories of heritage are recounted and celebrated. Engaging with the wisdom and experiences of ancestors serves as a guiding force, providing insight and support in the lives of practitioners today.

Finally, the impact of Viking history on modern Norse spirituality cannot be overstated. The fascination with Viking culture has inspired a resurgence of interest in Norse mythology, leading to a revival of traditional practices alongside a reevaluation of gender roles and environmental ethics within Asatru. As practitioners navigate their spiritual identities, they often embrace the feminine divine, recognizing the importance of goddesses like Freyja and Frigg in their worship. Additionally, contemporary Asatru is increasingly intertwined with environmentalism, as followers seek to honor the natural world through rituals that celebrate the interconnectedness of all life. This holistic approach reflects a broader trend in modern spirituality, where ancient beliefs are adapted to address pressing contemporary issues, further enriching the tapestry of Asatru today.

## The Role of Deities in Personal Spirituality

The role of deities in personal spirituality within the context of Asatru is multifaceted, reflecting not only the historical narratives of Norse mythology but also the individual experiences of practitioners today. Deities such as Odin, Freyja, and Thor serve as archetypes and symbols through which practitioners connect to their spiritual heritage. Each god or goddess embodies specific traits and powers, providing a framework for followers to explore their own identities and values. This connection goes beyond mere reverence; it invites practitioners to engage in a dynamic relationship with these figures, fostering personal growth and understanding.

In modern Asatru, the understanding of deities has evolved. While historical texts like the Poetic and Prose Edda provide foundational knowledge, contemporary practitioners often reinterpret these figures to align with their own life experiences. This personal interpretation allows individuals to select deities that resonate with their personal journey, creating a spirituality that is both rooted in tradition and adaptable to modern values. For example, Odin's quest for wisdom may inspire followers to pursue knowledge and self-improvement, while Freyja's embodying of love and fertility can guide those exploring relationships and creativity.

Rituals and celebrations in Asatru often center around specific deities, further enhancing their role in personal spirituality. Seasonal festivals such as Yule and Ostara not only commemorate significant events in the mythological calendar but also offer opportunities for practitioners to honor the deities through offerings, prayers, and communal gatherings. These rituals serve to reinforce the connection between the individual and the divine, providing a sense of belonging and community. By participating in these traditional practices, individuals can experience a profound sense of continuity with their ancestors and cultural heritage.

Ancestor worship also plays a crucial role in the spiritual framework of Asatru, often intertwined with the veneration of deities. Practitioners believe that their ancestors can influence their lives and that honoring them brings strength and guidance. This relationship is often expressed in rituals that include not just the deities, but also the spirits of ancestors, creating a holistic spiritual experience. Such practices reflect a deep respect for lineage and heritage, allowing individuals to draw strength from both their familial connections and the divine.

Furthermore, the role of deities in Asatru is not static; it evolves as practitioners incorporate contemporary values and beliefs into their practices. Issues of gender roles and environmentalism, for instance, have prompted many to reassess the roles of female deities and their relevance today. The feminine divine, represented by figures like Freyja and Frigg, is increasingly celebrated and valued in contexts that address modern gender dynamics and challenges. Likewise, the reverence for nature and the environment resonates with the attributes of deities associated with the earth, encouraging a spiritual practice that honors both the ancient and the contemporary. In this way, the role of deities in personal spirituality continues to adapt, reflecting the ongoing journey of Asatru from its historical roots to its modern expressions

# Unlocking the Secrets of Viking Runes: A Comprehensive Guide to Their Meaning and Use

## Chapter 1: Introduction to Viking Runes

### Definition and Overview

Viking runes, a system of writing used by the Norse peoples, hold a significant place in the tapestry of historical linguistics and cultural expression. Originating primarily from the Elder Futhark, the oldest runic alphabet, these symbols served not only as a means of communication but also as a conduit for deeper meanings and spiritual beliefs. The runes themselves are more than mere letters; they represent sounds, concepts, and, in many cases, the very essence of the world around the Vikings. Understanding this complex system requires an exploration into its historical origins, linguistic structure, and the cultural context in which it thrived.

The historical origins of Viking runes can be traced back to the early centuries CE, influenced by various cultures, including the Roman and Germanic tribes. The Elder Futhark, consisting of 24 characters, reflects this blend of influences and was primarily used in Scandinavia. Over time, the runes evolved into different variants, such as the Younger Futhark, as the Vikings spread across Europe and adapted to new environments. This adaptation not only showcases the dynamic nature of the runes but also highlights the interconnectedness of cultures during the Viking Age. Understanding these origins provides critical insights into how the Vikings viewed language and communication.

Each rune carries its own unique meaning, often tied to natural elements, deities, or concepts integral to Norse culture. For instance, the rune "Fehu" symbolizes wealth and prosperity, while "Thurisaz" represents protection and challenge. Learning to interpret these symbols involves not just recognizing their phonetic sounds but also delving into the rich mythology and lore surrounding each character. This interpretative layer adds depth to the understanding of runes, transforming them from simple letters into powerful symbols that resonate with the beliefs and values of the Viking people.

Runes were utilized in various aspects of Viking life, including communication, rituals, and even warfare. They were carved on stones, weapons, and personal items, often serving as talismans for protection or good fortune. Rune casting, a form of divination, allowed individuals to seek guidance from the runes, tapping into their perceived mystical properties. This practice not only reflects the Vikings' spiritual beliefs but also their understanding of fate and the interconnectedness of all things. The use of runes in daily life illustrates their importance beyond mere writing, embedding them deeply within the social and spiritual fabric of Viking society.

In contemporary spirituality, the fascination with Viking runes has seen a resurgence, as many seek to incorporate their meanings into modern practices. From meditation and personal reflection to artistic expression, the application of runes has evolved, bridging ancient wisdom with present-day insights. Additionally, the comparative analysis of runes with other ancient scripts, such as the Greek or Latin alphabets, reveals intriguing parallels and distinctions in how different cultures approached writing and symbolism. As individuals embark on the journey of learning and crafting their own runes, they not only honor the legacy of the Vikings but also unlock the profound secrets that these ancient symbols continue to offer.

## Historical Context

The historical context of Viking runes is deeply intertwined with the broader narrative of the Norse peoples and their interaction with the world around them. Originating from the Germanic tribes in the early centuries CE, runes were not merely a writing system but a complex symbol system rich with cultural significance. The earliest known runic inscriptions date back to approximately the 2nd century CE, highlighting their long-standing presence in Northern Europe. The Elder Futhark, the oldest runic alphabet, consists of 24 characters and was primarily used in the regions that are now Scandinavia and parts of modern-day Germany. Understanding these origins is crucial for grasping both the linguistic and cultural significance of runes within Viking society.

As Viking culture flourished from the late 8th century through the 11th century, so too did the use and interpretation of runes. The Vikings were not only seafarers and warriors but also traders and settlers who engaged in extensive cultural exchanges with other civilizations. This interaction led to the adaptation and evolution of rune usage, as they began to incorporate influences from the Latin alphabet and other writing systems. Runes were often inscribed on stones, weapons, and personal items, serving as markers of ownership, memorials, or expressions of identity. The historical context of runes reflects a dynamic interplay of adaptation and preservation, revealing much about the Viking worldview and their societal values.

The interpretation of individual runes is steeped in both linguistic and esoteric meanings. Each rune carries phonetic value as well as symbolic representations that reflect natural elements, concepts, or deities. For example, the rune "Fehu" symbolizes wealth and abundance, while "Uruz" denotes strength and health. This dual nature of runes as both letters and symbols allowed for layered meanings in communication, whether in everyday use or in ritualistic contexts. The historical understanding of these meanings can provide insight into how the Vikings perceived their world, their beliefs, and the values they held dear, often reflected in their art and storytelling.

In addition to their practical uses, runes held a significant role in Norse mythology and spiritual practices. The mythological associations of runes, such as Odin's discovery of them during his quest for wisdom, imbue them with a sense of sacredness that transcends mere written language. Runes were utilized in divination practices, allowing practitioners to seek guidance from the cosmos. This aspect of rune usage illustrates the Vikings' belief in interconnectedness between the material and spiritual realms, influencing their decisions in both personal and communal spheres. The historical context surrounding these practices sheds light on the spiritual landscape of the Viking Age and its enduring legacy.

Today, the fascination with Viking runes continues, as modern interpretations and applications emerge in various spiritual and artistic contexts. Individuals seeking to connect with ancient wisdom often turn to runes for guidance in personal development and self-reflection. The crafting of runes in contemporary art and literature reflects an ongoing dialogue with history, allowing for creative expressions that resonate with both past and present. By understanding the historical context of Viking runes, we can appreciate their significance not just as artifacts of a bygone era, but as living symbols that continue to inspire and inform our understanding of identity, culture, and spirituality.

# Chapter 2: What Are Viking Runes?

## The Elder Futhark

The Elder Futhark stands as the oldest known runic alphabet, consisting of 24 characters known as runes. This script, which dates back to the 2nd to 8th centuries, derives its name from the first six runes: F, U, Þ, A, R, and K. The term "Futhark" itself is a combination of these initial letters. The Elder Futhark is believed to have been used by the Germanic tribes of Northern Europe, including the early Vikings, as a means of communication, trade, and ritualistic expression. Understanding the structure and phonetics of this ancient writing system lays the foundation for exploring its applications and meanings across various aspects of Viking culture.

Historically, the Elder Futhark likely evolved from earlier alphabets, possibly influenced by the Etruscan or Latin scripts. The runes were not merely letters but held symbolic significance, often associated with specific concepts and deities. Each rune corresponds to a sound but also carries its own mythology and meaning, reflecting the interconnectedness of language and culture in Norse society. Archaeological findings, such as inscriptions on stones and artifacts, provide insight into how these runes were used in rituals, memorials, and even in everyday life, showcasing their importance in both the mundane and the sacred.

Interpreting individual runes requires an understanding of their meanings, which can vary depending on context. For instance, the rune "Þurisaz" symbolizes the thorn or giant and can represent protection or conflict. In contrast, "Wunjo" signifies joy and harmony. This duality of meaning enriches the practice of reading runes, allowing for a nuanced interpretation that can be applied in various situations, from personal reflection to divination. The interplay of these meanings is crucial for practitioners who seek to use runes for guidance or insight, particularly in a spiritual or personal development context.

Rune casting and divination practices have long been a part of the Viking tradition, where runes served as tools for seeking wisdom from the divine. Techniques such as casting runes onto a cloth or drawing them from a bag allow for a dynamic interaction with the symbols. Each cast reveals messages that resonate with the individual, often interpreted through the lens of intuition and personal experience. This practice continues to thrive in modern spirituality, as individuals seek connections to their ancestry and a deeper understanding of their lives through the ancient wisdom embedded in these symbols.

In contemporary times, the Elder Futhark has transcended its historical roots, finding applications in art, literature, and personal expression. Modern artists and writers draw inspiration from the runes, weaving them into their work to evoke a sense of mystery and connection to the past. Moreover, the study of runes has become a popular avenue for exploring identity and heritage, with many individuals learning to read and use them as a form of self-expression and spiritual exploration. By recognizing the rich tapestry of meanings and uses associated with the Elder Futhark, we can appreciate its enduring legacy and relevance in today's world.

## The Younger Futhark

The Younger Futhark represents a refined version of the earlier Elder Futhark, consisting of only 16 runes. It emerged around the 9th century and reflects the cultural and linguistic shifts occurring in Scandinavia during the Viking Age. The reduction in the number of runes was likely driven by the evolving Old Norse language, which required a more streamlined representation. Each rune in the Younger Futhark carries significant phonetic value, aligning closely with the sounds in Old Norse. Understanding this transition is crucial for those interested in the broader context of Viking runes and their historical progression.

Historically, the Younger Futhark is divided into two main variants: the long-branch and short-twig styles. The long-branch style is characterized by elongated shapes and was primarily used in inscriptions, while the short-twig variant features more compact forms suited for practical use, such as on everyday objects. This distinction highlights the adaptability of the rune system to various contexts, illustrating how Vikings employed runes for both ceremonial and utilitarian purposes. The choice of style often depended on the medium and the message, emphasizing the versatility inherent in runic writing.

Interpreting the individual runes of the Younger Futhark involves understanding not just their phonetic values but also their symbolic meanings. Each rune carries a wealth of lore and connotations, deeply rooted in Norse mythology and the cultural psyche of the time. For instance, the rune "Fehu" represents wealth and prosperity, while "Berkano" symbolizes growth and fertility. Such associations reveal how the Vikings viewed their world and the qualities they aspired to embody. This symbolic framework allows modern practitioners to derive personal meaning from runes, fostering a connection to Viking heritage and spirituality.

The uses of the Younger Futhark in Viking culture were diverse, extending from communication and record-keeping to magical practices. Runes were inscribed on stones, weapons, and personal items, serving both practical and ritualistic functions. In warfare, they were believed to invoke protection or favor from the gods. Additionally, the practice of rune casting for divination purposes became prevalent, as individuals sought guidance and insight through the interpretation of runes. This multifaceted application underscores the central role of runes in both everyday life and spiritual practices among the Vikings.

In contemporary contexts, the Younger Futhark continues to resonate, finding relevance in various modern spiritual practices and artistic expressions. Many individuals today engage with runes as tools for personal reflection and spiritual growth, employing them in meditation and ritual. The aesthetic appeal of runes has also inspired a resurgence in crafting and artistic endeavors, as individuals create personalized rune sets or incorporate them into artwork. This revival illustrates how the ancient symbols of the Younger Futhark can bridge past and present, allowing for a meaningful exploration of identity, heritage, and the enduring quest for understanding in an ever-changing world.

## Differences Between Runic Alphabets

The study of runic alphabets reveals significant differences that reflect the diverse cultural and historical contexts from which they emerged. The two primary runic systems, the Elder Futhark and the Younger Futhark, demonstrate distinct variations in both structure and usage. The Elder Futhark, consisting of 24 characters, was predominantly used during the early centuries of the Common Era, serving as the foundational script for Germanic languages. In contrast, the Younger Futhark, which evolved later, contains only 16 characters, reflecting a shift in linguistic needs and the simplification of the writing system as Viking society developed.

One of the notable differences between these alphabets lies in their phonetic representation. The Elder Futhark encompasses a broader range of sounds, accommodating the phonetic richness of early Germanic languages. Conversely, the Younger Futhark's reduction in characters led to a more limited representation of sounds, which necessitated the use of context and linguistic adaptation for accurate communication. This adaptation is evident in inscriptions where a single rune could represent multiple sounds, showcasing the fluidity and evolution of language among the Norse people.

In addition to phonetic differences, the cultural contexts surrounding the runes also vary significantly. The Elder Futhark was primarily used in inscriptions that served various purposes, including memorials, trade, and magical practices. These inscriptions often reflect the beliefs and values of the communities that used them. The Younger Futhark, on the other hand, emerged during the Viking Age and was frequently employed in a wider array of contexts, such as runestones and everyday objects, indicating its role in both practical and ceremonial aspects of Viking life.

The interpretation of individual runes also varies between the two alphabets. Each rune carries its own meaning and significance, which can differ depending on the alphabet in which it appears. For instance, the rune "Berkano," representing growth and fertility, appears in both systems but may have evolved interpretations influenced by societal changes. Such nuances highlight the importance of understanding the historical and cultural backdrop when studying runes, as meanings can shift over time and across different regions.

Lastly, the modern applications of runes, influenced by their historical origins, further illustrate the differences between the alphabets. Contemporary spirituality and artistic practices often draw upon the symbolic meanings of both the Elder and Younger Futhark, adapting them for personal interpretation and use. This blending of ancient and modern interpretations underscores the enduring significance of runes, revealing how their differences can enrich our understanding of Viking culture and its legacy in today's world.

# Chapter 3: The Meaning of Viking Runes

## Symbolism in Runes

Symbolism in runes is a profound aspect of their use, reflecting a complex interplay between language, culture, and spirituality in Viking society. Each rune is not merely a letter but a symbol imbued with specific meanings, often extending beyond the written word. The runes of the Elder Futhark, for example, represent not only phonetic sounds but also concepts, natural elements, and deities. This duality allows for a richer understanding of their significance, as each rune can convey multiple layers of meaning depending on its context.

The symbolism in runes is deeply rooted in Norse mythology and cosmology. Many runes are associated with particular gods and mythological stories, which provide a narrative framework for their interpretation. For instance, the rune Fehu, representing wealth and prosperity, is linked to the god Freyr, who embodies fertility and abundance. This connection highlights the importance of wealth not just in a material sense but also as a reflection of spiritual and social well-being. Such associations enrich the interpretative depth of the runes, making them more than mere symbols of communication.

In addition to their mythological connections, the runes also symbolize various elements of nature and the human experience. For example, the rune Mannaz represents humanity and the self, emphasizing themes of cooperation and social structure. Meanwhile, the rune Raido symbolizes travel and movement, reflecting the physical journeys undertaken by the Vikings as well as their spiritual quests. This naturalistic symbolism indicates the Vikings' deep connection to their environment and the significance they placed on personal and communal journeys.

The functionality of runes in divination practices further showcases their symbolic richness. When employed in rune casting, the symbolism of each rune can provide insight into an individual's life circumstances, challenges, and potential futures. The act of casting runes becomes a dialogue between the seeker and the symbolic meanings embedded within each rune. This spiritual practice illustrates how the Vikings utilized runes not just for communication but as a means of connecting with the divine and understanding their place in the cosmos.

In contemporary contexts, the symbolism of runes continues to evolve, finding relevance in modern spirituality and artistic expressions. Many people today draw upon the rich symbolism of runes for personal empowerment, meditation, and creative inspiration. The integration of runes into modern art and spiritual practices exemplifies how these ancient symbols can transcend time, offering insight and resonance in a contemporary setting. As individuals continue to explore the multifaceted meanings of runes, they unlock a deeper connection to both their historical roots and personal journeys.

## Cultural Significance

The cultural significance of Viking runes transcends their practical applications and delves deep into the identity and worldview of the Norse people. Runes were not merely a system of writing but a vital part of the social, spiritual, and artistic fabric of Viking culture. Each rune carried not only a phonetic value but also symbolic meanings that reflected the beliefs and values of the society. This duality – a means of communication and a vehicle for deeper meaning – highlights how runes served as a bridge between the mundane and the mystical, embodying the collective consciousness of the Viking Age.

In the context of Norse mythology, runes are frequently associated with the gods, particularly Odin, who is said to have discovered them while hanging from Yggdrasil, the World Tree. This mythological backdrop lends an air of sacredness to the runes, as they are thought to be imbued with divine wisdom. The act of carving or reading runes was often shrouded in ritualistic significance, reinforcing their importance in spiritual and communal practices. In many instances, runes were used in ceremonies, from rites of passage to agricultural blessings, reflecting the community's reliance on and reverence for these symbols.

The interpretation of individual runes further emphasizes their cultural relevance. Each rune not only represents a sound but also embodies concepts such as protection, fertility, and fate. Runes like Fehu (wealth) and Raido (journey) were more than letters; they were symbols that articulated aspirations and challenges faced by the Vikings. The meanings associated with these runes were not static; they evolved alongside the culture, influenced by the changing social dynamics and interactions with neighboring societies. Thus, runes became a living language of sorts, capturing the essence of the Viking experience throughout their history.

Moreover, the use of runes in Viking warfare and communication highlights their practical importance. Runes were inscribed on weapons, shields, and stones, serving both as a means of identification and as protective charms. This practice illustrates the belief that runes possessed inherent power, which could influence the outcomes of battles or provide blessings for the warriors. The inscriptions served to instill confidence and convey messages among warriors, reinforcing bonds within the community and ensuring that the collective memory of their exploits was etched in both stone and spirit.

In contemporary times, the cultural significance of runes persists, reflecting their adaptability and ongoing relevance. Modern practitioners of spirituality often turn to runes for guidance and insight, drawing upon their ancient meanings for personal reflection and divination. The resurgence of interest in Viking heritage has led to a revival in the crafting and artistic expression of runes, as they are incorporated into modern art and design. This blend of historical reverence and contemporary interpretation illustrates how runes continue to resonate with individuals seeking to connect with their ancestry while exploring their own personal journeys. Thus, the cultural significance of Viking runes remains a dynamic and evolving aspect of both historical study and modern spirituality.

# Chapter 4: How to Read Viking Runes

## Basic Principles of Rune Reading

Rune reading is an ancient practice rooted in the rich tapestry of Norse culture, where each symbol carries profound meaning and significance. The foundational concept of rune reading lies in understanding that these symbols are not merely letters of an alphabet but powerful representations of cosmic forces, life experiences, and spiritual insights. The first principle is to approach each rune with an open mind, allowing intuition and personal interpretation to guide the reading. Each rune resonates with specific energies, and acknowledging these vibrations can lead to deeper connections with the symbols.

Another essential principle is the contextual nature of rune reading. Runes do not exist in isolation; their meanings can shift based on the surrounding runes in a cast or the specific question posed. This interplay creates a dynamic landscape for interpretation, where individual runes can take on new dimensions. To engage with rune reading effectively, one must consider the relationships between runes and the broader narrative they weave together. This requires a thoughtful examination of each rune's position and its potential influences on the others.

Understanding the historical origins of Viking runes adds another layer to the practice. Runes were used by the Germanic tribes, with the Elder Futhark being the most recognized system, comprising 24 characters. Each rune not only represents a sound but also embodies a concept or idea. Familiarity with the historical context of each rune enhances the reader's ability to interpret them accurately. The roots of these symbols are intertwined with mythology, nature, and the cosmos, providing a rich backdrop for personal and spiritual exploration.

In addition to historical knowledge, the interpretation of individual runes is crucial. Each rune has its own unique meaning, often reflecting attributes such as strength, protection, love, or change. For instance, the rune Fehu symbolizes wealth and prosperity, while Thurisaz represents protection and conflict. When reading runes, it is important to consider both the traditional meanings and how they resonate with the reader's personal experiences. This personalized interpretation fosters a connection that can reveal insights into current life situations or future possibilities.

Finally, the practice of rune casting as a form of divination serves as a bridge between ancient wisdom and modern spiritual practices. Many practitioners utilize rune stones or cards, casting them in specific layouts to seek guidance. This method emphasizes the importance of intention when approaching a reading. Whether for personal insight or communal rituals, rune casting encourages a dialogue with the self and the universe. As adults explore the principles of rune reading, they can unlock a deeper understanding of not only the runes themselves but also their own inner landscapes, leading to transformative experiences and enhanced self-awareness.

## Common Misinterpretations

One of the most prevalent misinterpretations of Viking runes is the belief that they were exclusively used for magical or mystical purposes. While it is true that runes held significant spiritual meaning and were often employed in rituals, their primary function was as a writing system. Runes were used for practical purposes such as recording important events, marking property, and communicating messages. This functional aspect is sometimes overshadowed by the more sensationalized depictions of runes in popular culture, which emphasize their supposed magical properties.

Another common misconception is the idea that all runes possess inherent meanings that are universally understood. In reality, the interpretation of individual runes can vary significantly based on contextual factors such as the time period, geographical location, and cultural influences. For instance, a rune might symbolize one concept in a particular region while conveying an entirely different meaning in another. This variability underscores the importance of considering the historical and cultural contexts when interpreting runes, rather than relying solely on a fixed set of meanings.

Additionally, many people assume that Viking runes are a monolithic system without any evolution or change over time. In truth, the runic alphabet, known as the Futhark, underwent several transformations as it spread across different regions and cultures. The Elder Futhark, used primarily in the early Viking Age, later gave way to the Younger Futhark and even other regional variations. Each iteration reflects the linguistic and cultural shifts of the communities that utilized them, making it essential to recognize the dynamic nature of runes throughout history.

The association of runes with divination practices is another area prone to misunderstanding. While rune casting and divination were indeed practiced by some, they were not the primary function of runes in Viking society. Many modern interpretations of runes as tools for fortune-telling can lead to a skewed perception of their historical significance. It is important to differentiate between the historical use of runes for writing and communication and their later adaptations in contemporary spiritual practices.

Finally, there is a tendency to equate runes solely with Norse mythology and literature, overlooking their broader cultural implications. Runes were woven into the fabric of everyday Viking life, influencing aspects such as trade, communication, and even warfare. Their inscriptions on weapons and monuments reveal their practical applications beyond the mythological narrative. Understanding the multifaceted role of runes in Viking society allows for a more nuanced appreciation of their significance, transcending the simplified interpretations often found in modern retellings.

# Chapter 5: Historical Origins of Viking Runes

## Early Development and Use

The early development of Viking runes is deeply intertwined with the cultural and linguistic evolution of the Germanic tribes in Northern Europe. Runes are part of the Elder Futhark, a script that emerged around the 2nd to 3rd century CE. This alphabet consists of 24 characters, each known as a "rune," which not only served phonetic purposes but also held symbolic meanings. The creation of runes likely drew inspiration from earlier scripts such as the Etruscan and Latin alphabets, adapted to suit the sounds of the Germanic languages. The need for a writing system arose as these tribes began to establish trade routes and more complex social structures, necessitating a method for record-keeping and communication.

The meanings behind the individual runes reveal much about the values and beliefs of Viking society. Each rune embodies specific qualities, concepts, or natural elements, reflecting the interconnectedness of their world. For example, the rune "Fehu" symbolizes wealth and cattle, illustrating the importance of livestock in Viking culture. Similarly, "Thurisaz" represents giants and chaos, hinting at the dual nature of existence in Norse belief systems. Understanding these meanings is crucial for interpreting runic inscriptions accurately, as each rune can provide insight into the cultural and spiritual life of the Vikings.

In addition to their linguistic applications, runes played a significant role in Viking culture through their use in rituals, divination, and magic. Runes were often inscribed on stones, weapons, and personal items, serving both protective and commemorative purposes. This practice reflects a belief in the power of words and symbols to influence the physical world. Rune casting, a form of divination, involved drawing runes from a bag or casting them on a surface to seek guidance or insight. This method demonstrated the Vikings' reverence for fate and the unseen forces that governed their lives.

The historical significance of runes extends beyond their practical uses; they are also embedded in Norse mythology and literature. Runes are often associated with the god Odin, who, according to myth, discovered them while hanging from the World Tree, Yggdrasil, as a sacrifice. This narrative underscores the mystical aspect of runes, suggesting that they are not merely tools for communication but also gateways to deeper spiritual understanding. Many sagas and poems reference runes, illustrating their integral role in storytelling and the transmission of cultural heritage.

In contemporary times, the fascination with Viking runes has led to their resurgence in various modern applications, particularly within spiritual and artistic communities. Many individuals seek to unlock the meanings of runes for personal growth, meditation, and self-reflection. Additionally, artists incorporate runes into their work, blending ancient symbolism with modern creativity. This revival not only honors the historical significance of runes but also highlights their enduring relevance, as people continue to explore the depths of their meanings and applications in today's world.

## Influence of Other Cultures

The influence of other cultures on Viking runes is an essential aspect of understanding their development and significance. As the Norse people ventured beyond their homelands through trade, exploration, and conquest, they encountered a variety of cultures that left indelible marks on their rune tradition. The interaction with Celtic, Roman, and Germanic societies, among others, facilitated a rich exchange of ideas, symbols, and writing systems. This mingling of cultures not only broadened the Norse worldview but also enriched the runic alphabet, allowing it to evolve and adapt over time.

Celtic culture, with its intricate knot patterns and symbolic imagery, played a notable role in shaping Viking artistic expression. The Celts had their own form of written language, known as Ogham, which, while distinct from runes, shared the common goal of conveying meaning through symbols. As Vikings came into contact with Celtic tribes in the British Isles, they likely absorbed some of the artistic styles and spiritual concepts that influenced their use of runes. This blend can be seen in the decorative elements of Viking artifacts, where runes often appear alongside Celtic motifs, suggesting a fusion of cultural identities.

The Romans, too, significantly impacted the Viking understanding of writing and communication. The Latin alphabet, recognized for its efficiency and clarity, introduced the concept of standardized writing to the Norse people. While Vikings primarily used runes for their unique phonetic qualities, the encounter with Roman literacy may have encouraged the adaptation of certain runic characters. This interaction highlights the practical needs of the Norse as they navigated trade routes and established political alliances, necessitating a more sophisticated means of record-keeping and communication.

Furthermore, the Germanic tribes, sharing linguistic and cultural roots with the Vikings, contributed to the foundational aspects of runic development. Proto-Germanic influences are evident in the very structure of the Elder Futhark, the oldest runic alphabet. As tribes migrated and intermixed, the runes themselves began to reflect a broader spectrum of sounds and meanings, illustrating the dynamic nature of cultural exchange. This shared heritage among Germanic peoples not only reinforced the significance of runes but also established a common framework for their use across different regions.

In contemporary times, the impact of these historical interactions can still be felt in how runes are perceived and utilized. Modern spiritual practitioners often draw from the diverse influences that shaped the runic tradition, interpreting them through various cultural lenses. This multi-faceted approach allows for a richer understanding of runes in personal practice, as individuals explore their meanings and applications in a modern context. By recognizing the influence of other cultures, enthusiasts can appreciate the depth and complexity of Viking runes, unlocking their secrets in ways that resonate with both historical and contemporary significance.

# Chapter 6: Interpretation of Individual Runes

## Overview of the Runes

Runes, the ancient script of the Vikings, serve as a fascinating gateway to understanding their culture, beliefs, and practices. Rooted in history, these symbols were not merely a means of communication but encapsulated a rich tapestry of meaning and significance. Viking runes are primarily derived from the Elder Futhark, a set of 24 characters that each hold distinct interpretations and uses. This subchapter will explore the origins, meanings, and applications of runes within Viking society, while also considering their relevance in modern spirituality and art.

Historically, runes are believed to have emerged around the 2nd to 3rd century AD, likely influenced by other ancient scripts such as Latin and Greek. The word "rune" itself is derived from the Proto-Germanic term "rūna," meaning "secret" or "mystery." Viking runes were carved into wood, stone, and metal, serving various purposes from inscriptions on grave markers to practical messages. The historical context of runes is essential for understanding their significance, as they reflect the values and beliefs of the Norse people, including their connections to nature, the divine, and the cosmos.

Each rune in the Elder Futhark carries its own meaning and associations, often linked to specific concepts or elements of life. For instance, the first rune, Fehu, symbolizes wealth and abundance, while others, such as Thurisaz, are associated with challenges or protection. As one delves deeper into the interpretation of individual runes, it becomes clear that they can convey complex messages and insights. This interpretative layer adds depth to the understanding of runes and their application in various aspects of Viking life, from daily activities to spiritual practices.

In Viking culture, runes were not only used for writing but also played a crucial role in divination and spiritual rituals. Rune casting, a practice that involves drawing runes to gain insight or guidance, demonstrates how these symbols transcended mere communication. The act of casting runes connects practitioners to their ancestors and the natural world, allowing for a profound exploration of fate and personal destiny. This spiritual dimension of runes continues to resonate today, as modern practitioners often turn to runes for guidance in their personal and spiritual journeys.

The relevance of runes extends beyond their historical and cultural roots into contemporary applications. In modern spirituality, many individuals use runes as tools for meditation, self-reflection, and artistic expression. Runes have also been compared to other ancient scripts, revealing similarities and differences that enrich our understanding of writing systems and their roles in various cultures. Techniques for learning to read and interpret runes have evolved, making them accessible to a broader audience. This resurgence of interest in runes reflects a growing appreciation for ancient wisdom and its application in the modern world, bridging the past and present in meaningful ways.

## Detailed Meanings of Each Rune

The study of Viking runes reveals a profound complexity in their meanings, each symbol encapsulating layers of interpretation that reflect the beliefs, values, and experiences of the Norse people. The runes, originating from the Elder Futhark, consist of 24 characters, each with its unique phonetic sound and symbolic significance. Understanding these meanings allows for a richer appreciation of their historical context as well as their applications in modern spirituality and art. Each rune serves as a conduit to the past, linking the contemporary seeker to the ancient wisdom of the Vikings.

The first rune, Fehu, symbolizes wealth and cattle, representing not just material prosperity but also the idea of abundance and the flow of resources. This rune embodies the foundational aspects of Viking society, where livestock and wealth were indicators of status and survival. In contrast, Uruz represents strength and vitality, often associated with the aurochs, a wild ancestor of domestic cattle. This rune conveys the importance of physical power and endurance, essential traits for the Viking warrior and farmer alike. Together, these runes illustrate the duality of material and personal strength in Norse culture.

Continuing through the runic alphabet, we find Thurisaz, a symbol of protection and conflict, often interpreted as a giant or a thorn. This rune signifies the challenges faced by the Vikings, whether in battles or in their daily lives, and reflects the necessity of resilience. Conversely, the rune Ansuz represents wisdom and communication, linked to the gods and the power of language. It highlights the significance of storytelling and the oral tradition in Viking culture, emphasizing how knowledge and insight are vital for navigating both personal and communal challenges.

The runes also encompass themes of fate and destiny. For instance, the rune Kenaz symbolizes illumination and knowledge, representing the light that guides one through darkness. It encourages the pursuit of understanding, suggesting that enlightenment is a continuous journey. Meanwhile, the rune Gebo, which signifies gifts and partnership, speaks to the interconnectedness of individuals within a community. This rune underscores the value of relationships and mutual support, essential for the survival of Viking society in an often harsh environment.

In modern applications, the meanings of these runes have evolved but remain rooted in their historical origins. Today, practitioners may use them for divination, meditation, or artistic expression, drawing upon the ancient insights they offer. Understanding each rune's detailed meaning not only serves as a portal to the past but also enriches contemporary spiritual practices. By exploring the depths of these symbols, individuals can engage with the wisdom of the Vikings, integrating their lessons into modern life while preserving the heritage of this fascinating script.

# Chapter 7: Uses of Runes in Viking Culture

## Runes in Daily Life

Runes permeated various aspects of daily life in Viking society, serving not only as a means of communication but also as symbols imbued with deep cultural significance. Each rune carried its own unique meaning, often linked to specific aspects of life such as health, prosperity, and protection. The Vikings utilized runes in practical ways, inscribing them on tools, weapons, and everyday items to invoke blessings or to mark ownership. This practice provided a tangible connection to their beliefs and values, making the runes an integral part of their daily existence.

In addition to marking possessions, runes were frequently used in rituals and ceremonies. The Vikings believed that certain runes could influence outcomes in their favor, so they incorporated them into their spiritual practices. For example, during agricultural events like planting and harvesting, runes might be carved into wooden staffs or stones to ensure a bountiful crop. This intentional use of runes reflected a profound understanding of the interconnectedness between the natural world and their spiritual beliefs, showcasing how runes were woven into the fabric of their lives.

The Vikings also relied on runes for communication, both in practical terms and as a means of storytelling. Carvings on stones and wood often conveyed messages or commemorated significant events. These inscriptions could serve as records of achievements, memorials for the deceased, or as warnings for travelers. The ability to read and write in runes was a valued skill, and those who mastered it held a respected place within their communities. This emphasizes the role of literacy in shaping social status among the Vikings, distinguishing those who could harness the power of the written word.

Beyond their daily uses, runes played a crucial role in the oral traditions of the Vikings. Runes were often linked to mythology and folklore, with each symbol representing stories, gods, and cosmic forces. This connection to narrative enriched the cultural landscape, allowing individuals to explore their identity and heritage through the lens of runic symbolism. As a result, runes became a bridge between the mundane and the mystical, imbuing everyday life with a sense of purpose and connection to the past.

In contemporary society, the fascination with Viking runes continues, with many seeking to incorporate them into their daily lives. Modern interpretations of runes often emphasize personal empowerment and spiritual growth, allowing individuals to engage with these ancient symbols in new ways. Whether through art, meditation, or divination practices, the legacy of runes endures as a source of inspiration and guidance. By understanding the historical significance of runes in Viking culture, people today can unlock their potential to enrich their own lives, drawing from the wisdom of the past.

## Runes in Trade and Commerce

Runes played a significant role in trade and commerce during the Viking Age, serving not only as a means of communication but also as a tool for marking ownership and facilitating transactions. Merchants and traders utilized runes to inscribe their names, the names of their goods, and the terms of trade on various materials such as wood, stone, and metal. This practice helped ensure clarity and trust in business dealings, which was crucial in a time when oral agreements could be easily contested. The use of runes provided a tangible record of agreements, thereby reducing the potential for disputes and misunderstandings among traders.

The inscriptions often contained essential information about the items being traded, including their origin, quality, and price. For instance, a rune stone might bear the name of the trader, the item being sold, and an indication of its worth. This practice not only facilitated smoother transactions but also contributed to the establishment of trade routes and networks. Merchants could signal their reputation and reliability through their rune inscriptions, which helped in building relationships with customers and other traders across different regions.

In addition to practical uses, runes also held a symbolic significance in commerce. The Vikings believed that certain runes possessed protective qualities or could invoke prosperity. For example, the rune "Fehu," associated with wealth and cattle, often appeared in commercial contexts. Merchants might carve this rune on their goods or business documents, hoping to attract good fortune and successful transactions. This blend of practicality and spirituality reflected the deeply intertwined nature of Viking life, where the mundane and the mystical coexisted.

The archaeological record shows that runes were not only used in local trade but also in more extensive economic exchanges across the Viking world, including connections with other cultures. Runes found on artifacts in places like England and Ireland indicate that Viking traders were not only consumers but also influencers in the trade networks of their time. The ability to inscribe runes allowed them to leave their mark on foreign lands, thereby integrating their culture into the broader tapestry of European commerce.

Today, the study of runes in the context of trade provides valuable insights into the economic practices of the Viking Age. By examining the inscriptions and understanding their meanings, modern scholars gain a clearer picture of the social and economic dynamics of the time. This exploration of runes in commerce highlights the Vikings' advanced understanding of trade and their innovative use of language as a tool for facilitating relationships, ensuring fairness, and promoting prosperity in their interactions, both locally and internationally.

# Chapter 8: Rune Casting and Divination Practices

## Traditional Methods of Rune Casting

Traditional methods of rune casting have their roots deep in the practices of the Norse people, who utilized these ancient symbols not only for communication but also for divination and spiritual guidance. The act of rune casting often involved a set of runes, typically carved from wood or stone, which were used in various rituals to gain insight or predict future events. The casting process was steeped in tradition, requiring a deep connection to the runes and an understanding of their meanings. Practitioners would often prepare themselves through meditation or prayer to attune their minds to the spiritual energies at play.

The casting itself usually involved throwing or drawing runes from a bag or a container, allowing for a randomness that many believed opened a direct line to the divine. Each rune, with its unique symbolism and phonetic value, was interpreted based on its position and orientation after being cast. For example, runes that landed face up might signify positive influences or affirmations, while those that were reversed could indicate challenges or obstacles. This method of interpretation not only relied on the individual meanings of the runes but also on their relationships to one another, creating a complex web of significance that could guide the seeker's inquiries.

In Viking culture, rune casting was not merely an esoteric practice; it was often intertwined with everyday life. Runes were used for various purposes, including marking territory, commemorating the deceased, and even invoking protection in battle. This duality of function means that rune casting was accessible to different segments of society, from the everyday farmer to the shamanic practitioner. The communal aspect of these practices often involved gatherings that reinforced social bonds and shared beliefs, creating a rich tapestry of cultural significance around the runes.

Additionally, the historical origins of rune casting can be traced back to the Elder Futhark, the oldest form of runic alphabet. Each rune in this system carries both a letter and a meaning, often linked to Norse mythology and the natural world. For instance, the rune "Fehu" represents wealth and prosperity, while "Tiwaz" symbolizes honor and justice. Understanding these roots is essential for practitioners today, as it provides a context for the meanings and uses of the runes, enhancing the depth of their interpretations during casting.

In modern spirituality, traditional methods of rune casting continue to evolve, blending ancient practices with contemporary beliefs. Many practitioners now incorporate elements from other spiritual traditions, creating a more eclectic approach to rune divination. This fusion has led to a resurgence in the interest surrounding runes, as people seek to unlock their secrets for personal insight and guidance. By embracing both the historical significance and the modern applications of rune casting, individuals can connect with a timeless practice that resonates across the ages, bringing the wisdom of the Vikings into the present.

## Modern Adaptations of Rune Divination

Modern adaptations of rune divination have evolved significantly from their ancient origins, reflecting both contemporary spiritual practices and the ongoing fascination with Norse culture. In today's world, individuals seek to connect with the wisdom of the past while integrating it into their current lives. This has led to the emergence of various methods and interpretations that blend traditional rune casting with modern spiritual needs, allowing practitioners to explore personal insights and guidance through these ancient symbols.

One notable adaptation is the incorporation of runes into holistic and therapeutic practices. Many modern practitioners use runes not just as tools for divination, but also as instruments for self-reflection and personal growth. Workshops and online courses often teach individuals how to utilize runes in meditation or journaling, encouraging a deeper understanding of their meanings and how they can apply to one's life. This approach emphasizes the psychological and emotional aspects of rune interpretation, allowing participants to navigate their life's challenges through a symbolic lens.

Furthermore, the aesthetic appeal of runes has led to their integration into contemporary art and design. Artists and craftspeople create rune sets that not only serve as divinatory tools but also as decorative pieces. These modern rune sets often feature unique materials and artistic styles, appealing to a broader audience that appreciates both the historical significance and the aesthetic value of the runes. This trend has expanded the accessibility of rune divination, inviting individuals who may not have previously engaged with Norse mythology or spirituality to explore its depths.

Technology has also played a crucial role in the modern adaptation of rune divination. Mobile applications and online platforms now provide users with instant access to rune meanings, daily readings, and interactive casting methods. These digital tools allow for a more convenient and immediate experience, catering to the fast-paced lifestyles of contemporary society while still honoring the ancient practices. Additionally, online communities foster a shared space for discussion and interpretation, enabling practitioners to exchange insights and experiences across geographical boundaries.

Lastly, the resurgence of interest in pagan and spiritual practices has created a vibrant community focused on the exploration of runes and their meanings. Workshops, retreats, and online forums offer abundant opportunities for learning and collaboration. This modern renaissance not only preserves the knowledge of ancient rune practices but also encourages a re-examination and evolution of their meanings in today's context. As individuals continue to unlock the secrets of Viking runes, they affirm their relevance and adaptability in navigating the complexities of modern life, bridging the historical with the contemporary in meaningful ways.

# Chapter 9: Modern Applications of Runes in Spirituality

## Runes in Contemporary Spiritual Practices

Runes have seen a resurgence in contemporary spiritual practices, becoming a significant tool for personal growth, introspection, and divination. Modern practitioners often view runes not merely as historical artifacts but as living symbols imbued with spiritual significance. This revival is rooted in an increasing interest in ancient wisdom and a desire to connect with ancestral traditions. Today, individuals engage with runes in various ways, from meditation and ritualistic practices to psychological exploration, thereby bridging the gap between ancient Viking culture and contemporary spirituality.

The use of runes in divination has gained particular popularity, with practitioners casting runes to gain insights into personal dilemmas or life paths. This practice often involves drawing a set number of runes, each representing different aspects of the question posed or the situation at hand. The interpretation of these runes is not merely a matter of referencing their traditional meanings; it also incorporates intuitive insights and personal associations that the practitioner may have developed. This dynamic engagement with the symbols allows for a personalized spiritual experience that resonates with the individual's current life circumstances.

Moreover, modern spiritual communities have adapted rune practices to suit contemporary needs, incorporating them into various holistic healing modalities. For instance, runes may be used in combination with yoga, meditation, or energy healing practices. In these contexts, they serve as focal points for intention-setting and mindfulness. Practitioners often create rune grids or altars, using the symbols to enhance their spiritual work and to invoke specific energies or qualities associated with the runes. This integration reflects a broader trend in spirituality that values the merging of ancient wisdom with modern therapeutic practices.

In addition to their use in divination and healing, runes have also found their way into artistic expressions. Many contemporary artists incorporate runic symbols into their work, using them to convey meaning and evoke a sense of mystery and connection to the past. This artistic engagement not only celebrates the historical significance of runes but also invites viewers to explore their own interpretations and emotional responses. Crafting and using runes in modern art can facilitate a deeper understanding of the symbols while simultaneously serving as a vehicle for personal expression and creativity.

Finally, the exploration of runes in contemporary spirituality often leads to a broader examination of identity and heritage. Many individuals are drawn to runes as a way of reconnecting with their ancestral roots, fostering a sense of belonging and continuity. This connection to the past can be a powerful source of empowerment, as individuals seek to understand their place in the world through the lens of ancient wisdom. As such, runes are not only seen as tools for divination or art but also as instruments for personal transformation and a deeper engagement with one's cultural heritage.

## Runes as Tools for Personal Growth

Runes, the ancient characters used by the Germanic peoples, particularly the Vikings, serve as more than mere symbols etched on stones or wood. They can be viewed as powerful tools for personal growth, enabling individuals to explore their inner selves and navigate life's challenges. The rich history behind each rune provides a unique context that can inspire self-reflection and personal transformation. By understanding the meanings and associations of these runes, individuals can harness their energies to foster personal development and create a deeper connection with their own lives.

Each rune in the Elder Futhark, the oldest known runic alphabet, carries its own distinct meaning and symbolism. For example, the rune Fehu represents wealth and prosperity, while Thurisaz signifies protection and defense. By learning to interpret these runes, adults can engage in a process of introspection, identifying areas in their lives where they seek growth or change. This understanding allows for a more targeted approach to personal development, as individuals can select runes that resonate with their current life circumstances and goals, guiding them toward a clearer path forward.

Incorporating runes into daily practices can also enhance self-awareness and mindfulness. Adults can create rituals around rune casting, where they draw specific runes to gain insights into their situations or emotional states. This practice can encourage contemplation and provide clarity, helping individuals to confront their fears, aspirations, and challenges. By regularly engaging with runes in this way, people can develop a routine that fosters continuous growth and reflection, ultimately leading to a more balanced and fulfilling life.

Additionally, the historical context of runes enriches their potential for personal growth. The Vikings used runes not only for communication but also for magical purposes, believing in their power to influence fate and protect against misfortune. Understanding this cultural backdrop can inspire adults to view their personal growth journey as part of a larger narrative, one that connects them to ancient wisdom and practices. This sense of continuity with the past can empower individuals, reminding them that they are part of a long tradition of seeking knowledge and self-improvement.

Finally, the artistic aspects of runes provide another avenue for personal expression and growth. Crafting runes or incorporating them into art can serve as a therapeutic practice, allowing individuals to channel their emotions and experiences into tangible forms. This creative engagement not only reinforces the meanings of the runes but also fosters a deeper connection to one's inner self. By exploring runes in both their traditional and modern contexts, adults can unlock new dimensions of personal growth, leading to a richer understanding of themselves and their place in the world.

# Chapter 10: Comparative Analysis of Runes and Other Ancient Scripts

## Similarities with Other Scripts

Viking runes, while distinct in their origin and application, share several similarities with other ancient scripts, particularly in their structural and functional aspects. One notable parallel can be drawn with the Latin alphabet, which, like the runes, consists of characters that represent both sounds and meanings. Runes, part of the Elder Futhark system, were not only used for communication but also served ritualistic purposes, similar to how Latin was employed in religious and scholarly contexts. This dual function of script highlights a common practice among ancient civilizations, where writing transcended mere record-keeping and entered the realm of the sacred and the symbolic.

Another script that bears resemblance to Viking runes is the Greek alphabet. Both systems evolved in response to the specific cultural and linguistic needs of their societies. The Greeks developed their script to accommodate the phonetic nuances of their language, much as the Norse people adapted runes to capture the sounds of Old Norse. Furthermore, both the Greek letters and the runes were often inscribed on various materials, including stone and wood, serving as both practical tools for communication and as artifacts imbued with cultural significance.

In addition to structural similarities, the use of runes and other scripts often reflects a shared cultural context. For instance, the Phoenician script, which is considered one of the precursors to many alphabets, influenced the development of writing systems throughout the Mediterranean, including Greek and Latin. Similarly, the runic system, believed to have been influenced by the Italic scripts, embodies the interconnectedness of ancient cultures. The dissemination of these writing systems was often facilitated through trade and conquest, leading to the exchange of ideas and practices that shaped their evolution.

The interpretative nature of runes also finds common ground with scripts such as Egyptian hieroglyphs and Chinese characters, where symbols carry deeper meanings beyond their phonetic sounds. Runes were often imbued with magical connotations, and their inscriptions were thought to convey not just language but also power and intention. This mystical aspect can be seen in various ancient texts where symbols serve as conduits for spiritual or divine communication, suggesting that the human desire to imbue writing with meaning is a universal trait across cultures.

Finally, the modern interpretations of runes echo the ongoing relevance of ancient scripts in contemporary spirituality and art, akin to how the Greek and Latin scripts are still studied and utilized today. Just as scholars and practitioners draw on the rich history of Greek philosophy or Latin literature, modern enthusiasts of Viking runes engage with their meanings and uses in personal and collective spiritual practices. This enduring legacy illustrates how ancient scripts, including Viking runes, continue to resonate in today's world, bridging the past and present through their shared human experiences.

## Unique Characteristics of Runes

The unique characteristics of runes extend beyond their function as an ancient writing system; they embody a rich cultural heritage that intertwines language, mythology, and practical use. Originating from the Germanic tribes, specifically the Norse and Anglo-Saxon peoples, runes were etched into stone, wood, metal, and other materials, making them durable and versatile. Each rune is not merely a letter but a symbol packed with meaning. The Elder Futhark, the oldest known runic alphabet, consists of 24 characters, each representing phonetic sounds as well as concepts and deities. This duality reflects a profound connection between language and the cosmos, offering insights into the worldview of the Vikings.

One of the most striking characteristics of runes is their connection to the natural world and the spiritual realm. Many runes are associated with specific elements, animals, and forces of nature, allowing practitioners to tap into these energies for various purposes, including divination and protection. For instance, the rune "Uruz" symbolizes strength and vitality, often linked to the aurochs, a powerful wild ox. This association with nature extends to the entire runic tradition, where each symbol can serve as a conduit for understanding human experience in relation to the environment. This intrinsic connection enhances their use in both practical applications and spiritual practices.

The interpretive nature of runes adds another layer of uniqueness. Unlike more straightforward alphabets, each rune carries multiple meanings that can shift depending on context. This flexibility allows for personal interpretation and encourages deeper reflection. For example, the rune "Algiz" can signify protection, but it may also represent a connection to the divine or a call to embrace one's instincts. This multifaceted interpretation is integral to rune casting and divination practices, where the layout and position of runes can shift their meanings, creating a dynamic interplay between the symbols and the seeker's intentions.

Culturally, runes were not only used for communication but also played a vital role in rituals, magic, and warfare. Runes were inscribed on weapons, amulets, and stones to invoke protection or to ensure victory in battle. This functional aspect illustrates how runes served practical needs while simultaneously fulfilling spiritual and symbolic roles. The act of carving or casting runes was imbued with intention, making the process a ceremonial practice that connected the user to their ancestry and the spiritual world. The blend of practicality and spirituality highlights the importance of runes in Viking society.

In contemporary times, the unique characteristics of runes continue to resonate with individuals seeking spiritual growth or artistic expression. Modern applications involve using runes for personal insight, meditation, and creative endeavors, allowing a new generation to explore their meanings and symbolism. As people engage with runes, they often find a bridge connecting ancient wisdom with contemporary life, further enriching their understanding of this powerful script. The evolving relationship with runes reflects an enduring fascination with the past and a desire to integrate these ancient symbols into modern spiritual practices and artistic expressions.

# Chapter 11: Techniques for Learning to Read Runes

## Resources for Beginners

For those new to the study of Viking runes, a wealth of resources exists to facilitate understanding and interpretation. Beginner guides offer foundational knowledge about the Elder Futhark, the runic alphabet used by the Vikings, and provide insight into the historical context from which these symbols emerged. Texts such as "Runes: A Handbook for Beginners" and "The Viking Runes Explained" serve as excellent introductory materials, presenting the meanings of individual runes alongside their cultural significance. These resources can help demystify the symbols and prepare readers for deeper exploration of their meanings and uses.

To effectively read and interpret runes, beginners can benefit from online courses and workshops that specialize in runic studies. Many platforms offer structured learning paths that cover key concepts such as rune pronunciation, meanings, and the historical background of their use in Norse culture. These courses often include practical exercises and community forums, allowing learners to engage with others who share their interest. Additionally, instructional videos can provide visual context and demonstrate techniques for rune reading, making it easier to grasp the nuances of this ancient script.

Books dedicated to rune casting and divination practices are invaluable for those interested in applying runes in personal spiritual or introspective work. Titles like "The Book of Runes" by Ralph Blum can guide beginners through the process of casting runes for guidance and insight. These texts often include instructions for creating sacred spaces, conducting readings, and interpreting the results. Beginners may find it helpful to keep a journal to document their experiences with rune casting, as this practice not only enhances understanding but also encourages personal reflection.

Comparative analysis resources can offer insights into the similarities and differences between runes and other ancient writing systems, such as the Roman alphabet or Greek scripts. This understanding can enrich a beginner's appreciation for the uniqueness of Viking runes and their role in communication and culture. Academic papers and textbooks that explore linguistic connections can provide a broader context for the study of runes, while online forums and discussion groups allow for the exchange of ideas among enthusiasts and scholars.

Finally, incorporating modern applications of runes into creative projects can also enhance learning. Crafting runes for personal use or artistic expression can solidify their meanings and significance. Resources such as online tutorials for rune carving or crafting can inspire beginners to explore their creativity while deepening their connection to the symbols. Engaging with runes through art not only makes the learning process enjoyable but also fosters a personal relationship with these ancient symbols, bridging the gap between historical significance and contemporary relevance.

## Advanced Reading Techniques

To effectively engage with Viking runes, readers must adopt advanced techniques that enhance comprehension and interpretation. One of the most important methods is contextual reading, which involves understanding the historical and cultural backdrop of the runes. This technique requires delving into the Norse mythology and literature, where runes were not merely letters but symbols rich with meaning. By examining the stories and beliefs that surrounded these symbols, readers can uncover deeper insights into their applications and significance in Viking life.

Another critical approach is comparative analysis. This technique encourages readers to explore similarities and differences between Viking runes and other ancient scripts, such as the Latin alphabet or Egyptian hieroglyphs. By situating runes within a broader linguistic context, one can appreciate their unique characteristics and functional roles. This not only aids in learning how to read the runes but also fosters an understanding of their evolution and adaptation through time, revealing how they served as a vital means of communication in different cultural landscapes.

Practicing rune interpretation is another advanced technique that requires both analytical and intuitive skills. Readers should engage with individual runes, considering their phonetic values, symbolic meanings, and the cultural contexts in which they were used. This can involve creating personal associations and combining historical knowledge with modern interpretations. Engaging in discussions or joining study groups can further enhance this process, as sharing insights can lead to a more nuanced understanding of the runes and their myriad meanings.

Rune casting and divination practices are also valuable techniques for those interested in the spiritual applications of runes. This method encourages readers to experiment with casting runes for guidance, fostering a personal relationship with the symbols. By interpreting the runes cast and reflecting on their meanings in relation to one's own life, individuals can develop a deeper connection to the runic traditions. This practice not only serves as a tool for self-discovery but also bridges ancient wisdom with contemporary spiritual exploration.

Finally, crafting and using runes in modern art is an advanced technique that encourages creativity and personal expression. By designing and creating runes, individuals can engage with the symbols on a tactile level, fostering a deeper appreciation for their beauty and significance. This hands-on approach allows for an exploration of the aesthetic aspects of runes while simultaneously grounding them in personal experience. As readers blend historical techniques with contemporary methods, they contribute to the ongoing legacy of Viking runes, ensuring their relevance in modern spirituality and artistic expression

.

# Chapter 12: Runes in Norse Mythology and Literature

## Mythological References to Runes

Mythological references to runes are woven throughout Norse cosmology, emphasizing their significance beyond mere symbols. In the Eddas, particularly the Poetic Edda and the Prose Edda, runes are often associated with the gods and the creation of the world. One of the most notable figures linked to runes is Odin, the chief of the Aesir gods. According to myth, Odin sacrificed himself by hanging from Yggdrasil, the World Tree, for nine days and nights to gain the knowledge of runes. This act highlights the runes as not only a tool for communication but also as a means of accessing deeper wisdom and understanding of the universe.

The lore surrounding runes often portrays them as imbued with magical properties. They were believed to hold the power to influence fate, heal, and even bring prosperity. In several myths, runes are depicted as gifts from the gods to humanity, enabling mortals to connect with the divine and manipulate their destinies. The narrative of the runes being carved into wood or stone reflects the deep-rooted belief that language carries intrinsic power, a sentiment echoed in various cultures throughout history. This connection reinforces the idea that runes were not merely an alphabet but a sacred system of communication that bridged the human and the divine.

One of the most famous references to runes in Norse mythology is found in the story of the death of Baldur, the god of light and purity. His death, prophesied by the enigmatic mistletoe, illustrates the duality of fate and the limitations of knowledge, even among the gods. After Baldur's death, the attempt to resurrect him can be seen as a quest for understanding the runic language's deeper meanings. The interplay of life, death, and rebirth in this myth encapsulates the complex relationship the Vikings had with runes, viewing them as tools that could unlock the mysteries of existence while simultaneously recognizing their limitations.

The use of runes in Viking culture extended beyond personal significance; they were often inscribed on stones, weapons, and artifacts, serving as both memorials and markers of power. Runes were believed to convey messages from the past and to communicate strength, protection, and identity. This practice reflects a collective understanding of runes as a medium for storytelling and a means to immortalize important events and figures within their society. The connection between runes and mythology serves to reinforce their cultural importance, linking the past to the present through shared narratives and collective memory.

In modern contexts, the fascination with runes continues, drawing from their mythological roots to inspire contemporary interpretations. Many people turn to runes for personal insight, spiritual guidance, and creative expression, often referencing the rich tapestry of Norse mythology in their practices. The mythological references to runes provide a foundation for understanding their significance today, illustrating how these ancient symbols can be applied to contemporary spiritual practices and artistic endeavors. Through this lens, the runes serve not only as remnants of a bygone era but as living symbols that continue to resonate with individuals seeking connection and meaning in their lives.

# Runes in Sagas and Eddas

Runes hold a significant place in the Norse sagas and Eddas, serving as more than mere characters but as symbols imbued with cultural and spiritual meaning. These texts, which comprise a vast body of literature from the Viking Age, reveal how runes were interwoven into the fabric of Norse identity, mythos, and daily life. The sagas often depict runes as tools of communication, magic, and even divination, illustrating their multifaceted role in Viking culture. In particular, the Poetic Edda and the Prose Edda recount tales where runes are used to invoke power, foresee the future, or express profound truths, emphasizing their importance in shaping the worldview of the Norse people.

The historical origins of Viking runes trace back to the Germanic tribes of Northern Europe, with the earliest inscriptions believed to date from the second century. The runic alphabet, known as the Futhark, consists of 24 characters, each assigned specific phonetic values and symbolic meanings. The sagas often reflect this depth, attributing mystical qualities to individual runes. For instance, the rune for "F" (Fehu) symbolizes wealth and prosperity, while "T" (Tiwaz) represents honor and sacrifice. The careful selection of runes in saga narratives often conveys layers of meaning, revealing the values and beliefs of the Viking society that produced them.

In addition to their individual meanings, runes were frequently combined in various ways to enhance their power or convey more complex ideas. The sagas illustrate how these combinations could create protective charms or invoke specific deities, demonstrating the practical applications of runes in Viking life. Runes were also employed in the crafting of amulets and talismans, believed to provide the wearer with strength, guidance, or protection. The narratives often highlight the significance of these objects, portraying them as integral to the lives of warriors, travelers, and seers who sought to harness the power of runes for their own purposes.

Divination practices utilizing runes, as depicted in the sagas, further illustrate their spiritual significance. Rune casting, a method of seeking guidance from the divine, involved drawing runes from a bag or set and interpreting their meanings based on their orientation and position. This practice was often performed by practitioners or seers who claimed to possess a special connection to the mystical realm. The sagas recount instances where characters consulted runes for insight into their fates, revealing a deep-seated belief in the runes' ability to bridge the gap between the earthly and the divine, a belief that resonates with modern spiritual practices as well.

In contemporary society, the influence of Viking runes continues to manifest in various forms, from art to literature and spirituality. Modern interpretations of runes often draw upon the rich narratives found in the sagas and Eddas, adapting ancient wisdom to contemporary contexts. Artists and spiritual practitioners alike incorporate runes into their work, using them as symbols of personal empowerment and connection to heritage. This ongoing engagement with runes not only reflects a fascination with Viking culture but also underscores the timeless allure of these ancient symbols, inviting individuals to explore their meanings and applications in today's world.

# Chapter 13: Crafting and Using Runes in Modern Art

## Artistic Expression with Runes

Artistic expression with runes transcends mere inscription; it embodies a profound connection to history, spirituality, and personal creativity. Runes, as the ancient script of the Germanic peoples, particularly the Vikings, are imbued with meanings that extend beyond their phonetic representations. Each rune, with its unique shape and symbolism, serves as a canvas for artistic exploration, allowing modern creators to tap into the rich tapestry of Norse culture. This interaction with runes can be seen in various forms, from traditional carvings to contemporary adaptations in visual arts, where artists reinterpret these symbols to convey messages that resonate with both the ancient and modern worlds.

The artistic allure of runes lies in their historical origins, which date back to the early centuries of the Common Era. The Elder Futhark, the oldest form of the runic alphabet, consists of 24 characters, each with specific meanings derived from the natural and spiritual realms. Artists often draw inspiration from these meanings, creating works that reflect the essence of each rune. For instance, the rune "Tiwaz," associated with the god Tyr and concepts of honor and justice, may inspire a piece that explores themes of bravery and sacrifice. This process of interpretation allows artists not only to express their understanding of the symbols but also to engage viewers in a dialogue about the values and beliefs of Viking culture.

In addition to its historical context, the use of runes in artistic expression frequently intersects with modern spirituality. Many contemporary practitioners incorporate runes into their spiritual practices, using them as tools for meditation, manifestation, and self-discovery. Artistic representations of runes can serve as focal points for these practices, inviting individuals to reflect on the deeper meanings behind the symbols. In this way, runes become not just remnants of the past but living symbols that inspire personal growth and transformation. The act of creating art with runes can also be a spiritual journey, allowing artists to explore their own narratives while honoring the traditions of their ancestors.

Moreover, the versatility of runes lends itself to various artistic mediums, from painting and sculpture to textiles and jewelry. Crafters and artists often experiment with different materials, incorporating runes into their work through carving, engraving, or painting. This hands-on approach not only preserves the ancient art of rune crafting but also revitalizes it for contemporary audiences. The aesthetic appeal of runes, combined with their rich meanings, creates opportunities for artists to produce pieces that are both visually striking and deeply significant, fostering a renewed appreciation for these ancient symbols in modern society.

The intersection of runes and art ultimately encourages a deeper understanding of their role in Viking culture and beyond. Runic art serves as a bridge between the past and present, allowing individuals to engage with the stories and wisdom of the Norse people. Through artistic expression, runes are transformed into vessels of communication, carrying forward the legacy of an ancient script while inviting new interpretations and meanings. This ongoing dialogue between the historical and the contemporary highlights the enduring power of runes as symbols of creativity, spirituality, and cultural heritage.

## Incorporating Runes into Contemporary Art

Incorporating runes into contemporary art bridges the gap between ancient symbolism and modern creativity, allowing artists to explore the rich heritage of Viking culture while expressing personal narratives. Runes, with their distinct shapes and profound meanings, offer a wealth of inspiration for artistic endeavors. Artists can use these characters as visual elements, embedding them within paintings, sculptures, or mixed media projects. This integration not only enhances the aesthetic appeal but also invites viewers to engage with the historical and cultural significance of the runes.

The historical origins of Viking runes provide a foundation for their use in contemporary art. Runes originated in the Germanic tribes of Northern Europe, with the earliest examples dating back to the 2nd century. Each rune carries with it a story, a meaning, and a connection to the past. Contemporary artists who incorporate runes into their work often delve into this history, researching the Elder Futhark, the runic alphabet used by the Vikings. By understanding the context in which these symbols were created, artists can infuse their work with depth and resonance, making the ancient symbols relevant to today's audience.

In modern applications of runes within art, the interpretative potential of individual runes becomes a focal point. Each rune embodies specific themes, such as protection, prosperity, and transformation. Artists can select runes that align with their creative intentions, using them as talismans or motifs that reflect personal journeys or societal reflections. For instance, the rune Fehu, symbolizing wealth and abundance, might inspire a piece that explores themes of prosperity and community, while the rune Algiz, representing protection and safety, could be woven into a narrative about resilience in the face of adversity.

The role of runes in contemporary art also extends into the realm of spirituality and personal exploration. Many artists view runes not just as historical artifacts but as tools for divination and introspection. By incorporating runes into their artistic practice, they create spaces for reflection and connection, where the viewer can encounter the spiritual dimensions these symbols evoke. This practice often blends traditional rune casting techniques with modern artistic methods, allowing for a unique dialogue between the viewer and the artwork, fostering a deeper understanding of both the self and the ancient wisdom embedded in the runes.

Finally, the comparative analysis of runes with other ancient scripts reveals the universality of symbolic language in human expression. By studying how various cultures have utilized symbols for communication and meaning-making, contemporary artists can draw parallels and contrasts that enrich their work. This comparative approach not only enhances the artistic narrative but also situates runes within a broader context of human creativity and expression. Ultimately, incorporating runes into contemporary art serves as a powerful means of honoring Viking heritage while simultaneously inviting fresh interpretations and dialogues in today's artistic landscape.

# Chapter 14: The Role of Runes in Viking Warfare and Communication

## Runes as Tactical Tools

Runes, the characters of the ancient Germanic alphabets, were not only a means of communication but also served as tactical tools in Viking culture. Their significance extended beyond mere written language; they were imbued with magical properties and used strategically in various aspects of life, particularly in warfare. The Vikings believed that runes held power, and when inscribed or invoked correctly, they could influence outcomes, provide protection, or instill courage in battle. Understanding the tactical deployment of runes offers insight into how the Norse people viewed their world and the forces at play within it.

In the context of warfare, runes were often carved onto weapons, shields, and helmets. It was a common practice to inscribe runes that symbolized strength, protection, or victory. For instance, the rune "Tiwaz," associated with the god Tyr, represented honor and victory in combat. Warriors believed that these inscriptions would not only enhance their physical capabilities but also provide divine favor during conflicts. By utilizing these symbols, the Vikings created a psychological edge, instilling fear in their enemies while bolstering their own morale.

Beyond the battlefield, runes played a vital role in communication, particularly in conveying messages between warriors and their leaders. Runes were carved on stones or wood to relay important tactical information or to mark territory. The clarity and brevity of runic inscriptions made them an efficient means of communication during raids or while navigating unfamiliar terrain. This practical application of runes highlights their dual purpose as both a sacred script and a functional tool for coordination and strategy.

Furthermore, the use of runes in divination practices added another layer to their tactical significance. Vikings often consulted runes to gain insight into future events or to make crucial decisions. This practice, known as rune casting, involved drawing or tossing runes to interpret their meanings in relation to specific queries. The outcomes of these divinations could influence battle plans or personal choices, demonstrating how the Vikings integrated mystical elements into their strategic thinking. The interplay between fate and free will was central to their worldview, and runes provided a tangible means to navigate these complexities.

In contemporary contexts, the legacy of runes endures, particularly in modern spiritual practices and artistic expressions. Many people today explore runes not only for their historical significance but also as tools for personal growth and understanding. The tactical nature of runes, rooted in Viking culture, serves as a reminder of how symbols can carry profound meaning and influence human behavior. By studying these ancient tools, individuals can unlock insights into their own lives while connecting with the rich tapestry of Norse history and mythology. The exploration of runes as tactical instruments thus bridges the gap between the past and present, offering a unique lens through which to view both ancient and modern strategies for navigating life's challenges.

## Runes in Messages and Insignia

Runes in messages and insignia were integral to Viking communication, serving not just as a means of conveying information but also as a reflection of cultural beliefs and social values. The runic alphabet, known as the Futhark, consisted of various characters, each with its own unique sound and meaning. Vikings used these characters to inscribe messages on stones, wood, metal, and other materials, often in contexts ranging from personal expressions to declarations of ownership or memorials for the deceased. The significance of runes extended beyond mere writing; they were imbued with magical properties, believed to hold power and influence over the natural and supernatural realms.

In the Viking Age, the act of writing runes was often accompanied by ritualistic practices. Insignia carved into weapons or shields frequently included runes intended to invoke protection or to signify allegiance to a particular chieftain or clan. The inscriptions served both practical purposes—marking possessions to deter theft and asserting ownership—and symbolic ones, expressing the identity and values of the individuals or groups involved. This duality highlights the multifaceted role of runes in Viking culture, where they were not only tools for communication but also potent symbols of power and identity.

The interpretation of individual runes is essential for understanding the broader context of runic messages. Each rune carries its own inherent meaning, often tied to natural elements or mythological symbolism. For instance, the rune Fehu, representing wealth and prosperity, could be used in messages related to trade or abundance, whereas the rune Tiwaz, associated with honor and warfare, might appear in inscriptions related to valor in battle. This layered meaning allows for a rich tapestry of interpretations, where the context of the message further nuances the significance of the runes used.

Modern applications of runes have seen a resurgence, particularly in spiritual and artistic contexts. Many practitioners of modern spirituality utilize runes for divination, drawing upon their historical meanings to gain insights or guidance. Artists have also embraced the aesthetic and symbolic qualities of runes, incorporating them into contemporary works to evoke themes of heritage, identity, and empowerment. This revival illustrates the enduring fascination with runes and their capacity to bridge ancient traditions with modern expressions of belief and creativity.

In comparative studies, runes can be analyzed alongside other ancient scripts, illuminating their unique characteristics and cultural significance. While many writing systems served primarily utilitarian purposes, runes were often intertwined with the spiritual and mythological aspects of Viking life. This distinction underscores the importance of understanding runes not just as a form of communication but as a complex system that embodies the values, beliefs, and experiences of the Viking people. Through examining runes in messages and insignia, we gain deeper insights into the intricate tapestry of Viking culture and its lasting impact on the modern world.

# Chapter 15: Conclusion and Future of Rune Studies

## The Ongoing Interest in Runes

The ongoing interest in runes can be attributed to their rich historical significance and multifaceted applications throughout time. Rooted in the early Germanic and Norse cultures, runes have transcended their original purpose as mere letters of an alphabet to become symbols steeped in esoteric meaning and spiritual significance. Modern enthusiasts and scholars alike delve into the depths of these ancient characters, exploring their historical origins, individual interpretations, and the cultural practices surrounding their use. This enduring fascination serves as a bridge connecting contemporary society with the enigmatic world of the Vikings and their belief systems.

Understanding the meaning behind each rune is a key aspect of this interest. Each character in the runic alphabet, known as the Futhark, carries its own unique symbolism and historical connotation. For example, the rune 'Fehu' represents wealth and prosperity, while 'Thurisaz' embodies the primal force of chaos. As individuals seek to unlock the personal and collective meanings behind these symbols, they often turn to the interpretation of individual runes for guidance in their own lives. This exploration not only sheds light on ancient wisdom but also encourages a deeper understanding of oneself and the world around them.

The uses of runes in Viking culture further fuel this ongoing interest. Runes were not merely used for writing; they held power in rituals, magic, and even warfare. Viking warriors would often inscribe runes on their weapons or shields, believing that these symbols would invoke protection or victory. This intersection of language and the metaphysical realm continues to captivate modern practitioners who seek to incorporate runes into their own rituals or as tools for divination. The practice of rune casting, where individuals draw runes to gain insight into their lives, has seen a resurgence as more people explore spirituality and self-discovery.

In addition to their historical and cultural significance, runes have found a place in contemporary spirituality and art. Many modern spiritual practitioners utilize runes as a means of connecting with ancient wisdom, employing them in meditation, manifestation, and personal development. This renewed interest is mirrored in the arts, where the crafting and incorporation of runes into contemporary works serve not only as a nod to Viking heritage but also as a means of personal expression. Artists and crafters are increasingly using runic symbols to convey messages or invoke emotions, demonstrating the adaptability and relevance of these ancient symbols in today's creative landscape.

Finally, the comparative analysis of runes with other ancient scripts enriches our understanding of their place in the broader context of human communication. By studying the similarities and differences between runes and scripts such as the Greek or Latin alphabets, scholars can uncover deeper insights into the cultural exchanges and influences that shaped these writing systems. This ongoing scholarly dialogue not only preserves the legacy of runes but also ensures that their meanings and applications continue to evolve, capturing the imagination of new generations eager to unlock the secrets of the past.

## Potential Directions for Future Research

Future research on Viking runes can take several promising directions, particularly in the area of historical origins. Scholars should delve deeper into archaeological findings, examining artifacts that bear runic inscriptions. By utilizing advanced dating techniques and materials analysis, researchers can establish a more precise timeline for the emergence and evolution of runes. Additionally, a comparative study of runic inscriptions found in different geographical locations could illuminate how regional variations influenced their development and usage. This would provide a richer context for understanding the cultural exchanges that occurred during the Viking Age.

Another fruitful area for exploration is the interpretation of individual runes. While much has been written about the meanings attributed to each rune, these interpretations often vary among sources. Future studies could focus on a more systematic approach to decoding runic symbols by incorporating linguistic methodologies and examining the context in which specific runes were used. This could lead to more nuanced understandings of how meanings shifted over time and how they were influenced by contemporaneous languages and cultures, further enriching our comprehension of Viking runes.

The uses of runes in Viking culture also warrant further investigation, particularly regarding their role in daily life beyond the mystical or spiritual applications. Research could explore how runes were employed in practical contexts, such as trade, navigation, and communication. Analyzing runic inscriptions found on everyday objects might reveal insights into the socio-economic structures of Viking society. Such studies could also highlight the interplay between the mundane and the sacred in the use of runes, thereby providing a more comprehensive picture of their significance in Viking life.

In the realm of modern applications of runes, a growing interest in their use within contemporary spirituality presents an intriguing avenue for research. Scholars could investigate how modern practitioners reinterpret ancient runic traditions and adapt them to fit modern spiritual practices. This could involve qualitative studies, such as interviews with practitioners, as well as quantitative surveys to assess the popularity and perceived efficacy of these practices. Understanding the motivations behind modern rune casting and divination methods could bridge the gap between ancient beliefs and contemporary spiritual needs.

Finally, a comparative analysis of runes and other ancient scripts could yield fruitful insights into the broader context of writing systems. By examining similarities and differences in the structure, function, and cultural significance of runes alongside other scripts like the Greek or Roman alphabets, researchers can better understand the unique features of runes. This comparison could also extend to their influence on each other, especially in the context of the Viking Age's extensive trade networks and cultural exchanges. Such research would not only enhance our understanding of runes but also contribute to the larger field of historical linguistics and writing systems.

# Echoes of the North: Unraveling the Icelandic Sagas

## Chapter 1: Introduction to the Icelandic Sagas

### Definition and Overview of the Sagas

The term "saga" derives from the Old Norse word "saga," meaning "to say" or "to tell," and refers to a distinct genre of prose narratives that originated in medieval Iceland. These narratives, primarily composed in the 13th century, recount the lives and deeds of early Norse settlers, their descendants, and the legendary figures of the Viking Age. The sagas are characterized by their blend of historical fact and fiction, often illustrating the complexities of human relationships, moral dilemmas, and the harsh realities of life in a challenging environment. This genre captures the ethos of Norse culture, emphasizing values such as honor, loyalty, and the importance of lineage.

Icelandic sagas can be broadly categorized into two main types: the family sagas and the legendary sagas. Family sagas, or "Íslendingasögur," focus on historical figures and events within specific families, detailing the intricate relationships, conflicts, and resolutions that arise over generations. These sagas are rooted in historical events and provide insight into the social structures and legal practices of early Icelandic society. In contrast, legendary sagas, or "fornaldarsögur," often incorporate mythological elements and legendary heroes, presenting tales of supernatural events and epic journeys. Both types of sagas serve as vital sources for understanding the sociocultural landscape of medieval Scandinavia.

The historical context in which the sagas were written plays a crucial role in their narratives. Composed during a period of relative peace and stability in Iceland, the sagas reflect the concerns and aspirations of a society transitioning from a nomadic lifestyle to settled agricultural communities. The authors, often anonymous, drew upon oral traditions to craft these narratives, infusing them with both historical accuracy and creative embellishment. This duality allows the sagas to serve not only as entertainment but also as a means of preserving history and cultural identity, illustrating the values and beliefs of a society grappling with its past.

Character analysis in the sagas reveals a rich tapestry of archetypes that resonate throughout the narratives. The protagonists often embody traits such as bravery, cunning, and a deep sense of duty to their kin, which reflect the ideals of the Norse warrior ethos. Female characters, while sometimes relegated to subordinate roles, frequently display strength, intelligence, and agency, challenging traditional gender norms. The interplay between these characters often drives the plot, revealing the complexities of human nature in the face of fate and moral challenges.

Through their struggles and triumphs, the sagas provide timeless insights into the human condition.

The influence of Norse mythology on the narratives of the sagas is profound, as these tales weave together historical events with fantastical elements. The presence of gods, mythical creatures, and supernatural occurrences serves to enrich the sagas, grounding their themes in a broader cosmological framework. Norse mythology informs the characters' motivations and the moral lessons embedded in the stories, illustrating the interplay between fate and free will. As readers delve into the sagas, they encounter a world where the boundaries between reality and myth blur, culminating in narratives that are both historically significant and deeply resonant with the timeless themes of human experience.

## Historical Significance and Cultural Impact

The historical significance of the Icelandic sagas lies not only in their narrative value but also in their role as crucial documents of the medieval Norse world. These sagas, composed in the 13th and 14th centuries, reflect the social, political, and cultural landscapes of Iceland and Scandinavia during a time of great change. They provide insights into the lives of early settlers, their conflicts, and their value systems. By chronicling events from the Viking Age to the establishment of the Icelandic Commonwealth, the sagas serve as essential historical texts that inform our understanding of Norse society, law, and family dynamics. They reveal how sagas were intertwined with the fabric of daily life, offering a lens through which we can examine the societal norms and customs of the time.

In addition to their historical context, the cultural impact of the sagas has been profound and enduring. They have influenced not only Icelandic literature but also the broader literary tradition of Europe. The narrative techniques, character development, and thematic complexity found in the sagas have inspired countless writers and artists. From the romanticism of the 19th century to contemporary adaptations, the Icelandic sagas continue to shape storytelling practices across various mediums. Their portrayal of heroism, morality, and the human condition resonates with audiences, making them timeless works that transcend their historical origins.

Character analysis within the sagas reveals a rich tapestry of archetypes that reflect the values and struggles of Norse culture. Figures such as the heroic warrior, the cunning strategist, and the wise elder embody universal themes of honor, loyalty, and vengeance. These archetypes not only serve as narrative devices but also offer commentary on the complexities of human nature and the societal expectations of the time. The interplay between characters often highlights the tension between fate and free will, a recurring motif in Norse mythology that underscores the sagas' philosophical depth. By examining these figures, readers can gain a deeper understanding of how the sagas articulate the human experience through the lens of their historical context.

The influence of Norse mythology on saga narratives is another critical aspect of their cultural significance. Mythological elements are woven throughout the sagas, enriching the stories with layers of meaning and resonance. Themes such as the struggle against fate, the presence of supernatural beings, and the importance of honor and revenge are deeply rooted in Norse mythological traditions. This intersection between myth and history not only enhances the sagas' narrative complexity but also reflects the beliefs and values of the Norse people. By incorporating mythological references and motifs, the sagas create a dialogue between the historical and the divine, allowing readers to explore the intersections of everyday life and the extraordinary.

Ultimately, the historical significance and cultural impact of the Icelandic sagas extend far beyond their narrative content. They serve as a crucial bridge between the past and present, offering insights into the values, beliefs, and experiences of a society that has shaped much of Northern European culture. Through their exploration of human nature, societal norms, and the interplay of myth and history, the sagas continue to resonate with modern audiences. Their legacy endures not only in literature but also in the collective memory of a people who have preserved their stories through the centuries, echoing the timeless struggles and triumphs of humanity.

## The Oral Tradition and Literary Evolution

The oral tradition served as the fundamental foundation for the Icelandic sagas, shaping their narratives long before they were inscribed in written form. These tales emerged from a society where storytelling was not only a means of entertainment but also a crucial method of preserving history, culture, and identity. The oral tradition allowed for a dynamic evolution of stories, where details could shift and characters could be embellished or simplified according to the audience's reactions. This fluidity contributed to a rich tapestry of narratives that reflected the values and experiences of the Norse people. As the sagas transitioned from oral recitation to written text in the 13th century, the influence of this tradition remained palpable, imbuing the sagas with a sense of immediacy and communal relevance.

The process of literary evolution in the Icelandic sagas was significantly influenced by the historical context in which they were composed. The establishment of a written literary culture coincided with the Christianization of Iceland and the consolidation of chieftain power, which brought about a new social order. This transformation introduced new themes and motifs into saga narratives, as writers sought to reconcile pagan traditions with Christian values. The resulting texts reflect a complex interplay between old and new beliefs, showcasing how authors adapted the oral traditions to align with contemporary societal norms while preserving the essence of their ancestral stories.

Character analysis within the sagas reveals a rich array of archetypes that resonate with universal human experiences. Heroes and anti-heroes alike populate these narratives, embodying traits such as bravery, loyalty, and vengeance. Figures like Egill Skallagrímsson and Njáll Þorgeirsson stand out not only for their distinctive characteristics but also for the moral dilemmas they face, making their journeys relatable and timeless. The sagas often explore the consequences of personal choices, illustrating how individual actions can lead to both personal glory and tragic downfall. Through this exploration, the sagas provide profound insights into the human condition, all while maintaining a connection to their oral roots.

Norse mythology plays a pivotal role in shaping the narratives found within the Icelandic sagas. The sagas frequently incorporate mythological elements, weaving them into the fabric of historical accounts and personal stories. Deities, supernatural beings, and mythical events serve as both motifs and catalysts for character development, influencing decisions and outcomes. For instance, the presence of fate and prophecy looms large in many sagas, echoing the Norse belief in a predetermined destiny. This integration of mythology enriches the storytelling, offering layers of meaning that enhance the reader's understanding of the cultural worldview from which these sagas emerged.

Ultimately, the interplay between oral tradition, historical context, character archetypes, and Norse mythology culminates in a literary legacy that continues to resonate today. The sagas stand as a testament to the resilience of storytelling, showcasing how narratives evolve while preserving core themes that speak to the human experience. As we delve into these texts, we uncover not only the stories of the past but also the enduring echoes of a culture that valued memory, identity, and the shared bonds of community. The Icelandic sagas serve as a bridge between worlds, inviting readers to explore the depths of their narratives and the timeless truths they convey.

# Chapter 2: Historical Context of the Sagas

## The Viking Age and Settlement of Iceland

The Viking Age, spanning from the late 8th century to the early 11th century, marked a significant period of exploration, trade, and settlement for Norse seafarers. This era was characterized by the expansion of Norse culture across Europe and beyond, leading to the establishment of settlements in various territories. Among these territories, Iceland emerged as a particularly fascinating case of Viking settlement. The discovery and subsequent colonization of Iceland by Norse settlers in the late 9th century not only transformed the island's landscape but also played a crucial role in shaping the narratives found in the Icelandic sagas.

The settlement of Iceland began around 874 AD, when Norsemen, primarily from Norway, began to arrive on the island. This migration was driven by a combination of factors, including overpopulation, political strife, and the search for new lands. The most notable figure from this period is Flóki Vilgerðarson, who is traditionally credited with the first discovery of Iceland. His journey, along with others who followed, introduced a new chapter in Norse history, as these settlers brought with them their customs, beliefs, and a rich oral tradition that would later be captured in the sagas.

As the Norse settlers established their homes, they adapted to the harsh Icelandic environment, relying on their seafaring skills and agricultural practices. The social structure that developed mirrored that of their Scandinavian roots, with chieftains and clans forming the backbone of Icelandic society. This setting provided a fertile ground for the development of the sagas, which often featured themes of heroism, family loyalty, and the struggle against the forces of nature. The challenges faced by these early settlers are reflected in the sagas, where characters are frequently depicted navigating both personal and external conflicts, embodying the archetypal traits of bravery and resilience.

Iceland's unique geographical isolation allowed for a distinct cultural evolution that influenced the sagas profoundly. The interplay between the harsh natural environment and the settlers' Norse mythology is a recurring motif in these narratives. The sagas often incorporate elements of Norse beliefs, such as the significance of fate and the presence of gods, which shaped the moral frameworks and decision-making processes of the characters. As the settlers faced the unpredictable Icelandic climate, their reliance on mythological narratives provided a means to understand and cope with their realities, infusing the sagas with a rich tapestry of cultural significance.

The legacy of the Viking Age and the settlement of Iceland endures in the Icelandic sagas, serving as a testament to the resilience of the human spirit in the face of adversity. These narratives not only document the historical events of the time but also reveal the complex character dynamics and archetypes that continue to resonate with contemporary audiences. Through the lens of Norse mythology and the experiences of the early settlers, the sagas offer a profound exploration of identity, community, and the enduring echoes of a bygone era in the North.

## Political and Social Structures in Medieval Iceland

Medieval Iceland, particularly during the period from the settlement in the late ninth century to the establishment of the Althing in 930 CE, was marked by unique political and social structures that set it apart from contemporary European societies. The absence of a centralized monarchy allowed for the development of a system of chieftains, known as goðar, who wielded significant influence over their local regions. These chieftains were often landowners who held authority through personal loyalty rather than coercive power, leading to a complex web of allegiances and rivalries. The political landscape was characterized by a decentralized model, where power was distributed among various families and clans, each vying for dominance while simultaneously relying on social bonds to maintain their standing.

The Althing, established as one of the world's oldest parliaments, served as a crucial institution for political discourse and conflict resolution in medieval Iceland. It was convened annually at Thingvellir, where chieftains and free men gathered to discuss legal matters, settle disputes, and enact laws. This assembly represented the collective interests of the Icelandic population and provided a platform for negotiation and consensus. The legal system was heavily influenced by customary law, with an emphasis on oral tradition and local customs. The lack of formal written laws meant that the sagas often reflect the social norms and values of the time, illustrating how legal disputes and resolutions were embedded in the cultural fabric of Icelandic society.

Social stratification in medieval Iceland was relatively fluid compared to other European societies, with the potential for social mobility, particularly through successful trade or notable achievements in battle. The primary social classes included the aristocracy, represented by the goðar, the freemen or karlar, and the lower class known as thralls, or slaves. While thralls were at the bottom of the hierarchy, their status could be improved through manumission, and they sometimes played significant roles in the narratives of the sagas. The sagas often featured characters who transcended their social standing, highlighting the importance of individual agency and the potential for personal transformation within the socio-political framework of the time.

Gender roles in medieval Iceland were also nuanced, with women enjoying a degree of autonomy that was uncommon in many parts of the world. Women could own property, initiate divorce, and engage in legal proceedings, which is often reflected in the sagas through strong female characters who maneuver through the patriarchal structure. Figures like Guðrún Ósvífrsdóttir from the Laxdæla saga exemplify the complexities of female agency in a predominantly male-dominated society. The sagas' portrayal of women reveals a society that, while patriarchal, allowed for significant female influence in both domestic and political spheres.

The interplay between political and social structures in medieval Iceland is further enriched by the influence of Norse mythology and cultural traditions. The sagas frequently incorporate elements of myth and legend, intertwining historical events with the fantastical, which reflects the collective psyche of the Icelandic people. The reverence for the Norse gods and the belief in fate and honor shaped not only the narratives within the sagas but also the societal values that governed personal conduct and community relations. As such, the political and social frameworks of medieval Iceland were not merely administrative or hierarchical; they were deeply embedded in a rich tapestry of mythological and cultural narratives that continue to resonate in the contemporary understanding of Icelandic heritage.

## The Role of Christianity and Paganism

The interplay between Christianity and paganism in the Icelandic sagas reflects a complex cultural transition that shaped Icelandic identity and narrative traditions. As Iceland converted to Christianity in the year 1000, the sagas began to emerge as a literary form that captured the essence of both pagan beliefs and the new Christian ethos. This duality is evident in the sagas, where characters often grapple with moral dilemmas that reflect their pagan heritage while simultaneously navigating the principles of Christianity. The resulting narratives highlight the tension between old and new beliefs, illustrating a society in flux as it reconciled its past with the emerging Christian worldview.

Paganism in the sagas is prominently characterized by a rich tapestry of Norse mythology, where gods, goddesses, and mythical creatures play significant roles. Characters such as Odin, Thor, and Freyja are not only central figures in the mythological landscape but also serve as archetypes that inform the human experience depicted in the sagas. The sagas often reflect the values of the Viking Age, including honor, bravery, and fate, which resonate with the pagan belief system. These themes are intricately woven into the narratives, allowing readers to explore the moral complexities faced by the sagas' protagonists against the backdrop of a polytheistic culture.

As Christianity took root in Iceland, the sagas began to incorporate Christian themes and values, leading to a rich dialogue between the two belief systems. Characters in the sagas often exhibit traits that align with Christian virtues, such as compassion, forgiveness, and humility, while still being deeply influenced by their pagan origins. This synthesis is particularly evident in the portrayal of figures like Snorri Sturluson, who worked to preserve the sagas while also aligning them with Christian ideals. The sagas thus serve as a reflection of the societal values of their time, illustrating how individuals navigated their identities in a world where both paganism and Christianity coexisted.

The role of Christianity is further emphasized in the sagas through the incorporation of Christian symbols and moral lessons. The narrative structure often mirrors biblical stories, drawing parallels between saga characters and Christian saints or figures. This blending of traditions not only enriched the saga narratives but also provided a framework for understanding the moral landscape of medieval Iceland. The transformation of characters from pagan warriors to Christian heroes illustrates a broader narrative arc of redemption and moral evolution, making the sagas a vital source for understanding the cultural dynamics of the time.

In conclusion, the relationship between Christianity and paganism in the Icelandic sagas is a profound testament to the cultural and spiritual evolution of medieval Iceland. The sagas encapsulate the struggle between old and new beliefs, allowing readers to witness the gradual shift in values and identity. Through character analysis and thematic exploration, the sagas reveal how these two influences shaped not only the narratives themselves but also the society from which they emerged. As such, they remain a critical component of Icelandic heritage, echoing the complexities of a culture in transition.

# Chapter 3: Influences on the Icelandic Sagas

## Scandinavian Literary Traditions

Scandinavian literary traditions have played a pivotal role in shaping the cultural and narrative landscape of the Nordic countries, particularly through the lens of the Icelandic sagas. These prose narratives, originating in the 13th century, offer a unique insight into the social, political, and mythological contexts of medieval Scandinavia. The sagas not only reflect the historical realities of the Viking Age but also serve as vessels for the values, beliefs, and conflicts that characterized the Norse worldview. Understanding these literary traditions is essential for appreciating the depth and complexity of the sagas themselves.

The historical context of the Icelandic sagas is deeply intertwined with the political and social changes of the time. The transition from a nomadic, tribal society to a more settled, agrarian one created a fertile ground for storytelling. The sagas often depict the lives of chieftains and their families, exploring themes of honor, loyalty, and revenge. This focus on individual and familial dynamics mirrors the shifting power structures of medieval Iceland, where local leaders vied for influence and status. Moreover, the sagas were often composed in contexts of political unrest, reflecting the tensions and struggles of their era, which adds layers of meaning to their narratives.

Character analysis in the sagas reveals a rich tapestry of archetypes that resonate with universal human experiences. Protagonists and antagonists often embody traits such as bravery, cunning, and moral ambiguity, making them relatable to contemporary readers. Figures like Grettir the Strong and Njáll from Njáls saga are emblematic of the heroic ideal, yet they also reveal the vulnerabilities and flaws that accompany their strengths. The sagas frequently explore the consequences of characters' actions, emphasizing the themes of fate and personal agency. This complexity allows for a nuanced examination of human nature, where characters are not merely heroes or villains but rather intricate individuals shaped by their circumstances.

Norse mythology significantly influences the narrative structure and thematic content of the sagas. The intertwining of mythological elements with historical events creates a rich narrative tapestry that elevates the sagas beyond mere historical accounts. Gods, giants, and mythical creatures often appear alongside human characters, blurring the lines between the mortal and the divine. This interplay serves to reinforce the sagas' exploration of fate, destiny, and the supernatural, highlighting the belief systems that permeated Norse culture. The sagas thus become a reflection of the collective psyche of the Norse people, allowing readers to glimpse their fears, aspirations, and understanding of the cosmos.

The legacy of Scandinavian literary traditions, particularly through the Icelandic sagas, continues to influence modern literature and popular culture. Their themes of heroism, tragedy, and the human condition resonate across time and space, inspiring countless adaptations and reinterpretations. As contemporary readers engage with these ancient texts, they find not only a connection to their historical roots but also a deeper understanding of the universal themes that bind humanity. The enduring nature of the sagas attests to the power of storytelling, reminding us that the echoes of the North still reverberate in our collective consciousness today.

## The Influence of European Literature

European literature has profoundly influenced the development and evolution of the Icelandic sagas, intertwining the cultural narratives of the Norse with broader literary traditions. The sagas, originating in the medieval period, were not created in isolation; they emerged within a rich tapestry of European literary forms and motifs. The intricate storytelling techniques and thematic explorations found in the sagas reflect a dialogue with the literary currents of their time, particularly those stemming from the broader Scandinavian and continental European literary landscape. This influence is evident in the sagas' structure, character development, and the moral dilemmas faced by their protagonists.

The sagas often incorporate narrative elements that resonate with European literary traditions, such as chivalric ideals and the concept of heroism. In many ways, the sagas reimagined these themes through a Norse lens, focusing on the values of honor, loyalty, and vengeance that were paramount in Viking society. This adaptation can be seen in the characterization of figures like Grettir and Njáll, whose journeys echo the complexities of both personal and communal obligations, reflecting universal themes that transcend cultural boundaries. The significance of fate and free will, prevalent in European narratives, also finds a prominent place in the sagas, where characters grapple with their destinies against the backdrop of Norse mythology.

Moreover, the influence of classical literature cannot be understated. The sagas exhibit a familiarity with Greco-Roman literary traditions, particularly in their use of rhetoric and the exploration of tragic themes. The presence of fate, as embodied by the Norns in Norse mythology, parallels the Greek concept of Moira, suggesting a shared understanding of human existence's inherent uncertainties. This intertextuality enriches the sagas, allowing them to engage in a broader conversation about the human experience, morality, and the inexorable nature of fate.

Character analysis within the sagas reveals archetypes that resonate with both Norse and European literary traditions. The conflicted hero, the wise old man, and the treacherous antagonist are figures that appear across various cultures, suggesting a shared understanding of human psychology and social dynamics. For instance, the character of Egil Skallagrimsson embodies the archetype of the tortured genius, a figure who navigates the complexities of societal expectations and personal ambition. This archetypal resonance not only highlights the sagas' connections to European literature but also underscores their unique contributions to the understanding of character and narrative in literary history.

The impact of Norse mythology on saga narratives cannot be overlooked in the context of European literary influence. The sagas frequently draw upon mythological themes and figures, integrating them into their narratives in ways that enhance the drama and depth of the human experience. This interplay between the mythic and the historical creates a rich narrative tapestry that speaks to the collective consciousness of the Norse people while simultaneously inviting comparison with other European mythologies. Through this lens, the sagas serve as a testament to the enduring power of storytelling, illustrating how European literature shaped and was shaped by the vibrant cultural exchange that characterized the medieval world.

## Historical Events as Narrative Catalysts

Historical events serve as pivotal narrative catalysts within the Icelandic sagas, fundamentally shaping the plotlines, character developments, and thematic explorations that define these literary works. The sagas are deeply rooted in the historical context of the Norse society during the Viking Age, reflecting the values, struggles, and aspirations of their time. By intertwining fictional narratives with actual events, the sagas not only preserve the memories of past generations but also offer insight into the social structures, conflicts, and cultural dynamics of medieval Iceland. This interplay between history and narrative enhances the sagas' relevance, allowing them to resonate with readers across centuries.

One of the most significant historical events that influenced the sagas is the establishment of the Althing, one of the world's oldest parliaments, in 930 AD. This political development fostered a sense of community and governance among the settlers and became a crucial backdrop for many saga narratives. The Althing served as a platform for resolving disputes, enacting laws, and discussing matters of communal importance. Consequently, characters in the sagas often navigate the complexities of law and justice, reflecting the broader societal implications of their actions. The portrayal of such events adds layers of depth to character motivations and conflicts, making the narratives rich in both historical and moral significance.

Moreover, the Viking Age's expansion, marked by exploration and conquest, provides a dynamic context for the sagas. The encounters between Norse settlers and indigenous peoples, as well as the resulting cultural exchanges, influence character interactions and the evolution of saga themes. For instance, narratives of adventure and exploration often highlight the tension between the allure of the unknown and the ethical dilemmas faced by the protagonists. Characters like

Erik the Red and Leif Erikson embody the spirit of adventure while also grappling with the consequences of their actions, illustrating how historical events shape personal narratives and moral choices.

In addition to political and exploratory events, the sagas also reflect the impact of feuds and conflicts that characterized Norse society. Blood feuds, often ignited by personal grievances or honor disputes, serve as central motifs in many sagas. These historical realities are not merely background elements; they drive the narratives forward, catalyzing actions, choices, and transformations in characters. The emphasis on honor, revenge, and reconciliation echoes broader themes of loyalty and familial duty, allowing readers to delve into the intricate web of human relationships influenced by historical circumstances.

Finally, the integration of Norse mythology with historical events enriches the narratives of the Icelandic sagas. Mythological references often serve as metaphors for real-world events, providing a deeper understanding of character motivations and societal values. The sagas frequently invoke mythological archetypes, aligning historical figures with legendary heroes or gods to enhance their significance. This interplay between myth and history not only serves to elevate the narratives but also reinforces the cultural identity of the Norse people, illustrating how historical events can transcend time through the lens of storytelling. In this way, the sagas not only recount history but also weave it into the fabric of cultural memory, making them timeless narratives that echo through generations.

# Chapter 4: Character Analysis in the Sagas

## Heroic Archetypes and Their Development

Heroic archetypes in the Icelandic sagas serve as crucial vehicles for exploring the complexities of human nature, societal values, and the cultural context of Norse life. These archetypes often embody traits such as bravery, honor, and vengeance, reflecting the societal ideals of the Viking Age. Characters like Njáll and Gunnar exemplify the warrior ethos, while others, such as Hallgerður and Guðrún, represent the nuanced roles of women who wield significant influence within their narratives. Through their journeys, these figures not only engage in personal quests but also illuminate the collective identity of the Norse people, illustrating how individual heroism intertwines with community values.

The development of these heroic archetypes is deeply rooted in the historical milieu of early medieval Scandinavia. The sagas were penned during a time when the Norse were transitioning from a predominantly oral culture to one that embraced written forms of storytelling. This shift allowed for a more nuanced exploration of characters, as authors could delve into their inner thoughts and motivations. The sagas reflect the tensions of their time, such as the clash between pagan traditions and the encroaching influence of Christianity, which contributed to the evolving definitions of heroism. As characters navigate these tensions, their development mirrors the broader cultural shifts occurring within Norse society.

Central to the narratives are the themes of fate and free will, presenting a dichotomy that shapes the development of heroic archetypes. The concept of "wyrd," or fate, looms large in the sagas, suggesting that heroes are often bound by destiny. However, the choices they make in confronting their fates reveal their character and moral fiber. This interplay between predetermined destiny and individual agency becomes a hallmark of the sagas, leading to a rich tapestry of character development. For instance, characters may initially appear as straightforward heroes, only to reveal complexities as their stories unfold, prompting readers to reconsider their initial perceptions.

The influence of Norse mythology on these archetypes further enriches their development. Mythological elements often seep into the sagas, providing a framework through which characters grapple with the divine and the supernatural. The heroes' interactions with gods, giants, and other mythological beings often serve as catalysts for their growth, pushing them toward self-discovery and transformation. For example, encounters with figures from the pantheon can lead to moments of enlightenment or profound loss, underscoring the idea that true heroism often comes at a personal cost. This blending of myth and narrative illustrates the sagas' role as both entertainment and moral instruction, guiding audiences toward deeper reflections on virtue and vice.

In examining heroic archetypes within the Icelandic sagas, one discovers a rich landscape of character development that resonates beyond its historical context. These figures encapsulate the struggles and triumphs of the human experience, inviting readers to explore their own values and beliefs. The sagas, steeped in the complexities of Norse mythology and societal expectations, provide a lens through which to understand not just the past, but also the timeless nature of heroism itself. As such, the heroic archetypes in these narratives continue to echo, offering insights into the enduring quest for identity, purpose, and legacy in a changing world.

## Female Characters and Their Roles

The Icelandic sagas, rich in narrative complexity and cultural significance, feature a diverse array of female characters whose roles challenge traditional gender norms of their time. These women often find themselves in positions of agency, navigating a world dominated by male figures. Their characterizations reflect not only the societal values of the Viking Age but also the multifaceted nature of femininity in a harsh, often unforgiving environment. The presence of these characters adds depth to the sagas, illustrating how women influenced social dynamics and familial ties within their communities.

One of the most striking aspects of female characters in the sagas is their involvement in key plot developments. Figures like Gudrun Osvifrsdottir from "Laxdaela Saga" exemplify how women wield influence through their decisions, relationships, and even vengeance. Gudrun's journey through love, loss, and revenge highlights the complexities of emotional resilience and the power women could exert in a patriarchal society. Such portrayals resonate with themes of loyalty and betrayal, showcasing women as central figures in the moral and ethical dilemmas faced by characters in the sagas.

Moreover, the sagas often depict women as the keepers of lineage and heritage. Characters like Brynhildr from "Völsunga Saga" serve not only as pivotal players in their own narratives but also as symbols of the cultural and familial legacy that women upheld. Their roles as mothers, wives, and sisters illustrate the importance of familial bonds while also emphasizing the burden of these connections. The sagas frequently explore the tension between personal desire and familial duty, a theme deeply rooted in Norse mythology and its teachings on fate and destiny.

The influence of Norse mythology on these female characters cannot be overlooked. Many women in the sagas embody traits associated with goddesses and mythological figures, reflecting the intertwining of myth and reality within Icelandic culture. For example, the character of Freyja, who is associated with love and war, can be seen mirrored in the actions and motivations of saga heroines. This connection adds layers to their character arcs, as they navigate the divine expectations alongside the earthly challenges they face, reinforcing the idea that women were viewed as both powerful and vulnerable in the societal hierarchy.

Overall, the exploration of female characters in the Icelandic sagas reveals a rich tapestry of roles that challenge conventional perceptions of women in historical narratives. Through their agency, emotional depth, and connections to mythology, these characters enrich the sagas and offer a lens through which to understand the complexities of gender dynamics in the Viking Age. As modern readers engage with these texts, they uncover not only the stories of these women but also the broader implications of their presence and influence in a world shaped by both human and divine forces.

## Villains and Antiheroes in the Sagas

The Icelandic sagas are renowned for their intricate characterizations, particularly of villains and antiheroes, who often occupy central roles in the narratives. These figures are not merely obstacles for the protagonists but are crafted with depth, reflecting the complexities of human nature and moral ambiguity. The sagas often depict these characters as embodiments of traits such as pride, vengeance, and ambition, illustrating a nuanced understanding of morality that resonates with the audience. Their motivations and actions compel readers to grapple with the shades of gray in morality, challenging the traditional dichotomy of good versus evil.

One notable archetype of the villain in the sagas is the blood feuder, often driven by a desire for vengeance following a perceived wrong. Characters like Egil Skallagrimsson, from Egil's Saga, exemplify this archetype, where personal honor and familial loyalty propel them into cycles of violence. Such narratives reveal the societal importance of reputation and revenge in Viking culture, where honor was paramount. The antihero, on the other hand, emerges in characters who exhibit morally ambiguous traits yet garner sympathy from the audience. These figures, such as Grettir the Strong, showcase the struggle between individual desires and societal expectations, inviting readers to explore the complexities of heroism beyond traditional valor.

The influence of Norse mythology is evident in the portrayal of these villains and antiheroes. Many saga characters draw on mythological tropes, embodying traits found in gods and mythical creatures. Figures such as Loki, with his cunning and deceit, find parallels in saga villains who manipulate circumstances for personal gain. This interweaving of mythology and narrative enriches the sagas, providing a framework through which readers can understand the characters' motivations and actions. The sagas serve as a reflection of the cultural beliefs and values of the time, where the line between heroism and villainy is often blurred, mirroring the unpredictability of fate itself.

Moreover, the sagas often depict the consequences of villainous actions, emphasizing the cyclical nature of violence and revenge. Characters who engage in treachery or betrayal find themselves ensnared in a web of retribution, leading to a relentless cycle of bloodshed. This theme serves as a cautionary tale about the destructive nature of vengeance, suggesting that the pursuit of personal honor can ultimately lead to one's downfall. The sagas highlight the inevitable consequences of actions, reinforcing the interconnectedness of characters and their fates within the narrative landscape.

Ultimately, the exploration of villains and antiheroes in the Icelandic sagas offers profound insights into the human condition. These characters challenge readers to reflect on their own moral compass and the complexities of ethical decision-making. By delving into the motivations and consequences of these figures, the sagas reveal the intricate tapestry of human relationships and the often tumultuous paths individuals traverse. In doing so, they not only entertain but also provoke contemplation about the nature of good and evil, positioning the sagas as timeless narratives that continue to resonate with contemporary audiences.

# Chapter 5: Common Themes in the Sagas

## Honor and Revenge

In the Icelandic sagas, the themes of honor and revenge are intricately woven into the fabric of the narratives, reflecting the cultural values of Norse society. Honor, often equated with personal and familial reputation, serves as a driving force behind the actions of many characters. The sagas illustrate how one's standing in the community is paramount, and any affront to that honor necessitates a response, often through acts of vengeance. This societal expectation creates a cycle of retribution that can escalate conflicts, leading to feuds that span generations. The complexities of these themes reveal much about the moral framework guiding the characters, illuminating the ways in which honor dictated social interactions and personal choices.

The concept of revenge in the sagas is not merely a personal vendetta but also a means to restore balance and justice within the community. Characters often feel compelled to act in accordance with their understanding of honor, leading them to seek retribution for perceived slights or wrongs. This pursuit can take various forms, from calculated schemes to outright violence, and the sagas often depict the consequences of such actions. The deep-seated belief in the necessity of avenging wrongs highlights the tension between individual desires and communal expectations, illustrating how personal grievances can intertwine with broader societal norms.

Examining key characters within the sagas reveals the archetypal roles that honor and revenge play in shaping their identities and destinies. Figures such as Grettir and Njáll embody the struggle between personal integrity and societal pressures. Grettir, for instance, grapples with his sense of honor while facing relentless foes, illustrating the burdensome legacy of vengeance. Conversely, Njáll's story underscores the tragic ramifications of revenge, where the quest for honor leads to devastating losses. Through these characters, the sagas explore the complexities of human motivation, revealing how the pursuit of honor can lead to both noble and destructive outcomes.

The narratives of the sagas are deeply influenced by Norse mythology, which provides a backdrop for understanding the significance of honor and revenge. The myths often explore themes of fate, destiny, and the moral implications of one's actions, reinforcing the belief that individuals are bound by a code of honor that governs their lives. Deities such as Odin and Freyja exemplify the dual nature of honor, representing both the nobility of valor and the destructive power of revenge. As characters navigate their quests for honor, they often invoke mythological precedents, drawing parallels between their struggles and those of the gods, thereby enriching the narrative with layers of meaning.

Ultimately, the interplay of honor and revenge in the Icelandic sagas offers profound insights into the human condition, reflecting the values and beliefs of a society that revered both. The sagas serve as a mirror, revealing the complexities of personal and communal identity while illustrating the often tragic consequences of pursuing vengeance. Through their exploration of these themes, the sagas not only entertain but also provoke contemplation about the nature of honor, the cyclical nature of violence, and the enduring impact of myth on cultural narratives. As readers engage with these stories, they are invited to reflect on the age-old dilemmas of honor and revenge, echoing through time from the Norse past to contemporary life.

## Fate and Free Will

Fate and free will are central themes woven throughout the Icelandic sagas, reflecting the complex interplay between predestined outcomes and individual agency. The sagas often portray characters caught in the inexorable grip of fate, suggesting that their lives are governed by forces beyond their control. This deterministic view is heavily influenced by Norse mythology, where the concept of wyrd, or fate, plays a crucial role. In the sagas, characters frequently confront their destinies, grappling with the knowledge that their actions may lead them toward predetermined ends, thus raising questions about the nature of choice and responsibility.

The saga heroes often embody the tension between fate and free will, navigating their paths with a mix of courage and resignation. For instance, figures like Egil Skallagrimsson exhibit a fierce independence and a strong sense of personal agency, yet they are also portrayed as being bound by the inescapable threads of fate. Their struggles demonstrate a nuanced understanding of human existence; while they strive to assert their will, they remain aware of the celestial forces that shape their fates. This duality reflects the broader cultural beliefs of the Norse, where individuals were expected to act honorably despite the inevitability of their destinies.

The sagas also explore the impact of familial and societal expectations on individual choices. Characters often find themselves in situations where their actions are driven not just by personal desire but by the obligations imposed by kinship and community. This societal context complicates the notion of free will, suggesting that while characters may possess the ability to make choices, those choices are frequently constrained by their relationships and societal norms. The sagas depict the struggle to balance personal ambition with loyalty to family and tradition, emphasizing that even the most resolute individuals are often entangled in the web of their obligations.

Moreover, Norse mythology further enriches the dialogue between fate and free will in the sagas. The presence of gods and supernatural beings serves as a reminder of the cosmic forces at play, influencing human lives in ways that are often mysterious and inscrutable. Characters may receive prophecies or omens, which they interpret as a guide or a curse, illustrating the tension between accepting one's fate and attempting to alter it. The gods themselves exemplify this struggle, as they are powerful yet subject to the same fates as mortals, reinforcing the idea that no one, regardless of their strength or status, can escape the fabric of destiny.

In conclusion, the theme of fate and free will in the Icelandic sagas invites readers to contemplate the nature of human existence and the forces that shape our lives. Through character analysis and the exploration of archetypal figures, the sagas reveal a rich tapestry of human experience, where the quest for autonomy is often met with the recognition of inevitable fate. This interplay offers profound insights into the cultural psyche of the Norse people, illustrating how their understanding of destiny and choice continues to resonate in contemporary discussions about free will and moral responsibility.

## Family and Kinship Dynamics

Family and kinship dynamics in the Icelandic sagas serve as a critical lens through which to understand the social fabric of Norse society. The sagas often depict a complex web of relationships, underscoring the importance of lineage, loyalty, and honor. These narratives reveal that family ties were not merely personal connections but essential to one's identity and societal standing. In the sagas, characters frequently navigate conflicts that arise from familial obligations and rivalries, illustrating how kinship could be both a source of strength and a catalyst for strife.

The portrayal of family in the sagas often reflects the historical context of the Viking Age, where clans and kin groups played a significant role in community dynamics. Extended families, or "ætt," were vital in providing support and protection, influencing everything from property rights to marriage alliances. The sagas highlight how these kinship ties could lead to feuds, as seen in the legendary conflicts between the families of Njáll and Gunnar. Such narratives not only serve to entertain but also provide insight into the cultural values of the time, where loyalty to family was paramount and often dictated one's actions.

Character analysis within the sagas reveals archetypes that are frequently tied to family roles. The figures of the wise elder, the vengeful brother, and the courageous daughter emerge against the backdrop of familial loyalty and conflict. These archetypes resonate with readers as they reflect universal themes of love, betrayal, and the struggle for honor. Characters like Guðrún, who balances her personal desires with her familial obligations, exemplify the intricate dance between individual agency and collective responsibility that defines the sagas. Such portrayals invite deeper contemplation of how these dynamics shape characters' fates within the narrative framework.

The influence of Norse mythology on familial and kinship dynamics in the sagas cannot be understated. Myths often serve as a backdrop for understanding the moral and ethical frameworks within which these families operate. The gods and goddesses frequently embody familial qualities, such as loyalty and vengeance, which reverberate through the actions of the saga characters. For instance, themes of fate and destiny—common in mythological narratives—play a crucial role in shaping the outcomes of family disputes. This intertwining of myth and kinship creates a rich tapestry that deepens the reader's engagement with the sagas.

In conclusion, the intricate family and kinship dynamics in the Icelandic sagas highlight the interplay between personal relationships and broader social structures. Through these narratives, we gain insight into the values and beliefs that defined Norse culture, illustrating how families were both a source of identity and a battleground for honor and revenge. The exploration of these dynamics not only enriches our understanding of the sagas but also invites reflection on the enduring nature of family ties in shaping human experience across cultures and time.

# Chapter 6: The Impact of Norse Mythology

## Mythological Figures in the Sagas

The Icelandic sagas are rich tapestries woven from the threads of history, culture, and myth. Among the most compelling aspects of these narratives are the mythological figures that populate their pages, serving as both direct influences on the characters and embodiments of themes pervasive in Norse culture. Gods, giants, and other supernatural beings not only enhance the dramatic tension but also reflect the societal values and existential dilemmas faced by the saga protagonists. This interplay between mythology and narrative structure offers a depth of understanding regarding the sagas' commentary on human nature, fate, and the cosmos.

Central to the sagas is the pantheon of Norse mythology, with figures such as Odin, Thor, and Freyja often echoing through the character arcs and plot developments. Odin, with his quest for knowledge and mastery over fate, resonates with saga heroes who seek power and wisdom at great personal cost. Thor's embodiment of strength and protection aligns with the sagas' portrayal of male heroes who navigate battles and conflicts. Freyja, representing love and war, captures the duality of female figures in the sagas, who may embody nurturing qualities while also wielding significant influence over the destinies of men. Such mythological figures serve not only as archetypes but also as mirrors reflecting the complex interplay of human desires and divine intervention.

The presence of giants and other creatures of folklore further enriches the narrative landscape of the sagas. These beings often symbolize chaos and the natural world, challenging the human characters to confront their own limitations and vulnerabilities. For example, encounters with trolls or giants may represent not just physical battles but also the internal struggles of the saga heroes against their own fears and doubts. This thematic layer underscores the sagas' exploration of the human condition, revealing how mythological figures act as catalysts for character development and moral inquiry.

Moreover, the sagas are steeped in a historical context that intertwines with these mythological elements. As the Norse culture evolved, the sagas began to reflect the shifting beliefs and values of society. The incorporation of mythological figures into saga narratives can be seen as a means of connecting past traditions with contemporary issues faced by the authors and their audiences. This historical lens provides insight into how the sagas functioned not only as entertainment but also as vehicles for cultural reflection and continuity, helping to preserve the values and lessons of Norse mythology amid changing times.

Ultimately, the mythological figures in the Icelandic sagas serve as vital components that enhance the narratives' complexity and emotional depth. By embodying fundamental human archetypes and dilemmas, these figures offer readers a profound engagement with themes of fate, identity, and morality. The sagas invite adults to reflect on their own lives through the lens of these timeless characters, suggesting that the echoes of the past continue to resonate within the modern human experience. Through this exploration of mythological figures, readers gain a richer understanding of the sagas and their enduring relevance in the fabric of storytelling.

## Cosmic Order and Chaos

The interplay of cosmic order and chaos is a central theme in the Icelandic sagas, reflecting the Norse worldview that intertwines fate, divine influence, and human agency. In this context, cosmic order represents the established norms and laws that govern both the natural and social worlds, while chaos embodies the unpredictable elements of life that disrupt this order. The sagas frequently depict characters navigating the tension between these two forces, illustrating the struggle to maintain balance in a world filled with uncertainty and strife. This duality not only serves as a narrative framework but also as a philosophical exploration of existence, morality, and the human condition.

Norse mythology profoundly influences the sagas, providing a rich tapestry of archetypes and symbols that reflect the cosmic order. Central to this mythology is the concept of Yggdrasil, the World Tree, which connects the nine realms and serves as a metaphor for the interconnectedness of all beings. The sagas often draw on this imagery to illustrate how individual actions resonate within the larger cosmic framework. Characters such as gods, giants, and heroes are imbued with traits that align with these archetypes, representing the ongoing struggle between order and chaos. This relationship between character and cosmic significance allows readers to understand the sagas not just as historical narratives but as reflections of a broader metaphysical landscape.

The sagas also examine the concept of fate, or "wyrd," which plays a crucial role in determining the course of events. Characters often confront their destinies with a sense of inevitability, grappling with the tension between their desires and the overarching structure of fate. This exploration of free will versus predestination is emblematic of the Norse belief in the fragility of human agency against the backdrop of an indifferent universe. The sagas illustrate how characters attempt to assert control over their lives, often leading to tragic outcomes that underscore the chaos inherent in existence. The interplay between personal choices and the cosmic order creates a rich narrative tension that captivates readers.

In many sagas, the arrival of chaos often serves as a catalyst for transformation. Conflicts, betrayals, and the intrusion of supernatural elements disrupt the established order, forcing characters to adapt and evolve. This chaotic intrusion can be seen as a necessary force, prompting growth and resilience as characters confront their vulnerabilities. The sagas highlight the importance of responding to chaos with courage and ingenuity, suggesting that while order is desirable, it is through chaos that true character is revealed. This thematic exploration encourages readers to reflect on their own lives, contemplating how they navigate the unpredictable nature of existence.

Ultimately, the dynamic between cosmic order and chaos in the Icelandic sagas offers profound insights into the human experience. The narratives compel readers to consider the balance of forces at play in their own lives, prompting reflections on how order and chaos shape personal identity and societal norms. By engaging with these themes, readers gain a deeper understanding of the sagas as not merely historical accounts but as timeless explorations of the complexities of life, inviting them to ponder the eternal dance between structure and upheaval that defines the human journey.

## The Influence of Myth on Character Motivations

Myth plays a pivotal role in shaping character motivations within the Icelandic sagas, weaving a complex tapestry that intertwines historical events with the rich fabric of Norse mythology. The sagas, often regarded as a reflection of the social and cultural ethos of medieval Iceland, draw heavily from mythological narratives that provide not only a backdrop but also a framework for understanding characters' actions and decisions. The interplay between myth and character motivation reveals deeper insights into the values, beliefs, and existential dilemmas faced by individuals in these narratives.

Characters in the sagas often embody archetypal traits derived from mythological figures, which influence their choices and interactions. For instance, the heroic ideals present in figures like Odin and Thor manifest in the sagas' protagonists, who frequently grapple with themes of honor, fate, and personal sacrifice. The influence of these myths instills a sense of purpose in characters, driving them to seek glory or retribution in accordance with the heroic code. This alignment with mythological archetypes not only enriches character development but also creates a resonance with the audience, as they recognize familiar motifs that transcend time and culture.

Moreover, the sagas often reflect the Norse belief in fate, or "wyrd," as a powerful force guiding character motivations. Characters frequently confront their destinies with a mix of acceptance and defiance, mirroring the struggles of mythological heroes who contend with the whims of the gods. This tension between free will and predestination is a central theme that motivates characters to engage in quests for revenge or reconciliation, often leading to tragic outcomes. The sagas illustrate how characters navigate their predicaments within the constraints of fate, revealing a profound connection to mythological narratives that emphasize the inescapable nature of destiny.

The moral and ethical dilemmas faced by characters in the sagas are also deeply influenced by mythological themes. The sagas often explore concepts of loyalty, betrayal, and justice, reflecting the complex moral landscape of Norse mythology. Characters are frequently placed in situations where they must choose between personal loyalty and societal obligations, echoing the conflicts faced by mythological figures. These decisions highlight the struggle between individual desires and communal responsibilities, showcasing how myth serves as a moral compass that guides characters through their trials.

In conclusion, the influence of myth on character motivations in the Icelandic sagas cannot be overstated. The intertwining of mythological elements with character arcs enriches the narrative, providing readers with a deeper understanding of the cultural and ethical landscape of medieval Iceland. By examining how characters are shaped by myth, we gain insights into the fundamental human experiences of struggle, identity, and the quest for meaning within a world governed by both fate and personal agency. Through this lens, the sagas emerge not merely as historical accounts but as timeless explorations of the human condition.

# Chapter 7: Case Studies of Prominent Sagas

## Njáls saga

Njáls saga, one of the most celebrated of the Icelandic sagas, offers a profound insight into the complexities of human relationships, legal customs, and the moral dilemmas faced by its characters in the medieval Norse world. Set against the backdrop of Iceland's early settlement period, the saga chronicles the life of Njáll Þorgeirsson, a wise and astute man whose life intertwines with the fates of several key figures, including his friend Gunnar Hámundarson. The narrative unfolds with a blend of historical events and legendary embellishments, illuminating the social fabric of Icelandic society during the 10th and 11th centuries. This period was marked by a unique legal system known as the Althing, which plays a crucial role in the saga, highlighting the significance of law, honor, and revenge in Norse culture.

The characterization in Njáls saga is particularly noteworthy, as it presents a rich tapestry of personalities, each embodying various archetypes that resonate throughout the narrative. Njáll himself represents the archetype of the wise counselor, exhibiting traits of foresight and prudence in contrast to the impetuous nature of Gunnar, who embodies the classic hero archetype. Their friendship, characterized by mutual respect and loyalty, becomes a focal point of the saga, illustrating the intricate dynamics of masculinity and honor in Viking society. The saga delves into themes of friendship, betrayal, and the consequences of vengeance, showcasing how personal relationships are often tested by external conflicts and societal expectations.

Norse mythology significantly influences the narrative structure and themes within Njáls saga. The characters frequently invoke the gods and fate, illustrating the pervasive belief in supernatural forces that govern human affairs. The saga also reflects the Norse concept of honor and the inevitability of fate, captured in the recurring motif of blood feuds that escalate throughout the story. Njáll's prophetic dreams and the ominous omens that precede key events serve to remind readers of the intertwined nature of human agency and divine will, enhancing the saga's depth and complexity. This interplay between mythology and reality underscores the belief systems of the Norse people, revealing how these elements shaped their understanding of life and death.

The historical context of Njáls saga is critical to understanding its narrative and thematic richness. The saga emerges from a time when Iceland was transitioning from a society of clan-based loyalties to one that increasingly emphasized individualism and legal governance. This evolution is mirrored in the saga's exploration of personal honor versus communal responsibility. The characters navigate a world where the legal system is both a means of conflict resolution and a source of further discord, reflecting the challenges of establishing justice in a society where blood feuds are commonplace. The saga thus serves as a historical document, offering insights into the social, political, and legal landscapes of medieval Iceland.

In conclusion, Njáls saga stands as a testament to the enduring power of storytelling in reflecting the human experience. Through its intricate characterizations, profound themes, and historical significance, the saga not only entertains but also invites deep contemplation of the values and beliefs that shaped Norse society. As readers engage with the narrative, they are drawn into a world where the echoes of the past resonate, illuminating the complexities of honor, friendship, and the inexorable weave of fate that governs human lives. This exploration of Njáls saga enriches the understanding of the Icelandic sagas as a whole, revealing their capacity to illuminate both individual and collective identities in a rapidly changing world.

## Egils saga

Egils saga, one of the most esteemed narratives from the Icelandic sagas, presents a rich tapestry of themes encompassing heroism, familial loyalty, and the complexities of human emotions. This saga centers around the life of Egill Skallagrímsson, a historical figure whose exploits and character have fascinated audiences for centuries. Set against the backdrop of the Viking Age, the saga intricately weaves historical events with folklore, allowing readers to glimpse the societal values and challenges of 10th-century Iceland. The text serves not only as a narrative of individual achievements but also as a reflection of the broader cultural and historical currents of its time.

The saga is notable for its exploration of the interplay between personal identity and societal expectations. Egill, often portrayed as a fierce warrior and a skilled poet, embodies the archetype of the tragic hero. His journey reveals the tension between personal ambition and familial duty, as he grapples with the consequences of his actions on his family and community. The character of Egill is multifaceted; he is both a protector and a destroyer, illustrating the complex nature of human motivations. This duality resonates throughout the saga, emphasizing the moral ambiguities faced by individuals in a harsh and unforgiving landscape.

Norse mythology heavily influences the narrative structure and themes of Egils saga, enriching the story with layers of symbolic meaning. The saga incorporates mythological elements, such as the presence of supernatural beings and the significance of fate, which reflect the Norse belief system. The idea of fate, or wyrd, plays a crucial role in shaping the characters' destinies, often suggesting that their paths are preordained. This belief in fate is mirrored in Egill's life, where his extraordinary abilities and tragic flaws converge, ultimately leading to his triumphs and downfalls. The saga thus serves as a vehicle for exploring how mythological themes inform human experiences.

The historical context of Egils saga also merits examination, as it captures the essence of the Viking Age's cultural dynamics. The saga reflects the tensions between Iceland's settlers and their Scandinavian roots, highlighting issues like land ownership, power struggles, and the negotiation of loyalty among clans. The historical figures and events that populate the narrative ground Egill's story in a specific time and place, yet the themes of honor, vengeance, and kinship resonate universally. This blend of fact and fiction aids in understanding the complexities of Viking society and the moral frameworks that governed their actions.

In conclusion, Egils saga stands as a pivotal work within the landscape of the Icelandic sagas, encapsulating the intricate interplay of personal and societal narratives. The character of Egill Skallagrímsson serves as a compelling lens through which to explore themes of heroism, fate, and the human condition. Through its rich narrative and mythological underpinnings, the saga not only entertains but also invites reflection on the values and beliefs that shaped the lives of its characters. The enduring legacy of Egils saga continues to illuminate the cultural heritage of Iceland and offers profound insights into the timeless questions of identity, morality, and the complexities of human relationships.

## Laxdæla saga

Laxdæla saga, one of the notable sagas from medieval Iceland, presents a compelling narrative that intertwines the lives of its characters with themes of love, revenge, and the complexities of human relationships. Set in the late 9th and early 10th centuries, it chronicles the lives of the Laxdalir family, primarily focusing on the character of Gudrun Osvifrsdottir, a woman of remarkable depth and strength. Through her story, the saga explores the roles of women in Viking society, their agency, and the influence they wield within familial and societal structures. Gudrun's relationships with the men in her life, including her three husbands, serve as a lens through which readers can examine gender dynamics and the expectations placed upon individuals in a patriarchal society.

The historical context of Laxdæla saga is essential for understanding its narrative. Composed in the early 13th century, it reflects the values, beliefs, and conflicts of earlier times, particularly during the Age of Settlement in Iceland. The saga not only recounts tales of individual families but also mirrors the broader societal issues of the time, including land disputes, social status, and the emerging sense of Icelandic identity. By situating the personal stories of the characters within the larger framework of Iceland's history, the saga becomes a rich text for examining how personal and communal identities are shaped by historical events and cultural shifts.

Character analysis in Laxdæla saga reveals archetypes that resonate with timeless human experiences. Gudrun, for instance, embodies the archetype of the tragic heroine, whose choices lead to both personal triumphs and devastating consequences. The saga also introduces other archetypes, such as the wise old man in the form of her father, Osvif, who provides guidance yet is ultimately unable to shield his family from the turmoil that ensues. The interplay of these archetypes not only enhances the narrative but allows readers to engage with the characters on a deeper level, prompting reflections on their own lives and relationships.

Norse mythology significantly influences the narrative structure and themes of Laxdæla saga. The saga is imbued with references to fate, the supernatural, and the gods, reflecting the belief systems of the time. Characters often grapple with the concept of fate, as their lives seem to be governed by forces beyond their control. This interplay between human agency and divine influence is a critical aspect of the saga, raising questions about free will and destiny. The inclusion of mythological elements enriches the story, allowing for a nuanced exploration of the characters' motivations and the moral dilemmas they face.

Ultimately, Laxdæla saga stands as a testament to the enduring power of storytelling in shaping cultural narratives. Its intricate character development, historical context, and mythological underpinnings provide a multifaceted exploration of life in medieval Iceland. The saga not only serves as a window into the past but also invites contemporary readers to reflect on the universal themes of love, conflict, and the search for identity. As part of the larger tapestry of Icelandic sagas, Laxdæla saga continues to resonate, offering insights into the human condition that remain relevant today.

# Chapter 8: Modern Interpretations and Adaptations

## The Sagas in Contemporary Literature

The contemporary landscape of literature has been significantly shaped by the echoes of ancient narratives, particularly those found within the Icelandic sagas. These medieval texts, composed primarily between the 12th and 14th centuries, offer a rich tapestry of human experience, exploring themes of heroism, conflict, and identity. In recent years, authors have drawn upon the sagas, not merely as historical artifacts but as living texts that resonate with modern readers. This engagement has resulted in a renewed appreciation for the sagas, revealing their enduring relevance and the ways in which they continue to inform contemporary storytelling.

One of the most profound ways the sagas influence modern literature is through their complex character archetypes. Readers are often drawn to the multifaceted portrayals of figures such as the fierce warrior, the cunning strategist, or the tragic hero. Contemporary authors have adopted and adapted these archetypes, infusing them with new life while maintaining their foundational traits. This interplay between past and present allows for a deeper exploration of character psychology and moral ambiguity, inviting readers to reflect on the timeless nature of human struggles. As a result, the legacy of the sagas continues to shape character development in various genres, from fantasy to historical fiction.

The historical context of the sagas also serves as a fertile ground for contemporary writers seeking to explore themes of cultural identity and heritage. Modern narratives often grapple with the legacies of colonization, migration, and the search for belonging, mirroring the sagas' own preoccupations with kinship, land, and loyalty. Authors are increasingly using saga-inspired frameworks to examine contemporary societal issues, creating a dialogue between the past and present. This historical lens not only enriches storytelling but also prompts readers to consider how echoes of the past inform their own identities and experiences in an ever-changing world.

Moreover, the impact of Norse mythology on saga narratives continues to be a powerful source of inspiration for contemporary literature. The rich tapestry of gods, creatures, and cosmic battles found within Norse mythology is frequently woven into modern narratives, providing a mythical backdrop against which characters' struggles unfold. Authors harness these mythological elements to explore themes of fate, free will, and the cyclical nature of existence. By integrating these mythological motifs, contemporary writers pay homage to the sagas while simultaneously crafting new myths that resonate with today's audiences.

In conclusion, the Icelandic sagas remain a significant influence in contemporary literature, serving as a wellspring of inspiration for character development, thematic exploration, and narrative structure. As modern authors engage with these ancient texts, they not only revive the sagas' rich narratives but also invite readers to reflect on the complexities of the human condition. The ongoing dialogue between the sagas and contemporary writing underscores a shared human experience, bridging the gap between past and present, and ensuring that the echoes of the North continue to resonate in the literary world.

## Film and Television Adaptations

Film and television adaptations of the Icelandic sagas have emerged as significant cultural artifacts, reflecting contemporary interpretations of these ancient texts. The sagas, rich in historical context and character complexity, present a fertile ground for filmmakers and screenwriters seeking to explore themes of honor, fate, and the human condition. As adaptations proliferate, they often reshape the narratives to resonate with modern audiences while striving to maintain the essence of the original stories. This delicate balance raises questions about fidelity to source material and the creative liberties taken to enhance dramatic effect.

The historical context of the sagas is crucial for understanding their adaptations. Originating in the medieval period, these narratives encapsulate the values, beliefs, and struggles of Norse society. Filmmakers frequently draw upon this backdrop to provide authenticity to their adaptations. However, the challenge lies in translating a predominantly oral tradition, characterized by its episodic nature and intricate character dynamics, into a visual medium that demands a cohesive and engaging storyline. The resulting adaptations can sometimes oversimplify complex narratives or alter character arcs to fit a cinematic structure, which may lead to a departure from the source material's nuances.

Character analysis plays a pivotal role in the adaptations of the Icelandic sagas, where archetypes such as the hero, the anti-hero, and the tragic figure often come to the forefront. In film and television, these archetypes may be amplified or reinterpreted to create relatable or compelling figures for audiences. For instance, the depiction of characters like Egil Skallagrimsson or Njáll from Njáls saga can vary dramatically, with adaptations sometimes emphasizing their moral dilemmas or internal conflicts to engage viewers more deeply. This character-driven approach not only enhances the narrative but also invites viewers to reflect on the timeless themes of identity, loyalty, and vengeance that permeate the sagas.

Norse mythology serves as a fundamental layer within the saga narratives and significantly influences their adaptations. Elements of myth, such as the presence of gods, fate, and the supernatural, often find their way into modern retellings, whether through direct representation or thematic echoes. Filmmakers may incorporate these mythological aspects to enrich the story's depth and to highlight the sagas' connection to a broader cultural and spiritual heritage. By intertwining myth with the saga's historical elements, adaptations can create a compelling interplay that resonates with audiences familiar with both the ancient tales and contemporary storytelling techniques.

Ultimately, film and television adaptations of the Icelandic sagas are not merely retellings but reimaginings that reflect current societal values and artistic sensibilities. They serve as a bridge between the past and present, illuminating the relevance of these ancient narratives in today's world. While some adaptations may stray from the original text, they often succeed in capturing the spirit of the sagas, inviting new generations to explore and appreciate the rich tapestry of Icelandic history and mythology. As these adaptations continue to evolve, they contribute to the ongoing dialogue surrounding the interpretation of the sagas, ensuring their enduring legacy in popular culture.

## The Sagas in Popular Culture

The Icelandic sagas have transcended their medieval origins to find a significant place in modern popular culture, influencing literature, film, art, and even video games. These narratives, which chronicle the lives and exploits of Norse heroes and their families, resonate with themes of honor, fate, and the struggle against the elements. As adaptations emerge across various media, the sagas serve not only as sources of inspiration but also as mirrors reflecting contemporary societal values and conflicts. The portrayal of Viking culture and mythology continues to captivate audiences, revealing a persistent fascination with the past and its storytelling traditions.

In literature, authors have drawn upon the rich tapestry of the sagas to create works that echo the original narratives while infusing them with modern sensibilities. Novels such as "The Long Ships" by Frans G. Bengtsson and "The Half-Drowned King" by Linnea Hartsuyker reimagine the Viking Age, weaving together historical authenticity with character-driven stories. These authors engage with the archetypes found in sagas, such as the noble warrior, the cunning woman, and the tragic hero, allowing readers to explore complex moral landscapes that resonate with contemporary themes of identity and belonging. The sagas' exploration of family dynamics and societal obligations continues to inform character development in modern storytelling.

Film and television adaptations have further broadened the reach of the sagas, bringing their tales of adventure and conflict into the visual realm. Productions like "Vikings" and "The Last Kingdom" have sparked renewed interest in Norse mythology and the historical context of the sagas. These adaptations often take creative liberties, yet they capture the essence of the sagas' themes, such as loyalty, betrayal, and the inexorable passage of time. By portraying larger-than-life characters and epic battles, these visual narratives not only entertain but also invite viewers to reflect on the historical and cultural foundations of the Viking Age, intertwining them with modern narratives of heroism and struggle.

The impact of Norse mythology on saga narratives is another aspect that has permeated popular culture, shaping the way these ancient stories are interpreted and retold. The gods, monsters, and mythical creatures that populate the sagas have found new life in various forms of media, including graphic novels, video games, and even blockbuster films like the Marvel Cinematic Universe's "Thor." These interpretations often simplify or alter the original myths to fit contemporary storytelling frameworks, yet they maintain a connection to the themes of destiny, conflict, and the human condition. The interplay between mythology and saga narratives enriches the understanding of Norse culture, inviting audiences to engage with its symbols and archetypes in new and dynamic ways.

As the Icelandic sagas continue to inspire diverse forms of expression, they also raise questions about authenticity and representation in popular culture. The challenge lies in balancing the rich historical context of the sagas with the demands of modern storytelling. While adaptations can sometimes stray from the original narratives, they also serve as a testament to the sagas' enduring relevance and adaptability. As new generations encounter these stories, the sagas remain a vital thread in the tapestry of cultural history, encouraging exploration and dialogue about identity, heritage, and the timeless nature of human experience.

# Chapter 9: Conclusion: The Enduring Legacy of the Sagas

## Relevance to Modern Society

The Icelandic sagas, composed between the 12th and 14th centuries, hold significant relevance to modern society, transcending their historical context to offer insights into contemporary themes such as identity, morality, and community. These narratives, originating from a time of exploration and cultural exchange, provide a rich tapestry reflecting the complexities of human experience. As societies grapple with issues of belonging and cultural heritage, the sagas serve as a reminder of the enduring nature of these themes, encouraging readers to explore their own identities in a rapidly changing world.

In the realm of character analysis, the sagas present a diverse array of archetypes that resonate with modern audiences. Figures like the wise leader, the tragic hero, and the cunning trickster offer timeless lessons about human behavior and societal dynamics. For instance, the saga of Grettir the Strong showcases the internal struggles of its protagonist, whose battles against both external foes and personal demons highlight the quest for personal integrity in a world rife with conflict. Such character studies not only enrich our understanding of human psychology but also encourage introspection regarding our own life choices and moral dilemmas.

The influence of Norse mythology permeates the narratives of the sagas, imbuing them with a sense of the divine that continues to fascinate contemporary readers. Myths such as the tales of Odin and Thor are interwoven with the sagas, reflecting the cultural values and beliefs of the Norse people. This integration of mythology serves as a lens through which modern readers can examine the interplay between fate and free will, a theme that remains relevant as individuals navigate their own paths in a world often governed by unpredictability. The sagas prompt reflection on how ancient beliefs shape current perspectives on destiny and human agency.

Furthermore, the historical context of the sagas sheds light on the development of societal norms and legal structures in medieval Iceland, offering parallels to present-day societal issues. The sagas depict a society that valued honor, kinship, and justice, themes that resonate with ongoing discussions about social responsibility and the rule of law. In an era where the foundations of democracy and justice are frequently challenged, the sagas remind us of the importance of community and the consequences of individual actions. They provide a framework for examining how historical legal practices can inform modern legal systems and ethical considerations.

Finally, the enduring legacy of the Icelandic sagas can be seen in their influence on literature, art, and popular culture today. From adaptations in film and television to their presence in academic discourse, the sagas continue to inspire new generations. Their narratives offer a wealth of material for exploration and reinterpretation, making them not just relics of the past but living texts that engage with contemporary issues. As modern society seeks to understand its roots and navigate future challenges, the sagas serve as a bridge connecting the past with the present, illustrating the timeless nature of storytelling in shaping human experience.

## Continued Scholarship and Research

Continued scholarship and research into the Icelandic sagas remain vital for understanding their historical context and cultural significance. These narratives, composed between the 12th and 14th centuries, reflect the complexities of medieval Norse society and the unique Icelandic landscape that influenced their creation. Scholars have made significant strides in analyzing the socio-political climate of the time, revealing how external factors, such as the Christianization of Iceland and the influence of the Old Norse legal system, shaped the sagas. This exploration not only enhances our comprehension of the texts but also provides insight into the values, beliefs, and struggles of the Icelandic people during this transformative period.

Character analysis and archetypes within the sagas offer yet another rich avenue for scholarly inquiry. The sagas are replete with multifaceted characters who embody various archetypal roles, such as the hero, the anti-hero, the wise old man, and the strong woman. Researchers have delved into how these archetypes serve to reflect and critique societal norms, familial obligations, and personal honor. By examining the motivations and actions of key figures, such as Grettir the Strong or Njáll, scholars can uncover deeper themes of loyalty, revenge, and the human condition that resonate across time and culture.

The impact of Norse mythology on the narratives of the sagas cannot be overstated. Mythological elements permeate the sagas, influencing plot structures, character development, and thematic depth. Ongoing research has illuminated how these mythological frameworks inform the sagas' portrayal of fate, the supernatural, and the relationship between gods and humans. Scholars have sought to understand how these mythological references serve not only to enrich the storytelling but also to create a dialogue between the sagas and the broader Norse cosmology, thus situating the narratives within a larger mythic tradition.

In recent years, interdisciplinary approaches have emerged within saga studies, incorporating insights from archaeology, anthropology, and literary theory. This convergence of disciplines has led to new interpretations of the sagas, as researchers draw connections between material culture and textual evidence. For instance, archaeological findings related to burial practices and settlement patterns provide a tangible context for the social dynamics depicted in the sagas. Such interdisciplinary research enriches our understanding of the sagas, revealing the interplay between text and context, and challenging traditional notions of authorship and narrative reliability.

As scholarship continues to evolve, the Icelandic sagas remain a fertile ground for exploration and discovery. The richness of their narratives beckons both seasoned scholars and newcomers alike to engage with these texts, encouraging a deeper appreciation for their artistry and their profound insights into the human experience. Continued research not only preserves the legacy of these remarkable stories but also ensures that future generations can uncover the echoes of the North that resonate through time, deepening our understanding of both the sagas and the world from which they emerged.

## Future Directions in Saga Studies

As the field of saga studies continues to evolve, scholars are increasingly focusing on interdisciplinary approaches that draw from various academic disciplines, including anthropology, history, and literary theory. This trend allows for a more nuanced understanding of the Icelandic sagas, as researchers examine not only the texts themselves but also the cultural and social contexts in which they were created. Future research may delve deeper into how oral traditions influenced written narratives, exploring the interplay between performance and text. By integrating insights from folklore studies, scholars can better understand the sagas' origins and their role in shaping Icelandic identity throughout history.

Another promising direction in saga studies is the examination of character archetypes and their development throughout the sagas. As scholars analyze key figures such as heroes, anti-heroes, and female characters, there is potential for a richer understanding of gender dynamics and social roles within the narratives. Comparative studies that align saga characters with those from other mythologies and literary traditions can reveal universal themes and cultural specificities. This approach not only enhances character analysis but also situates the sagas within broader literary and historical frameworks, fostering an appreciation of their complexity and relevance.

The impact of Norse mythology on saga narratives is another area ripe for exploration. Future studies may focus on the ways in which mythological elements are woven into the fabric of saga storytelling. By analyzing specific instances of mythological references and their functions within the sagas, scholars can illuminate the relationship between myth and narrative structure. This exploration can also extend to the role of supernatural beings and the moral implications of their interactions with human characters, providing a deeper understanding of the sagas as reflections of Norse beliefs and values.

Digital humanities tools are increasingly being utilized in saga studies, offering innovative methods for analyzing text and context. These tools allow researchers to perform quantitative analyses of language, themes, and intertextual connections that were previously difficult to identify. Future research may involve the creation of digital databases that compile various versions of the sagas, enabling comparative analyses across different manuscripts and textual variants. The application of machine learning and other advanced technologies promises to uncover patterns and relationships within the sagas that can lead to new interpretations and insights.

Finally, the ongoing interest in global perspectives on the Icelandic sagas suggests a need for studies that engage with non-Western interpretations and influences. As scholars seek to understand how the sagas resonate in a contemporary global context, there is an opportunity to explore their adaptations in modern literature, film, and popular culture. This approach not only revitalizes interest in the sagas but also highlights their enduring relevance, inviting new audiences to engage with these ancient narratives. By embracing diverse methodologies and perspectives, future directions in saga studies can continue to enrich our understanding of these complex texts and their place in world literature.

# Echoes of Asgard: Analyzing the Prose Edda's Mythological Tapestry

## Chapter 1: Introduction to the Prose Edda

### Overview of the Prose Edda

The Prose Edda, a seminal work of Old Norse literature, stands as one of the primary sources of knowledge regarding Norse mythology and the ancient Scandinavian worldview. Compiled in the 13th century by the Icelandic scholar Snorri Sturluson, the text serves not only as a repository of myth but also as an instructional guide for poets of the time, elucidating the complex poetic forms and allusions prevalent in earlier Norse poetry. Divided into several sections, including the Gylfaginning, the Skáldskaparmál, and the Háttatal, the Prose Edda intertwines mythological narratives with practical guidance on poetic composition, reflecting Sturluson's dual aims of preserving cultural heritage and fostering literary creativity.

The Gylfaginning, or "The Tricking of Gylfi," presents a mythological framework through a frame story that depicts King Gylfi's quest for knowledge. In this section, Gylfi encounters the gods in disguise and learns about the creation of the world, the pantheon of deities, and the eventual doom of these gods in the cataclysmic event known as Ragnarök. This narrative not only serves to introduce the major figures and themes of Norse mythology but also encapsulates the cyclical nature of existence, a theme that resonates throughout the text. The interplay of fate and free will depicted in these stories creates a rich tapestry of characters and moral dilemmas that reflect the complexities of human experience.

In contrast, the Skáldskaparmál focuses on the art of poetry itself, offering a lexicon of poetic terms and techniques. This section provides insight into the cultural significance of skaldic poetry, highlighting how language and metaphor were pivotal in conveying meaning and emotion in Norse society. Sturluson meticulously catalogs various kennings—metaphorical phrases that enrich the language of poetry—illustrating the depth and creativity of Norse literary traditions. The emphasis on poetic form serves as a bridge between the mythological content of the Prose Edda and its role in the literary culture of medieval Scandinavia.

The Háttatal, the final section of the Prose Edda, serves as a compendium of metrical forms, showcasing Sturluson's expertise in poetic structure. By categorizing and exemplifying various verse forms, it offers a practical resource for aspiring poets while simultaneously reinforcing the cultural importance of storytelling in Norse society. This focus on form and technique highlights the intricate relationship between content and structure in the Prose Edda, revealing how literary techniques contribute to the overall impact of the myths and stories presented.

The Prose Edda's influence extends far beyond its immediate historical context, permeating modern interpretations of Norse mythology and fantasy literature. Its themes and characters have inspired countless adaptations in popular culture, from literature to film and video games. The enduring nature of the Prose Edda lies in its ability to convey universal themes of heroism, fate, and the human condition, making it a timeless source of inspiration. As scholars continue to analyze its intricate symbolism and character dynamics, the Prose Edda remains a pivotal text for understanding not only ancient Norse beliefs but also their lasting impact on contemporary narratives and cultural expressions.

## Historical Background and Authorship

The Prose Edda, composed in the early 13th century, serves as a vital source of Norse mythology and a significant literary work in the realm of medieval literature. Authored by the Icelandic scholar Snorri Sturluson, the text reflects both the rich oral traditions of the Norse culture and the literary conventions of the time. Sturluson, who was also a politician and historian, aimed to preserve and systematize the vast array of Norse myths and legends that were at risk of being forgotten due to the increasing influence of Christianity. His work is not merely a collection of stories; it is a deliberate effort to create a cohesive narrative that connects the past with the present and to establish a literary canon for a people grappling with their cultural identity.

The historical context surrounding the creation of the Prose Edda is essential to understanding its themes and motifs. Written during a period of significant transformation in Iceland, the text emerges from a society transitioning from paganism to Christianity. This shift is evident in the duality present within the Prose Edda, as it simultaneously honors the old gods while subtly accommodating the new faith. The tensions between these two belief systems are reflected in the characters and narratives Sturluson presents, allowing readers to explore the complexities of cultural change and identity. The Prose Edda thus serves as a mirror to a society in flux, encapsulating the struggles and adaptations of its people.

Sturluson's approach to authorship also merits attention, as it reveals his intentions as both a storyteller and a scholar. He employed various literary techniques that enhanced the narrative's depth, including alliteration, kennings, and a sophisticated use of foreshadowing. By structuring the Prose Edda into distinct sections—comprising the Gylfaginning, Skáldskaparmál, and Háttatal—Sturluson not only organized the myths but also created a layered text that invites analysis and interpretation. His skillful weaving of myth and history underscores the importance of literary craftsmanship in preserving cultural heritage, reflecting a conscious effort to elevate Norse mythology to the status of classical literature.

Character studies within the Prose Edda reveal profound insights into Norse values, ethics, and the human condition. Figures such as Odin, Thor, and Loki embody a spectrum of traits, from wisdom and strength to cunning and chaos. These characters are not merely archetypes; they are complex beings whose actions and motivations reflect the moral quandaries faced by their worshippers. The interplay between the gods and their interactions with humans further illustrates the intricate nature of fate, power, and sacrifice in Norse thought. Through these character studies, the Prose Edda provides a rich tapestry of narratives that resonate with universal themes, making them relevant even in contemporary discourse.

The influence of the Prose Edda extends far beyond its historical and literary significance, permeating modern fantasy literature and popular culture. Its rich mythological framework has inspired countless authors, filmmakers, and artists, serving as a foundation for the creation of new worlds and narratives. The archetypes and themes found within the Prose Edda continue to resonate, providing a wellspring of creativity that shapes contemporary storytelling. This enduring legacy underscores the importance of the Prose Edda not only as a historical artifact but also as a living text that continues to echo through the ages, influencing how we perceive mythology and its role in our understanding of human experience.

## Importance in Norse Literature

The Prose Edda stands as a cornerstone of Norse literature, offering profound insights into the cultural, religious, and social values of the Viking Age and beyond. Written by Snorri Sturluson in the early 13th century, this text not only serves as a repository of myths and legends but also functions as a vital source for understanding the cosmology and worldview of the Norse people. The importance of the Prose Edda lies in its ability to bridge the gap between oral tradition and written narrative, preserving a vast array of mythological stories that continue to resonate with audiences today.

One of the most significant contributions of the Prose Edda is its role in the preservation of Norse mythology. Through its detailed accounts of gods, giants, and heroes, the text codifies myths that may have otherwise been lost to time. Furthermore, the Prose Edda provides context and commentary on these myths, illuminating the societal norms and values embedded within them. This comprehensive approach allows modern readers to engage with the narratives not merely as stories but as reflections of the historical and cultural milieu from which they emerged.

The literary techniques employed by Snorri Sturluson are also crucial to the significance of the Prose Edda. His use of frame narratives, poetic devices, and rich symbolism enhances the storytelling, making complex themes more accessible. The interplay between prose and poetry in the text demonstrates a sophisticated understanding of narrative structure, inviting readers to appreciate the artistry behind the myths. Moreover, these literary techniques have influenced countless writers, establishing a framework that continues to inspire contemporary fantasy literature and beyond.

The Prose Edda's exploration of themes such as fate, heroism, and the relationship between gods and mortals resonates deeply with modern audiences. These universal themes transcend cultural boundaries, making the text relevant in a world where questions of existence and morality persist. Through character studies, readers can analyze figures like Odin and Thor, whose complexities and struggles mirror the human experience. This exploration fosters a deeper connection to the material, allowing for personal interpretation and engagement with the mythological tapestry woven throughout the text.

Lastly, the cultural impact of the Prose Edda extends into popular culture and media, showcasing its ongoing relevance. From adaptations in literature and film to influences in video games, the myths encapsulated within the Prose Edda have permeated various forms of entertainment. By examining these adaptations, one can see how ancient narratives continue to shape modern storytelling, reinforcing the idea that the echoes of Asgard remain vibrant and influential in contemporary discourse. The Prose Edda not only preserves the past but actively participates in the ongoing evolution of narrative art, ensuring that its importance in Norse literature endures.

# Chapter 2: Mythological Analysis of the Prose Edda

## Creation Myths

Creation myths serve as foundational narratives that explore the origins of the cosmos, humanity, and the divine, offering insights into the cultural psyche of the Norse people. In the Prose Edda, these myths are not merely stories but complex frameworks that intertwine with themes of fate, chaos, and order. Central to this exploration is the account of the world's creation from the primordial void known as Ginnungagap, where the interactions between fire and ice give rise to the first beings. This narrative not only establishes a cosmological structure but also reflects the Norse understanding of the balance between opposing forces, a theme that resonates throughout the mythology.

The role of Ymir, the first being born from the icy realms, is pivotal in understanding the Norse creation narrative. His body is eventually used to forge the world, embodying the theme of sacrifice that permeates Norse mythology. The dismemberment of Ymir represents a transformation of chaos into order, symbolizing the cyclical nature of life and death. This act of creation through destruction serves as a powerful metaphor for the Norse view of existence, where the cosmos is continually reshaped by the conflicts and resolutions among its inhabitants. Such themes illustrate the complex relationships between gods, giants, and humans, highlighting the interconnectedness of all beings within the mythological framework.

Moreover, the creation myths in the Prose Edda are rich with literary techniques that enhance their depth and significance. The use of alliteration, kennings, and vivid imagery creates a tapestry of language that elevates these narratives beyond simple storytelling. The personification of natural elements and the incorporation of allegorical figures serve to engage the audience, inviting them to reflect on their own place within the cosmos. Additionally, the oral tradition from which these myths emerged is evident in their rhythmic quality, which would have facilitated memorization and recitation, ensuring their preservation through generations.

Examining the historical context of the Prose Edda reveals how these creation myths were not only a means of entertainment but also a way to convey cultural values and societal norms. As the Norse people navigated their environment, the myths provided explanations for natural phenomena and moral guidance. The relationship between humanity and the divine is articulated through these narratives, establishing a framework for understanding the human condition in the face of an unpredictable world. This interplay between myth and reality underscores the significance of creation myths in shaping the identity of the Norse culture.

The influence of these creation myths extends beyond the confines of the Prose Edda, permeating modern fantasy literature and popular culture. Contemporary authors draw upon these rich narratives, reinterpreting them for new audiences while maintaining their core themes of conflict, transformation, and resilience. The enduring legacy of the Norse creation myths can be seen in various media, from literature to film, where the archetypes and motifs continue to resonate. As such, the Prose Edda's creation myths not only provide a window into the ancient Norse worldview but also serve as a testament to the timelessness of these universal themes.

## The Role of Gods and Goddesses

In the Prose Edda, the gods and goddesses serve as central figures that embody the complexities of human existence, morality, and the natural world. Each deity is intricately woven into the fabric of Norse mythology, representing various aspects of life and the universe. From the wise Odin, who seeks knowledge at great personal cost, to the nurturing Frigg, who embodies love and motherhood, these divine characters reflect the values, fears, and aspirations of the Norse people. Their stories not only provide insight into the ancient belief systems but also illustrate the cultural significance of these figures in shaping societal norms and behaviors.

The gods and goddesses of the Prose Edda are often depicted as flawed and relatable, making them accessible to the human experience. This anthropomorphism allows readers to engage with the deities on a personal level, as they navigate their own challenges and triumphs. The conflicts and alliances among the gods mirror the complexities of human relationships, illustrating themes of loyalty, betrayal, and redemption. This dynamic interplay among divine characters serves to emphasize the moral lessons embedded within their narratives, fostering a deeper understanding of the ethical frameworks that guided Norse society.

Symbolism plays a crucial role in the portrayal of gods and goddesses within the Prose Edda. Each deity is associated with particular symbols that convey their attributes and powers. For instance, Thor, the god of thunder, is often depicted with his hammer, Mjölnir, signifying strength and protection. Similarly, Freyja, the goddess of love and fertility, is linked to the fertility of the earth and the cycles of life. These symbols not only enhance the visual imagery of the myths but also serve as metaphors for broader themes such as fertility, war, and the balance of nature. The interconnection of these symbols with the characters enriches the narrative, allowing for a multi-layered exploration of meaning.

The historical context of the Prose Edda reveals the role of these deities in the transition from paganism to Christianity in Scandinavia. As the Norse culture encountered Christian influences, the portrayal of gods and goddesses began to adapt, reflecting the changing beliefs and values of the time. This evolution highlights the resilience of Norse mythology, as it incorporated elements of new faith while retaining its core narratives. The gods' adaptability serves as a testament to their enduring relevance, allowing them to be reinterpreted in various cultural contexts throughout history.

The influence of the Prose Edda's gods and goddesses extends beyond historical and literary analysis; they have permeated modern fantasy literature and popular culture. Contemporary authors draw inspiration from these mythological figures, reimagining them in new narratives that resonate with today's audiences. The enduring legacy of these deities can be seen in films, television series, and literature, where they continue to capture the imagination and inform contemporary storytelling. This ongoing engagement with the gods and goddesses of the Prose

Edda highlights their timeless appeal and underscores the importance of preserving and studying this rich mythological tapestry.

## The Concept of Destiny and Fate

The concepts of destiny and fate are central to the narrative structure and thematic depth of the Prose Edda, reflecting a worldview that intertwines human agency with a predetermined cosmic order. In Norse mythology, these ideas are often embodied by the Norns, the three female figures who govern the fates of both gods and men. Their existence emphasizes the belief that while individuals may strive for agency, their paths are ultimately influenced by forces beyond their control. This interplay between free will and predestination creates a rich tapestry of conflict and resolution throughout the Edda, inviting readers to explore the implications of fate in their own lives.

The Prose Edda presents fate as an inescapable reality, a theme that resonates throughout its various tales. Characters such as Odin and Loki grapple with their fates, often leading to tragic outcomes that highlight the limitations of their power. Odin, in particular, is depicted as a seeker of wisdom who sacrifices much in an attempt to alter his own destiny. Yet, even his profound knowledge cannot shield him from the inevitability of Ragnarok, the prophesied end of the world. This fatalistic perspective serves as a reminder of the ancient Norse belief that all beings are bound by the threads of fate, shaping their actions and reactions within the mythological framework.

Literary techniques employed in the Prose Edda further underscore the themes of destiny and fate. The use of foreshadowing, for instance, is prevalent throughout the text, often signaling the inevitable downfall of characters or events. This technique not only builds tension but also reinforces the notion that fate is immutable. Additionally, the narrative structure itself reflects a cyclical understanding of time, where beginnings and endings are interwoven, suggesting that destiny is not a linear journey but a complex interplay of interconnected fates. Such literary choices invite readers to ponder the implications of their own choices within a world that often feels predetermined.

Symbolism plays a crucial role in the exploration of destiny and fate within the Prose Edda. Various elements, such as the Yggdrasil tree, serve as powerful symbols of interconnectedness and the cyclical nature of existence. The branches of Yggdrasil reach into different realms, representing the myriad paths that individuals can take, yet its roots are deeply embedded in the ground, symbolizing the inescapable foundation of fate. This duality captures the essence of the Norse perspective on life—one that acknowledges the significance of personal choices while simultaneously recognizing the overarching influence of destiny.

In a broader context, the themes of destiny and fate in the Prose Edda resonate with contemporary audiences, particularly in modern fantasy literature. Many contemporary authors draw inspiration from Norse mythology, weaving similar themes into their narratives. The struggle against fate, the quest for agency, and the acknowledgment of cosmic forces remain relevant across genres and cultures. The Prose Edda's exploration of these concepts not only enriches our understanding of Norse religion and mythology but also offers timeless insights into the human condition, echoing through the ages and continuing to inspire generations of writers and readers alike.

# Chapter 3: Historical Context of the Prose Edda

## The Viking Age and Its Influence

The Viking Age, spanning from the late eighth to the early eleventh century, was a period marked by extensive exploration, trade, and cultural exchange that significantly influenced the development of Norse mythology as encapsulated in the Prose Edda. This era saw the Norse people venture beyond their homelands, establishing settlements in various regions including the British Isles, parts of France, and as far east as Russia. These interactions not only facilitated the spread of their beliefs and stories but also allowed for the integration of foreign elements into their own mythological framework. The Prose Edda, compiled by Snorri Sturluson in the thirteenth century, serves as a crucial literary artifact that reflects these cultural exchanges and the evolving nature of Norse mythology during and after the Viking Age.

The Viking Age was characterized by a rich tapestry of oral traditions that were eventually transcribed into written form, culminating in the Prose Edda. The oral storytelling practices of the Vikings played a vital role in preserving their myths, legends, and historical narratives. As the Vikings encountered different cultures, they assimilated new ideas and motifs, which later found their way into the Prose Edda. This cross-pollination of stories enriched the Norse mythos, allowing for a more nuanced understanding of characters and themes. The Prose Edda not only documents these mythical tales but also serves as a commentary on the societal values and beliefs prevalent during the Viking Age.

Literary techniques employed in the Prose Edda, such as allegory, alliteration, and metaphor, have their roots in the oral traditions of the Viking Age. Snorri Sturluson's narrative style reflects the rhythmic and mnemonic qualities of oral poetry, which were essential for storytelling in a predominantly oral culture. The use of kennings—compound expressions that convey complex ideas—exemplifies the intricacy of Norse linguistic artistry. Moreover, the Prose Edda's structure, which intertwines myth with narrative, mirrors the way Viking skalds would weave history and mythological elements into their performances, illustrating the seamless blend of fact and fiction that characterized the Viking worldview.

The themes explored in the Prose Edda, such as fate, heroism, and the cyclical nature of existence, resonate deeply with the experiences of the Viking Age. The concept of wyrd, or fate, highlights the Norse belief in predetermined destiny, reflecting the uncertainties faced by a seafaring people. Characters like Odin and Thor embody the virtues and struggles of the Viking spirit, serving as archetypes that resonate with both the historical and mythological narratives of the time. The Prose Edda not only preserves these themes but also invites readers to reflect on the moral and ethical dilemmas faced by its characters, offering insights into the human condition as perceived by the Vikings.

The legacy of the Viking Age, as captured in the Prose Edda, continues to influence modern interpretations of mythology and fantasy literature. The rich characterizations and complex themes found within the Prose Edda have inspired countless authors, filmmakers, and artists, shaping contemporary portrayals of Norse mythology. The resurgence of interest in Viking culture in popular media further underscores the timeless appeal of these ancient narratives. By analyzing the Prose Edda within the historical context of the Viking Age, we gain a greater appreciation for its enduring impact on modern storytelling and the cultural echoes that persist in today's literary landscape.

## Christianity's Impact on Norse Mythology

Christianity's introduction to Scandinavia in the late first millennium had profound implications for the indigenous Norse belief systems, particularly as reflected in the Prose Edda. This synthesis of religious ideas resulted in a complex interaction where Christian concepts began to permeate Norse mythology. The Prose Edda, compiled by Snorri Sturluson in the 13th century, serves as a pivotal text in this transitional period, illustrating how Christian values and narratives were woven into the fabric of traditional Norse myths, reshaping their meanings and interpretations.

One significant impact of Christianity on Norse mythology is the reinterpretation of gods and their roles within the mythological narrative. Figures such as Odin and Thor, once revered as powerful deities, began to be viewed through a Christian lens, often portrayed with moral complexities or diminished statuses. Snorri's descriptions of these gods exhibit a certain ambivalence, reflecting a shift towards a more ethical framework aligned with Christian teachings. This recontextualization not only altered the perception of these gods but also infused the narratives with themes of redemption and morality, aligning them with Christian ideals.

The Prose Edda also showcases an adaptation of mythological themes to reflect Christian dogma. Stories that previously celebrated the heroism and valor of pagan warriors gradually incorporated elements of Christian morality. For instance, the concept of fate, or wyrd, which was central to Norse cosmology, began to intersect with the Christian notion of divine providence. This blending of fate and free will introduced a new layer of complexity to the characters and their journeys, suggesting that their struggles were not merely against the whims of fate but also engaged with a higher moral order.

Literary techniques employed in the Prose Edda further illustrate the impact of Christianity on Norse mythology. Snorri's use of allegory and symbolism reflects a desire to bridge the gap between the old and new belief systems. By redefining the narratives with allegorical meanings that resonate with Christian doctrine, Snorri enabled his audience to find familiar moral teachings within the ancient tales. This literary approach not only preserved Norse mythology but also facilitated its transformation, ensuring that it could coexist with the burgeoning Christian faith.

In conclusion, the interplay between Christianity and Norse mythology as seen in the Prose Edda reveals a fascinating transition marked by reinterpretation and adaptation. This confluence of beliefs not only reshaped the narratives of Norse gods and heroes but also enriched the thematic depth of the text. As these ancient stories evolved, they reflected the changing cultural landscape of Scandinavia, presenting a complex dialogue between the old ways and the new faith that would ultimately influence the trajectory of Nordic identity and mythology for centuries to come.

## Socio-Political Structures in the Edda

The Prose Edda, a cornerstone of Norse literature, intricately intertwines mythological narratives with socio-political structures reflective of the time. These structures are not merely backdrops but serve as fundamental elements that shape character motivations and plot developments. The Edda captures the essence of a society where power dynamics, familial ties, and tribal affiliations dictated the lives of its characters. Within its pages, we observe how figures such as Odin and Thor navigate their roles not only as deities but also as representatives of the societal values and hierarchies prevalent in medieval Scandinavia.

The portrayal of gods and goddesses in the Prose Edda often mirrors the leadership and governance systems of Norse society. For instance, Odin embodies the archetype of the wise ruler, whose quest for knowledge and power underscores a societal reverence for wisdom as a form of authority. His interactions with other deities and mortals reveal the importance of alliances and loyalty, reflecting the intricate web of relationships necessary for maintaining social order. This dynamic is further emphasized through the concept of kinship, which serves as a pivotal theme throughout the Edda, illustrating how familial bonds influence political decisions and conflicts.

Moreover, the Edda's narratives often delve into the themes of conflict resolution and justice, both vital components of any socio-political structure. The tales of vengeance and reconciliation among gods and giants highlight the complexities of maintaining peace in a world fraught with rivalry. For example, the story of the Aesir-Vanir war not only showcases the interplay of power between different divine factions but also serves as an allegory for the necessity of negotiation and compromise in governance. This theme resonates with the historical context of Viking Age societies, where warfare and diplomacy were inextricably linked.

The literary techniques employed in the Prose Edda further enhance its exploration of socio-political themes. The use of allegory and symbolism allows for a deeper understanding of the moral and ethical dilemmas faced by the characters. The symbolism of Yggdrasil, the World Tree, for instance, represents the interconnectedness of all beings and realms, mirroring the social fabric of Norse society. This literary device not only enriches the narrative but also invites readers to reflect on the implications of their own societal structures, drawing parallels between ancient and contemporary governance.

Finally, the influence of the Prose Edda on modern fantasy literature cannot be overstated. Many contemporary works draw upon its socio-political themes, crafting narratives that explore power, loyalty, and conflict within their own fictional realms. This intertextuality not only preserves the legacy of Norse mythology but also highlights the enduring relevance of its socio-political insights. As readers engage with these modern adaptations, they are reminded of the Prose Edda's rich tapestry of characters and conflicts, which continue to resonate within the socio-political landscapes of today.

# Chapter 4: Literary Techniques in the Prose Edda

## Narrative Structure

Narrative structure in the Prose Edda is a complex framework that intertwines myth, history, and cultural identity, serving as a foundational text for understanding Norse mythology. The Prose Edda, attributed to the 13th-century Icelandic scholar Snorri Sturluson, employs a unique narrative technique that juxtaposes various mythological tales with a systematic approach to storytelling. The interlacing of different narratives not only provides a rich tapestry of characters and events but also reflects the oral traditions that preceded its written form. This structure enables readers to navigate the intricacies of Norse mythology, allowing for a deeper comprehension of its themes and symbols.

At the heart of the Prose Edda's narrative structure is the use of a frame story, which serves to contextualize the myths within a broader cultural narrative. This framing technique is evident in the way Snorri introduces various tales through the lens of an instructional narrative aimed at preserving the wisdom of ancient myths for future generations. Each section of the text, from the Gylfaginning to the Skáldskaparmál, unfolds in a manner that guides the reader through the complexities of Norse cosmology and theology, establishing connections between deities, heroes, and the natural world. This approach not only emphasizes the interconnectedness of these stories but also reinforces the educational purpose of the text.

Characterization within the Prose Edda is another critical aspect of its narrative structure. The text presents a diverse array of figures, from the mighty gods like Odin and Thor to the cunning giants and the fateful Norns. Each character embodies specific traits and motivations that drive the narrative forward, allowing for a multi-dimensional exploration of their roles within the mythological landscape. The often tragic arcs of these characters highlight the themes of fate, honor, and the struggle between order and chaos. By employing rich character studies, the Prose Edda invites readers to reflect on the complexities of human nature as mirrored in its divine counterparts.

Symbolism plays a vital role in the narrative structure of the Prose Edda, enriching the text with layers of meaning that extend beyond the surface of the stories. Objects, actions, and settings often carry significant symbolic weight, reflecting deeper cultural beliefs and existential themes. For instance, Yggdrasil, the World Tree, symbolizes the interconnectedness of all beings and the cyclical nature of life and death. Through these symbols, Snorri weaves a narrative that resonates with the spiritual and philosophical inquiries of his audience, encouraging them to engage with the text on a more profound level.

The influence of the Prose Edda's narrative structure can be seen in contemporary literature and media, where its themes and character archetypes continue to resonate. Modern fantasy authors frequently draw upon the rich narrative techniques established by Snorri, adapting the mythological elements of the Prose Edda to create their own fantastical worlds. The enduring popularity of these stories, along with their adaptation in films, video games, and novels, underscores the lasting impact of the Prose Edda's narrative structure. By analyzing these elements, readers can appreciate not only the historical significance of the text but also its ongoing relevance in shaping modern interpretations of myth and heroism.

## Use of Symbolism

The use of symbolism in the Prose Edda serves as a critical lens through which the intricate layers of Norse mythology can be understood. Symbolism imbues the narrative with deeper meanings, allowing characters, objects, and events to resonate beyond their literal interpretations. For instance, the portrayal of Yggdrasil, the World Tree, is not merely a physical entity but symbolizes the interconnectedness of all realms—gods, giants, and humans. This tree embodies the axis mundi, representing the universe's structure and the cyclical nature of life, death, and rebirth. Through such symbols, the Edda invites readers to explore profound philosophical questions about existence and interdependence.

Additionally, the use of animals as symbols within the Prose Edda enhances the thematic richness of the text. Ravens, particularly those associated with Odin, symbolize wisdom and the omnipresence of the god, while wolves reflect the duality of nature—both nurturing and destructive. The character of Fenrir, the monstrous wolf, signifies chaos and the inevitability of fate, embodying the tension between order and disorder that pervades Norse thought. These animal symbols serve to illustrate the cultural significance of nature in Norse society, where animals were often seen as manifestations of divine will or omens for the future.

Moreover, the symbolism of treasures and artifacts plays a pivotal role in the narratives of the Prose Edda. Objects such as Mjölnir, Thor's hammer, symbolize protection and power, while the ring Draupnir represents prosperity and the cyclical nature of wealth. These artifacts are not merely tools or possessions; they convey the values and beliefs of the Norse people, reflecting their understanding of fate, honor, and the transient nature of life. Through these symbols, the Edda articulates themes of sacrifice and the quest for knowledge, reinforcing the idea that true power lies in wisdom and moral integrity.

The colors and elements associated with various characters also contribute to the rich tapestry of symbolism. For example, the fiery nature of the giant Surtr symbolizes destruction and the inevitable end during Ragnarök, while the brightness of the Aesir reflects ideals of order and civilization. This duality of light and dark illustrates the Norse worldview, where life is a constant struggle between creation and destruction. The Prose Edda uses these symbolic contrasts to explore complex themes of morality, fate, and the human condition, inviting readers to reflect on their own lives in relation to the cosmos.

In conclusion, the symbolism woven throughout the Prose Edda not only enhances the narrative's depth but also provides a framework for understanding the cultural and religious beliefs of the Norse people. Each symbol, be it a character, an object, or a natural phenomenon, serves as a gateway to exploring fundamental human questions about existence, morality, and the universe. As contemporary readers engage with these ancient texts, the enduring power of symbolism continues to resonate, allowing for a richer appreciation of the mythological heritage that has shaped modern fantasy literature and popular culture.

## Characterization and Dialogue

Characterization and dialogue in the Prose Edda serve as critical tools for understanding the complex relationships and motivations of its characters. The Edda, attributed to the Icelandic scholar Snorri Sturluson in the 13th century, presents a rich tapestry of Norse mythology that is not only steeped in historical context but also vibrant with literary techniques that enhance character development. Figures such as Odin, Thor, and Loki are not merely archetypes; they embody specific traits and undergo transformations that reflect the intricate interplay of heroism, cunning, and folly characteristic of Norse culture. Through direct and indirect characterization, Sturluson crafts personas that resonate with the audience, allowing readers to engage deeply with their narratives.

Dialogue plays a pivotal role in revealing character dynamics and thematic depth within the Prose Edda. The conversations between gods, giants, and mortals are often laden with subtext, showcasing their motivations and relationships. For instance, Odin's interactions with other deities highlight his wisdom and desire for knowledge, while Loki's banter often underscores his trickster nature. This interplay propels the narrative forward, illustrating how dialogue can serve both as a vehicle for plot progression and as a lens for character analysis. Each exchange not only conveys information but also enriches the emotional landscape of the story, inviting readers to explore the nuances of Norse mythology.

The historical context in which the Prose Edda was written significantly influences its characterization and dialogue. Emerging during a time of cultural transition in medieval Scandinavia, the text reflects a society grappling with the remnants of pagan beliefs and the encroachment of Christianity. As such, characters may embody conflicting values, and their dialogues often reveal tensions between old and new ideologies. For example, discussions surrounding fate and heroism illustrate the Norse belief in destiny, while also hinting at the moral complexities introduced by emerging Christian thought. This duality enriches the characters, making them not only products of their time but also timeless figures that resonate with contemporary audiences.

Symbolism is intricately woven into the characterization and dialogue of the Prose Edda, enhancing its thematic complexity. Each character often symbolizes broader concepts, such as Thor's embodiment of strength and protection or Loki's representation of chaos and change. Dialogue frequently serves to reinforce these symbols, as characters engage in discussions that reveal their inherent traits and the roles they play within the mythological framework. These symbolic layers invite readers to delve deeper into the text, prompting them to consider how each character's journey contributes to the overarching themes of fate, power, and morality that permeate the Edda.

In evaluating the influence of the Prose Edda on modern fantasy literature, it is evident that its characterization and dialogue have left an indelible mark. Many contemporary works draw inspiration from the complex personalities and rich dialogues found within the Edda, utilizing similar techniques to craft their characters and narratives. As readers engage with these modern adaptations, the echoes of Sturluson's original prose remain palpable, illustrating how the Edda's characters and their dialogues continue to resonate across time and culture. This enduring legacy not only highlights the literary prowess of the Prose Edda but also underscores its relevance in the ongoing exploration of mythology and storytelling in contemporary media.

# Chapter 5: Character Studies in the Prose Edda

## Odin: The All-Father

Odin, known as the All-Father, occupies a central role in the Prose Edda, serving as a complex symbol of wisdom, war, and death. As a multifaceted deity, Odin embodies the paradox of a ruler who is both a seeker of knowledge and a harbinger of chaos. This duality is reflected in his relentless pursuit of wisdom, often leading him to extreme measures, such as sacrificing his eye at Mimir's well to gain insight into the secrets of the cosmos. The narratives surrounding Odin illustrate not only his power but also the moral ambiguities inherent in his character, suggesting a deeper commentary on the nature of authority and sacrifice within Norse mythology.

The Prose Edda, compiled by Snorri Sturluson in the 13th century, provides a rich framework for understanding Odin's character. The text presents him as a leader of the Aesir, the principal pantheon of Norse gods, while also exploring his relationships with other deities and beings, such as his sons Thor and Baldr. The dynamics between these figures reveal the complexities of familial loyalty and the burdens of leadership. Odin's interactions with figures like the wise giant Völundr and the prophetic seeress reveal layers of his character, illustrating how wisdom often comes at a significant cost, reinforcing the theme of sacrifice that permeates the Prose Edda.

Odin's symbolism extends beyond his immediate actions and relationships; he represents the archetype of the wandering hero. His journeys across realms, often in disguise, serve as metaphors for the quest for knowledge and understanding that transcends mere power. This aspect of his character resonates with the broader themes of exploration and discovery prevalent in Norse culture. The tale of his descent into Hel to retrieve the poet Bragi's wife, for instance, highlights not only his determination but also the inevitability of death and the afterlife, core themes in Norse beliefs. Such narratives contribute to the understanding of death as a transition rather than an end, emphasizing the importance of legacy, particularly through the art of storytelling.

The literary techniques employed in the Prose Edda further enhance the portrayal of Odin. Snorri's use of alliteration, kennings, and vivid imagery crafts a tapestry of interconnected tales that enrich the reader's experience. The deliberate narrative structure, which intertwines myth with historical context, allows for a deeper analysis of Odin's character as both a mythic figure and a reflection of Viking Age societal values. This blending of genres not only preserves the mythology but also invites contemplation on the nature of fate, destiny, and the human condition, themes that resonate with audiences across time.

Odin's influence extends into modern fantasy literature and popular culture, where his archetype continues to inspire characters and narratives. Contemporary works, from novels to films, often draw upon the complexities of Odin's character to explore themes of power, sacrifice, and knowledge. This enduring legacy illustrates how the Prose Edda's portrayal of Odin has shaped the archetypal hero's journey, affirming the All-Father's role not only in Norse mythology but as a vital figure in the broader landscape of mythological studies. As scholars and enthusiasts continue to analyze these themes, Odin remains a poignant symbol of the eternal quest for understanding in a world fraught with uncertainty.

## Thor: The God of Thunder

Thor, the God of Thunder, is one of the most prominent figures in the Prose Edda, encapsulating the essence of strength, protection, and the elemental forces of nature. He is primarily known for his formidable power and his role as a protector of both gods and humans against various adversaries, particularly the giants, who symbolize chaos and destruction. Thor's character embodies the duality of nature itself; he is both a nurturing figure and a fierce warrior. His hammer, Mjölnir, serves as a powerful symbol of his might and is often interpreted as a representation of both destruction and regeneration, reinforcing the theme of cyclical renewal present in Norse mythology.

The narratives surrounding Thor in the Prose Edda highlight his relationships with other gods, notably Odin and Loki. These interactions provide a rich tapestry of character dynamics that explore themes of loyalty, betrayal, and the complexity of divine relationships. Odin, as the Allfather, often contrasts with Thor; while Odin embodies wisdom and cunning, Thor represents brute strength and straightforwardness. Loki, on the other hand, serves as a catalyst for many of Thor's adventures, often leading him into perilous situations that test his resolve and character. This interplay reveals the multifaceted nature of Thor's persona, allowing readers to engage with the psychological dimensions of mythological figures.

Symbolism plays a crucial role in Thor's depiction within the Prose Edda. His hammer, Mjölnir, is not merely a weapon but a sacred tool associated with fertility, protection, and the sanctification of oaths, illustrating Thor's role as a guardian of order. The storms he conjures are emblematic of both rage and cleansing, reflecting the unpredictable forces of nature. Additionally, Thor's journey to the land of giants and the trials he faces symbolize the struggle between civilization and chaos, making him a quintessential hero in the mythological landscape. The recurring motifs of strength in adversity and the quest for balance resonate throughout the stories, aligning with broader themes in Norse culture.

Analyzing the historical context of Thor's character provides insight into the social and religious values of the Norse people. His worship likely stemmed from agrarian societies that relied on the natural elements for survival. The reverence for Thor can be seen in archaeological findings, such as amulets depicting Mjölnir, indicating that he was a central figure in the spiritual lives of the Norse. The Prose Edda's portrayal of Thor reflects the collective consciousness of a society that valued strength, bravery, and the protection of community against external threats. This historical lens enriches our understanding of his role as not just a mythological figure but a symbol of cultural identity.

Finally, the influence of Thor and the Prose Edda on modern fantasy literature and popular culture cannot be overstated. Thor has transcended his mythological roots to become a staple in contemporary storytelling, particularly within comic books and films, where he is reimagined and adapted for new audiences. This transformation speaks to the enduring power of myth and its ability to evolve while retaining core elements that resonate with human experience. The character of Thor serves as a bridge between ancient beliefs and modern narratives, illustrating how mythological archetypes continue to shape our understanding of heroism, morality, and the complexities of the human condition.

## Loki: The Trickster

Loki, often characterized as the quintessential trickster in Norse mythology, embodies the complexity and duality of human nature, serving both as a catalyst for chaos and a figure of profound insight. His presence in the Prose Edda, particularly in the narratives woven by Snorri Sturluson, reflects a multifaceted character whose actions provoke thought on themes of identity, morality, and the fluidity of allegiance. Unlike many other figures in the pantheon, Loki is neither wholly good nor entirely evil; rather, he exists in a liminal space that challenges conventional moral boundaries. This ambiguity makes him a compelling subject for analysis, allowing for deeper exploration of the underlying themes in Norse mythology.

The character of Loki is intricately linked to the concept of transformation, not only in his physical form but also in his relationships with other gods and beings. He is notorious for his shapeshifting abilities, which he employs to navigate various situations, often resulting in both humorous and catastrophic outcomes. This transformation can be viewed symbolically, representing the unpredictable nature of fate and the chaos that underlies the order established by the Aesir. Loki's role as a trickster is not merely for entertainment; it serves to illuminate the precarious balance between creation and destruction inherent in the cosmos, a theme that resonates throughout the Prose Edda.

Loki's relationships with other characters, particularly with Odin and Thor, further exemplify the tension between loyalty and betrayal. While he is often seen as a companion to the Aesir, his actions frequently undermine their authority and stability. The myth of the theft of Idun's apples, for example, showcases how Loki's deceit leads to dire consequences for the gods, emphasizing the theme of the trickster as both a friend and foe. This duality invites readers to reflect on the complexities of trust and betrayal, prompting questions about the nature of alliances and the potential for discord within even the closest relationships.

Loki's narrative arc culminates in the events leading to Ragnarok, where he emerges as a pivotal figure in the destruction of the gods. His betrayal, culminating in the death of Baldur, illustrates the tragic consequences of his trickster nature, transforming him from a seemingly benign companion into a figure of chaos that threatens the very fabric of the world. This transition underscores the theme of inevitability in Norse mythology, where even the gods are not immune to betrayal and loss. The portrayal of Loki in the Prose Edda serves as a reminder of the cyclical nature of creation and destruction, a theme that profoundly impacts the narrative structure of the text.

In the context of modern interpretations, Loki's character continues to captivate audiences, influencing contemporary literature and media. His representation in various adaptations, from comic books to films, often highlights his complexity and allure as a trickster figure. The enduring fascination with Loki reflects broader themes of identity, morality, and the human

517

experience, resonating with audiences seeking to understand the darker aspects of themselves and society. Thus, Loki stands as a testament to the power of myth in shaping cultural narratives, illustrating how the Prose Edda's rich tapestry of characters and themes continues to echo through time, influencing both historical understanding and modern storytelling.

# Chapter 6: Symbolism and Themes in the Prose Edda

## The Significance of Yggdrasil

Yggdrasil, the immense and central cosmic tree in Norse mythology, serves as a pivotal symbol within the Prose Edda, embodying the interconnectedness of all realms and the cyclical nature of existence. Its branches extend into various worlds, including Asgard, Midgard, and Hel, linking the divine, human, and underworld realms. This connection illustrates the Norse understanding of the universe as a complex web of relationships, where actions in one realm can significantly impact others. The tree's significance is further emphasized through its role in the creation myths and its presence in the narratives surrounding gods and heroes, acting as a constant reminder of the interconnected fates within the Norse cosmology.

The depiction of Yggdrasil also highlights the themes of life, death, and rebirth prevalent in the Prose Edda. The tree is not merely a passive element of the landscape; rather, it is a living entity that undergoes its own trials and tribulations. The presence of the Norns, who water Yggdrasil and shape the fates of gods and men, signifies the intertwining of destiny and the natural world. This relationship underscores the Norse belief in fate, emphasizing that while individuals may strive for agency, they remain ensnared in a larger cosmic order governed by the Norns' decrees. Thus, Yggdrasil becomes a symbol of the inevitable cycles of life, reinforcing the idea that every beginning carries within it the seeds of its end.

Moreover, Yggdrasil serves as a narrative device that facilitates the exploration of various characters and their journeys throughout the Prose Edda. As gods and heroes traverse its branches or seek solace beneath its shade, the tree becomes a backdrop for pivotal moments of growth, conflict, and resolution. The interactions of these characters with Yggdrasil often reveal deeper insights into their personalities and motivations, showcasing literary techniques such as symbolism and foreshadowing. For instance, Odin's sacrifice at Yggdrasil to gain wisdom parallels the tree's own sacrifices, emphasizing the theme of knowledge as a double-edged sword that demands great cost.

The historical context of Yggdrasil also sheds light on the cultural significance of trees in Norse society, reflecting the importance of nature and its reverence within the mythology. In many ancient cultures, trees symbolized life, wisdom, and connectivity, and Yggdrasil embodies these values for the Norse people. Its portrayal in the Prose Edda can be seen as a reflection of the Viking Age's relationship with the natural world, where the environment played a crucial role in shaping beliefs, practices, and social structures. Understanding Yggdrasil within this framework allows for a richer interpretation of the text and its themes, illustrating how mythology can serve as a mirror for societal values and concerns.

Finally, the influence of Yggdrasil extends beyond the Prose Edda into modern fantasy literature and popular culture, where it has become a symbol of interconnected worlds and complex narratives. Authors and creators frequently draw upon the imagery of Yggdrasil to evoke themes of destiny, sacrifice, and the cyclical nature of life in their own works. Its enduring legacy is evident in various adaptations, from literature to film, echoing the timelessness of the narratives found within the Prose Edda. As such, Yggdrasil not only anchors the mythological tapestry of the Edda but also serves as a bridge connecting ancient beliefs to contemporary storytelling, illustrating the continuing relevance of Norse mythology in today's cultural landscape.

## Themes of Heroism and Sacrifice

The themes of heroism and sacrifice are intricately woven throughout the Prose Edda, reflecting the ideals and values of Norse culture. Central to this tapestry is the notion of the hero as not merely a figure of strength and valor but as a character defined by their willingness to confront fate, often at great personal cost. These heroes, such as Sigurd and Odin, epitomize the complexities of bravery within a framework that acknowledges the inevitability of death and the pursuit of honor. The narratives encapsulate how heroism is often interlinked with the understanding that sacrifices made in the name of duty or love resonate beyond the individual, impacting the larger community and the cosmos.

Sacrifice in the Prose Edda is portrayed not only as a physical act but also as a moral imperative. Characters frequently face dilemmas that test their loyalty, courage, and ethical boundaries. The story of Odin, who sacrifices his eye for wisdom, underscores the theme that true knowledge often comes at a significant personal price. This willingness to relinquish something of great value for a greater understanding or purpose highlights a recurring motif in the text, where the pursuit of knowledge and power demands sacrifice. Such narratives serve to elevate the concept of sacrifice from the mundane to the sublime, suggesting that the act itself is a pathway to transcendence.

The interplay between heroism and sacrifice is further illuminated through the relationships between characters. The bonds formed through shared struggles often lead to profound sacrifices, as seen in the loyalty between warriors and their chieftains. The tales of fallen heroes, who choose to protect their kin or uphold their honor at the cost of their lives, resonate with the audience, reinforcing the idea that heroism is best displayed through selflessness. This collective ethos speaks to the Norse cultural understanding of fate and legacy, where the deeds of the living echo into the future, creating a profound sense of responsibility toward one's community and progeny.

In addition to character-driven narratives, the Prose Edda employs various literary techniques to enhance the themes of heroism and sacrifice. Symbolism plays a crucial role, with objects such as swords and shields representing not only physical strength but also the weight of responsibility that comes with power. The use of foreshadowing often hints at the sacrifices that characters must make, creating an atmosphere of inevitability that permeates the text. These techniques invite readers to engage deeply with the characters' motivations and the consequences of their choices, allowing for a richer understanding of the themes.

The exploration of heroism and sacrifice in the Prose Edda also resonates beyond its historical context, influencing modern interpretations of these themes in literature and media. Contemporary fantasy narratives often draw on these archetypes, reflecting the timeless nature of the human experience as portrayed in the Edda. As modern audiences engage with these stories, they find echoes of their own struggles with duty, honor, and the sacrifices required in the face of adversity. Thus, the themes of heroism and sacrifice not only define the characters within the Prose Edda but also establish a lasting legacy that continues to inspire and challenge readers today.

## The Cycle of Life and Death

The cycle of life and death, a central theme in the Prose Edda, reflects not only the beliefs of the Norse people but also the intricate narrative structure employed by its authors. This cyclical concept is prevalent throughout the various stories, illustrating a worldview where death is not an end but a transition, an essential part of existence. The tales of gods, humans, and even giants weave a tapestry that emphasizes this inevitability, showcasing how life and death are interconnected. The narratives often illustrate that every life has its purpose, and death is merely a stepping stone to another form of existence, reinforcing the idea that endings are merely beginnings in disguise.

In the Prose Edda, the character of Odin stands as a profound representation of this cycle. His quest for knowledge leads him to sacrifice himself, hanging on Yggdrasil, the World Tree, where he experiences death and rebirth. This act not only grants him wisdom but also exemplifies the necessity of facing death to attain greater understanding. Odin's narrative echoes through the tales of other figures, such as Baldr, whose death serves as a catalyst for the events of Ragnarok, the end of the world in Norse mythology. His demise signifies not only loss but also the promise of renewal, reinforcing the belief that through death, new life and opportunities arise.

The symbolism surrounding death in the Prose Edda is multifaceted. The concept of Valhalla, where warriors who die in battle are taken, represents an idealized afterlife that rewards bravery and valor. This notion encapsulates the warrior ethos of Norse culture, where death in combat is glorified and seen as a pathway to eternal honor. The contrast between Valhalla and Hel, the realm of the dead, further emphasizes the dichotomy of life and death, suggesting that not all endings are equal. Each fate reflects the characters' choices and actions during their lifetimes, showcasing a moral framework where deeds are weighed in the balance of existence.

The historical context of the Prose Edda contributes significantly to its exploration of life and death. Written during a time when Norse society was transitioning from pagan beliefs to Christianity, the text captures the tension between these worldviews. The cyclical nature of life and death in the Prose Edda can be seen as a response to the emerging Christian doctrine, which often depicted death as a finality rather than a transition. This cultural shift is mirrored in the text's narratives, where the acceptance of death as a natural part of life coexists with the looming influence of a more linear, judgment-based afterlife.

In contemporary literature, the themes of life and death derived from the Prose Edda resonate strongly within modern fantasy narratives. Many authors draw upon the cyclical motifs present in Norse mythology, using them to enrich their storytelling. The complexities of life, death, and rebirth offer fertile ground for character development and plot progression, allowing modern tales to explore the same fundamental questions that the Prose Edda addressed centuries ago. As a result, the echoes of these ancient beliefs continue to shape contemporary culture, illustrating the enduring power of the cycle of life and death as a theme that transcends time and remains relevant in today's literary landscape.

# Chapter 7: The Prose Edda and Norse Religion

## Rituals and Worship Practices

Rituals and worship practices in Norse mythology, as depicted in the Prose Edda, serve as vital windows into the spiritual life of the Norse people. These practices were not merely ceremonial; they were deeply embedded in their understanding of the cosmos and the divine. The Prose Edda, primarily authored by Snorri Sturluson in the early 13th century, reflects a time when the old pagan traditions were beginning to be documented in a Christian context, highlighting the tension between the two belief systems. This subchapter explores the intricacies of these rituals, which included offerings, sacrifices, and seasonal festivals, all aimed at appeasing the gods and ensuring harmony in both the human and divine realms.

Central to Norse worship was the practice of blót, or sacrifice, which involved offering animals, food, or other valuables to the gods in exchange for their favor. The Prose Edda describes various contexts in which these sacrifices occurred, often coinciding with significant agricultural cycles or important life events, such as births, marriages, and deaths. The act of blót was not only about the material offerings but also about establishing a reciprocal relationship between humans and the deities. This mutual dependence is a recurring theme in the Edda, illustrating how the Norse viewed their existence as intertwined with the divine forces that governed their world.

In addition to blót, the Prose Edda also highlights the significance of festivals, such as Yule and Álfablót, which served to reinforce community bonds and cultural identity. These gatherings were marked by feasting, storytelling, and rituals that honored the gods and the spirits of the ancestors. The communal aspect of these festivals underscores the importance of social cohesion in Norse culture, where shared beliefs and practices fostered a sense of belonging and continuity. The Edda captures the essence of these moments, showcasing how they contributed to the collective memory and identity of the Norse people.

The literary techniques employed in the Prose Edda further illuminate the rituals and worship practices of the time. Snorri Sturluson's use of poetic language, allegory, and mythological references enriches the descriptions of these practices, transforming them into narratives that resonate with deeper meanings. The interplay between myth and ritual is evident in the way characters like Odin and Freyja are portrayed as both divine figures and archetypal representations of human desires and fears. This duality invites readers to reflect on the complexities of faith and the human experience, bridging the gap between ancient practices and contemporary understandings of spirituality.

Lastly, the legacy of Norse rituals and worship practices, as preserved in the Prose Edda, continues to influence modern interpretations of mythology and fantasy literature. The rich tapestry of these ancient beliefs informs contemporary narratives, offering a source of inspiration for authors and creators who seek to explore themes of sacrifice, community, and the divine. As modern audiences engage with these ancient texts, the rituals encapsulated within the Prose Edda resonate with timeless questions about existence, morality, and the human connection to the sacred, ensuring that the echoes of Asgard remain relevant in today's cultural discourse.

## The Pantheon of Gods

The Pantheon of Gods in the Prose Edda serves as a complex reflection of Norse belief systems, embodying both the cultural values and existential dilemmas faced by the society that created them. Central to this pantheon are deities such as Odin, Thor, and Freyja, each representing distinct aspects of life and the human experience. Odin, the Allfather, is a figure of wisdom and sacrifice, often depicted as a seeker of knowledge at any cost. Thor, the thunder god, symbolizes strength and protection, while Freyja embodies love, beauty, and fertility. These gods not only govern their respective realms but also interact with humans, revealing a reciprocal relationship between the divine and mortal worlds.

The narrative structure of the Prose Edda showcases the gods' personalities and actions through various myths and legends, illustrating their dynamic roles within the cosmos. For instance, Odin's quest for wisdom, which involves sacrificing an eye at Mímir's well, highlights the theme of sacrifice as a pathway to enlightenment. The trials faced by Thor, particularly in his encounters with giants, serve as allegories for the struggles between order and chaos. This interplay of character-driven stories strengthens the reader's understanding of the pantheon as not merely a collection of gods but as active participants in a larger mythological framework that reflects the fears, hopes, and values of the Norse people.

Symbolism plays a significant role in the Prose Edda's representation of the gods, with each deity often associated with specific attributes and natural phenomena. For example, Thor's hammer, Mjölnir, is not just a weapon; it symbolizes protection and the sanctity of the home, embodying the warrior's duty to safeguard his community. Similarly, Odin's raven companions, Huginn and Muninn, represent thought and memory, emphasizing the importance of wisdom and reflection in decision-making. Such symbols enrich the narrative by providing deeper layers of meaning, inviting readers to engage with the text on both an intellectual and emotional level.

In examining the historical context of the Prose Edda, it becomes evident that the pantheon of gods reflects the societal structures and values of the Viking Age. The reverence for warrior culture, as seen in Thor's exploits, mirrors the importance of strength and honor among the Norse people. Conversely, Odin's multifaceted nature can be interpreted as a response to the existential questions posed by a harsh and unforgiving environment, where knowledge and foresight were paramount for survival. Thus, the pantheon is not static; it evolves alongside the culture that venerates it, illustrating the dynamic interplay between mythology and historical reality.

The influence of the Prose Edda's pantheon extends beyond its original context, permeating modern literature and popular culture. Contemporary fantasy narratives often draw inspiration from these archetypal figures, reinterpreting their stories and attributes to fit new contexts. The resurgence of interest in Norse mythology in films, television series, and literature demonstrates the enduring legacy of these gods. As audiences explore the complexities of the Pantheon of Gods, they not only engage with the mythological tapestry of the Prose Edda but also uncover the fundamental human experiences that these ancient stories continue to resonate with in today's world.

## Myths as Religious Texts

Myths have long served as a foundation for religious thought and cultural identity, and the Prose Edda stands as a critical text in understanding Norse mythology's role within the broader context of religious narratives. Unlike canonical religious texts that often present a singular, authoritative voice, the Prose Edda encapsulates a diverse array of myths that reflect the complexities of Norse cosmology, ethics, and societal values. These stories are not merely fictional tales; they are imbued with spiritual significance, offering insights into the beliefs and practices of the Norse people. The characters and events depicted within these myths illustrate the interplay between the divine and the mortal, revealing how ancient Scandinavians understood their world and their place within it.

The Prose Edda's format, combining narrative storytelling with poetic elements, enhances its role as a religious text. This duality allows for a more nuanced exploration of themes such as fate, heroism, and the relationship between gods and humans. The use of literary techniques, such as kennings and alliteration, not only enriches the text but also serves to elevate the narratives to a sacred status. By presenting these myths in a structured yet fluid manner, the Prose Edda encourages readers to engage with the material on both intellectual and emotional levels, fostering a deeper understanding of the underlying spiritual principles that govern the Norse worldview.

Character studies within the Prose Edda are essential for appreciating how these figures embody the values and beliefs of Norse society. Gods like Odin and Thor represent archetypal qualities such as wisdom, sacrifice, strength, and protection, serving as both relatable figures and lofty ideals. Their interactions with one another and with humans reveal moral and ethical dilemmas that resonate across time and culture. These characters are not simply mythological entities; they are representations of the human condition, grappling with issues of power, loyalty, and mortality. Such portrayals provide a framework for understanding the complexities of Norse spirituality and the societal norms that shaped it.

Symbolism and themes within the Prose Edda further underscore its significance as a religious text. The recurring motifs of creation, destruction, and rebirth reflect the cyclical nature of existence as perceived by the Norse people. The concept of Ragnarok, the prophesied end of the world, illustrates not only the inevitability of fate but also the hope for renewal and continuation beyond destruction. These themes invite readers to contemplate their own beliefs about life, death, and the cosmos, positioning the Prose Edda as a text that transcends mere myth and enters the realm of philosophical inquiry.

In examining the Prose Edda alongside the Poetic Edda, one can appreciate the multifaceted nature of Norse mythology and its religious implications. While both texts offer a wealth of narratives, their differing styles and purposes provide complementary insights into the Norse spiritual landscape. The Prose Edda's prose format allows for a more straightforward exposition of mythological themes, while the Poetic Edda's verse invites a more interpretive engagement with the material. Together, they create a rich tapestry of belief that continues to influence modern fantasy literature and popular culture, affirming the enduring legacy of Norse mythology as a source of inspiration and reflection on the human experience.

# Chapter 8: Comparative Studies with the Poetic Edda

## Key Differences in Structure and Style

The Prose Edda, composed by Snorri Sturluson in the early 13th century, is a seminal work in Norse literature that diverges significantly from its poetic counterpart, the Poetic Edda. One of the key differences in structure is the Prose Edda's organization into distinct sections, including the Gylfaginning, the Skáldskaparmál, and the Háttatal. This division allows for a systematic presentation of myths and poetic forms, contrasting with the more fragmented and often anonymous verses found in the Poetic Edda. The Prose Edda serves as a manual for understanding the myths and poetic traditions of the Norse, providing context and commentary that enhance the narrative flow and accessibility for readers.

In terms of style, the Prose Edda exhibits a preference for prose narrative, which results in a more straightforward and direct storytelling approach. This contrasts sharply with the highly stylized and metaphorical nature of the Poetic Edda, where kennings and alliteration create a rich, layered text that requires careful parsing. Snorri's prose is often descriptive and explanatory, aiming to clarify the complexities of Norse mythology for an audience that may not be familiar with its intricacies. This difference in style reflects Snorri's intention to preserve and elucidate the cultural heritage of the Norse people during a time of significant change.

Another critical difference is found in the treatment of characters and their development. The Prose Edda tends to focus on a more defined characterization of gods and heroes, offering background stories and motivations that shape their actions within the narrative. Characters such as Odin, Thor, and Freyja are fleshed out with histories that illuminate their roles within the mythological framework. In contrast, the Poetic Edda often presents these figures in a more episodic manner, emphasizing their actions and the consequences without the same depth of character exploration. This distinction affects how audiences engage with the figures of Norse mythology, as the Prose Edda invites a more intimate understanding of their personalities and relationships.

Symbolism and themes are also articulated differently between the two texts. The Prose Edda often contextualizes symbols and themes within its narrative, providing clear explanations and interpretations that guide the reader's understanding. For example, the symbolism of the world tree, Yggdrasil, is elaborated upon in a way that connects it to the overarching themes of fate and interconnectedness in the cosmos. Conversely, the Poetic Edda leaves much of this symbolism open to interpretation, relying on the reader to draw connections and meanings from the more abstract poetic forms. This difference highlights the Prose Edda's role as a didactic text, while the Poetic Edda remains a rich source of enigmatic imagery.

Ultimately, the influence of the Prose Edda on modern fantasy literature cannot be overstated. Its structured narrative and character depth have inspired countless authors and creators in the genre, providing a template for world-building and mythological storytelling. The clear exposition of Norse myths has allowed contemporary audiences to engage with these ancient stories in a way that is both entertaining and educational. In contrast, the Poetic Edda's more ambiguous style continues to inspire artists and writers seeking to capture the essence of myth through a lens of mystery and poetic beauty. The interplay between these two texts has enriched the understanding of Norse mythology, ensuring its relevance in both historical and modern contexts.

## Thematic Parallels and Divergences

The Prose Edda stands as a cornerstone of Norse mythology, intricately weaving a tapestry of themes that resonate through time and across various cultures. Within its narratives, thematic parallels and divergences emerge, offering a rich field for analysis. Thematically, the Prose Edda shares common ground with the Poetic Edda, particularly in the exploration of fate and heroism. Both texts depict characters grappling with their destinies, yet they approach these themes differently. The Prose Edda's more structured narrative style often highlights the inevitability of fate, while the Poetic Edda employs a more lyrical and fragmented approach, allowing for a broader interpretation of heroism and personal agency.

One significant divergence lies in the representation of the gods, particularly Odin, who emerges as a complex character in the Prose Edda. While he embodies the archetype of the wise and all-knowing deity, his actions often reveal a more ambiguous moral compass. This complexity is less pronounced in the Poetic Edda, where Odin's character tends to reflect a more straightforward heroic ideal. The Prose Edda emphasizes the costs of wisdom and the sacrifices made in the pursuit of knowledge, thereby presenting a more nuanced view of divinity that resonates with adult audiences seeking deeper philosophical inquiries into morality and power.

Symbolism plays a crucial role in both texts, yet the Prose Edda utilizes it in ways that reflect the historical and cultural context of the time. For instance, the recurring motif of the mead of poetry not only symbolizes inspiration and creativity but also serves as a commentary on the nature of knowledge and its accessibility. This contrasts with the Poetic Edda, where symbolism is often more direct and less intertwined with the societal implications of the time. The Prose Edda's layered symbolism invites readers to delve into the socio-political landscape of medieval Scandinavia, revealing much about the cultural values and beliefs held by its audience.

Moreover, the thematic exploration of conflict and resolution is treated differently in the two Eddas. In the Prose Edda, conflicts often arise from the gods' interactions with humans and each other, leading to a more complex interplay of relationships and consequences. In contrast, the Poetic Edda tends to focus on individual heroism and the personal struggles of its characters, which can create a more singular narrative arc. This distinction highlights the Prose Edda's emphasis on interconnectedness and the broader implications of conflict within a societal framework, providing fertile ground for comparative studies that examine the evolution of Norse literary traditions.

Finally, the influence of the Prose Edda on modern fantasy literature cannot be overstated. Its themes of heroism, fate, and the struggle for knowledge have echoed throughout contemporary narratives, shaping genres and character archetypes. The thematic parallels and divergences found within the Prose Edda not only enrich our understanding of Norse mythology but also illustrate how these ancient tales continue to inform and inspire modern storytelling. As we explore these thematic dimensions, we uncover the enduring legacy of the Prose Edda, revealing its significance as both a historical document and a timeless source of inspiration for creators across various media.

## Influence of the Poetic Edda on the Prose Edda

The Poetic Edda serves as a foundational text for understanding Norse mythology and influences the Prose Edda in numerous ways. Composed of a collection of Old Norse poems, the Poetic Edda predates the Prose Edda and provides a wealth of mythological narratives, character archetypes, and thematic elements that are woven into the fabric of the later prose work. The interplay between these texts is evident in the way the Prose Edda, authored by Snorri Sturluson in the 13th century, draws upon the poetic traditions established in the Poetic Edda to create a more structured and cohesive narrative.

One of the most significant influences of the Poetic Edda on the Prose Edda lies in the characterization of mythological figures. The Prose Edda elaborates on the characters introduced in the Poetic Edda, providing deeper psychological insights and motivations. For instance, figures such as Odin, Thor, and Loki are explored with greater complexity in the Prose Edda, where Snorri's interpretations often reflect a nuanced understanding of their roles within the mythological hierarchy. This expansion of character depth not only enriches the narrative but also allows for a more profound exploration of themes such as fate, power, and the duality of good and evil.

The thematic elements prevalent in the Poetic Edda also find resonance within the Prose Edda. Concepts such as the inevitability of fate, the transient nature of life, and the interplay between gods and humans are prevalent in both texts. Snorri Sturluson's work often echoes the sentiments expressed in the poems, reinforcing the idea that the myths serve as reflections of human experience. The Prose Edda not only preserves these themes but also reinterprets them through a more philosophical lens, encouraging readers to engage with the underlying moral questions raised by the stories.

Furthermore, the literary techniques employed in the Poetic Edda heavily influence the narrative style of the Prose Edda. The use of kennings, alliteration, and vivid imagery in the poems serves as a model for Snorri's prose. While the Prose Edda employs a more straightforward narrative style, it retains the poetic essence of the earlier text through its descriptive language and rhythm. This stylistic continuity allows readers to appreciate the cultural significance of the myths while also recognizing the evolution of storytelling techniques from poetry to prose.

Ultimately, the influence of the Poetic Edda on the Prose Edda extends beyond mere content and style; it shapes the very understanding of Norse mythology as a whole. By connecting the two texts, scholars can trace the development of mythological themes, characterizations, and narrative structures that have persisted through centuries. The Prose Edda not only acts as a bridge between ancient Norse beliefs and modern interpretations but also solidifies the Poetic Edda's role as a critical source for the preservation and evolution of Norse mythological heritage.

# Chapter 9: Influence of Prose Edda on Modern Fantasy Literature

## Inspirations for Contemporary Authors

Contemporary authors draw from a myriad of sources for inspiration, and the Prose Edda stands as a particularly rich wellspring of mythological narrative and thematic complexity. This collection of Old Norse tales, compiled in the 13th century, offers insights into the cultural and religious fabric of Norse society. Modern writers often find themselves fascinated by the multifaceted characters and their struggles, which reflect timeless human experiences such as love, betrayal, and the quest for knowledge. The vivid imagery and dramatic conflicts present in the Prose Edda serve as a framework that authors can adapt and reinterpret, allowing them to infuse their own narratives with depth and resonance.

The Prose Edda's exploration of themes such as fate, the cyclical nature of life, and the intricate relationships between gods and mortals provides contemporary authors with a foundation to delve into philosophical inquiries. The text's portrayal of the inevitability of Ragnarok, the end of the world as foreseen in Norse mythology, can inspire narratives that tackle ideas of destiny and the human condition. By weaving these themes into their work, authors can create stories that resonate with readers on both an emotional and intellectual level, prompting reflection on the nature of existence and the choices that define us.

Literary techniques employed in the Prose Edda, such as foreshadowing, symbolism, and allegory, offer valuable tools for modern writers. The use of vivid metaphors and rich descriptive language in the Prose Edda not only enhances the storytelling but also serves to convey deeper meanings and cultural significance. Contemporary authors can learn from these techniques to enhance their own prose, crafting narratives that are not only engaging but also layered with meaning. The way the Prose Edda interweaves myth with history provides a model for authors interested in creating worlds that feel both fantastical and grounded in reality.

Character studies within the Prose Edda reveal a complex tapestry of personalities, each embodying various archetypes that continue to resonate with modern audiences. Figures like Odin, Thor, and Loki are not merely mythological beings; they represent aspects of humanity, from wisdom and strength to chaos and trickery. By examining these characters and their motivations, contemporary authors can create their own multidimensional characters who reflect both the struggles and triumphs of the human experience. This approach allows for a richer narrative that invites readers to explore their own identities and moral dilemmas.

The influence of the Prose Edda on modern fantasy literature is undeniable, serving as a cornerstone for many contemporary works. Authors such as J.R.R. Tolkien and Neil Gaiman have drawn heavily from Norse mythology, integrating its elements into their own fantastical worlds. This connection between the ancient and the modern illustrates how mythological narratives can transcend time, continually inspiring new generations of writers. As contemporary authors engage with the Prose Edda, they not only pay homage to its legacy but also contribute to the ongoing dialogue between past and present, ensuring that these ancient tales continue to echo through the ages.

## Adaptations in Popular Fantasy Series

Adaptations of the Prose Edda into popular fantasy series exemplify the enduring influence of Norse mythology on contemporary storytelling. Several modern works draw inspiration from the characters, themes, and narratives found within the Edda, transforming these ancient tales into dynamic narratives that resonate with today's audiences. Series such as "American Gods" by Neil Gaiman and "The Witcher" by Andrzej Sapkowski showcase how elements from the Prose Edda have been reinterpreted and woven into new mythological frameworks, allowing for a fresh exploration of timeless themes such as destiny, power, and the human condition.

In these adaptations, characters from the Prose Edda often undergo significant reinterpretation. For instance, the Norse god Loki, originally depicted as a complex figure embodying both mischief and wisdom, is reimagined in various narratives to embody more contemporary archetypes. His role as an antihero in modern fantasy reflects a shift in societal values and a fascination with flawed characters. Similarly, Thor, traditionally portrayed as a protector and warrior, is infused with new characteristics that emphasize his vulnerability and fallibility, broadening the audience's emotional connection to these mythic figures.

The themes present in the Prose Edda also find new life in popular fantasy series. Concepts such as fate, sacrifice, and the cyclical nature of life and death resonate within the framework of contemporary storytelling, often serving as the backbone for character motivations and plot developments. The interplay between gods and mortals, as seen in the Prose Edda, is mirrored in these adaptations, where human struggles are often juxtaposed with divine interventions, allowing for a rich exploration of existential questions that remain relevant in modern society.

Symbolism and motifs from the Prose Edda are frequently employed in fantasy narratives to deepen the thematic content. For instance, the world tree Yggdrasil serves not only as a literal connection between realms but also as a metaphor for interconnectedness and the complexity of existence. Adaptations often utilize such symbols to evoke a sense of history and depth, reinforcing the idea that modern tales are not merely new stories but continuations of an ancient dialogue about the human experience. This layering of symbolism enriches the narrative and invites audiences to engage with the material on multiple levels.

Finally, the influence of the Prose Edda on popular culture is evident in various media, from television adaptations to video games, which frequently draw upon its rich mythological tapestry. These adaptations not only serve to entertain but also to educate audiences about Norse mythology and its historical context. As modern creators reinterpret these ancient stories, they contribute to a broader understanding of the Prose Edda's significance, ensuring that its echoes resonate within the fabric of contemporary fantasy literature and beyond, preserving its legacy for future generations.

## The Prose Edda's Legacy in Modern Media

The Prose Edda, composed in the 13th century by the Icelandic scholar Snorri Sturluson, has left an indelible mark on modern media, influencing a wide range of creative expressions. Its rich tapestry of Norse mythology, characterized by intricate narratives and vibrant characters, has provided a fertile ground for contemporary authors, filmmakers, and video game developers. These modern interpretations often draw on the original themes and motifs found in the Prose Edda, breathing new life into ancient tales while exploring universal human experiences, such as heroism, fate, and the struggle between chaos and order.

In literature, the Prose Edda's legacy is particularly prominent in the fantasy genre. Authors such as J.R.R. Tolkien and Neil Gaiman have acknowledged the influence of Norse mythology on their works. Tolkien's Middle-earth, for instance, is imbued with elements reminiscent of the Eddaic cosmos, showcasing a world populated by gods, elves, and other mythical beings. Gaiman's retellings in "Norse Mythology" directly engage with the stories of the Prose Edda, highlighting the relevance of these ancient narratives in contemporary storytelling. The themes of transformation and divine intervention resonate with modern readers, allowing them to connect with the mythological past in meaningful ways.

The impact of the Prose Edda extends beyond literature into the realm of film and television. The recent resurgence of interest in Norse mythology has led to a plethora of adaptations, from Marvel's Thor franchise to the critically acclaimed series "Vikings." These adaptations often take creative liberties but frequently root their narratives in the foundational stories and character archetypes established by Snorri. By showcasing gods like Odin and Thor, along with the complexities of their relationships, modern media invites audiences to engage with these figures, reinterpreting their significance for contemporary society.

Video games have also emerged as a significant medium for exploring the Prose Edda's legacy. Titles such as "God of War" and "Assassin's Creed Valhalla" integrate Norse mythology into their gameplay, allowing players to immerse themselves in a world inspired by the Eddaic narratives. These games not only entertain but also serve as a gateway for players to discover the underlying myths and legends, often leading to increased interest in the original texts. The interactivity of video games enhances the experience, enabling players to navigate the moral complexities and epic conflicts that define the mythological landscape.

Finally, the preservation and translation efforts surrounding the Prose Edda have facilitated its integration into popular culture. As scholars continue to analyze and reinterpret these ancient texts, new translations make the material accessible to broader audiences. This accessibility, combined with the enduring themes and characters, ensures that the Prose Edda remains relevant. Its legacy continues to evolve, demonstrating that the echoes of Asgard resonate in modern media, inspiring creativity and fostering a deeper understanding of our shared mythological heritage.

# Chapter 10: Manuscript Preservation and Translation of the Prose Edda

## Historical Manuscripts and Their Importance

Historical manuscripts, particularly those containing the Prose Edda, serve as vital artifacts that bridge the past and present, allowing contemporary audiences to engage with Norse mythology in profound ways. The Prose Edda, attributed to the 13th-century scholar Snorri Sturluson, encapsulates a wealth of mythological narratives, poetic forms, and intricate literary techniques. By studying these manuscripts, scholars can unlock insights into the cultural and societal values of the Viking Age, revealing how these stories shaped the worldview of their original audience. The preservation and careful translation of these texts are paramount, ensuring that the echoes of Asgard resonate through time, providing context for the myths that continue to influence modern literature and popular culture.

The significance of historical manuscripts extends beyond mere storytelling; they represent a complex interplay of language, culture, and identity. The Prose Edda not only preserves mythological tales but also functions as a source of historical context for understanding the Norse pantheon and its relationship with the surrounding world. Through character studies, one can examine figures like Odin, Thor, and Loki, analyzing their roles and the symbolism embedded within their narratives. The manuscripts reveal how these characters embody human traits and societal ideals, effectively making the myths relatable to audiences across generations. This aspect of the Prose Edda emphasizes the continuity of human experience, showcasing how timeless themes of heroism, fate, and morality are interwoven into the fabric of these ancient stories.

Literary techniques employed in the Prose Edda also merit examination, as they reflect the artistry of medieval Scandinavian literature. The use of kennings, alliteration, and narrative structure in the manuscripts showcases a sophisticated understanding of language and poetic form. These techniques not only enhance the aesthetic quality of the texts but also deepen their thematic richness. Analyzing these literary elements allows for a greater appreciation of how the Prose Edda conveys complex ideas and emotions, inviting readers to engage with the myths on multiple levels. The manuscripts thus serve as a testament to the creativity and intellectual prowess of their time, illustrating how literature can shape cultural identity and collective memory.

Moreover, the Prose Edda's influence extends into modern fantasy literature, where its motifs and characters have inspired countless works. The manuscripts provide a foundation for understanding how contemporary authors reinterpret these ancient myths, weaving them into new narratives that resonate with current audiences. This connection between historical manuscripts and modern storytelling highlights the enduring legacy of the Prose Edda, demonstrating its role as a source of inspiration for writers seeking to tap into the rich tapestry of Norse mythology. Analyzing these influences offers valuable insight into the ways in which ancient texts can continuously inform and transform literary landscapes.

Finally, the preservation and translation of the Prose Edda are crucial for ensuring its accessibility to future generations. As scholars work to maintain the integrity of these historical manuscripts, they also navigate the challenges of translation, striving to convey the nuances of the original language while making the text comprehensible to modern readers. This delicate balance is essential for fostering a deeper understanding of Norse mythology and its relevance today. By appreciating the importance of these historical manuscripts, we can better grasp the cultural significance of the Prose Edda, recognizing it as a vital resource that enriches our understanding of the past and informs our interpretations of the present.

## Challenges in Translation

Challenges in translation of the Prose Edda arise from its intricate blend of mythological narrative, historical context, and linguistic nuance. The original Old Norse text encapsulates a worldview profoundly different from contemporary perspectives, making it difficult for translators to convey not only the literal meaning of the words but also the cultural and emotional resonance behind them. The subtleties of Norse mythology, with its rich symbolism and complex characters, often resist straightforward translation. Each term, metaphor, and phrase is laden with significance that can be easily lost or misconstrued when rendered into modern languages.

One of the primary challenges lies in the Old Norse language itself, which possesses grammatical structures and vocabulary that do not have direct equivalents in English or other modern languages. The inflected nature of Old Norse means that word endings convey a wealth of information about tense, case, and number, which can lead to ambiguity in translation. Additionally, many words carry connotations that are deeply rooted in the cultural and religious practices of the Norse people, necessitating extensive footnotes or explanations that can disrupt the flow of the narrative. The translator must strike a delicate balance between fidelity to the original text and readability for the modern audience.

Cultural references and mythological allusions present further obstacles. The Prose Edda is steeped in the lore of Norse gods and heroes, and many references may be obscure to readers unfamiliar with Scandinavian mythology. Translators must decide whether to retain these references, risking alienation of the reader, or to provide additional context, which could detract from the immediacy of the storytelling. This challenge is compounded by the fact that some mythological concepts may not have direct counterparts in modern belief systems, requiring translators to find creative solutions to convey the intended meaning.

Another significant challenge is the preservation of the poetic structure and stylistic elements inherent in the Prose Edda. The text employs a variety of literary techniques, including alliteration, kennings, and compound words, which contribute to its rhythmic quality and aesthetic appeal. Translating these elements while maintaining the original's poetic essence is a daunting task. Many translators opt for prose translations that sacrifice poetic form for clarity, while others struggle to replicate the original's beauty, often resulting in translations that feel stilted or forced.

Finally, the historical context in which the Prose Edda was written plays a crucial role in its interpretation and translation. The text reflects the sociopolitical landscape of medieval Iceland, including its oral traditions and the transition to Christianity. Understanding these dynamics is essential for translators, who must navigate the nuances of historical interpretation while ensuring that the essence of the text remains intact. In doing so, they contribute to a richer understanding of the Prose Edda's impact on both its own time and its enduring legacy in modern culture and literature.

## Modern Interpretations and Editions

Modern interpretations and editions of the Prose Edda have significantly shaped the understanding of Norse mythology and its literary heritage. Contemporary scholars and translators have sought to make the text accessible to a wider audience while maintaining fidelity to its original context. This effort includes not only translations but also critical analyses that explore the layers of meaning within the text. The Prose Edda, written by Snorri Sturluson in the early 13th century, serves not only as a repository of mythological tales but also as a complex work of literature that reflects the values and beliefs of its time. The evolution of these interpretations highlights the dynamic nature of myth as it adapts to modern sensibilities.

One of the most notable modern editions is the translation by Jesse Byock, which aims to provide clarity and readability while preserving the poetic elements of the original. Byock's work emphasizes the narrative structure and character development within the Prose Edda, facilitating a deeper understanding of the relationships between figures like Odin, Thor, and Loki. This approach also underscores the text's role in Norse religion, illustrating how these deities embody cultural values and human experiences. By presenting the Prose Edda through a contemporary lens, modern translators invite readers to engage with the material in ways that resonate with current cultural themes.

The impact of the Prose Edda on modern fantasy literature cannot be overstated. Authors such as J.R.R. Tolkien and Neil Gaiman have drawn heavily from its narratives, weaving Norse elements into their own fictional worlds. Modern interpretations often highlight the Prose Edda's archetypal characters and themes, allowing new audiences to appreciate its influence on the genre. This intertextual dialogue not only revitalizes ancient stories but also encourages a re-examination of their significance in contemporary storytelling. The blending of traditional myth with modern creativity illustrates the enduring power of these narratives to shape cultural imagination.

In addition to translations and adaptations, the scholarship surrounding the Prose Edda has expanded to include comparative studies with the Poetic Edda. Such analyses reveal the intertextual connections between the two works, highlighting differences in style, tone, and thematic focus. By examining these texts side by side, scholars can better understand the evolution of Norse mythology and its literary forms. This comparative approach enriches the discourse on Norse literature and its significance within a broader historical and cultural framework, providing deeper insights into how these stories reflect the human condition.

Finally, the preservation and translation efforts surrounding the Prose Edda are crucial for its survival in the modern world. As interest in Norse mythology continues to grow, so does the need for accurate and accessible editions. Manuscript preservation initiatives ensure that future generations can study the original texts, while modern translations bridge the gap between ancient language and contemporary comprehension. The increasing presence of the Prose Edda in popular culture and media, from films to video games, highlights its relevance today and underscores the importance of ongoing scholarship and interpretation. These modern engagements with the Prose Edda not only honor its historical significance but also affirm its place in the ever-evolving tapestry of literature and myth.

# Chapter 11: Prose Edda in Popular Culture and Media

### Film and Television Adaptations

Film and television adaptations of the Prose Edda have played a significant role in shaping contemporary perceptions of Norse mythology. These adaptations often draw upon the rich narrative tapestry woven by Snorri Sturluson, highlighting key characters such as Odin, Thor, and Loki, while also introducing new audiences to the complex relationships and moral quandaries present in the original texts. By translating these ancient stories into visual formats, filmmakers and showrunners have the opportunity to explore the themes of heroism, fate, and the divine, which resonate deeply with modern viewers.

One of the most notable adaptations is the Marvel Cinematic Universe's portrayal of Thor and his companions. While it takes considerable liberties with the source material, this adaptation has successfully popularized the character of Thor, transforming him into a symbol of heroism and strength. By merging elements of the Prose Edda with contemporary storytelling techniques, the films have generated interest in the mythology and encouraged audiences to explore the original texts. This blend of ancient and modern resonates particularly well with younger audiences, making Norse mythology accessible and engaging.

Television series such as "Vikings" and "The Last Kingdom" have also contributed to the discourse surrounding Norse mythology and its historical context. These series often incorporate figures and events from the Prose Edda, albeit through a lens that emphasizes historical narrative over mythological fidelity. The dramatization of Viking culture, including their beliefs and interactions with the gods, provides a vivid backdrop that allows audiences to appreciate the cultural significance of these myths. In doing so, these adaptations foster a greater understanding of how Norse religion and mythology influenced daily life in the Viking Age.

Adaptations often emphasize visual storytelling techniques that can highlight the symbolic elements found in the Prose Edda. The use of special effects to depict the fantastical aspects of the myths—such as battles between gods and giants or the creation of the world—serves to enhance the viewer's experience. Moreover, the portrayal of mythological themes such as sacrifice, destiny, and the cyclical nature of existence can be visually compelling, allowing audiences to engage with these concepts in a new way. As filmmakers strive to encapsulate the grandeur of the original tales, they also reinterpret the deeper meanings embedded within them.

Ultimately, the influence of the Prose Edda on modern adaptations reflects a broader trend of reimagining ancient narratives for contemporary audiences. As adaptations continue to emerge across various media, they not only entertain but also educate viewers about the rich mythological tradition of the Norse. By weaving together historical context, character studies, and thematic explorations, these adaptations encourage a reevaluation of the Prose Edda and its relevance in today's cultural landscape. As interest in Norse mythology persists, it remains essential to consider both the fidelity of these adaptations to the source material and their broader implications for understanding the myths that have endured through centuries.

## Video Games and Interactive Media

Video games and interactive media have emerged as powerful platforms for storytelling, allowing players to engage with narratives in ways that traditional literature cannot. The Prose Edda, as a foundational text of Norse mythology, has found its way into various video game narratives, creating a bridge between ancient lore and modern interactive experiences. Titles such as "God of War," "Hellblade: Senua's Sacrifice," and "Assassin's Creed Valhalla" draw heavily from the rich tapestry of gods, giants, and heroes found within the Prose Edda, reinterpreting these characters and myths for contemporary audiences. This interaction not only revitalizes interest in the original text but also encourages a deeper exploration of its themes and characters.

The adaptability of the Prose Edda in video games illustrates the timeless nature of its stories and their relevance in modern culture. Game developers often utilize the complex relationships and moral dilemmas faced by figures like Odin, Thor, and Loki to create compelling narratives that resonate with players. For instance, the character of Loki, often portrayed as a trickster and complex anti-hero, invites players to explore themes of identity, deception, and the consequences of one's actions. This nuanced portrayal invites comparisons to traditional character studies in literature, highlighting the depth of the Prose Edda's characterizations and their potential for exploration in interactive formats.

Interactive media also offers a unique means of highlighting the symbolism and themes prevalent in the Prose Edda. Many games incorporate elements such as fate, honor, and the struggle between chaos and order, mirroring the philosophical underpinnings of the original texts. The choice-driven nature of video games allows players to engage with these themes actively, leading to different outcomes based on their decisions. This interactivity can foster a greater understanding of the moral complexities present in Norse mythology, encouraging players to reflect on their own values and choices in a way that passive consumption of literature does not.

Moreover, the influence of the Prose Edda extends beyond individual titles; it has shaped the broader landscape of fantasy literature and media. The archetypes and narrative structures established in the Edda have informed countless works, from J.R.R. Tolkien's Middle-earth to contemporary fantasy series. Video games stand at the forefront of this evolution, often serving as a modern extension of the mythological storytelling tradition. By engaging players in immersive worlds that draw from the Prose Edda, these games contribute to a renewed appreciation for Norse mythology, influencing how it is perceived and understood in popular culture.

Lastly, the preservation and translation of the Prose Edda have been critical in facilitating its integration into modern media. As new translations and interpretations emerge, they provide fresh perspectives that can inspire game developers and writers alike. This ongoing dialogue between ancient texts and contemporary media not only ensures the survival of these myths but also enriches the gaming experience. As players navigate the worlds shaped by the Prose Edda, they are not merely participants in a game; they become part of a larger narrative that honors the past while forging new pathways in storytelling.

## Merchandise and Fan Culture

Merchandise associated with the Prose Edda and its mythological themes has evolved significantly, reflecting the growing interest in Norse mythology and its narratives. From replicas of Viking artifacts to clothing emblazoned with runes and images of gods, the commercialization of these ancient stories has created a tangible link between contemporary culture and the mythological past. This merchandise not only serves as a means of artistic expression but also functions as a medium through which fans can engage with the stories and characters that have captivated audiences for centuries. The proliferation of such items signifies a broader trend where ancient myths are woven into the fabric of modern identity, allowing individuals to connect with their heritage or simply to participate in a cultural phenomenon.

Fan culture surrounding the Prose Edda is marked by a vibrant community that thrives on sharing interpretations, artwork, and adaptations of the text. Social media platforms and online forums enable enthusiasts to discuss their favorite characters, such as Odin, Thor, and Loki, fostering a sense of belonging among fans. This active engagement often leads to creative expressions, including fan fiction, artwork, and even role-playing games. The blending of ancient myth with contemporary storytelling not only enriches the original narratives but also demonstrates the adaptability of these tales to modern sensibilities. As fans reinterpret and reimagine these stories, they contribute to an ongoing dialogue that bridges the gap between the past and the present.

The impact of merchandise and fan culture extends to the realm of modern fantasy literature, where the Prose Edda has inspired countless authors. Elements from the Edda's rich tapestry of characters and themes can be seen in contemporary works, where writers draw on Norse mythology to craft their own narratives. This influence is particularly evident in fantasy series that feature gods, mythical creatures, and epic quests, echoing the structure and motifs found in the Prose Edda. As these stories gain popularity, they further the commercialization of Norse mythology, leading to the creation of themed merchandise that appeals to both new readers and long-time fans.

In addition to literary adaptations, the Prose Edda has permeated various forms of media, including film, television, and video games. This cross-media presence not only reinforces the appeal of the source material but also introduces the myths to audiences who may not be familiar with the original texts. Merchandise tied to these adaptations—such as collectibles, clothing, and game expansions—serves as a testament to the enduring relevance of these ancient stories. Through these products, fans can express their enthusiasm and connect with others who share their passion for Norse mythology, creating a dynamic community that celebrates and perpetuates the myths of Asgard.

The preservation and translation of the Prose Edda also play a crucial role in shaping merchandise and fan culture. As scholars work to make these texts accessible to broader audiences, the interest in Norse mythology continues to expand. Modern translations often come with annotations and interpretations that enhance the reader's understanding, making the tales more engaging and relatable. This scholarly work not only supports the creation of merchandise but also enriches the fan experience, as individuals explore the deeper meanings and historical contexts of the myths. Ultimately, the intersection of merchandise, fan culture, and scholarly analysis contributes to a vibrant ecosystem that keeps the echoes of Asgard alive in contemporary society.

# Chapter 12: Conclusion

## Recap of Key Insights

The Prose Edda stands as a cornerstone of Norse literature, weaving together myth and history with intricate narrative techniques. This work, attributed to Snorri Sturluson in the 13th century, serves not only as a guide to the mythology of the Norse gods but also as a crucial repository for understanding the cultural values and beliefs of the Viking Age. Through its detailed character studies, the Prose Edda illuminates the complexities of figures like Odin, Thor, and Loki, showcasing their multifaceted nature and the moral dilemmas they navigate. These characterizations reflect broader human experiences, allowing readers to draw parallels with contemporary life.

Symbolism and themes within the Prose Edda are rich and varied, often intertwining elements of fate, power, and the cyclical nature of existence. The concept of wyrd, or fate, plays a central role, emphasizing the inevitability of destiny while simultaneously highlighting the agency of the characters. The recurring motifs of creation and destruction, as seen in the tales of Ragnarok, serve as a reminder of the transient nature of life. This duality reinforces the idea that every end is also a beginning, a theme that resonates deeply in both ancient and modern narratives.

The historical context in which the Prose Edda was written cannot be overlooked, as it was a time of significant cultural transition in Scandinavia. The conversion to Christianity and the decline of pagan practices influenced Snorri's approach, as he sought to preserve the rich oral traditions of his ancestors while navigating the changing religious landscape. This tension between old and new beliefs is evident throughout the text, providing insights into the societal shifts occurring during the medieval period. The Prose Edda thus acts as both a literary artifact and a historical document, offering valuable perspectives on the era's worldview.

Literary techniques employed in the Prose Edda, such as alliteration, metaphor, and vivid imagery, enhance the storytelling and contribute to its enduring appeal. Snorri's use of prose interspersed with poetic elements allows for a dynamic reading experience, inviting readers to engage with the text on multiple levels. This blending of forms not only showcases Snorri's skill as a writer but also reflects the oral traditions from which these stories emerged. The influence of the Prose Edda extends beyond its pages, inspiring generations of writers and artists in the realm of modern fantasy literature and beyond.

Finally, the Prose Edda's impact on popular culture is profound, permeating various media, from literature and film to video games and art. Its themes and characters have been reimagined in countless ways, highlighting the timeless nature of these stories. As contemporary creators draw on the rich tapestry of Norse mythology, the Prose Edda continues to resonate, inviting new audiences to explore its depths. The ongoing preservation and translation efforts ensure that these ancient tales remain accessible, allowing for a renewed appreciation of their significance in both historical and modern contexts.

## The Prose Edda's Enduring Relevance

The Prose Edda remains a cornerstone of Norse mythology, serving as a key text that informs our understanding of the ancient Norse worldview. Written in the 13th century by Snorri Sturluson, this literary work not only preserves the stories of gods, giants, and heroes but also reflects the sociopolitical landscape of medieval Iceland. Its structure, which combines narrative with poetic elements, provides a rich tapestry that continues to resonate with readers and scholars alike. The enduring relevance of the Prose Edda can be seen through its exploration of themes such as fate, honor, and the interplay between chaos and order, which are as pertinent today as they were in the Viking Age.

One significant aspect of the Prose Edda's relevance lies in its role as a source for understanding Norse religion and mythology. The text serves as both a historical document and a guide to the beliefs and practices of the Norse people. By analyzing the myths and their underlying symbolism, contemporary readers gain insights into the values and ideals that shaped Norse culture. The Prose Edda also facilitates comparative studies with other mythological traditions, allowing for a deeper appreciation of universal themes in human storytelling. This comparative approach enriches our understanding of mythology as a cultural phenomenon that transcends geographical and temporal boundaries.

Literary techniques employed by Snorri Sturluson, such as alliteration, metaphor, and narrative framing, contribute to the Prose Edda's enduring appeal. The text's intricate storytelling weaves together various mythic elements, creating a dynamic interplay between characters and their destinies. These literary strategies not only enhance the aesthetic experience of reading but also serve to reinforce the thematic depth of the narratives. As modern readers engage with these techniques, they uncover layers of meaning that speak to the human condition, making the Prose Edda a timeless work that continues to inspire literary analysis and creative expression.

The influence of the Prose Edda on modern fantasy literature is another vital aspect of its relevance. Authors such as J.R.R. Tolkien and Neil Gaiman have drawn heavily from Norse mythology, often integrating elements from the Prose Edda into their own works. This adaptation of mythological themes and characters into contemporary narratives demonstrates the text's capacity to inspire new generations of storytellers. The fusion of ancient myths with modern storytelling not only keeps the Prose Edda alive in popular culture but also invites a re-examination of its themes in the context of current societal issues.

Finally, the preservation and translation of the Prose Edda play a crucial role in maintaining its relevance. As scholars continue to translate and interpret the text, new insights emerge, shaping our understanding of its significance. Furthermore, the Prose Edda's presence in popular culture—from films to video games—ensures that its stories reach a wider audience. This interaction between the ancient and the modern reinforces the idea that the Prose Edda is not merely a relic of the past but a living text that continues to echo through time, inviting exploration and engagement in an ever-evolving cultural landscape.

## Future Directions for Study and Exploration

Future directions for study and exploration of the Prose Edda present exciting opportunities across various dimensions of mythological analysis, historical context, and literary techniques. Scholars should consider deepening their investigations into the socio-political influences that shaped Snorri Sturluson's writings. Understanding the historical milieu of 13th-century Iceland could yield insights into how power dynamics, cultural exchanges, and prevailing beliefs informed the structure and themes of the Prose Edda. By situating the text within its historical framework, researchers can illuminate the ways in which Norse mythology served not only as a source of entertainment but also as a political tool in the consolidation of power and identity.

In addition to historical context, future studies could enhance our understanding of the literary techniques employed within the Prose Edda. A focused analysis on narrative structure, character development, and the use of poetic devices can reveal how Snorri crafted a complex tapestry of interwoven stories. Examining how he balances prose and poetry, as well as the implications of his stylistic choices, can deepen our appreciation of the text's literary artistry. Furthermore, comparative studies with the Poetic Edda could provide a richer perspective on how different formats convey mythological themes and character arcs, potentially leading to new interpretations of familiar tales.

Character studies within the Prose Edda offer another fertile ground for exploration. Analyzing the motivations, conflicts, and transformations of central figures such as Odin, Thor, and Loki can yield insights into larger themes of heroism, morality, and the human condition. Future research could delve into the psychological dimensions of these characters, exploring how their narratives reflect the values and fears of medieval Scandinavian society. By applying modern psychological theories to these ancient characters, scholars can uncover the enduring relevance of these myths and their impact on contemporary understandings of identity and agency.

The symbolism and themes prevalent in the Prose Edda warrant further examination, particularly in relation to their implications for Norse religion and cosmology. Future studies could explore how symbols such as Yggdrasil, the World Tree, and the various realms of existence articulate a coherent worldview that reflects the Norse understanding of life, death, and the cosmos. Additionally, the interaction between mythology and ritual practices in Norse culture can be a compelling area of study, as it may reveal how these narratives were not merely stories but integral components of religious life and community identity.

Lastly, the influence of the Prose Edda on modern fantasy literature and popular culture continues to be a vibrant area for scholarly inquiry. As contemporary narratives draw heavily on Norse mythology, understanding how the Prose Edda has shaped these modern interpretations can illuminate the enduring power of myth. Research into manuscript preservation and translation efforts can also contribute valuable perspectives on how accessibility and interpretation have evolved. By examining adaptations in film, literature, and gaming, scholars can assess the cultural resonance of these ancient stories and their capacity to inform contemporary ethical and existential questions.

# Beyond the Shield Wall: Disentangling Asatru from Racism

### The Origins of Asatru

The origins of Asatru can be traced back to ancient Norse beliefs and practices, rooted in the pre-Christian era of Scandinavia. As a polytheistic faith, it was characterized by the worship of a pantheon of gods such as Odin, Thor, and Freyja, alongside a deep reverence for nature and ancestral spirits. Early practitioners engaged in rituals that honored these deities, often linked to agricultural cycles, seasonal changes, and community gatherings. The transition to Christianity in the 10th and 11th centuries saw a gradual decline in these practices. However, the resurgence of interest in Norse mythology and Viking heritage during the 19th century laid the groundwork for modern interpretations of Asatru, often divorced from its original context.

The misinterpretation of Norse mythology and its association with racism can largely be attributed to the distortion of historical narratives. During the 19th and early 20th centuries, nationalist movements in Europe began to co-opt Norse symbols and myths as part of a broader agenda that emphasized ethnic purity and superiority. This appropriation contributed to the erroneous belief that Asatru is inherently linked to white supremacy. In reality, the mythology itself is rich with themes of diversity, community, and mutual respect among different beings, including gods, giants, and elves. These narratives reflect a complex understanding of existence rather than a narrow ethnocentric view.

Modern Pagan movements have significantly influenced the inclusivity of Asatru, promoting a more open and diverse interpretation of the faith. Many practitioners today emphasize the importance of personal choice, individual spiritual journeys, and community building that transcends ethnic boundaries. This shift has led to a more welcoming environment for individuals from various backgrounds who seek to engage with Norse spirituality. Notable efforts within the Asatru community highlight the need for inclusivity, recognizing that the essence of the tradition can be enriched through diverse perspectives and experiences.

Asatru also places a strong emphasis on personal responsibility and community, which serves as a counter-narrative to the misappropriation of its symbols by extremist groups. Practitioners are encouraged to take ownership of their actions and to contribute positively to their communities, fostering connections that are grounded in mutual respect and support. This ethical framework inherently challenges the notion that Asatru can be aligned with racist ideologies. Instead, it reinforces the idea that the practice is about building a shared identity based on values and principles rather than ethnicity.

Finally, the role of Norse symbols in contemporary anti-racist movements provides a powerful lens through which to view Asatru's evolution in a globalized context. Many practitioners advocate for a reinterpretation of these symbols as representations of unity and resilience rather than division. The participation of diverse practitioners in Norse pagan traditions further enriches the tapestry of Asatru, illustrating that it can thrive in multicultural settings. As a living tradition, Asatru continues to evolve, demonstrating that its core values can resonate with individuals from all walks of life, ultimately debunking the myths that seek to tether it to racism and exclusion.

## Common Misunderstandings

Common misunderstandings about Asatru and Norse Paganism often stem from historical misinterpretations and the appropriation of symbols by extremist groups. A prevalent misconception is that Asatru is inherently linked to racism or white supremacy. This notion arises from the misuse of Norse mythology and symbols by certain factions who distort these beliefs to promote a narrow, exclusionary agenda. However, the core tenets of Asatru emphasize respect for all individuals and the celebration of diversity. It is crucial to separate these ideological misapplications from the authentic spiritual practices of Asatru, which prioritize personal responsibility and community cohesion.

Historical interpretations of Norse mythology frequently contribute to these misunderstandings. Many individuals approach these ancient texts without sufficient context, leading to skewed perceptions of what Norse beliefs entailed. The sagas and Eddas reflect a rich tapestry of culture and values that are often misrepresented as advocating for racial superiority. In reality, Norse mythology encompasses a variety of deities and narratives that celebrate the human experience in all its complexity. Recognizing the nuances within these texts can help dismantle the simplistic associations made between Norse mythology and racial ideologies.

Modern Pagan movements have made significant strides toward inclusivity, challenging the narratives that link Asatru with exclusivist ideologies. Many practitioners actively work to redefine these traditions in a manner that embraces multiculturalism and diversity. The growing number of practitioners from various ethnic backgrounds engaging in Asatru highlights its appeal beyond racial identity. This evolution reflects a broader understanding that spirituality can transcend ethnic boundaries and that the values of respect, honor, and community are universal.

At the heart of Asatru is an emphasis on personal responsibility and community involvement. Practitioners are encouraged to take ownership of their actions and contribute positively to their communities. This focus on individual accountability fosters an environment where inclusivity thrives. By championing the well-being of all community members, Asatru practitioners create spaces that reject racism and embrace a shared humanity, reinforcing the idea that spirituality can unite rather than divide.

The role of Norse symbols in contemporary anti-racist movements further complicates the narrative around Asatru. Many symbols that have been co-opted by extremist groups are also reclaimed by those advocating for equality and social justice. The reinterpretation of these symbols serves as a powerful statement against hate and division. Additionally, the contribution of diverse practitioners to Norse Pagan traditions enriches the spiritual landscape, demonstrating that Asatru is not monolithic but rather an evolving practice welcoming of all who seek its wisdom. This complexity illustrates that the path of Asatru can coexist harmoniously within a multicultural framework, fostering understanding and respect across diverse communities.

## The Impact of Misinterpretation

Misinterpretation has significantly shaped the perception of Asatru and Norse Paganism, often leading to unfounded associations with racism and white supremacy. These misconceptions typically stem from historical interpretations that overlook the complex cultural and spiritual dimensions of Norse mythology. The Viking Age, often romanticized in popular culture, has been co-opted by extremist groups who selectively draw from these narratives to promote exclusionary ideologies. This misapplication of history not only distorts the original meanings behind symbols and practices but also perpetuates a false narrative that inaccurately represents the beliefs of contemporary practitioners.

The historical misinterpretations of Norse mythology often fail to recognize the fluidity of cultural identity in ancient societies. Norse myths and sagas were not static; they evolved over time and were influenced by various cultures through trade, conquest, and migration. These narratives were shaped by the experiences and beliefs of diverse groups, reflecting a tapestry of interactions rather than a monolithic ethnic identity. Misunderstanding this historical context can lead to the erroneous belief that Norse Paganism is inherently tied to racial identity, when in fact, it is a spiritual path that can be embraced by individuals of all backgrounds.

Modern Pagan movements have made significant strides toward inclusivity, actively working to dismantle the association between Norse spirituality and racist ideologies. Many practitioners emphasize the values of community, personal responsibility, and mutual respect, fostering an environment where individuals from different cultural backgrounds can come together. This shift toward inclusivity is not merely a reaction to past misinterpretations but a conscious effort to redefine what it means to practice Asatru in today's diverse society. By acknowledging and celebrating multicultural contributions, these movements enrich the spiritual landscape and challenge the narrow narratives often perpetuated by extremist factions.

The role of Norse symbols in contemporary anti-racist movements further complicates the narrative surrounding Asatru. While some groups have attempted to appropriate these symbols for their own agendas, many practitioners reclaim them as representations of unity and strength in diversity. This reclamation serves as a powerful counter-narrative, illustrating that Norse imagery can embody values of inclusivity and resistance against oppression rather than exclusion and hatred. As more individuals recognize the potential for these symbols to serve as a bridge between cultures, the landscape of Norse Paganism continues to evolve, reflecting a broader spectrum of identities and experiences.

In examining the intersection of Asatru and multiculturalism, it becomes clear that the evolution of Norse Paganism in a globalized context is marked by the contributions of diverse practitioners. Asatru is not confined to a single ethnicity or culture; its practices are adaptable and can resonate with individuals from various backgrounds. This adaptability encourages a rich dialogue about identity, spirituality, and community, challenging the misconceptions that have long plagued this tradition. By embracing a more nuanced understanding of Norse Paganism, we can move beyond the shield wall of misinterpretation and appreciate the depth and breadth of its true essence.

# Chapter 2: Historical Misinterpretations of Norse Mythology

## The Viking Age and Its Legacy

The Viking Age, spanning roughly from 793 to 1066 CE, served as a pivotal period in European history characterized by exploration, trade, and cultural exchange. Vikings, known for their seafaring abilities, ventured far beyond their Scandinavian homelands, reaching as far as North America, the Mediterranean, and the Middle East. This era was not solely defined by raids and warfare; it also saw the establishment of settlements and trade routes that facilitated interaction with diverse cultures. The legacy of the Viking Age is multifaceted, encompassing not only the historical narratives of conquest but also the rich tapestry of cultural exchange that influenced language, art, and social practices across Europe.

The misconceptions surrounding Norse mythology often stem from a limited understanding of its historical context. Many modern interpretations have been skewed by the lens of nationalism and racism, which have attempted to co-opt Norse symbols and deities for exclusionary purposes. However, original Norse beliefs were not founded on notions of ethnic superiority. Instead, they emphasized a connection to the land, community, and shared experiences, which allowed for a more inclusive understanding of identity. This is crucial in disentangling Asatru from the misinterpretations that link it to white supremacy, as the mythology itself is rooted in a worldview that transcends modern racial constructs.

In recent years, modern Pagan movements have increasingly embraced inclusivity, recognizing the importance of diverse voices within spiritual practices. Asatru, as a contemporary expression of Norse paganism, has evolved to reflect this inclusivity. Practitioners from various backgrounds contribute to the richness of traditions, reshaping rituals and interpretations of mythology to better align with a multicultural society. This evolution not only honors the historical context of Norse beliefs but also fosters a sense of belonging for individuals who may have been historically marginalized within these spiritual spaces.

A key tenet of Asatru is the emphasis on personal responsibility and community. This principle encourages individuals to take ownership of their actions while fostering a supportive environment for collective growth. Such an approach inherently contradicts the divisive ideologies often associated with extremist groups that misuse Norse symbols. Rather than promoting a singular ethnic identity, Asatru invites a diverse range of practitioners to engage with the traditions in a manner that resonates with their own experiences and cultural backgrounds. This aspect of the faith highlights the potential for unity in diversity, challenging the notion that Norse paganism is tied exclusively to a specific racial or ethnic identity.

The role of Norse symbols in contemporary movements reflects a broader societal commitment to anti-racism and inclusivity. While certain extremist groups have attempted to appropriate these symbols for their agendas, many practitioners actively reclaim them as representations of community, resilience, and cultural heritage. This reclamation underscores the importance of understanding the historical and cultural significance of these symbols, separate from their misappropriation by hate groups. Ultimately, the evolution of Norse paganism in a globalized context serves as a testament to the enduring nature of these beliefs and their capacity to foster connections among diverse communities, dispelling the myths that seek to confine them to a singular, exclusionary narrative.

## Myths Versus Historical Facts

The belief that Asatru and Norse Paganism are inherently tied to racism or white supremacy is a misconception that has been perpetuated through historical misinterpretations and modern narratives. Historically, Norse mythology and the beliefs surrounding it were diverse and fluid, practiced by various groups across Scandinavia and beyond. These early practitioners did not adhere to a rigid ethnic identity; rather, their beliefs were shaped by local customs, social structures, and interactions with neighboring cultures. By examining the historical context of Norse beliefs, it becomes clear that the association with racial ideologies is a modern construct that distorts the rich tapestry of past practices.

Modern pagan movements have significantly influenced the understanding and practice of Asatru today. Many contemporary practitioners emphasize inclusivity and community, actively working to dismantle the stereotypes that have emerged around Norse spirituality. These movements often engage with social justice issues, aligning their practices with broader values of equality and respect for all individuals, regardless of their ethnic background. Asatru is increasingly seen as a spiritual path that welcomes diverse practitioners and encourages personal responsibility, challenging the notion that it is exclusive to any one race or ethnicity.

The emphasis on personal responsibility and community within Asatru further debunks the myths linking it to racism. Practitioners are encouraged to take ownership of their actions and to contribute positively to their communities. This focus fosters a sense of belonging that transcends ethnic boundaries, promoting a model of spirituality that values individual integrity and collective support. In this framework, the teachings of Norse mythology can be interpreted to advocate for harmony among diverse groups rather than division.

The role of Norse symbols in contemporary anti-racist movements highlights the potential for these images to be reclaimed and redefined. While some extremist groups have co-opted symbols such as the Valknut or the Mjölnir for their agendas, many practitioners are actively working to reclaim these symbols for positive representation. These symbols can serve as reminders of the original values of strength, protection, and unity that are central to Norse mythology. By engaging with these symbols in a way that promotes inclusivity, practitioners can challenge the narratives that seek to align them with hate.

Asatru is evolving in a globalized context, where diverse cultural expressions contribute to a richer understanding of Norse pagan traditions. Practitioners from various backgrounds bring their interpretations and practices into the fold, creating a dynamic and inclusive community. This intersection of Asatru and multiculturalism demonstrates that Norse beliefs can thrive in a diverse world. It is essential to recognize that the historical roots of Norse spirituality do not support a singular ethnic identity, but rather celebrate the shared human experience and the bonds that connect us across cultures.

## The Role of Romanticism in Shaping Perceptions

Romanticism played a pivotal role in shaping modern perceptions of Norse mythology and Asatru, significantly influencing how these traditions are understood today. Emerging in the late 18th and early 19th centuries, Romanticism emphasized emotion, nature, and the glorification of the past. This movement fostered a renewed interest in folk tales, myths, and ancient traditions, which included Norse mythology. As scholars and artists sought to reconnect with what they perceived as a more authentic cultural heritage, they often romanticized these ancient practices, sometimes distorting their meanings and connections to contemporary issues, including race.

The misinterpretations that arose from this romanticized view of Norse culture often intertwined with the rise of nationalist sentiments, particularly in Europe and the United States. Many individuals and groups began to selectively adopt elements of Norse mythology to construct narratives that supported a racial or ethnic identity, erroneously linking Asatru to concepts of racial superiority. This misappropriation has led to the unfounded association of Norse paganism with white supremacy, overshadowing its core values of community, personal responsibility, and a deep connection to nature. Such oversimplifications ignore the complexities and nuances of Norse traditions and their historical practices.

Contrary to these misconceptions, the modern Pagan movements, including Asatru, have increasingly embraced inclusivity and diversity. Practitioners from various backgrounds are reclaiming these traditions, focusing on the universal themes present in Norse mythology that resonate with people across different cultures. Asatru emphasizes personal responsibility and community, inviting individuals to interpret their spiritual journeys without being confined by narrow ethnic definitions. This evolving understanding of Norse mythology allows for a broader interpretation that champions multiculturalism, challenging the narrative that associates these practices exclusively with a specific racial identity.

Furthermore, the use of Norse symbols in contemporary anti-racist movements highlights the capacity of these symbols to transcend their historical contexts. Activists have repurposed imagery once co-opted by extremist groups, recontextualizing it to signify resistance against oppression and a commitment to inclusivity. This reclamation serves as a reminder that symbols can evolve and take on new meanings, often reflecting the values of those who wield them. Asatru, at its core, advocates for a connection to heritage that is not limited by skin color or ethnicity, promoting a vision of community that is inclusive and diverse.

The contribution of diverse practitioners to Norse pagan traditions further enriches this dialogue. Asatru practices have been embraced by individuals from various racial and cultural backgrounds, each bringing their unique perspectives and experiences to the tradition. This blending of ideas fosters a more comprehensive understanding of Norse spirituality, emphasizing that it is not a monolithic practice but one that can be adapted and redefined in a globalized context. The evolution of Norse paganism reflects a broader trend of spiritual practices becoming more inclusive and representative of diverse communities, reinforcing the notion that heritage and identity are complex and multifaceted concepts.

# Chapter 3: Modern Pagan Movements and Inclusivity

## The Rise of Contemporary Paganism

The contemporary resurgence of Paganism, particularly in the form of Asatru and Norse Paganism, reflects a significant shift in how these ancient traditions are interpreted and practiced today. The rise of these movements must be understood against a backdrop of historical misinterpretations that have erroneously linked Norse mythology with notions of racism and white supremacy. In reality, Asatru emphasizes personal responsibility, community engagement, and a deep respect for nature, values that are universally applicable and not confined to any particular ethnic identity. This chapter aims to disentangle these misconceptions and highlight the inclusive nature of contemporary Norse Paganism.

Norse mythology has often been misrepresented in popular culture and academic discourse, leading to a distorted understanding of its principles. Historical texts and sagas have been selectively quoted or interpreted to promote a narrative that aligns with extremist ideologies. However, the original stories are rich with themes of cooperation, diversity, and the importance of community, which contradict the divisive interpretations often associated with them. By examining the full scope of Norse mythological texts, one can appreciate the complexity of these narratives and the values they espouse, which are inherently inclusive rather than exclusive.

Modern Pagan movements have actively worked to redefine and reclaim these ancient traditions, fostering an environment that welcomes practitioners from diverse backgrounds. This inclusivity is not merely a contemporary trend but a fundamental aspect of what it means to engage with Norse spirituality today. Many practitioners recognize the need to create spaces that celebrate multiculturalism, allowing for a broader understanding of how Norse practices can coexist with various cultural identities. This evolution is indicative of a larger movement within Paganism that seeks to embrace diversity and challenge the exclusionary narratives that have plagued these traditions.

Asatru's focus on personal responsibility and community serves as a powerful counter-narrative to the associations with racism. The practice encourages individuals to take ownership of their actions and contributions to their communities, irrespective of their ethnic backgrounds. This emphasis fosters an environment where all practitioners are seen as equal, promoting a sense of belonging that transcends racial and cultural boundaries. By engaging in rituals and community activities, practitioners find common ground and shared values, reinforcing the idea that Norse Paganism can be a unifying force rather than a divisive one.

Furthermore, the contemporary use of Norse symbols in anti-racist movements illustrates a significant reappropriation of these images away from extremist groups that have attempted to claim them for their agendas. Many activists draw upon Norse symbols to represent resilience, strength, and community solidarity, consciously rejecting the racist interpretations that seek to co-opt these ancient traditions. By embracing a more inclusive interpretation of Norse imagery, practitioners and activists alike can actively challenge the narratives that have historically linked these symbols to exclusionary ideologies. In this way, the rise of contemporary Paganism represents not only a revival of ancient practices but also a commitment to fostering inclusivity and understanding in a multicultural world.

## Asatru's Place in the Modern Pagan Landscape

Asatru occupies a unique position within the modern pagan landscape, often misunderstood due to the lingering misinterpretations of its roots and practices. The incorrect assumption that Asatru is inherently tied to racism or white supremacy has persisted, perpetuated by extremist groups that misappropriate Norse symbols for their own agendas. This distortion not only undermines the true essence of Asatru but also casts a shadow over the rich tapestry of Norse mythology and its diverse interpretations. In reality, Asatru emphasizes values such as personal responsibility, respect for nature, and community cohesion, which are universal and can be embraced by individuals from various backgrounds.

Historical misinterpretations of Norse mythology have further complicated Asatru's modern identity. Many narratives surrounding Norse deities and legends have been oversimplified or stripped of their cultural context. The complexity of these stories often reflects a broader understanding of human experience, exploring themes of fate, honor, and interconnectedness. By engaging with these myths in their entirety, practitioners can gain a deeper appreciation for their significance beyond the narrow lens of racial identity. This understanding allows for a more inclusive practice that welcomes individuals regardless of their ethnic backgrounds.

Modern pagan movements have made significant strides towards inclusivity, challenging the outdated notions that have historically plagued Asatru. Many contemporary practitioners actively reject any association with racism, emphasizing that Norse spirituality is about personal growth and communal ties rather than ethnic exclusivity. This shift is reflective of a broader trend within paganism, where the focus is increasingly on shared values and the celebration of diversity. Asatru practitioners today often engage in dialogues about inclusivity, aiming to create spaces where everyone feels welcome to explore and connect with Norse traditions.

The emphasis on personal responsibility and community within Asatru serves as a foundation for its practice, promoting a sense of accountability that transcends ethnic lines. This principle encourages individuals to take active roles in their communities, fostering connections that are based on shared values rather than heritage. Asatru thus becomes a spiritual path that invites diverse practitioners to contribute their perspectives and experiences, enriching the tradition as a whole. This communal aspect reinforces the idea that Norse paganism is not confined to a single ethnic identity but is instead a living, evolving practice open to all.

The intersection of Asatru and multiculturalism reflects a growing recognition of the contributions of diverse practitioners to Norse pagan traditions. Asatru's practices are increasingly visible in non-white cultures, demonstrating that the essence of these beliefs can resonate across different backgrounds. This evolution is crucial in debunking myths surrounding Norse paganism and ethnic identity, highlighting that spirituality can be a source of unity rather than division. Additionally, the role of Norse symbols in contemporary anti-racist movements illustrates a reclaiming of heritage that stands against the misuse of these symbols by extremist groups. In this context, Asatru emerges as a pathway not only to reconnect with ancient traditions but also to foster a more inclusive future within the broader pagan community.

## Efforts Toward Inclusivity and Diversity

Efforts toward inclusivity and diversity within Asatru and Norse Paganism are increasingly recognized as essential to countering the harmful narratives that associate these traditions with racism and white supremacy. For many practitioners, the core tenets of Asatru emphasize community, respect for nature, and personal responsibility, which inherently reject the exclusionary practices often mistakenly attributed to these spiritual paths. As modern practitioners engage with their traditions, they actively seek to dismantle the incorrect assumptions that have historically clouded the understanding of Norse mythology and its cultural significance, fostering a more inclusive environment for all who wish to partake in these beliefs.

Historical misinterpretations of Norse mythology have played a significant role in the association of Asatru with ethnonationalism. Scholars and practitioners alike are working diligently to clarify these misconceptions by emphasizing that Norse mythology is a rich tapestry of stories that transcends race and ethnicity. By focusing on the universal themes of honor, courage, and kinship found within these myths, practitioners are recontextualizing these narratives to promote a message of inclusivity. This shift encourages individuals from diverse backgrounds to explore their connections to these ancient stories, fostering a sense of belonging within the broader Asatru community.

The influence of modern pagan movements has also contributed significantly to the push for inclusivity within Asatru. Many contemporary pagan groups explicitly prioritize diversity, advocating for the inclusion of voices from various racial and cultural backgrounds. This has led to a re-examination of traditional practices and beliefs, allowing for a more multifaceted understanding of spirituality that honors the complexities of individual experiences. As practitioners share their diverse interpretations of Norse mythology and engage in dialogues about cultural appropriation, they collectively work towards a more inclusive practice that respects both heritage and personal identity.

In this evolving landscape, the emphasis on personal responsibility and community plays a crucial role in fostering inclusivity. Asatru practitioners often highlight the importance of individual actions and ethical choices as foundational to their beliefs. This focus empowers individuals to take a stand against racism and discrimination, reinforcing the idea that personal conduct shapes the community's values. Through community initiatives, educational programs, and open discussions, Asatru groups can actively combat the negative associations that have emerged over the years, promoting a culture of acceptance and understanding.

The contribution of diverse practitioners to Norse pagan traditions cannot be overlooked. As individuals from various racial and cultural backgrounds engage with Asatru, they enrich the tradition with new perspectives, rituals, and interpretations. This dynamic evolution reflects the globalized context in which Norse paganism exists today, allowing for a more inclusive and multifaceted practice. By embracing multiculturalism and recognizing the value of diverse voices, Asatru can continue to grow and adapt, ensuring that it remains a spiritual path accessible to all, free from the shadows of extremism and exclusion.

# Chapter 4: Asatru's Emphasis on Personal Responsibility and Community

## The Core Tenets of Asatru

The core tenets of Asatru emphasize a deep connection to nature, reverence for ancestral traditions, and a commitment to personal responsibility. At its heart, Asatru is a polytheistic belief system that honors the Norse gods, goddesses, and the spirits of the land. This framework encourages practitioners to develop a personal relationship with the divine, fostering a sense of spirituality that is both individual and communal. Unlike the misconceptions that often link Asatru to racism or white supremacy, its focus is on the ethical and moral responsibilities of the individual and the importance of community ties. The teachings advocate for respect, honor, and integrity, which form the foundation of a harmonious society.

Asatru's historical interpretations of Norse mythology reveal a rich tapestry of cultural narratives that transcend the simplistic and often distorted views promoted by extremist groups. Norse myths are not merely tales of gods and heroes; they are complex stories that explore themes of fate, honor, and the human condition. Acknowledging the multifaceted nature of these narratives allows practitioners to embrace their spiritual heritage without falling into the trap of racial essentialism. Furthermore, the historical context of these myths shows that Norse culture was not monolithic; it evolved through interactions with various peoples and traditions, highlighting the importance of inclusivity.

Modern pagan movements have significantly influenced the practice of Asatru, promoting values of inclusivity and diversity. Many contemporary practitioners come from varied ethnic backgrounds, enriching the tradition with their unique perspectives and practices. This evolution reflects a broader understanding of spirituality that values personal experience over rigid dogma. By fostering an environment where all are welcome, Asatru can serve as a platform for dialogue and understanding among diverse communities. This inclusive approach challenges the outdated notion that Norse Paganism is the exclusive domain of any one ethnic group.

Personal responsibility is a key aspect of Asatru, encouraging individuals to take ownership of their actions and their impact on the community. This principle promotes a healthy sense of agency, urging practitioners to engage positively with their surroundings. The emphasis on community ties fosters a supportive network where individuals can share experiences and learn from one another. Through communal rituals and gatherings, practitioners strengthen their bonds while celebrating the diversity within the tradition. This focus on accountability and connection serves as a counter-narrative to the misappropriation of Norse symbols by extremist groups, who often ignore these foundational values.

In the globalized context of today, Asatru continues to evolve, drawing from a wide array of cultural influences while maintaining its core principles. Practitioners from non-white cultures actively contribute to the tradition, enriching it with their own beliefs and practices. This dynamic exchange not only challenges the associations of Asatru with racism but also demonstrates its adaptability and relevance in contemporary society. By embracing multiculturalism, Asatru can transcend its historical roots and emerge as a truly global faith, one that celebrates diversity and shared humanity while honoring its ancestral past.

## Community Building in Asatru Practices

Community building in Asatru practices serves as a vital foundation for creating inclusive spaces that reject the misconceptions linking Norse Paganism to racism or white supremacy. At its core, Asatru emphasizes the importance of kinship and camaraderie among its practitioners. The tradition encourages individuals from diverse backgrounds to come together, fostering a sense of belonging and mutual respect. This collective spirit counters the narratives propagated by extremist groups that attempt to claim Norse symbols and mythology for exclusionary purposes, revealing the true essence of community within Asatru as one that celebrates diversity rather than division.

Historical misinterpretations of Norse mythology have often contributed to a skewed understanding of the tradition, leading some to erroneously associate it with racial superiority. However, the authentic practice of Asatru is rooted in the ancient stories that emphasize virtues such as honor, courage, and integrity, devoid of any inherent racial bias. By engaging in community activities such as group rituals, storytelling, and educational workshops, practitioners can reclaim the narratives of their ancestral past, highlighting the shared human experiences that transcend racial boundaries. This approach not only nurtures a communal identity but also dispels harmful myths that have plagued the tradition.

The influence of modern Pagan movements on inclusivity within Asatru cannot be overlooked. Many contemporary practitioners actively strive to adopt practices that reflect a broader understanding of community, incorporating elements of multiculturalism and collaboration. These movements promote the idea that spirituality can be enriched by drawing from various cultural backgrounds, thus allowing Asatru to evolve and adapt in a globalized context. Such inclusive practices encourage dialogue among practitioners of different ethnicities, fostering a richer communal experience that honors both individual and collective heritage.

Asatru's emphasis on personal responsibility enhances the concept of community by encouraging individuals to take an active role in shaping their spiritual and social environments. This principle cultivates a sense of accountability among practitioners, motivating them to engage with one another in meaningful ways. By working together on communal projects, supporting each other's personal journeys, and addressing societal issues, Asatru communities can forge strong bonds that reflect their shared values. This commitment to personal and collective growth further strengthens the fabric of the community, making it a welcoming space for all who wish to participate.

In examining the contributions of diverse practitioners to Norse Pagan traditions, it becomes evident that Asatru is not a monolithic belief system but rather a vibrant tapestry woven from various cultural influences. Asatru practices in non-white cultures exemplify this diversity, showcasing how the tradition can be interpreted and expressed in multiple ways. By embracing these varied expressions, Asatru communities can continue to grow and evolve, ensuring that the practice remains relevant and inclusive. This evolving landscape not only enriches the tradition but also serves as a powerful counter-narrative to those who would misuse Norse imagery for divisive purposes, reinforcing the notion that Asatru is a path for all who seek connection with the sacred.

## Personal Responsibility as a Guiding Principle

Personal responsibility is a foundational principle within Asatru, guiding practitioners toward ethical living and community engagement. This concept emphasizes that individuals are accountable for their actions and decisions, promoting a framework of integrity and respect. Unlike the distorted perceptions that link Asatru to racism or white supremacy, personal responsibility encourages adherents to reflect on their beliefs and behaviors in a way that is inclusive and respectful of diverse backgrounds. This principle not only fosters personal growth but also strengthens community bonds, highlighting the importance of mutual support and understanding among practitioners.

In the historical context, Norse mythology and traditions were often misinterpreted or romanticized by extremist groups seeking to appropriate cultural symbols for their own agendas. These misinterpretations overlook the rich tapestry of Norse beliefs that advocate for honor, courage, and the interconnectedness of all people. By embracing personal responsibility, Asatru practitioners can combat these historical inaccuracies and work towards a more authentic understanding of their heritage. This approach allows individuals to engage critically with their traditions and to reject any narratives that promote division or hatred.

Modern Pagan movements have made significant strides in promoting inclusivity and diversity within their practices. Asatru, in particular, has evolved to welcome practitioners from various ethnic backgrounds, reflecting a more globalized understanding of spirituality. Personal responsibility serves as a catalyst for this inclusivity, encouraging individuals to challenge exclusionary practices and to actively participate in creating a welcoming space for all. This evolution signifies a broader recognition that spirituality transcends ethnic identity and is accessible to anyone who seeks a meaningful connection to the past.

The intersection of Asatru and multiculturalism is further enriched by the contributions of diverse practitioners who bring their unique perspectives to the traditions. These individuals often reinterpret Norse symbols and stories in ways that resonate with their own experiences, thereby enriching the practice. Personal responsibility plays a crucial role in this process, as it empowers practitioners to honor their own cultural backgrounds while engaging with Norse traditions. This dynamic exchange fosters a vibrant community that values diversity and recognizes the importance of shared humanity.

In contemporary society, the role of Norse symbols has been redefined through their association with anti-racist movements. Activists often reclaim these symbols, emphasizing their original meanings and promoting unity rather than division. Within this context, personal responsibility becomes a guiding principle for Asatru practitioners who wish to engage with these symbols meaningfully. By acknowledging the historical misuse of Norse imagery, practitioners can actively participate in the narrative of reclamation, ensuring that their beliefs and practices are aligned with values of inclusivity and respect for all. This commitment to personal responsibility ultimately paves the way for a more just and equitable practice of Asatru in a diverse world.

# Chapter 5: Debunking the Myths: Norse Paganism and Ethnic Identity

## The Myth of Racial Exclusivity

The notion that Asatru and Norse Paganism are inherently tied to racism and white supremacy is a pervasive myth that requires thorough examination. This misconception often stems from historical misinterpretations of Norse mythology, where characters and narratives have been appropriated to serve exclusionary ideologies. In reality, Norse myths are rich in complexity and diversity, reflecting a wide array of human experiences and values. They emphasize virtues such as honor, courage, and community, which can resonate across cultural boundaries. A careful reading of these texts reveals that they do not endorse racial exclusivity, but rather celebrate the human experience in all its forms.

The influence of modern pagan movements has also played a significant role in shaping the understanding of Asatru as an inclusive practice. Many contemporary practitioners actively reject the notions of racial purity that have been misapplied to these traditions. Instead, they promote an Asatru that welcomes individuals from various backgrounds, emphasizing shared values and mutual respect. This shift has led to a more expansive interpretation of what it means to honor Norse gods and goddesses, allowing for a rich tapestry of cultural influences to shape personal and communal practices. Inclusivity has become a hallmark of many Asatru communities, challenging the outdated notions of exclusivity.

Asatru's emphasis on personal responsibility and community is another critical aspect that counters the myth of racial exclusivity. The practice encourages individuals to take ownership of their beliefs and actions, fostering a sense of accountability that transcends ethnic boundaries. This focus on personal integrity and communal well-being invites a diverse range of practitioners to engage with the tradition meaningfully. Asatru teaches that one's worth is not determined by ethnic background, but by one's actions and contributions to the community. This principle facilitates the inclusion of practitioners from various cultures, enriching the tradition as a whole.

The role of Norse symbols in contemporary anti-racist movements further challenges the misconceptions surrounding Norse Paganism. Many symbols traditionally associated with Norse culture, such as the Valknut and the Mjolnir, have been reclaimed by activists who seek to promote unity and inclusivity. These symbols serve as reminders of the shared heritage that can exist outside the confines of racial identity. The intersection of Asatru and multiculturalism highlights that these symbols can foster dialogue and understanding among diverse groups, creating a space where all are welcome to participate in the celebration of shared values and histories.

Finally, the contribution of diverse practitioners to Norse Pagan traditions illustrates the evolution of Asatru in a globalized context. As more individuals from various backgrounds adopt and adapt these practices, the tradition becomes enriched by their unique perspectives and experiences. This dynamic evolution challenges the static notions of ethnicity that some may attempt to impose upon Norse Paganism. By embracing a broader definition of community and identity, Asatru can continue to thrive as a living tradition that reflects the diverse tapestry of human culture, ultimately debunking the myth of racial exclusivity.

## Ethnic Identity in Norse Traditions

Ethnic identity in Norse traditions is often misinterpreted, leading to the erroneous association of Asatru and Norse Paganism with racism and white supremacy. Historically, Norse culture was not monolithic; it encompassed a range of ethnicities and tribes across Scandinavia and beyond. The Vikings engaged in trade, raiding, and cultural exchange with numerous peoples, including the Celts, Slavs, and even those in the Mediterranean. This diversity was reflected in their mythology, which included a multitude of gods, goddesses, and heroic figures, many of whom were worshipped and revered across different regions and ethnic groups. The idea that Norse identity is strictly tied to a singular ethnic lineage is a modern construct that oversimplifies the complex interactions and influences that characterized the Norse world.

Modern Pagan movements have taken significant steps to foster inclusivity within their practices, challenging the notion that Norse traditions are exclusive to individuals of Northern European descent. Many contemporary practitioners actively work to reclaim Norse spirituality as a path that welcomes individuals from various backgrounds. This inclusivity is evident in the emphasis placed on personal responsibility, community building, and shared values rather than ethnic heritage. Asatru, in particular, encourages individuals to forge connections based on mutual respect and understanding, creating a space where diverse practitioners can come together to honor the traditions of their ancestors while also recognizing the importance of cultural multiplicity.

Debunking the myths surrounding Norse Paganism and ethnic identity requires a critical examination of how symbols and practices have been co-opted by extremist groups. While certain Norse symbols, such as the hammer of Thor or the Valknut, have been appropriated by white supremacist organizations, their original meanings within Norse mythology are far removed from these ideologies. These symbols represent strength, protection, and the interconnectedness of life and death rather than racial superiority. Understanding the historical context of these symbols and their rightful place in Norse traditions allows practitioners to reclaim them in a manner that aligns with the core values of Asatru, including respect for all individuals, regardless of their ethnic background.

The intersection of Asatru and multiculturalism highlights the evolving nature of Norse Paganism in a globalized world. Diverse practitioners contribute to the richness of Norse traditions, infusing them with their unique cultural perspectives and practices. This evolution is a testament to the adaptability of spirituality and the ability of ancient traditions to resonate with contemporary values of inclusivity and acceptance. Asatru practices are not confined to any one ethnicity; rather, they can be embraced by individuals from various backgrounds, fostering a sense of community that transcends racial boundaries.

In contemporary anti-racist movements, the reclamation of Norse symbols plays a crucial role in countering the narratives propagated by extremist groups. By embracing Norse heritage as a space for all, practitioners can effectively challenge the misconceptions that link these ancient traditions to modern racism. This recontextualization allows individuals to celebrate their ancestry while also standing firmly against any ideologies that seek to divide based on race. The ongoing dialogue surrounding ethnic identity in Norse traditions is vital for ensuring that Asatru remains a path of inclusivity, unity, and respect for all people, emphasizing the shared human experience over divisive categorizations.

## Asatru Beyond Ethnic Boundaries

Asatru, often misconstrued as an exclusively Nordic or white-centric belief system, transcends ethnic boundaries, inviting practitioners from diverse backgrounds to engage with its rich tapestry of mythology and spirituality. The misconception that Asatru is inherently tied to racism or white supremacy stems from historical misinterpretations and the appropriation of Norse symbols by extremist groups. Historically, Asatru and Norse mythology have been misrepresented, leading many to associate the faith solely with a homogenous ethnic group. However, the essence of Asatru lies in its core values, which emphasize personal responsibility, community, and a deep connection to nature, rather than ethnic identity.

Modern Pagan movements have significantly influenced the inclusivity of Asatru. Many contemporary practitioners actively seek to dismantle the racist narratives that have plagued the tradition. This evolution reflects a broader cultural shift toward recognizing and honoring diverse identities within spiritual practices. By embracing the idea that Asatru can be a spiritual path for individuals of various backgrounds, modern practitioners highlight a collaborative approach that values shared human experiences over ethnic exclusivity. This inclusivity reshapes Asatru into a global tradition, welcoming those who resonate with its principles.

Asatru emphasizes personal responsibility and community engagement, principles that resonate universally and are not confined to any single ethnic group. These tenets encourage practitioners to take an active role in their communities, fostering connections that transcend cultural boundaries. The practice of honoring one's ancestors does not necessitate a narrow ethnic focus; rather, it invites individuals to explore their familial histories, regardless of their racial or ethnic backgrounds. This approach reflects a broader understanding of heritage, enhancing the communal aspect of Asatru and its relevance in a multicultural society.

The role of Norse symbols in contemporary anti-racist movements further illustrates the disconnection between Asatru and extremist ideologies. Many practitioners reclaim these symbols, emphasizing their original meanings and promoting messages of unity and respect. For instance, symbols like the Valknut and Yggdrasil are often reinterpreted in ways that celebrate diversity and challenge oppressive narratives. By participating in social justice movements, Asatru practitioners demonstrate that the tradition can be a source of empowerment and inclusivity rather than division.

The contributions of diverse practitioners to Norse Pagan traditions showcase the evolution of Asatru in a globalized context. As more individuals from various cultural backgrounds engage with Asatru, they bring unique perspectives and practices that enrich the tradition. This dynamic interplay of ideas allows for the development of a more inclusive understanding of Norse spirituality, where practices in non-white cultures are acknowledged and celebrated. Ultimately, the future of Asatru lies in its ability to adapt and grow within a multicultural world, proving that its principles can resonate across all ethnicities and backgrounds.

# Chapter 6: The Role of Norse Symbols in Contemporary Anti-Racist Movements

## Symbols of Resistance

Symbols of resistance have emerged within the context of Asatru and Norse Paganism, challenging the pervasive misconceptions that link these traditions to racism and white supremacy. In historical narratives, symbols such as the Valknut and the Yggdrasil have been appropriated by extremist groups to promote a narrow, exclusionary ideology. However, it is essential to reclaim these symbols for their original meanings rooted in spirituality, community, and resistance against oppression. This reclamation process highlights how Norse symbols can serve as powerful emblems of unity and inclusivity, rather than division.

The historical misinterpretation of Norse mythology often leads to a distorted understanding of its symbols. Many narratives have focused solely on the warrior ethos and bloodlines, neglecting the rich tapestry of stories that emphasize wisdom, hospitality, and interconnectedness among all beings. The myths encourage a broader interpretation of identity that transcends ethnicity, illustrating the potential for these tales to inspire resistance against racism and xenophobia. By re-examining the stories behind the symbols, practitioners can cultivate a more inclusive understanding that honors the diversity of those who engage with Norse traditions.

Modern Pagan movements have increasingly emphasized inclusivity, reshaping the landscape of Norse Paganism. Many practitioners actively challenge the misconceptions associated with Asatru, promoting a vision that includes individuals from various backgrounds. This shift reflects a growing awareness that spirituality is not tethered to ethnicity but is a shared human experience. Symbols like the hammer of Thor, often misappropriated, are now being reinterpreted as tools for empowerment and solidarity among diverse communities. This transformation showcases how Norse symbols can be utilized in contemporary anti-racist movements, fostering a sense of belonging that transcends racial boundaries.

The emphasis on personal responsibility and community within Asatru further strengthens its position against racism. Adherents are encouraged to cultivate virtues such as courage, honesty, and generosity, which can be seen as a direct counter to the divisive ideologies perpetuated by extremist groups. This focus on ethical living promotes a communal spirit where individuals actively resist societal injustices. By embodying these principles, practitioners demonstrate that true strength lies in unity and the celebration of diverse identities, allowing the symbols of their faith to become beacons of hope and resistance.

Finally, the evolution of Norse Paganism in a globalized context reflects a vibrant tapestry of practices that incorporate the contributions of diverse practitioners. Asatru is no longer confined to a singular narrative; instead, it has absorbed influences from various cultures, leading to a richer and more multifaceted practice. This inclusivity challenges the notion that Norse symbols are exclusive to a specific ethnic identity. By examining the ways in which Norse imagery and practices have been embraced by non-white cultures, it becomes clear that these symbols can represent resilience, solidarity, and a collective struggle against the forces that seek to divide us.

## Reclaiming Norse Imagery

Reclaiming Norse imagery is essential in dismantling the misguided association of Asatru with racism and white supremacy. Historically, Norse symbols and mythology have been misappropriated by extremist groups seeking to promote a narrative that aligns with their xenophobic ideologies. This distortion not only undermines the rich cultural heritage of Norse traditions but also alienates those who genuinely engage with these beliefs in a spirit of inclusivity and respect. By confronting these misinterpretations head-on, practitioners of Asatru can reclaim their heritage from those who would wield it as a weapon of division.

Norse mythology, with its rich tapestry of gods, heroes, and cosmic narratives, has often been subject to oversimplification and historical inaccuracies. Many of the interpretations used by white supremacist groups draw from a selective reading of the past, cherry-picking elements that fit their agenda while ignoring the broader context of Norse culture, which was inherently diverse and interconnected with various peoples. By highlighting the complexity of Norse myths and the historical realities of the Viking Age, modern practitioners can challenge these misrepresentations and illuminate the inclusive nature of ancient Norse society.

The influence of contemporary pagan movements has catalyzed a shift toward inclusivity within Asatru. Many modern practitioners actively seek to create spaces that honor the traditions of the past while embracing a multicultural present. This has led to a growing recognition that Norse spirituality is not confined to a single ethnicity but can be practiced by individuals from various backgrounds. Such inclusivity reflects a broader understanding of spirituality that transcends racial boundaries, emphasizing shared values and communal bonds over ethnic identity.

Asatru places a strong emphasis on personal responsibility and community, principles that resonate deeply with anti-racist movements. This perspective encourages individuals to take ownership of their beliefs and actions while fostering a sense of belonging that is open to all. By promoting values such as honor, respect, and mutual support, practitioners can counter the narratives perpetuated by extremist groups and instead, cultivate a community that is rooted in shared humanity. This focus on ethical conduct aligns seamlessly with the principles of social justice and equality, reinforcing the idea that Norse traditions can be a source of empowerment for diverse populations.

The role of Norse symbols in contemporary anti-racist movements illustrates the potential for these ancient images to serve as unifying forces rather than divisive ones. Many activists have reclaimed symbols like the Valknut and the Thor's hammer, using them to promote messages of solidarity and resistance against hate. This reclamation process illustrates that Norse imagery can embody values of unity, strength, and resilience when appropriated thoughtfully. Furthermore, the contributions of diverse practitioners to Norse pagan traditions enrich the narrative, demonstrating that Asatru is not a monolithic faith but a dynamic, evolving practice that thrives on the contributions of all who seek to engage with it authentically.

## The Intersection of Symbols and Social Justice

The intersection of symbols and social justice within the context of Asatru and Norse Paganism reveals a rich tapestry of meanings that often defy the oversimplified narratives associated with racism and white supremacy. This complexity is rooted in historical misinterpretations of Norse mythology, which have been manipulated to serve exclusionary ideologies. Contrary to the belief that Asatru is inherently tied to racial identity, the tradition itself encourages a broader understanding of heritage that is inclusive of diverse backgrounds. By examining the origins of these symbols and their meanings, one can uncover how they can serve as powerful tools for social justice rather than instruments of division.

Modern Pagan movements have significantly influenced the conversation around inclusivity, challenging the notion that Norse symbols are synonymous with racism. Practitioners today are actively reinterpreting historical texts and symbols to promote a message of unity and acceptance. This shift in perspective not only embraces the multicultural dimensions of contemporary society but also reclaims these symbols from extremist groups that have co-opted them for their own agendas. Asatru emphasizes personal responsibility and community, encouraging individuals to engage with their heritage in a way that honors diversity and fosters mutual respect.

Debunking the myths surrounding Norse paganism and ethnic identity is crucial in understanding its true essence. The practice of Asatru is not confined to a single ethnic or racial group; rather, it is an evolving tradition that welcomes individuals from various backgrounds who seek connection with the ancient ways. This openness allows for the integration of diverse practices and beliefs, enriching the tradition and expanding its relevance in today's multi-ethnic societies. The contributions of practitioners from various racial and cultural backgrounds highlight the adaptability of Norse paganism and its capacity to resonate across different communities.

Symbols associated with Norse mythology have found a place in contemporary anti-racist movements, showcasing how these emblems can serve as vehicles for progressive change. Activists reclaiming these symbols challenge the narratives imposed by extremist groups, reaffirming their meaning as representations of resilience, community, and justice. By doing so, they not only honor the historical significance of these symbols but also redefine them in a modern context that prioritizes inclusivity and social equity. This reclamation is a powerful reminder that symbols can evolve and be recontextualized to align with the values of a diverse society.

The evolution of Norse paganism in a globalized context underscores the importance of fostering an inclusive dialogue within the community. Asatru practices in non-white cultures demonstrate that the tradition transcends geographic and racial boundaries, emphasizing shared human experiences over divisive identities. This globalization of Norse paganism invites a rich exchange of ideas and practices, encouraging a more comprehensive understanding of what it means to engage with these ancient beliefs today. By recognizing and celebrating the contributions of diverse practitioners, the Asatru community can further distance itself from the stigmas of racism and white supremacy, paving the way for a more equitable future rooted in shared values and mutual respect.

# Chapter 7: Intersection of Asatru and Multiculturalism

## Embracing Diversity in Belief Systems

Embracing diversity in belief systems is essential for understanding the true essence of Asatru and Norse Paganism, particularly in the face of pervasive misconceptions linking these traditions to racism and white supremacy. Historically, the interpretation of Norse mythology has been manipulated to serve the agendas of exclusionary ideologies, which often distort the rich tapestry of the Norse spiritual heritage. By recognizing that Asatru is rooted in a diverse array of beliefs and practices, we can challenge these misinterpretations and reclaim the narrative surrounding these ancient traditions. It is crucial to acknowledge that the essence of Asatru transcends any singular ethnic identity, embracing instead a broader spectrum of human experience.

The modern Pagan movements have significantly influenced the inclusivity within Asatru, fostering an environment where individuals from various backgrounds can find resonance with Norse spirituality. This inclusivity is reflected in the practices and rituals that draw from a wide range of cultural influences, demonstrating that spirituality can be both personal and communal, irrespective of ethnic origin. As contemporary practitioners incorporate diverse perspectives, the evolving nature of Norse Paganism becomes evident, revealing how these belief systems can adapt and grow while maintaining their foundational principles. This evolution showcases the potential for a pluralistic approach to spirituality that honors the past while remaining open to new interpretations.

Asatru emphasizes personal responsibility and community, principles that can bridge divides and foster understanding among practitioners from different backgrounds. This focus on individual agency not only empowers personal growth but also encourages a collective commitment to inclusivity and respect. By engaging in dialogue and shared practices, practitioners can cultivate a sense of belonging that transcends racial and cultural barriers. Such engagement is vital in dispelling the myths that have historically surrounded Norse Paganism, emphasizing that the path of Asatru is not confined to any one identity but is instead an open invitation to all who seek to explore its teachings.

The role of Norse symbols in contemporary anti-racist movements further illustrates the potential for Asatru to serve as a unifying force. Various symbols, once co-opted by extremist groups, have been reclaimed by activists advocating for social justice and inclusivity. This reclamation challenges the narrative that these symbols are inherently tied to racism, instead highlighting their broader significance within a multicultural context. By embracing these symbols for their original meanings and recontextualizing them within a framework of unity, practitioners of Asatru can actively engage in dismantling the harmful associations that have emerged over time.

The contribution of diverse practitioners to Norse Pagan traditions enriches the spiritual landscape, demonstrating that Asatru is not a monolithic belief system but a dynamic, evolving practice shaped by its followers. Asatru practices in non-white cultures reveal that the appreciation for Norse mythology can extend beyond traditional boundaries, fostering a more global understanding of these ancient beliefs. In a globalized context, the intersection of Asatru with multiculturalism presents an opportunity to celebrate diversity while honoring the core values of the tradition. This approach not only broadens the appeal of Norse Paganism but also reinforces its relevance in a world where inclusivity and understanding are increasingly vital.

## Stories of Multicultural Practitioners

The practice of Asatru, often mischaracterized as racially exclusive or aligned with white supremacy, is, in reality, enriched by the contributions of practitioners from diverse backgrounds. This subchapter highlights the stories of multicultural practitioners who embody the true spirit of Norse Paganism, demonstrating its inclusivity and adaptability across different cultures. These individuals illustrate how Asatru can thrive in a globalized context, breaking down the barriers erected by historical misinterpretations and modern misconceptions about the faith.

One notable practitioner is a Black woman from the United States who discovered Asatru through her studies of Norse mythology. She found resonance in the values of honor and community that permeate the tradition. By blending her cultural heritage with her newfound beliefs, she has created a unique practice that honors both her ancestry and the Norse gods. Her journey exemplifies the potential for Asatru to serve as a spiritual framework for those outside traditional Northern European demographics, fostering a sense of belonging and shared values among diverse practitioners.

Similarly, a Latinx man in South America has integrated elements of Norse mythology with indigenous spiritual practices, forming a syncretic approach to worship. His rituals combine traditional offerings to the gods with local customs, emphasizing the universal themes of nature, respect, and community. This fusion not only honors his lineage but also showcases how Norse mythology can be relevant and meaningful across different cultural landscapes, further debunking the notion that Asatru is exclusively tied to a specific ethnic identity.

The stories of these practitioners highlight the importance of personal responsibility and community within Asatru. Many have engaged in local initiatives that promote inclusivity and understanding, often leading workshops and discussions that challenge the misconceptions surrounding their faith. By openly sharing their experiences and knowledge, they contribute to a broader narrative that emphasizes responsibility not only to oneself but also to the community, fostering connections that transcend racial and cultural divides.

Lastly, the involvement of diverse practitioners in Norse Pagan traditions enriches the tapestry of Asatru, allowing it to evolve in a contemporary context. The intersection of Asatru and multiculturalism is not merely a theoretical concept; it is alive and dynamic, driven by individuals who seek to honor the past while embracing the present. Their narratives serve as powerful counterpoints to extremist interpretations of Norse imagery, demonstrating that the symbols of this tradition can be repurposed to advocate for inclusivity and solidarity among all people, regardless of their background.

## The Future of Asatru in a Diverse Society

The future of Asatru in a diverse society hinges on a collective understanding that the practice is not inherently tied to any racial or ethnic identity. Historically, misinterpretations have often conflated Norse mythology with concepts of racial superiority, largely fueled by the appropriation of these traditions by extremist groups. This distortion has overshadowed the inclusive tenets of Asatru, which celebrate individual connection to the divine, ancestral respect, and communal bonds. As practitioners and scholars strive to reclaim the true essence of Norse spirituality, it is essential to recognize that the richness of Asatru can thrive in a multicultural context, where diverse backgrounds contribute to its evolution.

Modern Pagan movements have increasingly emphasized inclusivity, creating spaces for practitioners from all walks of life. This shift has been particularly vital in dismantling the erroneous belief that Norse traditions are exclusive to people of Northern European descent. The adaptation and reinterpretation of Asatru by individuals from various ethnic backgrounds not only enriches the tradition but also reaffirms its core values of respect, honor, and personal responsibility. By fostering a community that celebrates diversity, Asatru practitioners can collectively combat the stereotypes that have long plagued their traditions.

Furthermore, the emphasis on personal responsibility within Asatru serves as a foundation for ethical living in a diverse society. Each individual's journey in understanding their place within the universe and their community can lead to a greater appreciation of cultural differences. As practitioners engage with the tenets of Asatru, they are encouraged to reflect on their actions and their impact on others, fostering a sense of accountability that transcends ethnic boundaries. This focus on personal accountability can be a powerful tool in promoting dialogue and understanding among diverse communities.

The role of Norse symbols in contemporary anti-racist movements illustrates the potential for Asatru to become a symbol of unity rather than division. While certain extremist groups have sought to co-opt these symbols for their own agendas, many practitioners are reclaiming them as representations of resilience, strength, and community support. By engaging in discussions about the true meanings behind these symbols, Asatru can position itself as a faith that champions inclusivity while honoring its historical tapestry. This reclamation process is vital in ensuring that Norse spirituality is not misrepresented or weaponized against marginalized communities.

As Asatru continues to evolve in a globalized context, the contributions of diverse practitioners will play a crucial role. The interplay between various cultural practices and Norse traditions can lead to innovative expressions of spirituality that honor both the past and the present. By embracing multiculturalism, Asatru can emerge as a dynamic and inclusive faith that resonates with individuals across the spectrum of human experience. The future of Asatru lies in its ability to adapt, grow, and foster connections among its practitioners, ensuring that it remains a vibrant and relevant path for all who seek its wisdom.

# Chapter 8: Analyzing the Use of Norse Imagery by Extremist Groups

## Historical Context of Symbol Usage

Historical usage of symbols in Norse culture has often been misinterpreted and co-opted by various groups throughout the ages. The symbol of the swastika, for instance, has ancient roots in Norse and Indo-European traditions, representing good fortune and well-being long before it was appropriated by the Nazi regime. This distortion exemplifies how symbols can evolve in meaning over time, often becoming associated with ideologies that starkly contrast with their original significance. Understanding this historical context is crucial to disentangling Asatru and Norse Paganism from the misconceptions that link them to racism and white supremacy.

In the early 20th century, the romanticization of Norse mythology led to a resurgence of interest in Viking culture, which was often framed within a narrow ethnic identity narrative. This period saw the rise of movements that sought to connect modern national identities to ancient Norse heritage. However, such interpretations frequently overlooked the complexities of Norse mythology and its rich tapestry of cultural exchanges. As Norse mythological symbols were appropriated by these movements, they became tools for promoting exclusionary narratives, thereby distorting the inclusive and diverse nature of historical Norse societies.

The modern pagan movements have worked actively to reclaim and reinterpret Norse symbols in ways that promote inclusivity and community. Many practitioners of Asatru today emphasize the importance of personal responsibility and the interconnectedness of all individuals, regardless of their ethnic backgrounds. This evolving perspective challenges the notion that Norse Paganism is inherently tied to a singular ethnic identity. Instead, contemporary Asatru communities often celebrate the diversity of their members, recognizing that the values of honor, courage, and community transcend ethnic lines.

Moreover, the role of Norse symbols in contemporary anti-racist movements has gained attention in recent years. Activists have sought to reclaim these symbols from extremist groups that have misappropriated them, emphasizing their original meanings and advocating for a broader understanding of Norse heritage. This reclamation reflects a growing recognition that Norse mythology and symbols can serve as a bridge rather than a barrier, fostering dialogue about inclusivity, multiculturalism, and shared values among diverse groups.

Finally, examining the contributions of diverse practitioners to Norse pagan traditions reveals a rich and varied landscape that counters the notion of a monolithic Norse identity. Asatru practices have evolved in non-white cultures, demonstrating that these beliefs can be embraced and adapted by individuals from various backgrounds. This globalization of Norse Paganism not only enriches the tradition but also reinforces the idea that spirituality and cultural practices can flourish in an inclusive manner, ultimately challenging the historical misinterpretations that have linked Norse symbols to racism and exclusion.

## Misappropriation of Symbols

Misappropriation of symbols is a critical issue in the discourse surrounding Asatru and Norse Paganism, particularly when addressing the misconceptions that link these traditions to racism or white supremacy. Symbols such as the swastika and the Valknut have been co-opted by extremist groups, distorting their historical significance and transforming them into emblems of hate. This misappropriation clouds the true essence of Norse mythology and spirituality, which is rooted in concepts of honor, community, and personal responsibility. Understanding the original meanings of these symbols is essential to disentangling them from modern misinterpretations that serve agendas of oppression and division.

Historical misinterpretations of Norse mythology have often fueled the erroneous connection between Asatru and racism. Many narratives have been shaped by selective readings of history, emphasizing the warrior culture and ethnic exclusivity of ancient Norse societies while ignoring the complexities and multicultural interactions of the Viking Age. The Norse people engaged in trade, exploration, and cultural exchange across vast regions, leading to a rich tapestry of influences that contradict the notion of a homogeneous ethnic identity. Recognizing this historical context helps dismantle the simplistic and inaccurate associations made between Norse spirituality and racial ideologies.

The influence of modern pagan movements has been significant in promoting inclusivity within Asatru. Contemporary practitioners increasingly emphasize the importance of community and shared values over ethnic identity. This shift reflects a broader understanding of spirituality that welcomes individuals from diverse backgrounds, fostering an environment where shared beliefs take precedence over racial or ethnic origins. Such inclusivity not only honors the original tenets of Norse paganism but also counters the narratives perpetuated by extremist groups that seek to limit the practice of Asatru to a specific racial demographic.

Asatru's emphasis on personal responsibility and community further distances it from any association with racism. Central to Asatru is the idea that individuals are accountable for their actions and must strive to better themselves and their communities. This focus promotes a sense of belonging and mutual respect among practitioners, regardless of their backgrounds. By prioritizing ethical living and communal bonds, Asatru encourages a worldview that transcends racial divisions, fostering a more inclusive understanding of what it means to practice Norse spirituality in the modern world.

The role of Norse symbols in contemporary anti-racist movements illustrates the potential for reclamation and reinterpretation of these images. Many practitioners and activists are working to redefine symbols like the Valknut as representations of unity, strength, and resilience against oppression. This reclamation serves as a powerful counter-narrative to the misappropriation by extremist groups, reinforcing the idea that Norse traditions can be a source of empowerment for all individuals, irrespective of their racial or ethnic identities. As Norse paganism continues to evolve in a globalized context, it becomes increasingly clear that these traditions can embrace multiculturalism while remaining true to their historical roots.

## The Response from Within Asatru

The response from within Asatru to the misconceptions linking the tradition to racism and white supremacy is multifaceted and grounded in a deep understanding of both historical context and modern practices. Many practitioners assert that the core tenets of Asatru, which emphasize personal honor, community responsibility, and respect for the earth, are fundamentally at odds with ideologies that promote racial superiority. This internal dialogue seeks to clarify that the essence of Asatru is not about ethnic exclusivity but about a shared reverence for nature, the gods, and the cultural heritage of the Norse peoples as a whole.

Historical misinterpretations of Norse mythology have often provided fertile ground for racist ideologies. These misinterpretations tend to focus on a selective reading of ancient texts, stripping them of their rich cultural contexts. Within Asatru, there is a concerted effort to educate both practitioners and outsiders about the complexities of Norse mythology, which includes diverse narratives that highlight the values of wisdom, bravery, and community rather than division based on ethnicity. The belief that Norse myths inherently support racial supremacy is increasingly recognized as a distortion that undermines the true spirit of these ancient stories.

The influence of modern pagan movements has led to a growing emphasis on inclusivity within Asatru. Many contemporary practitioners actively seek to create spaces that welcome individuals from various backgrounds, recognizing that spirituality can be a unifying force rather than a divisive one. This movement has been bolstered by dialogue among diverse groups within the pagan community, promoting the idea that Norse spirituality can coexist with multicultural perspectives. Such an inclusive approach allows for a richer, more nuanced understanding of Asatru that honors its roots while embracing the diversity of today's practitioners.

Asatru's emphasis on personal responsibility and community further distinguishes it from extremist ideologies. Practitioners are encouraged to take ownership of their actions and to contribute positively to their communities, fostering an environment of mutual respect and support. This principle aligns closely with the values of equity and justice that reject racial hierarchies. Asatru communities are increasingly focused on building relationships across cultural lines, demonstrating that personal and communal growth can occur in a diverse setting.

In the face of the appropriation of Norse symbols by extremist groups, there is a strong movement within Asatru to reclaim these symbols for their original meanings. Many practitioners engage in activism that aligns with anti-racist efforts, using Norse imagery to promote messages of unity and resistance against hate. This reclamation reflects a broader understanding of how Norse traditions can evolve in a globalized context, embracing not only the historical aspects but also the contributions of diverse practitioners. By highlighting the role of non-white Asatru practitioners and showcasing their experiences, the community continues to redefine its identity, ensuring that it remains a space for all who seek to connect with the ancient traditions in a modern, inclusive manner.

# Chapter 9: The Contribution of Diverse Practitioners to Norse Pagan Traditions

## Voices from Various Backgrounds

The narrative surrounding Asatru and Norse Paganism is often overshadowed by the misguided perceptions linking these spiritual practices to racism and white supremacy. However, practitioners from diverse backgrounds have come forward to share their experiences, revealing the rich tapestry of beliefs that transcend ethnic boundaries. Individuals of various heritages, including Black, Latino, and Indigenous practitioners, have embraced Asatru, finding meaning and spiritual fulfillment without subscribing to the narrow ideologies that some extremist groups promote. Their voices challenge the misconception that Norse mythology is exclusively tied to whiteness, demonstrating that these traditions can be inclusive and enriching for people of all backgrounds.

Historical misinterpretations have often fueled the erroneous association of Norse mythology with racial identity. Many practitioners highlight that the ancient Norse did not view the world in terms of modern racial constructs. They celebrated their gods and goddesses through a lens that emphasized community, loyalty, and respect for nature rather than ethnicity. By examining the historical context of these myths, it becomes evident that the true essence of Norse spirituality lies in its connection to personal growth and the natural world, rather than any rigid adherence to racial or ethnic identity. Practitioners today strive to reclaim these narratives, emphasizing their universal themes of honor, courage, and kinship.

Modern pagan movements have increasingly embraced inclusivity, allowing for a broader interpretation of ancient traditions. The intersection of Asatru with multiculturalism has fostered an environment where diverse practitioners can contribute their unique perspectives. Workshops, gatherings, and online communities have emerged, encouraging discussions around the importance of inclusivity within these spiritual practices. This evolution not only enriches the Asatru tradition but also creates a welcoming space for those who might otherwise feel alienated by the historical misuse of Norse symbols. By sharing their interpretations and rituals, practitioners from various backgrounds help redefine what it means to be part of the Asatru community.

Asatru places a significant emphasis on personal responsibility and community, which resonates deeply with practitioners from all walks of life. This focus encourages individuals to reflect on their actions and their impacts on others, fostering a sense of accountability that transcends racial and cultural boundaries. Community rituals and gatherings often highlight shared values, drawing people together in celebration of their collective heritage and beliefs. The diverse voices within these communities remind us that Asatru can be a unifying force, promoting mutual respect and understanding among its practitioners, regardless of their backgrounds.

In contemporary society, Norse symbols have also been reclaimed by anti-racist movements, further distancing them from their extremist misuse. Many practitioners actively engage in discussions about the appropriation of these symbols and work to educate others on their true meanings. The contribution of diverse practitioners adds depth to this conversation, as they share their perspectives and experiences in navigating their identities within Asatru. This ongoing dialogue serves to dismantle the myths surrounding Norse Paganism, illustrating that it is not a monolithic practice tied to any one ethnicity. Instead, it is a vibrant and evolving tradition that celebrates diversity, encouraging all to find their place within its rich heritage.

## Innovations in Practice and Belief

Innovations in practice and belief within Asatru and Norse Paganism present a compelling narrative that counters the pervasive assumptions linking these traditions with racism or white supremacy. Historically, these belief systems have been misinterpreted, often due to a lack of understanding about their core tenets and practices. Rather than promoting exclusion, many modern practitioners emphasize a belief system that is rooted in personal responsibility, communal bonds, and respect for all individuals, irrespective of their ethnic backgrounds. This shift in focus encourages a more inclusive interpretation of Norse mythology and spirituality, demonstrating that Asatru can be a framework for unity rather than division.

Modern Pagan movements have significantly influenced the inclusivity of Asatru, leading to a re-examination of traditional practices and beliefs. Many contemporary practitioners actively challenge historical misinterpretations by highlighting the importance of diversity within the Norse mythological landscape. The notion that Norse deities and mythic narratives are exclusively tied to a singular ethnic identity is being dismantled, allowing for a broader application of these beliefs. This progressive approach is fostering spaces where individuals from various cultural backgrounds can explore and express their spiritual identities without fear of racism or cultural appropriation.

Asatru inherently emphasizes personal responsibility and community engagement, principles that resonate deeply with the values of inclusivity and mutual respect. Practitioners are encouraged to take ownership of their beliefs and actions while fostering connections with others. This communal aspect serves to reinforce the idea that spirituality is not confined to one ethnic group but is instead a shared human experience. By engaging with diverse communities, practitioners can enrich their understanding of Norse traditions and create a tapestry of beliefs that reflects a multitude of perspectives.

The contemporary application of Norse symbols in anti-racist movements further illustrates the evolving nature of Asatru and its disconnect from extremist ideologies. Symbols such as the Valknut and Yggdrasil are being reclaimed and redefined by diverse groups advocating for social justice and equality. This reclamation serves as a powerful counter-narrative to the appropriation of these symbols by hate groups, demonstrating that the core values of Norse spirituality can be aligned with principles of inclusivity and multiculturalism. Such efforts highlight the potential for Norse imagery to represent solidarity and resistance against oppression.

Diverse practitioners contribute significantly to the ongoing evolution of Norse Paganism in a globalized context. As Asatru and its related traditions become increasingly accessible to people of various ethnicities, the discussions surrounding their practices and beliefs expand. This intersection of Asatru with multiculturalism encourages new interpretations and adaptations that honor both ancestral traditions and contemporary sensibilities. By embracing a broader, more inclusive understanding of Norse spirituality, practitioners are not only preserving their heritage but also actively engaging in a dialogue that promotes unity and understanding across different cultural landscapes.

## Celebrating Diversity within Tradition

Celebrating diversity within the context of Asatru and Norse Paganism is essential to dispelling the misconceptions that link these ancient practices to racism or white supremacy. Historically, Asatru has been understood through a narrow lens, often misinterpreted as a movement solely for people of Northern European descent. This perspective overlooks the rich tapestry of cultural influences and practices that have emerged over centuries. Asatru, at its core, is about honoring the traditions and values of the past while embracing the diverse identities that practitioners bring to the faith today.

The historical misinterpretations of Norse mythology often arise from a failure to recognize the complexity of the myths and their interpretations. Norse stories feature a myriad of characters and themes that transcend racial and ethnic boundaries. Many tales highlight virtues such as honor, bravery, and wisdom, which are universal ideals applicable to all people. By celebrating these narratives in their entirety, practitioners can create a more inclusive understanding of Norse mythology that resonates with individuals from various backgrounds, reinforcing the notion that Asatru is not racially exclusive but rather accessible to all who seek its wisdom.

Modern pagan movements have significantly influenced the inclusivity of Asatru, encouraging a reexamination of traditional practices and beliefs. This evolution reflects a broader societal shift toward recognizing the importance of diverse voices within spiritual communities. Many contemporary practitioners advocate for a version of Asatru that is rooted in personal responsibility and community engagement, emphasizing that the practice is about building connections across cultures rather than adhering to a singular ethnic identity. This approach not only enriches the tradition but also fosters a spirit of cooperation and mutual respect among practitioners from different backgrounds.

Debunking the myths surrounding Norse paganism and ethnic identity requires a critical analysis of how symbols and imagery have been appropriated by extremist groups. While some have attempted to co-opt Norse symbols for divisive purposes, it is crucial to understand that these symbols originally represented concepts of honor, courage, and kinship that can be reinterpreted in an anti-racist context. The role of Norse symbols in contemporary anti-racist movements illustrates how these images can serve as tools for unity rather than division, emphasizing the need for practitioners to reclaim these symbols and redefine their significance in a modern, multicultural context.

The contribution of diverse practitioners to Norse pagan traditions highlights the evolution of Asatru in a globalized world. Practitioners of various ethnicities and cultural backgrounds are engaging with Norse mythology and rituals, infusing them with their unique perspectives and experiences. Asatru practices are being adapted and embraced in non-white cultures, demonstrating that the tradition is not confined to a singular narrative but is instead a living, breathing faith that evolves with its practitioners. By celebrating this diversity, Asatru can continue to grow and adapt, fostering an inclusive environment that honors both heritage and contemporary multiculturalism.

# Chapter 10: Asatru Practices in Non-White Cultures

## Global Perspectives on Norse Paganism

Global perspectives on Norse Paganism reveal a rich tapestry of beliefs and practices that extend well beyond the confines of racist ideologies. Historically, the association of Asatru and Norse mythology with white supremacy has emerged primarily from misinterpretations and distortions of the original traditions. This misconception has often overshadowed the diverse and inclusive nature of contemporary Norse Pagan practices, which draw upon a broad range of cultural influences and emphasize personal responsibility, community, and respect for all individuals, irrespective of their ethnic backgrounds.

Modern Pagan movements have significantly contributed to the re-examination of Norse traditions, fostering an environment of inclusivity that stands in stark opposition to extremist ideologies. Many practitioners actively work to dismantle the associations with racism, emphasizing that Norse mythology and Asatru are spiritual paths that can be embraced by people of all backgrounds. This shift reflects a growing acknowledgment that the sacred narratives and symbols of Norse culture are not inherently tied to any particular ethnicity but rather speak to universal human experiences.

The emphasis on personal responsibility within Asatru further distinguishes it from ideologies that promote division or supremacy. Practitioners are encouraged to reflect on their actions and their impact on their communities, fostering a sense of accountability that transcends ethnic lines. This focus on individual character and communal wellbeing promotes a holistic understanding of what it means to honor the gods and the natural world, encouraging a diverse practice that includes various interpretations and expressions of faith.

Debunking myths surrounding Norse Paganism's alleged ties to ethnic identity is crucial in reclaiming these traditions from the clutches of extremist narratives. Norse symbols, once co-opted by hateful groups, are being reappropriated by anti-racist movements that recognize their potential for unity and resistance against oppression. This reclamation showcases the ongoing evolution of Norse imagery in a contemporary context, emphasizing its capacity to symbolize solidarity rather than division.

As Norse Paganism continues to evolve within a globalized framework, its practices are increasingly embraced by diverse communities. This blending of cultural influences enriches the traditions, allowing for a broader interpretation of what it means to practice Asatru in today's world. In doing so, practitioners from various ethnic backgrounds contribute to a dynamic and inclusive understanding of Norse spirituality, reinforcing that these ancient beliefs are not the exclusive domain of any one group but are available to all who seek to connect with them in a meaningful way.

## Case Studies of Non-White Practitioners

Case studies of non-white practitioners of Asatru reveal a rich tapestry of diverse experiences that challenge the notion that Norse Paganism is inherently tied to racism or white supremacy. One notable example is the involvement of African American practitioners who have embraced Asatru as a spiritual path that resonates with their quest for identity and belonging. These individuals often draw parallels between their ancestral spiritual practices and the values espoused in Norse mythology, emphasizing the universality of themes such as honor, loyalty, and the connection to nature. Their experiences illustrate that Asatru can serve as a means of cultural reclamation and personal empowerment, rather than a tool for exclusion.

The journey of Latinx practitioners in Asatru further underscores the inclusivity of this spiritual tradition. Many Latinx individuals have found solace in Norse mythology's emphasis on personal responsibility and community. They often engage in rituals that blend their own cultural heritage with Norse practices, creating a vibrant expression of spirituality that honors both traditions. For these practitioners, Asatru represents a break from the constraints of mainstream religious narratives, allowing them to forge a unique path that is both personal and communal. Their contributions highlight the adaptability of Norse Paganism in a multicultural context.

Asian practitioners of Asatru also provide compelling case studies that dispel myths about racial exclusivity in Norse Paganism. By embracing the values and stories within Norse mythology, these individuals challenge the idea that Norse spirituality is reserved for those of European descent. They actively participate in discussions around the ethical use of Norse symbols, promoting a message of inclusivity and understanding. Their presence in the Asatru community reflects a growing recognition that spirituality transcends ethnic boundaries and that the teachings of Norse mythology can inspire individuals from all backgrounds.

The role of non-white practitioners in contemporary anti-racist movements illustrates the potential for Norse symbols to serve as tools for unity rather than division. Many of these practitioners reappropriate symbols that have been misused by extremist groups, emphasizing their original meanings related to strength, resilience, and community. This reclamation effort not only confronts the narrative that associates these symbols with racism but also fosters a more profound understanding of their significance within a broader context of social justice. By actively engaging in discourse around these issues, non-white practitioners contribute to the ongoing evolution of Asatru as a diverse and inclusive spiritual path.

The evolution of Norse Paganism in a globalized context is significantly influenced by the contributions of diverse practitioners. As they bring their own cultural perspectives and experiences into the fold, they enrich the tradition and challenge prevailing stereotypes. This intersection of Asatru and multiculturalism demonstrates that the practice of Norse Paganism is not static but rather a dynamic and evolving expression of spirituality. By celebrating the diverse narratives within the Asatru community, we foster a more inclusive understanding that honors the complexity of identity and the shared human experience.

## Cultural Exchange and Adaptation

Cultural exchange and adaptation are pivotal concepts in understanding the evolution of Asatru and Norse Paganism, particularly in dispelling the misconceptions that link these traditions to racism or white supremacy. Historically, Norse mythology and practices were localized, but as globalization intensified, the interactions among diverse cultures became more prevalent. This exchange provided opportunities for people from various backgrounds to reinterpret and incorporate Norse symbols and beliefs into their own spiritual practices. As a result, Asatru has evolved beyond its geographic origins, fostering a more inclusive approach that embraces individuals from different ethnic and cultural backgrounds.

The historical misinterpretation of Norse mythology often fuels the erroneous assumption that Asatru is intrinsically tied to racial ideology. Many narratives have emerged that misrepresent the mythological texts and their original contexts, leading to a skewed perception of Norse culture. By examining the stories and symbols within their historical framework, we can appreciate the richness and complexity of Norse mythology, which, far from being racially exclusive, offers a plethora of themes relevant to all humanity. This understanding aids in dismantling the false equivalence drawn between Norse traditions and modern extremist ideologies.

Modern pagan movements have significantly influenced the inclusivity of Asatru. Many practitioners today actively seek to create spaces that welcome individuals of all backgrounds, challenging the traditional narratives that have sometimes confined Norse spirituality to a singular ethnic identity. This shift reflects a broader trend within paganism, where diverse spiritual expressions are celebrated and encouraged. The emphasis on personal responsibility and community within Asatru further supports this inclusive ethos, as practitioners are urged to engage thoughtfully with their beliefs and to respect the diverse interpretations that arise from cultural exchange.

Debunking myths surrounding Norse paganism and ethnic identity is essential to fostering a more accurate understanding of these traditions. The notion that one must be of Scandinavian descent to practice Asatru ignores the reality that spirituality transcends ethnic boundaries. Diverse practitioners have contributed to the evolution of Norse traditions, enriching them with their unique perspectives and practices. This multicultural approach not only enhances the tradition but also challenges the narrow definitions imposed by extremist groups that seek to hijack Norse symbols for their own agendas.

As the role of Norse symbols continues to evolve, their use in contemporary anti-racist movements illustrates the potential for these images to foster unity and resistance against oppression. Many individuals and communities are reclaiming these symbols to promote inclusivity and social justice, countering the narratives propagated by extremist factions. The intersection of Asatru and multiculturalism is thus not only a reflection of historical exchanges but also a dynamic response to modern societal challenges, demonstrating that Norse paganism can thrive in a globalized context while remaining committed to its core values of respect, honor, and community.

# Chapter 11: The Evolution of Norse Paganism in a Globalized Context

## Historical Evolution of Asatru

The historical evolution of Asatru is a journey that spans centuries, rooted deeply in the ancient traditions of the Norse people. Originally, Asatru was a polytheistic belief system that celebrated a pantheon of gods and goddesses, revering nature, ancestors, and the cycles of life. As Christianity spread throughout Scandinavia from the 8th to the 12th centuries, many of these pagan beliefs were marginalized and often demonized. However, remnants of Asatru survived, preserved through folklore, customs, and oral traditions, allowing the essence of Norse spirituality to endure despite external pressures and the imposition of a dominant faith.

The revival of Asatru in the late 19th and early 20th centuries marked a significant turning point, as interest in Norse mythology and folklore surged during the Romantic movement. Scholars and enthusiasts began to reinterpret ancient texts, often infusing their work with contemporary ideas about nationalism and ethnicity. These interpretations, while reflective of their time, frequently misrepresented the inclusive nature of Norse paganism. The conflation of Norse identity with ethnic identity laid the groundwork for the misappropriation of Asatru by extremist groups that sought to use its symbols and narratives to promote racial superiority, fundamentally distorting the original tenets of the faith.

In contrast to these historical misinterpretations, modern pagan movements have increasingly emphasized inclusivity and community. Many contemporary practitioners of Asatru actively work to reclaim the tradition from extremist ideologies, promoting a version of Norse spirituality that welcomes individuals from diverse backgrounds. This shift reflects a broader trend within modern paganism that recognizes the importance of personal responsibility and community cohesion. Asatru encourages its followers to engage with their spirituality while fostering an environment of mutual respect and understanding, allowing for a rich tapestry of beliefs and practices that transcend ethnic boundaries.

Debunking the myths surrounding Norse paganism and ethnic identity is critical to understanding its modern manifestations. Asatru is not inherently tied to any specific race or ethnicity; rather, it is a spiritual path that can be embraced by anyone who resonates with its principles. This understanding is further supported by the contributions of diverse practitioners who have enriched Norse traditions, infusing them with their cultural perspectives and experiences. As a result, Asatru today reflects a broader and more inclusive understanding of spirituality, breaking away from the limitations imposed by historical misinterpretations.

The role of Norse symbols in contemporary anti-racist movements highlights a significant evolution in the perception of Asatru. Many activists have reclaimed these symbols, advocating for their original meanings that celebrate community, courage, and resilience rather than the divisive narratives propagated by extremist groups. This intersection of Asatru and multiculturalism demonstrates a collective effort to redefine what it means to be a follower of Norse paganism in a globalized context, showcasing a belief system that is inherently adaptable and welcoming. As Asatru continues to evolve, it stands as a testament to the power of community and spirituality that transcends racial and ethnic divides.

## Modern Challenges and Opportunities

Modern challenges and opportunities surrounding Asatru and Norse Paganism primarily stem from the persistent mischaracterization of these spiritual practices as inherently tied to racism or white supremacy. This misconception often arises from historical misinterpretations of Norse mythology, where ancient tales are erroneously framed to support exclusionary narratives. Scholars and practitioners must confront these misunderstandings head-on, emphasizing that the core tenets of Asatru focus on personal responsibility, community, and respect for all individuals, regardless of their background. Engaging in dialogue and education is crucial to dismantling these harmful stereotypes that have taken root over decades.

The influence of modern pagan movements has made strides toward promoting inclusivity within Asatru. Many contemporary practitioners actively seek to broaden the understanding of Norse spirituality, moving away from the ethnocentric views that have plagued its image. This shift not only reflects a growing awareness of the diverse backgrounds of practitioners but also showcases the adaptability of Norse traditions in a multicultural context. By embracing inclusivity, Asatru can evolve into a more vibrant, relevant spiritual practice that resonates with a wider audience while remaining true to its historical roots.

Asatru places significant emphasis on personal responsibility and community involvement, principles that are especially relevant in today's diverse societies. Practitioners are encouraged to engage with their communities, fostering relationships that transcend racial and cultural boundaries. This commitment to personal accountability allows individuals to navigate their spiritual paths while contributing positively to the world around them. By embodying these values, Asatru can serve as a model for how spiritual practices can unite people rather than divide them, creating opportunities for collaboration and understanding across various cultural contexts.

Debunking the myths surrounding Norse Paganism and ethnic identity is another vital aspect of addressing modern challenges. Many practitioners assert that Norse mythology and its associated practices are not limited to any single racial or ethnic group. In fact, the traditions have evolved over centuries, influenced by various cultures and communities. This evolution underscores the fact that Asatru is not a monolithic practice; it welcomes diverse interpretations and expressions that reflect the richness of human experience. Recognizing this diversity is essential for dismantling the false narrative that links Asatru to racial exclusivity.

The role of Norse symbols in contemporary anti-racist movements further illustrates the potential for Asatru to serve as a force for good in today's society. Many practitioners and activists have reclaimed these symbols, using them to promote messages of unity and resistance against hate. By actively engaging with the historical context of these symbols and reinterpreting them through an inclusive lens, Asatru can play a significant role in fostering a more equitable society. This intersection of tradition and modern values presents an opportunity for Asatru to not only redefine its identity but also contribute meaningfully to the broader dialogue on race, culture, and spirituality in a globalized world.

## The Future of Norse Paganism in a Global World

The future of Norse Paganism in a global world is poised for significant transformation as practitioners increasingly recognize the importance of inclusivity and diversity. The historical misinterpretations that have often framed Asatru as inherently tied to racism are being challenged by a growing body of evidence and scholarship. This shift allows for a more accurate understanding of Norse mythology and its relevance to contemporary life, free from the distortions imposed by extremist ideologies. As awareness spreads, many practitioners are actively working to dismantle the erroneous associations between Norse traditions and white supremacy, promoting a more nuanced view that embraces the richness of Norse heritage as part of a broader human experience.

Modern pagan movements have played a crucial role in fostering inclusivity within Norse Paganism. Many practitioners now prioritize personal responsibility and community engagement, emphasizing that Asatru is not a doctrine of exclusion but rather a path that invites individuals from diverse backgrounds to explore their spiritual journeys. This evolving perspective is supported by the recognition that the core values of Asatru—honor, truth, and loyalty—can resonate with a wide array of cultural identities. As practitioners share their stories and experiences, they contribute to a more vibrant and multifaceted understanding of what it means to engage with Norse traditions today.

The debunking of myths surrounding Norse Paganism and ethnic identity is essential for its future in a multicultural landscape. While some groups have attempted to appropriate Norse symbols for their agendas, the larger community of Asatru practitioners is reclaiming these symbols to reflect their true meanings. This reclamation process involves acknowledging the historical contexts of these symbols while also emphasizing their universal values. By fostering dialogue and education, practitioners can combat the misconceptions that have led to the association of Norse imagery with extremist beliefs, ultimately reinforcing the idea that Norse Paganism is accessible to all who seek it.

In the current globalized context, Asatru is evolving as practitioners from various backgrounds incorporate their cultural perspectives into their practices. This intersection of Asatru and multiculturalism enriches the tradition, allowing for a more comprehensive exploration of Norse mythology and customs. Diverse practitioners bring unique insights and interpretations that can deepen the collective understanding of Asatru, making it a living tradition that reflects the experiences of a global community. As this evolution continues, it becomes increasingly evident that Norse Paganism can thrive in a pluralistic society, promoting harmony and mutual respect among different cultures.

The future of Norse Paganism will depend on the community's ability to foster inclusivity while honoring its roots. By actively engaging with the legacies of Norse mythology and addressing the historical misinterpretations that have tainted its image, practitioners can cultivate a space where all individuals feel welcomed. The ongoing dialogue about the role of Norse symbols in contemporary anti-racist movements further underscores the commitment to dismantling oppressive narratives. As the community grows and evolves, it may serve as a beacon of hope, demonstrating that spiritual practices can transcend boundaries and work toward a more equitable and just world for all.

# Chapter 12: Conclusion: Moving Beyond the Shield Wall

## Bridging Gaps and Building Understanding

Bridging gaps and building understanding in the context of Asatru and Norse Paganism requires a nuanced examination of historical interpretations and modern realities. Many people mistakenly associate these spiritual practices with racism and white supremacy due to misinterpretations of Norse mythology and the appropriation of symbols by extremist groups. It is essential to recognize that Asatru, at its core, emphasizes personal responsibility, community, and a deep connection to nature, which can be embraced by individuals of all backgrounds. By dissecting these misconceptions, we can foster a more inclusive understanding of Norse spiritual traditions.

Historical interpretations of Norse mythology have often been skewed, leading to a misunderstanding of its core principles. Ancient texts and sagas reflect a rich tapestry of beliefs that focus on honor, bravery, and the interconnectedness of all life. These stories were not written to promote racial superiority; rather, they served as a means of imparting values that resonate across cultures. By returning to the original texts and their meanings, we can counteract the erroneous narratives that have emerged over time and highlight the universality of their teachings.

The influence of modern pagan movements has played a significant role in promoting inclusivity within Asatru and Norse Paganism. Many contemporary practitioners actively seek to dismantle the association of these traditions with racism by emphasizing diversity and acceptance. Asatru communities are increasingly welcoming individuals from various ethnic backgrounds, recognizing that spirituality transcends race. This shift is not merely a reaction to external pressures but a genuine effort to create spaces where everyone can explore their connection to the divine and to nature, regardless of their heritage.

573

Debunking the myths surrounding Norse Paganism and ethnic identity is crucial in building a more inclusive narrative. Asatru does not inherently prescribe a specific ethnic identity; rather, it is a spiritual path that can be followed by anyone who resonates with its principles. This understanding is further complicated by the appropriation of Norse symbols by extremist groups, which often distort their meanings and intent. It is vital to reclaim these symbols and contextualize them within their original cultural significance while celebrating the contributions of diverse practitioners who enrich these traditions through their unique perspectives.

In a globalized context, the evolution of Norse Paganism reflects broader themes of multiculturalism and intersectionality. Practitioners from non-white cultures have incorporated Asatru practices into their spiritual lives, enriching the tradition and enhancing its relevance in today's diverse world. This interplay of cultures not only challenges the notion that Norse Paganism is exclusive to a single ethnic group but also illustrates the adaptability and resilience of these ancient beliefs. By creating dialogues between different cultural expressions of Asatru, we can bridge gaps and build understanding, fostering a more harmonious coexistence among all who seek truth and fulfillment within these venerable traditions.

## The Path Forward for Asatru

The future of Asatru lies in a conscious effort to disentangle the faith from misconceptions that have long been associated with racism and white supremacy. This path forward begins with an acknowledgment of the historical misinterpretations of Norse mythology that have contributed to these erroneous associations. By emphasizing the original context of the Eddas and sagas, practitioners can reclaim Asatru as a spiritual practice rooted in respect for nature, community, and personal responsibility rather than in exclusion or division. This reclamation is critical in countering narratives that have distorted the essence of Norse beliefs to serve extremist ideologies.

Modern Pagan movements have increasingly focused on inclusivity, offering a framework that allows Asatru practitioners to engage with diverse cultures and perspectives. By fostering open dialogue and collaboration among various traditions, Asatru can evolve beyond narrow ethnic confines. This inclusive approach not only enriches the practice but also highlights the universal themes present in Norse mythology, such as the importance of honor, courage, and kinship. It is essential for practitioners to recognize that these values transcend racial and ethnic boundaries, allowing for a more holistic understanding of Asatru that welcomes individuals from all backgrounds.

Personal responsibility and community are central tenets of Asatru, and these principles can guide the movement toward a more inclusive future. Practitioners are encouraged to take an active role in their communities, fostering environments that celebrate diversity and mutual respect. This emphasis on communal responsibility can help dispel the myths that link Norse paganism to ethnic exclusivity. By working together, practitioners can create spaces that honor the traditions of Asatru while embracing the contributions of diverse practitioners, thereby enriching the faith and its practices.

The use of Norse symbols in contemporary anti-racist movements serves as a powerful reminder of the potential for these symbols to unite rather than divide. Asatru practitioners can reclaim symbols like the Valknut and Yggdrasil, emphasizing their positive meanings and connections to community and nature. This reclamation is vital in countering the appropriation of these symbols by extremist groups that seek to distort their significance. By actively engaging with and promoting the positive aspects of these symbols, Asatru can position itself as a faith that stands firmly against racism and exclusion.

In a globalized context, the evolution of Norse paganism must reflect the realities of an interconnected world. Asatru practices are already being observed in non-white cultures, demonstrating the adaptability and relevance of these traditions beyond their historical origins. Embracing this multicultural aspect allows Asatru to thrive as a dynamic faith, drawing from a rich tapestry of experiences and insights. By fostering an environment where diverse voices can contribute to the ongoing narrative of Norse paganism, practitioners can ensure that the path forward for Asatru is one that is inclusive, respectful, and rooted in shared human values.

## A Call for Inclusivity and Awareness

A growing number of individuals are recognizing the need for inclusivity and awareness within the Asatru community. The misconception that Asatru and Norse Paganism are inherently linked to racism or white supremacy stems from historical misinterpretations and the appropriation of Norse symbols by extremist groups. It is crucial to clarify that these beliefs distort the rich tapestry of Norse mythology and traditions, which have always emphasized values such as honor, courage, and community rather than racial exclusivity. By confronting these assumptions head-on, practitioners can reclaim the narrative and foster a more inclusive environment that honors the true essence of Norse spirituality.

Historically, interpretations of Norse mythology have often been skewed by a Eurocentric lens, leading to a simplistic understanding of complex cultural narratives. This reductionist view has contributed to the erroneous belief that Norse traditions are exclusive to specific ethnic identities. However, the essence of these myths transcends ethnicity, highlighting universal themes of human experience. By educating ourselves and others about the depth and diversity of Norse mythology, we can dismantle the barriers created by historical misinterpretations and promote a more nuanced understanding that welcomes practitioners from all backgrounds.

Modern Pagan movements have made strides towards inclusivity, emphasizing the importance of community and shared values over ethnic identity. Asatru, in particular, places a strong emphasis on personal responsibility and collective well-being. This framework encourages practitioners to engage with their communities in meaningful ways, fostering connections that celebrate diversity rather than division. By promoting inclusivity, Asatru can serve as a model for how ancient traditions can adapt and thrive in contemporary society while embracing multiculturalism and understanding.

The role of Norse symbols in contemporary anti-racist movements further underscores the need for awareness and inclusivity. While some extremist groups have attempted to co-opt these symbols for their own agendas, many practitioners actively challenge this narrative by reclaiming the symbolism for positive social change. This reclamation serves as a powerful reminder that Norse imagery can represent unity, resilience, and the fight against oppression. By participating in movements that promote social justice, those within the Asatru community contribute to a broader dialogue about inclusivity and the true meaning of their spiritual practices.

Finally, recognizing the contributions of diverse practitioners to Norse Pagan traditions enriches the community as a whole. Asatru practices are not limited to any one culture or ethnicity; they have evolved and been embraced by individuals from various backgrounds. This evolution reflects the globalized context in which we live, where cultural exchange and dialogue are more prevalent than ever. By celebrating the diverse expressions of Asatru and acknowledging the roles that practitioners from different backgrounds play, we can create a vibrant, inclusive community that honors the legacy of Norse spirituality while remaining relevant in today's multicultural world.

www.ingramcontent.com/pod-product-compliance
Lightning Source LLC
Chambersburg PA
CBHW081131020726
47504CB00010B/2043